THE DAUGHTERS OF
HARWOOD HOUSE

TRILOGY

THE DAUGHTERS OF
HARWOOD HOUSE

TRILOGY

*Three Romances Tell the Saga of Sisters
Sold into Indentured Service*

SALLY LAITY
& DIANNA CRAWFORD

BARBOUR
PUBLISHING

Rose's Pledge ©2012 by Sally Laity and Dianna Crawford
Mariah's Quest © 2012 by Sally Laity and Dianna Crawford
Lily's Plight © 2013 by Sally Laity and Diana Crawford

Print ISBN 978-1-63058-157-2

eBook Editions:
Adobe Digital Edition (.epub) 978-1-63058-614-0
Kindle and MobiPocket Edition (.prc) 978-1-63058-615-7

All scripture quotations are taken from the King James Version of the Bible.

Cover Image: Dennis K. Johnson / GettyImages

Published by Barbour Books, an imprint of Barbour Publishing, Inc., P.O. Box 719, Uhrichsville, Ohio 44683, www.barbourbooks.com

Our mission is to publish and distribute inspirational products offering exceptional value and biblical encouragement to the masses.

 Member of the
Evangelical Christian
Publishers Association

Printed in the United States of America.

Rose's Pledge

Daughters of Harwood House
Book One

ACKNOWLEDGMENTS

The authors gratefully acknowledge
the generous assistance provided by:

Abigail Andrews
Washington County Free Library
Hagerstown, Maryland

Sandy Weston
Grafton Library
Grafton, West Virginia

These individuals helped us gather necessary period data
and shared their extensive knowledge of various settings
used in this story. To you we express our sincere appreciation.

Special thanks to fellow writers and friends:

Delia Latham
Sue Rich

Your tireless critiquing of our work in progress,
together with suggestions and comments along the way,
were an immense help. May the Lord bless you both.

DEDICATION

This book is lovingly dedicated to our Lord and Savior, Jesus
Christ, who blessed this magnificent nation from its founding,
and to our families, whose love and support makes our writing
possible.

Chapter 1

Bath, England, 1753

The *rat-tat-tat* of the brass door knocker echoed eerily through the spacious house.

Kneeling on the kitchen's stone floor, Rose Harwood started. *Oh no. Please, not now.* She dropped the scrub brush into the bucket and scrambled to her feet, wiping her hands on her long work apron. The pungent odor of lye soap clung stubbornly to them, but she could do nothing about that at the moment. Perhaps the caller would not notice the smell—or worse, her red hands. Never before had she undertaken such menial labor.

Even as she tore off the soiled apron, her frantic gaze searched worktables and shelves until it landed on the spice chest. Mexican vanilla beans could mask the scent. But no. . .she could not justify the ruination of something so costly to replace.

Especially now.

The knocker rapped several more times. Louder. More insistent.

"Do calm yourself, Rose." Clasping her hands together, she hiked her chin with new resolve. "I simply shan't go to the door."

But that wouldn't do either. Under normal circumstances, if none of the Harwood family happened to be in residence, the hired girl would answer a summons. But circumstances were no longer normal. Several weeks past, Rose had been forced to let Hildy go. Word must not get out, lest people begin to suspect.

Expense be hanged. She lifted the spice chest from a niche beside the hearth oven and opened it, releasing myriad exotic fragrances into the air. Without so much as a second to savor the sweet perfumes, she snatched the small pouch of vanilla beans, shook two brown stalks out, and rubbed them vigorously over her hands.

A third, more demanding, tapping resounded through the rooms.

Was this to be the day of the family's undoing? Inhaling a troubled breath, Rose hurried to the front door and opened it. "Constable Bradley." She swallowed her angst and bobbed a curtsy. "Good morning to you, sir."

"Good day to you, Miss Harwood. I trust you are in good health." He touched his hat in a polite gesture. "Is your father at home?"

Rose had never noticed how huge the local official was. In his great winter coat, he quite filled the entry. She shook off the wayward thought. "I am most sorry, sir, he is not. May I be of service?"

"'Tis gentlemen's business, miss." Clutching the edge of the warm fur hat he'd removed, the aging man turned to leave. "I'll fetch him down at his shop."

Fetch him? The constable had come to place Papa under arrest! Her worst fears realized, Rose caught hold of the man's arm. "My father keeps no secrets from me. Pray, do come inside. I'm sure there must be another answer."

His bushy eyebrows dipped as he frowned down at her. "Forgive me, miss. I have me duty."

"Please, sir. I ask but five minutes."

He hesitated then exhaled in a huff. "Very well. But not one minute more."

As she stepped aside for him to enter, she glanced up and down the lane. No one seemed to be about, but that didn't mean that some snoopy neighbor wasn't peeping out from behind lace curtains. Bath most certainly had its share of busybodies.

She closed the door and turned to the official, who dwarfed the small, tastefully furnished parlor. "Do warm yourself at the fire."

Moving to the marble hearth, the constable thrust forth his beefy hands toward the comforting glow. But despite his seeming compliance in giving ear to her request, the expression on his heavily jowled face remained dour.

Rose attempted a bit of light conversation, desperate to establish some measure of rapport. "I shall be exceedingly heartened when April brings a bit of spring weather, will you not?"

It was wasted effort, as her visitor did not deign to reply. Instead, he shot her a worried look. "Be assured, Miss Harwood, 'tis all legal and final. I've the papers right here in me pocket." He patted his coat. "I'm duty bound to take your father into custody."

"But if you please, sir, Papa is seeking a loan even as we speak. Tomorrow or the next day he's certain to have the money. See if he won't."

The constable shook his head. "Forgive me, miss, but Merchant Solomon, of Bristol, will wait no longer. I've been ordered to collect either the money owed by Henry Harwood or the man himself this day. So I'd best get meself down to his shop."

Rose twisted her hands together and bit down hard on her lip. She could not let such a thing happen. Not to Papa. Especially since none of this was his fault.

She stepped in front of the constable, blocking his path. "You said you were told to arrest him today. Yet the day has scarcely begun. I beg you, please give me until the last hour. I pledge most sincerely that I shall satisfy Papa's account with Supplier Solomon before the sun sets."

The officer absently brushed back strands of his graying hair and plunked his beaver hat atop his head once again.

Rose sensed the man was contemplating her proposal and therefore pressed her advantage. "Constable Bradley, you've known me my whole life. You know I am a responsible person. I've run this household since I was a mere thirteen years of age, taking care of my brothers and sisters, never once straying from my obligations. If I say I will do this, you can be most assured that I will."

His expression softened. "Ye've been a blessing to your pa, that's certain. A comely lass such as yourself, sacrificing your courting years to help your family. Nevertheless, if your father is unable—"

"I vow I shall see to the matter. I mean this most sincerely." She met his gaze squarely, despite the fact he'd as much as called her a spinster. She had to remain strong. Do what Papa could not bring himself to do.

The constable sighed. "Very well, Miss Harwood. Ye have 'til nightfall. Not a moment more."

Vastly relieved, Rose ushered the official out then returned to take mental inventory of the room. Each familiar article of furniture, every table decoration, and even the exquisite carpets had been carefully, lovingly, selected by her mother. The family had basked in its beauty over the years. But alas, sentiment no longer had a place here. All must be sold. Now. Today. But where? Market day wasn't until Friday.

In a rise of panic, she pressed her hands to her temples. "Where? Where?"

The Bristol docks.

"Of course!" Several ships were certain to be in port, with captains looking for quality merchandise to take abroad and sell for profit. Since she must journey there to deal with Mr. Solomon anyway. . .

She plucked a Chinese jade figurine from the mantel. So much to pack and load. So little time. La, why had Mariah and Lily chosen this day of all days to go visiting? She needed their assistance desperately. With no time to waste, she'd simply have to go and fetch them.

But reality stopped her in her tracks. Mariah was on a mission of her own, to gain a wedding proposal from Lawrence Wirkworth before their family's calamitous reversal of fortune became common knowledge. Rose shook her head. How typical of Mariah to think only of herself.

In truth, however, Rose had to concede it was essential for her sister to find swift success. Once the family's finest goods were loaded onto the cart and hauled out of town, all of Bath would see *and know* that something was amiss at Harwood House.

"May God help us all."

———

Chilled to the bone and exhausted from a day of dickering and bartering, Rose trudged up to the front entrance in the last faint light of eventide. The thirteen-mile distance from Bristol had seemed more like a hundred on the rutted, ice-crusted roads, despite the fact that, partway, a kind passerby had provided a ride in his wagon. The elements had been the ruination of her best shoes, and several spots on her feet burned as if a hot poker had tormented her heels and toes. But her return to Bath before nightfall had been imperative.

Thank Providence, the wax-sealed envelope from Mr. Solomon now lay in the hands of the constable. She'd obtained a reprieve for Papa. Gotten him another month to pay the remainder of his debt.

With a weary sigh, she reached for the door latch. The threat of this day had been conquered, albeit at great cost. Far greater than she would ever have foreseen.

She swallowed her trepidation and pushed the door open.

A cluster of relatives—her entire family—turned to face her, their grim faces snatching from her mind the fine speech she'd concocted along the way. Papa stood beside Mariah, a comforting arm about her, both looking as if they'd just returned from a funeral. In sweet contrast, her youngest sister, Lily, greeted Rose with a gentle smile. Next to Lily stood Tommy, the baby of the family. Only a scant spark of his usual mischief glowed in the twelve-year-old's eyes.

Even Charles, their married brother, was present. By this hour of the evening, he should have been in his own home with his wife and children. In the erratic light of an untrimmed lamp wick, his lean face seemed much older. Much harder.

Mariah broke from the group. "Just where, might I ask, have you been?" Anger contorted the family beauty's delicate features into an ugly accusation as she rushed toward Rose. Her deep blue eyes flashed fire, and her mass of black ringlets bobbed in disarray. "Look about you, Rose. We have been robbed. Our family home has been ransacked. Everything of value is gone—even the money Papa set aside for my dowry." She paused, and her expression became accusing. "Tell me this is not your doing. If it is, I demand you explain yourself." She planted a hand on either hip, her lips pressed into a grim line.

Rose had hoped for a moment or two to rest before facing her loved ones, but it was not to be. Somehow she would have to relate the sordid details of this trying day.

Henry Harwood, the kindest of fathers, now loomed before her, more agitated than she'd ever seen him. He grasped her by the shoulders. "I must ask what you know of this, daughter. Speak up. Tell us all."

Rose felt the bite of his fingers through the thickness of her woolen cloak. She lifted her gaze to the beloved face that had aged noticeably in the past few weeks since the financial trouble erupted—when the flamboyant Sir Gordon Ridgeway had met an untimely death in a duel mere days after taking possession of fifty signature brooches he was in the habit of passing out to his lady friends. The gentleman had begged off paying for the jewelry, promising to return in a fortnight with the money. Papa could not have refused the young bachelor, his best customer. But now Sir Ridgeway's uncle refused to honor the debt, refused even to acknowledge a debt existed, leaving her father, the finest goldsmith between Oxford and Bristol, in ruin.

Surely he would understand her actions of this day and forgive her desperate deeds. She fervently prayed it would be so. Hadn't she proved how much she cared for her family these past twelve years since her mother's death on the childbed? She'd taken charge of newborn babe Tommy, as well as the other children, run a well-ordered household. Putting the needs of her dear ones first, she'd unselfishly set aside even her own chances to wed.

Of course her father would understand. He knew her heart as she did his. She reached past the folds of her cloak to smooth a crease alongside his tight mouth. "I've aided the family in the one way I knew you could never bring yourself to do, Papa."

She looked past him to Charles, who bore a strong resemblance to their lank-boned father, down to an identical trim mustache. "I know you'll all see the wisdom in what I've done. I'll tell you everything. But first—" Rose shifted her attention to her youngest sister, who had yet to venture forward. "Lily, dearest, would you mind fetching me a cup of tea? I've had a most tiresome day."

The growing worry in Lily's dove-gray eyes melted away, replaced by a simple trusting goodness that never ceased to lift Rose's spirits. "I shan't be a minute," she said in her airy voice. "The kettle is already heating."

As the girl hastened out of the parlor, Rose noticed how tall the lass had grown this past year. The child had become a maiden last month, on her fourteenth birthday. She was now old enough, Rose fervently hoped, to do without her big sister. Older than she herself had been when their mother passed from this life.

"Rose." Her father pulled her attention back to him. "I must ask you to explain yourself. I came home from the shop to find the house stripped of everything we hold dear, and your sister Mariah in high dudgeon."

"Aye." Tommy nodded. "You'd have thought she was musket shot the way she wailed and clutched herself." With an exaggerated moan, the twelve-year-old grabbed at his shirtfront and staggered toward the nearest wing chair, where he collapsed into its confines. The merry scamp could always be counted upon to lighten the gloomiest of moments.

Despite herself, Rose's lips curled into a smile as she moved across the room and gratefully took a seat in the companion silk brocade chair. The larger pieces remained in the room only because the pony cart had been too full to fit any more items.

Obviously Mariah had derived no humor from their younger brother's imitation of her. She shot him a scathing glower before lighting on the settee and eyeing Rose with naked malice. "If you intended to rob me of my dowry, I must know why you waited until Lily and I had gone to the Wirkworths'. I wasted hours smiling and cooing over their horse-faced heir. Had you an ounce of common discretion, you should have allowed me this one last chance to make a successful match before people learned of Papa's huge debt. And I had Master Lawrence so close to pledging himself to me. So close," she grated through clamped teeth. Angrily she tossed her head, sending her midnight curls to bouncing like so many coiled springs. "I shan't be surprised were he to come here this very eve to ask Father for my hand. Can you imagine anything more dreadful? One look at this room bereft of so many fine furnishings and he'll surely draw the most shocking conclusions. That is, if one of our neighbors doesn't enlighten him first. Soon enough everyone will be aware of the shame that has befallen this family. We shall never be able to hold our heads up again."

Rose got up and stepped toward her sister with an outstretched hand. "Please, Mariah, you must trust that the Lord will see us through this valley of misfortune. Today I had no choice but to act immediately and choose the only open path to reverse our tragic circumstances. Surely you will all come to understand it was the prudent one."

"Daughter." From her father's tone and unyielding expression, Rose realized he had reached the end of his patience.

"Why don't we be seated?" She pulled loose her cloak ties and carefully lifted the hood from her head, tucking a loose strand of amber-colored hair into the heavy coil resting low at the base of her neck. "I'm afraid this day's sad happenings touch us all."

As her father and Charles settled in the hard-backed armchairs flanking the settee, Rose's gaze roved the room. This once cozy parlor of their neat quarried stone house now appeared stark and spartan, devoid of most of the lovely furnishings that had made it home. It was as if she saw it for the first time.

None of them had the slightest suspicion it would be her last.

But no tender memories would she take from this bare skeleton of a room, no comfort. Mariah had voiced the truth when Rose first stepped inside. Their home had indeed been robbed—of all its grace and charm.

Every wall hanging and crystal lamp, every porcelain piece, stitched tapestry, and doily had been stripped from the parlor. Even the prized Chippendale table. Rose had managed to find room in the pony cart for that one last elegant piece. And should Papa but open the music cabinet, he would discover the absence of Mariah's violin, Lily's flute, and her own mandolin. The windows stood bereft of their fine Belgian lace curtains; only the heavy velvet drapes remained for privacy's sake.

The room looked as utterly cold and dreary as her journey home had been.

Charles's voice interrupted her brief reverie, sounding every bit as overwrought as their father's. "You should be aware, sister, that we arrived here just in time to prevent Mariah from going after the constable."

A tremor coursed through Rose. She clasped her hands to steady them as she turned to her father. "'Twould not have been his first visit here this day."

Paling frightfully, Papa sat up rod straight and clutched his knees.

Rose's brothers and Mariah also stiffened as if frozen in place. Only their eyes moved as they looked from one to the other. They had not realized how desperate their situation truly was.

Lily returned at that moment, carrying a tea tray with cups for all. Her guileless expression gave no import to the everyday crockery used in place of the fancy china now missing from the kitchen. "I thought we all might enjoy tea." She placed the tray on the low table in front of the settee and began to pour from the pot.

Rose appreciated the few moments' reprieve while Lily served everyone. But before she managed even a second sip of the comforting brew, her father interrupted. "Rose. We've waited quite long enough. Enlighten us now, daughter."

Slowly, deliberately, Rose set her cup and saucer on the table beside her, placing the spoon just so along the side in vain effort to delay the telling. After inhaling deeply, she began. "'Tis most fortuitous that our house sits on the line between the jail and your shop, Papa. Constable Bradley stopped here first, on the chance you were still at home."

As she related their exchange and explained her promise to the official, Tommy broke in, wariness ringing in the boyish pitch of his voice. "I did not see the pony cart in its normal place. Where is it?"

"I'm most sorry to say I had to sell it, Tommy."

"Surely not!" He sprang to his feet, his fists knotted. "But Corky! Surely you did not sell Corky along with it!"

"Sit!" Papa commanded with uncharacteristic harshness.

Rose's chest tightened with pity for her father. This terrible trouble should not have befallen such a kind, gentle man, much less her baby brother. The pony had been the lad's pet, his bonny companion. She attempted a sympathetic smile.

"Not Corky." Tommy crumpled into his seat, his chin quivering.

Charles cleared his throat, looking as if his passion hovered on the verge of erupting. "Continue, Rose."

"As your eyes can attest, I loaded everything I could carry and drove down to the Bristol docks, hoping to sell it. This could not wait for market day."

"Or for Father's approval, I daresay." Charles's accusatory tone effectively placed the blame squarely on Rose's shoulders.

She ignored his comment. "Nonetheless, I was able to make more of a profit than I had even hoped. As Providence would have it, three ships were in port. They were loading cargo for the American colonies, and you know how eager the colonists are for some of our more civilized articles. Oh and Mariah, I'm very sorry to confess I also had to sell our few pieces of jewelry and our most fashionable gowns."

Her sister gasped so violently, Rose surmised that had a crystal lamp remained in the room, its dangling pendants would have been set to tinkling.

Notching her chin a touch higher, she continued. "Some healthy competition started between the captains, and by the time all the bartering and dealing ended, I walked away with forty-three pounds sterling, two shillings, and a sixpence for our possessions."

Papa let out a weary breath. "I say, my dear. You did exceedingly well to obtain such a goodly sum. However, I must avow 'tis barely a third of what I owe the gold supplier."

"So Mr. Solomon informed me. He refused to accept any less on account than seventy pounds. So Mariah's dowry of twenty pounds had to be sacrificed as well. He left me no other choice."

A low, mournful whimper issued from her sister.

Perhaps Mariah was at last beginning to comprehend the necessity, Rose decided as she tore her gaze from her middle sister and rested it on young Tom. "You do understand we couldn't allow the constable to take Papa to debtors' prison. Such a horrid fate would be punishment far beyond what should be imposed upon him." She then turned to Charles, whose stone-hard expression had yet to yield to the gravity of the situation. "Brother, even on the chance that you possessed enough of Papa's skills to fashion most of the pieces on order, no supplier would give you credit for gold bullion or for cut gems once they learned of Papa's imprisonment. And you know the only way to get someone out of that unspeakable place would be to pay off all creditors in full. No more bargaining, no more promises. We would be out on the street, forced to sell the very roof over our heads."

Charles turned to Papa. "See what comes of your relying so much on Rose." He wheeled back to her, his jaw set tighter than before. "Had you come to us before running off in typical female panic, we would have told you Father was in the midst of arranging a mortgage."

Papa raised a hand, effectively silencing any further outburst. "Son, I had hoped to spare you, now that you've your own family to be concerned about. I did obtain a loan, that much is true. But not nearly as much as I requested. And since the gem cutter was pressing harder at the moment, I had to use the funds to pay him."

Rose hurried to further her own defense. "So you see, there was no recourse left to me but to sell even the pony and cart, as well as. . .as. . ."

Every eye focused on her, waiting.

She took firm hold of the chair arms for support and met her father's stare as the remainder of the news poured from her lips like water over a precipice. "I suppose there is no easy way to tell you this, Papa. After I sold the cart and pony, I still lacked four pounds. And Mr. Solomon was not to be bargained with. He'd accept no less on account than the agreed upon sum. The constable was waiting. The afternoon was dwindling away. So I—" She swallowed. When she spoke again, she could barely manage a whisper. "I. . .sold myself."

Chapter 2

It took the huge vessel *Seaford Lady* six interminable weeks and four days to carve a passage through the vast, dark waters of the cold Atlantic Ocean. Rose doubted she would ever forget them. But once she'd recovered from the seasickness that laid her low for the first week, she found the voyage somewhat more enjoyable as she watched the crew dealing efficiently with monstrous sails, changing winds, and strong sea currents. Yesterday's first glimpse of land had thrilled her, and on this last night aboard ship, she wished she had more time to prepare herself for what lay ahead. . .four years of servitude as an indentured servant.

At least the crossing had been without mishap. Surely that was a good sign. She had to trust that this voyage to the American colonies was God's will, not merely her own rash choice. She could hardly bear to look back on the pain and sorrow in her father's eyes when he bade her a last farewell. Even now she blinked away stinging tears and suppressed the lingering doubts that had plagued her during the entire trip.

The fragile promise of dawn began to show through the porthole of the overcrowded ship's cabin. In the faint light, Rose slipped from the bottom bunk and onto the narrow wooden floor between two sets of cots stacked three high. The thought of a few moments of solitude on deck, breathing air she did not have to share with five other travelers, left her almost giddy. She plucked her cloak from the foot of her narrow bed and snugged it around her, then pulled on her slippers and tiptoed out the door, careful to close it without waking her cabinmates.

She padded along the lantern-lit passageway then out onto the wide deck of the three-masted merchant ship. A chilly breeze billowed the huge sails, which swelled and flapped, their gentle motion causing little stress to the scores of ropes and spars. The vessel plowed slowly north into the deepest reaches of Chesapeake Bay, heading toward the tobacco port of Baltimore.

When the *Seaford Lady* first entered the bay yesterday, one of the seamen had informed Rose that the inlet cut between the mainland and a peninsula for a good two hundred miles. He certainly had not lied, because after these many hours, the ship had yet to reach its destination.

She stepped to the starboard railing to view the coming dawn. A pale pink glow illuminated the treetops along the ragged eastern shoreline. So close she could almost smell the scent of pine. The cool air that brushed past her cheeks felt surprisingly pleasant for the first week of May, reminding her that the ship sailed the same latitudes as southern Spain.

Spying a dot of light onshore, Rose felt her pulse quicken. Not so far away, some woman had likely risen in the quiet hush to begin another day. No doubt she was in the kitchen stirring banked embers at the back of the hearth, bringing the morning's cook fire to life. By tomorrow, Rose might very well be tending just such a hearth, if the captain had spoken truthfully. According to him, colonials always came to the dock whenever his vessel arrived to bid for the bondservants he'd contracted.

"Good morn to ye, Miss Harwood." A lone sailor made his way from the bow. He sidestepped some lashed-down barrels, a jovial grin revealing a gap in his front teeth.

"Good morning, Seaman Polk." Rose quickly tucked her long night braid inside her hood. Remembering her state of undress, she scrunched in her toes in her bed slippers beneath the dark folds of her cloak's hem. He would think her most common indeed, with barely covered feet.

"We should make port in an hour or so." He paused beside her. "Ye might be wantin' to tell the other womenfolk to start gatherin' their belongings together. Soon as the cap'n reports to the harbor master, he'll be wantin' to. . .to see you folks on yer way."

Rose knew the seaman wanted to spare her feelings by avoiding the plain truth: that Captain Durning would soon be auctioning off the lot of them to the highest bidder as if they were nothing but cattle or sheep. She managed a smile. "We packed our things last eve, but I suppose I should awaken them soon. They'll all want to look their best."

The sailor's sunburned face brightened. "That won't be no work a'tall for you and your sisters, Miss Harwood. 'Specially Miss Mariah."

"That's most kind of you to say," Rose assured him, though the words came hard as she turned back to the railing. She had argued bitterly against Mariah and Lily accompanying her to this new land. But indeed, their contention had been as sound as her own when she had bargained away the family assets. Mariah insisted that if she and Lily left with Rose, Charles would be able to move his young family to Harwood House, thereby eliminating the need for Papa's business to support two homes. Contemplating their logical, if somewhat disheartening reasoning, their father finally relented.

Rose smiled to herself as she recalled Lily's personal reason for coming along. The girl could not suffer the thought of her older sister going to the colonies all alone. After all, Rose had mothered her from her earliest memories.

Mariah, on the other hand, had a far more practical purpose. She had heard that the lines between the classes were less distinct in America and more crossable. She felt she might do quite well for herself amongst what was rumored to be a rather *provincial* people. Despite her own impoverished circumstance, she truly believed her beauty and charm alone to be a more than sufficient dowry. She'd spoken of little else from the moment the three had set sail.

No doubt about it, Mariah would have to be closely watched.

"Rose! Mariah!" Lily rushed through the cabin doorway, her cheeks positively glowing. "Captain Durning says it's time for us to go ashore. I daresay, I cannot abide such excitement."

"Nevertheless," Rose said quietly to calm the younger girl, "he advised us to remain here until his business with our cabinmates and the German family from the adjoining quarters has been concluded." She recalled with distaste the conspiratorial wink he had given Mariah as he related his reputation for "saving the best for last." Rose would have much preferred being present during the earlier transactions for some idea of what she and her sisters might expect, but the man had been most insistent.

Now that the moment to disembark had arrived, her insides quivered uncontrollably. Her one slim comfort was the promise she had extracted from Captain Durning to sell the three of them together.

She glanced around the cabin, noticing how much less crowded it appeared once their luggage had been taken ashore. "Search under the cots, Lily. We shouldn't want to leave anything behind."

Mariah, already in the doorway, swung back. "For pity's sake, Rose. Don't be such a mother hen. We've checked the room from floor to ceiling, and as you can see, not a lock of our hair is out of place, nor has a single wrinkle dared crease our skirts." She whirled out into the corridor with Lily chasing after her.

Compelled to make her own final inspection of the cramped quarters, Rose could only agree. Both her sisters were impeccably groomed. Mariah was stunning in her royal blue taffeta, shawled in white lace—a combination which enhanced the deep indigo of her eyes and her shining black hair. Her wide-brimmed bonnet sat at a tilt as blithe as the girl herself. The blue satin ties and white under-frills would help contain her bountiful curls.

Lily's finely woven wool in muted pink accented her more delicate features and light gray eyes. Her hair had yet to darken from flaxen to golden brown as Rose's had by the time she'd reached her fourteenth year. Mayhap Lily's would remain blond, since her eyes were several shades lighter than Rose's blue gray, and her complexion so fair it burned and freckled in the slightest sunshine. The two of them favored the taller, slender Harwood side, unlike Mariah, who had their mother's more rounded figure.

Rose sighed. What would Mother have thought of her daughters' present circumstances? She'd had such high expectations, such fine hopes for all her children. Her last words had concerned them as she'd extracted a vow from Papa to see the girls safely through the pitfalls of this earthly walk, and she expressly urged Rose, as the oldest, to remain faithful to her Christian upbringing as an example to her siblings.

Now such unforeseen changes lay ahead. But no matter what they entailed, Rose intended to keep that solemn pledge. In this she would not fail her mother.

With a last smoothing of her gloved hands over a daygown of nut-brown linen edged with natural lace, she left the safety of the ship's cabin in search of her sisters. Surely they hadn't gotten too far ahead in the few moments' time since they'd dashed off.

Descending the wooden walkway from the ship to the quay, Rose surveyed the sprawling city with amazement. From the accounts she'd read in the English newspapers, she'd expected the ports to be little more than provincial villages. Yet from this high vantage point, she could see rows and rows of substantial buildings stretching inland. On either side of the *Seaford Lady* a veritable forest of masts jutted up from their moorings, while seagulls circled and darted low, their cries piercing the salt-laden air.

The wharf itself teemed with as much activity as any Bristol dock. Such clamor greeted her after so long at sea, and such an array of smells. Loaded wagons rumbled and groaned beneath heavy loads as they rattled across the wooden planks. Horses clomped and whinnied, while their drivers yelled curses and hawkers shouted their wares. Rose had to smile. On a wharf, every day was market day.

Unable to find her sisters in the crowd, she stepped aside for dockworkers busily off-loading the ship, while a customs agent inspected the cargo manifest. Amid all the hustle and bustle, red-coated king's men kept order. This new land was every bit as civilized as her own England, Rose concluded. She relaxed and took a deep breath, catching her favorite smell, a whiff of the hundreds of hard rolls being baked to supply the outgoing ships.

Rose's gaze lighted on a cluster of men dressed in the attire of tradesmen and merchants. In the center stood Captain Durning and her sisters. She hardly recognized the man, decked out in his best powdered wig, ruffles, and feathered, three-cornered hat. Obviously he wanted to impress the more simply dressed gathering. How sad that his ill-fitting coat puckered between its brass buttons, spoiling the image. With curt motions, he beckoned Rose to join them.

Hesitant to leave the safety of the ship, she waited for the captain's more insistent gestures. When she could delay no longer, she moved toward him. . .toward a very uncertain future. Her pulse quickened upon reaching the landing. *Have faith. The Lord is looking after us.* Papa always said that—even when the opposite seemed true. Squaring her shoulders, she made her way through the gathering to join her sisters.

Captain Durning leaned close, looking none too happy with her. "Tardiness is not a virtue," he rasped into her ear. He pursed his thick lips and stepped onto a platform made of sturdy boards placed on nail kegs. Head and shoulders above the crowd, he scanned his customers as his loud voice rang out. "Gentlemen! As I promised, I have saved the choicest for last. These three young lasses have been schooled in all the social graces, as well as the art of fine cooking. They can also read and do sums. Any one of 'em would make an ideal lady's companion or children's governess."

"Put up the one in blue," a portly man hollered. He wore no frock coat, merely an unadorned vest over his blouse as if he'd just come from a trades shop. "I'll bid on her."

"I'll expect a starting bid of no less than twenty-five pounds for this one." The captain reached down to help Mariah onto the stage.

Rose's gasp went unheard beneath the audience's appreciative comments as they ogled Mariah, who stood up there for all to see. The miser had begrudged Papa the mere six pounds he'd shelled out for Mariah. For Lily he'd refused to go higher than five—scarcely more than a half a pound a year. Out of that stingy sum, their good father had sacrificed two pounds to each of his daughters in the event some calamity should befall them. And this vile man intended to profit a despicable fourfold!

A sudden realization penetrated Rose's consciousness. The captain was offering Mariah separately. This was not to be borne! He'd promised all of them *and Papa* that he'd keep them together. "Captain Durning!" She raised her voice above the confusion. "You agreed to sell us as a family."

Ignoring her protests, he went on with the proceedings. "What do I hear for a first bid?"

"I'll give ye twenty pounds," the portly fellow said. "Not a pence more."

"Twenty-one," another yelled.

"Twenty-two," shouted yet another.

Rose shot a look at Mariah. The girl's eyes fairly danced, and a half smile graced her lips. For some unfathomable reason she actually seemed to be *enjoying* her moment onstage. All the more incentive for Rose to take further action. She stepped directly in front of the captain and raised her voice. "*Mister Durning!* I shall be forced to call the authorities if you do not honor the agreement you made with our father."

The man's florid complexion darkened. His eyes narrowed menacingly as he leaned toward her and thrust a clenched fist beneath her nose. "We have no written contract, wench. I'll thank ye to keep yer mouth shut."

Rose felt Lily edge closer, and the girl's small hands clutched Rose's arm. She could not let the child or her other sister down. Her own hands curled into fists. "And I'll thank you to honor your word as a gentleman, sir."

His mouth twisted into a smirk, and he jutted out his fleshy neck. "What we have, shrew, is yer name on a legal document that says I have the right to sell the three of ye to whomever I please. And if ye don't keep quiet, I'll have ye locked in the hold of me ship until I've completed the rest of me business."

"Not before I summon the port authorities." Rose whirled around. The blackguard would see she was no ignorant street urchin.

"Good sirs," the captain cried, "lay hold of this baggage and hold her whilst I fetch my men."

No sooner had the request been voiced than two men clamped hands on to her, pinning her in place.

She tried to wrench free, but to no avail. Far worse, the ruffians seemed to enjoy their task most thoroughly. "Don't fret, Cap'n," one of the audacious pair called brightly. "We'll see the lass stays put."

"And I'll see you and your manhandling cohorts brought up before the magistrate," Rose countered with equal force. She then felt a tugging on her ruffled half sleeve.

"Please, Rose," Lily urged. "Don't say anything more. They'll take you away."

Rose's heart went out to her baby sister. Only the men restraining her prevented her from pulling the girl into her arms. Looking beyond Lily to Mariah, she saw that her other sister's attention was occupied elsewhere. Up on the platform, Mariah's bold stare was fixed on a young, raven-haired gentleman on the outskirts of the crowd. He sat astride a long-legged bay.

Wearing naught but a loose shirt and tight breeches tucked into tall boots, the smoothly tanned man was as handsome as Mariah was beautiful. And he beheld her with the same blatant interest.

Flirting! Rose acknowledged. *The pair of them! How disgraceful!*

The young man did not take his eyes off Mariah. "I'll bid thirty pounds on the beauty in the blue frock."

The gathering grew quiet. The gentleman had bid quite a tidy sum for a mere four years of household servitude. . .if that was all he thought he was purchasing.

"Thirty-one," came from another quarter.

Grinning lazily, the horseman hooked his leg over his saddle's pommel, as if prepared to stay for the duration. "Forty."

At the enormous bid, murmurings of amazement spread through the crowd. Then expectant silence. All eyes turned toward the challenger— another young jack-a-dandy. At his shrug of defeat, attention shifted to the man who'd opened the bidding.

He rubbed a hand over his paunch and looked from Mariah to the young mounted gentleman. His expression soured and his bushy brows formed a V over his slitted eyes. He did not take kindly to losing.

Observing his stubborn glare, Rose suspected him to be the sort who would be an abuser of servants. She held her breath and sent a fleeting prayer heavenward that the older man would concede.

Abruptly, he grunted and stomped off, shoving past anyone in his path.

"Sold!" The captain's triumphant shout grated on Rose's frayed nerves. He sounded more than pleased with himself and his good fortune. "To the gentleman on the fine stallion."

The man laughed and spurred his mount forward. Edging the animal alongside the makeshift platform, he scooped up a very willing Mariah, whose arms were already outstretched and waiting.

Rose fumed. *The hussy*. Furious, she broke free from her captors' grasps and lunged toward her sister, grabbing a handful of Mariah's stiff taffeta skirt. "Come down from there this instant."

"Miss Harwood has a point. Set the lass down."

The captain's words surprised Rose. Renewed hope flowed through her.

"Ye'll not be taking her anywhere until there's hard cash in me hand and ye put yer signature on the indenturement." He slid a satisfied glance to Rose. "Everything proper and legal."

Rose could not abide such a display of impudence. He should be thrashed. She jerked once more on her sister's blue taffeta.

Mariah gifted the handsome rider with an apologetic smile then complied by allowing him to lower her to the ground, which he did much too slowly.

So appalled she could not speak, Rose tugged Mariah to a spot between her and Lily. But before she could deliver a scathing reprimand, the captain seized Lily beneath the arms and deposited her on the platform.

"There ye go, child," he said sternly.

Rose's heart jolted as her sister's eyes grew round with fright and her face lost all color. Hiking her skirts, Rose stepped a foot onto the stage. "Mr. Durning. Lily and I *must* be sold together. She's far too young to go forth alone. I beg you to reconsider."

Durning booted her foot off the platform. "Stay put and hold yer tongue, or I swear I'll clap ye in chains and sell ye in another port a few days' sail from here."

Rose ignored the vehemence in that statement and met his glare. She would not be intimidated by this blighter of honest dealings.

Gradually his expression eased, and he glanced away. "If someone wants the both of ye, he'll not be prevented from bidding on *yerself* next. In the meantime, I advise ye to mind yer manners." He placed an arm around Lily and ushered her a few steps farther away.

Shy, timid Lily pleaded silently with Rose, her soft silvery eyes clouded with fear.

Rose had to clamp her hands over her mouth to keep from crying out. This was all wrong. So wrong. The villainous captain had lied to her, to Papa. To all of them.

Durning again raised his voice to the gathering growing steadily in the midmorning sun. "This young lass is also of the merchant class. She's had the finest education a maiden of her advantages could receive. She can read and write and has been taught all the latest stitchery designs. She's a good-natured girl and quick to learn."

Unable to bear so many eyes upon her, Lily slid behind the captain. He dragged her forward again, this time holding her in place with a firm grip. "She may look a bit frail, I'll avow," he went on, "but I assure ye she didn't suffer a day of illness on the long voyage here. She's—"

"The little thing don't look like she'd stand up to much hard work," someone behind Rose challenged. "But I'll give ten pounds for her—if her teeth are sound."

Durning took hold of Lily's chin. "Open your mouth, girl. Let's have a look."

"How dare you!" Utterly insulted by the blackguard's thoughtless ill treatment of her poor sister and humiliated for her as well, Rose hoisted herself onto the stage, only to be immediately plucked off by the same ruffians who had restrained her moments before. She had no choice but to stand by as the younger girl closed her lashes over tears. Helplessly she watched them roll down her sister's pale cheeks. Her own followed suit.

Durning made a show of peering into Lily's mouth then smiled with benign assurance. "As perfect as the queen's own pearls, I must say."

"Ten pounds, one shilling."

The firm but gentle voice came from quite near Rose. Swiping the moisture from her eyes, she noted that this man did not wear the tailored clothing of a city businessman. Wearing plain-spun and simply made attire, he was rather tall and lean, with a build similar to that of their father. He had a kind face.

"Ten and two shillings," came from the vile man who'd wanted to see Lily's teeth.

Frowning, the man beside Rose reached into his pocket and pulled out a fistful of funds. He opened his hand, displaying a heavily calloused palm filled with paper and coin, which she counted silently along with him. Ten and six. He stepped forward. "Ten pounds, three shillings."

His competitor spoke again. "Eleven pounds. That's my final offer."

The gentle-voiced man's shoulders sagged. He glanced at Rose, his disappointment unmistakable. "I was hoping I could get a nice young girl like her for my Susan. She's been poorly for quite a spell now." He turned to leave.

The mere thought of the teeth-inspecting reprobate taking Lily away, having her at his mercy, was more than Rose could accept. She reached out and caught the kind-faced man's sleeve. "Bid more. Please."

He smiled sadly down at her. "I would if I could, miss. Alas, I cannot."

Before he finished speaking, Rose had one of her two precious pounds out of her small purse. She pressed it into his hands. "Please."

Moments later, to her everlasting gratification, she heard the captain award dear Lily to the gentle-faced man. She breathed a quick prayer of thanks. Her baby sister had been properly placed in a good home.

"Hie thyself up here, wench." Captain Durning's voice lacked even a smidgen of gentleness.

Consumed by concern for Lily, Rose had forgotten her own turn would come. She refused to budge.

The two ruffians hooted with laughter and hoisted her onto the platform.

She swung around to give them a piece of her mind but met only more guffaws and clapping from the onlookers. She'd become a spectacle. The morning's entertainment. How she wished she had contracted with a different ship's captain, but it was far too late for remorse. She clamped her jaws together and faced the lying, cheating peddler of flesh who had betrayed her trust.

As the laughter faded, Durning's singsong rang out across the crowd. "Now if ye want a full day's labor for yer money, this *spinster* here is the one ye're lookin' for. The female's five and twenty. In her prime. She's run an entire household since she was thirteen. Raised her four sisters and brothers, and ye've all seen how at least two of those lasses turned out." He cocked an eyebrow for emphasis.

Rose was sorely tempted to announce that she would give no buyer more than eleven pounds' worth of labor during the next four years—the six that Captain Durning paid her and five for the expense of her passage. She loathed the thought of that cur profiting any more than he already had. But no doubt the captain would lock her in the hold and carry out his threat. Should he cart her off to a different port, there'd be no way of keeping track of Mariah and Lily. How could she endure that? They needed her. Especially Mariah, whether or not the flirt would agree.

With her mind in such turmoil, it took a moment for Rose to become aware that every man within twenty yards was staring at her. Scores of eyes raked her from head to toe and back again. The prospective buyers nodded and chatted amongst themselves. A few pointed as they discussed her attributes.

These strangers in this strange land. . .appraising her worth.

Rose had never felt so exposed in her life. Or so helpless.

Chapter 3

T he wench's sisters may have virtues enough," a bystander hollered. "But this one's got the tongue of a fishwife!"

Laughter again erupted from the men gawking at Rose. They'd become a merry crowd, and at her expense. She struggled to retain what little dignity remained to her. If honoring a promise to one's parent and protecting one's family was termed being a "fishwife," so be it. She searched around for the two girls.

Lily stood near her new master, gazing up at Rose with heartfelt sympathy.

Mariah, however, seemed not in the least offended by the derisive levity aimed at her older sister. Her smile was as broad as anyone else's as she and her fancy gentleman-owner stood beside his elegant horse.

Once the revelry died down, the captain continued his spiel. "Ye've merely seen the woman act the way of any mother hen worth its feathers. She's tryin' to keep her little chicks tucked beneath her wings. Of the three of 'em, I'd say she's by far the most experienced worker." He paused. "Now, who'll give me a startin' bid?"

A newcomer attired in a gold-trimmed burgundy frock coat shouldered between two other prospective customers standing just below Rose. "I need to look over them hands of hers."

Rose was tempted to refuse, considering his request was only a little less degrading than being asked to display her teeth. Yet from the man's dress and expression, he appeared quite successful and even earnest, especially compared to the more seedy types who made up much of the gathering. She held out her trembling palms as he and several onlookers crowded closer to examine them.

"Look pretty soft to me," one commented.

"Aye," someone else agreed. "All three of them sisters are wearin' right fine frocks. Mayhap the lasses are more used to givin' orders than takin' 'em."

The captain let out a huff of disgust. "'Tis true, the Harwoods come from excellent stock on t'other side of the water. To see any of 'em put to work as mere scrubwomen would be a pure waste. This one in particular is accomplished in preparin' tasty foods. She can put every spice ever brought to the British Isles to proper use."

Rose found the captain's praise of her talents a bit excessive; nevertheless, she appreciated his generous words on her behalf. Cooking indeed had been the one household duty she truly enjoyed and had never relinquished to a servant.

A shout came from the left. "Fifteen pounds. A good English cook beats any of those Frenchies hired by folks over on the Potomac. Can't abide their runny sauces."

"Sixteen," another called out.

"Seventeen."

"Eighteen."

"Nineteen."

Bids came in such swift succession Rose could no longer ascertain the individuals speaking. Glancing at the captain, she realized the insufferable toad was actually deriving a perverse sort of pleasure from her distress. She clamped her teeth together, determined to bear the shameful outrage with fortitude.

A wagon rolled to a stop at the edge of the crowd, and the driver, an older man with a scraggly, graying beard rose to his feet. The ill-fitting clothes on his short and squat figure looked rumpled and soiled beneath the droopy-brimmed hat he wore. His high-pitched voice rang out above the din. "Did I hear tell the lass is a good cook?"

"Aye." Captain Durning nodded.

"I'll gi' ye fifty pounds fer her."

"Sold!" The captain allowed no time for reconsideration on the part of his customer.

Rose looked at Durning, who grinned like a pirate with a newly captured treasure on this most profitable of days. When he snagged her hand and dropped down to the splintery wharf, she lost her will to resist. Meekly she followed as he pulled her toward the wagon driver ambling his way through the crowd.

Close up, the squat newcomer looked even more shabby and unkempt. His ruffled shirt bore a profusion of smudges and food stains, and he reeked of sweat and other indefinable odors. Rose could not venture a guess as to when he'd last seen a bath, if ever. The mangy, untidy ne'er-do-well was to be her owner? How would she suffer such a fate? Her throat clenched as dismay crushed her soul.

Oblivious to the obnoxious smells resonating from the wagoneer, Captain Durning grasped the man's grubby hand and pumped it with fervor. "Come with me. I've a quill and ink on yon barrelhead. Once ye settle up, I'll give ye her papers to sign." He checked around and gestured to his other two successful buyers. "Ye men that bid on the other lasses come along, too."

Still held in Durning's strong grip, Rose woodenly followed the group now making their way to the barrels lining the customhouse.

Lily rushed over and hissed into her ear, "What are we to do, Rose? You cannot go with that foul man. He's—he's *horrid*."

Mariah whispered in her other ear, "We must not allow that disgusting creature to take you off to heaven knows where. I shall have Colin speak to the captain on your behalf."

"Colin, is it?" Rose swung toward her sister. "And I suppose *Colin* is already addressing you by your given name as well?" She could only wonder what philandering purpose the man had in mind when he'd purchased Mariah.

The other girl's lips drooped into a pout. "Upon my word, Rose. This is not the time for such trivial nonsense." In a rustle of taffeta, she whirled away to join the stylish gentleman and his bay stallion.

Rose traipsed after her. She would have a word with this *Colin* while the opportunity presented itself. Catching up with her sibling, she hooked an arm about Mariah's shoulders and stared up at the interloper. "Sir, before you sign my sister's papers, I'll thank you to relate exactly what duties will be expected of her in your employ."

Not at all intimidated by her question, the bounder smiled. "To be quite truthful, Miss Harwood, I have no duties in mind for her whatsoever. But I assure you, my mother shall be most pleased at my finding someone of your sister's refined qualities to be her companion."

His reply stunned Rose. "You. . .you bought her for your mother?"

"Why, yes. Of course. Surely you didn't think me the sort to have something else in mind for the lass." His forehead creased in amusement.

Surely she had, and in fact, still did. "Then I'm sure you will not mind pledging to see my dear, virtuous sister placed into your mother's watch-care before the sun sets this day. And you'll see to her religious instruction as well?"

"Rose!" Twin spots of color sprung forth on Mariah's indignant face, but her new master placed a staying hand on her arm and met Rose's gaze in all candor. "You have my most solemn word, miss."

"I thank you, sir. I shall rest easier knowing she is with trustworthy folk." From the pocket of her skirt she withdrew a shard of lead and a scrap of paper. "Might I ask where to post my sisterly correspondence? I should hate to lose touch with one of the only two relatives I possess on this continent."

He gave a polite nod. "To Barclay's Bay Plantation at Alexandria. On the Virginia side of the Potomac."

"Virginia? But isn't that another colony? How far away is your plantation?"

"Rest easy, miss. 'Tis within a day's ride."

"A day's ride?"

Mariah eased out of Rose's grasp and turned to Mr. Barclay. "Pray sir, forgive me, but I'm afraid my sister and I have a matter of much deeper concern. We must not let that swarthy old man take her. Would you please speak to the captain? Implore him to withdraw these proceedings?"

He grimaced slightly. "My dear Mariah, the man bid fifty pounds."

"Yes, I'm quite aware of that." She employed her most persuasive smile. "But if you would just try."

Colin Barclay shook his head with sad finality. "I regret to say all closing bids are final. I do find it rather astounding that one so unkempt should have that amount of ready cash. One can only wonder how he came by such funds."

Her last flicker of hope gone, Rose assured herself that her new owner could be set to rights easily enough with a bit of soap and some hot water. Very hot water and lots of it. But Mariah? She sighed and prayed fervently that Mistress Barclay would be a most conscientious guardian to her new charge.

Impulsive, flighty Mariah, an entire day's ride away.

And what about Lily? To what distance might she be taken? *Not so far, dear Lord. Please, not so far.*

Leaving Mariah and Mr. Barclay, Rose approached the farmer who waited in line for his turn with Captain Durning. "Sir, I trust you live nearby?"

"The name's John Waldon, miss. And may I express again my sincerest appreciation for your assistance." He cast a worried glance toward the uncouth fellow leaning over Rose's papers. "'Tis my deepest regret I was unable to return the favor. I've just come from building our new house up in Pennsylvania's Wyoming Valley. Within the week we'll be departing Baltimore."

"Wyoming Valley? Pennsylvania?" Rose's chest began to tighten beneath the heaviness pressing on her spirit. She had read of vast tracts of land existing in the Americas, but she'd been told most people lived along the seaboard. "Pray, good sir, how far from here is that? I'm afraid I'm not familiar with these colonies and how they relate to each other. I must know where my sister will be living."

The sadness she'd seen earlier when he'd mentioned his ill wife deepened. "Several days upriver, miss." He took her hand. "I wish it were closer. But I vow to you, your sister will be kindly treated in my household, and you may consider yourself most welcome to come visit us whenever your master can spare you."

The invitation was hardly comforting. Why had she ever agreed to allow the girls to accompany her to the colonies? Instead of beginning a new life together, the three of them were being scattered like chaff on the far winds. This was such a crucial time in their young lives, yet there'd be no seeing to her dear sisters' spiritual instruction if they did not dwell in close proximity to herself. Mariah, in all likelihood, could easily go astray.

Why has this horrid fate befallen us, dear Lord?

"Rose Harwood." The captain held out a plumed quill to her. "Step forward and put your name under Mr. Eustice Smith's."

The longest week of Rose's life dragged slowly by on the swift, dark currents of the Potomac River. A vast array of birds, many of which Rose had never seen before, soared and swirled overhead in the bluest of skies. Others flitted among the topmost branches of the trees lining the wide banks, their cheery twitterings barely penetrating her gloomy thoughts. Why were those insignificant creatures free of earth's constraints, while she was being carried farther into the unknown?

On either side of her, virgin forest tangled with such density she could scarcely peer more than a few feet into its growth. Strangely, as she rested atop several meal sacks in the confines of a cumbersome keelboat Mr. Smith had hired, the foliage—like great green walls, high and impenetrable—seemed almost protective, except when the feral screech of some unseen, unknown animal carried to her ears. Then the hairs on her arms stood on end.

Nevertheless, Rose resolved to remain as calm as the duck she spied floating in the shallows with a brood trailing placidly behind. Rose's composure was one of the few things she still clung to as the rough-hewn boat distanced her from everyone dear to her.

She and Mr. Eustice Smith were not entirely alone. The man had hired another riverboat like the one she was on, each being poled upriver by a crew of five—two on each side manning the poles and one at the rudder. Purposely tuning out the annoying din of unseen peepers and tree toads whose endless chorus filled the air, Rose disregarded the good-natured chatter exchanged by the men. She preferred the solitude of her thoughts, however depressing and hopeless they might be.

After the party had taken leave of Baltimore, she had felt safe enough as they passed the array of towns and settlements speckling the region. In between, there'd been vast plantations of tobacco fields. Great manor houses overlooked the river, attesting to the prosperity of the region. She couldn't help but wonder if Mariah would be dwelling somewhere among them.

Traffic at first seemed brisk on the busy waterway. But all too soon the river left the flatlands and began cutting through hill country. This morning she'd seen only one other string of rivercraft. The passing flatboats heading downstream were piled high with what she learned were beaver pelts. Such carnage, she mused, took place in those dark, distant woods—and all for making fashionable men's hats.

A thunderous boom roared across the water. Rose sprang to her feet and searched in all directions as the sound echoed back and forth between the ridges framing the narrow valley.

"Nothin' to fret about, missy." A shabby boatman walking his jammed pole to the rear of the boat nodded toward the noise and spit a brown streak of tobacco juice in that direction. "'Tweren't nothin' but a big ol' tree sayin' its last good-bye."

Rose sat down again, settling her charcoal gray skirt over her ankles. "I thank you for putting my mind at ease."

Her thanks sparked a grin from the rawboned man, his body straining as he maintained pressure on the pole. "Didn't want ye thinkin' a pack o' wild Injuns was swoopin' down on us."

"Indians! I thought the Indians sold all their land on this side of your mountains and moved out to the west."

"Aye," he grunted with a glance back at her. "They did. Fer the most part."

Rose chose not to linger on his last words or question him further, no matter how strong her curiosity. Being a lone woman among so many men, it seemed prudent to refrain from engaging them in conversation, even on the most basic of topics. From their uncommon interest in her every move, a person would think her as fascinating as Mariah.

With her sister once again on her mind, Rose had to admit it now seemed almost laughable how worried she had been that her siblings would be taken away from Baltimore. The irony that she was the one going who-knew-where was not lost on her. And after more than a week traversing this river, Rose had pressing questions for Mr. Smith—questions he seemed adept at sidestepping.

All she had learned from the evasive man was that he purchased her for the sole purpose of relieving his wife of mealtime chores—and that not out of kindness for his missus, but because he deplored the woman's cooking. He'd been extremely closemouthed as to the actual location of their home. She'd gleaned little more from him than the knowledge that the supplies stacked high for transport were to replenish his store. The vague address she'd been able to provide her sisters at their tearful parting was to write her in care of the Virginia and Ohio Company office in Alexandria. . .yet was not Alexandria one of the towns they'd left behind?

As the party traveled northward, Rose could only wonder if she was anywhere near where Lily would be living. But rather than poling into the settlement, the men veered onto the river's southern fork. There'd been no sign of civilization along the banks since. With every endless mile, Rose was being carried deeper into the wilderness.

And nothing could be done about that for four interminable years.

Seized by a sense of desperation, she searched ahead along both banks. If only Mr. Smith's store would soon come into sight, she might be positioned within a day of her baby sister—indeed even less if heading downstream in one of those narrow native boats the men called canoes. They seemed to glide by faster than a man could run.

It was high time she received a straight answer from the storekeeper. Rose hoisted herself off the sacks and, careful not to trip over her bothersome skirts, gingerly navigated toward the front of the keelboat, where the man sat. He could be found easily enough at any time of the day or night merely by following her nose, she conceded wryly. Surely when he reached their destination his wife would make certain he had a good soak in a bathtub. Rose yearned for that luxury herself. . .along with the safety of female company.

Her owner slouched on a crate, his hands clasped between his knees. With his floppy hat shading most of his face, he seemed to be searching ahead with intense interest.

She stopped and placed her feet apart to balance herself on the moving craft. "Mr. Smith, I should like a word with you, if I might."

He looked up and blinked. "Oh, good. Yer here." His high, thin voice rose in stark contrast to his coarse features. "We'll be dockin' 'round the next bend. It'll be the end of our ride on this here river, and I'll expect ya to haul off all that truck ya insisted on cartin' along with ya. I'll not be payin' the men extra fer that."

She bristled. "I've done so at every portage, sir, have I not?"

He grunted like a mean-tempered pig. For a man who had paid such a goodly sum for her person, he seemed unaccountably stingy in the matter of her belongings—one trunk and two valises, leaving her to lug and drag them along herself whenever necessary. But they were all she had left in this world, and she was not about to leave a single piece behind.

Suddenly the import of his last words struck her. "You say we're about to dock? Oh, splendid! Splendid!" Turning away, she could not suppress a huge grin, and she did not care if the other men misread it. They had arrived at last—mayhap she would be within a few days' journey of where at least one of her dear sisters would be located.

Even as Rose cautiously made her way to where her large black chest sat with the valises strapped on top, a horseshoe curve came into view. She could see a wide sandy strand stretching across its inward side, and fingering out from that, a sturdy deck. Two overturned canoes rested in the sand, a pleasing sight.

As the craft moved closer, Rose noticed that inland of the short pier lay a clearing dotted with log buildings, corrals, pens, and fenced pastures housing a number of horses and other animals. The tiny settlement appeared similar to the last place they'd stopped to unload and portage around a small waterfall, but here the current ran smoothly as far as the eye could see.

Beyond the clearing, an endless stand of thick forest closed off further view of the region. Could this isolated outpost be the location of Mr. Smith's store?

On land, an individual charged out on the dock, waving and yelling words that became somewhat jumbled as they echoed off the layered rock walls on the other side of the river.

The men pushing the poles hollered back, "Halloo the landing!" Laughing, they walked their poles toward the rear.

Rose saw people streaming out of the closest cabin and running to the dock. They wore dreary, coarse-spun shirts, and their sagging knee-high breeches met none-too-clean stockings.

With one exception. Tall, stalwart, and ruggedly built, a fine figure of a man strode forth. Appearing quite prosperous in a white ruffled shirt and brocade vest, which he wore with indifferent grace, he had a midnight blue frock coat draped over one arm.

Rose's spirits lifted. Perhaps there was a village of substance nearby after all. She glanced down at her simple linsey-woolsey spotted with pine pitch. She'd worn it for the past week to prevent spoiling any of her better gowns. Even the shawl collar she'd placed atop her bodice was her oldest. But perhaps the straw bonnet with its wide black ties was none the worse for wear and would add a bit of style. She sincerely hoped to make a good impression on Mr. Smith's good wife.

Nearing the dock, one of the crewmen tossed a rope to a waiting fellow who quickly looped it around a thick post and drew the craft alongside. The lumbering conveyance thudded against the pilings and shuddered heavily before another worker caught and fastened a second rope, snugging the rear of the vessel. The other keelboat was tied in similar fashion.

Mr. Smith and the crew hopped ashore and exchanged boisterous greetings with those on the landing.

To Rose's dismay, she saw a brown jug making swift rounds. She could only pray it contained cider. But spirited contents or no, the matter was out of her hands. With the men no longer underfoot, she took advantage of the moment and grabbed the handle of her trunk, dragging it toward the side.

Before she'd gotten halfway there, she felt the boat dip as someone came aboard. She looked up at the man attired in finer clothing who strode steadily toward her in his neat buckle shoes.

"If you please, miss." He kept his voice pleasingly low in timbre as he removed his three-cornered hat and placed it on a crate. "Let me be of assistance." A broad smile revealed straight, healthy teeth, and dark, softly curled hair framed sincere hazel eyes. A jovial crinkling of his brow further disarmed her. Rose found something quite stirring about his appearance. Even though his long face was far too rugged for genteel handsomeness, its hollows and angles had a compelling quality one could not easily dismiss. There was no way to guess his age. Not with skin bronzed by constant exposure to wind and weather. But despite his elegant attire, he carried a sense of recklessness about him, of adventure. And for some reason, the warm friendliness in his eyes made her sense instinctively that she could trust him.

She felt fleeting regret for having lacked foresight enough to begin the day in a more presentable fashion. For the first time since selling herself into bondage, she truly felt the part of the dowdy servant. She managed only a weak smile as the man continued to hold her in his gaze.

The breeze caught a tendril of her hair and whipped it across her cheek. With him staring so intently, should she brush the strand free of her lashes or pretend it didn't exist? Unaccountably light-headed under his scrutiny, she felt her heart quicken beneath her laced bodice.

He bent down and caught hold of the trunk handle with hands as hard and brown as those of any riverman she'd yet encountered. He seemed to Rose a man of substance, yet one unafraid of honest labor, and his assistance was more than appreciated. She preceded him off the boat.

With solid ground beneath her feet at last, Rose assessed the settlement more closely, noting the weathered but sturdy cabins speckled here and there within the wide clearing. Large corrals teemed with horses, while additional pens housed several cows. A few rumpled men and a ruddier individual who she assumed could easily pass for an Indian lurked about, watching the keelboats being unloaded. Aware of the more-than-interested attention her arrival caused the residents, she ignored their grins and suggestive stares and hiked her chin.

"You sir!" Mr. Smith hollered. "Stop!" Despite the straggly beard shrouding most of his face, the trader's displeasure was unmistakable, even from a distance.

Her chivalrous helper glanced over his shoulder. "You yammerin' at me, Eustice, you ol' river rat?" A lazy sort of American accent softened his rumbly voice.

Mr. Smith cocked his head, squinting in the glare of the sunshine. Then he let out a hoot. "Nate Kinyon? That you?"

"Aye. Headin' down to Conococheague to see if Ma's still holdin' up. It's been nigh two years or so since I was back that way."

"Well, you look purty enough t' be a reg'lar party cake."

Mr. Kinyon turned a shade redder above the ruffles at his throat, and a corner of his mouth quirked as he eyed the storekeeper. But he made no response. He hoisted the hefty trunk and the two valises onto his shoulder as if they weighed next to nothing and strode toward the front of the boat.

Trader Smith jabbed a stubby finger at him. "That's jes' what I meant. I want the girl to haul that truck off on her own."

Rose blanched as the onlookers ceased talking among themselves and centered their attention on her, each curious ear perked.

Either her rescuer didn't notice or he didn't care. Without hesitation he leaped onto the dock with her belongings.

Rose shriveled inwardly in discreet silence, knowing—hating—the next words sure to come out of Eustice Smith's mouth.

Her unaware hero, heavily muscled shoulders straining the brocade fabric of his vest, marched right up to the storekeeper and dropped the burden mere inches from his feet. "And why shouldn't I help the lass?"

Rose's throat began to close.

"'Cause she's a stiff-necked female, that's why. Needs to be taught a thing or two."

Knowing Mr. Smith wouldn't leave the matter half told, Rose wished she could crawl inside her trunk and close the lid. In truth, there was no shame in insisting on what few rights she had, or even in being a bondservant. The difficulty lay in making herself believe that.

One of the raftsmen butted in. "She belongs to Smith, Nate. He bought the woman to cook fer him."

Mr. Kinyon's square jaw went slack, and he looked from the storekeeper to her.

Rose detected a subtle change in the way he now viewed her, and she abhorred it. But what could she say? Every word was true. She'd been purchased like any other sack of goods off the ship.

The man's brows knitted over a sharp gaze that seemed to pierce right through her. Then he leveled a glare at Mr. Smith. "He's jestin', right?"

The storekeeper took a small step back. For the first time since she laid eyes on the little man, he seemed unsure of himself. Then he stiffened. "Paid good money for her, Nate. Hard cash. The contract says I'm to provide her with food, shelter, an' two sets of clothes a year. And at the end of her four years, she gits sent on her merry way with a month's supplies an' four pounds sterling. The papers didn't mention nothin' about where that food and shelter was to be provided."

What did he mean, where? Rose trembled as a chill ran down her spine. Something was very wrong. She somehow found her voice. "Where exactly are you taking me, Mr. Smith?"

"Nowhere, that's where." Towering head and shoulders above Mr. Smith, Nate Kinyon widened his stance and challenged her sulky owner with a withering glower. "You ain't takin' this pretty little lass no three hundred miles into Indian country. An' that's that."

Chapter 4

Rose's blood turned cold. *Indian country!* Her lips fell open, and her arms dropped like rocks to her sides. Her gaze darted from Trader Smith to Nate Kinyon and back again. "Surely you're not considering taking me off to where wild Indians live. I cannot— You cannot—"

Smith's slitted eyes hardened. "I can an' I will. An' you can an' you will. You have no say in the matter, seein' as how yer bought an' paid for." He turned to Nate. "My stomach's gone right sour on me lately. I'm in sore need of some good English puddin's an' such to sweeten it up. You can understand that. Hear tell she's a real good cook."

Astonishment clouded Mr. Kinyon's expression, and his jaw went slack. "You mean to say you're draggin' this gentle lass all the way out to that tradin' post of yours just so she can make you up some puddin'? That's plumb crazy, Eustice. Plumb crazy."

"It ain't neither." He bristled, a sneer twisting his grizzled face. "You must not a'heard, but me and my partner, we ain't been hittin' it off these days like we used to. So Branson's fixin' to set up his own post down on the Little Kanawha."

Nate frowned and tucked his chin in disbelief. "How can he do that? I happen to know the fur company requires two men to be posted at each store. Besides, what's that got to do with puddin'?"

The trader sniffed in disdain, as if Nate possessed the thickest skull since the dawn of time. "He's the only one what could make it right—when we was able to get ahold of some milk. But I seen to that." He gestured toward the penned cows.

Nate glanced in the direction indicated. "I did hear you was takin' them beasts overmountain with you. Ought'a be a challenge, I'd say." He smirked.

Her irritation mounting as she stood by listening to the bizarre turn of the conversation, Rose planted her fists on her hips. "Pudding! Cows! I cannot believe any of this. It's simply not to be endured."

"Quiet, woman!" The trader returned his attention to Kinyon. "Me an' Branson figgered we wouldn't say nothin' to the comp'ny. More profit for us both that way. 'Sides, I got my wife's brothers to help me keep an eye on the place."

Kinyon kneaded his chin. "Looks like you two have things all worked out between you, then." He shook his head, appearing to mull something over in his mind. "Well, think on this. What say I get you a couple puddin' recipes an' trade 'em an' whatever you paid for the woman—plus a little profit, a'course—an' that'll make us all happy. How much *did* you lay out for her, anyway?"

For one brief moment, Rose felt a ray of hope that this trustworthy-looking man wanted to save her from her fate. Then she realized she was merely being bartered for again. Hopelessly outmatched, she gave a huff and turned in proud defiance to stride away.

Smith grabbed her arm, halting her midstep, and glared at Nate. "Even if the gal was for sale at any price—and she ain't—when did you ever have fifty pounds jinglin' in that pouch of yourn, I'd like ta know?"

"Fifty pounds?" Kinyon hiked his brows. "You paid fifty pounds for her?" He eyed Rose up and down with an intensity that made her cringe.

Humiliated beyond belief, Rose knew she must look a fright, having worn the same clothes for days. Even her once-fashionable hat was droopy, and when had she last run a brush through her tangled hair? She lowered her gaze to her hands, noticing that Smith's grubby fingers still gripped her arm. She felt as if she was in the middle of a nightmare—only this bad dream was all too real and had barely begun. Hearing the jingling of some coins, she raised her lashes, not entirely ready to relinquish all hope.

Nate Kinyon emptied his leather pouch into his open palm, fingering through the contents as he mentally tallied the sum. "I can give you eleven pounds, two shillings, sixteen Spanish dollars, and four bits on account. How's that? I'll have the rest next spring after trappin' season." He stole a quick glance at Rose then looked at the trader. "I'm good for it. You know I am."

Smith gave a dubious half smirk, a sly spark in his beady eyes. "I'm sure ya are. Only those promises won't do my innards one lick'a good." He shifted his stance and glanced around the settlement. "So where's that huntin' partner of yourn? Thought you two was joined at the hip."

He shrugged. "Black Horse Bob ain't comin' out with me. Right now he's over playin' cards with some of your boys. Said he'd wait there till I get back."

Nodding, Smith cocked his head. "You two'd have more spendin' money if you'd stop throwin' it away at cards. Never did put much stock in gamblin' meself."

A sheepish hue tinged the tips of Kinyon's ears as he looked at Rose. He straightened to his full height. "Spent most of my purse on these city duds I'm sportin'. Didn't want Ma to think I'd gone all woodsy."

Surmising that someone with the name "Black Horse Bob" must have a long, horsey-looking face, Rose peered over the tall man's shoulder and up the bank toward the buildings, trying to spot someone of that description. A jolt of alarm whipped through her when she saw as many Indians as white men milling about now—heathens who, she'd heard, scalped people, skinned them, and ate their hearts. A nervous chill went through her.

Oddly enough, no one else seemed uneasy. She drew a measure of comfort from that. Perhaps the things she'd heard back in England were just talk. After all, Mr. Smith wouldn't be so interested in acquiring a "puddin' maker" if living in Indian country was so very dangerous. His own wife was there, wasn't she? Nevertheless, Rose couldn't help recalling Mr. Kinyon's words: *"You ain't takin' this pretty little lass no three hundred miles into Indian country."*

Indian country. Three hundred miles from civilization.

More than three hundred miles from her sisters.

Lily. Mariah. Stark despair crept into Rose's heart.

Bringing the discussion to a timely end, Trader Smith pivoted on his heel and started up the sloped bank from the river as the boatmen traipsed back and forth, toting cargo off the vessels and piling it in stacks. He raised his voice to a yell. "One of ya go fer the horses I bartered for. We still got half a day's light left, an' we need all of it."

Horses! As if she hadn't endured sufficient indignities already, the sickening dread that now she'd be expected to continue this journey on horseback sank into Rose's heart with a thud. She'd never been on a horse in her life—not even Timmy's pony, Corky. She didn't have the slightest notion how to climb in skirts and petticoats way up onto some hairy, smelly beast and perch there for some interminable length of time, much less control the animal and make it go in the right direction.

"Hey! Bondwoman!" Smith's nasally voice cut into her musings. "Git yerself an' that truck of yourn up here. Time's a'wastin'.' "

Swallowing her angst, Rose felt an empathetic hand come to rest on her shoulder.

"Don't worry about your things. I'll fetch 'em for you." Nate Kinyon turned then swung back around. "Did Eustice speak true? Did he actually pay fifty pounds for you?" A skeptical dip of his straight brows indicated disbelief.

"Aye. He did indeed, sir."

Kinyon pursed his lips in thought. "For that skinflint to lay out that kind of money for a cook, that stomach of his must be worse off than he says. Not that a good cook wouldn't be worth a hefty price, mind you, if a fellow has it to pay." He glanced up the hill at the trader occupied with stacks of unloaded cargo. "Still, he just shoulda hired a man, is all." He reached down for her belongings and hefted them onto his shoulder.

Not bothering to agree with sentiments that matched her own, Rose had little choice but to follow after her rescuer. Creepy chills made the hairs on the backs of her arms prickle when they passed close by sullen-looking Indians who made no effort to disguise their meaningful ogling as they followed her with their eyes. She could only imagine what the guttural sounds passing between them were saying about her. She straightened her spine and clung to whatever composure still remained as they reached one of the packhorses.

Nate cut her a sidelong glance and set her luggage on the ground. "Don't fret yourself about the Indians, miss. Smith forked over quite a purse for you. He's not about to let no one give you trouble. Soon's I get back from my family's homestead, I'll come out an' check on you myself. Who knows? I might be able to talk some sense into him by then."

Rose didn't know how to respond. This strange land, these strange people with their unknown language, and the fearsome possibilities lying ahead filled her with trepidation. Everything was happening so fast. Nothing was under her control. She was completely at the mercy of Eustice Smith. Nevertheless, she raised her lashes and met Kinyon's kind gaze. "I do thank you for your concern, Mr. Kinyon. 'Tis most appreciated, I assure you."

A gentle smile tweaked the corners of his mouth. "An' I thank you for bein' such a pleasurable sight for these poor, deprived eyes. We don't get to see many womenfolk out here in these parts."

Nor had she. Her sisters were the last women she'd spoken to since the three of them had stepped onto colony soil, adding even more to her loneliness. "No doubt you'll see many more pleasing sights as you travel back into civilization. I shall pray for your safety, as I allow you'll pray for mine."

He opened his mouth as if to reply then rubbed his jaw. "Hmm. Well.

Sure thing, lass. Oh, by the by, what might I call you, if you don't mind my askin'?"

"Miss Harwood. Rose Harwood. And if perchance you should happen to pass through the Wyoming Valley settlements, where my sister Lily has been bonded to a family by the name of Waldon—or travel by Alexandria, where my other sister Mariah is to live on the Barclay Plantation—please be kind enough to inform them you've seen me and that I am. . .safe." *So far, at least,* her mind added as a leering Indian moved noiselessly past her.

Mr. Kinyon tilted his head. "I hadn't planned on goin' downstream as far as Alexandria, but if it'd help you rest easier, I'll make every effort to do so. As for the other lass, I fear goin' off in that direction ain't in my plans right now."

Shoulders sagging in disappointment, Rose knew she'd asked too much of the man, however kind he might seem to be. "That valley. . .'tis farther upstream, then?"

"Well, miss, it's upstream, that's the truth of it, but we're not talkin' this stream. She'll be near the Susquehanna River, likely somewheres around the Wilkes-Barre settlement."

The news quenched Rose's spirits. "Where is that river? I believe Mr. Waldon spoke of it being near Baltimore."

"If I had my map on me, I could show you that the mouth of the Susquehanna is a mite north of Baltimore, an' the Potomac dumps into the bay a few miles south of the city. From its headwaters up in New York, the Susquehannah flows right through Pennsylvania an' on into Maryland. What we're standin' in is Virginia territory."

"Oh my." It was too much to take in, and her mind whirled with the realization of the immeasurable distance that likely would stretch between her and the other girls. Her throat closed up with disappointment, and tears sprang to her eyes, trembling upon the tips of her lashes. She could hardly speak. "The last thing I told our papa before we sailed for these colonies was that I wouldn't let them out of my sight." She cast a despondent glance in the direction of the river that had already carried her far, far from Mariah and Lily. "I promised. Made a solemn pledge that I'd remain strong in my faith and look after them. Somehow I must keep my word."

Kinyon raised a calloused hand and squeezed her shoulder. "Are you sayin' you only just got here from across the water? I vow you're a long way from home, Miss Harwood. But I hope you'll take comfort from knowin' you'll never be outta my thoughts."

Just then Eustice Smith's boots clomped toward them over the uneven ground. "Thought you was on your way downstream, Nate. Ain't that what ya said?"

Aware that Mr. Kinyon's gaze remained on her damp eyes, Rose lowered hers.

"Aye, that I am. That I am." He let go of her shoulder and closed his fingers around one of her hands, and she felt a strange combination of strength and gentleness as he lifted her hand to his lips. "Till we meet again, pretty lass." A last long look and he took his leave.

Rose could not bear to watch him go.

Plunked unceremoniously by her owner atop a mammoth beast with a tangled mane of hair, Rose had no idea how she was supposed to steer it. Fortunately the animal seemed to know what was expected, as it followed Mr. Smith's horse behind the settlement and into a forest of thick trees sporting every shade of green imaginable. Only the palest semblance of sunlight, obscured and fragmented by the canopy of leafy branches overhead, lit the trail. . .a trail so primitive it was hardly more than a deer path.

Rose stole a last backward glance toward the river, where the solicitous Mr. Kinyon had paddled away in one of those swift canoes less than an hour ago. Even though she'd barely met the man, she realized he was the first person who had befriended her in these colonies, and now he, too, was gone—just like Mariah and Lily. Here she was: a lone woman perched on a smelly creature with her smelly master and six equally smelly Indians—*Indians!*—traveling a brush-lined trail leading into the vast, deeply shadowed wilderness to some unknown destination. Would she ever feel truly safe again? As the party plodded along in silence, she resigned herself to her disheartening fate, praying for the grace to endure whatever lay ahead.

Her thoughts reverted back to her arrival at the tiny river settlement a scant two hours ago, to meeting Nate Kinyon. From the first moment he stepped into her life, he'd shown nothing but kindness. . .the only modicum of human decency she'd encountered since disembarking the ocean vessel. She'd felt instinctively that he had a trustworthiness about him, that he was a man of his word. He'd said he'd come to Mr. Smith's store and try again to rescue her. The promise in his voice, in his eyes lingered in her heart after he walked away.

Even now she replayed the scene in her mind, allowing it to fill her with hope. Was it possible that the Lord sent him for the very purpose of reuniting her with Mariah and Lily? Or had he merely acted the part of a gentleman to go along with his fine clothes? Perhaps this whole predicament was the Almighty's punishment for rashly having taken control of her family's situation without so much as a prayer for wisdom and guidance, and now God was leaving her to stew in this mess she'd brought on herself and her sisters. The possibility was too horrid to dwell on, and her heart ached with the pain of loss.

Not liking the direction her thoughts were taking, Rose turned around and met the face of the feathered savage directly behind her. Clad in buckskin trousers similar to Mr. Smith's, he wore no shirt but had a decorative thing made of colored beads around his neck. His hair, parted in the middle, had been plaited and tied with leather strips.

In the shadowed foliage, the mounted Indian appeared darker than ever as a sly, unpleasant smirk brought a sinister glint to his coal-black eyes.

Rose pretended not to notice and gazed beyond him to the rest of the pack train traversing along a path so narrow it could accommodate only a single horse at a time. Each of the five Indian riders trailed a string of four loaded animals behind them. Taking up the rear, another whip-wielding Indian, this one in buckskin trousers and an open buckskin vest, drove a bull, two cows, and a calf. Feathers adorned his braided hair, also. For such a ragtag, motley party of travelers, they made quite an impressive assemblage, Rose decided. Perhaps Mr. Smith's establishment was not nearly so primitive as he and his native helpers appeared.

The Indian at the rear gave a smart crack of his whip, and Rose jumped at the unexpected sound. The rider behind her chuckled under his breath, adding to her already strained nerves. She sat up straighter, determined not to appear like some weak, simpering female as they forged ever deeper into woods so thick with growth hardly a breath of wind stirred through the treetops.

A spot on one of her thinly pantalooned legs began to chafe. Not wanting to draw undue attention, she casually tucked a bit of petticoat between the hard leather saddle and her knee. Traveling at this slow pace had enabled her to adjust quickly enough to riding horseback, but she feared the animal's swaying and bumping would inevitably take its own toll.

Suddenly from off to the side, wild snapping and cracking echoed through the dense brush. Rose's heart pounded, and she tightened her grip on the saddle's pommel. A doe plunged out of the growth in a blur of brown, missing her by mere inches as it leaped across the trail and clattered into the undergrowth on the other side.

Some other wild creature must be chasing after it! Rose held her breath, waiting, listening, but when she heard nothing but the blowing and *clop-clop* of the horses, the straining of leather, and an occasional birdcall or tree toad, her panic eased. Ahead of her, Mr. Smith continued on as though nothing out of the ordinary had occurred, while she still trembled from head to foot—and this journey into the notorious unknown had only just begun.

A familiar phrase popped into her mind. *"Yea, though I walk through the valley of the shadow of death. . ."*

That's where I'm going, dear Lord. As she felt herself losing the last shred of control, she recalled the rest of the verse: *"I will fear no evil: for thou art with me."*

Are You with me, Father? Will You come with me into this dark, mysterious land? Please don't forsake me, Lord. I'm so alone.

Chapter 5

The woodland trail made a gradual ascent to higher ground as the afternoon slipped away. Now and then an occasional break in the dense forest growth provided Rose with a brief glimpse of a nearby stream paralleling the trail. Occasionally she heard disturbing and unfamiliar wild cries emanating from deep in the forest on either side. Determined not to let them affect her, she governed her emotions and watched Mr. Smith for his reaction. Nothing seemed to disturb him.

His horse whinnied then, as did the others. The trader reined his animal to a stop and pulled a pistol out of his belt.

Rose's horse came automatically to a stop behind Mr. Smith's, its ears perked and flicking from side to side. Rose tensed, wishing she had a firearm of her own for protection. She detected the sound of hooves coming toward them from the opposite direction and turned to glance at the Indian in back of her.

He, too, had drawn a weapon. A big, long musket.

From around a curve rode two bearded, scraggly, lean men attired in the fringed garb Rose had become used to seeing since her arrival in the backcountry. They also held weapons at the ready.

"That you, Smith?" the lead rider hollered. "Thought fer sure the buzzards had picked them bones o' yers clean by now."

"It's me, all right. An' still in the flesh, to boot." He tucked away his pistol. "You boys headed in to spend yer money?"

The man in front grinned, drawing up alongside Mr. Smith. "That's the plan. Gonna have me a high ol' time with—" Catching sight of Rose, his mouth gaped open. "Horsefeathers, Eustice. You got yerself a young white woman there!"

He straightened in the saddle and lifted his bearded chin. "No. What I got me is a cook there. An' don't none of you yahoos forget it."

Dragging his eyes off Rose, the man swung around to the rider in back of him. "You see that? Smith's got hisself a—a cook!" Turning again to the trader, his mouth went into a slack grin. "If'n you say so."

"I do." His tone took on a defensive edge, and no smile softened his demeanor. "The gal's me bondservant, bought an' paid for with hard cash."

"Well, I'll be dogged." The newcomer's eyes raked over Rose in a slow survey. "Where 'bouts could a body find a cook like that, I'd like ta know."

"On the docks in Baltimore. That's where." The trader nudged his mount into motion and maneuvered it around the first rider. "Don't have no time to chew the fat with you boys. We're losin' daylight. See y'all later."

Rose's horse started dutifully behind him. As she passed the riders, she was extremely conscious of the way they filled their eyes with her as if they hadn't seen a female in years. But then, all she'd seen for the past several days was men. The sight of another woman would be just as welcome to her. She'd be glad to reach Mr. Smith's store and meet his wife. She was in dire need of feminine companionship herself at this point.

In the waning daylight, Mr. Smith guided his mount off the path and into a small, level clearing, where he came to a stop. He swung down and approached Rose. "We'll make camp here fer the night. My stomach's not farin' so good. I'll have the boys get a fire started fer ya an' fetch the fixin's fer some mush whilst you go milk the fresh cow."

Still perched on her horse, Rose swept a glance around. "I'm sorry. I don't see a place to cook in."

With an incredulous grimace that scrunched up one side of his scruffy face, he shrugged. "Place! There ain't no place. Just pick a spot." He shook his head in disgust.

She stared dumbly down at the man. "Surely you're not saying we'll be staying here! On the ground!"

"That's right, missy. Right here on the ground. Now get yerself down. I'm hungry." He started to walk away.

"Wait!" Rose tried to come up with some graceful way of getting off her mount while renewed panic filled her. "I'm not sure I know what mush is, and I've never milked a cow before in my life."

Smith stopped in his tracks and turned to gawk at her then narrowed his eyes. "Ya said ya was a cook. Were ya gullin' me?"

"No, sir. Not at all."

"Then it's best ya get busy, ain't it?" He reached up without so much as a by-your-leave and hauled her right off the horse.

It was most fortunate that he kept hold of her momentarily, because her legs felt really strange after riding on a saddle all afternoon. It was all she could do not to sink to the ground in a graceless heap. Doing what she could to gather herself together, she gave him her most forthright look. "I daresay I'm considered quite a fine cook. . .in an actual kitchen. . .with milk already waiting in a pail. And what, might I ask, is mush?" She waved aside a pesky fly.

The trader rolled his eyes and muttered something unintelligible under his breath as he wagged his head in scorn—actions he repeated numerous times over the course of the next quarter hour while he demonstrated how to dispense milk from a cow's udder.

Rose found the squeeze-and-pull chore a touch more difficult than it looked—especially with so many muscles in her lower regions aching while she stooped. And the fact that her Indian audience grinned and snickered at her clumsy efforts didn't make it any easier. Apparently they considered her as inept as Mr. Smith did—these Indians who were supposed to be so dangerous. Though she still felt a bit ill at ease in their presence, they had yet to do anything threatening other than leer in her direction from time to time. Again she concluded that their exploits must have been exaggerated back in England. She purposely disregarded them and continued doing her best while they unloaded several items from the packhorses. She was glad to have a bit of space between her and them. Whenever they were near, she detected a stench she couldn't identify.

After she'd managed to acquire a reasonable amount of milk from the soft-eyed cow, Mr. Smith directed Rose to a blazing campfire, where a tripod fashioned from sturdy sticks held a blackened pot suspended above the heat.

"Watch." If he'd said that once during the last half hour, he'd said it a dozen times. He poured water from his flask into the kettle then opened a gunnysack slumped nearby along with several others. More than a little exasperated, he rammed his filthy hand into the bag and pulled out a fistful of gritty yellow powder. "Cornmeal." Eyeing her pointedly, he tossed the grain into the pot then added a second handful.

It took all of Rose's fortitude to restrain herself from giving the man a piece of her mind, but knowing it would be wiser to hold her tongue, she clamped her lips together. After all, she needed no reminder that she was in the middle of nowhere—a lone female with seven men—a precarious situation if ever there was one.

The trader grabbed a stick from a pile of kindling off to the side and rubbed it across his grubby pants as if that would do more to clean it than recent rains could have done, then used it to stir the contents of the pot. After that, she surmised, he no doubt expected her to eat the nasty mess.

"See?" Straightening from the fire, he turned to her with a smug grimace. "Nothin' to it. Course it'll need a pinch o' salt, an' I'm partial to some sweetenin'. After the water boils down some, pour in some o' that rich milk. That's all there is to it. Mush." He handed Rose the stir stick. "Just don't let it get lumpy."

Determined to remain in the man's good graces, Rose spoke in a casual tone. "I'll do my best. But where might I find the salt and sugar?"

He squinted as if his patience had reached the painful limit and stepped directly in front of her, his foul breath almost smothering her. She held her ground despite the inclination to step back from the stench. "Don't try playin' dumb with me so's I'll send ya back, gal. It ain't gonna happen." He kicked at another large sack. "Salt." And the one next to it. "Sugar." With a "humph" of disgust, he stomped away to where the Indians were rigging tarps between trees.

Despite her intentions not to upset the trader any more than necessary, Rose gulped in dismay. Surely those flimsy bits of cloth would not constitute their only shelter for the night! The very thought made her ill. Mosquitoes had voracious appetites after dark, and already she had more bites than she could count. Each evening during the trip upriver, the trader had managed to secure food and lodging for the party at various villages along the way, so they'd been protected from insects. Tonight would be different.

How many more nights in the open lay ahead? Small wonder that when she questioned him about their destination he'd been so vague. The man was scarcely more than a sneaky weasel. But then she was probably every bit as stupid as he thought she was. Hadn't she gotten herself in this untenable predicament in the first place? Even convicts balked at being sent to America as indentured servants to pay their sentences. She should have thought of that before undertaking such a rash course of action. Had she saved her father from prison only to condemn herself to an even worse fate?

As another mosquito sang in her ear, she swatted it away.

Observing her action, the trader chuckled. "If ya ask one o' them Injuns fer some o' that bear grease they smear on their bodies, ya won't have none o' them bugs botherin' ya."

Bear grease. So that accounted for the stench around them. Rose didn't respond.

~~~

Assorted night sounds magnified in the fading twilight around the camp, adding to Rose's heightened anxiety as she tried to dislodge a piece of dried meat from between her teeth with her tongue. Losing a battle with persistent mosquitoes that seemed drawn to the light, she appreciated the swift bats cavorting overhead, making a meal of the loathsome insects. Across the fire from her, Mr. Smith sipped from a tin mug of steaming tea, straight from a beat-up old pot, leaves and all. She ignored his steady perusal of her, unable to envision what tasteless gruel he expected her to concoct next.

He pointed with a grubby finger toward one of the stained tarps now stretched out about three feet above the rocky, leaf-strewn ground. The poorest excuse for a red blanket she had ever seen had been tossed beneath, apparently for her use. "Over there's where you'll bed down fer the night."

Rose slid a troubled glance from the makeshift bed to the Indians crouched around another campfire a scarce stone's throw away.

Smith gave a snort. "Don't bother frettin', little missy. Them redskins know yer my property, an' they'll think twice b'fore triflin' with anything what b'longs to me."

Thus far the trader had shown no inclinations of a trifling nature either, but Rose dreaded having to attempt sleeping on hard ground that in all likelihood would be damp and lumpy with rocks. Far worse, that disgusting blanket quite possibly housed lice, bedbugs—or some other night-crawling vermin known only to the colonies. A shiver coursed through her at the unwelcome possibility.

Thankful she'd had foresight enough to pack some necessities for the journey from England, Rose got up from the chest she'd used for a seat and dragged it over to the tarp. She'd use the scant bedding she'd brought with her, along with her cloak, to ward off the night chill. Her shawl would do for a pillow, and the trunk itself would provide whatever privacy she could hope for in such a situation. As to whether she'd get a wink of sleep in the company of so many strange men was yet to be determined—especially with unseen forest creatures prowling about. After heading for a nearby bush to answer nature's call, she returned to her designated sleeping spot, swallowing her fear as the mournful howl of wolves filtered through the trees.

Surely Mr. Smith and the others would keep their weapons at the ready, she assured herself as she tried to ignore the incessant chirping of crickets. The men seemed to be used to making their way through the wilderness. Down on her knees while she created her own small haven in the dark, Rose heard the hobbled horses in the meadow whinny as they'd done that afternoon, when they'd signaled the approach of riders. She paused in her work and peered over her trunk.

Mr. Smith snatched up his musket and stepped out of the glow of the campfire, and the Indians melted silently into the shadows.

Rose's pulse throbbed in her throat. She'd heard tales of land pirates— and of savage Indians who tortured and murdered unsuspecting folks. Now she could only wait to see what sort of fate awaited this camp in the wilds. The temperature had dipped lower once the sun was no longer dominating the daytime hours, and a cool, pine-scented breeze wafted through the clearing, adding to her shivers.

"Halloo the camp!" came a shout from the direction of approaching horse hooves. "It's us. Nate Kinyon and Black Horse Bob."

Releasing a slow breath, Rose eased up in her hiding place behind the trunk as Mr. Smith and the Indians moved back into the firelight, their weapons now lowered. The silhouettes of two riders on horseback, followed by a couple of packhorses, met her eyes. And foolish though she knew it was, Rose had never been so glad to see anyone in her life.

Mr. Smith, however, appeared none too pleased to have visitors. His expression in the erratic firelight resembled a scowl as the two riders in fringed buckskin dismounted. Rose couldn't discern the newcomers' features in the dark, but she recognized the taller of the pair as Mr. Kinyon. She focused on his familiar form, still appealing and muscular in the brushed leather clothing as he towered over her owner.

"Thought you was headed downriver," the trader said, his tone somewhat accusing.

Kinyon shrugged, moving closer into the fire glow. "Been gone from home so long I figgered Ma wouldn't recognize me anyway."

Rose noticed that the other frontiersman wore dark braids and had a lithe build similar to those of the Indians at the other fire. He gave a hearty whack to Kinyon's back. "'Specially in them fancy duds. Ol' Nate looked like one of them parrots I once saw down in York Town. All bright colored and struttin' up an' down on some ol' sea captain's shoulder like he was the king of the realm."

Apparently still put off by their unexpected arrival, Mr. Smith gave a grudging grunt at the man's levity.

Mr. Kinyon swept a glance around in the darkness, taking measure of the camp. "Where's our Miss Harwood, Eustice?"

"She ain't *your* anything," the trader rasped. "Don't be gettin' any notions about her in yer head. But seein' as how you two are here, yer welcome to stay. The more weapons the better."

Listening to the exchange, Rose felt silly crouched down in the shadowed confines of the tarp, but she wasn't certain it would be prudent to stand and present herself.

Mr. Smith made the decision for her. "As fer my cook, my property, she's already abed." He didn't bother to gesture in her direction.

The braided fellow tilted his dark head. "Now that's a real shame. I was lookin' forward to seein' this *property* of yours. Reckon it can wait'll mornin'. Think I'll mosey over and see what our Shawnee brothers think of the new gal. That might be pretty interestin'." He flashed an amused grin.

Rose watched from her haven as the man left his friend and joined the Indians sitting cross-legged around the other campfire. From what she could tell in the limited light, he appeared to have a darker complexion than either Smith or Kinyon. Possibly he was an Indian himself, though the easy way he had of speaking like a white man surprised her. She returned her attention to the trader and their other visitor.

"I drunk up most of the tea, but I believe there's some dregs left in the pot," Smith said. "There's cups in that sack by yer foot."

Deciding his tone had taken on a smidgen of friendliness, Rose eased down on her makeshift bed and laid her head on her wadded-up shawl. An owl hooted from not far away, and as she leaned out from the tarp toward the sound, her breath caught at the beauty of the night sky. Millions of stars twinkled like diamonds against the cobalt blue, reminding her of the awesome power of God and His tender care for His creation. She hoped He hadn't forgotten her and her plight. Deep in thought, she breathed in the night air bearing traces of woodsmoke, damp earth, and the ever-present pine.

The firelight reflecting on the tarp was blocked momentarily then reappeared as Mr. Kinyon moved between her sleeping spot and the fire to settle down with her owner. "Don't s'pose you heard anything new from up New York way while you was down in Baltimore."

"Like what?"

"I don't know. I'm just wonderin', since the French sent that large force down from Fort Frontenac on the Ontario. Hear tell they're plannin' to build forts down as far as the Ohio. The Federation's gettin' real nervous."

"You talkin' the Iroquois Federation? What difference would it make to them, I'd like ta know. If anybody should start worryin', it should be us English traders."

"The Mohawks especially are concerned about the Senecas. Pretty much all the Seneca villages have pulled up stakes an' are now hangin' out at the French posts. Lots of gifts an' promises have been made to 'em. The other tribes are afraid the French'll woo 'em into attackin' the English tradin' posts along the rivers."

Listening to the news, Rose edged forward a bit and tugged her cloak more closely around herself. She'd hoped the conflict between the Indian tribes and the settlers had eased long ago as the colonies became more populated.

Kinyon continued in his even tone. "Since the Federation chiefs signed agreements to support the English, you'd better believe they ain't happy. If there's trouble, they say they won't attack their Seneca brothers. They figure that'd destroy their own treaties."

The trader snorted. "Aw, just more of the same ol' gossip. Most of the Iroquois tribes are partial to our trade goods. They'll stick with us.

'Sides, it don't have nothin' to do with me. My store's in a Shawnee town. Way south of all that squabblin' betwixt the governor of New York an' the Frenchies."

Shawnee town? Weren't the Shawnee a tribe of Indians? Why, that awful man was carting her off to the wilds to live in an Indian town! Rose's spirits sank to a new low. Each piece of information she'd heard this day was worse than the one before. She settled into her uncomfortable, lumpy bed, her thoughts awhirl in her head. This whole thing had to be a really bad dream. Soon she'd wake up to find all would be well.

Lord God in heaven, please make this circumstance merely a horrible nightmare. Ever since Mother passed away, I've been faithful to do my duty. I took care of my family just as I was supposed to. I ran a fine household. I lived the life You ordained. But now. . .I feel as if I've been thrown out to be devoured by wolves.

Hot tears trailed down her cheeks, and Rose curled into a ball, pulling her cloak over her head. It was bad enough having had to dispose of treasured family possessions and be forced to leave her beloved homeland to endure endless days of seasickness and weeks on a ship tossed about on angry waves. Then to be humiliated before leering strangers on an auction block and parted from her sisters for an interminable time. But now this! This was far worse. Here she was in the midst of some frightful, unknown wilderness with an uncouth man dragging her off to a village of heathens who spoke a tongue she did not understand—and who might invariably decide to murder her in the end. What had she done to deserve such a horrid fate?

Chapter 6

A cacophony of birdsong drew Rose out of deep slumber. Surmising she must have left the window open, she snuggled deeper into her warm haven for a few more moments of sleep before rising to prepare breakfast for her family.

The raucous *rat-a-tat-tat* of a woodpecker brought her fully awake, to the realization that there was no window, there was no family. She was in the middle of nowhere, a lone woman in a camp full of men, most of whom were heathen Indians.

As she rolled over to take a look beyond her trunk, every bone in her body ached, and muscles she'd been completely oblivious to all of her life protested. The mere thought of having to get on that blasted mangy horse again made her want to groan aloud. Nevertheless, she managed a painful roll onto her side and raised her head enough to peek out at the camp.

The faint blush of dawn was just beginning to make an appearance through a break in the trees. Rose barely made out two men slumbering beneath furry hides near the dead campfire, likely Mr. Kinyon and his friend. Off to one side of them, loud snoring interspersed with the occasional snort drifted from beneath a strung tarp. She smirked.

Mr. Smith, of course.

A number of yards away, the Indians occupying the other camp also lay sleeping. At least it would allow her time to go down to the creek and make herself more presentable. Perhaps more than presentable. She needed to look as good as humanly possible so Mr. Kinyon would feel compelled to do all in his power to redeem her from Mr. Smith and reunite her with her sisters.

She eased gingerly to her knees and crawled out from under her tarp then forced herself to stand, biting her lip at the aches and pains the slightest movement caused. Cautiously picking up her valise so as not to disturb the others, she tiptoed on stiff legs out of the camp toward the sound of the rushing creek.

But. . .fifty pounds. That was a fortune indeed, an insurmountable amount of money for someone to acquire. *Father, it cannot be Your will that I be taken into a land of wild savages. The Bible says that nothing is too hard for You. Surely You can get me back to civilization.*

Detecting movement back at the camp, Rose looked over her shoulder and saw one of the Indians beginning to stir. Once again she was reminded of her precarious situation. She hoped the God who made the heavens truly knew about her. And truly cared.

Nate shifted position on his sleeping mat to alleviate the annoyance of the sharp pebble poking into his hip. The rock wasn't the only thing irritating him. He should be halfway to his mother's by now, sleeping in a soft, warm bed and waking to the smell of bacon and biscuits at some friendly inn. But no. One brief encounter with a single female—an Englishwoman, at that—and here he was, sleeping out in the open on the rocky ground. He stifled a disgusted groan at his insanity.

Lifting his head slightly, he surveyed the camp and surrounding pasture in the faint daylight. Cows! Smith was bringing along cows to go with his new cook! There seemed no end to the man's foolhardiness. At the other camp, he saw one of the trader's hired Shawnee braves at work coaxing a new fire to life. Rumbling snores emitting from a nearby tarp announced Eustice Smith's sleeping presence.

He could not see around Miss Harwood's trunk at the other strung tarp. But maybe if he got up and gathered sticks for a fire he might "accidentally" catch a peek at the lady. He kicked aside his buffalo robe and rose with a stretch onto his moccasined feet. Then, realizing the possibility she might see him at the same time, he smoothed his rumpled buckskins and untied the thong holding his hair at the back of his neck. Using his fingers, he tamed the unruly mess as best he could and retied the leather strip around his queue again. After all, the fact that most women seemed to consider him handsome was not lost on him. No sense spoiling the image. He felt a smug grin tug at his lips.

As he began gathering wood from deadfall at the edge of the camp, he caught a flash of motion coming from the trees. He thought in reflex of his musket's location then realized it was merely the woman returning from the direction of the mountain stream. The same dress she'd worn before still clung enticingly to her young, womanly curves, and he noticed that the brown shade was as soft as that of a fawn and matched her coiled hair. Her complexion, still pink from the cold water, made her gray-blue eyes appear large and luminous. He remembered then why he'd come back.

She walked—or limped, to be more precise—out of the forest and came to an abrupt stop when she saw him. Realizing he'd been gawking unabashedly, he stepped forward. "Excuse me, miss. I musta forgot my manners. I'll get you a cook fire goin' before I go wash up."

"Thank you, Mr. Kinyon. That's very kind of you," she said softly. She turned and dropped her valise on the trunk.

Reveling in the sound of that lovely, refined voice of hers, Nate caught himself staring at her trim figure again. Any man worth his salt would be most fortunate to bask in her attributes. Not that he was of a mind to forfeit his adventurous life just to settle down, but he could understand why others might be so inclined. Giving himself a mental shake, he turned his attention to gathering enough kindling to start a fire.

Moments later, kneeling down to feed dry grass to some banked embers while he coaxed a spark to flame, he sensed rather than heard her light step behind him. He turned on his heel.

She gazed down at him. "No doubt you'll think this sounds silly, but I've not the slightest idea what sort of meal is required of me or what is to be done."

"Meal, miss? When we're on the trail we usually just finish off the game we shot an' roasted the night before. I notice you got a pot of somethin' sittin' on that firestone. What's in there?"

She grimaced. "Some sort of a cornmeal mixture he called 'mush.' Disgusting concoction, I thought."

Nate had to smile. He opened his mouth to reply, but movement on the far side of the campfire interrupted him.

Where he lay on a sleeping mat, Bob propped himself up on an elbow with a lazy grin and peered up at Miss Harwood. "Now I see what the big hurry was all about."

Ignoring the barb he knew was directed at him, Nate gave his full attention to nursing the tiny flame again.

Miss Harwood moved to his side. "How do you do," she whispered to the half-breed Indian. She put a finger to her lips then pointed to the tarp where Mr. Smith still sawed wood. "I don't believe we've been properly introduced. I'm Rose Harwood."

He sprang to his feet, an eager gleam in his dark eyes. "That's a real purty name," he said in a much quieter tone. "From now on, ever' time I see a rose, it'll put me in mind of you." Taking a step closer, he bowed at the waist. "My name is Robert Bloom Jr., Miss Harwood. But if you prefer, my ma's people call me Boy on a Black Horse."

Tucking his chin at his partner's overt display of interest, Nate let out a small huff. "An' the rest of us call him Horse Bob or just Bob most of the time." Glancing up at her, he remembered to smile.

She returned his smile then switched her attention to his partner. "I believe I shall call you Mr. Bloom. If you don't mind, of course."

"No, miss. I'd be pleased. It's got a real respectful ring to it, don't it?"

The guy was taking a real shine to the Englishwoman, Nate realized. Gritting his teeth, he tossed a few sticks on the growing fire then stood to his feet. "I'll take the teakettle down to the stream an' fill it whilst Bob an' me wash up." He nailed his partner with a glare.

Watching after the pair as they took their leave, Rose felt renewed hope blossoming in her chest. Perhaps she could glean some much-desired information from those two frontiersmen if she invited them to breakfast. She sensed that even the dusky-skinned man seemed intent on making a good impression on her. He might be another ally in her effort to return to civilization. With that thought in mind, she stirred some extra cornmeal and water into the pot. With any luck, there'd be sufficient milk left from last eve, and a touch of extra sugar should make it better than yesterday's.

She worked quietly, hoping Mr. Smith would sleep longer. At the other camp, however, she noticed that more of the Indians were up and about. She wished they'd stop ogling her. . .but comforted herself with the assurance that they simply weren't used to seeing many fair-skinned women.

Rose added more wood to the fire and positioned the pot of mush over the flames. As she stirred the mixture, she saw that her hands were now soiled with soot and dirt. Not only that, but a loose wisp of hair was flying about on the breeze. Noticing the two tall, leather-clad men striding out of the trees toward her, she wiped her hands on the smudged apron she'd worn last eve then tucked the strand of hair back into proper order. She focused on Mr. Kinyon, hoping her assessment did not appear anything beyond casual interest. To her own amazement, she decided buckskin suited the man far more than did proper English garb. In that comfortable clothing he appeared infinitely more capable of keeping her safe.

As the two passed her trunk, they each grabbed an end and brought it over near the fire. "For milady to sit on," Kinyon announced quietly. He placed the teakettle among some outer embers.

From his quiet tone, Rose concluded she wasn't the only one who wanted to delay the trader's awakening. "Thank you again. The mush will be ready in a few minutes. I'd be most pleased if you both would join us for breakfast this morn."

Mr. Bloom smiled, the whiteness of his teeth brilliant against his dark skin and much tidier braids. "We were hopin' you'd give us an invite."

"Then do have a seat, gentlemen." Rose felt a rush of heat in her cheeks at the awareness that there were no chairs to be had.

The men didn't seem to notice. They dropped down onto the ground and crossed their legs, while she perched on her trunk. "I have a question to ask of you. . .if you wouldn't mind answering."

"Anything," they answered in unison, then swapped peculiar looks.

Rose did her best to squelch a smile. "Mr. Kinyon, I couldn't help overhearing you speaking to Mr. Smith last eve. About the French and a tribe of Indians, I mean, attacking English trading posts. I—"

Kinyon raised a hand, stilling her. "You needn't be worryin' about that sort'a thing. Where you're goin' is way to the south of the area we were discussin'—unless I figger out a way to talk ol' Eustice into sendin' you back out with me first."

"That's just it, don't you see?" She inclined her head. "I've asked the man at least a dozen times where it is he's taking me. But he has yet to answer me."

"No wonder." Mr. Bloom chuckled.

Glaring at his partner, Mr. Kinyon picked up a small stick and smoothed out the dirt before him. He drew a large square then pointed the stick at the center. "Think of that space as bigger'n your whole England. To the west are these mountains we're crossin'." He sketched a rough map in the dirt. "At the north end are some huge inland seas of freshwater that are as far west as the Mississippi River an' run into each other until they empty into the St. Lawrence River that dumps into the Atlantic. Along them lakes an' both rivers is where the Frenchies have forts an' fur tradin' posts."

"I've read about the Mississippi. Doesn't it flow all the way down to New Orleans, the port on the southern coast?"

"Right." He pointed to the far bottom corner of his dirt map. "An' the French have decided they want everything in the center area that New York an' Virginia have claimed. Them Frenchies are a greedy bunch, so they brought in some soldiers an' established a store. . .about here." He indicated a spot not far below the most eastern lake.

"And just where is Mr. Smith's trading post located?"

He pointed farther south with the tip of the stick. "I'd put it here. On the Muskingum River just before it pours into the Ohio."

"Well, that doesn't look so very far to me," Rose said, trying to sound hopeful despite the niggle of dread spreading through her.

"It might not *look* far on a map," Mr. Bloom cut in. "But what with all the rivers an' creeks we'll be crossin' to get there, it'll take four, maybe five weeks through some not-so-friendly Indian country. 'Specially with the horses an' all Smith's trade goods."

"Not so friendly?" Purposely overlooking the proposition of spending four or five interminable weeks on the trail, Rose mouthed her main concern.

Mr. Kinyon quickly stepped in. "Bob means not so friendly to the French, lass. The English have made treaties with most of the tribes where Smith's store is located. An' the tribes want English goods as much as the English want the furs the Indians provide."

Only slightly comforted by his elaboration, Rose had to be sure. "So then everything is fine at Mr. Smith's trading post, just as if he were in a foreign country like Spain or Portugal." It was more question than statement.

Kinyon cocked his head back and forth. "More or—"

Following his gaze, Rose saw that the trader had risen.

Smith peered at the two men then at her. "I see ya got breakfast goin'. Good. We'll be hittin' the trail soon as we've et." He strode toward the Indian camp. "You boys start loadin' the horses."

"Reckon we better get to ours, too." Kinyon stood to his feet. "No sense keepin' Eustice waitin.'"

As far as Rose was concerned, the later they broke camp and left, the better, because nothing Mr. Kinyon or Mr. Bloom had said made her feel any more at ease about what lay in her future. She'd overheard the frontiersman tell the trader last eve that several hundred French soldiers were heading south. . .and they had Indian allies aiding them in their intentions.

Chapter 7

Rummaging through the sacks by the campfire, Rose unearthed enough spoons, wooden bowls, and cups for herself and the three men to use for breakfast. Now she had to figure out where to set things. What she would give for a proper table covered with pristine linen and lovely china, a real home. She'd taken such niceties for granted back in England, where she had no difficulty acting the hostess and serving guests. But out here in the woods, nearby logs and stones would have to suffice.

The ever-present awareness that the men in both camps observed her slightest movement both perplexed her and filled her with a strange sense of worth. Back home in Bath, most locals had considered her only goldsmith Henry Harwood's spinster daughter. Those who knew how she'd taken her mother's place and cared for her family members looked on her with pity that she'd never experience the benefits bestowed by matrimony.

Lifting the kettle away from the fire to pour in tea leaves for steeping, Rose glanced up to see how far along the men were with tying the bundles onto the packhorses. Obviously this was the accepted mode of transporting goods in the colonies, as normal and common as the freight wagons that rumbled along the cobblestone streets of Bath to deliver wares to the city's wealthy inhabitants.

One particular detail set the Indians apart from the English, however, and that was the variety of ways they dressed their straight black hair. Two of the braves wore braids. Another had his head shaved except for a short, narrow strip running from front to back, and a fourth let his hair flow loose, except for a small braid on each side. The one herding cows had the front portion pulled up in a topknot that exploded with feathers. But all of them used beads and feathers in assorted ways to decorate their hair.

And one of them leveled a bold stare right at her.

Diverting her gaze, Rose walked purposefully over to her bedding, gathered it up, and carried it to her trunk. Except for Mr. Smith's disgusting blanket, she folded each item and packed it away so her things would be ready to be picked up when the men carted off the foodstuff. Thank goodness the trader hadn't required her to load her chest onto a horse. It was one thing to drag her property along on the ground, as she'd done when they'd traveled by flatboat, but quite another to have to lift the heavy belongings over her head.

After she finished packing the chest, she locked it and laid the folded tarp and red blanket on top. Another glance toward the men revealed Mr. Kinyon, Mr. Bloom, and Mr. Smith heading toward her. She reached up and gave a quick pat to her hair to make certain no stray wisps had worked loose before pouring the tea.

"Everything's ready," she said on their arrival. She fixed a cup of half tea, half milk and handed it to the odorous trader.

Slightly out of breath, as if he'd just completed backbreaking labor, he dropped down on a log, eyes closed, and took a sip of the hot brew.

Rose flicked a glance at the other two men. "Would you care for milk in yours as well?"

"No, it's fine like this." Mr. Bloom reached out a hand for his.

Mr. Kinyon nodded as he accepted the one offered to him. "Same here. We don't wanna be no bother."

"An' I'll be holdin' ya to that," the trader announced in his weary tone. He opened his narrow eyes enough to glare at them.

Rose leaned over the pot and scooped a portion of mush into a wooden bowl, adding some crushed sugar, milk, and a spoon. She handed it to her owner. "'Tis such a lovely morn." She dished out a second bowl. "The sun has come up, the birds are singing, and the hand of Almighty God kept us safe through the long night. I do believe we would be remiss if we forgot to ask Him to bless our food and today's journey."

The three swapped dubious looks. Mr. Smith put down his spoon.

Rose handed Mr. Kinyon the next bowl, oddly aware that he didn't meet her gaze this time. He just stood there, cup in one hand, bowl in the other. As she scooped out Mr. Bloom's portion, an awkward sort of silence permeated the air. Nevertheless, Rose was not about to retract her request. If her lot was to accompany these men into the wilderness, she was determined to take the Lord along with her.

Finally the trader cleared his throat. "I b'lieve Nate here's the one who usually gives the blessing, don't you, boy?" He winked at Mr. Bloom.

Mr. Kinyon's eyes flared wide. He glanced from Mr. Smith to his partner, who was losing his battle against a grin. Adjusting his stance, the frontiersman inhaled a sharp breath and turned to Rose. "Once you're settled, I'd be glad to do the prayin'."

＊＊＊

Though he'd given in to the woman to be polite, Nate felt as if he'd just been cornered by a pack of ravenous wolves. Nobody had asked him to say grace over food in—in—how many years? Not as far back as he could recall. And both those jokesters knew it.

Miss Harwood remained calm, as if she'd just asked the most natural thing in the world, then she sprang to her feet. "Oh! I've forgotten to bring out the dried meat." She set down her bowl and hurried to retrieve some from one of the sacks.

Given a moment's blessed reprieve, Nate racked his brain for the words his father always said before meals. *Father in heaven. . .Father in heaven. . .bless the food. . . .* What else?

All too soon the woman was back, passing strips of jerky to each of them.

His partner and that snake-in-the-grass Smith still sported mocking grins.

Miss Harwood retook her seat on the trunk and looked expectantly up at him with those luminous blue eyes, eyes filled with so much hope they stole his breath.

Nate shot a quick glance to see if the Shawnee were watching, but they were occupied with their own meal and not paying them any mind. Relieved, he filled his lungs and let out all the breath at once. All right. He could do this. How hard could it be?

Three heads bowed. Waiting.

Nate removed his broad-brimmed hat and cleared his throat. He swallowed. "Father in heaven, bless this food, an'. . .an' thank You for . . .for a cloudless day an'. . .a pretty woman to look at." *Couldn't hurt to be charming.* "Oh, an' amen." Then, realizing he was the only one still standing, he slapped his hat back on, plopped onto his buffalo robe, and balanced his mush along with the cup of tea, glad the ordeal was over.

A snicker issued from the log as Mr. Smith hiked his shaggy brows. "Didn't know ya had it in ya."

Nate branded him with a glower. "There's a lot about me folks don't know, Eustice."

The trader gave a grudging nod. "A lotta truth in that. You long hunters spend most of yer time braggin' and lyin' about how you can shoot out the eye of a squirrel at a hundred yards, or how you outwrestled some she-bear. We never hear the real stuff."

A span of uncomfortable silence magnified the sounds of forest creatures coming to life. Already the tree toads' chorus drowned out the trill of the birds cavorting from branch to branch in the nearby thicket. Overhead a hawk circled against the blue sky, on the hunt for a warm, tasty morsel to carry off in its talons and devour.

Miss Harwood's gentle voice broke into the quiet. "Mr. Kinyon, I believe you spoke of going to visit your mother yesterday. Pray, where does she live?"

Glad for the change of subject, Nate felt his tension ease. "A couple days downriver from where you docked, miss. My older brother took over my pa's place after he passed on. Ma stayed there with him an' his young'uns."

"Then I'm sure she's well cared for." She took a spoon of mush and swallowed it. "It must give you great comfort to know your mother's in good hands when you're deep in the wilderness."

He spoke in all candor. "Never gave it much thought, to tell you the truth. With the farm goin' to the oldest son, I figger the duty of lookin' after Ma fell to him, too. Besides, she's real partial to his offspring. Young Nathan, the one they named after his handsome, adventurous uncle, he's a real corker." Feeling the tips of his ears heat up at the outrageous boast, Nate gave her a lopsided grin. "An' I myself was named after someone in the Bible, Miss Harwood. Ma was pretty fond of a couple of the prophets an' liked to read their writin's over an' over."

At this, Bob set his empty bowl aside and chimed in. "Far as names go, I got Nate's beat by a mile. I was named after Scotland's greatest king, Robert the Bruce."

She smiled. "How splendid. That man was a great leader, freeing the Scots from an oppressive English king." She looked back at Nate. "And Nathan in the Old Testament was a brave prophet indeed to stand up to King David and cause him to face the dreadful sin he'd committed by taking another man's wife. I should like you gentlemen to know I think it's marvelous that you both honor your heritage. . .as I do mine."

Smith snorted under his breath, but Nate ignored him. "From your manner an' speech, Miss Harwood, I can tell you came from a fine family. Whereabouts is it, exactly, that you hail from?"

"Why, thank you, Mr. Kinyon. I do indeed come from fine, God-fearing folk. And had it not been for the untimely death of a young lord who owed my father a great deal of money, I allow I'd still be living in the bosom of my family in Bath, England. But alas, many sacrifices had to be made to spare our family from total ruin."

The trader guffawed with such relish, mush spewed out of his mouth. He wiped his chin on his sleeve. "Woman, I'd say any family what has to sell off its daughters is already in ruination."

She hiked her chin and arched her brows higher, answering him with a tinge of vexation in her voice. "I should have you know, Mr. Smith, that my sisters and I gladly took it upon ourselves to sell our services for a mere four years to save our family's home and livelihood. I've not the slightest doubt that our father will have saved enough funds to send for us by the time we have completed our terms, if not before."

Intrigued by her story despite the limited details she'd provided, Nate wanted her to be sure he was on her side. "Know that I'm at your service, lass, for as long as you need me."

She returned an appreciative gaze to him and opened her lips to speak but was interrupted.

"Me, too," Bob injected. Nate glared at his irritating partner for butting in.

The trader shook his head in disgust and got up from the log, not bothering to dust off his backside. "Just remember, both of ya, she's at *my* service and *in* my service. . .which reminds me. Get done eatin', woman, and git this mess cleaned up. Day's a'wastin'." Swinging around, he stalked off toward the heavily laden packhorses.

Fifty pounds. Glaring after him, Nate bit his tongue at the man's churlish treatment of such a refined young woman. Somehow, some way, he had to get his hands on fifty pounds. And a profit.

Chapter 8

Settled again on the horse she'd ridden the day before, Rose did her best to ignore her aching thighs—which doubtless would feel added torture by day's end. Ahead of her, Mr. Smith's mount lumbered along, the muscles of its rump twitching, its straggly tail swishing away blackflies. The steady plodding of the horses' hooves, along with their blowing and nickering, made time pass slowly. From time to time a break in the forest canopy overhead allowed a view of fluffy clouds floating across the expanse of blue. Colorful birds flew among the branches, and the occasional squirrel scampered up a nearby tree trunk. In other circumstances, this could be a pleasant day's diversion from one's daily life. Alas, these circumstances were far from that.

Rose reflected back on the panic she'd experienced at the start of the journey. No amount of praying had calmed her fears about accompanying a strange man and five Indians into deep, dark wilds filled with unidentifiable sounds. This morn, however, she had two knights in shining armor—well, not so shiny, attired in buckskin instead of hammered mail—but still, they were in attendance and hopefully would protect her from harm. She smiled thinly, feeling a bit safer.

The ache in her heart, though, she could not dismiss. How were her sisters faring? Had Mariah settled into her life at the Barclay Plantation? Did she get along with Colin Barclay's mother? And was she remembering to act ladylike and not be a flirt?

And what of dear, sweet Lily? Had she reached her new home? Mr. Kinyon said she'd be located quite a distance from Baltimore. Was she safe now and providing the needed care for her new owner's sickly wife? *Please take care of both my sisters, Father. . .and please hasten the day when we'll be together again.*

The trail broadened, and Robert *the Bruce* Bloom moved alongside Rose on his sleek black horse. Strange, he appeared every inch as much the savage as Smith's Indians, yet he seemed as endearing to her as her youngest brother, Tommy. With skin several shades deeper than a white man's, his features were pleasant, his form tall, lean, and honed. Since he and Mr. Kinyon had joined the party, one or the other would ride next to her whenever space allowed, each regaling her with exploits that outshone his partner's.

As Mr. Bloom approached, Rose planned to take charge of the conversation. His civilized ways fascinated her, and she wanted to learn more about his unusual past.

"Miss Harwood." He greeted her with a broad grin.

She started right in. "Mr. Bloom. I'd like to ask you something, if I may."

"What is that?" Concern furrowed his dusky brow, making his dark brown eyes appear almost black.

To put him at ease, she offered him a small smile. "I'm curious regarding your parents. Having just arrived from across the water, I've never had occasion to meet someone with your background."

His smile fell flat. "You mean about me bein' a half-breed?"

"Not at all. That term hardly describes your heritage. You've actually had the advantage of having parents from two different continents. . . a man of two worlds."

His jovial grin reappeared, and he sat straighter in the saddle. "That does have a more pleasurable ring to it." He paused then continued. "My ma was captured and sold as a slave when she was young, and my pa took it on hisself to marry up with her an' take her to live on his farm. So you're right about the two worlds. Trouble is I never feel like both my feet are welcome in either one, an' no matter where I go, seems part of me's left on the outside."

Rose gave a light laugh. "I know exactly what you mean. From the moment I stepped foot on this continent I've felt as if neither of my feet is touching solid ground. In my wildest girlhood dreams, I never expected to be here in the colonies, let alone find myself traversing a wilderness trail to an unknown destination."

"You came as a surprise to us, too." He chuckled along with her. "It's different with me an' Nate, though. His pa's place bordered ours, so him an' me grew up together as boys, playin' together, fishin' together, best friends. I even had me some schoolin' along with him. When we go out on our own, explorin' some new piece of country, my feet's jest where they wanna be. A'course, there was a spell when the two of us was separated for some years, when Ma run off with me back to her own people."

"Mercy. I'm sure going to a whole new world must have been difficult for a young lad."

He shrugged a shoulder. "Not too bad. They was more willin' to accept my English blood than the white man was my Indian side. I got used to bein' looked down on or just plain ignored by folks. But I had some catchin' up to do with Ma's people, learnin' to hunt with a bow an' such. A lot of their ways seemed strange. Pa's Presbyterian teachin's pulled one way and theirs the other."

"I can understand that." But she wanted to know more, so she plunged on. "How were you able to reconcile the two different teachings?"

He laughed. "If you'd a'knowed my pa, you wouldn't ask that. When I was near sixteen, I came back out to see how him an' Nate was doin', an' Pa wouldn't let up on me till he set me straight. He took down his big ol' Bible ever' night an' read it out loud at the supper table after we finished eatin'. An' once when that preacher Reverend Whitefield come through our town, Pa drug me to the meetin' place to hear him. That Reverend

Whitefield was one powerful preacher, a true man of God, an' like they say, I 'saw the light.' I like to think of myself as one of them New Lights. Nate doesn't b'lieve like me yet, though. I'm still workin' on him."

Rose wondered what Nate's beliefs were. He'd prayed that rather odd prayer at breakfast this morn, but it seemed to come from his heart. She barely restrained herself from turning around to look at him. Instead, she moistened her lips and inhaled deeply. "George Whitefield has also preached to great crowds in my country. I never sat under his teaching myself, however. My family's in good standing with the Church of England. And from what I understand," she added with diplomacy, "the Reverend Whitefield's beliefs differ somewhat from our own."

"That makes you an Anglican, don't it?"

"Yes. In my deepest heart."

He nodded his dark head, gazing off into the distance before turning to her once again. "I always wondered about the difference between you Anglicans an' us Presbyterians but never knowed anybody I could ask about things. Would ya be of a mind to talk to me about it some evenin'?"

Rose couldn't believe her good fortune! A true Christian believer traveling with her! *"Oh, ye of little faith. . ."* God had not deserted her after all. "'Twould be my pleasure, Mr. Bloom."

"Hold up!"

Almost lulled into semiconsciousness by the gentle rocking of her horse, Rose jerked fully awake when Mr. Kinyon yelled from behind. She swung in her saddle to see the men of the party bringing their animals to a halt.

"Why are we stopping?" Barely twenty minutes had elapsed since the group had stopped to rest the horses.

"Riders comin' after us." He pulled his long-barreled musket from its scabbard and checked its load, as did the others.

Rose scanned the forest trail they'd been steadily climbing. Despite its rustic beauty, she couldn't forget the possibility of real danger lurking along the route. If shooting started, should she race ahead? Hop down and take cover behind a tree? Or. . .

When she saw Mr. Smith dismount at the front of the train, she swung a leg over the saddle.

"Stay put," Mr. Kinyon ordered, passing by with his rifle in hand. "Prob'ly nothin' to worry about."

Probably. She turned on her mount to watch then realized she was the only one still on horseback—a perfect target. Not an ideal situation.

Two white men and a pair of brown-skinned Indians rode up to the end of the column and reined in their horses. Without having drawn weapons, the riders remained on their mounts as they conversed with the travelers in her party, all of whom had congregated at the rear.

One of the newcomers flicked several glances in her direction, making Rose uneasy. Had they come because of her? Had Mr. Smith broken some law by forcing her to accompany him into Indian territory? A tiny ray of hope lessened her fear.

The group talked for several minutes, leaving her to sit and wonder about the proceedings. Finally, the members of her party headed back to their horses, and the strangers slowly worked their way past them on the narrow trail. She didn't know what to think and drew a nervous breath.

Nate Kinyon and Mr. Bloom reached her first. The latter nodded a greeting. "Sorry to tell ya this, but I gotta leave. I'll catch up with ya at Smith's tradin' post soon as I can."

"You're leaving?" Distraught, she cut a glance to his partner. "And you. Are you leaving as well?"

He shook his head and flashed an easy smile. "No, miss. Don't worry yourself none. I ain't goin' nowhere. Bob has to go with these fellows down to a Catawba village. Seems a white boy was brought there to be ransomed back to his folks, an' they need my pal to translate for 'em. The two braves they sent out to make a deal don't talk English so good."

A touch more at ease since Mr. Kinyon wasn't going to desert her, Rose checked back toward the approaching white men.

Their demeanors remained serious, even determined. "Hurry up and say your good-byes," one said to Bloom as they came alongside. "Who knows what them savages already done to Billy—and what all they want from us to get him back."

Rose could easily understand their angst, but she couldn't help remembering that Robert Bloom was the only person with whom she'd been traveling who professed to be a Christian—and now he was leaving her behind to go to the aid of a boy some savages had taken captive. But she couldn't help but identify with the lad—who was probably scared to death being held prisoner by wild Indians—and she empathized with the strangers. "I shall pray for you and the boy, that he'll be safe and unharmed, and that your journey homeward will be without peril."

One of the men took off his hat and bowed his head to her. "Thank you for that." He swept a glance around at her motley group then extended his hand, giving hers a warm squeeze. "We'll be prayin' for you, too, miss. May the good Lord keep you safe in His hand as that devil Smith carts you off into that hellish heathen land of his." He flicked a disgusted glance to her owner, who at that moment was lumbering up the trail from the rear.

Rose felt renewed trepidation as the stranger wagged his head and led his party and Robert Bloom away.

Chapter 9

Determined not to cry as the newcomers and Robert Bloom took their leave, Rose watched after them until they reached the top of the ridge and vanished from sight. How frail was hope, she mused, when it could vanish so quickly. She'd grown accustomed to having Bloom around, had counted on his presence, and his unexpected departure filled her with emptiness.

In front of her, Mr. Smith turned in his saddle, a smug smirk twisting one corner of his mouth. "Now I'll only have one o' them moonstruck jaspers to keep an eye on, Miss Harwood." With a glance encompassing Nate and the others, he raised an arm high, heeling his horse into motion. "Forward, ho."

The flame of embarrassment burned Rose's face. Mr. Kinyon had to have heard the trader's comment. What must he think? Without checking behind to gauge his reaction, she nudged her mount to a walk. But the creaks and plods coming from the caravan as it started up did not muffle the low chuckle that rumbled from the frontiersman's chest. Why, the man actually found the crude remark humorous! She pursed her lips and straightened her shoulders.

As they gained the top of the rise and started down a steep incline, it dawned on Rose that Smith—uncouth and tactless though he may be—may have bought her to be a cook, but had assumed the responsibility of being her chaperone. The smelly trader possessed at least a spark of human decency. At this, Rose nearly laughed herself. Who could have imagined that after the monotonous, predictable life she'd endured in her motherland, her world was destined to be turned upside down?

It would be awhile before Nate would be able to erase the memory of the desolation he'd detected on Miss Harwood's face when Bob rode off to help fetch the kidnapped boy. And the leader of the group's parting remark about praying for her safety had only made things worse. Despite her brave front, the woman had fears enough regarding her uncertain future without some stranger adding to her misery. But leave it to Smith to lighten the mood. He chuckled again.

The trader's attempt at levity sure caught the little gal off her guard, though. Her spine went as straight as a ridgepole, and her neck turned beet red. Nate would look for an opportunity to talk to her, ease her mind a bit. She'd fare well enough if she were prepared for what might lie ahead. They'd come to the Cheat River soon, where they'd raft across the water a few at a time. There might be a chance then to allay some of her misgivings.

The sound of rushing water made it to Rose's ears before the river came into view. It grew gradually louder as they ambled steadily downward, drowning out the usual forest sounds. It must be a river of some size, like the Ohio. That name had been bandied about during the trek, and it was reported to be quite large. The group had been traveling for days already. Perhaps the men hadn't exaggerated about the journey requiring weeks. Mr. Kinyon himself had said they'd be venturing three hundred miles into the wilderness. Had even twenty of those miles been covered yet? It felt like a hundred to her backside.

Soon they came to a break in the forest growth, providing Rose her first glimpse of a wide, swift-flowing river. A number of tall trees had been cut down and used to construct a crude wooden dock jutting out over the water's edge. Two layers of rope stretched from the dock across to the other side, where they wound around a pulley, and a raft made of logs attached at both ends to the lower rope bobbed on the current.

"Blast!" Mr. Smith whacked his hat against his thigh, dislodging a puff of trail dust. "We gotta haul the fool thing over to us."

Rose startled. *The man must be mad if he thinks that pitiful-looking bit of wood can bear the weight of horses and goods—and us!* She observed the rapid swells coursing past the dock. Hearing a horse moving up alongside hers, she slanted a nervous glance at Nate Kinyon.

His expression remained even. "We'll be waterin' the stock before we cross. I'll take your mount down to the river whilst you stretch your legs a bit."

"Surely you don't mean we're expected to cross that wild torrent on that useless conveyance!" She pointed toward the raft, hoping her voice didn't sound as frightened as she felt. When she looked back at Nate, he was actually grinning. She let out a silent huff of displeasure. Did he find everything humorous, for pity's sake?

His countenance never did turn serious. "I reckon the ferry does look a mite puny, but don't be frettin' your pretty self. It's sturdier than you think. Besides, I'll be right there with you to see you don't lose your footin'."

Rose drew little comfort from his words or his smile. Anyone with sense could see that such an ill-crafted thing could very well be the end of them all. Should she find herself in the churning water, her limited ability to swim would be no match for the river's power, especially if she had to contend with cumbersome skirts and petticoats.

When they reached the dock, the frontiersman reined in and dismounted. He caught up the traces and strode to the front of Rose's horse. "Time to get down, miss. I'll be waterin' the animals now."

Gracefully as possible, Rose acquiesced, counting it a blessing that she didn't collapse at his feet. At least the practice of getting on and off the beast over the past few days had been of some benefit, though her legs still retained an awkward, wooden feel and ached after riding for hours. As the shuffle and clomp of the rest of the caravan surrounded her, she dodged her way to the edge of the river and gazed across to the other side. The men and horseflesh surged down to the water for a drink, and the thirsty cows mooed as they lumbered past in a cloud of dust. No one else appeared concerned about the crossing, so Rose tamped down her own foreboding. She vowed she'd give no further hint of her disquiet but couldn't help gauging the swiftness of the current all the same. *Be with us, Father. See us safely to the other side. . .somehow.*

Mr. Kinyon returned moments later with the horses. He handed Rose a leather flask. "You must be thirsty. Have some cool mountain water whilst we wait for the men to haul the ferry across."

"Thank you." Taking the container, she lifted it to her lips and let the refreshing liquid cool her tongue. How she longed for a much-needed bath after the dusty ride. She lowered the flask and watched the raft moving slowly through the current as a couple of the Indians hauled on the lower ferry rope.

The frontiersman cleared his throat. "There's somethin' you need to know."

What else? she wanted to scream. But considering the new vow she'd made not to reveal her emotions, she took a breath for patience and turned to him. "What is it, Mr. Kinyon?"

He grimaced, crimping up one side of his face. "It's all the *mister* an' *miss* business. Don't you think it's time we get past that nonsense? Could you see fit to call me just Nate, or even Kinyon? An' I'd be purely pleased to call you Rose. If you wouldn't mind."

She gazed beyond him to where the rumpled Mr. Smith was checking the straps and tie-downs on a packhorse. Raising her eyes to meet those of the frontiersman, she was lost in the sincerity she saw in the hazel depths, and her insides went still. "I suppose, under the circumstances, it might not be improper for us to address one another by our given names.

'Tis not as if we are among the gentry out here."

That infectious grin she'd grown accustomed to seeing popped into place again. "No, miss, we surely ain't. Now that we got that outta the way, *Rose*, there's another matter I'd like to set your mind to rest about."

Certain it could only be the "moonstruck jaspers" remark Mr. Smith had made earlier, she steeled her expression and waited for him to elaborate.

"About them Indians kidnappin' that boy. You don't need to worry about that none. Long as you don't go wanderin' off by yourself out here, nothin' like that'll happen to you."

A small shiver went through Rose. "Surely you're not telling me that boy took a walk by himself and got captured by sheer chance!"

"No, not a'tall. His pa said the boy an' his brother an' another lad was out coon huntin' with their dogs after dark. Chasin' after the hounds, they prob'ly got themselves too deep in the woods, and considerin' all the racket dogs make, it would'a been easy for some Cherokee huntin' party to hear 'em." He shrugged a shoulder. "Likely the Indians figgered the boys was trespassin' on their huntin' grounds, so they went after 'em. I expect they must'a killed the two older boys who might'a given 'em trouble an' took the young one to their village. Prob'ly figgered he was young enough to retrain, make him part of their tribe, if his kin didn't offer enough of a price to get him back."

Rose's brows arched in shock. "You're saying that Indians do not consider murder or kidnapping an evil act, then?"

"Not like we do." Nate shifted his stance. "They got different ideas on what's right an' what's wrong. Sometimes they capture a person to replace one of their own who might'a been killed by a white man."

That sort of logic didn't sit well with Rose. She glanced toward the dock at the Indians chatting back and forth between themselves as they worked. She then looked again at Nate. "Indeed, they truly are as savage as I've been told, even if 'tis not apparent at first glance."

He tilted his head and studied her. "No more savage than what's been goin' on in Europe for a thousand years, kingdom against kingdom. The word *Indian* is the one Columbus tagged 'em with when he thought he'd discovered the route to India. These people have their own nations an' clans just like in Europe. Actions that might be considered evil in their own towns an' villages are quite acceptable against other tribes. That includes killin' an' takin' hostages. Indians have their own territories an' languages an' rules of conduct just like in Europe an' the rest of the *civilized* world." He stopped talking abruptly and flashed a sheepish grin. "Sorry. Reckon I was speechifyin' a touch."

Rose smiled. "'Tis quite all right. I suppose the more I'm able to understand regarding this foreign land I'm in, the less apprehensive I'll be. So I gather I'll be going to a town where the neighbors are friendly and business is conducted similar to the way it is in the shops at home in Bath. Is that right?"

"Not exactly." His grin broadened, and he rested an elbow on his horse's saddle. "More like the bargainin' that goes on in the weekly markets or down on the docks in Baltimore, I'd say."

Baltimore. Thinking back on her experience there, Rose recalled seeing a ship of African slaves in chains being off-loaded as she was leaving the wharf. The phrase *savage Indian* lost some of its sting. Their actions couldn't hold a candle to the cruelty of the English slavers who captured and sold other humans into a lifetime of bondage just to line their own pockets with gold. "I do thank you for your frankness, Mr.— Nate. I shall look forward to more of your *speechifyin'*. As I gather more information about the daily lives of the natives here, I'm less befuddled about what I might face when we reach our destination." She paused. "Pray, what is the name of the town I'm going to?"

Nate rubbed his chin. "Don't know as it has a proper name. Some Shawnees an' Delawares started raisin' their wigwams an' longhouses in the area when the fur company contracted for Smith an' his partner to set up their store there. Us longhunters call it Muskingum-at-the-Ohio. . . or just plain Muskingum."

"Muskingum. What an odd name. Whatever does it mean?"

"I ain't rightly sure. I think the word comes from the Erie tribe, or mebbe the Senecas. You see, along the Ohio's been mostly free huntin' and trappin'. No tribe in particular claims that territory. Leastways, not yet."

"Hmm. How odd. In England—as well as all of Europe, I believe— every foot of land in existence is claimed by some individual or some government."

Nate chuckled. "Us humans tend to be a greedy bunch, don't we?"

A laugh bubbled up out of Rose before she could catch herself.

The frontiersman tipped his head, studying her, then stepped closer. "You know, that's the first time I heard you laugh. Don't mind sayin' I like the sound of it."

Rose felt unwelcome heat climb her neck and warm her cheeks as she stared back at him. For a moment all thought fled except how very much she admired his stalwart presence, his face, his smile. . . .

"Yo! Kinyon!" Mr. Smith's bellow from the riverbank halted her midthought. "Stop your moonin' an' git down here. We need to git these skittish horses aboard."

Mooning! The trader had no end of ways to humiliate her. Rose felt her face grow even warmer, especially when Nate's grin widened from ear to ear. Then, recalling the rest of her owner's words, she turned toward the dock and watched the men struggling to coax a loaded horse onto the wobbly raft. Ears back, the brown gelding's eyes walled to the side, and the terrified animal went stiff legged. It would not budge. *I know exactly how you feel, poor thing.*

Reaching the others, Nate whipped off his linen hunting shirt and tossed it over the packhorse's eyes. Almost immediately, the animal began to relax. Rose watched the frontiersman lean close to its ear and speak a few words then lead it slowly from the dock onto the gently rocking ferry, where two other horses had already boarded. Once the gate bars dropped into place, Nate and two of the Shawnee braves tugged on the rope that would take the Indians and the first three horses to the other side of the river.

She knew it was less than ladylike to stare at the man's broad back, but Rose could not deny Nate Kinyon made a rather dashing figure without his shirt. Finely honed muscles stood out with his movements, and the June sunshine lent a glow to his bronzed skin. He truly was quite capable when he put his mind to it. Recalling his promise—or almost promise—to take her back to her sisters, she had no doubt he was a man who'd move heaven and earth to stand by his word.

Watching the raft make its slow passage, a mental image made Rose smile. If she balked about setting foot onto that pathetic, rickety raft, would Nate throw his shirt over her eyes and lead her onto it?

No indeed. A gallant champion like Nate Kinyon would scoop her up into those strong arms of his and carry her aboard bodily.

Chapter 10

Nate focused his attention on loading the raft time and again, then watching it cart animals and various members of the party across the river. But he also observed Rose Harwood from the corner of his eye. Each successful crossing seemed to alleviate her fears a little more, and as old Eagle Eye Smith finally left for the other side, Nate knew her trip would be more enjoyable without the man's presence. Now only one cow and a calf remained to be ferried across, along with Rose, himself, and the last Shawnee, who would help pull them to the other bank.

When the wooden raft returned to their side, Nate turned to Rose. "I believe it's our turn."

"So 'twould appear."

He held out a hand, and she placed her fingers in it.

"Thank you." She managed an uncertain smile.

Though bravely spoken, a slight tremor in her hand belied her spunk. It felt small engulfed in his, small and silky as a flower, and he realized how fitting the name Rose was for her.

He also realized with no small shock that he was becoming completely besotted with the woman! A woman who'd likely cost him at least fifty pounds—and possibly considerably more—if he ever succeeded in convincing Eustice Smith to release her. The trader hadn't hesitated to part with that hefty sum to buy her, and all he'd wanted was a cook. Nate had known Rose but a few short days, and for some illogical reason, she occupied most of his waking hours. He'd lived a footloose life for years, picking up and moving on whenever the notion struck, always anxious to see what lay beyond the next mountain, around the next bend in the trail. Why did this pert little female kindle within him thoughts of home and hearth? He needed to thwart those inklings right now!

But as he led her to the railing near where he'd assist the Indian in working the rope, he found it hard to release that delicate hand enclosed in his.

A glance past her shoulder revealed a knowing smirk on the brave's sun-browned face. Nate offered him a weak grimace and reached for the rope, nodding for the two of them to pull in unison.

Rose stood wide eyed, watching the current with a modicum of acceptance, if not enjoyment. And Nate enjoyed watching her.

In midstream, she turned to him. "Cheat River. Are you acquainted with how it came to have such a curious name?"

"Aye." He huffed with effort as he yanked on the rope. "But first, I'd like to hear how you got your name. It suits you fine."

"My name?" She focused her gaze off into the distance, a tiny smile on her lips. "Actually, while my mother was awaiting my birth, she came across a term in her Bible: 'Rose of Sharon.' She thought it was the loveliest name ever, so that's what she and my father decided to call me."

"Rose of Sharon—"

"Kinyon!"

At the Indian's sharp tone, Nate realized he'd stopped pulling. He immediately got back to work, but not before catching the grin Rose tried to contain as she turned her attention to the water. It didn't bother him in the least. She needed to know he was truly interested. "Your parents must care a great deal for you an' miss you sorely."

She gave a sad shake of the head, the brim of her bonnet dipping on the breeze. "I'm afraid Mum went to be with the Lord when my youngest brother came into the world. I've no doubt that Papa misses my sisters and me a great deal, however. We were quite close."

"I'm sure he does." Nate gave the hemp two sharp yanks. "Especially you."

"And my cooking. Let's not forget about that." The teasing lilt of her voice faded along with her smile, and she turned serious. "Ironic, is it not? 'Tis that very skill that has thrust me upon this tiresome journey." She filled her lungs and let the air out in a slow breath. "Speaking of journeys, this small part of it has almost come to an end. So do tell me from whence this river got its name."

"Oh, that." Nate checked ahead to the dock as the small conveyance neared the wooden structure then gave a hearty pull on the rope. "Hear tell this particular river got its name when some hunters left their gear along the bank while they were off yonder dressin' out a buck. They weren't gone too long. But when they came back, that cheatin' river had made off with all their truck. Swept it away while they weren't lookin.'"

"You can't be serious." Rose slanted him a look of disbelief.

"Sure as I'm standin' here. This river's known to be real tricky. It can wash right up onto its banks and steal a pretty little thing like you away before you know it. And that surely would be a cheat if ever there was one."

Rose closed her eyes and shook her head. "Nate Kinyon. As they say in Ireland, I do believe you've kissed the Blarney Stone."

He chuckled. "Mebbe a time or two." And gazing at those tempting lips on his Rose of Sharon, he knew something else he'd like to kiss.

⌐——

After making the successful river crossing, the party lined up again to travel onward, and Rose found herself in the middle of the pack train. She found the change unsettling, as the Indians' relaxed behavior took on an ominous change. No longer did they chat back and forth in the low tones of their strange tongue. Instead they became silent and watchful, constantly looking about. Often their hands would come to rest on a rifle or sheathed knife—particularly when a birdcall or the screech of some wild animal echoed through the forest growth.

Added to that, Nate Kinyon, whom she looked upon as her protector, no longer rode directly behind her. He'd taken the lead position, ahead of Mr. Smith. At times he rode even farther beyond, out of sight, sometimes for half an hour or more.

Rose couldn't help remembering the frontiersman's explanation regarding the territory they were entering. No tribe had laid claim to it, he'd said. The land lacked a governing force of any sort, and here young boys could be captured and killed or carted off by roaming Indians and ransomed without fear of reprisal. She could tell from the tension in the backs of the men in the party that unspoken dangers of other kinds could be lying in wait anywhere, anytime in this vast, untamed place.

No one had to remind her that the pack train was a prime target. She was riding in the midst of twenty heavily laden horses weighted down with goods and treasures every Indian coveted—or Mr. Smith wouldn't be hauling them these many, many miles. Remembering how readily he had plunked down fifty pounds for her alone, she surmised his store must be a profitable enterprise. She sent yet another silent prayer for safety aloft.

Late afternoon sunlight through the treetops speckled the rustic deer trail as the party lumbered on, single file. Humidity magnified the woodland scents as they passed rocky outcroppings covered with moss, and as always, Rose's nostrils detected the smell of the horses as they plodded onward. Her thoughts drifted back in time to her English home, where she'd have had a perfumed handkerchief tucked in her sleeve for use at a moment's notice to disguise unpleasant odors. How sweet was the scent of the summer roses that climbed the garden trellis in back of their home, the inviting aroma of fresh-baked bread and raisin scones that filled the house. And the lovely tea Lily would brew. What she'd give for a soothing cup right now on this seemingly endless day!

At the sound of approaching hoofbeats, Rose tensed, gradually relaxing as she spotted Nate returning.

Passing the front of the group, he came to join her, a weary smile intensifying tired lines around his eyes. "We'll be stoppin' for the night soon, but not lightin' any fires, sorry to say." His quiet tones set her on alert again. "We'll just eat up some of those hard buns an' jerked meat we brought with us. Mebbe some of that fresh cow's milk would taste mighty good. Oh, an' I happened across a few berries awhile back, so I picked some."

"No fire, you say?" Wishing he'd elaborate further, Rose decided she'd really rather not know what put him on guard. She'd have to trust God to look after this vulnerable, mismatched group forging ever deeper into the unknown.

Nate untied a juice-stained sack from a saddle ring and handed it to her. "If it's any comfort, you'll be takin' it kind of easy for a spell. There'll be no cookin' tonight or any other night for a couple days." He tipped his head in Mr. Smith's direction and chuckled.

Rose laughed with him. "Quite right. I fear poor Mr. Smith and his tender stomach are hardly getting his money's worth out of me."

A frown crinkled the frontiersman's forehead, and he kneaded his chin. "That purely puzzles me. Ol' Eustice has always been a shrewd dealer. I wonder if a sour stomach is his whole reason for wantin' you so bad."

With a glance at the trader, Rose shivered as a chill shot through her.

Nate's broad hand covered hers on the pommel. "Like I told you before, I'm here, and I ain't goin' nowhere."

Gritting her teeth against the pain caused by riding hours on horseback, Rose hobbled back toward the camp, carrying milk from the cow that now grazed placidly on meadow grass. The hem of her fawn skirt swished with her movements, and she gazed down in despair at how dusty and dismal the daygown now looked after having been worn day after day. It had snagged countless times on protruding brambles. Inhaling the delicate scent of wildflowers dancing in the meadow, Rose wished she looked as fresh and smelled so sweet. She recalled with chagrin her uncivil thoughts regarding the odorous Mr. Smith and realized she could be close to such rankness herself now. But she would not sacrifice another daygown. How long had it been since she had sunk into a tub billowing steam and soaked until the water grew tepid? Or climbed between crisp bed linens of pristine white that still carried the fragrance of the summer wind? Would she know such luxuries again?

Reaching the clearing, where food sacks sat propped against a fallen log, she set down the bowl of milk and retrieved the items for the evening's spartan meal. Not far away, the members of the party worked in harmony while she removed wooden trenchers and cups for her threesome. The men had to be as travel weary as she, yet no one complained as they freed horses of their burdens and hobbled them.

One of the Indians paused in his work and eyed the sky with concern. Rose glanced up and sighed at the sight of clouds rolling in. She'd already had to forfeit the promise of stimulating conversation regarding faith with 'New Light' Robert Bloom and would not be allowed the simple comfort of herbal tea this night. Now a storm loomed. The injustice of it all stung her. But rather than allow herself to sink into the mire of self-pity, she refused to give in to tears that would make her appear weak in the presence of all these men. Lifting her chin with renewed purpose, she resumed her chore, setting out the trenchers and cups and gathering the needed food items Nate had mentioned.

The sounds of repeated thwacking and chopping made her glance toward the thicket, where Indians were cutting branches from fir trees and tossing them into piles. There was to be no fire this eve. What purpose lay behind such a waste of energy? Other men were busy removing tarps from the packs and stringing them between trees. This time the worn canvases were more in number and strung at a slant, likely to provide runoff from the imminent rain. But what would keep water from blowing in from the sides?

The unusual pile of fir branches continued to grow. Then the men gathered them and spread them out, layering some beneath the tarps and leaning some upright against the sides, layer after layer. Primitive shelters took form before Rose's eyes. The fir branches that seemed to have no purpose would surely keep their bedding off the damp ground, as well as keep out blowing rain.

When Nate Kinyon placed her trunk and valises inside one of the crude huts, Rose appreciated his constant concern for her personal welfare—despite her fear that she no longer smelled as sweet as her namesake flower.

From out of nowhere the story of the Nativity drifted into her mind, reminding her of the way the Lord had looked after Mary and her baby when a situation seemed impossible. God provided the unwed peasant girl a confidante in her relative Elizabeth, and a husband who, instead of giving her a certificate of divorce, married her and then lovingly cared for her and her unborn child. When King Herod sought to destroy her baby, the Lord compelled Joseph to take his family and flee to Egypt. Always there were angels to guide and protect them. God truly did care for His own.

Hearing footsteps, Rose glanced up to see Nate walking toward her with that endearing grin that warmed her heart. Was he her own personal angel sent by God when she needed help the most? *Don't be such a goose!* Even after all these days, the man turned red as ever when he offered the prayer at breakfast.

But still, it was an interesting thought. She returned his smile.

Chapter 11

Grateful for the chance to sit down at day's end, Nate sank onto a fallen log at the campsite and stretched out his legs.

Across from him Rose lowered herself with her usual grace onto a slumped flour sack and drew her ivory shawl about her shoulders. She always dispensed with her bonnet when preparing a meal, and wisps of honey-gold hair—though somewhat tangled from travel—formed little curls around her face, giving her an enchanting innocent charm as she looked up at him and Eustice. "Would either of you care for the honor of blessing our food—such as it is—this eve?"

"Sure thing," Nate blurted without thought. He'd been stewing all afternoon about Smith and his covert plans for Rose, and neither a humbling request for prayer from her nor a taunt from the trader would deter him from the questions he intended to level on the man once they were out of Rose's earshot. Alone on his horse earlier, he'd searched his mind for snatches of blessings from his childhood that his deceased father had offered at mealtimes. Drawing on those memories, he spoke with fortitude that had been sorely lacking in his earlier efforts. "Heavenly Father, we thank You for this quiet day an' for the meal we're about to partake. We also ask You to be with Bob on his errand of mercy for the unfortunate lad an' work out the details so things can be put right. . . ."

Wondering if any of the Indians over in their circle might have understood enough English to know he performed a religious rite, he sneaked a peek in their direction while Rose and Eustice had their heads bowed. The redskins were a superstitious lot, and who knew what they might think? But seeing they were involved in their own concerns, he relaxed and concluded the prayer. "In Jesus' name, Amen."

He sniffed in confidence for having discharged the duty adequately and raised his head. Rose still hadn't looked up but wore a sweet smile as she took a sip of milk. He'd gained a little ground with her, sure enough, and the thought pleasured him. But Smith was another matter entirely. The surly man sat rigid as a totem pole on a rock nearby. Nate snatched one of the hard buns off the trencher Rose had set out and tore off a chunk with his teeth. The sooner they all chewed down this tough-as-a-boot excuse for a meal, the sooner she'd be able to leave for her shelter and find the rest she sorely deserved. Then he would see about getting some straight answers from that old geezer.

"Woman," Smith said, "fetch me a bowl. I need to sop my bread in some o' that milk ya' got us."

"Of course." Swallowing down a bite of her own bun, she turned to Nate. "Would you care for some milk as well?"

He shook his head. "Naw. My teeth could use the workout." Glaring at the trader, Nate's ire for him grew as he watched the submissive young woman waiting on a wretch not fit to wipe her shoes.

Holding her wrap closed with one hand, she served Smith the requested bowl of milk and retook her seat, settling her skirts about her. "Mr. Smith? I should like to inform my sisters of my whereabouts. How many days do you assume it will take us to reach your store?"

He shot a wary glance up at the sky. "Depends on the rain. If a lot of it gets dumped on us and the rivers start swellin' we'll have to give 'em time to smooth out b'fore we can cross 'em."

"Rivers? There are more of them ahead?" Her face paled noticeably.

"Yep."

"How many are there?"

Nate snickered. "Go on, Smith. Tell the lady how many rivers, cricks, an' streams we still have to cross." A bit shocked by the animosity he could hear in his own voice, Nate determined to rein it in.

The trader cut him a sullen look. "However many it takes us to get there. That's how many." He went on dunking his bun.

Intense silence settled over the campsite, leaving only night sounds and the murmured conversation of the Shawnee at the other circle to go with the sounds of chewing dried meat and the crunching of hard bread. The wind was picking up, stirring through the treetops as churning clouds darkened the sky and the low rumble of distant thunder echoed. A mosquito whined near Nate's ear, and he brushed the pest aside.

Finally Rose broke the stillness, her voice still amazingly patient. "Mr. Kinyon. I've heard that the colonies abound with opportunities for farming and the trades. Why would an obviously capable man such as yourself choose to leave those things behind to hunt for wild game in the wilderness? Every farm we passed along the Potomac had an abundance of farm animals."

Nate prickled. So that was her intent? To get him to forsake his wanderlust and agree to hitch himself up to some old plow on some old ramshackle farm for the rest of his life? Off to the side he heard Smith cackle around a mouthful that puffed out his bearded cheek, and it galled Nate no end. "What me an' Bob do is more important than huntin'. We hunt so we can fill our stomachs or trade with the tribes for other food an' furs. Furs is as good as cash money anywhere in the nations."

"I see." But the way her slender brows dipped toward each other indicated she was no less puzzled.

Nate explained further. "Me an' Bob, we're explorers, like Columbus. The colonies are sittin' on the edge of a vast continent, an' we chart the rivers an' lakes an' such for folks that'll come after us. There's great tracts of open land that scarcely a man, white or red, has ever set foot on. Folks need to know what's out there, so they can find places to settle an' make lives for themselves."

Her features calmed. "Oh. I see. You're providing a service of true import, then. . .at the sacrifice of comforts offered by home and hearth."

How did she manage to get back to him farming? Nate rolled his eyes. This was not going well. But she had to realize that he would never be tied down. Not to her, not to anybody. Not now, not ever. "I do my best to get home to see Ma a couple times a year. More, if I have good reason." That said, he added his most charming smile.

Rose lowered her lashes without responding.

Good. She was starting to take to the notion. Nate slid a glance at Eustice Smith, eyeing him from unkempt head to scuffed toe. A serious talk with that man was overdue. Long overdue.

In the fading light of day, Nate watched Rose clear away the meal trappings. He couldn't help but admire her for not voicing a single complaint about the many discomforts she'd suffered during the long journey. Anybody with eyes in his head could tell she was worn out by each day's end. After hours on horseback, she hobbled about on stiff legs to see to her own needs and theirs as well.

The dress he'd thought so comely at the start of the trip was wrinkled from top to bottom, bore a liberal amount of stains and trail dust, and showed numerous snags from bramblebushes she'd scraped past. And her skin, though she managed a quick wash at the creek now and again, looked smudged. He'd wager the gal had never been so rumpled or dirty in her life. She had real spunk. Spunk and grit. He watched her limp to her shelter, where she stretched a kink out of her back before crawling inside.

A light mist was just beginning, and from the look of the dark clouds shrouding the sky, it was a mere portent of the impending storm that would make a royal mess of things. Thunder and lightning would make the horses skittish also, so the Indians would need to stay close to them through the storm and keep them from bolting. Switching his attention to Smith, who sat on a boulder nursing a cup of milk, Nate noted that the man was looking particularly slovenly. But the trader did little but sit around in his trading post between infrequent trips out to civilization. A trivial detail like his appearance wasn't high on his list of concerns.

Lumbering to his feet, Smith rubbed his belly.

Nate cleared his throat. "I'd like a private minute with you, Eustice."

He grimaced, easing back down. "Don't tell me you're fixin' to shove off, too."

"I'm not sure. You still set on draggin' that poor gentlewoman off to that godforsaken Shawnee settlement of yours?"

Smith narrowed his beady eyes. "Look here, Kinyon. I didn't buy that gal just so's I'd have a skirt around to gawk at. Like I tol' ya, I'm in dire need. Her comin' with me's a matter of life and death. Mine."

"Aha. Just like I figgered."

"What're ya talkin' about?"

Nate shook his head in disdain. "Some chief's got it in for you, an' you bought her for him as a way of atonement. Well, I'm here to tell you, that ain't gonna happen." He snatched his hunting knife from the scabbard hooked to his belt and raised it to make his point. "I'll do you in myself first."

The man's eyes flared, and he jerked to his feet, spilling his cup to the ground. "Wait just a minute!" He stretched out a hand to ward Nate off. "Ya got it all wrong. I bought her papers so's she could cook fer me, an' that's the plain truth. My stomach's been ailin' me sore most all the time, and sometimes"—he peered around and lowered his voice— "I even pass some blood now an' again. If I don't get me some soothin' food soon, I could up an' die."

Nate sat back and eyed him closely in the growing darkness. Though grime and the man's frizzled beard hid most of his face, Smith did look a mite poorly, and his eyes had a yellowish tinge.

The trader continued. "I got me some chickens off a passin' raidin' party awhile back, an' now with the cows I'm bringin' home, there'll be milk an' eggs a'plenty. Enough to see me through till my stomach gets put to rights. I even bought some good English spices and healin' herbs the gal knows how to use. So as you can see, no price in this world's gonna buy her off me till I'm in fine fettle again."

Serious raindrops began spattering them as they stared each other down. Nate grimaced and dried his knife on his pant leg then shoved it back inside its sheath. He'd just have to wait Smith out, one way or the other. "Well then, Eustice, I reckon my answer to that question of yours is I'll be ridin' with you the rest of the way." He got up and strode to his own shelter.

Rain, rain, rain. Slogging along the muddy trail, Rose looked woefully up at the gloomy sky and shook her head. At least the thunder and lightning had ceased sometime during the wee hours. From the time she'd left the leaky shelter of the crude hut where she'd slept last night, they'd all sloshed through mud or been splattered by it as the caravan trudged up one ridge and down the other side. Then it was start up yet another mucky ridge and face the inevitable swollen stream they needed to cross at the bottom. All the while, water poured from the sky as if angels were emptying barrels of it at a time.

Whenever Mr. Smith gave the order to rest the horses, Rose hopped down into ankle-deep mud, which saw to the swift ruination of her soft leather shoes. The soles barely allowed her to keep her footing, especially on any sort of grade. Going downhill was hard even on the animals, who also struggled to keep their footing beneath their heavy loads.

Gritting her teeth as the rain continued to pummel her, Rose clutched her soggy cloak closer. Soaked through, its hue was more violet than burgundy. She turned her head slightly to peer around, and the limp brim of her bonnet drooped like a funnel, pouring a stream of cold water down her nose and hands. She winced. If there was anything that smelled worse than a wet horse, it was her smelling like a wet horse!

She knew the rest of the party looked as bedraggled and smelled as odorous as she did. The decorative feathers the Shawnee braves sported in their braids and on their clothes now drooped as sadly as everyone's expressions. Thank heaven it was June and only mildly cool, or they'd all be shivering and covered with gooseflesh.

Up ahead, she saw Nate on his horse, coming back from scouting after nearly an hour. She wondered if anyone—Indian or bandit—possessed gumption enough to lie in wait to ambush a caravan in such abysmal weather. After he stopped to converse with Mr. Smith, he headed down the line to her.

"You look like a drowned chicken." A sympathetic smile curved one side of his lips.

She snickered. "I beg to differ. The Indians with all their soggy feathers look like drowned chickens. I, on the other hand, look and smell rather like a drowned skunk." The sad truth of her words made her grimace.

A teasing spark lit his eyes as he leaned closer, the brim of his hat spilling rainwater onto the ground. "I'd say in that wet wool, you smell more like a dead sheep." He reached around and untied his bedroll, shaking out the fur blanket he slept in. He handed it to her. "Shed that wet cloak of yours and wrap this around you instead. The rain won't get through it."

Rose was touched by his kind offer. "Are you sure you don't need it?" A dollop of water dropped on her hand from overhead branches.

He smiled as she glared up at the tree. "Actually, I'm used to weather like this. Been traipsin' around out in nature nigh onto ten years now. Like it says in Ma's Bible, 'This, too, shall pass,' and all that."

Rose only hoped it would. As gracefully as possible, she shed her sodden cloak and accepted his covering. It was heavier than she'd expected—far heavier than her wet cloak. She took measure of the thick fur, which held little resemblance to the coveted wraps and muffs displayed in the elegant shop windows at Bath. "What type of fur is this?"

He shrugged. "Buffalo. Keeps a body dry when it needs to."

"Dry? Is there such a thing?" Laughing, she pulled it around her soaked clothes.

Nate reached over to help her. The weight of the wrap was no match for his strength, and he hefted it as if it weighed no more than a feather.

But what surprised Rose even more was his gentleness. Suddenly she was acutely aware of how very close he was. She could feel the warmth of his breath feathering her cheek, and it sent a tingly sort of pleasure through her being, the likes of which she'd never felt before. But then, he was the sort of man the likes of which she'd never encountered before. Nate Kinyon was like a protecting angel. Her own protecting angel.

He fiddled with the fur wrap until he had it snugly about her shoulders. His hazel eyes, very near, met hers and lingered there for a breathless moment. Finally he centered himself again on his saddle and gathered his reins. Cocking his head to one side, he flashed a grin. "Keep it warm for me till I get back."

Without further word, he spurred his horse on.

Now, whatever did he mean by that? Uncertain whether or not she liked that particular smile, she couldn't help staring after him. Then she straightened her spine. *The man was such a flirt.*

Chapter 12

The rain gradually slowed and came to an end. Rose swept a thankful gaze up at the sky as late-afternoon sunshine broke through the clouds, slanting shafts of light into the forest. Familiar with Britain's wet climate, she was intimately acquainted with rain, but except for the drenching suffered on her homeward trek from Bristol during a downpour, she'd never felt like a drowned rat until now. And at least the road in England had been cobbled, not a slippery quagmire. Moisture still dripped from the trees onto the soggy trail, making travel precarious, but she knew several hours of strong sunshine would set things to right. As the pack train continued a descent that began half an hour ago, the pathway began to level out, making the journey a bit easier. Perhaps they were coming to the river Mr. Smith had mentioned last eve. She certainly hoped so. They were supposed to stop and make camp there.

The buffalo robe Nate Kinyon had loaned her had protected her from getting any wetter, but she longed to get out of her still-damp clothes and into something dry. How ironic that after fearing for her sisters and being concerned about their welfare, she was the one traveling into the unknown. The girls were undoubtedly warm and dry in substantial homes with tight roofs over their heads, while she herself could easily catch lung fever and slowly waste away.

Shrugging off the temptation to feel sorry for herself, Rose directed her thoughts across the ocean to her father and brothers. She hoped her and her sisters' sacrifices had indeed saved the rest of the family from ruin. But how marvelous it would be to go home again, be snuggled and toasty warm in her own feather bed with a blazing fire in the hearth, the wonderful smell of rich stew from supper permeating the dwelling. She should never have taken such blessings for granted. She breathed a prayer for her sorely missed loved ones, trusting them in God's hands, and vowed that if ever she found herself living a life of ease again, she would express her utmost thankfulness daily.

A sudden gust of wind chilled by the storm swirled around her, and Rose tugged the fur tighter about her. At least she still had that one small comfort, even if it was only a loan from Nate.

Where was Nate? Turning in her saddle, she searched past two of the Shawnee and their strings of horses and discovered him and Mr. Smith conversing as they rode side by side. The frontiersman must have ridden in while she allowed herself that brief moment of self-pity. She didn't dare dwell for long on how truly miserable she felt, lest she fall apart, and when the reality of her situation occasionally did intrude, she strove to quash it as quickly as possible. She had to remain strong—or at least appear to.

Now that the storm had passed and the last of the heavy clouds scudded from view, the bright sunlight cheered her up. But her optimism quickly faded as she detected the ominous roar of a river ahead growing louder by the moment. Rain had probably swollen the volume of water, as Mr. Smith had predicted. Remembering the last crossing, which had been tentative enough to give any brave soul pause for thought, she hoped they wouldn't attempt to cross an even mightier river this eve.

The party emerged into an open meadow, and Rose feasted her eyes on the variegated greens sprinkled liberally with summer wildflowers. Everything looked fresh and clean, and leftover raindrops sparkled like diamonds amid the tall weeds. Even the cool breeze smelled sweet. Then she saw more red men.

A cluster of nearly naked Indians with shaved heads stared at them from the riverbank. They looked nothing like the Shawnee she'd grown used to seeing. Attired only in loincloths and bedecked with feathers, they sported piercings and strange-looking tattoos on various parts of their bodies. They smiled and waved, however, so Rose hoped Providence would find them friendly after all. Still, she couldn't shake off her anxiety.

The man ahead of her appeared at ease after spotting the braves, but Rose saw that his hand now rested on the butt of his musket.

Three long canoes lay upturned on the bank near a ferry raft similar to the one used at the last river crossing. The sight of crude shelters like the caravan had used last evening indicated the Indians must have camped there during the storm. Now they had a campfire to warm their chilled bones and some delicious-smelling meat roasting over the blaze. Rose breathed in the enticing aroma.

Reaching the unfamiliar group, the pack train came to a halt. Nate, Mr. Smith, and the first of the Shawnee riders dismounted and joined the strangers. Rose was not near enough to make out voices or words, but she noticed that as the men talked, they used their hands more than their mouths, communicating with grunts and broad gestures that looked somewhat comical.

Her first impulse was to get off her horse, but since the other Shawnee in the party had remained mounted while they watched the exchange, she resisted any thought of sliding down. Even though she sensed no hint of danger, she assured herself that the Indians at the camp didn't mean any harm.

After a few tense moments, Mr. Smith broke away from the group and headed toward Rose. He stopped at her side and spoke under his breath. "I want ya to stay put till we build ya a shelter. Then ya need to get in it and stay there. We'll bring over some food when it's done."

The thought of actual food, fresh and hot and tasty, sounded inviting, yet a sense of unease slithered through Rose. She glanced beyond the trader to Nate, who continued gesturing and nodding with the strange

Indians. "Surely you don't mean we must stay the night here. . .with these. . .other strange Indians."

"Aye. That's just what I'm sayin'. They come downriver with a mind to do a bit o' tradin'. An' as you'll learn soon enough, redskins don't get in no big rush about it. We might be up half the night dickerin' and parlayin' over what's tossed on the blanket. . .an' I don't want you throwed into the mix. Is that clear?"

Thrown into the mix! What did that mean? Rose wanted more of an explanation and opened her mouth to protest the whole affair but bit back her words. She'd already been auctioned off once, only to be dragged out to this uncharted expanse of emptiness, and she couldn't begin to imagine what horrors might await her were she to be purchased by one of those vicious-looking tattooed Indians. "Rest assured, Mr. Smith, I shall be only too happy to leave you gentlemen to your business."

"*Gentlemen*, eh?" The trader gave a wry chuckle. Then he winced and rubbed back and forth across his protruding belly. "Sure will be glad to get back to my place. This trip's takin' the starch clean outta me." The short, paunchy man took a step away then turned back. "Remember what I said. Stay outta sight."

Stay out of sight! As if Rose needed her owner to tell her that more than once. Despite the day's mild temperature, she huddled within the confines of Nate Kinyon's fur blanket and sat still as a post until the other horses in the pack train had been unloaded. With even her nose buried inside the hairy cover, she'd scarcely even peeked out of it, avoiding all eye contact with the peculiar Indians.

The sound of approaching footsteps made her pulse quicken, until she recognized them as Nate's.

"You can get down now, little missy. And don't worry none about stayin' safe. We'll all of us be keepin' watch."

Somewhat encouraged, Rose opened the fur wrap, but felt somehow as exposed as a flag on a pole. Missing its privacy, she shivered.

Nate reached up to her, and she gratefully accepted his help. Again she was impressed at the way gentleness tempered his strength, and part of her wished she could remain within the safe circle of those strong arms. A man of his ilk would make any woman feel secure and protected. But each nerve in her body sensed that everyone was watching. Her skin crawled as she felt dark, hooded eyes observing her every step on the way to her private shelter.

The low jabbering started up again. Already Rose regretted having parted with Nate's fur robe. She still felt vulnerable and exposed even inside the crude hut with the added protection of her belongings surrounding her. Any thought of shedding her damp clothing and changing into a dry outfit fled her mind. Instead she peered out the entrance toward the fire, watching the goings-on at the gathering.

The men from the pack train clustered around the Indians' campfire, drying out, with the exception of Nate, who occupied himself with the unsaddling of her horse. For ten minutes or more Rose kept an eye on the group. Finally she exhaled a bated breath as she saw them all settle down onto blankets around the fire. One of the Indians turned a spit, which held what appeared to be a wild turkey and perhaps a goose. The aroma of those roasting birds was almost more than her hungry stomach could endure.

She continued to observe the men for several more minutes to be sure no one was leaving the others. Then she hurriedly flung open her trunk and plucked out some bedding and some dry clothes, intending to be changed and have her bed made before anyone started moving about again.

Without Bob around, Nate was glad a Cherokee by the name of Two Crows spoke passable English. Nate fared well enough using sign language but preferred being able to talk in plain words whenever possible. The Indian had recognized Nate's name and even asked about Black Horse Bob.

But once they'd waded through all the polite questions regarding mutual acquaintances, the expression on Two Crows's face changed from friendly smiles to stony reserve.

Nate tensed. *Why the sudden change?*

"What you hear about Mohawk Chief Tiyanoga and English governor Clinton at Albany?" The Indian's black eyes narrowed as he studied Nate.

Nate and Eustice Smith swapped a glance and shrugged.

"We ain't heard nothin'," Smith replied evenly. "I been down in Baltimore. There was talk about some French soldiers an' a black robe movin' aways south of Lake Erie to build a fort. Nobody's happy about it. That's the last I heard." He sniffed.

The Indian hiked his chin. "Chief Tiyanoga say they build forts from big lake to Ohio River. He say to Clinton, 'We make treaty with you. Why you no go stop the French?' Then Tiyanoga say, 'Mohawk support English allies, but English allies no support Mohawk.' He say the Dutch buy small piece of land from Mohawk, but say piece is bigger." Two Crows spread his arms wide. "Tiyanoga say no more. He say he send wampum belt to the Six Nations, say chain is broken with the English."

Neither Nate nor Smith moved, but their eyes met and held for a brief second.

The trader shook his head offhandedly. "That bunch up in New York is always gettin' things wrong with the Nations. But them Indians up there got William Johnson to speak for 'em. He's a fair man. He'll sort things out sure 'nuff."

"Aye, that he will." Nate gave an emphatic nod. But inside, he knew that if Governor Clinton did nothing and allowed the French to gain control of the Ohio, Smith's trading post and every other English enterprise this side of the Alleghenies would be at risk.

Inhaling a troubled breath, he glanced around the circle of Indians, wondering if even the Shawnee and the Cherokee farther to the south would turn on them. If so, what would become of Rose. . .his Rose of Sharon?

Chapter 13

A canopy of stars twinkled in the blue velvet sky, while around the camp and off in the distance, fireflies flickered like so many more miniature stars. An occasional bat darted among the leafy treetops, and the hobbled horses stirred at the plaintive howl of a wolf. Used to nature's sounds, Nate chewed a bite of turkey and relaxed, enjoying the rush of the dark water not far away.

In the group ringing the campfire while they ate the roasted meat, Nate had the distinct impression the Cherokee seemed more inclined to be friendly toward the Shawnee braves than the Shawnee were toward the Cherokee. While the Cherokee talked with the help of hand signs, the Shawnee kept their replies short and blunt. Nate figured the Shawnee didn't want their red brothers to the south to think they could blithely intercept the pack train and get first pick of all the best trade goods. No doubt the Shawnee were already coveting a few particular items among the lot.

Switching his attention to Two Crows, Nate sensed the Indian's interest lay elsewhere—in the direction of Rose's haven—and the knowledge set him on edge. Nate had taken her a turkey drumstick moments earlier, and since then the interpreter seemed more occupied by the possibilities of what might be inside her small shelter than in the goods from the sacks and crates awaiting the group's inspection. He took another bite of the roasted turkey that had been flavored with some of Eustice Smith's seasonings, watching as the dark hooded gaze of Two Crows drifted often to Rose's hut.

The Indian wiped the back of his hand across his greasy mouth, puffing out his chest as he sat up straighter and turned to Nate, a frown rippling his tattooed forehead. "Why you serve woman? Why she no serve you, the man, like good squaw?"

Nate opened his mouth to reply, but Smith's voice cut him off. The trader leaned forward and cocked his grizzled head to one side. "The gal don't b'long to Kinyon. I bought her. She's my property, jest like ever'thing else on this here pack train." Having made the announcement, he sat back with a satisfied "harrumph."

Perhaps it was the man's stern tone of voice that caused the other Indians around the fire to cease talking and turn their attention to him, but Nate was quite sure they understood little, if anything, of what the trader had just said.

Not to be dissuaded from his question, Two Crows eyed Smith steadily. "If woman belong to you, why she not serve you?" His sullen eyes narrowed in confusion.

The trader raised his chin and stared hard at the Indian for several seconds before replying. "She's up there b'cause that's where I told her to stay, that's why. She don't need to be out here prancin' around fer you youngbloods to be gawkin' at. As it is, I'm already havin' to put up with more prancin' an' preenin' than a body should have to." He shot a surly glance at Nate as if challenging him to deny the accusation.

The interpreter still appeared perplexed, but he didn't comment further. His party had come many miles downriver with a load of furs to trade, and Nate was certain that, despite his curiosity about the ways of a white man, Two Crows knew better than to anger the trader who possessed the goods they hoped to barter for.

The other Cherokee began to stir restlessly—not a good sign. Then one of them said something in their language to Two Crows, who responded with a few words that seemed to mollify the Indian somewhat. He and his companions settled down again on their blankets and helped themselves to more meat from the roasted birds.

Nate decided it was time for a change of subject. "How is it that you braves knew we'd be comin' through here today? I find that mighty curious."

Two Crows let out a small huff. "Hunting party see when Smith go east. He take many horses loaded with furs for trade. We bring many prime furs in canoes. Wait at river crossing. Three suns." He held up a trio of greasy fingers. Then his gaze wandered again to Rose's hut with a knowing grin. "Smith's number-two wife, she make happy man under blanket."

Nate was sorely tempted to wipe that leer off the Indian's mouth but knew the prudent thing would be to refrain. They were crossing lawless Indian lands, and only an idiot would want to deliberately invite trouble.

Keeping the peace seemed the least of Eustice Smith's concerns, however. He leaned toward Two Crows with a meaningful glare and shook a turkey wing in the red man's face. "You'd best forget about the woman, or I won't so much as let ya get a sniff of what's in them packs of ourn." He gestured with a thumb toward the goods waiting to be displayed.

Two Crows's eyes widened for a second. He then composed his features into the more normal unreadable demeanor most Indians adopted and settled back on his blanket, eating as if nothing whatever had transpired.

Stifling a grin, Nate took another big bite himself. Up until now, he'd always assumed Eustice Smith would trade away his own mother if the price was right. But apparently that was not so when it concerned his stomach. Even more surprising, the man wasn't about to brook any vulgar insinuations about his lovely new cook. Would wonders never cease!

Then a more unwelcome realization dawned. Getting Rose out of

Smith's clutches was going to take a lot more effort than he'd figured on.

A lot more.

Having devoured the delicious turkey leg Nate had been kind enough to bring to her the previous evening, Rose still basked in the memory of the savory meat the next morning, wondering when she'd last enjoyed such a treat. Even without the roasted potatoes and fresh bread that would have accompanied it back home, it had been a most welcome change from the tiresome mush and cold jerked meat that made up most meals on the trail. Now what she would give for a spot of tea to warm her insides. But knowing there was little chance of that luxury, she disregarded the activity from the camp and concentrated on the lovely songs of the birds cavorting among the trees nearby. Already the tree toads were in fine harmony, and the steady drone of cicadas promised a hot day ahead. Meanwhile the ever-present river continued to surge and gush past the camp, though the volume had lessened somewhat from the previous day.

Rose's thoughts turned heavenward. *Dear Lord, how I thank You that Mr. Smith rode up to the auction when he did and not a moment sooner. I could not begin to imagine my sweet Lily being in my position here, not with her youth, her innocence. . . .*

On the heels of that notion, the mental picture of Mariah came to mind, and Rose felt a droll smile tug at her lips. Even a man as obstinate and stubborn as Mr. Smith would have sent someone as spirited as Mariah packing once she started whining and complaining at the sight of the first smudge on one of her gowns. And the dire comment she'd have made about his smell! La, either the man would have traded her off at first opportunity, or he'd have resorted to gagging her. Even then, however, the girl's nose would have curled in utter disdain at the odor whenever he passed by.

On the other hand, he might have traded Mariah off to those Indians he'd bargained with half the night. That realization sent a chill through Rose. And what if their dear father ever found out about such an unforeseen turn of events! How such disastrous news would break his heart. The poor beleaguered man had suffered trials enough, with the betrayal that left him in financial ruin. Surely the Lord would reward him in full measure for his patience and unfailing faith throughout the whole sorry affair.

She wondered if her family in England gave much thought to their loved ones who'd sailed across the wide ocean to the colonies. . .or for that matter, if Mariah even once wondered about her sisters' well-being. Perhaps she was consumed mostly with thoughts of herself and her own surroundings. Rose knew that Lily, having been so attached to both her sisters, undoubtedly kept her and Mariah in constant prayer. Rose suppressed a pang of longing for the dear girl. *Please keep her in Your tender watch-care, Father. I miss her so.*

As she sat in her shelter, observing the movements outside, Rose sighed. The early morning sun glistened off the river, casting golden outlines around the first members of the caravan making the crossing. Fortunately, the queer-looking Indians were hastening the trip by loaning their canoes to transport the goods, while the horses were hauled across the rapid water on another pitiful raft.

And here she still sat, relegated to stay out of sight as she had the night before.

Far from being the dull, overlooked spinster she'd been back home in England, it seemed the tattooed Indians considered her a lady of mystery. Now and again they'd pause in their work and glance toward her shelter, which grated on her nerves. How drastically her life had changed in such a short amount of time. Nibbling the inside corner of her lip, she wondered if it might have been wiser to display herself out in the open last eve in all her rained-on, rumpled glory. But when still another pair of beady black eyes flicked her way, she knew she had to trust that Mr. Smith and Nate knew best. After all, they'd had previous dealings with these natives of the land and knew some of the intricacies of their nature.

At last the goods and animals completed the tedious journey across the river. When the Cherokee began their slow paddle upstream with their load of pots, knives, bolts of cloth—and muskets—Nate came ambling up the bank toward Rose's hut. He waved, his friendly grin a most pleasing sight, as he called out to her, "Time to go, pretty lady."

His presence on the trip made it seem less of a trial and more like an adventure to Rose, especially since she knew he was making the journey for one reason only. For her. Smiling, she stood from her pallet and folded the blankets. Then after placing them and her other belongings inside her trunk again, she clicked it shut.

Time to go. . .into her still unknown future.

Chapter 14

On her very first seemingly endless day of travel, Rose had decided it was pointless to try to memorize passing landmarks in hopes of making her way back to Baltimore some future day on her own. Now that a fortnight had passed, she relinquished even the hope of escaping by her own efforts. As the caravan plodded up one mountain and down again, crossed another stream or creek or river like the one they'd forded a day or two or three ago, she concentrated on the beauty of God's untouched wilderness.

Her eyes beheld huge moss-covered boulders and majestic, sheer cliffs jutting out of the mountainside along the route. Strange new animals peeked from behind trees and shrubs and massive ferns, and bright red birds reminded her of Mariah dressed in all her finery. Just then a pair of orange-bellied birds resembling the orioles in England flitted among the trees, adding splashes of vivid color among the many blends of green.

Bluebirds with prominent crests and black, white, and red woodpeckers were also quite colorful, she admitted, but they had the annoying habit of breaking the blissful silence by making cacophonous calls and rapping on trees.

Inhaling the fresh scent of pine and the fragrance of the meadow flowers and tall grasses growing beside gurgling brooks, Rose couldn't help comparing the alluring perfumes of nature to the rank, odorous sewers of Bath, the acrid smell of smoke and falling ash from a thousand British chimneys. During the long voyage across the Atlantic, she had not experienced anything akin to the wonders of this new land, America. It was so filled with life, she felt exhilarated.

"Caught you smiling again." Nate surprised Rose as he guided his mount alongside hers.

"I'm afraid you did. I just saw a greedy little squirrel with the fluffiest tail ever trying to stuff one more acorn into his cheek. . .and all the while he's squealing at another squirrel in the next tree. See him?" She pointed up to a branch not far away.

He nodded, and that easy grin of his stretched across his face. "Thought you'd want to know we'll be reachin' the river in a couple of minutes."

"Another river?" She rolled her eyes. "And which one will that be, not that it makes the slightest bit of difference."

"Which one?" His straight brows sprang high on his forehead as he stared at her. "The Ohio. It's the one all the others we crossed drain into."

"Oh. Well, now that you mention it, I believe I can almost hear the roar. Did you not say the Ohio's near the river where Mr. Smith has his store?"

"Aye." His grin widened. "Where the Muskingum forks in. It's a mile or so downriver from here."

Rose felt her pulse quicken with excitement. . .and fear. "As I recall, you said a Shawnee and Delaware Indian village has formed near his enterprise."

"Right. But don't fret. Those Indians never gave him a lick of trouble, so they shouldn't bother you none. Like I said, they value the trader and the goods he supplies too much to give him reason to up an' leave here with all his merchandise."

After all this time, we shall finally reach our destination, then. Splendid! Still feeling some trepidation at the thought of being presented to the trader's wife, Rose schooled her features and did her best to dredge up a smile. Surely Mrs. Smith, another white woman, would be glad to have some female company around.

Rose cast a despairing look down at her hopelessly faded and worn brown dress, which she'd sacrificed rather than spoiling any of the few other daygowns she'd brought with her. All the natural lace that had adorned it at the start of the trip had frayed and worn away, and with all the snags and tears and stains the pitiful garment now bore, its best fate lay in the burn barrel. While the men were occupied with constructing the rafts the party would need, there had to be time to spruce up before meeting the trader's wife. Rose decided to don the indigo blue gown she'd worn briefly while her rain-saturated clothes dried. She'd prevail upon Nate to get her trunk down from the packhorse.

How odd, though, that Mr. Smith had not volunteered a single piece of information about his wife during this journey—except that he didn't like her cooking. Whenever Rose attempted to bring up the subject, mentioning that the woman must be very lonely with him gone for such a long time, he'd merely shrugged and said that her brothers were there to keep her company. *More men.* Rose supposed she'd be cooking for them, too.

Within moments, the midnight blue of an immense river came into view, certainly much larger than any of the others they'd crossed along the way. Dark and deep, it moved so massively that scarcely a ripple disturbed its surface.

"I've never seen such a wide, powerful river," Rose murmured.

Nate emitted a chuckle from deep inside. "I canoed down it once as far as the Mississippi, an' as big as you think the Ohio is, the Mississippi's a good four or five times bigger."

Rose gasped. "Mercy me. This surely is a wondrous new land." She turned to him.

As he gazed at her, Nate's eyes took on a warmth she'd never before glimpsed in them. Then he looked off into the distance. "That it is, Rose. That it is."

Could she possibly have been the cause for such a tender gaze, or was it merely evidence of how much he loved his frontier life? She reined in the romantic fancy lest he read something in her own expression. "I do hope Mr. Smith's store is on this side of the river. I can't imagine a rope long enough to ferry us to the other shore."

He threw back his head and laughed. "Now that would be a powerfully long chunk of hemp, wouldn't it? Unfortunately, his store does happen to be on the other side, so we'll have to build us some rafts for crossin'. By the time we rudder our way across, we'll probably have floated down to just about where the Muskingum town is. I'd say we should have enough trees downed an' cleaned an' the rafts put together before the day's out."

Looking about as men began chopping down trees, Rose knew this would be far from just one more crossing for them—it would be crossing the hard way. With Britain being tamed and settled from shore to shore, bridges, walls, buildings, tradesmen, and exotic trade goods were all a matter of course. Though her life had been quite busy there, compared to the American frontier it had been quite easy. Food was as near as the local marketplace, clothing as close as the nearest seamstress. And Papa's livelihood hadn't involved providing a necessity like food or shelter or clothing. He made adornments for the frivolous rich folk to wear about as they attended socials and parties.

Yes, life had been much easier in Britain, more tranquil, and shamefully taken for granted by everyone. Rose breathed in her surroundings. Perhaps circumstances had been more comfortable there, but in some strange way, she'd never felt so alive as she did now.

She looked up at Nate. "While you men are building the rafts, is there something I might do to help? I cannot sit about doing nothing."

He gave a decisive nod. "Food. Lots of food. I know the Shawnees'd appreciate whatever you fix, same as the rest of us. Choppin' down trees for rafts is real hunger-makin' work."

"As you wish. I shall make the lot of you a royal feast. . .even if it is jerked meat and mush and beans. And could you possibly get me my trunk when you have a moment?"

Raft construction took longer than expected, and rather than attempt a night crossing, Nate was glad when Smith decided they'd make camp one last time. Some of the men had gone hunting and returned with a pair of fat geese, which Rose immediately prepared and roasted for supper. They were quickly devoured, fresh game always being appreciated much more than dried jerky. Nate admired the outdoor cooking skill his very refined Rose had acquired along the journey. She'd come a long way from having to depend on a proper hearth.

The following morning, the log rafts were loaded and launched one by one. Eustice Smith oversaw the loading of the first two, figuring that by taking one in the middle of the line, he'd be able to keep an eye on all his goods and be onshore when they were unloaded. Now on the third one with Rose and the trader, Nate watched Rose observing the lead raft as it slowly made its way across and downstream, aided by the river.

"We'll reach the village just before the Muskingum merges," he told her, "an' be at the tradin' post soon enough." Keeping a steady hold on the rudder, he studied the slender English beauty perched on her trunk as she looked ahead, her expression heart-wrenchingly expectant. The dark indigo of the new gown she'd put on added depth to the blue-gray of her eyes. Even her hair had been washed and brushed and lay in shiny, silky amber waves he wished she hadn't tied back with a ribbon. She looked so feminine and delicate, yet he'd witnessed her strength of character and determination dozens of times. If only she knew what lay ahead. . .

Nate swallowed a huge chunk of guilt. He should have prepared her for her first visit to a Shawnee village instead of allowing her to believe Smith's store sat in the middle of a civilized town. But she had so many fears to work through already, he didn't have the heart to cause her more worry. Things were sure to come as a shock to her. He eyed the trader slouched on a flour sack with his grubby hands dangling between his knobby knees. Just what would the old geezer take to let her go back where she belonged?

Catching the eye of the Indian riding with them, Nate motioned for him to take over. The brave obliged and handed Nate his pole then took control of the rudder stick while Nate made his way gingerly across the logs to Smith. He cleared his throat.

The man peered up at him and grunted.

Speaking in tones Rose would not overhear, he met the trader's narrowed eyes. "Look, Eustice. You know an' I know that Indian village is no place for a proper lady like Rose Harwood. Tell me what I can give you to let her go back to her kind. Do the decent thing for once in your life."

The man fingered his beard as if considering the matter and let out a deep huff. His bony shoulders rose with a shrug, then he looked up at Nate in all seriousness. "The truth of it is, if I had me enough furs or cash money ta quit sellin' stuff to folks an' go off where I'd be able ta live in comfort the rest o' my life, I'd take it. This trip's prit'near been the end o' me, Kinyon. It's all I can do to put one foot in front o' the other. I'm too old to be gallivantin' back east for goods ta sell then hike over mountain trails an' sleep on the hard ground in all kinds o' weather. Thing is, right now I need that gal to cook me some good food till I'm able ta consider packin' up an' leavin'. That's all I can tell ya."

A tide of discouragement swept over Nate. *Enough furs or cash money to live on for the rest of his life! How could a body come up with that?* Awhile back, he remembered hearing rumors about silver, about some Shawnee chief downriver toward the Mississippi having a secret silver mine. Could it be true? Well even if it was, rumor had it that some Frenchies had set up a trading post of their own down there, and they sure wouldn't want any competition. Still. . .one never knew. He turned to admire Rose again. Somebody had to do something, and there was nobody to do anything but him. He'd just have to find a way, that's all there was to it.

Chapter 15

Rose didn't know what she expected to see when she arrived at the settlement where Mr. Smith's trading post was located, but it wasn't anything remotely compared to what she found. Before her lay fenced, cultivated fields that flanked a goodly number of dome-shaped and cone-shaped dwellings covered with bark and animal hides, and even some long, low lodges. When the raft passed some of the conelike structures near the riverbank, bronze-skinned men, women, and naked children had charged out of them, whooping and yelling as they ran alongside, keeping pace with the raft. Others, many attired in pale deerskin, streamed from other huts to join them. Her anticipation mounted with the excitement of the gathering throng.

Scanning the enthusiastic revelers, Rose searched for Mrs. Smith among the mass, but to no avail. Obviously the woman was shy or perhaps used to such displays and reluctant to be jostled by such an eager crowd. She grabbed hold of the railing as the raft floated next to one of the others and dug into the moist riverbank. Nate's strong arm saved her from pitching forward as it lurched to a stop.

Mr. Smith hollered some harsh orders in the Indian language, and the crowd backed away, though they continued to chatter in their guttural way and laugh among themselves, pointing at the newcomers. Most of their attention centered on Rose.

Uncomfortable with their unbridled ogling, Rose gasped as Nate scooped her up into his arms and jumped ashore. Amid the ear-splitting racket going on all around them, she could barely make out his explanation about not wanting to ruin her shoes as he set her on dry ground and returned to the raft.

Left on her own, she found herself instantly surrounded as a mob of Indians of all ages closed in around her, babbling in their foreign tongue. The stench of bear grease on their shiny bodies filled her nostrils. Eager voices of men, women, and children drowned out every other sound as frantic hands shot forth from all directions to touch her, grabbing at her clothing, her skin, and her hair. The stylish bonnet was torn away, and her hair tumbled from the pins she'd so carefully placed in order to look nice for Mrs. Smith. As locks of it were yanked one way and then another, some fell before her eyes, nearly blocking her vision. Overcome by mounting panic, she couldn't even speak. She wanted them all to stop touching her and step away. *Dear Lord, help me. Protect me. I do not know what to do.*

From behind, someone suddenly whisked her up, and her heart nearly exploded from fright. Recognizing Nate, she regained her senses, and her heightened breathing slowed to normal. He'd come back, saved her again, and bullied his way through the crowd. To Rose's utmost relief, the Indians did not follow after them as he carried her away from the melee.

This was not the welcome she'd expected. Wanting no more than to relax into the comfort of his embrace, Rose knew it was not proper to do so. Instead she assessed more of the settlement, amazed at its size and the extensive array of crops. But as Nate strode away from the cluster of dwellings and headed toward the outskirts, she looked ahead and saw they were coming to a building completely different from the rest. Made of logs piled one on top of the other on three sides, the open front had only a canvas covering, which had been pulled to the side. Rose blew a wisp of hair out of her disbelieving eyes and her heart stopped. *This—this decrepit hut—was the profitable enterprise the trader owned?* She didn't know whether to laugh hysterically or burst into tears. Shocked beyond words, she could only gape at the wretched structure, where a pair of unfamiliar braves who looked younger than she by a few years sat on the ground, cross-legged, leaning back against posts flanking either side of the entrance, their black eyes glittering. Peering as hard as she could within the shaded confines of the store, she could not make out Mrs. Smith anywhere.

"Sorry I left you alone like that, Rose," Nate said as he set her down. "I should've figgered they'd be meddlesome, seein' somebody so pretty as you outta the blue. Anyway, looks like Eustice can get along fine without my help." He motioned with his head toward the crowd, where the trader was directing the unloading of his merchandise. Following Nate's gaze, she saw horses and cows being led ashore, goods hauled off, and workers being greeted and hugged by loved ones. The accumulating piles of supplies drew considerable attention as curious inhabitants of the village craned their necks to peer inside the crates, while Mr. Smith continued to yell at them in their language. Obviously he didn't want anyone making off with any of his precious cargo.

Considering everything she'd endured since her arrival in this land, Rose wondered why any of these circumstances surprised her. It was actually a fitting ending for an incredibly unbelievable journey. After all, the trader had sloughed off every question she'd asked regarding his store.

Even Nate, *her protector*, had given only the barest hint of a response when she inquired about specific details, she reminded herself. But having known him long enough to appreciate his stalwart character, she gave him the benefit of the doubt, surmising that he'd only been trying to be merciful. She moistened her lips and took a deep breath, doing her best to smooth her hair into some semblance of order with her fingers as she looked up at him. "I had no idea that they were like this. I'd heard so many stories about the noble savage, I thought they'd all be. . .proud.

Self-controlled. Instead, they bring to mind the poor street urchins in the slums of London. Wild, smelly, and loud."

Nate's hazel eyes radiated gentleness, and a sheepish half smile played across his mouth. "I'm truly sorry for bein' so remiss. I shoulda warned you not to dress so fancy-like. Most of 'em have never seen such fine women's clothes. Thing is, I was so caught up feastin' my eyes on how pretty you look, I just plumb forgot. I hope you'll forgive me."

At Nate and Rose's approach, the unsmiling Indians at the store's entrance unfurled their legs and sprang to their feet, catching up muskets as their ferret eyes squinted with suspicion. Both men had tattooed arms and wore their hair loose with cloth bands tied above their brows, and they were attired differently from the braves Rose had ridden with for the past weeks. Instead of wearing long buckskin trousers, they had on only breechcloths and beaded moccasins, leaving their legs bare. Each wore an intricate breastplate of beads over their hairless chests. Trying not to gape, she nodded a polite greeting then started into the trading post to see if she might have missed Mrs. Smith behind a stack of kegs or barrels. Moving past the braves, she felt their intent gaze following her.

A touch roomier than it appeared at first glance, the trading post had several kegs and barrels occupying its corners. She noted some cooking pots and kettles hanging on hooks, along with wooden bowls of different sizes. Crates of tomahawks and hunting knives sat on the dirt floor beside half-a-dozen muskets. A rustic shelf fastened to one of the log walls held yard goods, folded blankets, and an open box containing an array of mismatched buttons. Brass looking glasses nearby reflected light from the entrance onto a variety of colored beads, and the odor of cured animal hides stacked almost waist high permeated the structure.

She heard Nate greet the pair from the open doorway where he stood. "Running Wolf, Spotted Elk. How're things goin' for you boys?"

"No trouble," one muttered, his tone more cool than friendly.

Rose stopped to glance over her shoulder. None of the Indians she'd traveled with had spoken a word of English in her presence, though they seemed to understand whatever Mr. Smith said to them.

"We let no one in," the young brave continued. "Trade only on blanket out here. No one steal from Fawn Woman when Smith not here."

Nate nodded. "That should please Eustice. I'm sure he'll reward you and Fawn Woman with somethin' real good for bein' so diligent. By the way, Miss Harwood here would like to meet Eustice's wife. Where might she be?"

The brave pointed toward the crowd surrounding the rafts being unloaded. "She waits to see what gifts husband bring."

Hearing that information, Rose turned and came forward to look toward the crowd. So Mrs. Smith had been there all the while. Strange that she couldn't be seen amid the onlookers pressed shoulder to shoulder at the river. And where were the woman's brothers? Becoming aware that neither stone-faced brave had smiled as yet but stood erect, eyeing her, Rose thought they reminded her of the Royal Palace Guard at London's Windsor Castle. Ignoring their leering stares, she searched the milling throng chattering near the trade goods, but she still could not spot the trader's wife among them. Obviously the woman must be quite comfortable around the Indians, or she wouldn't mingle so closely with them. No doubt after living among these people she'd become rather fluent in their language the way her husband had. As yet unable to make out even the simplest of words, Rose marveled. Would she ever be able to converse with them herself?

As Rose wandered again among the goods in the store waiting for the trader and his wife, Nate moved closer to the guards. "Do you boys know if any of the Miamis or Illinois from downriver have come up this way with metal bracelets to trade?"

The pair exchanged wordless glances; then one of them shook his head. "Metal bracelets come from over great sea, not from setting sun. English make good bracelets." He rubbed his tanned fingers over the wide brass circlet clasped around his upper arm. "French bracelets no good."

"Aye. The English ones are best." Gratified that no one here had become aware of the silver discovery farther west, Nate glanced toward the river where supplies from the rafts were being carried to the store. He leaned inside the entrance. "They're bringin' stuff up from the river now, Rose. Come outside an' have a seat. I'd like a word with you."

"Of course. I shouldn't want to be in the way while the goods are being stored." She followed him to a log in front of a dead campfire and sank down onto it.

He propped a foot alongside her, and they watched the parade of crates and sacks being transported into the trading post. "In a few days I'll be headin' out," he said at last.

"I beg your pardon?" A flicker of fear sparked in her eyes as she met his gaze.

He gave a nod. "I spoke to Eustice, an' I believe I can get him the price he wants to sell you to me."

Her fear evaporated. Anger took its place. Her mouth dropped open in a look of shock, and her face grew white.

Her reaction floored him. Hadn't it been clear all along that he'd come on this journey with the intent of getting her free of Eustice Smith? He reared back with a frown. "What's the problem? I thought that's what you wanted."

Chapter 16

Rose's fists closed around handfuls of her skirt, and she clenched her teeth together so hard they hurt. This man—this *rescuer* she had counted on all this time—wanted to *buy* her, not free her. She did want to be out of here, but not as merely another man's property. Surely the bounder did not expect to purchase her from Mr. Smith so he could drag her off somewhere for his own amusement!

She fought for words to express her fury so Nate Kinyon would have no doubt as to how despicable a cur she thought him to be. But before she could verbalize her opinion of him and that plan of his, Mr. Smith emerged from the group of Indian workers toting cargo to the trading post and strode over to her. He gestured with his thumb toward the rear of the store.

"Back there, woman, there's a pen o' chickens. An' off to the right o' that you'll find my wife's garden. Make me up a pot o' rich chicken soup with plenty o' cooked-down vegetables. My sleepin' quarters are in that wigwam left o' here. There's a dutch oven inside ya can use. Oh, an' milk the cow first off. I need some milk to soothe my innards right quick."

Rose stared at him, completely dumbfounded. She was quite capable of plucking chicken feathers, but he expected her to go and kill the poor bird herself? The swine! Already in high dudgeon over Nate Kinyon's announcement moments ago, she felt her stomach tighten further. This was all too much.

"Well, get to it, gal." His scowl darkened. "Now."

"But—I've yet to meet your wife. I'd hoped—"

He rolled his squinty eyes and shook his head. "Ain't no use. You'll get no help from her."

"Please."

His bony shoulders sagged. "Oh, all right." He swung on his heel and turned to Running Wolf or Spotted Elk—Rose didn't know which was which—who stood speaking to a squaw. "Fawn Woman! Get over here."

In total disbelief, Rose felt the single wish that had sustained her throughout the endless journey crumble to ashes as a slender Indian woman grimaced to the young brave and approached on silent feet. Near Rose's own age, the dusky-skinned woman with a beaded leather headband above long, shiny braids and a beaded dress of soft doeskin would have been considered quite a beauty, were it not for the obstinate expression of sheer disgust that hardened her features. She cut a wordless glance to Mr. Smith, then to Rose.

Her husband tilted his head toward Rose. "This here's Rose Harwood. I brung her to cook fer me. Miss Harwood, this is my wife, Fawn Woman Smith."

Too devastated to utter a response, Rose merely stared as the woman raked her head to toe with her deep brown gaze and grunted. She reached out and felt Rose's gown. "Want gown." She pouted at her husband.

That Indian woman wants my clothes! Not only is she not English, she wants my clothes! Rose all but choked.

Mr. Smith steered his wife away. "Ya don't need that rag o' hers, Fawn. I brung you a gown of yer own. Better an' much grander than hers. You'll see."

"Hmph." Only slightly mollified, the squaw crossed her arms in defiance. "She cook for you. I no eat pale-woman food. Woman no sleep in my wigwam."

"She won't have to," the trader agreed, "soon as ya build her one next to ours."

"Me?" The squaw raised her chin and sneered.

"Aye, woman. You."

She huffed and pursed her lips. "Want gown. Give now."

Smith appeared noticeably weary of the situation, but his determined stance showed he wasn't about to give in to his wife or any other female. "First ya build the wigwam. Then ya get the gown. That's final." Shaking his grizzled head, he turned to Rose and lifted a hand palm up in question. "What're you still standin' there fer? Git a move on. I need that soup quick. I got a powerful ache in my belly."

Rose fully understood. Her own stomach wasn't feeling so wonderful at the moment, imagining the chicken she'd have to butcher with her own hands.

Having witnessed the conversation, Nate cleared his throat and stepped up beside Rose. "Think I'll give the little lady a hand, if it's all the same to you, Eustice."

The trader shrugged and stomped away, while his wife cast a scathing glare over her shoulder at both of them and went to see to her task.

Rose gave the frontiersman a wavering smile. He'd come to her aid again. How could she stay mad at him? Once again God had shown His faithful presence, His mercy. As Papa always said, *God is a sure help in time of need.* She sent a thankful prayer aloft and followed Nate behind the trading post to the chicken pen, her feet dragging the entire way.

⚊⚊

The village lay quiet. Night sounds from the surrounding forest drifted across the area as the moon shed its light on the sleepy settlement. Lounging on his sleeping pallet with a cup of tea at the campfire in front of Rose's thrown-together wigwam, Nate shook his head, wondering when a gust of wind would blow the pitiful thing clear out over the next ridge. Fawn Woman had put the least effort possible into its construction, her disdain for Eustice's new cook almost tangible.

He redirected his thoughts to Rose, already asleep inside the structure's barely adequate shelter. This day had been a hard one for her, likely the first of many. He'd make her hovel more secure in the morning. Sure had been a sight to behold, though, her chasing after that poor squawking chicken earlier. A smile twitched his lips. How could she be that old without ever having killed a chicken before? Must be because city folk had butchers and bakers at their beck and call. Proper little Rose Harwood was out of her depth, but she did have pluck. She stuck to something till she saw it through.

Hearing footsteps coming out of the woods, he glanced up to see Eustice Smith returning from answering nature's call. Nate sprang to his feet and went to intercept the man before he entered his wigwam. "I'd like a private word with you."

"What? Now?" Smith let out a weary breath.

"It'll only take a minute." He handed him his leftover tea. "Let's sit over on your log."

Lumbering beside Nate till they reached the fallen wood, Smith sank onto it. "Make it quick. I'm bushed."

Uncertain about how to start, Nate decided to go for broke and blurt out the words plain and simple. "Far as I know, Bob still has most of his money from the furs we traded, an' I'll be gettin' some mighty fine pelts myself for that fancy suit I bought before the trip. If you'll take all of that, plus whatever money I still have on me in trade goods, me an' Bob'll go downstream and do some sharp tradin' in some of the tributaries that don't have no store. Mebbe get enough in those untried areas so you could retire to that life of ease you was talkin' about."

The old man chuckled. "Ya really do want that little gal I bought, don't ya'?"

Not relishing being made sport of, Nate felt his hackles go up. "That's why I'm here."

"That's French territory you'll be headin' into, ya know." Smith took a sip of the tepid tea.

Nate shrugged. He'd discerned a hint of interest in the trader's voice, a good sign. "All the better. Think on it, Eustice. You got finer quality cloth an' weapons than those Frenchies do. Besides, me an' Bob can take care of ourselves."

Rubbing his shaggy beard in thought, Smith grunted. "Do what you want. I don't see as how I can lose. I wasn't much cottonin' to ya hangin' around here, distractin' my cook, anyway."

"Distractin'? That what you call help? You should be thankin' me, man. If it wasn't for me showin' her the how-to, Rose'd still be out back tryin' to catch that chicken you had for supper, an' you know it."

Smith sputtered into a laugh then clutched his belly with a wince and glanced over at Rose's deplorable wigwam. "That ol' bird gave her a run fer her money, eh?" He handed the empty cup back to Nate. "Well, there's no denyin' the gal cooked me up a fine meal. These innards o' mine don't feel near as bad as before. I knowed she'd do me some good." He nodded in thought and got up.

Nate watched the man amble away to his wigwam, holding his midsection.

On his way back to his sleeping pallet, he looked across the moonlit Indian village. It had swelled in size since he'd come through last spring. There had to be thirty-five or forty wigwams now, and at least three longhouses. He could see light streaming from one of those gathering places. Some tribe members must be inside tossing bone dice. Indian men weren't so different from most footloose men he came across in his travels. They all liked to gamble.

For a few seconds, he toyed with the idea of joining them. He'd probably get a lot more for his fancy clothes with several men vying for each piece. But then he glanced over at Rose's shelter and knew she wouldn't like him gambling. Shaking off the unwonted conviction, he recalled his promise to sleep near her entrance tonight. She'd been pretty jumpy, this being her first night in such a foreign environment. Besides, he really didn't want to chance losing the few pounds he possessed, not when he needed so much more than that to fulfill his plan.

He wondered how much money Bob had on him. That partner of

his was such a miser, he habitually sent most of his money to his father's sister for safekeeping. Nate glanced toward the river. Bob should have beaten the caravan and been here long before the party arrived. What was taking him so long? The sooner the two of them went looking for that silver he'd heard about, the sooner they'd get back. . .and the sooner he'd get his Rose, his Rose of Sharon.

A small shaft of light fell across Rose's eyes, awakening her. Blinking against the brightness, she peered up to see sunshine streaming through one of several holes in the cone-shaped wigwam Fawn Woman had slapped together. Rose grimaced, thankful it hadn't been rain that disturbed her sleep. When she found some free time, she'd patch those spots. Sitting up on the sleeping pallet of furs, she vowed to save up chicken feathers until she had enough to make a softer bed. She took a leisurely stretch as she took stock of the cramped living quarters, half of which was cluttered with sacks and kegs and small chests containing Mr. Smith's personal foods. There had to be a way to stack them neatly so she'd have more room.

Sounds from outside drifted to her ears as the village residents began to stir. Rose bolted up from her pallet and opened her trunk, snatching from the contents the now-stained brown gown and its equally spotty apron. No one could possibly envy those. She dressed quickly and ran a brush through her hair before tying it back with a ribbon. Then she opened the flap of her wigwam.

As he'd promised, Nate slept nearby. His thoughtfulness touched her, and she tiptoed quietly past him to take care of her morning needs at the bubbling creek she'd discovered yesterday in a shallow gully behind the crude chicken coop and pen.

While at the brook, Rose wondered what day of the week had just dawned and calculated it must be Wednesday. She must not lose track again. Scanning the area around her, she found a sharp rock and used it to scratch a line into a nearby tree. She'd make one mark for each day so she'd always know when the Sabbath came.

In the morning's quiet freshness, she sat with her back against the beech tree and bowed her head. *Dear Father in heaven, thank You that my long journey has finally ended. I don't understand the reason You brought me here, but I ask for strength and patience as I fulfill my contract. Please help me to be an example of Your love to the Smiths and to remain faithful to my faith, as I promised Mum. And as always, I commit my loved ones into Your loving care.*

On her way back, Rose spied Mrs. Smith emerging from the much larger rounded wigwam in a gaudy red gown more suited for a theater performer than a respectable lady. Her husband's taste in women's fashions left much to be desired. Rose kept her features composed as she nodded a greeting to her owner's wife.

The Indian woman deliberately averted her face, ignoring her.

Rose tucked her chin. *Surely Fawn Woman Smith doesn't imagine I'm out to steal her husband. As if I'd be tempted by that filthy old goat!* With a shake of her head, she hoped that once the squaw realized there was no possibility of that particular danger, she might become friendlier. After all, they'd be living in close proximity to one another, with wigwams and campfires separated by no more than fifteen feet. With the wigwam belonging to the store's two guards on the other side of the store, the arrangement was actually quite cozy. A touch too cozy.

Not wanting to disturb the men, Rose nursed a fire from some banked coals then poured water into the kettle suspended above, all the while adding up how much time being a cook in this primitive setting was going to take. There were chickens to feed, a cow in the makeshift stable to milk, the growing calf and other cattle to drive out to graze in the large pen. Then, of course, there was the garden. That responsibility would probably fall to her as well. Yesterday Nate had mentioned gathering berries and nuts when they were in season. But she'd draw the line at chewing leather to soften it for clothing, as she'd seen an old woman doing in front of a village wigwam. That couldn't possibly be a cook's job.

Once she'd fed the chickens and gathered the eggs, she noticed that

Mrs. Smith had started her own fire and stood chatting with another squaw, no doubt showing off that silly red gown.

"Mornin', pretty lady," Nate called with a grin as he came out of the woods.

She smiled back. "Good morning to you. I'll have the tea steeping in no time." She started toward her wigwam for the supplies, intending to ply the frontiersman with a hundred questions. She'd done the same thing yesterday and hoped he wouldn't lose patience.

"I'm glad to help," he said, following after her.

He always seemed eager to assist her, and she wondered idly if he'd be so accommodating if they were married and he was sure of her. Her cousin back in England complained constantly about being taken for granted. Of course, actually marrying Nate was the furthest thing from Rose's mind. She got out the ingredients for biscuits and began mixing them. Besides, he seemed more interested in buying her.

"I'll see to the milkin'," Nate remarked. "You're busy."

"That would be wonderful." *And I know you're hoping to be invited to breakfast.* Rose smiled to herself. Mr. Smith wasn't the only man who appreciated good cooking.

Moments later, the salt pork sizzled in the pan, and Rose knew its aroma was a magnet, drawing Nate back with milk in a very short span of time.

"Cows are out grazin'." He gave a nod, looking rather pleased with himself as he handed her the milk pail, only a quarter full. "That's all that glutton of a calf left me."

"Thank you. It's plenty." Rose moistened her lips. "When winter comes, will I be expected to cook outside in the rain and snow?"

He shook his head. "Folks cook inside then. There's a flap up top of your wigwam you can open to let out the smoke. Works pretty good. 'Cept—"

She paused in her work and met his gaze.

"Well, you don't have to worry none about that. I'll see you're outta here before then."

Rose didn't want to think about how he planned to accomplish that little detail, and there wasn't time to dwell on it anyway. She caught a flash of red out of the corner of her eye. An unsmiling Mrs. Smith sauntered up to them, her dark eyes glinting with anger. She stepped right in front of Rose and grabbed her hand, drawing her along with her toward the store, where one of the guards sat slumped over, fast asleep. Fawn Woman gave him a swift kick with her moccasin, and he jerked awake as she tugged Rose past him into the store.

The woman stopped before bolts of material in a variety of colors and patterns. "You." She pointed to Rose then took hold of her skirt and shook it. "Me."

Confused, Rose frowned. "Yes, we both are wearing daygowns."

The squaw shook her head and pouted. She placed a hand on some shiny yellow satin.

"I believe she wants you to make her a new gown," Nate supplied, having come into the store without Rose noticing.

Mrs. Smith grabbed the bolt and thrust it at Rose. "Gown. Make."

Rose gave her a pleasant smile. "Of course. I shall make you a gown right after we've eaten breakfast."

She gave a decisive nod. "After eat." She whirled around, her red skirt flaring into the surrounding goods, then walked away, her nose in the air.

Nate chuckled.

"What's so funny?" Rose asked, fighting irritation.

"Your 'mistress' is makin' sure she ain't losin' her exalted position as the storekeeper's only real wife. She wants everyone to know you're not just Eustice's slave, but hers, too."

Rose sniffed in scorn. "I cannot imagine anyone would want to be that man's wife."

"Now, see? That's where you have it wrong." Nate put a hand on Rose's shoulder and steered her out of the store, back to the cook fire. "Fawn Woman doesn't want to be Smith's wife. Fact is, he bought her some time back. But the title does hold importance in this village, plus she has the protection of her two brothers Smith hired to come along when he brought Fawn Woman out here. The three are Susquehannock."

"Those two guards outside are her brothers?" Rose rolled her eyes. "Oh mercy. Classes exist even here in the wilderness, and she's an outsider who wants to be part of the aristocracy."

He nodded. "Somethin' like that. Just do like she says an' always stay close to Smith an' the Susquehannocks. No matter how Fawn Woman postures, none of 'em will let any harm come to the 'cook' while I'm gone."

"Gone?" He'd told her before that he was going to leave, and it remained in the back of her mind, but Rose had dismissed that fact.

"Any day now." Reaching the fire, Nate bent to turn the side pork with a long fork but avoided meeting her eyes. "Soon as Bob gets here." Straightening up again, he stared out over the wide river, his straight brows dipping together in a worried frown. "Funny, I was sure he'd beat us here."

Rose glanced from him to the village of people milling about now, all of them speaking words she would never understand. . .and Nate was going to leave her. How would she manage without him?

Chapter 17

Rose struggled to keep the slippery yellow material from snagging on the rough crate top she was using as a worktable to cut out Mrs. Smith's gown. No matter what ill opinion Fawn Woman held of her, Rose determined to do her finest work on the garment. There had to be a way to encourage friendship with the squaw, since they'd be living near each other for the next four years.

From several yards away, children's laughter drifted like music to her ear. Looking toward the youngsters at play, she spied three little Indian girls kneeling in the shade of an oak tree, putting together a miniature wigwam for dolls. Several naked boys with small bows and arrows shot at a thick tree trunk nearby. Rose smiled at the way girls always played house and boys always tried to outdo each other. They weren't so very different from white children.

Suddenly one of the boys dropped his bow and pointed toward the river. He bolted for the bank, and the others scampered after him.

Rose turned to see what had drawn his attention and spotted a lone Indian in a canoe paddling toward shore. Laying aside the scissors, she stood for a better look. "Robert Bloom!" Relieved that Nate's partner remained alive and well, she felt a twinge of sadness as well, since his coming would precipitate his and Nate's departure. But at least it was comforting to know Robert was a practicing Christian, unlike his pal. The short, perfunctory prayers Nate offered at mealtimes did please her, but she sensed that pleasing her was his motivation. She would have preferred seeing evidence of some real faith.

Perhaps the frontiersmen would remain at the village for a while. Rose dreaded being left here with Mr. Smith as the only other white person in residence. She remembered Robert's desire to have spirited conversations with her about the teachings of George Whitefield and other new Christian thinkers coming into prominence, like John and Charles Wesley. She hoped there'd be time for some good talks.

A deep sigh came from inside. If nothing else, Robert would have information about the lad taken hostage and how the Lord had answered their prayers. This eve she would make a delicious meal for the men. Out in the wilds they had to exist on whatever fish or game they found along the way—or worse, eat only cold jerky for days on end as the caravan had often been forced to do. Perhaps after some good English cooking, they wouldn't be so eager to head for parts unknown.

Finishing up his improvements on Rose's wigwam, Nate heard the commotion at the riverside and saw Bob paddling ashore. He dropped his tools and went to meet him. Half the village already swarmed the water's edge, and the Shawnee braves he and Bob had traveled with threaded their way to the front of the crowd as Nate waded into the water to pull in the canoe. "Glad to see you still have your scalp, buddy. But what'd you do? Swap your horse for this thing?"

Bob grinned. "No, I came across it hidden in some reeds." He hopped out and helped shove the bark-covered canoe onto the beach. "Knowin' how you love raft buildin', I thought mebbe you'd like to go back over with me to build one for my horse."

Chuckling, they strode together up the shallow rise. They scarcely gained the top before Indians and hired braves from the village crowded around them and started jabbering to Bob in their language. Words flew back and forth so quickly Nate could only pick up one or two but suspected they were discussing the hostage situation. Bob wore a satisfied expression as he answered questions, but oddly, the Indians seemed far more pleased than he was. A couple of them snickered and swapped knowing glances.

Nate elbowed his pal in the ribs. "I take it you were able to rescue the lad in question."

"Aye. But the Indians are happy about what all the Cherokees got in the trade."

"Good trade." One of the hired braves smirked.

Nate's brow furrowed. "What'd those men have to give up to get the boy back, anyway?"

"All their trade goods an' every cent they had with them, plus all the cash money I had on me."

"All of it?" Nate saw his personal plans for Bob's money evaporate like dew in the sunshine. "But you're talkin' only what was left after the funds you sent home for safekeepin', right?"

He nodded. "Aye. But the kid was lookin' real beat up. I had to help him. You'd've done the same."

"You're right." Nate felt the chink in his plan grow wider, but nothing could be done about that. "Well, let's get a couple of volunteers an' retrieve your horse before some wildcat gets wind of him."

"Good thinkin'." Bob cleared his throat. "How's Rose, by the way?"

Irritated by his partner's interest in her, Nate gave a curt response. "She's here an' she's fine. I'll tell you all about her on our way across the river. Think I've come up with a plan to get her away from Smith." *One that'll take a mite of adjusting, in the light of things.*

Bob laughed. "You haven't settled on killin' the man, I hope."

"Actually, the thought did cross my mind." Nate flashed a sheepish grin. "But the way these Shawnees love that store of his, I figured they'd scalp me for sure." *On the other hand, Smith might not go for the new plan. . . .*

From her position near the store, Rose watched in disappointment as Nate and Robert shoved the canoe back into the water then hopped into it. Two Indians joined them, and the four men began paddling back across the river. Nate said he and his partner would leave as soon as Robert returned, but how could they go so suddenly without so much as a brief farewell? Her throat closed up, and her chest began to ache as hot tears stung her eyes. She blinked them back, determined not to cry. She needed to stay strong before these village people.

Mr. Smith came up behind her. "Those two're prob'ly goin' over to fetch Bob's horse. The river's too deep fer it to swim across. They'll have to build a raft to get the mare to this side."

A wave of relief swept over Rose, but she was still confused. "Why did they not take one that's already beached here?"

He looked at her as if she were daft. "'Cause o' the swift current. They'd have a time of it tryin' to paddle one o' them lumberin' things upstream. It's too deep fer polin."

Rose tamped down her embarrassment. She should have known that, remembering how swiftly the raft moved yesterday when she arrived. At least she had hope that the men would soon return.

"Another lazy hunter to feed." The trader grimaced and started away then turned back. "Don't be killin' another chicken. I'll get ya some venison to cook fer 'em. I'll eat whatever's left o' last night's chicken stew. But make plenty o' puddin."

An hour later, Rose added a pinch more seasoning to the venison stewing in the kettle, hoping to make it smell and taste more like meat she preferred. To her nostrils it smelled worse than the bear grease the Indians lathered on themselves to fend off mosquitoes. She gazed out across the river yet another time, wondering how much longer it would be until the men returned. How she wished she could see past the bend where they'd paddled out of sight. Mr. Smith had never actually lied to her, but it would be nice to have proof he'd been right about their constructing a raft.

As if her thought had conjured the man up, the trader again strode up to her without her noticing, quiet as an Indian in the moccasins he now wore. "Don't be wastin' all my good flour on them upstarts. Make 'em some corn bread instead."

"As you wish." She slid a weary glance after him as he sauntered back to the store. Would he be that stingy with his food once the men had gone? *Gone.* Even the word was depressing. How she would miss the two once they left. She'd be entirely friendless then and would have God alone to turn to.

Chapter 18

After hours of felling trees and constructing a raft for his partner's horse, Nate wanted nothing more than to bed down for the night. But the enticing aroma wafting his way from Rose's kettle revived him as he and Bob climbed the rise to Smith's trading post. Not far from the store, Rose bent over the fire, stirring the suspended pot, and his gaze drank in the picture of grace and femininity she made with her honey-colored hair streaming over her slender shoulder.

Before they reached her, Running Wolf and Spotted Elk left their posts and came to greet Bob, eager to hear the details of his exploits.

Nate gave them a polite nod and looked again in Rose's direction. She'd seen him, too, and the surprise on her face warmed his insides. . . until her gaze shifted to his partner and really lit up.

"You're looking rather well," she told Bob when the four of them arrived. "Were you able to rescue that boy?"

He grinned from ear to ear. "Aye. He should be back in the arms of his ma by now. It'll prob'ly be a long time before he strays far from home again."

"Praise the Lord."

"Amen to that." He laughed and moved closer to her.

Rose continued to regard only him. "We must give a sincere thank-you to the Almighty when we bless the food this eve. 'Tis just about ready."

"And it smells mighty good." Nate managed to wedge into the conversation.

His partner glanced across the distance between Rose's cook fire and Fawn Woman Smith's, where the squaw tended her own pot. "Does she eat separate?"

Nate answered for Rose. "Her an' her brothers. That's how she wants it."

"Hmm." Leaving Nate and Rose, Bob walked over to her.

She looked up at him with a pleasant expression. Smiling warmly, she spoke to him in her language, gesturing toward her own cooked meal.

He gave a nod but responded in a voice too low to be heard at a distance.

The woman's smile flattened momentarily, but as Bob kept talking, her glum demeanor brightened, and she turned with a stiff smile toward Nate and Rose.

Grinning with satisfaction, Bob rejoined Rose and the men. "Mrs. Smith's invitin' us to join her. Help me tote this good-smellin' food over to her fire, boys."

Noticing how eagerly the braves grabbed up trenchers and cups, Nate suspected they'd been yearning to try some of Rose's good cooking.

As Bob snatched the board holding the corn bread and the pail of milk, Nate released a long, slow breath. He much preferred it when there'd been just Smith and him and Rose.

Or better yet, just him and Rose. But that was not to be. Yet.

Reluctantly, he plucked a rag to protect his hands from the hot kettle handle and unhooked the pot from the tripod then reached to pick up a smaller pot at the edge of the coals.

Rose looked up. "Oh, that one's not to be shared. 'Tis for Mr. Smith and his poor digestion."

"Don't forget to bring some fur robes to sit on," Bob called over his shoulder.

Rose had yet to move. Nate could tell she was no more thrilled about the unexpected arrangement than Mrs. Smith was. "It'll be all right," he assured her. "Bob always wants folks to get along, whether they want to or not. It's his way."

"Well, I'm afraid *she* has the opposite desire," Rose said wryly.

"Mebbe. But try to make the best of it. While we're gone, it'd be better to have her for a friend than an enemy." He tried to cheer her with a grin.

Rose looked all the more troubled and quickly turned away. "I'd best go tell Mr. Smith dinner's ready."

Watching after her, Nate could tell from the sad droop of her shoulders that she didn't want him and Bob to leave her. But he also knew that the sooner they left, the sooner he'd be able to come back for her and take her with them.

Rose found her owner trading with an Indian who'd come from downstream earlier that day. She waited for him to finish his business dealings before announcing supper, hoping his presence at the meal would lend the support she needed to face his unpleasant wife.

A touch of the day's heat still lingered in the early evening, and when Rose and the trader joined the group, everyone had gathered in a circle away from the cook fire. They'd piled food on their trenchers but had yet to begin eating. By the eagerness in their expressions as she and Mr. Smith approached, she assumed Robert had mentioned that most white people began their meal with a blessing, a custom not followed by Indians.

The brothers' nostrils flared as they inhaled the aroma of the food before them, and Rose hoped their eager display would not anger their sister. Fortunately all the men had been wise enough to take portions from both women's cooking pots.

Robert nodded to Nate. "If it's all the same to you, I'll do the prayin' this time."

"Sure, go ahead." Unsmiling, Nate gave a nod.

Rose saw a muscle work in his jaw. He seemed disappointed. Perplexed, she bowed her head along with the others as Robert began speaking.

"Thank You, heavenly Father, for Fawn Woman's kindness in askin' us to share some o' her fine cookin'. We ask You to bless it as we eat. Thank You, too, for allowin' Billy Wexler to be restored to his family. Now please protect me an' Nate as we leave tomorrow to visit new tribes. Make 'em curious to know about You. In Jesus' name, amen."

"Amen," Rose whispered. She needed a chance to collect herself after hearing of his and Nate's departure on the very morrow, so she took her time filling her trencher over both pots. When she turned back to take a seat on one of the pallets, all the men were eating with great gusto—especially Fawn Woman's brothers. Even more amazing, the woman herself took a gingerly sniff of Rose's stew, which encouraged Rose. She scanned the group. "Did you know that Rome was once saved from savage hordes from the north with pepper?"

Robert hiked his brows. "You don't say."

"'Tis true. The Romans bought them off with all the pepper they had in the city. It seems everyone enjoys a variety of spices." Mrs. Smith had yet to sample any of the meat from Rose's kettle, so Rose decided to plunge in and taste the squaw's stew to show her appreciation. She deftly avoided the fatty meat and tried the woman's greasy mixture of corn, beans, and summer squash. A grisly chunk of fat hid beneath the vegetables, but she managed to keep from gagging as she forced it down whole with a smile and a nod.

Alas, Fawn Woman wasn't even looking her way.

"Muskrat." Nate grinned. "Tasty, eh?"

The squaw gave a smug nod while Rose struggled to keep the food down. "Rat?" Her gaze darted across the fire, where Robert and Mr. Smith both sat chuckling.

Robert reached over and gave Rose's arm an empathetic pat. "It's not really a rat. More like a beaver. That robe you're sittin' on is made from muskrat pelts."

Her hand automatically went down to touch the brown fur and found it thick and soft to the touch. It was rather sweet of him to comfort her. How she wished she was attracted to the dedicated Christian instead of to Nate.

While the men took their time eating the meal, Rose and Fawn Woman picked at theirs. Rose noticed that her hostess continued to ignore her presence.

Nate broke the silence. He turned to the trader. "Eustice, when that boy got ransomed, his pa an' his companion didn't have enough goods or cash on 'em, so Bob had to use all his own money to help out. That got me to thinkin'. You front us a canoe loaded with trade goods, an' I'm sure we'll get a lot more prime pelts for the truck out where there ain't a tradin' post for a hundred miles."

The trader lazed back a moment, pondering the matter, then sported a sly smile. "If I git my cost back off the top, then I'm willin' to be generous. I'll split the profit with ya, since you boys'll be riskin' yer necks—or should I say scalps."

That last statement struck Rose hard. The caravan hadn't had any real trouble on the way here—but there'd been seven well-armed men in the party.

Nate looked from Robert to Mr. Smith. "We'll give you all the furs. All I want is Rose."

This time she really had to fight not to retch. How mortifying to have a man bartering over her—and in front of Mr. Smith's already haughty wife! A gleam in those sullen eyes proved the squaw understood quite a bit more English than she spoke.

The trader toyed with his beard. "It'll take more'n one measly little tradin' trip to set me up fer life, ya know. I 'spect you boys'll be paddlin' down there a whole lot more times than ya bargained fer."

Nate narrowed his eyes and studied the man. "Exactly how much do you figger you're gonna need to set yourself up, anyway?"

Rose wanted desperately to put a stop to this outrageous conversation, but the thought of bringing notice to herself at such a humiliating moment seemed even worse.

Mr. Smith rested an elbow on one knee and leaned his bearded chin on his fist, appearing to give the matter serious thought. "I'd say about five hundred pounds."

Nate set down his trencher. "Three's more like it."

"Not hardly. But I mebbe could squeeze by on, say, four hundred."

To Rose's astonishment, she saw the frontiersman reach over to the trader with his hand outstretched. "Deal. An' I'd like that in writin'."

Four hundred pounds! He'd never be able to earn such a fortune in ten years, much less one summer. Even two or three. "I must see to cleaning the kettle," she mumbled. She needed to leave before she broke down in front of them all. Rising, she snatched the pot from where it sat near the fire, not caring that the handle was still hot, and hurried away. For all Nate Kinyon's big talk, they both knew she'd be here for the full four years of her indenturement.

Tears blurred Rose's vision as Nate and Robert Bloom took their leave. To help with the unfamiliar dialect needed in the Wabash area, they hired a Miami lad who'd been stolen as a youth, and the three of them paddled downriver in a long canoe piled high with bundles of trade goods. *Please watch over them, Father. Keep them safe.*

When the boat vanished from sight around the river's bend, she inhaled a wavering breath and trudged slowly back to her wigwam. The fact that the return of the young brave would guarantee Nate and Bob a hearty welcome eased her mind a bit, but she couldn't help wondering if her two frontiersmen would come back alive. Mr. Smith's caustic remark about their scalps still rang in her mind.

From the corner of her eye, she spotted Fawn Woman coming her way.

The squaw didn't bother with any sort of greeting. "You. Go. Me gown."

Rose sighed and went to fetch her sewing, which had been interrupted by the men's departure. Nate had divulged a second reason why the Indian woman was so adamant about a new gown. Shawnee women didn't have the fine thread or needles Rose possessed. Instead, they used leather thongs and reed strands, along with what looked like hair or whiskers from animals. The clothing they made appeared sturdy, but they were also coarse. Mrs. Smith would be quite the envy of the others in the village, having not one, but two cloth gowns.

Rose briefly considered selling two of her own better gowns out of the mere four she had brought from England. If what Mr. Smith predicted turned out to be true and Nate came up short of pelts even after several trips, the money her gowns might bring in could help out. Once the other squaws caught sight of Fawn Woman's gown, they'd probably be willing to pay for one of their own.

Sinking down onto a log, Rose opened her sewing basket. Her thread supply was shrinking fast. She wished she'd had the foresight to bring much more along. Picking up the partially sewn gown, she set to work.

Her thoughts drifted to the possibility of leaving Mr. Smith's protection and riding off with Nate Kinyon. Could that actually happen? And if so, would it be a wise choice? What exactly were Nate's plans for her? Did he truly intend merely to return her to her sisters after everything he'd have to do to earn four hundred pounds? That was hard to believe. And he'd never even hinted at marriage. *Dear Lord, this is such a dilemma. I need Your wisdom to show me what to do.*

Just then a shadow moved across her basket, and Rose looked up.

Her heart froze.

Chapter 19

Rose's mouth dropped open in shock. A pitiful-looking white woman stood before her in a filthy, ragged daygown. Her puffy blue eyes were rimmed with red, her skin sallow and blotchy, and hair that once might have been the soft gold of a wheat field hung in matted strings. But far worse, cuts and bruises covered her face and all exposed skin. A whimpering infant was slung behind her slumped back.

Setting her work aside, Rose placed her sewing basket on the ground and stood, trying to compose herself. "What can I do for you?"

"Milk." The word came out in a croak. "For my baby. I dried up." With effort she drew a ragged breath. "I'm. . .dyin."

"That cannot be." Rose glanced out across the village, but no one was paying them any mind, as if a woman so obviously suffering didn't merit the slightest consideration. Swallowing her abhorrence, Rose motioned toward the sitting log. "Please, sit down. I'll get milk for both of you."

Trembling, the woman dropped down with a gasp.

Her heart crimping, Rose moistened her lips. "I'll take the baby for you." She lifted the infant out of the ragged sling, noticing that though the baby was thin and dirty, it seemed unhurt. She estimated its age to be four or five months at most. The little one gazed up with wide blue eyes, hungry eyes that made her wonder when it had last eaten.

Leaving the child's mother, Rose hurried down to the brook, where she kept a pail of milk cool in the water's flow, and fetched it back. She shifted the baby to one hip then plucked a couple of dipping gourds from her wigwam, along with one of the few small metal spoons Mr. Smith possessed and returned to the slumped woman. Setting down the pail, she quickly dipped some milk for her. "Here. This may make you feel a bit better."

She raised a discolored arm and pushed the gourd away. Her hand burned with fever. "Jenny needs it more."

Rose shook her head and thrust the milk back to her. "I've plenty for your baby girl. This is for you. Please drink it." Satisfied when the woman acquiesced and raised it shakily to her lips, Rose dipped the second gourd into the pail and took a seat on a nearby fur blanket within eyesight of the baby's mother. She began spoon-feeding the infant. The poor little thing slurped at it so greedily, Rose's eyes swam. She could hardly get it to her fast enough.

The mother looked longingly at the baby devouring the milk, and she tried to smile. "My name. . .is Hannah Wright." The strangled whisper seemed to sap much of her strength, but she took a sharp breath and went on. "I come from a homestead up near. . .the west fork of the Susquehanna." A pause. "My husband's name was Adam."

As Hannah Wright drew another breath, Rose felt a sudden ache in her throat. *Past tense. He must be dead.* The baby squawked and kicked its tiny feet, and Rose resumed feeding it.

"Adam's folks live east of there. . .near the main branch. Names are Edith and Chadwick Wright. Take Jenny Ann to them. Please." She coughed. "You. . .only hope."

"But you're a hostage, are you not? Will the Indians allow me to take the baby?"

The still half-full gourd slipped from the feverish hand, and Hannah moaned, rocking back and forth as if consumed by pain.

Seeing the poor woman's struggle to speak further, Rose propped the fur securely around the baby and stood to her feet. "We can talk later. First we need to take care of you. My name is Rose."

Hannah held up a hand and wagged her head. "It's. . .too late." Moving aside her ragged skirt, she exposed a swollen leg that looked as if it had been hacked at with a tomahawk. Discolored and covered with dried blood and oozing pus, it smelled like rotting fish.

The hideous sight almost caused Rose's stomach to heave. Unable to fathom such vile cruelty, she quickly inhaled to keep from fainting.

Mr. Smith ambled up to them. He stared at the woman but did not appear surprised or appalled upon seeing her. "Who's this?"

His indifference angered Rose. "We must get this poor woman out of this place."

"Too late," Hannah whispered again. She tried to raise a hand but barely succeeded. It fell back onto her lap. "Take my Jenny."

Furious now, Rose swept Hannah's skirt aside, displaying the putrid injury the unfortunate young woman had suffered. "Look at this, Mr. Smith. Have you medicine at the store that might help her?"

He took one look then shrugged and shook his shaggy head. Bending over, he gave the woman's shoulder a sympathetic pat. "Sorry as I can be, missy. It's past any helpin' at this point. Should'a been tended days ago."

Her reddened eyes filled with tears.

Rose stared at him in dismay. "But we *must* do something."

"Fawn Woman!" Smith hollered, straightening up.

The squaw looked over at him with a sour face as she sat stringing some shiny beads near their wigwam. She grudgingly got to her feet and came to join him.

He glared at her. "When was this gal brought here? Why weren't her wounds tended to?"

The baby began to fuss, so Rose stooped down and fed her a little more milk while Fawn Woman rattled off an explanation in her language. Then, as if Hannah didn't exist, she turned around and sauntered off to her beads again, obviously devoid of interest in the matter.

Such heartlessness and savage inhumanity revolted Rose. So the stories she'd heard about the hellish treatment whites received from Indians were true, after all. Hannah Wright was proof. The possibility that such vicious cruelty could one day be inflicted upon *her*, but for the trader's presence, made Rose's blood turn cold.

Mr. Smith turned to her. "This is how it is. The woman an' babe were brought here as slaves by the son-in-law of an old woman. He was replacin' his wife an' son, who both died during the birthin'. The brave's not real fond of his wife's mother, an' he decided to rid himself of havin' to care fer the ol' gal. Problem is, the girl was hurt pretty bad when she ran the gauntlet. Worse, the baby's not a boy, so the mother-in-law says she's been cheated. She threw this one an' her babe out an' is refusin' to claim them. Nobody else wants a dyin' woman, an' nobody wants the babe, either, 'cause there's already a lot more women than men in the village, what with all the warrin' betwixt the tribes. She's been draggin' herself around fer days, fightin' the dogs fer scraps to eat."

It was hard for Rose to get words past the clog in her throat. Tears coursed down her cheeks as she went to Hannah and wrapped her arms around the poor woman.

Hannah made an effort to stand, finally managing with Rose's help. She gasped for breath. "Now *I* understand."

Rose struggled to support the weakened girl's nearly dead weight. "Mr. Smith, help me to get her to my bed. I'll do what I can."

She began to cry. "Thank you, Rose," she whispered between gulps. "God bless you."

Giving little thought to her clean bedding, Rose and Mr. Smith lay Hannah gently down onto her pallet. Filth could be washed away. Help could not wait. Rose touched the burning brow. "I'll get some cool water and a washing cloth. We'll have you clean and comfortable soon."

"My baby."

"Don't you worry about Jenny. We shall tend her as well." She slanted a pointed look at Mr. Smith and arched a brow. "Will we not?"

"Aye." He grimaced. "Fawn Woman'll see to her right away."

Moments later, Rose brought some washrags and a bucket of water into the wigwam. Hannah appeared to be fast asleep but startled when Rose ran a cool cloth gently over one of her arms. She closed her bruised fingers around Rose's hand. "My name is Hannah Wright. My. . .husband's folks are near—"

"Shh," Rose crooned. "I remember. The Susquehanna. Rest now. You and your baby are safe here." But a new worry assailed Rose. Wasn't the Susquehanna the river up which Lily had been taken? Was any white person truly safe in this wild land? She breathed another swift prayer for God to watch over her little sister.

"Jesus promised. . .to send someone," Hannah whispered. "And He sent you." She closed her eyes, and the slightest smile played over her cracked lips.

The sentiment stunned Rose. *Me, sent by God?* Had God planned months ago, before she'd ever left England and sailed to America, that she would be here at this very place to help Hannah Wright? Freshening the rag in the cool water again, she felt renewed hope spring to life in her heart. God truly did have a purpose for bringing her here.

Hannah mumbled something unintelligible just then.

"What did you say, dear?"

Her eyes still closed, she drew a labored breath. "I don't mind dyin'. I'm goin' to my Adam. He's. . .waitin' for me." She smiled again, a real smile this time.

Blinded by her own tears now, Rose continued to wash the precious woman. She needed to be beautiful for her husband.

Chapter 20

Rose felt the little warm baby stir beside her as it breathed in soft content. Having gotten only snatches of sleep, she opened her eyes to the pitch-dark night and listened once again for Hannah's raspy breathing.

Ominous silence filled the air.

Pulling back the light cover over her and Jenny, Rose crawled across to where the child's mother lay. Her heartbeat throbbed in her ears as she reached out and found Hannah's face. Where there had been a raging fever, the skin was cool to the touch, and no breath issued from Hannah's lungs. Already on her knees, Rose sank the rest of the way down onto her folded legs with the realization that Jenny's mother had died. She'd put up a valiant struggle to stay alive until she knew her little one was safe, and once she had that assurance, she'd let herself go.

Tears Rose had banked earlier that day broke through her resolve and streamed down her cheeks. Hannah was the second young mother whose untimely death she had witnessed. Rose's own mother had been only a few years older than Rose was now and had been in the process of giving birth to a new babe when the angel of death had paid a visit. It seemed so senseless at the time—just as Hannah's dying seemed senseless now. And it, too, had left Rose in mourning and burdened with the responsibility of a baby.

She crept back to the slumbering little one and snuggled close to her softness, breathing in her little clean smell and seeking comfort for herself and for the tiny orphan.

Then terrible doubt surfaced. *Father God, the Bible says our times are in Your hand, but I cannot understand how You could allow such a tragic thing to happen to someone so undeserving of this horrid fate as Hannah Wright. She was Your child. Surely she must have cried out to You to save her. But You did not. Are You really there? Do You really care?*

A wracking sob swelled within her breast, and Rose sat up to stifle the sound before she disturbed Jenny. She clamped her hand tightly over her mouth as her cheeks and hand were washed with her tears.

Completely unexpected, a soothing sense of peace spread through her, and she recalled plainly the words of comfort her father had given her when her beloved mother breathed her last. *"The Bible tells us that our days are numbered by the Lord before we are born, Rosie-mine. It says there's a time to be born and a time to die. He alone knows when those times come to us. Even though there will always be suffering in this life, He knows all those who love and trust Him. He never leaves us or forsakes us. He stays by our side through all the hard times. And He will always see us safely through to the other side. God is waiting to welcome us home."*

The gnawing ache inside her lessened as her sorrow eased with hope. Hannah Wright's last words played across her memory. She was looking forward to being reunited with her Adam. . .and the two were probably even now embracing in the presence of the Lord, happier than they had ever been. Despite the evil torture the poor woman had endured, her ultimate victory was her everlasting joy in a place where sorrow and pain and death would never again intrude.

The baby made a sighing sound.

Rose lay back down and drew little Jenny close. The tiny girl was her sole responsibility now. God had put the precious child into her care. From this moment on, she must remember that her coming here— despite the hardships and fears she'd endured along the way—was no accident. The Lord had placed her here in His time and for His purpose. Whatever she had to face, she would be strong in her faith, just as she had promised her mother so long ago. Strong for God and strong for Jenny.

Rose chose a small knoll just out of sight of the Shawnee village where she felt Hannah would finally rest in peace. Mr. Smith had Running Wolf and Spotted Elk dig the grave in a spot shaded by a towering maple tree, and the two lowered her body, wrapped in a clean blanket, into the ground. Rose held Jenny close as she and the trader watched the braves fill in the gaping hole. Then Rose placed the few late wildflowers she'd found nearby atop the mound of fresh earth.

After the two Indians walked away, Mr. Smith pulled a thin book from inside his belted shirt and exhaled as he opened the worn volume. His high-pitched voice broke the silence as he began reading. " 'Jesus said unto her, I am the resurrection, and the life: he that believeth in me, though he were dead, yet shall he live: and whosoever liveth and believeth in me shall never die.' " Rose recognized the familiar passage from the apostle John's writings and looked up at the trader while he finished. "Ashes to ashes, dust to dust."

Astonished that the man actually had a New Testament in his possession and made sure Jenny's mother had a Christian burial, Rose tried not to let her surprise show.

Mr. Smith reached out with his gnarled hand and ruffled Jenny's silky hair. "We should bow fer a word o' prayer." He cleared his throat. "Almighty God, Ya know what took place here that put this young gal in an early grave. Ya say in Yer Word that vengeance is Yourn, an' I guess we have to leave it at that. I know Yer lookin' after her, an' we'll do our best to look after the little one she left behind. Amen."

Touched by the heartfelt prayer, Rose raised her head. . .only to be assaulted by laughter a short distance away. This unfortunate white woman died because no Indian deigned to tend her wounds, and these people found humor in something so despicable?

She swung toward the noise and saw three native girls about the same ages as her sisters playing some sort of game. Each had a short-handled paddle of sorts and repeatedly hit into the air what looked like a small ball with a tail of feathers.

Rose wiped perspiration from her brow and relaxed. At least the girls hadn't been laughing at the death of Hannah Wright. Nevertheless, it irked her that life in the village went on as usual. As she and Mr. Smith returned to the trading post, she could see older women seated in front of their wigwams weaving reeds into baskets or stitching leather. Another kneaded a lump of clay. A few collected vegetables in their gardens, while some of the men stood in the river casting nets for fish. Not far from them, youngsters splashed about in the shallows near the bank. No one cared a whit about the fact they'd caused mortal injury to an unprotected woman—an innocent baby's mother—and then allowed her to die an unspeakable death.

Still, Mr. Smith had cared. For all his gruff talk, the man truly cared. Rose's respect for him went up a notch.

From the corner of her eye, she caught him rubbing his stomach as he so often did of late. As she turned to him, he stretched out his arms. "Let me have that sweet little gal fer a spell. I had me four sons b'fore my Ellie passed on. Never did have us no little gal."

Rose smiled and handed the baby to him. "I didn't know that. Where are they now?"

He tossed his head as if it was of no import, but Rose didn't miss the spark of pride in his eyes. "Scattered about back in Virginny with fam'lies o' their own now. I seen to it they was all set up in a prosperous trade. Good boys, one an' all."

Listening to him imparting personal information, Rose realized she wasn't the only melancholy one today. Hannah's funeral must have brought back memories of the first Mrs. Smith's death. "Have you and your present wife been blessed with any children?"

He snorted. "No. An' we ain't likely to, neither." His jaw tightened.

Rose had more questions, but from the derision in his voice, she thought it best to drop the matter. "If you'd be kind enough to entertain little Jenny for a while, I'll go cook you both a nice rice pudding with raisins and cinnamon. How's that?"

He laughed and lightly tweaked Jenny's button nose, making the little one catch a breath and giggle. "We'd like that right 'nough, wouldn't we, sweet thing?"

Watching the two of them, Rose knew she had certainly misjudged Mr. Smith. He wasn't nearly the heartless man he'd led her to believe. It was all a big act.

During the long weeks that followed, Rose kept a number of pressing questions to herself. Days were growing noticeably shorter. Many of the village crops had been harvested and dried or stored for the coming winter. As the weather began to cool, the leaves started turning the magnificent colors of autumn. Yet Nate and Robert Bloom had still not returned.

Mrs. Smith now paraded before the other squaws in another daygown Rose had made her, a blue checked one. But the trader's wife couldn't hold a candle to her two brothers, who strutted around in matching green-and-yellow-striped shirts Rose had sewn for them.

Now besides caring for the baby and doing the cooking, Rose was learning the fur business—which animal furs were the most valuable and the subtle differences within a species that determined the quality of each pelt. Mr. Smith was her teacher, and he also had her bargaining with the Indians whenever they came to the trading post with canoes loaded down with bundles of furs. She still hadn't mastered any of the Shawnee language, much less the dialects of any of the other tribes, but she'd picked up on a primitive sort of sign language that was used in trade and got by fairly well with it.

Rose had never questioned the man regarding his reasons for these new duties, but she knew instinctively why he'd been so intent on having her learn his trade. He did not trust Fawn Woman, and no matter how mild and smooth the food was that Rose made for him, it was obvious he continued to suffer pain in his stomach. His straggly beard no longer hid the sunken cheeks bearing witness to a noticeable loss of weight. She suspected he was much worse off than he let on.

One day after an Indian who bore multiple scars and disfigurements left the trading post and headed back upstream with his goods, Rose could not contain her curiosity. She straightened some of the pelts the red man had left in trade and approached her owner as he jiggled the now healthy Jenny Ann on his knees. "Mr. Smith, how could one man be covered with so many scars, like that Indian was, unless—" She paused for breath. "When Jenny's mother was dying, you said she'd had to run a. . .a. . ."

"Gauntlet," he supplied. "An' yes, that brave might'a had to run it, too. Likely he was stole from his people by some other tribe. An' ya might say, runnin' the gauntlet is like bein' initiated. If ya make it through, yer good 'nough to be adopted into the tribe."

"What is a *gauntlet*, exactly? I've often heard that word." She noticed the baby's eyelids were growing heavy, and the trader did as well. He laid her gently down onto a plush pallet of furs they'd put between some crates and smiled as she put her thumb into her rosebud mouth and nodded off. Then he looked up at Rose.

He let out a slow breath. "It's like this. The whole tribe lines up in two rows facin' each other, an' they all got sticks. The captive has to run betwixt 'em whilst they're swingin' the sticks at 'em. They get a real kick outta tryin' to trip a poor fella up, 'cause then he has to start over again. Afterward, though, if he was brave 'nough to make it the whole way, they take him in and patch him up, an' he's part o' the tribe. Might be he's still a slave, though."

"But they didn't help Hannah Wright, even though Spotted Elk told me she actually did make it through."

He nodded. "I heard that, too. 'Fraid that little gal was unlucky enough to get herself caught in the middle of a family squabble."

Rose mulled over his response. "Well, if Nate or Robert was set upon by some other tribe, would they have to run the gauntlet?"

He rubbed his bearded chin. "That there's a different case. Them boys is down tradin' in country them Frenchies is tryin' to claim as their own. Those two would prob'ly get treated a mite rougher than Miz Wright."

Sobered by that statement, Rose felt the blood drain from her face. "Surely you don't mean. . . ."

He didn't answer right away. Then he shrugged a shoulder. "If them Frenchies get wind of 'em, those two could be in fer some real trouble. But don't start worryin' overmuch. Them boys is real good at takin' care o' themselves. They don't take no foolish chances, neither." He grimaced and pressed a hand atop that spot on his belly that seemed to give him the most trouble. "Reckon them eggs I had this mornin' didn't set so well. Think I'll go lay down fer a spell." He glanced lovingly down at Jenny Ann, sleeping sweetly on her soft pallet, then met Rose's gaze. "Keep an eye out fer customers."

"I will." Still awed by the tenderness he displayed around the baby, Rose sensed he was as attached to the child as she herself was. As she watched him head for his wigwam, she wished she'd managed to squeeze in a few more questions. Nate and Robert had been gone weeks now, much too long for them to dispose of one measly canoe load of goods— and they'd taken on that dangerous mission just for her.

To keep her mind off the plaguing thought, she began lining up knives and hatchets neatly on a crate top. Those items were some of their best sellers, and the stock was dwindling.

A voice from outside interrupted her chore. "Harwood."

Rose pivoted and glanced out the store's wide opening. Running Wolf, in his green-and-yellow shirt, pointed down toward the riverbank.

She followed the gesture with her gaze and saw two men beaching a canoe.

White men! Nate? Robert?

But as they looked up toward the store, her joy plummeted to her toes. Strangers. Merely strangers.

Chapter 21

Muskets in hand, the newcomers broke away from the curious villagers and started up the rise to the trading post. Rose saw their jaws go slack when they caught sight of her and knew they must be wondering how a white woman happened to be standing at the store entrance. No doubt they'd be full of questions. Well, she had questions of her own for them.

Both men were attired in the typical buckskin garb worn by hunters and frontiersmen alike, and both sported beards. The taller of the pair had a droopy mustache which moved when he spoke. "You sure don't look like most hostages I've seen."

Ignoring their lack of a polite greeting, Rose tilted her head slightly. "Welcome to our store. Miss Harwood at your service." She fingered the edge of the long apron she wore over her cobalt daygown.

Both quickly swiped their fur hats off their heads. "Beg your pardon, miss," the shorter, stocky man said. "I'm Mr. Gilbert. My partner's Mr. Townes." He blinked his hooded eyes as he and the other man stared unabashedly. "Where'd you come from?"

"As to your kind remark," she said in a businesslike tone, "I'm not a hostage. I'm Mr. Smith's servant."

"Servant! Are you saying Eustice Smith brought you, a woman, out to this wild place—and you agreed to come?" Hiking his brows, he eyed her up and down.

Rose regretted having to explain. She'd never get used to the sting of her lowly position. "I should have said I'm his bondservant. I had no choice but to come."

Their expressions hardened, and Mr. Townes spoke. "Where is the trader? We need to talk to him." They started to move past her.

Rose put up a staying hand. "Please. I'm afraid Mr. Smith isn't feeling well just now. He's abed, taking a nap."

"That's not our concern, miss. We have important business to discuss."

"Gentlemen, please. I shall go and wake him if I must, but first, I've a few questions to ask, if you'd be so kind as to indulge me."

Both men relaxed, and Mr. Gilbert even managed an obliging smile. "Of course, Miss. . .Harwood, was it? What do you need to know?"

Rose noticed by his manner of speech that he seemed more educated than many of the other white people she'd encountered in her travels into the wilderness, and she found it quite refreshing. She smiled, alight with hope. "I was wondering if you happened to come across Nate Kinyon and Robert Bloom on your way here. I believe you came upriver, did you not?"

He gave a negative shake of his head. "Sorry, miss, but no. We came downriver from up on the Allegheny."

Profound disappointment flowed through her.

"We've been checking on the infringement of the French up north," Mr. Townes added, "by order of Governor Dinwiddie. We just stopped by for fresh mounts so we could report back to him. We hoped Smith could provide us with a couple of good horses."

Rose focused on that disturbing information. "The French are to the north and east of us?"

Townes stepped forward and took her hand, a calming look in his eyes. "Don't you worry your pretty head. No officer, even a Frenchman, would allow harm to come to a lady like yourself. You can be sure of that."

Rose sensed the statement held little truth, if any, but remained silent.

"Now, if you don't mind," he went on, "we'd really appreciate a word with Trader Smith."

"Of course." She paused then searched their faces. "But might I ask a favor of both of you?"

"Anything, miss. What is it?"

"I'd appreciate it if you'd carry some missives with you when you go. I'd like my family to know I'm well. They've had no word from me for some time, and 'twould set their minds at ease."

Mr. Gilbert nodded. "I've pretty decent penmanship. Would you like me to write the words for you?"

Rose nearly smiled. They probably hadn't come across many bondservants who could write. "That won't be necessary. I have my own writing implements. I'll go and wake Mr. Smith, and while you conduct your business, I'll write my letters."

Putting quill to paper, Rose was careful not to cause her sisters needless worry. She did want them to know Mr. Smith had turned out to be a kind employer and that she was faring well in a village to the west. They didn't need to know it was a Shawnee village or that it was hundreds of miles to the west. She encouraged Mariah to remember to give priority to her spiritual well-being while she honored her commitment to her employer on the plantation. To Lily she mentioned that the Lord had placed a darling baby girl into her safekeeping, and she asked her to let the baby's relatives know that though the child's mother had passed away, the little one was fine and—

For a split second, Rose considered sending the baby back with the men but quickly discarded the notion. Even if they happened to be adept at caring for a baby, they'd be hard pressed to provide suitable food for her. Besides, Rose had already grown attached to Jenny Ann and wasn't ready to give her up just yet.

"Is that within Your will, Father?" Realizing she'd spoken aloud, she shot a cursory glance around to see if the braves at the entrance had noticed her talking to the air.

She needn't have worried. They sat with Mr. Smith and the others at his fire while Fawn Woman served them food and drink. Amazingly, the squaw hadn't demanded Rose come to help. A closer look indicated she was paying close attention to the conversation. Her posture suggested she was every bit as interested in the news the men brought as Rose had been.

Within the hour, the men selected two mounts. While the supplies they'd purchased were being loaded, Mr. Smith continued conversing with Mr. Gilbert.

Rose picked up her wax-sealed letters and a few coins and walked out of the store to Mr. Townes as the man stuffed the last of his purchases into a sack. "I do appreciate your taking my correspondence with you, sir. I don't know what the post might cost once you reach a town, but this should suffice." She handed him the money and the letters.

He looked down at them, then at Mr. Smith, who was speaking with his friend. Toying with his mustache, he met her gaze. "Miss Harwood," he said under his breath, "I don't know what Trader Smith has told you. But no court in the colonies would hold you to your indenturement bond if you'd leave this place with us right now. Just walk down to that raft with me and get on. I'll shoot the blighter if he tries to stop you."

Rose's heart took flight. Leave? This minute? Return to civilization and her sisters?

For a few seconds she entertained the thought. Then her gaze slid to Mr. Smith, who was wasting away by the day before her eyes. She could not desert him in his time of need. And Jenny Ann. . . The baby had been sleeping since the men arrived. In all likelihood the trader hadn't bothered to mention anything about her presence, or the visitors would have gone inside to see Jenny for themselves. If they took her with them, it would be weeks before the milk she was thriving on would be available again—and besides, Mr. Smith was so attached to her.

And Nate. She couldn't possibly leave before he returned. . .*if* he returned.

Rose exhaled a wistful breath and looked up at the man, wearing the most sincere expression she could muster. "'Tis a kind and generous offer. I thank you from the bottom of my heart. But I know for a certainty that the Lord placed me here, and I cannot and will not shirk my duties—no matter how tempting your offer may be."

He opened his mouth to object.

"Truly, kind sir." She placed a silencing hand on his arm. "My place is here. At least for now."

He stared hard at her then eased his stance. "As you wish, miss. I respect your decision, even if I don't agree with it. I'll not forget you in my prayers."

"That is all one can ask." Glad to learn he was a man who sought God, she tipped her head toward her employer. "And please add Mr. Smith's condition to your prayers. He's been poorly for some time. Pray that his recovery will be swift and complete."

Even as she spoke the words, Rose feared her request held little hope. She'd been trying to ignore the trader's rapidly failing health for days, telling herself it was her imagination, that he'd perk up soon. She was plying him faithfully with soups and broths and puddings, but they seemed to have lost their effect. Now she had to wonder what would become of her if Nate didn't come back and Mr. Smith were to die. Fawn Woman had never befriended her, and who knew how the Shawnee in the village would look upon her once Mr. Smith was no longer around to protect her.

Her troubled gaze followed the travelers as they walked their newly purchased mounts down to the raft, and a sudden panic gripped her in its icy fingers. What *would* become of her? It took every ounce of willpower she possessed to stay where she was and not run down to them and plead that they take her and Jenny with them.

As a last resort, she turned her face up to the cloudy sky. *Have I made the right decision, Father? Do You truly want the baby and me to stay here. . .or did You send those men to deliver us from this place? Please, I need to know Your will before it's too late.*

Jenny's airy giggles blended with Mr. Smith's nasally laughter, drawing Rose away from her sewing. She gazed over at the pair and watched Jenny Ann crawling all over the trader. Smiling at the enchanting sight, she tucked her cloak more securely around her legs against the cool draft finding its way past the store's partially covered opening.

Jenny Ann had begun to crawl and pull herself up to whatever happened to be within her reach. To Rose, she seemed to be early in her accomplishments—at least earlier than her brother Tommy had been at that age. To corral the active little one, Mr. Smith fashioned a little walled area from crates and grain sacks, and on this clear, crisp day the two of them sat inside it on a fur robe, his back propped against one of the crates.

A fire in the small fireplace nearby kept the back of the store fairly warm, and the trader sat near its heat most of the time now. Rose tried not to think about how much weaker he seemed with each day. . .yet he never tired of sweet Jenny. He called her his little bundle of blessing, his joy. It seemed the baby ate more solid food than he did, since he subsisted on nothing but milk and pudding now.

Rose had spent most of the morning sewing. To rest her strained eyes, she blinked and peered out of the store's opening toward the village. Since the episode with Hannah Wright, she still harbored the opinion that the Shawnee were savages, but she couldn't deny that their daily life proved to be pleasant. In some instances they seemed kinder than some English people she'd known. Rose rarely heard an angry shout from the village inhabitants and had never witnessed a hand being raised against a child, yet the children hardly ever misbehaved. The younger ones were quite happy as they mimicked their parents in their games, while the older ones seemed eager to learn needed skills from the grown-ups.

From out on the water, Rose heard echoing shouts and checked to discover the source. There she saw two village canoes bearing several enthusiastic young lads racing each other across the river, even on this chilly day.

She thought back on the surprise she'd felt upon learning that Indians bathed in the river quite regularly. And now that mosquitoes no longer presented a problem, the people ceased to wear that odorous bear grease.

How unfortunate that Mr. Smith had never taken up the habit of cleanliness. Rose wondered how Fawn Woman slept in the same wigwam with him. But then, perhaps that was one reason the squaw was unpleasant much of the time.

Aside from Mrs. Smith, most of the villagers seemed content. But despite their congeniality, Rose knew they could turn vicious and violent in an instant, becoming heartless and uncaring about any unfortunate soul they deemed their enemy.

She cut a glance at the trader's wife. Sitting at her own fire and adorning her yellow dress with an assortment of colored beads, the woman still treated Rose with loathing and spoke only when there was an order she wished to give.

Attired in doeskin leggings and shirts these cool days, Running Wolf and Spotted Elk sat with their sister, their moccasined feet stretched out toward the fire. They'd completed their chores with the stock and had milked the cow for Mr. Smith, so they were enjoying a few moments' relaxation.

It was hard to believe how gruff the trader had been when she first joined him, how angry he'd been to learn she'd never milked a cow or killed a chicken. He'd mellowed so much, especially since Jenny Ann had come along. Now he relegated only the care of the store and the baby to Rose and assigned the outside chores to the brothers. The two hadn't balked when ordered to take over those responsibilities, but Rose had noticed that the three siblings spent much of their time in covert conversation of late. As they happened to be doing now.

One of the braves saw her peering out at them and made a comment, and the talking stopped.

Rose wondered if Mr. Smith had been cognizant of their secrecy, or had he been so caught up with little Jenny and his bad digestion that the Indians' conduct didn't seem of import? Perhaps they'd always been that way. But how she wished she understood their language.

She looked over at the trader as he kissed Jenny's short, blond curls. "Mr. Smith?"

"What's up?"

"Nothing. I'm just curious. 'Tis one of my worst faults, I know."

He smirked. "So what bee do ya have in yer bonnet this time?"

"Actually, 'tis you and Fawn Woman. You don't seem to show much affection for each other. How is it that you married her? If you don't mind my asking."

He tossed his head and patted the baby's diapered bottom. "Ya might say it was mutual attraction."

Rose frowned in confusion, and he chuckled.

"I thought she was purty to look at, an' her pa was real partial to a new musket with fancy scrollwork I'd just brought into the store."

"Surely you don't mean you traded a musket for a wife!" The concept disgusted Rose. A woman was of far more value than that.

Adept at reading her expressions by now, Mr. Smith rolled his eyes. "That ain't no different from them English aristocrats an' all that business of swappin' lands and dowries an' such, is it?"

She mulled over his remark in her mind. "No, I suppose not. I just never thought of it that way."

"Besides," he went on, "Fawn Woman wasn't no innocent victim. She made her own requests. She went through my store pointin' to all manner of useless truck she just had to have." Jenny tugged at a handful of his beard, and he chuckled and pried her little fingers away. "All them beads an' shiny baubles she wanted is long since lost or traded off by now." His grin widened. "But she's still got this fine ol' man o' hers."

His words rekindled thoughts of Mariah and her desire for the better things. Rose hoped and prayed her sister would not turn out to be as foolish as Mrs. Smith. She picked up her sewing and resumed working on another warm dress she'd started for Jenny out of a bit of woven fabric.

The trader continued his tale, his voice thoughtful. "When I seen how unhappy Fawn was, 'specially since she never birthed a young'un, I was fixin' to divorce her. But then me an' my partner was ordered to leave her village an' head overmountain to set up a store out here on the Ohio. We figgered if we took her along, those two brothers o' hers could be persuaded to come along, too—fer a price, a'course. She's still ever' bit as greedy as she always was, an' them boys did love the new rifles we give 'em."

Pausing in her work, Rose slid a glance their way. The two were never without their muskets—or the knives and hatchets tucked in their waistbands. They looked formidable enough and seemed proud of being the store's guards. No doubt it gave them a sense of power. Rose was just glad they were there to protect this little encampment and not to attack it.

Nevertheless, something about their taciturn conversations and occasional sly looks made Rose feel apprehensive. . .particularly with Mr. Smith in his weakened condition.

Just how much did Fawn Woman hate Rose. . .and her own husband?

Chapter 22

"Harwood! Up!"

Someone was shaking her shoulder. Rose struggled to open her eyes. It was still dark. Still cold.

"Up."

Recognizing Fawn Woman's voice, Rose felt for the baby sleeping beside her then sat up. Something was amiss. "What is it?"

"Husband. Come." The squaw's shadowy figure hurried to the flap and pulled it back. "Come. Now."

Shoving her feet into her shoes, Rose collected her cloak off her trunk and threw it about herself as she followed after the woman. Since no unusual sounds or activity drifted from the village, Rose's worst fears filled her with dread. Only one thing would cause the trader's wife to summon her in the dark of night. Mr. Smith must have taken a turn for the worse. . .or—

She couldn't finish the thought.

Inside the larger wigwam, the fire pit blazed, providing welcome warmth that surrounded Rose. Fawn Woman stopped near the fire and stoked it with a stick.

"Rose?" Mr. Smith's faint croak came from the far end of the dwelling. The quaver in his voice made her heart lurch. She went immediately to where he lay among some furs and sank down to her knees beside his pallet. In the glow from the flames, she could see his face had lost all color. His eyes appeared sunken, and his breath came out in jerky rasps. Deep trepidation settled its weight on her heart.

"Rose?" he said again, even more weakly.

She leaned close. "I'm here. What can I do for you?"

"I need. . .my tin box. Get it."

She glanced around. "Tin box?" It seemed every available spot around the wigwam was stacked high with goods of all kinds. Nothing resembled a tin box.

Fawn Woman, now sitting opposite the fire, pointed with her stick. "There."

Rose crossed to it and picked it up then returned to him. Kneeling, she held it out to him.

He gave a slight shake of his head. "Open it."

She did as bidden and found it was filled with legal documents and writing paper, a couple of plumed quills, and a considerable number of coins in various denominations. In the corner was a bottle of ink.

"Take out. . .your indenture papers," came his halting whisper. "Dip a quill." He paused and took a breath. "I need to sign 'em off."

He was releasing her? As she followed his instructions, the trader struggled to roll onto his side and raise his head. With a shaky hand, he used his dwindling reserve of strength to scratch his signature. His head fell back to his pillow.

Overwhelmed at her owner's kind act, Rose tucked the papers inside an inner pocket of her cloak. Then, after returning the box to its proper place, she sank down at his side again. "Please, Mr. Smith, I want to help you. There must be something I can do."

"Nothin', child." She detected sadness, finality in his voice. "My innards must'a. . .popped a hole." Another pause. "I'm bleedin' out."

Rose's heart plummeted to her toes. She shot a frantic look at his wife. As though detached from the situation, the squaw sat staring at the fire, idly toying at it with the stick she held. A wicked twitch of her lips looked a whole lot like a sickening smile.

The trader's bony hand wrapped weakly around Rose's, drawing her attention away from the insensitive woman. "Give her brothers. . .another musket each. . .so they'll stay till. . .Nate comes to git ya outta here." The pressure of his hand waned. "Take any money I have. . .to get started on."

No. No. Rose's throat thickened with anguish. Panic raised gooseflesh on her arms. "Please don't die. Don't leave me." She barely choked out the words.

"Can't help it." He drew another laboring breath. "Should'a had them governor's men. . .take you an' the babe with 'em." Nodding sadly, he gave a wry grimace. "Didn't think I was this bad."

She cupped his icy hand in both of hers and held it to the warmth of her cheek. "I wanted to stay. I did. You needed me here. I wouldn't have left you."

The trader attempted a smile. "Yer my brave gal." With a groan, he blanched even whiter and let out a shuddering breath. "My boy Charlie. . .has a cooperage in Fredericksburg." Another pause. "Git word to him. He'll tell my other boys." He gave her hand a slight squeeze with his colder, weaker one. "Yer the daughter I never had." He peered up at her with a slight nod. "Good an' kind, ya are. . . . Knowed it when I first seen ya. . . . May the good Lord bless an' keep ya."

"But—Mr. Smith—"

"Git little Jenny fer me. . . . I need one more look at my joy."

When Rose brought the half-asleep little one to see Mr. Smith, she found with dismay that he'd stopped breathing. His passing left her completely bereft. That he had not lived long enough to set his eyes upon his sweet angel added sorrow beyond words. After Rose took the sleepy child back to their wigwam and settled her once again on her fur pallet, an emptiness beyond anything she'd yet experienced gnawed at her heart. She and Jenny were now the only white people left at the trading post on the edge of the Shawnee village and without the protection of Mr. Smith—a reality that brought deep unrest. But at least no one was around at the moment to see her cry. Rose no longer fought against the tears she'd been holding back. Sobbing quietly, she let them run unheeded down onto her pillow until she had no more left inside.

In the morning, the Susquehannock brothers took care of the burial. Speaking around the tightness in her chest, Rose read some scripture verses and said a prayer over the trader's grave. It took all the strength she possessed to maintain her composure in the braves' presence, when what she wanted more than anything was to give in to her grief and wail for all the world to hear, the way she'd heard an Indian woman grieve the loss of a family member last month. Heart aching, she placed a small bunch of lacy ferns atop the lonely mound near Hannah Wright's resting place.

After she and the brothers returned to the store, she offered Running Wolf and Spotted Elk the new muskets Mr. Smith wanted them to have so they'd stay and continue guarding the place. Nodding and smiling, they took them with obvious gratitude. They had always been friendly to her, especially after she made them the matching shirts.

But their sister was another matter entirely. Rose had no idea what Fawn Woman was thinking.

When Rose had asked for Mr. Smith's frayed New Testament to read at his grave, the woman had handed it over. . .but did not deign to come and see her husband's body laid to rest. With a very determined look on her face, the young woman took all of the trader's clothing and bedding and set them afire then swept out the wigwam with a vengeance. From a deerskin pouch she wore around her neck, she sprinkled some kind of powder across the floor.

For all that frenzy of work, Fawn Woman never demanded help from Rose, which made her even more leery. The squaw had always derived perverse satisfaction from ordering her around. She wondered if the woman was actually mourning her dead husband in her own way but knew that would be one huge stretch of the imagination. Fawn Woman had made no secret of the contempt she harbored for the trader. Or for Rose and Jenny.

Far more disturbing, all trading at the store ceased upon Mr. Smith's death. Groups of Indians would talk among themselves and stare now and then toward the trading post, but not one ventured forth to trade or do business. The few canoes that did arrive from up or down the river were intercepted and the goods or furs were taken to one of the longhouses instead.

Nightfall arrived all too soon, closing in on Rose with its strange sounds and black coldness. She feared having to cross the short distance from the trading post to her wigwam, but the canvas covering the storefront did little to keep out the cold after sundown. It was too chilly for Jenny. There was no other choice. She'd already started a fire in her wigwam, so carrying the baby with her, Rose banked the hot coals in the hearth. Then after collecting a musket and the fixings, plus a hatchet and a sharp hunting knife, she went at last to her meager dwelling and prepared for bed.

Lying on her sleeping pallet, she couldn't decide whether it was the occasional night sounds that kept her on edge. . .or the ominous silence. After lying awake for hours, she slept only fitfully, dozing then jerking awake at the slightest noise, real or imagined. She was now completely alone in this vast wilderness, and the stark realization made her shiver in the fearsome chill of night.

She had no one to turn to now.

No one but God.

Dear Heavenly Father, You promised never to leave me or forsake me. Please take away this fear I have inside. Help me to be brave. Please, give me rest. And please, please, bring back Nate.

Something pulled Rose's hair. She opened her eyes to see a smiling Jenny Ann with her tiny hand entwined in Rose's night braid.

Remembering the uncertainty of the night before, Rose felt for the loaded musket lying on the dirt floor beside her pallet, where she'd tucked it beneath the edge of her top blanket for protection. She'd caught only short snatches of sleep, and from the brightness of the light seeping past the flapped opening, she must have overslept.

She got up quickly, noticing she still wore her clothes from the previous day. She'd been too nervous to change into her nightshift, but here she was, just as safe as before Mr. Smith passed away. The Susquehannock brothers proved to be honorable men.

Once she got the banked embers going to warm the wigwam, she changed the baby's diaper layered with its crushed moss for a dry one while Jenny giggled and played with the braid dangling over Rose's shoulder. Then she bundled the little one up and walked out with her into the cold morning.

Rose had hoped to find someone else up and about to take the baby while she took care of her own morning needs. But no one else was around. She gave a small grimace. It seemed once the trader was no longer present, his widow and her brothers didn't see a necessity to rise early.

Rose sat Jenny in the little pen the child and Mr. Smith had played and napped in together the day before yesterday. In her mind, she could still hear the two of them laughing. The reminder of her and Jenny's loss assaulted her with sorrow as she headed for the woods.

On her way back, Rose heard the chickens squawking to be let out of their coop. She looked past their crude hut to the corralled stock. Unless it was her imagination, there didn't seem to be as many horses as there should be. She took a quick count. Sixteen—out of twenty-two! Six were missing—including a gelding Nate had left there for safekeeping.

She rushed to the brothers' wigwam. "Running Wolf! Spotted Elk! Come out! We've been robbed!"

There was no response.

Rose grasped the flap and tore it aside. The wigwam was empty!

She then dashed to Fawn Woman's wigwam and pushed that flap aside. The squaw—and most of her belongings—were gone. And Mr. Smith's metal box lay open, emptied of his money.

The scuffling sounds that had disturbed her restless sleep last night hadn't been forest animals scurrying about, after all. A quick check of the store revealed a number of items missing, the worst of which was the bundle of the best furs.

Rose stood seething for several moments. But gradually it dawned on her that Mr. Smith's widow was probably due an inheritance. After all, she had stayed with the man for six years. Whatever money he'd saved was rightfully hers. Rose could do nothing about the rest.

Knowing it was now her responsibility to look after the animals, she put Jenny into the baby sling the trader had fixed for her and slipped it on. Grabbing the sack of feed, she headed for the chicken pen.

Walking outside, she noticed a group of Indians standing at the entrance of one of the longhouses a short distance away. All were staring at her. The dire reminder came again that she was here in this Shawnee village alone, with no protector, and nothing between her and them but a single-shot musket.

Chapter 23

Afraid to let Jenny Ann out of her reach, Rose spent the morning with the child slung on her back while she took care of the chores. The entire time she worked, she kept one eye on the Shawnee in the village, aware of their furtive glances in her direction. What were they thinking, planning?

She alternated between praying for God's protection and debating whether or not to take Jenny and some supplies and ride away. But she'd need help to cross the river. . .and the Shawnee hadn't even tended Hannah Wright's wounds. What were the chances they'd be willing to aid her and Hannah's daughter?

Of course, there were plenty of goods available to pay for assistance, which might help. On the other hand, what would prevent the Indians from coming to the trading post at will and helping themselves to whatever they wanted?

Father, what should I do? Give me courage. . . . Please, God, please bring Nate back.

But no answer was emblazoned across the sky, and no assurance of what action she should take brought peace to her heart.

As Rose cooked oats with dried fruit for her and Jenny's noon meal, she spotted two Shawnee approaching. They carried no weapons, but considering she was a mere woman, would they even feel they needed them? Her pulse throbbed in her throat.

She glanced down at Jenny nearby, who was crawling after a bean-filled rattle Mr. Smith had made from a gourd. Then she checked to make sure her musket was still propped against the sitting log.

The two had warm fur robes wrapped around them against the cold. As they approached, Rose noted that along with the usual buckskin breeches most villagers wore, the round-faced older of the two sported an elaborate feather headdress adorned with an abundance of decorative beading. A necklace of bear claws peeked from an opening in the robe. She recognized him as one of the chiefs of the village. He raised a brown hand in greeting.

The action didn't seem hostile, but still. . . Forcing herself to relax, she returned his greeting.

"Harwood woman," the younger brave said.

She nodded, grateful that one of them spoke English. "Good afternoon." She checked to see Jenny was still nearby then motioned to the sitting log not far from the fire, where the warmth from the flames along with the sunshine would keep them comfortable. "Please, sit down." She'd learned early on that visitors were always invited to sit and always offered food or drink.

The two lowered themselves to the log, an indication they'd come to talk.

"Would you care for some tea?" She gestured toward the pot where she'd been brewing some for herself.

The young man spoke to the elder, then they both nodded.

Good. Rose managed a smile and rummaged through a sack for a pair of extra cups. There was no point in complicating things by asking if they wanted sugar or cream. She felt their eyes following her every movement as she removed the pan of cornmeal mush from the coals. She hoped the cooked mixture wouldn't get too lumpy before they took their leave—assuming they left peaceably.

After pouring tea into the three cups, she handed each Indian one then took hers and sat across the fire from them, waiting for them to say something.

They didn't. Not right away. They sat on the log, presumably enjoying their drink while steadily observing her.

Rose breathed a prayer for protection yet again while she took a sip and tried to appear calm. This time, however, she added a request for wisdom to her growing list of desperate needs.

At last the chief set his cup down and said something to the interpreter.

The younger man, elaborately tattooed, with earrings made from animal teeth dangling from his lobes, smiled. "Red Hawk say Susquehannocks no good. Steal horses. Run away. Shawnee no steal."

The chief spoke to him again and he continued. "Smith know he die. Smith make you good trader. Red Hawk say stay. Is good store. Red Hawk give guards. Keep store safe." He pointed to himself. "Cornstalk. Cornstalk stay. Fast Walker come, stay." He nodded, his straight brows raised in question. "Good?"

Rose couldn't believe what she was hearing. Not only were they not planning to harm her; they were going to protect her and the store. Astounded at God's mercy, her heart all but burst from thankfulness as she nodded and smiled at both of them. At least she'd learned one word to say in trading, so she used it now. *"Oui-saw."* Good. She hoped she pronounced it half as well as Cornstalk spoke English. Their languages were so different.

Jenny started fussing just then, and Rose immediately picked her up. She didn't want the child to cry, since Shawnee considered that to be rude behavior. From what Mr. Smith had told her, if a Shawnee baby persisted in crying, it would be strapped in its cradleboard, taken into the woods, and left alone to hang in a tree until it learned crying would not get it any attention.

The Indians raised their cups and drained them then stood to their feet and raised a hand in farewell.

The tattooed one gave a nod. "Cornstalk get Fast Walker. Come here."

Rose smiled with an answering nod. "Thank you."

As they walked away, relief surged through her. Moments ago she'd felt abandoned by everyone she knew. Now her circumstances had taken the opposite turn, and she'd be under the protection of the Shawnee. Better still, if she stayed and traded with the Indians until all the supplies were gone, she might possibly be able to save up enough money to buy back her sisters—perhaps even secure passage for the three of them back home to England.

But before she could revel in that unexpected prospect, unbidden thoughts of Nate Kinyon crowded in. . .of his hearty laugh, his teasing smile, his concern for her. Was returning to England and life as a spinster what she truly wanted? "Nate, where are you?"

Rose drew her cloak around herself and Jenny on the log as she gazed across the wide river. All afternoon, distant banging sounds had carried from the other side. Someone across the way must be building a raft. She didn't know whether to be glad or concerned. The only time a raft was used was to transport livestock, and Mr. Smith had mentioned that officials from the fur company sent men out every couple of years to check on the trading posts. Had the time come for that?

Jenny squealed and grabbed at Rose's arm.

"Forgive me, sweetheart. Mama stopped feeding you, didn't she?" With a shake of her head at her carelessness, Rose spooned some smashed beans and squash into Jenny's mouth and gazed lovingly at the child. How like a rosebud were the tiny lips that could smile so sweetly. No one could deny she was growing cuter by the day. And the little one's nearly white-blond hair now curled about her ears. Whenever Indian squaws happened into the store, they could not resist fondling Jenny's silky ringlets. All their babies had straight black hair.

Reaching for another spoonful of food, Rose realized she'd called herself "Mama" to the baby. She'd become far too attached to Jenny, which was not prudent since the day would soon come to hand her over to her grandparents. Rose tilted her head with a sigh and grinned at the infant. "But you're mine for now." She blew at one of those flaxen curls as she scooped in another bite.

A village dog began to bark. Then others joined in, and they loped down toward the water. Rose glanced across the river, where two men and four horses were making the crossing.

Mr. Smith's employers, perhaps? Surely they'd insist upon her leaving. No way on earth would they allow a lone female to run one of their stores. But would they at least give her recompense for the profitable trading she'd conducted during the weeks since Mr. Smith had passed away? They probably wouldn't be pleased by the small number of fur bundles that remained on hand or the amount of missing trade goods. Nate and Robert Bloom had taken a fully loaded canoe with them when they left, and the Susquehannocks had helped themselves to both goods and furs when they stole away in the dead of night. Fortunately she'd saved the remainder, pitiful lot though it was.

Rose glanced at the two Shawnee braves who had provided protection since the Susquehannocks deserted her. How she wished the men coming were Nate and Robert. As hard as it was to accept, she was beginning to believe they were never coming back.

Jenny cooed and smiled one of her sweet baby smiles, and Rose's heart crimped as she picked up the child and hugged her close. She'd never be able to erase from her mind the terrible condition Hannah Wright had been in before she died. . .nor could she dwell on similar thoughts of what might have happened to Nate and Robert. She sloughed off the morbid turn her mind had taken and caught Jenny's little fist with a playful shake. "We should find out who the visitors are, should we not?" Standing up with Jenny in her arms, she started down the slope.

Already the enthusiastic villagers were assembling on the riverbank, awaiting the newcomers' arrival. With the baby propped on one hip, Rose waited behind the noisy crowd, awed by the change in her perception of the Indians. At home in England, she'd believed them to be nothing but half-naked savages bent on butchering anyone who ventured into the frontier. Now, she kept a slight distance between them and herself merely because she didn't want to get jostled in their excitement.

After beaching their raft, two bearded men dressed in the rough attire of frontiersmen came toward her through the crowd, trailing their horses after them. Both halted at the sight of her then continued their approach. "Rose Harwood?" one asked, the eyes beneath his bushy brows squinting as if unable to believe what he saw. He nudged frameless spectacles higher on his hooked nose.

"Yes, I'm Miss Harwood." Her heart plummeted. They knew her name. Surely they had to be the fur-company men. But they looked scruffier than the last men who'd come through the village.

"I knowed I had letters to deliver to a Rose Harwood," the man with glasses went on. "But I never expected no white woman."

"Aye," his partner agreed, daylight glancing off a scar that ran down one cheek. "We thought it was an Indian wife or a half-breed. But you don't look like no half-breed I ever seen. An' with a towhead baby yet!"

The word *letters* dawned on Rose. "You have letters for me?" She stepped forward, holding out her free hand.

"Yes, ma'am, in one of our bags," the first said. "For you an' Trader Smith. When we stopped by the Ohio an' Virginia Fur Company they asked us to drop 'em by on our way in."

"Then you're not in the employ of the fur company."

"No, ma'am. We're trappers. Goin' downriver for winter beaver."

She breathed a sigh of relief. This meant she had more time to trade with the Indians for furs. More time to make money. "Please," she invited, "do come up to my fire. I've got chicken stew in the pot."

"Chicken! That does sound temptin'." Tugging on his horse's reins, the man started up the hill, past her and the baby. "Ho! Smith! Where you hidin' out, you ol' skinflint?"

Before Rose could say anything, the scarred man paused beside her. "One more thing."

"Yes?"

"Jest so's ya know, some men from the fur company are on their way. They was startin' out a couple'a days behind us."

Her chest tightened with dread.

He cracked a gap-toothed grin. "But don't ya go feedin' them no chicken. 'Possum's good enough for them greedy misers."

A few days after the trappers left, Rose heaved a sigh as she gazed down at Mariah's letter again. Would the girl never change?

Salutations, Rose, the missive began.

Salutations! How pretentious! One would think Mariah was composing business correspondence. But at least she'd taken the time to put plume to paper and had given her older sister some thought. She read further:

> *I was quite surprised to hear from you. I had been rather concerned about your welfare at first, considering the appearance and ghastly odor of your employer. But Colin assured me that any man who could hand over the sum of fifty pounds for you without batting an eye was surely a man of far greater prospects than he appeared. Since receiving your letter, I see Colin was correct.*
>
> *Although you must be living in quite remote circumstances without shops or other niceties, I assure you I am not much better off. I have been relegated to the lowly position of tutor to Colin's three sisters and secretary to Mr. and Mrs. Barclay. For as wealthy as these colonials are, the females especially lack most severely in penmanship.*
>
> *The girls tag behind me wherever I step, and Mistress Barclay is forever finding something for me to do, so I have precious little time to myself. Would you believe that the woman actually had me serve food at their annual summer gathering? I was sorely mortified!*

To make matters even worse, I am allowed only one day to myself a week, and Mrs. Barclay refuses to let Colin escort me anywhere. I have been to the shops only once since my arrival here, and that was as a companion to the old biddy and two of her spoiled daughters. I need not tell you how little money I have to spend. Fortunately, Colin slipped me a few coins. He really is a dear, as generous as he is handsome.

Alas, the mistress is calling me. I shall try to write more in a few days.

I remain your obedient sister,
Mariah

Rose laughed at the absurd ending. *Obedient? Rarely! Willful? Often! And quite often concerned only about herself.* But the girl did have her moments of generosity, and Rose knew she genuinely cared for her family.

Laying the letter aside, she picked up the one from Lily and pressed it to her heart. Sweet Lily. She unfolded the thick missive which she'd read so often she'd nearly committed it to memory. The words penned in her younger sister's fine hand were so like her, Rose could imagine Lily speaking them in her airy voice:

My beloved sister Rose,

I cannot express in words how unbearably deeply I miss you. I wish so very much that I could have gone with you that day we were all auctioned off. I was so distraught about your welfare I grieved for you daily, until I received your precious letter. But know that every night the Waldons and I pray for your safety and your happiness in your strange and scary circumstance.

When I read how you came to possess the baby of that unfortunate woman, it brought me to tears. Soon after we arrived here, we heard that a band of savages had swooped into the Wrights' farm, intent upon burning and destroying, as they are prone to do. It was no surprise to hear they took Mistress Wright and her baby hostage. How terribly sad that the poor woman died. However, Mr. Waldon assures his wife and me that we are in no danger. The Wrights lived at the very edge of the frontier on land sold to Mr. Wright by one tribe of Indians, while a different tribe also laid claim to that very land. Mr. Waldon is certain his deed for the property we dwell on is in no way questionable. Still, whenever I venture outside, I always check the woods. I am sure I shall grow more comfortable with my surroundings as time goes by.

I could not be happier here. Mr. Waldon is a kind and gentle husband, father, and employer. Mistress Waldon somewhat reminds me of you. She treats me like a younger sister, though she is not nearly as energetic as you, dear Rose. Some days she can scarcely walk, for the pain in her joints is severe. Other days she seems much improved. Before all our meals, we pray for her healing.

Smiling, Rose laid down the letter. She'd been right about giving Mr. Waldon the extra money he'd needed to purchase Lily's papers.

Or had she? It sounded like Lily lived far too close to where Indians had conducted a murderous raid. Rose flicked a glance to the store's front, where her guards relaxed just outside near their fire, their muskets and hatchets lying nearby to ensure her safety. . .these 'peaceful' people who decorated their dwellings with bloodied scalps and other severed body parts. She shuddered.

An icy breeze tugged at the lowered canvas at the front of the store, loosening the ties, and an edge began to flap. Rose left the limited warmth of the crude fireplace and checked on Jenny. All but swallowed by furs as she napped, the child had one tiny hand peeking out. Rose reached down and tucked it beneath the warm covering then went outside to retie the loose thong holding the canvas in place.

No one had come up the river to trade for several days, and even the Shawnee were staying inside their warm wigwams. Rose knew if she didn't have Jenny Ann to keep her company she'd be unbearably lonely.

The weather had turned much colder. Except for the evergreens, all trees and shrubs were devoid of their brilliant fall colors. Their bare forms looked forlorn, like so many skeletal fingers poking up at the sky. After tightening the flap's ties, Rose gazed toward the river. Crackly ice fringed the dark water, and overhead, a dull, gray cloud bank threatened snowfall.

Whatever had possessed her to remain here through the harsh winter with a little baby? Perhaps the men from the fur company would arrive soon and give her orders to leave. . .and hopefully escort her back to civilization.

Spying a canoe coming into view around the bend, Rose grimaced. Likely it was just some Indians willing to brave the cold to come and trade.

Cornstalk and Fast Walker straightened, alert at their posts. Rose felt at ease knowing the two had promised to keep her safe.

Stepping back inside the dimly lit store, she began straightening things, making certain the goods were displayed to their best advantage. She hoped Jenny, in her little warm cocoon, wouldn't be too fussy when awakened by the arrival of customers. From the shouting and hullabaloo of barking dogs that had already begun, the visitors would be surrounded by welcoming villagers any minute.

It would take time for the furs to be unloaded. Rose added water to the kettle over the fire and stirred the coals. The travelers would probably be chilled to the bone and would appreciate some hot India tea, always a treat from the usual bitter herb teas almost everyone here served. And a few leftover biscuits remained from noon. She'd get those out as well. Not quite an English high tea, but thought of serving afternoon tea as if she were at home in Bath brought a bubble of laughter. Rose clamped a hand over her mouth so she wouldn't disturb Jenny.

Sudden light flooded in from the front of the structure, and she swung toward it.

"Rose? You in here? It's me, Nate. I'm back."

Chapter 24

Out of breath after racing up the bank from the river, Nate searched frantically in the dim light of the log-built trading post. Then in a blur, Rose flew to him and threw her arms about his neck.

"You're alive! You're actually alive! Thank God!"

Wrapping his arms around her soft form, he hugged her tight. "So are you. When we got word that Eustice had died, I was so worried, I—"

An ear-piercing wail came from farther back in the store.

Going rigid, Nate pushed Rose to one side and went for his hunting knife.

The wail turned into sobs. He moved toward what sounded very much like a very unhappy little one. He couldn't believe his eyes. There, walled in by a few crates and sacks, sat a baby. A blond, blue-eyed, squalling baby.

He felt the blood drain from his face as he wheeled back to Rose. "You—you never told me you were with child."

"Me?" Rose's expression was one of shock. Then she burst into laughter. "I'm not her mother," she sputtered between giggles. "But she is mine to care for until I'm able to deliver her to her grandparents." She reached down and picked up the towhead, who stopped crying almost immediately. "Nate Kinyon, I'd like to introduce Jenny Ann Wright. Her mother, unfortunately, died after suffering grievous wounds while running the gauntlet. She asked me to look after her little one."

His brow furrowed. "That's really regrettable. . .but not unheard of."

Clinging to Rose, the child peered at him from rounded blue eyes as if taking his measure, then reached out a tentative little hand, still moist from her mouth.

Nate took hold of the slimy fingers, and the little curly-top gifted him with a darling, two-tooth grin. The little one was every bit as irresistible as the woman holding her.

"Robert Bloom is with you, is he not?" Rose searched his face.

"Aye. He's seeing that everything's unloaded. He's brought back quite the surprise. Wait'll you see." Nate chuckled then sobered. "It's true, then? Smith's dead? You were left here by yourself?" Concerned over her sad situation, he drew her and the baby close to him, burying his face in Rose's hair, breathing in her unique scent. She felt so good in his arms. He made a solemn vow not to let her out of his sight before he had her safely away from here.

After a long-spun moment, she leaned her head back and gazed up into his eyes with such warmth he thought he'd melt. "I feared you were dead. Whatever took you so long?"

The store's flap flung wide again, and Robert Bloom strode in, all smiles, with his arm around a slip of an Indian lass. A thick hat of rabbit fur hid most of her raven hair but not the perfect oval of her olive face with its huge, dark-chocolate eyes. Wrapped in a soft fur robe, she looked small and shy beside Robert's lean form as she lowered her lashes with a faint smile.

Robert drew the girl along as he came forward and took Rose's hand. "Rose, I'm so glad you're alive an' well. If you hadn't been, I reckon I would'a had to shoot Nate for leavin' you here in the first place."

Pleased they'd both finally returned, yet still surprised, Rose glanced from the Indian girl to Nate, who offered a sheepish shrug.

"And this must be the baby Red Hawk was telling me about down at the river." Robert reached over and ruffled Jenny's hair with his free hand. "Cute little thing." His gaze met Rose's again. "Praise the good Lord you were here for that little gal."

Rose nodded. "I feel the same way. I've no doubt Jenny Ann is the reason God allowed me to be brought here. He knew she'd be in dire need of someone to care for her."

"Aye. He does work in mysterious ways. Speakin' of that, look what the Lord gave me." He gazed lovingly down at the girl at his side. "This here is Swims with Otters, but I can't help myself. . . . I call her Shining Star 'cause I can't seem to take my eyes off her."

Smiling at his words, Rose lifted the willowy girl's hand, drawing her liquid brown eyes up to her. "I'm very pleased to meet you, Shining Star." She motioned toward the back of the store. "Would you like to take a seat by the fire? I've water heating for tea." She smiled at the men, including them in the invitation.

Robert quickly translated what Rose had said, and they all moved to the warmth of the back of the store, removing their outer clothing along the way. Without her hat, Swims with Otters's glossy braids, entwined with thin strips of leather, hung to the middle of her back. She brushed a few stray strands from her eyes.

Rose noticed the girl also wore an intricately beaded headband, which complemented her beaded doeskin Indian dress and calf-high deerskin moccasins. "While I prepare the tea," Rose said, "you men will have to tell me why you were gone so long. And Robert, how you happened to bring along this lovely girl."

<hr />

"It's a pretty sad story," Bob said, taking a sip of steaming tea as the four settled on grain sacks they'd pulled close to the fire.

Nate peered over the top of his cup and cut his friend a pointed look, a warning not to let the reason for their delayed return slip out. No sense frightening Rose any more than necessary.

Bob reached beside himself and squeezed the Indian maiden's hand. "You see, Rose, Shining Star's part of the Miami nation. She lived in a village not far from Mascouten territory, an' them two tribes've been feudin' back an' forth for some time. I reckon it got pretty bad, 'cause the Miami women outnumber the men a good four or five to one these days."

"Mercy." Rose hugged Jenny close. "How dreadful, all those widows and orphans." She gazed down at her own little orphan.

Nate chimed in, hoping to ease her mind. "The men take on more wives. That helps some."

Rose tucked her chin and arched her brows. "Surely you don't mean plural marriage. That's a rather pathetic solution to such a problem."

"Anyway," Bob said, "Shining Star's pa was killed in a raid last spring. Then when her brother never came back from huntin'. . ." He shrugged a shoulder. "What men are left already have more wives an' daughters than they can hunt for an' feed. So her mother came to me."

Looking from him to the Indian lass and back, Rose met Bob's gaze. "To ask you to marry her daughter."

He slid an uncertain glance to Nate before responding. "More like she wanted to sell Star to me." At Rose's gasp, he rushed on. "You see, if the widow had trade goods, she could bargain with the village hunters for meat now an' again. . .to see her an' her other little ones through the hard winter."

"So you bought her? You actually bought her?" Rose rolled her eyes and grimaced.

Nate could see this was not going well for his partner. Not well at all.

Bob offered a weak smile. "No, not at first. But her ma kept comin' back to me with her, pleadin'. An' I felt so sorry for my shy little girl, I gave in." He lifted his chin a notch. "But rest assured, Miss Rose, I won't be beddin' or weddin' her till she comes to know the Lord as her Savior."

Rose arched her brows. "Don't you mean, *if?*" she challenged.

Watching her reaction, Nate shifted uncomfortably on his seat. Rose Harwood was one stiff-necked woman, especially when it came to religion. A body would think she was one of them Puritans.

But Bob didn't seem the least put off by her remarks. "I already thought about that. A lot. I figger if she don't become a believer, then I'll look for a suitable husband for her among the other tribes."

Nate was pretty sure he discerned a hint of triumph in the smile that played across Rose's lips. "In that case, I shall make room for the girl in the wigwam with Jenny and me."

Looking from her to Bob, Nate released a tired breath. He couldn't believe he'd just risked life and limb for such a hardheaded woman. But he had to admit he was as besotted as Bob. No doubt about it.

Chapter 25

As they all continued sipping their tea, Rose rocked back and forth slightly with Jenny Ann asleep in her arms. She studied Swims with Otters, or Shining Star—whatever Robert wanted to call her—then glanced at Robert, seated beside the lass. "I must say your young lady scarcely appears older than my youngest sister."

He tipped his head. "She was born durin' the time of fallin' leaves, fifteen years ago. I know she's a little thing, but she's full growed."

"Fifteen." Rose shook her head. Papa wouldn't have considered an offer for any of his daughters until they were at least seventeen years of age. Thoughts of Mariah came to mind. The girl had been too picky for her own good. . .and then it was too late. And here sat a shy girl who reminded Rose so much of young Lily, already given to a man—*sold* was closer to the truth. The very concept was appalling.

Remembering the leftover biscuits, she used her free arm to reach behind herself for the covered plate then removed the cloth and offered one to Nate and then the girl.

The lass glanced from the plate to Rose, then to Robert, with questions in her dark eyes. He smiled and nodded, and she took one but held on to it and stared, as if she didn't know what it was.

Robert also took one, bit into it, and said something to her.

Finally the girl took a small nibble. After a few seconds she took another bite.

"Oui-saw?" Rose asked, using her one and only word of Shawnee.

The bashful smile appeared, and the lass nodded.

"So," Nate cut in, taking a second biscuit, "seems you been pickin' up a bit'a Shawnee."

Rose chuckled. "I'm afraid that's the extent of it. Mr. Smith taught me the word when he was training me in the business of trading."

Grinning, Robert gave a nod "That's what Red Hawk told us. About you in here dickerin' just like you knowed what you was doin.'"

"I actually do know what I'm doing." She flashed a wry smile. "Most of the time."

"Red Hawk said that when the Susquehannocks left, they run off with several horses an' a bunch of your best furs," Robert said.

She nodded. "Along with all the cash money, I'm sad to say."

"Well, no need to fret," Nate assured her. "Bob an' me did real good, all considered. An' with Smith gone, you ain't bound to him anymore."

Remembering the trader's final act of kindness, Rose smiled. "Quite right. In fact, before he died, he signed off on my papers to make everything legal. So I'm hoping to earn enough from the furs and trade goods still left in the trading post to buy my sisters' papers and free them, as well." Having divulged that information in a rush, she waited for their reaction.

Nate turned and surveyed the goods stacked against the side wall. "Don't look like that'll be a problem. We'll buy back your sisters, take that baby back to wherever she belongs, an' still have plenty leftover to have ourselves one fine time in Baltimore. Or mebbe you'd rather go to Philadelphia. Hear tell they got a lot more shops an' taverns an' playhouses an' anything else we fancy."

A fine time? That was his proposal? To offer her what some bigwig would offer a loose woman? Crushed and not wanting him to see the disappointment on her face, she stood with the sleeping baby and went to stoke the fire.

All those long days and weeks she'd spent longing for Nate Kinyon to return—wasted. So was her deepest hope—that he'd taken steps to strengthen his faith, since he knew how much it meant to her—so that when he asked her to marry him, she could say yes. But the horrid truth was her chances of wedding Nate were no better than Robert Bloom's were of marrying Star. Probably worse. Shining Star had yet to hear enough about the Lord to accept or reject Him. But Nate. . .

A plan formed in Rose's mind, and she swiveled on her heel, hardening herself as she looked at Nate. "I'm sorry, but your plans won't do. I'm not footloose as you are. I have serious responsibilities. Not only do my sisters need to be bought out of bondage, I need enough money to purchase their passage back to England, where they can be properly looked after by our father."

Nate reared back. "I thought the whole point in comin' to America was because your father couldn't look after you girls."

She gave a small shrug. "I'm sure he and my brother have managed to take care of the problem that beset our family by now. In any event, I plan to make money enough for each of my sisters to have a sizable dowry so they'll be able to make a good match." She knew she was probably overreaching, but she was too hurt to care.

Standing to his feet, Nate towered over her. "An' how do you propose to do that? If you don't mind me askin'."

Rose wished he weren't so much taller than she, but she did her best to straighten to her full height as she looked up at those steely hazel eyes of his. She mustered as much force in her voice as possible so he'd hear her determination. "By continuing to run this trading post as I've been doing since Mr. Smith passed on. The villagers want me to stay. The store is good business for them as well as for me, with people constantly coming and going. There's no reason for me not to go on looking after things until I've earned sufficient funds. I could not earn a fraction of what I'll make here anywhere else."

Still seated with his Indian maiden, Robert gave a light laugh. "Looks like she's been doin' fine so far. Course, on the other hand, there's the problem of restockin' an' such. Plus I don't see them boys out at the Virginia an' Ohio lettin' a woman run the place, when it comes right down to it."

"Well. . ." That was so true. How would she? An idea slowly surfaced. Rose took a deep breath and averted her gaze from him to Nate. "As it happens, a pair of trappers came through a few days before you arrived, and they told me representatives of the company would be here any day to check on things. And I thought. . ." She glanced at Robert. Noticing he was talking quietly to the girl, Rose drew a breath and stepped nearer to Nate so she could speak softly. "I thought if you two would stay on till they leave, you could pretend. . .to be. . .my husband." There. She'd said it.

Nate clamped a hand on her shoulder and pulled her closer, his mouth agape. "Did you say what I thought you said?"

⁓

Rose had no idea how she suffered through Nate's snickering and teasing. The maddening frontiersman was having a lot of fun at her expense. Granted, it took awhile for him to see the logic behind her scheme, but once she explained her reasoning, he was quick to come around—even if he did have a mischievous gleam in his eye. Surely he did not imagine he could attempt anything untoward during their little deception. In any event, she was more than glad to have *her protector* back again. . .along with Robert Bloom, of course.

She got up from her seat on the flour sack. "I'm sure the three of you must be hungry after paddling all day upriver in such cold weather." She moved toward Nate with an impish smile. "Here, let me have *our* baby. You need to bring in your pelts before one of the villagers takes a liking to them."

"You're right about that." With no indication that he'd noticed her suggestive statement, Nate rose to his feet and handed Jenny to her. After shrugging into his warm outer garment, he headed out.

Robert also came to his feet, and so did Shining Star. He turned to the lass and spoke quietly in her language first, repeating the words in English. "Stay here." He gestured toward Rose. "With Miss Rose." Obviously he was attempting to teach her some basic English, which Rose appreciated.

The Indian girl sank back down onto her seat and looked timidly at Rose. "Wi' Mi' Rose." She checked back at him with a tentative smile.

"Oui-saw. Good girl." He cupped her cheek in his palm and smiled into her eyes.

Observing the loving expressions passing between them, Rose felt a twinge of envy and, for a brief moment, felt like crying. But she'd been doing quite enough of that of late, she reminded herself, and sloughed off the emotion.

Robert grinned over at her. "I'm sure Star'd be happy to hold the baby while you tend to things."

"If you're certain. I could put Jenny in her little pen."

He shook his head and spoke a few words to the lass, and she got up. As Star approached Rose with her arms outstretched, he threw on his fur robe and started to leave. But reaching the flap, he stopped and turned. "Rose, what you really need is a cradleboard like Indian mothers use. Babies love 'em 'cause they never have to be left with someone else while their mothers work. I'll see if I can trade some squaw outta one."

"Thank you," she said in her most polite tone. Having given Jenny over to the Indian girl, Rose pondered the concept of cradleboards versus a cloth sling. She'd noticed babies strapped to their mothers' backs and thought the stiff contraptions looked too restrictive. Yet the wee ones all seemed happy, snuggled and warm inside their little cocoons. Perhaps Jenny would feel more secure in one. She glanced at the little one and saw her smiling and toying with one of Shining Star's braids while the lass sang softly in her ear.

Nate came back in on a blast of winter air, his arms straining with the weight of a large bundle. "Where do you want these?"

Rose quickly dragged a couple of crates away from the side wall. "Put them here. 'Twould be best to keep them separate from the others."

Dropping them with a thud, Nate bent over and pulled out what appeared in the dim light to be a beaver pelt. "Feel how thick this is, Rose." He held it out to her.

She smoothed her hand over it. "Oh yes. Very prime. A lovely pelt."

"Aye. We only traded for the best. That wasn't the main reason we went tradin', though. We heard rumors that one of the tribes had a secret silver mine, and we were hopin' to get our hands on some of that silver we heard about. Enough to satisfy even ol' Eustice." Taking the beaver hide, he caressed her cheek with the silky fur. "Almost as soft as your skin."

Gazing up at him, Rose couldn't move. There was such passion in his eyes it made her knees feel weak. She couldn't believe how easily she fell beneath his spell.

Robert strode in just then with his arms filled with furs, and the tension lightened noticeably. Rose moved out of his way. "Put them there with Nate's."

He dropped the load onto the first pile. "Did I hear Nate mention the silver?" He stepped nearer to Rose and grimaced as he pulled up a sleeve, displaying a bracelet. "One of the two we managed to get our hands on."

She gasped. "Then you did find the silver mine."

Both men laughed, and Robert elaborated. "Mighty strange, the way a story gets started an' grows into somethin' a whole lot bigger an' better with the tellin.'"

Smiling and frowning with confusion at the same time, Rose was all too aware that Nate had yet to take his eyes off her. She hoped her idea of pretending they were husband and wife before the fur-company officials wasn't giving him any more improper ideas. She found it difficult to focus on his partner's words.

"Turns out," Robert continued, "the bracelets came from Spanish Mexico. Been traded here an' there till they made it up to the Ohio Valley. All that way. Ain't that somethin'?"

"It truly is," she responded. Still feeling Nate's eyes on her, she steeled her emotions and faced him.

A one-sided grin emerged, and he rejoined the conversation. "Aye, and us paddlin' up one stream after another, like we was Ponce de León, searchin' for his fountain of youth."

So that's why they were gone so long. Rose looked from one grinning face to the other then decided to get their minds back on business. "Since Mr. Smith, may God rest his soul, has passed on, 'tis only right you should have all the profits from your venture. I have the bills of lading from the goods he purchased and the record of the items you took with you, so when the furs are taken to the company, it should be quite easy to figure."

"That'll help make up for the trouble we had," Robert muttered.

"What trouble?" Her heart skipped a beat.

"Nothin' to speak of," Nate blurted. He slid a significant glare to his friend.

That really piqued Rose's curiosity.

Nate's expression eased to one more innocuous. "Well, now. That's mighty nice of you, givin' Bob and me the profit. Speakin' of ol' Eustice, did he treat you decent after we left? I told him I'd—well, let's just say I told him to be nice to you."

Another bittersweet memory came to the fore, and Rose smiled. "Thank you. But I must say, once little Jenny Ann came to us, Mr. Smith became a different man. No matter how bad he felt or how his stomach pained him, he loved playing with her. We spent nearly all our time together after she came along—mostly here in the store, with him teaching me the business." Remembering her treasured book, she pulled the slim volume from her apron pocket and held it to her breast. "This New Testament was his. We read from it quite a lot, particularly toward the end."

"Well, I'll be." Nate's smug expression vanished.

Robert, however, looked pleased. "You have a copy of the scriptures!" His gaze veered from her to the Indian lass. "That'll make things easier. I won't have to rely on just the verses I know when I talk to Star about the Lord."

Seeing the delight in the man's demeanor, Rose appreciated the tenderness, the innocence of their new love. She glanced at Nate to gauge his reaction to his friend's comments. But there was no shared joy in his expression. He looked more like a cornered rat.

It was her turn to give him a smug smile.

Chapter 26

Nate and Bob left Shining Star settled in with Rose and the baby in Rose's wigwam and headed for the Shawnee council lodge, as Red Hawk had requested earlier. Nate's insides felt pleasantly sated after enjoying Rose's delicious cooking. It had been ages since he'd downed such tasty eggs and side pork—especially with the added treat of fluffy biscuits slathered with butter. Eustice certainly knew how to pick a cook! He stifled a grin at the ridiculous notion. Cooking was only one of Rose Harwood's many fine attributes.

As he and Bob reached the lodge and entered, most of the talking ceased between the villagers assembled in the immense ninety-by-fifty-foot structure. Always amazed by the size and spaciousness of a longhouse, Nate surveyed the toasty interior with interest. A sturdy framework of thick, upright poles, interlaced with a series of thinner poles, was overlaid with sheets of flattened elm bark. Shafts of waning daylight slanted through a number of smoke holes in the roof and cut through the gloomy, smoky interior, glinting off a grisly collection of scalps displayed on poles like trophies. Nate observed that though many sported black Indian hair, several were blond, red, and assorted shades of brown. Even a couple of gray ones. He caught a troubled breath, inhaling a blend of tobacco, wood, earth, and Indian.

Because of the cold weather, all the fire pits along the length of the lodge were ablaze, and what smoke didn't rise to the smoke holes above mingled with that coming from several long, decorative pipes making the rounds.

It appeared every man in the village had come to the gathering, along with several women who sat on pallets behind the circle of men. Obviously everyone wanted to hear the latest news.

Red Hawk motioned for Nate and Bob to be seated between him and another chief named Barking Dog.

While lowering themselves down onto the packed earth floor, Nate tried not to show his amusement over the second chief's name. He wondered if, as a boy, the chief had gone around barking like a dog, or had he merely teased the mangy camp dogs into incessant yapping? Judging from the rapid rate at which the man spoke, Nate guessed the first assumption was correct.

A pipe came his way, and Nate took it and drew a few puffs then passed it on and settled into a comfortable position. He knew from experience he and his partner would be here for quite some time, with Bob doing all their talking.

As always, conversation began with the polite blather regarding health, how the hunting and fishing had gone this fall, and the usual inane pleasantries. Then Bob's expression turned serious, and he leaned forward. Nate knew the important subjects had finally come up.

In seconds the men sitting around the circle began muttering in low tones to one another, their expressions sober, often bordering on sullen.

Nate decided it was high time he started learning enough Shawnee to make out the gist of what the Indians were discussing. He elbowed Bob. "What'd you say to them?"

He angled his head Nate's way. "I told 'em about the scores of canoes we saw beached where the Scioto River merges with the Ohio. An' that when we sneaked up on the camp, we saw almost as many French soldiers there as Indians."

Red Hawk frowned and said something to Bob.

Nate managed to catch the word *Miami*.

His pal gave a negative shake of his dark head and made a correction. "Mostly Seneca."

The others present relaxed visibly. Nate surmised it was because several of those gathered around the fire happened to be Miami braves.

An interminable hour or so dragged by before Bob finally stopped conversing with the leaders and turned to Nate. "We can go now."

Nate resisted the urge to rub his numb backside as he stood with his friend to shake hands with the men nearby. Then, smiling and nodding, he and Bob took their leave.

As they left the village and covered the short distance to the trading post, Nate drew in a deep breath of fresh air and let it slowly out. "Prob'ly if I took time to learn some Shawnee, meetin's like that wouldn't drag on so."

Bob laughed. "It would help, no doubt about it."

"Well, tell me. Did the Shawnees give you any idea of how they felt about the French movin' south from Fort Ouiatenon?"

His friend shrugged. "They weren't concerned about it. They said the French tried to go that far down the Scioto a few years back, and the Shawnee chiefs at Sinioto told them politely but firmly that they weren't welcome in the Ohio Valley. They kind of *suggested* they go back to their fort, where they'd be safe. What Red Hawk and the others didn't like was those northern tribes coming south into their huntin' grounds."

Recollecting their own recent experience in that area, Nate was thankful the two of them made it back in one piece. "Personally, what I didn't like was all the time we had to stay hidden once the French found out we were tradin' in those parts. We lost more'n a month before they finally moved on."

"Well," Bob said with a grin, "beats havin' our scalps hangin' on some Seneca's lodge pole, don't it?"

"Aye. That it does. I'm kinda partial to mine after all this time. I just hope them Frenchies keep themselves down that way, seein' as how Rose has her heart set on bein' a storekeeper. With me." He grinned and looked up the hill toward her wigwam silhouetted in the moonlight.

It was going to be a lot of fun getting that little gal off that high horse of hers.

Rose awakened to a mild sunny morning, a rarity for late fall. Feeling gloriously alive, she gave a languorous stretch. Nate and Robert were back! If that weren't bounty enough, she and Jenny now had the company of Shining Star in their wigwam, the baby slept soundly through the night, and by all calculation, today was Sunday!

Thank You, dear Lord, for my many blessings. Please, please don't give up on Nate. With both Robert and me pointing him toward You, he just might find his way.

She raised her head and peered across the cold fire pit to the mound of fur where only the top of the Indian girl's dark head was visible. *And please open Shining Star's heart and mind that she might see Your light. She seems like such a sweet girl. She reminds me so of Lily. And thank You for the safe return of the men. You know I'd all but given up on them.*

Easing slowly out of her bedding so she wouldn't disturb Jenny, Rose used a stick to dig to the bottom of the fire pit. After finding some live coals, she blew on them and added wood shavings until enough of a flame sprouted for her to add some thin sticks.

Movement across the wigwam revealed Shining Star beginning to stir. The girl opened her heavily lashed, doelike eyes. At first sight of Rose they registered panic; then she relaxed and smiled shyly as she started to get up.

Rose gestured for her to lie back down. Then, hugging herself tight, she made shivering motions. "Cold," she whispered.

"Cold," the lass repeated softly. With a soft giggle, she snuggled down once again into her lush coverings.

Rose had to smile. Star truly was a joy, just as Robert had said. Perhaps with her around, Rose wouldn't miss Lily so much. . .or the rest of her family. *God bless Papa, Tommy, Charles and his family. . .and do keep after Mariah, since I am not there to do it.*

What a treat, having an extra pair of hands, Rose mused, as she and the Indian girl walked with the baby to the store. Getting herself and Jenny dressed and bundled for the day had been only half as much work with Shining Star a willing helper.

They found a roaring fire already blazing in the hearth when they entered the trading post. Better yet, the water kettle already hung suspended above the heat. Emotion swelled within Rose at the touching surprises, but she reminded herself they were just small acts of kindness. Yet how she appreciated kind acts now. . .so much more than she had before Nate left with Robert.

She carried Jenny closer to the warmth of the fire, noting that neither of her knights in shining armor was present in the store's shadowy interior.

Shining Star also glanced around, appearing frightened as she caught Rose's hand. "Bob."

Knowing the men were most likely out tending the livestock, she smiled at Star. "Horses." She cupped her hand and put it to her mouth. "Feed horses."

"Horse." The girl nodded and turned toward the entrance.

Rose caught her hand. "Shining Star watch Jenny." She handed the baby to her then pointed to herself. "I cook. Feed bellies." She rubbed her own midsection.

An understanding smile curved Star's lips. She patted her stomach then the baby's. "Feed bellies."

Delighted, Rose laughed. They were going to get along just fine.

At that moment, Nate and a blast of sunshine burst through the opening. He held his hat upside down in his hands. "Mornin', ladies." He flashed that infectious grin of his. "Fed your chickens and collected the eggs." He tilted his hat slightly so Rose could see them nestled within what looked like some wilted weeds. "Loved the eggs so much last night, I sure hope you won't mind cookin' us up another helpin'. I pulled a onion outta the garden, too. Thought we could add some to the eggs."

"You did, did you?" She grinned at his enthusiasm.

"Aye. Them biscuits were mighty good, too. An' I dug up a turnip an' a couple carrots an'—"

Shining Star interrupted with a tug on his sleeve. "Bob."

Nate gave a nod and pointed toward the entrance. "Bob come." He switched his attention back to Rose. "He'll be in soon as he finishes milkin' the cow."

She shook her head in wonder. "The two of you are such a help. With my morning chores done, I can start on the biscuits right away, so we—"

The flap opened again, bringing Robert, along with another momentary shaft of sunshine.

"I'll get those biscuits going," Rose continued. "That way we'll have plenty of time for a nice leisurely church service. 'Tis the Sabbath, you know."

"Church service?" Bob set the milk pail on a crate and walked toward Shining Star. "Now, that's what I like to hear. We'll have some Psalm singin', too." He smiled down at the girl.

"Yes, we'll sing, as well." Rose glanced at Nate.

His grin had flattened, but the second he noticed her looking at him, he propped it up again. "Singin's fine with me. I like singin'." But the dull glint in his eye matched his forced enthusiasm.

Rose quickly pivoted back toward the flour sack. It wouldn't do for him to see her smirk.

⁓

"'From all that dwell below the skies,'" Nate sang as he and his friends sat outside, his voice determinedly joyful and robust, "'let the Creator's praise arise: Alleluia! Alleluia!'" Truth was, he did love to sing, and it wasn't as if he was a heathen. He'd been to Sabbath services every Sunday as a kid. "'Let the Redeemer's name be sung, through every land, in every tongue. Alleluia! Alleluia! Alleluia! Alleluia!'" Even as he belted out the words, he realized their little group truly had caught the attention of the villagers, since they, too, had come outside to enjoy the warmth of the winter sun.

Nate could feel Rose watching him before they started into the next verse of the hymn, and that was the most fun of all. He knew she had to be flabbergasted that he even knew the song. She'd barely squeaked out her alleluias.

He focused on the next stanza. " 'In every land begin the song, to every land the strains belong. Alleluia! Alleluia! In cheerful sound all voices raise, and fill the world with joyful praise. Alleluia! Alleluia! Alleluia! Alleluia!' "

Rose finally caught the spirit of the hymn and raised her voice. She sang the chorus in a surprisingly beautiful soprano, the perfect blend with his baritone, Nate thought. Fact was, the two of them went well together in a lot of ways. They'd have a great time of it, if only she would quit insisting on being such a Puritan and admit it.

As they started into the next verse, Nate feasted his eyes on her as she sat across from him on a crate with Jenny Ann in her lap, like a beautiful Madonna holding the babe. Then his gaze drifted to Bob's Indian girl. If anyone was uncomfortable in this impromptu church service, it was poor Shining Star. With her dark head lowered, she darted glances around the group then out to the villagers down the slope.

Nate couldn't help feeling sorry for her. He knew her bewilderment must be acute. When she looked at him at the start of the final stanza, he sent her a reassuring smile. Her transition into the white world was going to be hard. Bob's mother had never been accepted by the good people in the area where they lived. *Lord, if Shining Star comes out with us, please make them so-called Christians in our neighborhood treat her with the kindness she deserves.*

Realizing with no little shock that he had actually said a real from-the-heart prayer, it dawned on him that he hadn't joined in at the start of the third verse. So he jumped right in. " 'Alleluia! Thy praise shall sound from shore to shore. . . .' "

As the hymn came to an end, Bob held up Mr. Smith's New Testament and bowed his head. "May our Father God bless the reading of His Word, and may He open the ears of understanding to all who hear, in the name of our Lord and Savior, Jesus the Christ."

He then drew Shining Star down on the sitting log beside him, opened the Bible, and began reading aloud. Nate recognized the first verse of the Gospel of John as one often read in his childhood home. " 'In the beginning was the Word, and the Word was with God, and the Word was God.' " Marking his place with his index finger, Bob closed the Bible and turned to the lass, translating what he'd just read. She frowned in puzzlement and asked several questions.

Nate noticed that Rose wore a soft smile as she watched the exchange between the couple. She didn't appear to harbor even the slightest prejudice against the Indian maiden. She turned that lovely smile on him, and his heart grew suddenly warm. "I can see how confusing that first verse could be."

"Aye." Standing to his feet, he reached over for the fidgeting Jenny Ann. "Even if I knew enough of her language, I sure wouldn't wanna try and translate that to the girl. She wouldn't have no problem with the idea of two gods, but"—raising the baby aloft a bit, he then brought her to his chest and nuzzled her neck till the cutie giggled—"Star's problem'll be with the Father an' the Son bein' just one God with one set of purposes. Wait'll she hears about how we're supposed to love everyone, even our enemies!"

He sat down on the log beside Rose and set Jenny Ann on his foot to give her a horsey ride. The little one laughed even harder. "Star is used to war gods an' Mother Earth an' spirits in lots of different forms, like the raven, for one. It has the spirit of a trickster. An' the spirit of the bear? Now, that's big power. Tobacco smoke, that can be real special. The Indian holy men use it to call in the spirits whenever they feel the need. Come to think of it, they're a very spiritual people—in their own way."

The two of them glanced over at Bob and Star, who were still occupied with their discussion. Rose tweaked Jenny under her chin and gave her a motherly smile then looked up at Nate. "Robert has been praying that the Lord will give her understanding. And I know He will. The choice of whether to believe and, more important, to become a disciple, a follower of the Lord, is hers alone."

Nate knew inside that the *disciple* part was actually directed at him. But he knew something else, as well. If Rose wanted him to be one of those Christians who shunned anyone who came from another country or had darker skin, she was barking up the wrong tree. As far as he was concerned, his God didn't mind folks having a little fun now and then either. He opened his mouth to tell her just that, when two musket shots in rapid succession came from across the river. He sprang to his feet.

Rose stepped beside him. "What is it?"

He shrugged. "Folks wantin' some canoes sent over for 'em, I reckon."

"Most likely them fur company men," Bob added as he joined them. He and Nate peered toward the opposite riverbank, where a party of men stood waving their arms.

"Aye. Looks like." Propping their little fluffy-haired cherub in his one arm, Nate slipped his other one around Rose's waist and drew her close. "Just one happy family, right?" He glanced down at those blue-gray eyes of hers. "Time to start lyin'."

The scared-rabbit look on her face was priceless.

Chapter 27

Rose had been in Nate's arms before, when he'd helped her down from horses or carried her to and from rafts, but this was nothing like those occasions. She knew he was in high humor watching the Shawnee paddle three long canoes across the river to fetch the officials from the fur company. She could see the mischievous gleam in his eyes and sensed his tightly contained mirth just begging for release. She also detected a certain possessive quality about the way he tucked her close. Of course, they were *supposed* to look like a married couple—after all, it was her idea. But why did her silly heart go all fluttery as if it was real? And to think this farce was right after their church service, for pity's sake. He must think her a hypocrite.

She inhaled a shaky breath and eased from his grasp, opting for the coward's way out. "I'll go kill and pluck a couple of young chickens. No doubt those men would appreciate a hearty Sunday dinner."

"I'll kill 'em for you." Nate offered the baby to her, but she quickly stepped back.

"No. Keep Jenny with you. She looks perfectly happy, and I've become quite capable of doing a number of things since you were here last. You and Robert go down and greet our guests. 'Tis only right." She arched her brows and smiled, hoping he'd agree.

He did.

On her way to the chicken pen, however, her conscience wouldn't let her alone. Here she was, a stalwart Christian—so she'd thought— planning to deceive the fur company men. And much worse, enlisting the aid of the very person she was judging for his unchristianlike proposal! She truly was a hypocrite.

A familiar Bible verse floated across her mind. *"Judge not, that ye be not judged."* Rose wished she'd never heard it.

But Lord. . . She unlatched the gate and stepped into the small penned area. *Surely You can see I'm trying to set to rights the suffering I caused my family last spring when I acted rashly and took matters out of Papa's hands. Had I waited on You, Father, You certainly would have made another way for us. Just as You've made this way for me right now.* She gave a righteous nod. *Absolutely. I am doing the right thing. This small deception is for the greater good.* And it's not as if she and Nate couldn't be married. It was a harmless lie, really.

Having packed that irritating conscience away once again in its tidy little box, Rose started after a young red rooster.

The usual crowd of inquisitive Shawnee lined the bank above the river, awaiting the arrival of the men being paddled across from the other side with piles of goods. Weaving through the bystanders with Bob a mere step behind, Nate realized he hadn't informed his friend of his decision to help Rose out with the scheme she'd proposed. He shifted Jenny to his other arm and stopped, turning to face Bob. "I. . .uh. . .need you to go along with whatever I tell those company men."

He frowned. "What're you talkin' about?"

Hoping to come up with the right words, Nate motioned with his head for Bob to follow as he made his way to the edge of the people and their steady chatter. "It's like she told us. She's determined to stay an' work at the tradin' post till she can save up enough money to send her sisters back to England. She's mighty sure of herself now that she can hear the jingle of some money. A far cry from when she first started out here. But you an' I both know no company officials are gonna let a lone woman run a store, no matter how good she's been doin' it." He put a finger up for Jenny Ann to tug on while he worked up nerve enough to admit his willing duplicity. "So we decided to, well. . .pretend to be husband an' wife."

Bob snorted. "An' that's your way of wormin' your way into her good graces?"

"Nay. I'm tellin' you the whole thing was her idea."

Bob tipped his head in thought. "It don't sound a bit like her."

"I know." Nate grinned. *That's the beauty of it!* "But I have to help her out."

Bob studied him for a moment. "Well, for the time bein' I think I'll let your conscience *and hers* be your judge."

That wasn't exactly what Nate hoped to hear. "Does that mean you won't say nothin'?"

"I won't say nothin'. But don't expect me to be a party to this little plot."

"Whatever you say. Not sayin' nothin's all I ask." Breathing a sigh of relief, he changed the subject and edged closer with Jenny in his arms. "Ever see a cuter little gal?"

⁓

The Shawnee paddlers delivered five men in the first ice-crusted canoe—three officials from the fur company, attired like easterners, and two frontier guides. When the craft beached in the icy slush lining the edge of the water, the first newcomer gave dubious consideration to the short span he'd need to leap over to make it to the bank. Then, obviously certain his boots were tall enough to ford the shallows, he hopped out.

The next two, however, didn't fare so well. Nate couldn't squelch a snicker when the pair splashed water halfway up their backsides. They yelped and let out a few choice words as they dashed onto the shore.

Their guides weren't far behind. Instead of climbing up the rise, however, those men waited for the remaining canoes to come in.

The Shawnee didn't appear particularly interested in the white men. They focused on the two other canoes loaded with goods for the store.

Careful to maintain his own footing for the baby's sake, Nate gingerly stepped down the slick grassy bank with Bob to greet the visitors. "Welcome. You must be the fur company men we been expectin.'"

The first man peered over his long nose as he brushed slush from the bottom of his trousers. "Hawkes is the name. And who might you be, young man?" A suspicious note rang in his tone, and his expression registered surprise upon catching sight of the white baby.

"Kinyon. Nate Kinyon," he answered quickly. "We been lookin' after the place here since—"

"Where's Eustice Smith?" the official interrupted. "Our business is with him." He repositioned his fur hat atop his salt-and-pepper hair.

His two companions—the much younger one, short and stout, with a pasty complexion; the other tall and thin as a beanpole, with sleeves and trousers barely long enough to cover his limbs—joined him. Neither exuded the slightest hint of pleasantry in his posture or manner, but looked Nate up and down as if taking his measure and finding him in dire want.

Bob edged forward. "Sorry to have to say this, but Trader Smith passed away a few weeks back, may the good Lord rest his soul."

"So me and the missus has been keepin' the place goin' ever since," Nate cut in.

"You and the missus?" A sneer curled the edge of his thin lips as Mr. Hawkes exchanged a skeptical glance with his cohorts.

The little round fellow began to shiver. Remembering the young man's rather wet disembarking, Nate nodded to the threesome. "We got a nice fire goin' in the tradin' post. An' the wife keeps a pot of hot tea brewin.' Come up and dry off by the fire whilst we talk."

Once he and Bob had the damp newcomers wrapped in blankets and fur robes, each holding a steaming cup before the crackling fire, Nate related the story, keeping it simple. "So me and Bob went off to do some tradin' for Mr. Smith. My wife stayed behind to cook for him. Her and our baby, that is."

Rail-thin Mr. Parker tucked his chin. "I cannot believe you'd bring a white woman and an infant out here among these savages."

Nate flashed his most disarming grin. "My Rose, she has a real tender heart. Once she heard tell that Eustice was havin' so much trouble with his innards, she come along to cook him up some soups and puddin's to help him get back on his feet. But nothin' she did made him any better off. Poor ol' feller passed on whilst me an' Bob was downriver tradin'." Nate congratulated himself for not having uttered a single lie in that statement.

Hawkes had yet to crack a smile. "I haven't seen Smith's wife or brothers about. Where are they?"

"Them no-accounts?" Nate scoffed. "They hightailed it outta here. Snuck off in the night with a bunch of the best furs, all Smith's cash money, an' six of the horses—an' one of 'em was mine. Bob an' me brung in a load of real prime pelts from downriver, though. That sort'a makes up for their theivin'. Sort'a."

The explanation still did not satisfy the man. He looked askance at Nate. "What about that wife of yours? Where is she, if I might ask?"

Nate gave a proud smile and puffed out his chest. "Soon as she saw you comin', her and Bob's woman went out back to kill some chickens for dinner. She knowed you was travelin' in this cold weather an' wanted you to have a fine meal." Sneaking a quick look at his friend, Nate noticed Bob still wore a grim expression. No reason to make him suffer through any more of this. He glanced at the visitors. "Did you men leave your pack train across the river unattended?"

As Hawkes deepened his stare, stout young Mr. Jenkins spoke up. "We left three of our men with the horses."

"Well, I'm sure them boys'd feel a whole lot better if we sent over a couple braves to help guard 'em. Bob, why don't you ask Cornstalk an' Fast Walker to paddle over there an' spend the night?" He turned back to

Mr. Hawkes. "You fellas are stayin' the night, ain't you?"

Still steely-eyed, he nodded. "Yes. In fact, we are."

Shortly after Bob took his leave, the frontier guides and several braves arrived with supplies from the canoes.

"Put the goods anyplace in here," Nate said. "We'll sort through 'em later."

"*If* we decide to leave them here," the obstinate one said flatly.

Time for another change of topic, Nate decided. "Like I said, me an' Bob just come back from downriver. Things ain't lookin' good down thataway. A large party of Frenchies—plus some Indians from up north, Senecas maybe—was down on the lower Scioto where it merges with the Ohio. They caught wind of me an' Bob tradin' with the Miamis, an' we had us a bear of a time getting' shuck of 'em. Had to hole up for a couple weeks before they paddled down toward the Mississippi."

This news tidbit piqued interest from all three. "The Scioto, how far down is that?" Mr. Parker asked.

"Depends on which way you're goin'." Nate grinned. "Canoein' downstream, it takes near a week if you stay on the river most of the day. Upstream it takes more'n twice that long."

Stocky Mr. Jenkins wrapped his hands around his cup. "You say they went downstream."

"That's right."

"Yes," Hawkes added, "but you don't know how far downriver they went, do you?"

Nate wagged his head. "No, I sure don't, sir. And I'd appreciate it if you wouldn't be mentionin' it to my Rose. No need for her to be worryin' 'less there's real reason to. Me an' Bob had a palaver with the Shawnee chiefs here, an' none of 'em heard tell of Frenchies snoopin' around these parts."

"Well," he commented, "they're doing more than merely snooping around north of here. They seized Joe Frazier's trading post up on the Allegheny. At a Seneca village, by the by."

"You don't say." Nate straightened his spine at the disturbing news.

The Allegheny River flowed into the Ohio. "What about Frazier? What'd they do to him?"

"He didn't happen to be there at the time, but two of his men were captured."

"Aye," Parker added. "It's in territory claimed by Pennsylvania, but the only governor that seems to understand the seriousness of the situation is Governor Dinwiddie of Virginia. Mr. Hawkes"—he indicated the man with the long nose—"went to see him about it, and the governor immediately sent a letter to King George. Dinwiddie is sure His Majesty will grant him permission to act."

Nate's fingers clenched into fists. "You mean to tell me that governor's just sittin' there twiddlin' his thumbs till the king sends word all the way back across the ocean?"

"My sentiments exactly," Mr. Hawkes said with a negative shake of his bony head.

"When did the letter get sent?"

"In October." Hawkes let out a disgusted breath.

Nate snorted in disbelief. "So the answer's still weeks away. No wonder the French are bein' so bold." Peering out the canvas opening, he spied Rose and Shining Star coming from the direction of the chicken pen. A headless bird dangled from each of Rose's hands. Standing up, he met Mr. Hawkes's gaze. "Like I said, don't say nothin' about this to the womenfolk."

Chapter 28

Surely there'd been time enough for Nate to speak to the company men about her and him staying on as traders, Rose thought on her way back to the store. She put the dead chickens in a tub alongside the structure and hurried to the campfire for a kettle of heating water.

She knew three officials had arrived and were now in the trading post, but now two others, most likely their guides, warmed themselves outside at the fire. She'd forgotten there were more men. "Good day," she said pleasantly.

The pair in typically soiled frontier garb stared openmouthed at her. "Good day to ye," one managed.

"There's tea inside the trading post, if you'd like to have some."

"Nay, miss," one with a frizzy red beard said. "We'd just as soon do our restin' outta the way, if ye know what I mean."

"Aye." His ragamuffin partner chuckled.

"As you wish." She bunched a handful of her apron in one hand and grasped the water kettle suspended over the fire. "We'll be having our Sabbath meal in an hour or so."

"Sabbath meal," one murmured. "Ain't had one o' them in a coon's age."

Starting away with the hot water, Rose turned back with a smile. "Well, I'm pleased to say that today you shall have one."

She returned to the tub, where Shining Star stood staring at the lifeless carcasses. No doubt the Indian girl was curious about the English way of doing things. But Star wasn't the only one engrossed. The men at the fire circle also stared—at Rose. As if she wasn't already nervous enough about the businessmen inside.

She pretended not to notice their ogling as she poured the entire kettle of steaming water over the chickens to loosen the quills. Then she wiped her hands on her stained apron, removed it, and checked her hair. Taking the girl's hand, she headed toward the trading post and entered with Star in tow.

"Good Sabbath, gentlemen." She hoped her smile appeared cheerful.

The fur company officials sprang to their feet, along with Nate, who held Jenny in his arms.

"Good day to you, madam." A man with a long face and a nose to match gave her a slight bow of his head. His gaze made a swift assessment of her appearance but revealed nothing. "I presume you are Mistress Kinyon. Allow me to introduce myself and my companions. I am Mr. Hawkes. To my right is Mr. Jenkins, then Mr. Parker."

Each nodded his head in turn.

She bobbed a curtsy, surprised that Star followed her lead. "I'm pleased to meet all of you. This is Shining Star, our friend Robert Bloom's young charge. I hope you've had some tea. The days have been terribly cold of late."

"Yes," the stocky fellow named Jenkins agreed. "Your husband has already seen to our comfort."

"I was certain he would." Rose gave Nate an adoring glance. "He's always been quite the thoughtful type." She smiled at her frontiersman. "We'll have our Sabbath meal soon."

"Why, I've hardly had a decent meal since we left Virginia," the taller man named Parker mused.

"Nor have I," Mr. Jenkins commented wistfully. "My wife's a wonderful cook."

"Well, today you'll all share our Sabbath meal with us." Travelers—even well-dressed ones—were a sad reminder that men without the comforts of home were quite pitiful creatures. She flicked another glance at Nate, who obviously appreciated her performance. His grin softened his rugged features, adding a spark to his hazel eyes.

Rose returned his grin with flair as she hooked the kettle above the coals again. "Do be seated, gentlemen. And since it will be awhile until our meal is ready, I'm sure my husband will be only too happy to refill your cups, won't you, dear?"

"Of course. Only too happy," he mimicked sweetly.

Ignoring the incorrigible man, Rose could hardly restrain herself from asking the all-important question. Would they accept her as a trader for them or not? Regardless, if Nate had not as yet broached the subject, perhaps the officials would be in a better mood once their stomachs were full. "If you will excuse us, gentlemen, Shining Star and I need to return to our meal preparations. We want this dinner to be especially festive in your honor."

Mr. Hawkes remained standing. "Mistress Kinyon. Am I to assume you are the Miss Harwood for whom I've received letters?"

Rose's pulse throbbed. "Why, yes. Harwood was my maiden name. Have you mail for me? Perhaps a letter from my family in England?" The possibility of hearing from her father made her heart pound.

"No, madam. England, you say. I was quite certain I detected a refined accent in your speech. And you're wed to this. . .woodsman?" He frowned in puzzlement.

How to respond without adding to her guilt. She swallowed the growing lump in her throat. "Cupid's arrow takes the strangest paths, does it not?" Without daring to glance at Nate, she added a little laugh. "If you'll excuse us, we must get to preparing the chickens."

As Nate watched the two women sashay out to the deceased chickens, he had to admit he was quite impressed with his little actress-wife. Rose hadn't spoken a single lying word. Of course, the deception was still there. Smiling, he turned back to the men. "If you're all finished with your drinks, I'll show you the fine pelts we brought in."

Hawkes elevated a haughty brow. "Yes. And the ledger." Without further adieu, he set down his empty cup and stood to his feet. The others got up as well.

Jenny Ann had nodded off, so Nate laid her down in her little pen and covered her. Then he led the three officials to one side of the store, stopping near the pile of prime pelts. "I think you'll like what you see here. Once Eustice caught on to Rose's writin' skill, he had her keep the records."

Hawkes did not reply as his gaze briefly skimmed the bundle. He ran his fingers across Rose's neat display of trenchers filled with different-colored beads. "So where's that ledger?"

Nate plucked the volume off a stack of crates and handed it to the arrogant man. "You'll see everything's in order. After Smith's wife took off, Rose made a full inventory to see what all was missin'—not includin' my horse, that is. A good, sure-footed chestnut gelding. He has two notches in his right ear. If you run across him in your tradin', I'd sure appreciate you buyin' him for me. I'll even give you a profit."

"Yes, yes." The man did not bother to look up from the ledger pages while his cohorts inspected the piles of pelts. After a couple of minutes he raised his head. "Come over here, Jenkins. I say, it's a delight to see everything recorded so neatly and with proper spelling."

Both lackeys hurried to his side and peered over his shoulder at the columns of figures. "Quite right." They nodded in agreement.

"An' if you look around," Nate added, "you'll notice my Rose has a real eye for makin' things look nice. The customers are always sayin' how they like the way she keeps the place. When Eustice died an' them Susquehannocks took off, Chief Red Hawk sent some of his best braves over to protect her an' the store till me an' Bob got back. Everybody here's real pleased with her." He moved a touch closer and lowered his voice. "So we was wonderin' if we could take over for Eustice on a permanent basis. What d'you say?"

Plucking feathers at the tub, Rose craned her ears toward the canvas opening, trying desperately to hear what was transpiring inside the store. She'd sensed from Nate's tight expression that he had yet to speak to suspicious Mr. Hawkes about becoming the new proprietors of the trading post. But alas, the men's conversation was too indistinct for her to make out the words.

Even when Nate's voice ceased and the official began speaking, it was still too quiet to be heard. Waiting, hoping, Rose wished she was inside so she could see their expressions and hear what was being said about her, about the store, about the future.

Abruptly, Nate let out a burst of enthusiasm. "Thank you. You won't be sorry. You'll see." Her heart leaped with joy.

"Now let's have a look at those pelts you've been bragging about," Hawkes said distinctly.

Rose tried to contain the stubborn smile spreading from ear to ear. Leaving Shining Star scraping carrots and squash for the meal, she wiped her hands and approached the entrance, lifted the flap, and stepped inside. "I hope you found everything to be in order, Mr. Hawkes."

He turned to her with his first genuine smile. "Why, yes, Mistress Kinyon. I can certainly see the woman's touch here. It was not what I expected, to be sure. But perhaps I should induce more couples to man our trading posts." He shifted his attention to Nate and gave him a peculiar look.

Wondering if it was a doubtful one after all, Rose let out a breath. "I just came to fetch this kettle." She started toward the hearth. "'Tis delightful having all this company. And with this unexpected gift of a mild, sunny day, 'twould be wonderful to set up a long table outside so we can all share the meal together. Could you fix one up for us, sweetheart?"

Nate glanced around. "I reckon we could make a table out of some crates. Anything for you, honey-pie."

"And a bolt of color covering it would look rather festive, don't you think?"

As the men all came to their feet with ready grins, Rose had a comical thought. If only her ever-so-proper family could see her holding court for an assortment of well-dressed businessmen and their unkempt guides at a splintery crate table! A table covered with—she glanced across the bolts of material—turquoise cotton. Yes. Turquoise to go with today's brilliant sky.

By the time all was ready to serve at the crude dinner table which occupied a spot between the trading post and the outside cook fire, Rose caught a flash of deerskin from the corner of her eye. She saw Shining Star running down the hill to meet Robert Bloom, returning from escorting a pair of braves across the river to help guard the horses of the company men.

Thank You, Father, that he's back in time to join us. Since it was the Sabbath, it would be only proper to ask Bob to give a reading from the Bible. Travelers likely heard the scriptures read about as often as they partook of a proper Sunday dinner.

Stripping off her apron, she went to summon the men to the table. It amazed her to find them still gabbing in the trading post. Wasn't it women who were supposed to be the talkers?

"No," Mr. Hawkes was saying as she walked in. "Venango is—Oh, here comes our lovely hostess." He offered her a polite smile.

Rose couldn't help noticing the sudden halt to their conversation caused by her arrival and smirked. Most likely they'd been swapping naughty stories, as men at the taverns in Bath so often did. Strange, though, she heard none of the usual laughter in this case. "Gentlemen, I've come to announce our Sabbath meal is ready."

As the assembly got up from the sacks and crates on which they'd been sitting, she noticed that all of them had removed their hats and every last one had combed his hair and tied it neatly in a queue. How touching of them to put forth an effort to look presentable.

Outside, Rose hurried to greet Robert, who walked hand in hand with Shining Star, chatting with her.

"I seen that dinner table on my way across the water," he said with a grin. "Couldn't miss the tablecloth. Even the people in the village are gawkin."

Rose glanced toward the settlement, noting a number of Indians seated around a fire outside the council house, staring their way. "'Twould seem I've given them something new to talk about, have I not?" Smiling, she turned back to him and Star. "I'd appreciate it very much if you would read a selection of scripture before I ask Nate to give the blessing."

A grin broadened Bob's face. "You're askin' Nate to pray? In front of all them men?"

Rose couldn't stop her own smile from growing. "It seems only proper, since he's the head of the house, so to speak. You sit at one end of the table, and I'll be sure he takes the other."

"What about those company men?"

"Why, Mr. Hawkes will sit at Nate's right hand, of course, and Mr. Parker will sit at your right. They're the two older ones. Mr. Jenkins shouldn't mind."

A laugh rumbled from deep inside Robert, and Star looked up at him with a puzzled expression. Sobering, he spoke a few words to her in her language, and they started walking again. "Everybody's standin' 'round the table, Rose. You'd best get up there to that fancy little tea party of yours."

Chapter 29

B e careful for nothing,'" Bob read, "'but in every thing by prayer and supplication with thanksgiving let your requests be made known unto God.'"

Seated on a keg at the opposite end of the makeshift table, Nate's mind drifted from the scripture reading and floated to Rose, on his left, while Jenny, dozing on a pallet on the ground beside her, nuzzled with a handmade rag doll. Rose had accomplished so much in two hours. Not only had she put together a fine meal, but she'd found time to don a daygown he'd never seen before. The cornflower-blue material seemed to light up her azure eyes, and the faint scent of rose water she had used on her long, honey-colored hair danced across his nostrils on the light breeze. A few loose silky strands glistened in the firelight, free from the blue ribbon that tied the remainder at the nape of her neck.

The heady aroma of chicken and dumplings overtook her sweet scent and made his mouth water. He couldn't wait to taste them and the beans, carrots, squash, and biscuits lining the table, along with a metal pitcher of fresh milk and a container of butter.

Everything looked appealing on the sea of turquoise fabric, despite the mismatched trenchers, tin plates, and utensils that had been gathered for use. His English Rose had come a long way from the frightened young woman he'd first met. And glancing around the table, he realized his was not the only admiring glance she drew. When the men weren't staring wide eyed at the array of food, they were enthralled with Rose. His *wife*. To make certain everyone understood he had prior claim to the British beauty, he reached over and took one of her hands where it lay on the table.

Her gaze flew to his then quickly calmed. A soft smile lit her eyes, and she lowered her lashes.

Nate leaned close and whispered in her ear, "Everything's nice. Real nice."

Thank you, she mouthed then returned her attention to Bob.

Keeping hold of her hand for good measure, Nate made a real effort to shift his attention to his friend for the remainder of the reading.

" 'Finally, brethren, whatsoever things are true, whatsoever things are honest, whatsoever things are just, whatsoever things are pure, whatsoever things are lovely, whatsoever things are of good report; if there be any virtue, and if there be any praise, think on these things.' "

Nate wondered if Bob had deliberately chosen that scripture to chastise Rose or him. Most likely both. How much longer was the chapter, anyway?

" 'Those things, which ye have both learned, and received, and heard, and seen in me, do: and the God of peace shall be with you.' " Closing the Bible, Bob looked up with a satisfied smile. "May God bless the reading of His Word." His gaze moved to Nate. "And now our host will bless the food."

Caught completely off guard, Nate barely managed to keep his mouth from falling open.

Rose squeezed his hand, and an impish spark in her eyes went right along with her pleased smile.

Well, he played his games and she played hers. He could do this. Drawing a calming breath, he stood and bowed his head. "Our Father, which art in heaven, bless this food an' the lovely hands that prepared it, in Jesus' name, Amen."

A rather contrite "Amen" echoed around the table as he regained his seat and the men reached eagerly for bowls of food. Once everyone had filled their plates and commenced eating, compliments rained on Rose.

"I can't tell you," a guide named Davis gushed for about the dozenth time, "how good these here dumplin's be. I ain't had none like these in two, three years."

A slight pink tinge heightened Rose's coloring as she smiled. "I do thank you. When we've finished, I've a surprise for you all."

All eyes swung to her as the visitors continued to stuff themselves.

"There are trees in this area that bear a lovely red-orange fruit the Shawnees like to cook. Nate told me they're called persimmons. I've added some persimmon, along with nuts and spices, to a pudding I hope you'll find quite tasty."

One of the longhunters slid a sidelong glance toward Nate. "If'n you ever take a notion to get shed o' that useless man o' yourn, I'd be mighty pleased to take you to wife."

"And I'd be mighty pleased to crack that head of yours wide open," Nate grumbled. He started to get up.

Rose caught his arm. "Darling, he's merely jesting."

Uncoiling, Nate sank back onto the keg. He felt a little foolish, but her calling him "darling" did much to ease his ire. Too bad it was all for show.

Mr. Hawkes, on his other side, chuckled. "Being the husband of the only white woman in the whole of the Ohio Valley must be quite a challenge."

Turning to the man, Nate propped up a smile. "You might say that, especially since you brought this wolf pack here with you."

"And especially since you're wed to an exceptionally lovely lady." Hawkes gave Rose a gracious nod.

"Thank you, kind sir." She graced him with a smile then looked down the table toward Bob.

Nate caught her worried glance but breathed with relief when he saw his partner totally absorbed in quiet conversation with Shining Star.

Mr. Hawkes shifted his gaze toward the village. "I've noticed an unusual amount of attention coming from the Indians, as well."

Since most of the villagers were taking advantage of the unseasonably mild temperature, reminiscent of an Indian summer day, a good number of them did happen to be looking toward their festive gathering. "We never took our Sabbath meal at table before. Most of 'em have prob'ly never seen such a sight, us eatin' out here like this."

Rose touched his arm. "Sweetheart, we should invite the chiefs and their families to a Sabbath meal soon."

Hawkes returned his attention to her. "Ah. So your true goal, Mistress Kinyon, is to civilize the savages, then."

She shrugged a shoulder. "The Good Book says we're to love our neighbors, and they are my neighbors."

"We can only hope and pray it will always be that way." The official relaxed on his seat. Nate sensed a covert meaning hidden within those benign-sounding words and wasn't surprised when Hawkes turned to him. "I'm rather surprised that none of those *neighbors* dropped by the trading post as yet to look over the new goods we brought."

Nate cocked his head back and forth. "They'll hightail it up here once you leave."

"Mebbe the redskins don't like the way we smell." The red-bearded longhunter whacked his thigh in mirth then sobered. "Beggin' your pardon, ma'am."

Hawkes cut a glance to his partners then back at Nate. "I'll settle up with you, so we can load up the bundles of furs and be out of here at first light. And if I don't see you then, I want to thank you again for manning the trading post so efficiently since Mr. Smith's untimely death, and for locating so many prime pelts for the company on your trip downstream."

Rose came to her feet, and every man present started scrambling to his. "Please, gentlemen, remain seated. I'm merely going to fetch the spiced persimmon pudding."

"Spiced persimmon pudding," young Mr. Jenkins echoed on a wistful breath. "Sounds like music to my ears."

Kinda like her voice sounds to mine. Nate followed Rose's movements as she walked away. He liked the way she moved. In fact, he liked a whole lot of things about Rose Harwood. She seemed to grow on him more with each passing hour.

If only she'd change her mind about *him.*

As the sky darkened and bright stars spangled the clear, cool expanse overhead, Rose took the baby inside her wigwam to settle her down for the night. Nate was relieved and gladdened as he sat bundled in a fur robe around the outside fire with the three company men and Bob, and Bob's Indian maiden, of course. She was never far from him. The last of the counting in the trading post was done, of stock coming in and furs going out. And Nate had a cup of hot tea in his hand and plenty of coin jingling in his pouch. Rose would be real pleased.

Music from a reed flute drifted from the Shawnee village, with drums throbbing a beat.

"What does that mean?" Alarm rang in Mr. Parker's voice.

"Just makin' music." Bob's gaze gravitated to Shining Star. "Prob'ly just some young bucks tryin' to impress a shy maiden."

Nate chuckled. "Or they're lettin' us know we're not the only ones who can have a party."

Mr. Jenkins nodded. "They did seem quite interested in our dinner. They must have been curious about what we were all saying."

Leaning forward, Mr. Hawkes's expression looked deadly serious in the firelight. "There's something I forgot to mention earlier. The reason Joe Frazier wasn't at his trading post was because he was out looking for his villagers. They'd all disappeared during the night. They knew the French were coming and didn't want to get caught in the middle. Even though they prefer our goods, they're more than willing to trade with whoever sets up a post, English or French."

"That's good to know." Nate rubbed his chin in thought, wondering if these Shawnee villagers would prove to be as disloyal.

Shining Star seemed to detect the seriousness of the moment. Her slender brows knitted with concern, she quietly spoke to Bob. His answer seemed to satisfy her, and she relaxed against him again.

From the corner of his eye, Nate caught a flash of movement. "Here comes Rose," he said in a low voice, then raised the volume. "Has the Potomac started freezin' yet? The stream behind the corrals was frozen half the mornin' yesterday."

"No, not yet." Mr. Hawkes rose to his feet. "Mistress Kinyon, do join us."

"Why thank you." She came into the light, her heavy woolen cloak snug around her.

Nate flashed her a grin. "I take it you got our little Jenny-girl all settled down for the night, my love."

The smile she offered did look genuine as she plucked a cup off a nearby rock and poured some tea from the kettle. "Hopefully, yes."

Pulling back the robe covering his legs, he patted the spot next to him on the sitting log. "Come sit with me, sweetheart." He sure did like playing the part of her husband. Maybe soon. . .

As Rose complied, Nate draped an arm about her shoulders, surprised when she actually leaned into him—even if it was only ever so slightly.

She took a sip of her tea. "I've a fire going in all the wigwams to warm them up. And I've placed blankets and fur robes in the large one over there." She pointed to the one the Susquehannock brothers had used. "Of course, you may want to add your own bedding. It seems to be turning quite chilly."

"Thank you," Mr. Hawkes said with a polite bow of his head. "You've been a far more gracious hostess than we could ever have imagined."

"Well, I do hope your workmen won't mind staying in the trading post."

"That's better accommodations than they've had on the trail thus far."

Young Mr. Jenkins leaned forward. "Where exactly did you come from in England, Mistress Kinyon? I hope to go to Britain for a visit one day soon."

Rose smiled at him. "Were you to make port at Bristol, you'd not be far from my city, Bath."

"I've heard of that place. Isn't that where all the rich people go on holiday?"

"Why, yes, it is." She settled more comfortably at Nate's side. "They come to soak in the hot mineral springs and to take in the plays and balls, of course. But I prefer to think that more importantly, they come to see and be seen. I'm sure you'd enjoy a visit there most thoroughly."

Watching Mr. Hawkes, Nate perceived the man's suspicious nature coming again to the fore as he stared at Rose as if she were telling lies. He had the greatest urge to blacken that company man's judging eyes.

"And you left all that for *this*?" Hawkes made a wide arc with his arm.

She stiffened a bit. "I'm afraid you misunderstood me, sir. Bath was my home, not a place I visited. My father owns a small shop there."

Jenkins brightened. "Perhaps you could persuade your father to carry some of our furs."

"That sounds quite lovely, but for the shops in Bath they'd need to be fashioned into elegant wraps and other accessories."

Thin Mr. Parker finally entered the conversation. "No wonder Mistress Kinyon is well accomplished in the art of display, being the daughter of a shopkeeper."

Nate felt Rose relax again as a small laugh bubbled out of her. "Actually, I learned far more from visiting other shops, if you must know."

The statement puzzled Nate. He'd never thought of her as a spendthrift.

Jenkins looked from her to Nate and back to her. "From what I've heard, the English have the finest shops in the world, with treasures brought in from all the most exotic places around the globe. Coming to the colonies, and then out here to the wilderness, must have been quite a dramatic change for you."

Still smiling, she tilted her head. "More so for my sister. More often than not, I was accompanying her in her quest for the latest fabrics and trims."

"I see."

Mr. Hawkes frowned. "Your sister came to America with you?"

Even Nate felt Rose's sharp intake of breath, as if their nosy employer was beginning to wear on her the way he was on Nate.

"Quite right. She currently resides with a plantation family adjacent to the Potomac River."

"You don't say." His interest obviously piqued, Hawkes straightened. "Perhaps I know them."

"Are you acquainted with the Barclay family?"

"The Barclays! Of Barclay Enterprises?" He shook his head in disbelief. "Why in the world would a lady like yourself allow Kinyon to drag you this deep into Indian country?"

At this, Nate reached the boiling point. Employer or not, the bounder needed his face smashed in. Pulling his arm from behind Rose, he—

Her elbow jabbed sharply into his rib, effectively stopping him. Then she casually stood to her feet. "I prefer to think of my sojourn here as a wondrous adventure. It's been a rather long day, however, so if I don't see you before you leave in the morning, it's been a true treat having you visit us, even for such a short time."

All the men got up, and Nate put his arm around her again. "Aye. It's been a big day. Good evenin', gents."

Leaving the others behind, Nate escorted Rose to her wigwam. Reaching it, he pulled back the flap for her then entered behind her. He dropped the covering closed with a smile.

She swung to face him, hands on her hips, eyes flashing in the light of the fire. Her harsh whisper broke the silence. "What do you think you're doing?"

"Your *husband* is coming to bed," he countered in a blithe whisper of his own, definitely not wanting to wake Jenny.

She flung a look of panic in the direction of the others then turned back to him, her jaw set.

Just then the flap opened, and Shining Star slipped in.

Ruining the moment.

Nate had forgotten the girl stayed with Rose. Worse yet, Bob had probably sent her running in here. Black Horse Bob, the guardian of everyone's virtue.

His gaze returned to Rose. Her expression of panic was now one of renewed confidence as she tipped her head.

"You're absolutely right. We must not make our employers suspicious, must we?" A smile spread across her face. "You may sleep across the fire on Shining Star's pallet, Nate, and she"—Rose rested a hand on the girl's shoulder—"can sleep over here, with Jenny Ann and me."

Chapter 30

Rose felt something tickling her nose. *Nate?* Her eyes sprang open and met Jenny's sweet smile. Capturing the baby's little fingers, Rose kissed them. Was anyone else awake? She raised her head to peek over Star's sleeping form and saw Nate also asleep on the opposite side of the fire pit. It must be very early, or only a little past dawn on a gray morning. Her eyes roved over the fur-shrouded frontiersman as he lay there, and a smile tugged at her lips. After all his tossing and turning last night, he needed the extra sleep.

Still in her clothes from yesterday, she bundled Jenny, eased up off the sleeping pallet, and slipped outside with her.

Mr. Hawkes and his two companions sat with their backs to her around a roaring fire. They'd truly be off to an early start, Rose mused, heading for the woods.

After seeing to her morning needs, she plucked the covered milk pail from the thin film of ice surrounding it in the stream and started back. Jenny Ann would be patient for only so long.

She could see the workers loading bundles of pelts down at the river as she came up behind her three employers. "Good morning, gentlemen."

The threesome turned to her, all smiles, and spoke as one. "Good morning, Mistress Kinyon."

"I trust you slept well."

Mr. Hawkes nodded. "It was a pleasure not to have to erect tents. The fire kept us quite comfortable."

She smiled and set down the pail. As she reached into a sack and removed a small pan, he got up and came forward. "Let me hold your little one for you. She reminds me of my grandbaby back home."

"Why, thank you." She handed Jenny to him then poured milk into the pan and set it on one of the rocks surrounding the fire pit. "I like to warm her milk on cold mornings." She glanced up at the official. "What's your grandbaby's name, Mr. Hawkes?"

"Arthur. Arthur Hawkes. My daughter-in-law insisted on naming him after me. We call him Arty. He was seven months old when I left on this trip. How old is your little girl?"

"She's—what's the date? I'm afraid I've lost count." Rose felt her cheeks warm.

The man chuckled. "That's easy to do out here, so far away from everything. Today's the third of December." He patted Jenny's back then turned to his companions. "You two go join the others. I need to speak to Mistress Kinyon alone. I'll be along directly."

A niggle of unease made Rose's heart skip a beat. Had he discovered the deception?

His expression gave no indication of censure. After the men had left, he met her gaze. "I must ask you, are you truly here of your own free will, mistress? You may speak frankly to me."

Relieved that he was merely concerned for her welfare, Rose gave a polite nod. "Yes, of course. Point of fact, 'twas entirely my idea. A way for us to earn a goodly amount of money in a relatively short time."

A frown furrowed the man's forehead. "But a decision of that magnitude requires considerably more experience than you possess."

Rose's pulse increased. Surely he was not reneging! Not after all her and Nate's efforts to convince him of their capabilities.

"You came out here with Eustice Smith this summer, did you not?"

She reached down for the pan so he wouldn't see her face. "Yes.

'Tis true." Had Mr. Smith informed the fur company about her, his bondservant?

"Then you weren't here during the time of the spring raids, when captives are brought in, were you?"

Remembering Jenny Ann's mother, Rose barely kept herself from shuddering as she poured milk into a tin cup. Amazing how she'd blocked the poor woman's dreadful fate from her mind already.

Hawkes stepped closer. "Torture is the Indians' favorite entertainment. They delight in keeping their victims screaming for days on end before the poor devils finally die. They derive some kind of perverse pleasure in causing people to suffer unspeakable horrors."

Her chest tightening, Rose reached for Jenny and took her from the official. "I'm sure you must be exaggerating. I've heard of the gauntlet captives must run through to be worthy of joining the tribe. 'Tis an initiation, I believe. The lads at university do no less."

Mr. Hawkes wagged his head and scoffed. "Listen to me, you silly woman. That's only for the ones the Indians intend to adopt into the tribe. Captured braves and other unfortunate individuals are another matter entirely. Some of them are taken with the prior intent to *be* tortured for the tribe's amusement."

Stunned, Rose sank down onto the log to feed the baby. What a fool she'd been to excuse so lightly the mind-set of the Indian.

"I can understand your wanting to be here to trade when the trappers bring in the winter furs. Granted. But know this—" He flicked a gaze beyond her.

Giving the baby a sip, Rose looked up to see Robert striding toward them.

Hawkes gave him a courteous nod. "It's just as well you're here to hear this. I'll be sending replacements out here no later than April 1. I will not be party to having Mistress Kinyon and her babe around when the spring raids start. Is that clear?"

Robert glanced at Rose then back at the official. "I wholeheartedly agree. We'll be packed an' ready. Don't much relish bein' here myself then."

Hawkes tipped his hat to Rose. "I shall look forward to seeing you at our headquarters this spring." He pivoted on his heel and started to leave.

"I bid you Godspeed, Mr. Hawkes," she called after him. "We shall pray for your safety."

He stopped and swung back, looking from her to Robert and back again. "You look after yourself, too."

Rose sensed from the queer looks passing between her friend and the official that something serious was being left unsaid. But what?

Allowing grabby little Jenny to hold her own cup, Rose could wait no longer. She looked up at Nate's partner. "Robert, 'tis quite obvious you and Mr. Hawkes went to great lengths to keep something from me. I must know what it is."

From his demeanor, she could tell she had him cornered.

"I'm not— Oh look. Here comes Nate."

Approaching the fire, Nate gave a huge grin, directing his gaze at Rose. "Mornin'." Then he tipped his head in the direction of the riverbank. "I see the men are ready to push off. I'd sure hate to be out on that icy river before the sun has a chance to warm things up." He gave the departing company men a jaunty wave, then grabbing a cup from the sack, he poured himself some tea and came to sit next to Rose and the baby.

She took a slow, calming breath. "It seems Robert and Mr. Hawkes are keeping a secret from me, Nate. One I'm sure you must be privy to." She arched a brow.

He shot his pal a serious glower. "You don't say."

Robert shrugged. "Hawkes says he's sendin' replacements out here by the first of April. Looks like all that fine playactin' of yours didn't make much difference. You're still gonna be tossed out."

"'Twas not like that." Rose let out a huff. "Not like that at all." She took the cup from Jenny and wiped the child's face and neck with her apron. "Mr. Hawkes doesn't want me here in the spring when the Shawnees start bringing in captives."

Nate kneaded his chin in thought. "Ah yes, the spring raids. I'd say the decision's for the best. You an' Jenny Ann need to be away from here then. Somewhere safe."

Recalling Hannah Wright and her needless death, Rose couldn't fault any of them for their reasoning. "I suppose you're right." She picked up the baby and kissed her plump cheek. "But I shall hate having to give up Jenny. I'm afraid I've become quite attached to the little angel."

Nate ruffled the towhead's silky curls, making her giggle. "She is a cutie, no doubt about that."

"And then of course," Rose continued, "there are my sisters. I shan't have nearly enough money by April. Nor will I have this sort of opportunity ever again."

"Greedy, greedy." With a teasing smirk, Nate got up.

The accusation irked Rose. She stood to face him straight on. "'Tis not for me, and you very well know it."

"Aye. I know." His expression sobered. "Tell you what. I'm willin' to give you whatever I earn in tradin' between now an' then to help. How's that?"

She opened her mouth to protest, but he turned to his partner. "What say we go take care of the stock while the gals fix breakfast?"

Robert slid a longing look over at Rose's wigwam.

Clapping him on the back, Nate snickered. "Don't worry, pal. Your little darlin'll be up an' about soon enough. I saw her sneakin' peeks at me while I was gettin' up."

He grunted then started after Nate for the animal pens. "Shining Star knows you had no business spendin' the night in there."

Rose couldn't let that pass. "'Twas all my fault," she called after them. They swiveled to face her. "What webs we do weave when we try to deceive. . .or something to that effect." Blushing, she hung her head.

But not before she caught Nate's grin. "No. Exactly like that!" He gave a hoot over his shoulder as he continued toward the stock. "Exactly like that."

A cluster of Shawnee on their way to the trading post passed Nate and Bob as the two of them hiked toward the center of the village. "They're over there, in front of Red Hawk's wigwam." Bob pointed with his decorated Indian pipe.

"Good. Cornstalk's there, too." Nate picked up the pace. "Might as well get this over with."

Obviously having spied them approaching, Red Hawk raised his hand and motioned for Nate and Bob to come join him. "Greetings," he said, the word heavily accented as they reached the campfire. "Sit."

Nate knew that was pretty much the extent of Red Hawk's English, but he appreciated the attempt, since his own knowledge of the Shawnee language was equally lacking. "Greetings." He smiled and nodded at Cornstalk and a couple of older Indians as he took a seat alongside Bob on a coarse buffalo hide.

Bob took a tobacco pouch from his pocket, pouring and tamping a portion into the bowl of his pipe. He plucked a stick from the fire and lit the pipe, drawing a couple of puffs to get it going. He then handed it with both hands to Red Hawk.

As the chief took his time smoking the pipe, Nate sensed the man was particularly enjoying tobacco that had been cured on the plantations back east.

While Red Hawk was occupied, Bob started a conversation in Shawnee with Cornstalk. After the brave's response, he turned to Nate. "He says the music last night was as I figgered. One of the young bucks was tryin' to make time with a maiden by impressin' her with his skill on the flute."

"Oh, the webs their sweet smiles weave for us to get caught in." Nate chuckled, remembering Rose's remark.

Bob laughed also, and Cornstalk interrupted with a question. When Bob translated for him, all the Indians present laughed and nodded at Nate.

Once the pipe had made the rounds and returned to Bob, Nate nudged him. "Mebbe it's a good time to mention that invite to dinner for the chiefs an' their families."

"They're gonna consider it pretty strange, you know."

"Aye." Nate shrugged. "But no more strange than all of us sharin' the same pipe is to me, a white man."

Bob turned his attention to the two chiefs. Nate recognized Rose's name a time or two in the conversation and watched the older men exchange disbelieving glances.

Finally Red Hawk's feathered headdress bobbed as he met Nate's gaze with a nod and laughed.

Bob grinned along with them. "They say they'd be pleased to accept."

"Yeah, but what's so all-fired funny?" Nate frowned, looking around at all the amused expressions.

"I'll explain later. First, I'd better ask if they know anythin' about the attack on the tradin' post at the Seneca village at Venango."

Unable to understand the proceedings, Nate could only watch expressions and draw his own conclusions. The Indians seemed surprised that the French had seized Frazier's trading post, but he couldn't tell if it was an act being put on for his and Bob's benefit.

Nate was pretty sure he knew what Bob was relating, and he watched especially close for the slightest flicker of an eye, any telltale fidgeting. Still, nothing sinister seemed apparent while Cornstalk and Red Hawk both took turns answering. But then, red men were noted for being stoic when they wanted to be.

After a few moments of lighter conversation, Bob hiked his chin at Nate. "I reckon we better get back an' help Rose. There's prob'ly a crowd at the store by now."

Once they'd said their good-byes and were far enough away, Nate turned to his pal. "Well? What'd they say? Are they willin' to stay loyal to us, knowin' the French are both downriver an' upriver from here?"

He shrugged. "They gave me the same ol' speech. Our trade goods are better, an' the Shawnees are stronger an' braver than any Seneca ever thought of bein'. An' Cornstalk said the French bleed just like the Seneca."

"That sounds fine an' good. But did they come right out an' say they'd stay loyal?"

Coming to an abrupt halt, Bob looked him square in the eye. "Come to think of it, they never actually said those words."

Nate gave him a thoughtful nod. "Winter's almost on us. Not even the French should be out makin' trouble this time of year." He paused. "By the way, why were the Indians laughin' at me when you asked the chiefs to dinner?"

"Oh that." A grin crawled across Bob's irksome face. "They said Rose was—what was that word? Oh yeah. She's got you *henpecked* real good."

Nate drilled him with his most menacing glare. "An' who, might I ask, gave 'em that idea?"

Instead of showing the least amount of remorse, Bob threw back his head and howled with laughter. His next words came out in a sputter. "You're even startin' to sound all uppity, just like her."

Chagrined, Nate gave a resigned nod. "You're right, ol' buddy. But if I'm henpecked, you're nothin' but a flop-eared hound, moonin' after your Shining Star. That's some lovesick name you labeled her with, by the way."

Bob gave a helpless, palms-up shrug. "Right. Absolutely right. Looks like both of us have turned into nothin' but a couple of ol' lap dogs. But ain't it fun!"

Chapter 31

What a long, busy day. Though chilly from the store's flap being opened so often, Rose was elated at the number of Shawnee who'd come to check out the trading post's new stock. She waved good-bye to one of the few Shawnee squaws who'd actually made a purchase, as the woman left with yard goods and a pair of scissors. Rose had also sold her a needle and thread from her own sewing basket, knowing that when she returned to civilization in a few months, her sewing supply could be replenished.

She marveled at the bargain she'd made and entered the sale into the ledger. Then, as she folded a muskrat robe, a smile twitched her lips. Not long ago she'd eaten Fawn Woman's muskrat stew and envisioned a wiry-haired, beady-eyed rat was in her mouth. Rose shook her head at the memory. Fortunately she'd never had to eat muskrat stew again.

Laying the robe in the now empty corner where only yesterday huge bundles of furs had been stacked, she heard excited Shawnee voices at the other end of the store. She turned to see an older squaw talking animatedly to a younger Indian mother toting a baby in a cradleboard on her back.

Rose looked at Shining Star, who picked up Jenny Ann, and together they crossed to the chattering pair. Rose smiled as the older one held a pair of eyeglasses up to her face and moved her hand in front of them. "Ah, the eyeglasses." Rose plucked another pair from the basket and unfolded the arms then placed the glasses on her own face to demonstrate their purpose.

The squaw grinned and nodded then took the spectacles in her hand and held them out to Rose.

Rose cupped a number of beads in her palm and showed them to the woman, who laughed with joy and said something to the young mother and Shining Star. Rose wished she'd learned a little of the language so she could share in the woman's discovery.

The squaw turned to Rose again and pointed to a large wooden comb fastened above one of her coiled ebony plaits. A pair of deer were intricately carved across its width. She pointed to the spectacles, indicating her desire to trade the comb for the glasses.

Rose smiled sadly and gave a negative wag of her head.

At that, the older Indian looked herself over then scanned her young companion. Surely she didn't covet the spectacles so much she'd offer to trade the mother for them! But the squaw nudged the mother around and grabbed hold of the cradleboard instead.

Rose's mouth gaped in surprise. No one would offer a baby in trade!

Just then, Nate and Robert entered the store, their faces glowing from the cold. Rose was vastly relieved to have an interpreter. She looked up at Robert. "Is this woman hoping to trade the baby for a pair of eyeglasses?"

Robert spoke to the squaw in her language, and she laughed and shook her head vigorously. Her answer set Robert, Star, and the young mother all snickering.

Chagrined, Rose knew the joke was on her.

Still chuckling, Robert let her in on it. "Bird Woman wants to trade the cradleboard for the eyeglasses."

With a surge of relief, Rose sought Nate's advice. "Do you consider this a good trade, Nate? I'm not accustomed to trading in anything but furs."

He winked at her, a spark of devilment glinting in his eyes. "Honey-pie, a trade's always good if both parties're satisfied. Are you satisfied?"

In no mood for his antics, she ignored his playful tone and stuck to business. "Yes, of course. But we're partners, you and I. What profit would there be for you if I were to accept a cradleboard in trade? The fur company pays only for furs."

He grunted. "I know one thing for sure. My poor arms would profit. I must'a toted Jenny around half the day yesterday. What've you been feedin' her, anyway?"

With a good-natured glare, Rose relented. "Oh, very well." She turned to the squaw with a smile. "Oui-saw."

———

When the last customers finally left the store, Star took Jenny to the wigwam to change her diaper and lace her into the cradleboard.

Watching after the Indian maiden, Rose caught Robert observing his young charge's departure with longing and gave his arm a pat. "She's such a dear girl and so helpful. I do hope she comes to know the Lord. I'd be very disappointed if we had to leave her here."

He tilted his dark head at Rose, his expression serious. "That's somethin' I pray about all the time. But if I can't marry her myself, I should be checkin' out some of the unmarried Shawnee braves. I wouldn't want her with a man who already has another wife to lord it over her."

Warming himself at the nearby hearth, Nate swung around. "You ain't still thinkin' about leavin' that gal here, are you?"

His friend turned somber eyes on Nate. "I ain't mentioned anything about it to her yet, 'cause I'm afraid she'll pretend to become a Christian just to please me. I want her to become a true believer. It should come from her heart."

"But how could you just hand her over to some brave?" Nate tucked his chin. "You love her. Any fool can see that."

A long braid fell forward as Bob hung his head. "Aye. I love her. But it was wrong to let myself grow so fond of her. The Bible makes it plain that a Christian shouldn't be unequally yoked. I'm thankful I got Rose around here to keep me thinkin' straight." He narrowed his gaze and turned to her. "'Cept you're doin' a better job with me than I done with you over that playactin'."

Humbled by her own guilt, Rose nodded. "I'm so sorry. You're quite right. I now realize things would've turned out the same with those company men had I not resorted to lies. I shall do my best not to weaken again, no matter what." Her gaze gravitated to Nate. *No matter how hard it might be.*

Nate's eyes flashed with anger as he took her by the shoulders. "Are you tellin' me that unless I toe that holier-than-thou line of yours you won't ever marry me?"

Rose yearned to inch back from his accusation, but his strong hands clamped her to the spot. She inhaled a calming breath. Then the full meaning of his words dawned on her. She raised her lashes and peered up into his eyes. "You've never asked me to marry you."

His mouth opened with a confused sputter, and his expression became gentle. "Well, I am now." Releasing her from his grip, he lowered his arms to his sides and gazed into her soul. "Marry me, Rose."

Aching at his vulnerability, Rose moistened her lips and shot a helpless look to Robert but found no help there. She lifted a silent plea to heaven for the right words, words that she had to utter, even though she knew they'd wound Nate deeply. She tried to delay the inevitable. "I had no idea you actually wanted me for a wife."

He rolled his eyes and shook his head. "What do you think we been dancin' around all this time?"

"I was of the opinion you cherished your wanderlust too much to settle down in one place. You told me as much, if you recall."

Averting his gaze for a second, he shrugged. "I know, but I'm sure we could work somethin' out that'd make both of us happy."

"Possibly." Her pulse throbbed in her ears. He wanted to marry her! It was the deepest desire of her heart! Only. . .the time had come to lay out the truth. "But there's still the matter of my obeying the Lord's instructions not to be yoked to someone who hasn't put God first in his life. Expecting that standard from Robert but not myself would be unpardonably hypocritical, would it not? I must be true to my faith."

He took a backward step. . .inches that felt like a mile to Rose as he glowered at her through pained eyes. "You have the nerve to say that to me? After all the lyin' we done yesterday?" He let out an exasperated huff. "I gotta get outta here." Wheeling around, he stormed out of the trading post. The flap closed with a resounding *slap*.

The clog that formed in Rose's throat made it hard to breathe, hard to talk. Her first impulse was to sink to the floor and weep. But gathering all her strength, she turned to Robert. "He's right. I've been such a hypocrite. May God forgive me."

He came closer and wrapped an arm around her, hugging her close. "Ain't none of us gets it right all the time. I'm real glad Jesus died to pay the penalty for our sins, or we'd never get to heaven on our own."

The tears Rose struggled so hard to suppress spilled over her lashes and down her face, and it was all she could do to utter a reply. "But what I did was worse than mere lies. I became a stumbling block to someone who desperately needs the Lord. I made it even harder for Nate to seek after God."

Robert didn't respond for a few seconds. He tipped his head with a soft smile. "Well, missy, I reckon the two of us'll have to pray that the Lord'll keep after both Nate and Star, while we try harder to stay outta God's way. The Bible does say nothin's too hard for God."

⁓

Waking up *again*, Nate gritted his teeth. It wasn't bad enough lying wide awake on his sleeping pallet for hours, jumping at every night sound, before finally nodding off. Now he was fully conscious again. And it was all that blasted woman's fault. Staring into the pitch darkness, he gave a disgusted huff. Dawn was nowhere near coming.

If it was light out, at least he could get up and go chop wood—or better yet, wring Rose's neck. Anything to work off the rage churning inside him. Funny, he'd actually expected her to loosen up from her judging ways after living out here without all the stuffiness of the rigid do's and don'ts from back east. He snorted in scorn. Sure, he was good enough to come to her rescue and save her skin now and again, but not good enough to be her husband. She was nothin' but a user. A useless, mealymouthed user. That woman could give the worst hypocrite a few lessons.

He smirked. And wasn't she nice as pie at supper, smiling that timid little smile as she served him first, givin' him the biggest chunk of corn bread. Oh yeah, she wouldn't think of marryin' him, but she still wanted to keep him on her leash. She—

A scraping sound interrupted his musings. Scraping and crunching. . .ice crunching from the direction of the river. Like canoes coming ashore!

Lunging to his feet, Nate sprang to the wigwam's opening and peeked out.

The faintest silhouettes of several large canoes were gliding to shore, canoes holding a good twenty men each. Two had already come in, and the disembarked men were sneaking onto the beach.

Why hadn't the village dogs announced the arrival of strangers?

Moving away from the opening, Nate turned around and knelt beside Bob, placing a hand over his partner's mouth. "We're bein' attacked!" he rasped under his breath. "They're comin' ashore now!"

Chapter 32

Bob shot to his feet, fully alert. "Attacked! Who is it? French or Indians?"

"Can't tell."

Both men grabbed their moccasins and fur robes in one hand and their weapons with the other. Crouching low in the darkness, they bolted from their wigwam to the one housing the girls.

"Don't make a sound," Nate cautioned under his breath as he slipped inside.

A step behind him, Bob went immediately to Shining Star's pallet and murmured quiet words to wake her.

Nate knelt by Rose and gently shook her shoulder.

"What?" came her groggy voice.

"Shh. Get up!" he whispered. "Grab your shoes an' cloak. We gotta get out of here. Now." Stuffing his hatchet and knife in his belt, he gingerly lifted the sleeping baby and her coverings.

"But we're not dressed," Rose protested softly.

Nate tried not to lose patience. "Shoes, cloak, an' follow me. Now!"

Peering out the opening while the women grabbed what they could, he saw that the invaders onshore were waiting for the other canoes. He was thankful that the trading post's location, near the edge of the forest a good hundred yards from the beach, gave them the precious time needed to slip into the woods.

There was no moon to give away their presence, but that meant there was no light to guide their way either. Still in his bare feet, Nate handed the baby to Rose and tugged her along by the shoulder. "Keep low," he whispered, leading her behind the wigwam.

Hastening after him, Rose emitted a grunt of pain, and Nate regretted none of them had shoes on as yet. The ground was bitterly cold and damp from recent snow flurries, not the best for undetected flight.

They passed the chicken pen and skirted the corral.

Rose stopped. "Are we not taking horses?" she hissed.

"No. No time. Come on."

"But—we could go faster."

"And noisier. Anyway, they'll serve a better purpose right now."

He nodded to Bob and his friend opened the gate of the corral, shooing the horses out so they'd scatter and cover any trail they left behind. Feeling his way through the snagging brush and trees, Nate wished he had the luxury of a torch to light their way, but that was out of the question until they were sure they weren't being followed.

In back of him a twig snapped. "Try to step softly," he muttered to Rose without bothering to slow down.

From off in the distance they heard triumphant shouts and blood-curdling Indian yips.

Nate raised an arm to stop his small group. "Don't make a sound." As they halted, he craned his ears to the ominous melee echoing from their camp. The glow from several fires began to flicker through the forest growth.

"Our wigwams," Bob muttered. "Just ours, from the look of it. Has to be the French an' some of their Seneca buddies."

"Aye. And wasn't it nice of 'em to send us a beacon to keep us goin' straight," Nate grumbled bitterly.

"Well, let's get our shoes on whilst they're busy an' lace the baby in the cradleboard," Bob suggested.

"You brung the cradleboard?"

"Shining Star thought to grab it. That an' some extra blankets."

"Bless her," Rose said on a breathless whisper. "Someone take Jenny while I put on my shoes. Then Star can strap the carrier onto me."

Nate took the baby and hugged the sweet darling close. "I can't believe how quiet she's bein.'"

"She's always been a sound sleeper. But somehow," Rose mused, "I think she knows our lives depend on her silence."

In the gradual lightening of a misty predawn, Rose could see the ground in front of her a bit easier as she followed Nate. And having her stockings and shoes on did much to save her feet from further stubbed toes, scratches, and bruised heels. They'd crossed a couple of streams that were mostly frozen over, but enough water had gotten through the soft leather to keep her feet icy cold. Her toes felt numb and her shoulders ached from the unfamiliar weight of the cradleboard straps, but no one else had voiced a complaint, and she refused to be the first. The Lord and Nate were seeing them to safety. They hadn't detected sounds of anyone following. . .so far.

Fatigue was quickly overtaking her. Rose took a deep breath. How much farther must they go before Nate considered it safe for a few moments' rest?

As if reading her mind, the frontiersman stopped. He turned around and peered over her head at Robert. "There's a good-size stream up ahead. It's mostly frozen, but out in the center the ice looks thin. I'm goin' upstream a little ways. There's bound to be some boulders or a fallen log we can use to get across. Stay with the women. I won't be long."

Watching him go, Rose unhooked the straps from her shoulders and brought the baby around to face her.

Jenny Ann showed all four of her little white teeth in a big smile. Apparently the little imp was enjoying the ride. "Thank You, Lord,"

Rose said in a bright voice to the baby, "for bringing us this cradleboard yesterday." *Yesterday! The Lord provided the item exactly when He knew I'd need it.* The amazing thought awed her.

"Aye," Robert added, "an' thanks for Nate's keen ears last night."

Rose sank down on a decaying log then looked up at Star and patted the spot beside her. As the girl took a seat, Rose turned her gaze toward Robert and saw him retracing their footsteps.

Several feet into the brush, he went still, musket in hand, and swiveled around to check the rear, like the intrepid frontiersmen she'd heard stories about all the way back in England.

"Surely not even Indians could follow our trail in the dark," she ventured. "I could barely see my hand before my face."

"No, they couldn't," he answered over his shoulder. "Not without a torch. The horses probably did much to obliterate our footprints—at least in the beginning. But now that it's gettin' light, they'll pick up our trail soon enough. Then they'll track us. That's why we gotta keep movin'." He glanced in the direction his partner had taken.

His answer puzzled Rose, and she couldn't keep her emotion from creeping into her voice. "But why would they follow us? They've got the store. Is that not enough?"

He came back to join her and Star. "True, they have the store. But they ain't fixin' on lettin' us go tattle to the English. Leastways not till they finish sewin' up the rest of the Ohio Valley."

Shining Star made a comment to Robert and unhooked a bag from her belt that Rose hadn't noticed before.

Robert strode over to the girl with a smile and lifted her to her feet. He gave her a long hug—the kind Rose wished she'd get from Nate about now. But she knew better than to expect one after the way she'd offended him and the way he'd avoided her all yester's eve.

Releasing Star at last, Bob took the sack and handed it to Rose. "She brought along a bag of cornmeal."

Tears Rose had managed to keep banked throughout the hard night sprang into her eyes, and she gave Shining Star a grateful smile. "Thank you, thank you. Oui-saw." When it came to surviving in the wild, the lass knew ever so much more than she. "We'll be able to feed Jenny a bit of mush, albeit very cold mush."

Leaning the cradleboard against the log, she stood to search around. "What can I use to mix it in?"

"Here." Bob opened the flap of a pack he had strapped across his chest and pulled out a gourd cup.

Deeply appreciative, Rose felt even more inadequate as she took hold of the rustic handle. All of the others had possessed the foresight to bring necessities along, while she'd been so frightened when they'd fled the wigwam, she'd been grateful to discover she'd left her stockings from yesterday stuffed in her shoes.

Nate trotted back downstream along an animal trace shortly after leaving the others. Spotting them up ahead, a rush of relief shot through him to see they were still there and still safe. He slowed to a walk. Unwonted tenderness for Rose crimped his chest as he watched her feeding the baby from a gourd. Drawing closer, he saw mush smeared over half of Jenny's face. Thank goodness someone had thought to bring food for her.

Bob swung from guarding the rear as Nate approached, his expression easing noticeably. "Ain't heard nothin' so far."

All three girls turned their heads toward Nate, and the baby gave him a big smile. Rose and Star sprang to their feet.

"Finish feedin' the little one. I found a crossin' not too far from here." He motioned with his head for Bob to follow him a few feet away from the females, where he spoke in low tones. "How long do you think it'll take them boys to catch up to us?" He eyed the path they'd trodden through the woods. . .more than obvious in the moist ground.

Bob tipped his head. "Three, four hours at most."

"That's what I reckon. When we get up to the log I found, I don't think we'll be able to fool 'em no matter what we do. We can't keep from breakin' up the ice shroudin' it. They'll know we crossed there."

"Then we gotta get these women movin' a whole lot faster." Bob tossed a glance back at them.

"I think our best chance is to make it down to the Ohio as soon as we can."

"Aye. Once we're across, we can do some backtrackin', try to fool 'em then."

"In the meantime, keep on prayin' to that God of yours that we do."

"You, too."

Nate smirked. "I reckon your prayers'll carry a lot more weight than mine."

Bob shrugged. "Do it anyway."

Grunting his doubt, Nate shifted his attention to the women. "Let's go. They're up an' waitin'."

Knowing they had to get to the other side of the stream and down to the river before the trackers made it this far, he set a fast pace up the narrow trace. *If You're listenin', Lord, please let us find a canoe or a raft waitin' on the Ohio when we get there.* Nate knew it wasn't much of a prayer, but he meant every word.

Moments later they came to the pine log he'd found that stretched across the stream. A few thin, broken-off branches stuck up here and there along its length. He leaped off the bank then turned to lift Rose and the baby down to it.

Instead of accepting his assistance, however, she backed up, bumping into Star. She stared at the fallen tree trunk, pointing at the thing in horror. "But—it's covered with ice! Surely you don't expect me to cross on that!"

Rose heard Nate's exasperated huff as he scowled and motioned her forward. His demeanor hardened, and he spoke in a stern but even tone. "We got no choice. 'Sides, it's not as hard as it looks."

She knew he was lying. The likelihood of slipping off the log and crashing through the ice into the dark water beneath sent chills of sheer terror through her. She glanced over her shoulder.

"Go on," Robert urged as Shining Star nudged Rose's shoulder. "We don't have time to waste."

Trembling from head to toe, Rose clenched her teeth and dropped down into Nate's arms.

"I know you got on them slick, leather soles," he said, still holding her. "But I'll be crushin' the ice in front of you. Just hang on to my belt."

She still wasn't convinced. "But—I'm afraid. Not just for me. It's the baby. What if I fall?"

Robert spoke quickly to Star, and the Indian girl immediately unhooked the cradleboard from Rose's back then swung the baby up behind herself with Robert's help.

"Now come on." Nate grabbed Rose's hand and practically dragged her to the log, just past where the roots stuck out. "Stay right there." Leaping onto it with the help of a root, he reached down to her. "Give me your hand, Rose. Now."

Her panic continued to mount. "But. . .I cannot swim."

"You won't have to. You ain't gonna fall. Give me your hand—unless you want me to sling you up over my shoulder an' cart you across that way."

The poor man had come to the limit of his patience. Rose raised her trembling hand. He closed his around it and in one swift haul, had her on top of the log.

One of her feet slipped off the slick tree trunk. She wobbled.

Nate pulled her close. "You can do this."

She looked at him in a silent plea. Beneath her feet, she could tell the log was just as slippery with icy moss as she suspected it would be.

He exhaled a weary breath. "Look, sweetheart, I have my musket right here to help steady me. See?" His gaze softened to one of concern. "I won't fall. All you need to do is hang on real tight an' take one step at a time."

Aware that every moment she held the group up meant their pursuers would get that much closer, Rose swallowed. It had been rather comforting that he'd called her *sweetheart*. . . .

"I'm turning forward now." Nate let go of her hand.

"All right." Quickly she clutched on to the back of his thick leather belt, the knuckles of her cold hand turning white as snow. "I'm ready." *Please help me, Lord. Keep us safe. All of us.*

Nate slowly edged forward. And slippery as the going was, Rose amazed herself by managing to follow him as she carefully placed one foot in front of the other.

Nearing the halfway point, he stopped. "You're gonna have to let go whilst I get around this here branch."

Her heart stopped then pounded double time. Did she have good enough footing?

"Let go, Rose. It'll just take a second, then I'll help you around it."

She knew Robert and trusting little Shining Star watched her from behind, and she felt like such a coward. *Father in Heaven, I need Your help again.* She forced her fingers to uncurl from Nate's belt and stood there, holding her breath.

Using the broken-off branch for support, he stepped around it to the other side then balanced himself with his musket and reached for her.

Rose had to take a step forward on her own, over moss she knew was exceptionally slippery out here over the water. She was already bone tired, and now her whole body started to shake. Her legs felt rubbery.

He met her gaze straight on. "You can do it. Go for the branch. I'm here."

Afraid to take a breath lest she lose her balance, Rose determined to take the terrifying step. Gingerly she put her foot down then shifted her weight, leaving the safety of the previous spot. She reached for the branch. Her foot slipped! She felt herself starting to fall!

"I've got you." Nate caught her arm, pulling her back up. "Grab on to the branch."

Shaking like a leaf in the wind, she grabbed hold with both hands.

His big hand covered hers, and he flashed an encouraging smile. "Soon as we get to the other side, I'm slicin' some grooves in the bottom of them shoes of yours. That should keep 'em from slippin' so much."

He truly did know how difficult it was for her to keep her footing. He did care. The realization warmed her insides.

His voice brought her back to the moment. "Now, hang on to the branch with your left hand, an' I'll pull you around with your right. Don't worry about losin' your footing. I got you."

And Rose knew he did have her. Not just her hand. He had her whole heart. If only. . .

Chapter 33

Nate had to admire Rose. She'd managed to keep up with him for the past half hour as they followed a narrow trace downstream. It did help having Shining Star carrying Jenny Ann on her back. But Rose. His Rose. By the time he'd gotten her across the stream and off the fallen log, she'd been shaking so hard he'd wondered if he should pick her up and carry her. His compassion won out, and he pulled her into his arms, soaking in her nearness, never wanting to let go—until Bob gave him a playful shove.

Her strong religious convictions still taunted Nate, but no matter how desperately he tried to harden his heart toward her, the need in those dusky blue eyes drew him, tore at him. The thought of her being taken captive by the Senecas and made to suffer unspeakable horrors made his knees buckle. And little Jenny Ann. . .

He called himself every fool name he could think of for not insisting on taking the two of them back to civilization the minute he and Bob got back to the trading post. He knew what the French were up to, that they were closing in, and that it was only a matter of time before they had Smith's trading post in their sights.

He became aware of the sound of rushing water. They were coming up on the river at last. Eager to search the bank for a craft of some sort, he turned to his friends. "I'll run ahead an' see if I can find a canoe hidden in the reeds."

"Don't show yourself till you're sure no one's out on the water searchin' the banks," Bob cautioned.

In moments, Nate reached the edge of the trees overlooking the river. A quick visual scan of the area revealed no pursuers, but the river curved about a quarter of a mile downstream. Men could come paddling around that bend at any second.

In his urgency, he slid, more than scrambled, down the steep bank. It wasn't a likely spot for someone to stash a canoe, but he had to look anyway.

His moccasins became waterlogged in the ice-crackled edges as he slashed through reeds and cane in his frantic search for a craft of any kind. But by the time the others called down to him from above, he'd found nothing. Nothing! Not that he'd expected a real answer to that pathetic prayer of his.

They needed to get across the river and onto the trail back to civilization. Time was running out. He called up to Bob, "Send the women down to braid some reed strips into rope. Give Star your knife."

Rose didn't wait to be told twice. She slid down the muddy bank to him.

He pulled his own blade out of its sheath and handed it to her as she gained her feet.

"What are we doing?" She headed for the nearest reeds even as she asked the question.

"Buildin' a raft faster than you'll ever see, that's what."

She tucked her chin but set right to work without further questions.

"Baby's comin' down," Bob said as he lowered Jenny Ann in the cradleboard.

Nate caught hold of the bottom of the carrier and brought it the rest of the way, astonished at how good the tiny girl had been. He'd heard somewhere that babies loved being walked outdoors, and this little gal was sure proof of that. He propped the cradleboard against the bank and started crawling up to the top as Star slid past him.

Bob was already at work with his hatchet, slicing small branches off a fairly straight limb from a downed fir when Nate reached him. A second tree had fallen nearby, shearing branches from smaller trees on its way down. *As if God knew we'd need those limbs.* Nate scratched his head in wonder.

Maybe the Almighty had heard his prayer after all and knew there was no canoe to be found. Maybe that's why He'd allowed the trees to fall where they had. Nate reached for another limb to strip. God truly was with them! It wasn't for his sake, of course, but for Rose's and Bob's. . .and maybe even Shining Star's.

Bob tossed a stripped limb aside and reached for another with barely a pause. "I've been thinkin'. The village dogs weren't barkin' their heads off when those canoes came in. Did you notice that?"

"I did." Working swiftly, Nate stripped his branch and heaved it onto the steadily growing pile. "I'm thinkin' they might'a been muzzled. If you noticed, there was only three spots of light from fires. Our wigwams. Somebody must'a come in and made a deal with Red Hawk beforehand."

Pausing for a second, Bob met his gaze then resumed working. "When we was havin' our friendly little talk with 'em yesterday, do you s'pose they already knew what was comin'?"

"Who can say?" Nate didn't slow down as the unreadable Shawnee expressions came to his mind. "All I know is they didn't come right out an' make us any promises, did they?"

Bob glanced back toward the path they'd traveled. "No, they sure didn't." He sliced his hatchet down another limb. "But I guess we can't blame 'em. Why get kilt over who's gonna run the tradin' post?"

Nate mulled over his friend's words. "Right. But it still galls. Them gals could'a been torched in their sleep. Thank the good Lord we came back when we did."

A grin spread across Bob's face. "Right, Nate. Thank the good Lord."

⌒⌒

Rose gawked at the pitiful raft Nate and Robert were pushing across the shelf of ice to the frigid water and vowed not to panic the way she had earlier. The two frontiersmen had gotten them this far. They were all tired and hungry and cold, but they were still alive and relatively safe. She took a closer look at the newly built contraption. Limbs no more than three inches thick were tied together with reeds and leather strips cut from the men's leggings. Still, she had no choice but to trust it would hold together and not sink. Even if the rickety thing did manage to somehow stay atop the water, the fir fronds blanketing the raft weren't enough to keep them all from getting thoroughly soaked—but she refused to think about that.

Nate had been true to his word and ridged the soles of her shoes, so Rose stepped carefully behind the men on the slick ice without slipping. She glanced over at Jenny Ann happily bobbing along in the cradleboard on Shining Star's back. Hopefully the baby, at least, would stay out of the icy flow.

Nate motioned her forward. "Crawl to the front and lie flat."

As she did, Rose tried to convince herself it was a warm summer afternoon, and she was going punting on the Thames for the simple pleasure of it. She struggled to ignore her thrumming heart. Mustering a brave smile as she passed Nate, she followed his instructions, working her way to the front of a space that measured a scant five feet wide and had an uneven aft not more than seven or eight feet long.

Unbidden panic started to rise when Shining Star slid into place belly-down beside her. The cradleboard on the Indian maiden's back resembled an upturned cocoon. Jenny Ann looked over at Rose and grinned, innocently oblivious of the danger facing them all.

This was crazy! Someone needed to get the baby out of here! But just as she reached to snatch up the child, Nate and Robert shoved the makeshift craft out and dove onto it.

It dipped under the water! She gasped as shockingly cold waves rushed across her legs. Then the raft bobbed up again. It was actually floating!

Nate loomed above her. "Scoot to the center. I need room to paddle."

Paddle? The men hadn't even chopped off the ends of the branches for fear the noise would draw their pursuers. Still, she inched toward Star and looked back at Nate.

He dipped a slab of bark into the water and began using it to propel the rude craft.

Rose rolled her eyes. The current was dragging their little raft downstream, toward the trading post they'd just fled, yet they expected to get across this wide expanse before it reached the settlement—with those pieces of bark? They couldn't have covered more than five or six miles during the night before veering toward the river.

Glancing back to Robert, she saw that he'd wedged a slab of wood between two of the central limbs, like a rudder.

Slightly encouraged, she arched her upper half toward the side. Cupping her hand, she reached into the icy current, to help.

"Here." Nate handed her the bark. "Use this."

As she took it and began paddling, he picked up another chunk and paddled with her. On the other side, Robert did the same.

To her surprise, they started to make progress! But would they make it across to the other side before drifting down to the village? The river was so wide. And canoes could slice across to them in no time at all.

Oh man. . .this was a mistake. A big mistake. The farther out on the river the raft got, the more vulnerable they were. The realization sank in Nate's stomach like a boulder. A single canoe coming around the bend carrying armed men was all it would take to do them in.

Still, bad choice or not, they had to keep going. He and Bob could probably outrun persistent trackers, but not with two women and a baby along. *Lord, did I make the right decision? We're sittin' ducks out here.*

He kept a steady eye focused downriver. Ignoring his aching shoulder muscles as he dug his bark shard into the water time and again, he willed the sluggish raft to move faster.

"Let it drift downstream a little," Bob said. "Look. The ice juts farther out over there." He pointed at a spot not far away.

Hallelujah! Nate stopped paddling and let the river take them farther downstream, where a chunk of peninsula with overhanging trees had shaded that frozen stretch from the heat of the sun.

"Only fifty or sixty more feet! Paddle! Paddle!" he urged. They were going to make it!

Once they came to the solid ice, Nate indicated some roots poking up out of the frozen water. "Climb up them roots," he told Rose and Star. "We don't wanna leave no trace of where we came out."

Bob was already at work chopping the raft apart and tossing the remains into the current. Nate yanked out his own knife, and within a minute no evidence of their rude little craft remained. They swapped satisfied grins, and the two of them grabbed their muskets and mounted the roots to join the women.

As Nate climbed up behind his pal, Bob let out a hoarse whisper. "Duck!"

One foot still dangling off the edge, Nate flattened himself to the ground. He lifted his head a fraction and peered around the mound of roots out toward the river.

Out in the middle of the flowing current, a long canoe loaded with a dozen men, half of whom wore French uniforms, sliced silently upstream. One of the Frenchmen had a telescope but at the moment had it pointed at the opposite shore.

Nate slowly pulled his foot up and crawled behind some brush just as the soldier swung the long tube in his direction. Keeping low and peeking through the branches of the shrub, Nate held his breath, watching, watching, as the telescope focused on this shoreline. Had they left any visible sign? Would Jenny pick this moment to cry out?

The canoe sped on with no order to change course. When the soldier switched his attention to the far shore again, Nate hauled in a lungful of air, only now realizing he'd been too tense to breathe.

He scrambled up the rise to where the women lay beneath some low evergreen branches with the baby between them. Rose was kissing Jenny's eyes, one after the other. She'd been keeping the baby entertained and quiet.

Coming to his feet, Nate reached down and tugged Rose gently off the ground. Her hands were so very cold. Cupping them between his own, he rubbed them to generate some warmth and get the circulation going. "We're safe. For a while, anyway. Once we get far enough away from this river, I'll start a fire so we can dry off."

"And warm up," she breathed around chattering teeth as she shivered from head to toe. "That would be heavenly." Her eyes glowed with gratitude.

Nate couldn't stop looking at her. Even all bedraggled, her hair askew, her heavy cloak smelling of wet wool, why did she have to be so alluring? Knowing he had to get her warm, he picked up the cradleboard. "Here, let me help you get Jenny hooked on."

Chapter 34

Nate could hardly believe their good fortune. Surely God had a hand in leading them to the cavelike recess in the hillside. An outcropping of rock sheltered it overhead, and the natural shape of the concavity offered protection on three sides. When they found some dry wood scattered in back of the space, as if Someone knew they'd be coming, he was tempted to believe in miracles. Maybe all those prayers Bob and Rose kept sending up, to say nothing of his own pitiful pleas, really did make a difference.

Removing his partially dry fur robe, he spread it out on the ground for the women to sit on. Their quiet cooperation throughout the ordeal seemed to him another miracle. . .especially since Rose had never been too shy to express her opinion about things.

He and Bob were used to maintaining silence during these past years since they'd been exploring, and they worked together just as quietly now as they knelt down to get a fire going. While Bob struck his knife repeatedly against a piece of flint, Nate nudged fragments of dry moss beneath the flying sparks.

A tiny flame soon burst forth. Nate blew on it gently until it grew enough to add twigs.

Sighs of pleasure erupted from Rose and Shining Star, and he looked up to see admiration in their eyes. At least for the moment, it seemed he and Bob were their heroes.

"We should be safe here for a while," Nate said. "Long enough for our clothes to dry, anyway, an' maybe get something into our stomachs." He knew he shouldn't keep looking at Rose, but she seemed like a magnet to his eyes. He drank in the sight she made, cuddling Jenny Ann within the warmth of her damp cloak. Giving himself a mental shake, he tore his gaze away. "Have any jerky tucked away in that haversack, Bob?"

"Some, I reckon." He broke a twig in half. "I'll check once we get this fire goin' good." He added more sticks to the growing flames.

Nate nodded. "I prob'ly have some in mine, too. We're gonna want somethin' to flavor that cornmeal."

"I wish I'd have had the foresight to bring something as well." Rose's sad comment drew Nate's attention back to her.

He flashed an indulgent smile. "You looked after Jenny an' kept her quiet when it mattered. That was more than enough."

A tender glow of gratitude returned to her blue-gray eyes, and the sight was almost enough to be his undoing.

He shot to his feet. "You can handle this, Bob. I'll go down to the river for some water."

"Be careful, Nate," Rose called after him, her voice soft and low.

He opened his mouth to reply then clamped it shut and turned on his heel. Didn't the woman know that was what he was desperately trying to do?

⚊⚊

The overcast sky added dampness to the day, making Rose's search for dry moss difficult, since she'd been instructed to remain within sight of the camp. She moved aside a clump of dead leaves with her foot and found a small strand of green to add to the meager supply she'd already found. A gust of cold wind swirled her cloak open, and she used her free hand to tug it more closely about herself while she continued her search.

Detecting footsteps not far away, she glanced up to see Nate returning to camp, gingerly balancing his gourd cup and a small pan in either hand as he walked. She thought it odd that he'd used such little containers to tote water back to the shelter.

Even as she moved out of sight behind a tree trunk, she knew it was silly to not want him to know she was there.

He joined Robert at the rocky cave and set down both vessels with a faint *clink*. "Can't believe it. How could both of us go off without grabbin' our flasks?"

Smiling to herself, Rose tilted her head enough to peer out at them.

Suddenly Nate straightened with a start and swung around, accidentally bumping the gourd. Water sloshed to the ground.

She ducked behind the tree again.

"Where's Rose?" A distinct note of panic tinged the frontiersman's voice.

Robert snorted. "Calm down. She just went to find moss for the baby."

"Oh." Nate released a lungful of air. "You did caution her not to wander too far, right?"

"I did. Take it easy, pal. She's not gonna take any chances."

"Hmph." He paused. "Guess it's just as well she ain't here right now."

Rose inched forward and saw Robert look up at Nate in question.

"I saw some Senecas across the river runnin' along the bank. They're prob'ly the bunch that followed our trail. They must've found where we built the raft, and now they're searchin' the banks to see where we landed. They know we ain't stupid enough to let ourselves drift very far downstream."

Rose moistened her lips and let out an uneasy breath.

"You're right about that," Robert agreed. "Let's pray they don't find a canoe before gettin' back to the village an' spreadin' the word."

Nate lowered his voice, making his next words barely audible to Rose. "Don't mention nothin' to the women. They're scairt enough as it is."

As we have every right to be. Shrinking out of sight again, Rose thought about Nate, her knight in shining armor, always doing his utmost to protect her, always taking care of her—regardless of anything thoughtless or hurtful she said to him. Why, she'd even refused to marry him, all because she was *too good* for him. What a laugh. Truth was, she didn't deserve him! The very thought of how she'd berated him, how she'd so callously dismissed his proposal, made her loathe herself.

Still, the reasons for her refusal—no matter how tactlessly she might have expressed them—remained valid. She belonged to the Lord, and Nate Kinyon did not. God's instructions must stand. She could not be bound for life to a man who did not seek after the Lord. No matter how her heart ached about it.

God had seen them through thus far. She had to believe He'd continue to do so. *Please, Father, give Nate and Robert wisdom for whatever may lie ahead. Stay with us. Keep us safe.*

The foursome gathered around the tin pan of mush. Holding Jenny in her lap, Rose couldn't help thinking back on the sumptuous Sabbath meal they'd enjoyed a mere two days past. The roasted chicken had been tender and moist, the vegetables cooked to perfection. Yet this simple fare of mush with jerked meat could be no less appreciated. Nate and Robert had carved crude spoons from a couple of broad sticks they'd found, and Rose held hers poised and ready to attack the meal.

"We need to give thanks," Robert said, bowing his head. "Lord God, we thank You for providin' us with this food. I thank You for Shining Star, too, an' ask a special blessin' on her for rememberin' to bring the cornmeal. In Jesus' name, amen."

About to thrust forth her spoon, Rose stopped midmotion as Nate's voice interrupted.

"And one more thing, Lord," he added as she closed her eyes again. "We need to thank You for all You've been doin' to keep us safe." He chuckled. "The fact that You had Rose make me so mad I couldn't sleep was the first of 'em."

She sneaked a peek through her lashes at him, wondering if he was trying to get back at her, but the expression on his rugged face was the most sincere she'd ever glimpsed there.

"An' since then it's been one thing after the other," he went on. "You know better than me all You been doin' to look after us. I wanna thank You for that. Really thank You." Abruptly he raised his voice. "Well, eat up, y'all." He dug his makeshift spoon into the mush.

Still mildly stunned, it took a moment for Rose to remember to join the others scooping food from the communal pan. What was she to think about Nate's prayer? She simply didn't know what to make of it.

"Uhh. Uhh." Jenny reached out a little hand toward the food, returning Rose to the moment. She quickly dipped her spoon and gave the child the first bite then alternated with her, making sure Jenny had no reason to fuss again.

Across the campfire, Shining Star said something to Robert that sounded like a question. He answered, his voice casual as they spoke back and forth throughout the meal.

Rose could think of nothing worthy to say to Nate. Fortunately, he wasn't speaking to her either. Fact was, he seemed to be going out of his way not to look at her, even when he passed her the gourd of water. He kept all his attention on the food before them. So she did as well.

Eventually Robert broke the tense silence. "Shining Star asked me to thank you, Nate, for your prayer." A smile added a spark to his dark eyes. "She says it's a great comfort to know she's with men who seek the favor of our God. An' she believes that He must be very powerful."

Nate tipped his head to the Indian girl. "That was a real nice thing to say."

As Robert translated, Rose sprang to her feet, bringing the baby up with her. Truly overwhelmed with the incredible change in the frontiersman, she didn't want anyone to discover the tears brimming in her eyes. Wiping Jenny's mouth with her already-ruined cloak, she went to the cradleboard to fasten her in. Without chancing a look back at the others, she cleared the clog in her throat. "Time's a'wasting"—words she'd heard Nate say so many times during their journey to Muskingum.

"But you gals' clothes are still damp," Robert protested.

"They'll dry soon enough," Rose assured him airily as she laced the baby in her warm cocoon.

Nate stood up. "She's right. He used his foot to kick dirt over the fire, effectively snuffing it. Then he swung his gaze to Rose and locked with hers for the first time. He grinned. "Time's a'wastin.'"

Chapter 35

Rose scarcely noticed the weight of the baby and cradleboard digging into her shoulders. The seriousness of the pursuers chasing after them made even the discomfort of her battered feet of little import as she followed Robert and Shining Star into the woods, skirting leftover patches of dismal snow in their path. Nate had smiled at her. Sensing he was no longer angry, she walked on in silence, basking in the sweet memory of his grin.

No one had to remind her that two skilled frontiersmen like Nate and Robert could easily elude the French and Seneca trackers, were they on their own and had minds to do so. Instead they were willingly risking capture, torture, and even death just to protect their women. *Their women.* Rose didn't dare dwell on the significance of that thought.

She tossed a worried look over her shoulder, hoping to see Nate coming. He'd remained behind to cover any evidence of their presence at the cave. Her last view of him as the party left the campsite revealed him spreading moldy leaves across those they'd disturbed and raking over imprints of their feet with a leafless tree branch. *Watch over him, Father. Surround him with Your angels. . . .*

The image of his priceless smile drifted across her thoughts again. But dear as the sight of it had been to her, Rose hesitated to assign it much significance. He could easily have changed his mind about marriage, considering the heartless fashion in which she'd crushed him by voicing her strong religious convictions. Even now the memory tormented her. But at least he was back to his old teasing self again. . .and how she loved that side of him.

She loved *him*. The prospect of having to give him up in the near future while they went their separate ways was worse than torture. How would she ever find the strength to do it? *Dear Lord, help me to bear in mind that just because Nate turned to You in a time of dire need, it doesn't mean he won't revert to his old ways the minute the danger is past.* Slowing her pace to step over a protruding root in the path, she deliberately steered her mind onto a different course. *And thank You so much that Jenny has been quiet and happy all this time. She truly loves being outdoors and traveling. Were I a Shawnee mother, I'd give her the name Traveling Woman.* With a smile, Rose stepped cautiously through a low, muddy spot.

Somewhere behind her twigs snapped. She and Robert both halted and whirled around. He raised his musket to his shoulder.

Rose caught her breath as the clatter intensified, growing closer. Nate? Was he being chased?

Then, a few yards in back of them, a doe leaped out of the brush, its eyes wild with alarm as it crashed on and vanished into the forest growth, a young fawn clattering after it.

Something had frightened the animals. A shudder went through Rose as she detected the yipping of wolves echoing in the distance.

"Come along," Robert ordered, his voice low and sharp.

Her pulse still throbbing, Rose cast a fearful look around. Then she started up the hill after Robert and Star with a longer stride, dodging snags and whips from brambly bushes she pushed past. *Oh Lord, please don't let Nate get caught. Keep him safe.*

⸺

Nate grimaced as he half jogged, half walked, following the broken twigs and footprints the threesome had left in their wake. He'd done his level best to cover their tracks from the river so the Senecas would be unable to detect the point where they'd emerged from the water. Then he buried the campfire and cleared a good fifty-yard radius around the cave, hoping the sharp-eyed trackers would be unable to decipher signs of their resting place. Hopefully they'd be long gone before anyone stumbled upon this fresh trail.

It was taking him longer than expected to catch up to Bob and the others. But that was good. Obviously his friend had set a rapid pace as the party headed for Gist's Trail, a trace that would lead them back toward civilization. Both he and Bob knew they'd have to keep off the actual trail, but by staying within close proximity of it, they'd at least be going in the right direction.

He stopped now and then to cock an ear in the direction of the cave, listening for any signs they were being followed. So far he'd heard nothing unusual. *And don't let there be none, Lord,* he prayed for the dozenth time.

Nate had to concede that prayer was becoming the best weapon he and his friends had in these dire circumstances. He could no longer discount the amazing way they'd managed to elude capture thus far. The gut-wrenching fear that had clutched his insides through the first part of the day had gradually eased, and a sense of peace had taken its place. If it really was God looking after them, Shining Star had been right about the Lord being powerful. And Rose was right that He took care of His people. Surely God's hand had helped them cross that river, and it had to be Him keeping Rose and the others safe now till Nate could catch up to them. That was a mighty comforting thought. And quite humbling.

Continuing to follow the trail for an hour or so, Nate caught the scent of smoke in the air. A terrible sense of foreboding tightened his chest. The others couldn't be more than a mile this side of Gist's Trail. Why in the world would Bob start a fire? He had to know the smell would lead the Indians right to them!

He broke into a run. The blaze needed to be put out before the trackers behind them caught wind of it.

Suddenly someone darted into his path. Nate dove off to the side in reflex.

"Partial to dead ferns, are ya?" Bob asked quietly, a grin broadening his dusky cheeks.

It was quite tempting to illuminate his pal on his partialities, but Nate rolled his eyes instead as he picked himself up and dusted himself off.

Bob held a warning finger up to his lips and motioned for Nate to follow him. Not far away, he parted the low, straddling limbs of a fir. There beneath an evergreen canopy sat Rose and Star, sharing one of the blankets Star had brought, with Jenny Ann between them.

All three girls favored him with smiles, but Rose's was the one that warmed Nate's heart.

He was about to crawl in and join them, when Bob released the branches and motioned for Nate to go with him several feet away from the others. There Bob spoke under his breath. "There's some Senecas up on the trail. They must've figgered we'd head for it. But thank the good Lord they decided to make camp before we accidentally stumbled into their nest."

Nate clamped a hand on his friend's shoulder and gave a squeeze. "Aye. He's been watchin' out for us today. That's for sure."

"I figger we're far enough away from 'em here that even if the baby starts to fussin' they won't hear her."

"How close are we to the trail, anyway?"

Bob gave a casual shrug. "I snuck up a ways. I'd say 'bout half a mile."

As they turned and strode back to the fir tree, Nate checked the sky, gauging the remaining light. The day was almost over. Finally. This had been one of the longest of his life. He stopped near the tree and turned to his friend. "We need to save the cornmeal for Jenny. For now, I reckon we can get by on what cracked corn's in my haversack. Plus I found two small pieces of jerked meat. How much you got?"

"None." Bob winced. "Me an' the gals ate what little cracked corn I had. Baby's been fed, too. Tomorrow mornin' we better snare a critter of some kind."

"Right. Can't afford to make noise shootin' somethin'."

Pulling aside the floppy limb, Bob motioned Nate inside. "I'll take the first watch. You get some rest. The women already piled up a goodly amount of needles for beds."

"Ain't you tired? You been on the trail as long as me."

Bob gave a snort. "I already had plenty of sittin' time, waitin' for you to git your lazy self up here. Go ahead. I'll wake you in an hour or two."

Sleep. The very thought made Nate yawn. He let the branch swing back into place, effectively closing him inside the small haven.

He met Rose's gaze as she patted a welcoming pile of needles. "Here." Her sweet whisper lulled him even further. "Lie down and rest."

She was here. She was safe. He could rest now. He dropped down to the makeshift bedding and closed his eyes, warmed by her presence.

A long, miserable night dragged by. The bitter cold intensified when freezing rain began to fall from the heavens, drenching the branches of the fir tree and dripping relentlessly over the limited shelter. If not for the three shared fur robes, they'd have been soggy messes. In the wee hours the sleet turned to snow, whipped about by a sharp wind. By the time morning dawned, not a hint of a smile graced a face in the bedraggled group. Even Jenny squirmed restlessly in her cradleboard.

"Think I'll make us a fire." Forcing a note of optimism into his voice, Nate scanned the area for something that might burn.

Rose glanced up in alarm. "But—won't that give away our position?"

He shrugged. "Naw. At first light, I hoofed out to the spot where Bob an' me figgered the Senecas made camp, an' it was deserted. We're pretty safe now."

"You mean they returned to Muskingum?" Giving his sodden moccasins a cursory glance, she released a slow breath.

Shaking his head, he took the bundled-up baby from her when Jenny grunted and looked at him with rounded eyes. He nuzzled the little darling. "They left tracks in the snow. Headin' east."

Bob unwrapped a few pieces of dry wood from his haversack and knelt down with his knife and flint to coax a blaze to life. "That's what I expected. They'll prob'ly go up several miles an' wait for us to come to them." His gaze gravitated to Shining Star as she stepped past Rose, tying the end of her ebony braid. He said something to her, and she gave him a shy smile. "I should have a fire goin' in a minute or so," he said to no one in particular.

A concerned frown drew Rose's brows downward. "Are you quite sure a fire won't be dangerous?"

"Trust me," Nate said, drawing her attention to him. "The Senecas had a pretty good-sized one goin' through the night. They'll think any smoke that drifts their way is leftover from theirs."

Her gaze clung to his for a heartbeat before she let it slide to the babe in his arms.

As Rose wrapped her hooded cloak more tightly around her, Nate couldn't help but glimpse the muddied, ruffled edge of her flannel nightdress. Though at times she wrapped in one of the two blankets Star had brought, the nightdress and her damp cloak were all she had to ward off the morning's bitter cold, while the rest of them wore thick fur robes. He had to do something about that.

"Ya know. . .I've been covetin' that cloak of yours," he told her.

That brought her eyes back to his as she looked from him down to her limp wrap. "I can't imagine why." She gave a wry shake of her head.

"Well, think about it." He handed Jenny to Shining Star and tried to sound earnest as he nonchalantly stooped down beside Bob to help with the fire. "This here heavy robe of mine sorta gets in the way times when I need to be movin' real fast. Your cloak I could belt down good an' tight an'—" He watched a slow smile of disbelief add a twinkle in her eye. "What's so all-fired funny?"

She snickered. "The sleeves wouldn't even reach halfway down your arms."

The woman was making it hard for him to maintain a straight face, especially when he pictured himself in it. Without cracking a smile, he gave particular attention to feeding dry needles to Bob's tiny flame. "See? That's what I mean. They'd be outta the way for sure."

"You're right." Bob's lips twitched at the corners as he made an effort to quell his own grin. "Mebbe I'll outbid you for it."

Nate slanted him a meaningful glare. "It was my idea," he blustered to keep from laughing out loud.

"Well," Rose said ever so innocently, "if you're positive you must have it, then I'd welcome the extra warmth of yours."

"It's a deal." Managing to control his features, Nate stood up.

Rising, Rose pushed the burgundy-colored hood from her head. Her hand went to the messy night braid uncoiling down her back. "I really must do something with my hair. Perhaps if we've time before we leave."

"I'd be willin' to help out," Nate blurted. The teasing provided him an excuse to stop trying to hold back his grin.

She arched her brows. "Yes, I'm sure you would." She slipped out of her cloak and held it out to him.

Nate's heart crimped as she shivered before him in nothing but a loosely draped flannel nightdress. Wasting not a second, he whipped off his fur robe and wrapped her in its warm confines.

"This," she sighed, "is so much better." She lingered within his arms for several seconds before easing away.

Nate gulped. The way he felt right now, he doubted he'd need to put on her pitiful wrap for some time to come. He flicked a glance down at Bob.

His partner stared back, all trace of his former humor gone. Bob the chaperone was back.

Nate shifted his gaze away while he shoved his hands through the wide sleeve holes of Rose's cloak then strode off. "I'll go break through that pond ice down yonder and bring us back some water."

Chapter 36

Rose had never been more deeply thankful than she was the moment Nate wrapped her in his warm robe. Chilled to the bone, she'd begun to fear she'd never be able to keep up with the others on one more day's journey in this cold, much less ever reach civilization. But in the heavy fur wrap, she felt herself beginning to thaw. After taking care of her morning needs and getting Jenny tucked inside the cradleboard, she finger-combed her hair as best she could and fashioned it into long braids that would cover her cold ears.

Nate had yet to return with water from the pond they'd passed at the bottom of the last rise. What was causing the delay? She tried not to think the worst but couldn't stop her angst from building.

The marvelous blaze Robert had going dispelled the cold for a radius of several feet, and they all took advantage of the simple, yet vital pleasure. But Rose caught the repeated glances he flicked in the direction his partner had taken. His expression revealed nothing, but Rose sensed his concern over Nate's absence.

He cleared his throat and stood. "Think I'll go see what's keepin' Nate." As he retrieved his musket propped against a nearby tree, Rose noticed with a jolt that Nate's weapon remained there.

She watched Robert start down the hill.

Just then Nate came into view coming up the rise. Rose's knees nearly buckled with relief as he grinned and held up a dead rabbit by its hind legs.

Robert shook his head and joined him.

Meat! Fresh meat! Rose's mouth watered at the concept of actual food—fresh, hot, and glorious.

The frontiersman looked so comical with her too-small cloak belted around his muscular form, his gear dangling against his long legs as the men strode to the fire, but who could think of laughing at someone who'd part with his own garment out of concern for her? After they all ate, she'd insist they swap back. One blanket Star had brought along had been sacrificed as diapers for the baby, but the other, wrapped around the cloak, provided Rose sufficient protection from winter's cold.

Nate handed her the pan of water he'd brought from the pond and held the critter aloft. "This li'l fella took one look at me in this pretty cloak an' was so dumbfounded he stood there, stock still, starin' for all he's worth. I figgered it was only kind to put the poor confused fella outta his misery. One swift throw of my knife did it."

The man was proud of himself. . .but not half as proud as she was of him. He'd brought the food they'd need to make it through the day.

Shining Star, however, was more interested in getting to the necessities than in hearing about the daring deed. Snatching the creature from Nate's grasp and the knife from his sheath, she slapped the rabbit down and began skinning it right there.

Rose squelched her amusement by setting the water near some hot coals. Straightening, she changed the subject. "How long should it take us to get back to the Delaware River?"

The men traded glances before Nate answered. "Considerin' the snowfall an' the fact we won't have a cleared trail to walk on, I'd say two weeks. What's your reckonin', Bob?"

He cocked his head. "That an' mebbe a day or two more. . .unless we can get to usin' the trail fairly soon."

Rose looked from one to the other. "But isn't this the same one we came in on? It took more than a month to get here riding horseback."

"With a loaded-down pack train and cows," Nate added. "We had to load an' unload 'em every day, plus get all that truck across all them rivers. Then we had horses comin' up lame, an'—" He paused and stared at her. "Speakin' of comin' up lame, there's some tricky ground ahead. Lots of ups an' downs. I don't want you women takin' no chances. If you need help, holler."

"I seem to recall doing a bit of hollering while we crossed that slick log yesterday—for all the good it did me." Rose stifled a teasing smile.

"That does bring back a faint memory." Nate flashed a grin but quickly sobered. "I got you across that thing just fine. But up ahead there'll be holes for twistin' your ankle in an'—" He stopped and glanced into the woods.

Rose followed his gaze, wondering what he might have heard.

"Anyway"—his expression exhibited no new concern as he continued—"I'm gonna hunt you gals some walkin' sticks while you cook our breakfast. Me an' Bob'll have you all fixed up."

He turned on his heel and started away but swung back after taking only a few steps. "By the by, Miss Rose. You're lookin' mighty fine in that fur robe. Yessir. Mighty fine." A playful grin lit up his hazel eyes. "I'll make a mountain woman outta you yet."

For three tension-filled days, the men took turns hiking close to the trail, waiting, hoping, praying for the moment the Indian war party would give up searching for them and turn back. The weather remained bitingly cold, but at least there'd been no more snow after the last storm. The ground retained some drifts in spots, but where weak rays of sunshine managed to melt it away, the earth was frozen too hard to be muddy. . .or to leave their footprints. Whenever Rose was not within his sight, Nate had to remind himself continuously that the Lord was looking after them.

From time to time, however, discomfiting memories of periods in the distant past ate at him, times when Christians had been martyred for their beliefs or thrown to lions. He could only trust that his party would not meet such a fate.

As the overcast afternoon began to wane, Nate veered off the eastern trail and headed north in search of Bob and the others. Soon it would be time to make camp for another night—another cold night without a fire. Or maybe just a tiny fire, just big enough to roast the beaver he'd come across earlier that day. He'd heard a loud *snap* near a stream and discovered a beaver caught in the claws of a white man's trap. It seemed the Lord had once again provided supper for them as He'd done for Moses and the Israelites in the wilderness. Nate hefted the critter high to admire his catch, imagining the tasty feast it would make.

Perhaps instead of martyrdom, he should concentrate on manna. But try as he might to recall the Twenty-third Psalm, which he'd memorized as a child, he could only resurrect one phrase: *"though I walk through the valley of the shadow of death."* That part had really caught his imagination.

Bypassing a moldy reed bog, Nate reminisced on his days as a lad, remembering his pa. The big strapping man had set a fine example for his sons. He'd been a faithful, hardworking disciple of God, but that had not kept him from being taken from his family while they still needed him. And little Jenny's folks had both been cruelly torn away from her. So many happenings seemed to lack purpose. Unanswered questions kept challenging Nate's faith, and all the while he was away from Rose and the others, worry was a constant companion.

On his way here, he'd crossed a creek with noticeably thin ice. What if it broke open when Rose tried to cross it? He should be there to see her safely to the other side, not way out here where he couldn't help.

Movement on the edge of his vision interrupted his musings, as a group of people stepped stealthily through a stand of birch trees. They were too close to the trail to be his friends. Lowering the heavy beaver to the ground, Nate slipped behind a thick oak and raised his musket as they came steadily, silently, in his direction.

Had they found the rest of his party and killed or captured them?

Were they now searching for him?

Deftly, he inched forward to peer around the tree.

A huge whoosh of relief left his lungs. Rose. . .Bob. . .and Shining Star, toting the baby on her back! They'd made great time in this section.

Clutching the beaver more securely in his grip, he stepped out from the cover of the tree.

Instantly, Bob's musket swung toward him. Then, emitting a frosty cloud of breath, Bob lowered the weapon and strode to meet him.

Nate's attention went to Rose, who gave him a weary smile.

A hard lump centered inside his chest. If only they could afford to take a day to rest, but that was one luxury they could ill afford. Someday soon he'd make up to her for all she'd endured since arriving in America. . .or die trying. "What are you doing so close to the path?" he asked in the same quiet tone they'd used the past four days.

His partner gave a noncommittal shrug. "Couldn't be helped. The last ridge was too steep that far out an' covered with ice. How close are we to the trail, anyway?"

"'Bout a hundred yards, easy."

Bob's brown-black eyes clouded as he frowned. "Any sign of the trackers?"

"They're still on the move."

"Well, at least we know they're a ways ahead of us."

Nate huffed. "Only if they didn't decide to start backtrackin' today."

Concerned as he surveyed the area, Bob turned to him. "Since we're this close to the trail, let's cross over to the other side. They could easily figure out what we're up to and send some of their men down this side, like I'd do if I was leadin' 'em."

Nate kneaded his chin. "If we do go over to the other side, we could keep on goin' down to where Smith's partner set up his post on the Little Kanawha. Course, for all we know, the French could've sent men there, too. They've been pretty busy."

"Aye." Bob eyed the tired women. "Best we just keep workin' our way out where we know it'll be somewhat safe."

"Well. . ." Nate looked up, judging the remaining daylight. "If we're gonna cross, we better do it now."

"Aye." Bob gestured for Rose and Star to join them. "We're gonna move to the other side of the path."

"Why?" Rose's features scrunched up in puzzlement.

Leave it to her to always have to know the reason for everything. Nate slid an exasperated glance heavenward. "The trackers are less likely to look for us on the south side. That's why."

She nodded in chagrin then followed after Bob and Star, who had already started off. She smiled at Nate and pointed to the dead beaver as she walked past him.

He returned her smile and fell into step behind his Rose of Sharon. Just having her near again calmed him. And even if she did insist on knowing all the answers for everything, he knew her trust in him was growing with each passing day. He wondered if his trust in God would ever be that strong.

Lord, I suppose You know how hard it is for me to trust You when I don't know if Your plan for us is to be saved or martyred. An' You must know I got a powerful hankerin' to spend a whole lot of time lovin' that woman.

Chapter 37

Snow still shrouded the uphill terrain in spots the sickly December sun could not reach. In the week since they'd set out on this arduous journey on foot, Rose knew her legs and ankles had grown much stronger. Even her shoulders had become accustomed to the weight of Jenny's cradleboard when it was her turn to carry the child.

Little Jenny Ann was having the time of her life on her never-ending piggyback ride. She seemed to sense when everyone's mood was light, and then she'd coo and giggle during her waking hours. If the mood was tense, she'd clam up and look from one morose face to the next without making a sound. She seemed especially drawn to Nate and would tangle her fingers in the beard he'd acquired along the way. When he nuzzled her, the wiry hair on his chin made her laugh.

The Lord enabled the men to find meat every day now, and Rose began to look on the trek as an amazing adventure. *How do I thank You, dear Father, for allowing us all to witness Your wondrous workings? I pray that both Nate and Star will come to realize that You do care for Your people and are in control.* She emitted a tremulous sigh. If only she could be sure of Nate. He was becoming dearer to her with each passing day, and she knew her life would be empty if he weren't part of it.

An icy breeze whipped across her face, and she pulled his fur robe tighter around herself. The brawny frontiersman still swapped it for her cloak now and again, though it offered him pitiful protection from the elements. Even the bottoms of his leggings hung in shreds since he'd cut off strips to build the raft. But comical picture or not that he made, she loved her backwoods longhunter with every fiber of her being.

At the front of the group, Robert signaled for her and Shining Star to stop and hide. He raised his musket.

Rose felt only a modicum of concern. The men took this precaution whenever an unexpected sound or sight caught their attention. Detecting the noise herself, she scanned the area for a wild animal.

But it was Nate whose footfalls made the incredible racket as he came sprinting toward them through a stand of dense pines.

Had they been discovered? Her heart pounded hard as she crouched with Star behind a boulder hardly large enough to conceal one of them.

Panting as he caught up, Nate grinned from ear to ear. "The Indians turned back!" He gasped, gulping another breath. "Passed right by me about an hour ago."

Rose slowly stood from her hiding place. "Are you saying. . . ?"

"Aye." He came closer, his eyes sparkling in a way she hadn't seen in weeks. "We can get on the trail now."

Robert wasn't quite ready to relinquish all caution. "You're sure *all* of 'em went by? The whole search party?"

"Ever' last stinkin' one of 'em. I counted all eight Senecas trottin' on by me. An' they looked real eager to get back. I figger they must be as tired of this as we are."

His friend thumped him soundly on the back. "By tomorrow eve we should be able to do some real huntin' then."

"Not only that." Nate laughed as he caught Rose's face in his hands. "We can have us as big a fire as we want."

"Tonight?" she breathed, almost unable to speak for joy.

His smile faded and his shoulders sagged as he released his hold. "I should'a said tomorrow, love. Tomorrow night."

She took a deep breath and tipped her head. "Well, now. That's something for us all to look forward to."

"That it is." He drew her into a hug. "We got a whole lot of things to look forward to now."

He called me his love. Rose could hardly breathe.

"*Looking forward to* is more like what I expect you to keep in mind," Robert reprimanded from behind.

Easing away from her, Nate turned to his friend, who stood with his arm around Shining Star's shoulders. "Don't you think you oughta be takin' some of your own advice, *pal*?"

Rose covered a smile with her hand as Robert glanced from Star to Nate. "It's different with the two of us. We were married by the Miami chieftain."

"Well, you ain't married in the sight of almighty God."

Rose burst out laughing. The danger was surely over now—the men were bandying words back and forth, like old times.

~

Raising her mud-caked hem to step over a root on the trail as she walked alongside Nate, Rose noticed that the leather uppers of her shoes had become unrecognizable, though they'd somehow held together. The trusty walking stick Nate had fashioned for her did make walking easier.

Not even the cold could put a damper on her mood. A couple of hours from now, the men would build roaring campfires—one for toasting themselves and one for roasting whatever game they'd shoot. Better still, in a few more days they'd walk down to the Delaware River and beyond, to safety. She hoped the river wasn't frozen over. A time of drifting down its current would be a lovely change from walking.

Extending her once-creamy hands out before her, she grimaced at how rough they'd gotten, how browned by the sun. And she didn't have any clothing to wear, having left every last stitch behind in the burned wigwam. If her family could see her now, they'd be appalled.

"I'm glad I didn't write to my sisters and let them know exactly where

I was," she said, doing her best to match Nate's long-legged strides. "By now the colonies must know about the attack on Mr. Frazier's tradin' post. The girls would've been beside themselves with worry."

He looked down at her and took one of her hands in his. "Tell you what. When we deliver the baby to her grandparents in the spring, we'll go visit those sisters of yours an' see how they're farin'."

She felt comforted by his words but could only manage a sad smile. "I had so hoped to be able to buy them out of servitude. If only one of us had thought to bring the money Mr. Hawkes paid us."

Nate chuckled. "We had other pressin' matters at the moment."

"Quite right." She nodded thoughtfully. "But speaking of Jenny Ann, it's going to be terribly hard to give her up. I shall miss her so much."

He gave an empathetic squeeze to her hand. "Me, too. You know, we could write to her kin an' tell 'em how attached we are to her. Mebbe they'd let us keep her."

"What are you saying?" Surely he didn't mean he'd be willing to settle down in one place and help raise her!

Nate came to a halt, stopping her along with him. "I may not be as thick with the Lord as you'd like me to be, Rose, but me and Him's been havin' some real interestin' conversations lately."

Conversations? Was there no reverence? Did Nate assume he could treat almighty God like one of his pals? "Nate—"

He dropped her hand and stepped back, his eyes narrowing. "I can tell by the look on your face. You still don't think I'm good enough for you. Now that you're all free an' clear an' goin' back to civilization, you figger you don't need a rough guy like me no more. Figger you can snag yourself some bloke who's a whole lot more upstandin', more—"

Robert turned back abruptly, almost bumping into them. He glowered and held a finger up to his lips. "I hear horses up ahead. Get off the trail, Rose, till Nate an' me see who it is."

Seeing that Shining Star had already ducked into the woods with the baby, Rose felt her blood turn cold. "More Indians?"

"I doubt it." Nate's words came out on a harsh note as he sprinkled gunpowder into the flashpan of his musket. "Most likely trappers comin' in for winter pelts. Best not to take chances, though. Hurry!" Anger still sparked in his eyes.

Rose grabbed his shoulder. "Not till I tell you your *figuring* is a bunch of nonsense."

"Go!" He replugged his powder horn. "We'll talk later."

Nate and Bob positioned themselves behind trees on either side of the trail, waiting for the source of the creaks and groans of leather and the hoofbeats to crest the hill. Two bearded riders came into sight, each pulling a pack animal.

As they drew nearer, Nate let out an easy breath. "Looks like Reynolds an' Stuart," he called across to Bob. Stepping out onto the trail, he waved his rifle overhead in greeting as a relieved grin spread across his face.

The rawboned men, bundled in heavy fur wraps, gave a jaunty return wave. The first one shook his head. "Well, if it ain't Nate Kinyon an' Black Horse Bob. An' still sportin' their scalps, yet."

Nate grinned back. "Aye. Barely." He turned and hollered into the woods, "You gals can come out. They're friends."

Bob strode forward. "Howdy, boys. Sure is good to see a friendly face."

Rose emerged from the stand of trees, checking her hair and drawing her worn cloak snugly about herself. Nate had to chuckle at the sight. *Women. Always worryin' about their looks.*

"How—" The greeting died in Stuart's mouth as he spotted the women stepping onto the trail. A white woman never ceased to catch everyone by surprise. He and his partner dismounted and walked straight to Rose.

"Ya poor thing." Reynolds's bushy eyebrows dipped into a frown. "Don't ya be frettin' none, yer on yer way home now." He turned to Nate. "What'd you boys have to fork out to ransom the gal back?"

"I wasn't a hostage," Rose said. "I worked for Eustice Smith until he went to be with the Lord."

Reynolds whipped the coonskin cap off his wiry hair. "You was at Smith's tradin' post? Well, I'll be a –" He clamped his mouth shut before uttering something Nate was sure was not fit for feminine ears.

He and his partner crowded close. "Well, I'll be," they said in unison, wagging their shaggy heads.

Not appreciating the way the hunters were surrounding Rose, Nate edged to her side. "We're in a real hurry to get back to the Delaware."

"Aye." Bob nodded. "Some Frenchies an' a big party of Senecas from up north came sneakin' into Muskingum b'fore dawn a week ago. They been chasin' after us. They finally gave up an' turned back the day b'fore yesterday."

"Turned back, did they?" Surprise tinged Stuart's expression. He narrowed his beady eyes.

Nate slipped closer to Rose. "We covered our tracks real good when we left then did our best to stay off the trail, so they were never sure we was comin' this way. They passed us by that first day and kept right on goin'. They must'a waited up ahead, hopin' we'd come to them. When we never did, they gave up and went back. I'm sure they sent out trackers to the north and south, too. Figgered we might'a went thataway."

Reynolds scratched his head. "'Bout how far ahead of us would ya say them Injuns be?"

"Two, mebbe three days," Bob answered as Shining Star moved alongside him. "You should pick up their tracks in a couple'a miles." He helped unhook the cradleboard on Star's back and brought Jenny around to the front.

Both hunters gawked.

"Whose babe is that?"

"Mine." Nate blurted the word without thinking. He didn't like the way the pair kept ogling Rose. He caught Bob's glare and attributed it to the lie, but he still didn't correct the error. He maintained a steady glare.

Reynolds kneaded his scraggly beard and looked from Nate to Rose and back. "I didn't know ya had a young'un."

Stuart picked up on Nate's not-so-subtle warning and changed the subject. "So Smith's tradin' post was taken by the French, too. Make sure ya get word to Governor Dinwiddie. He'll be mighty interested. Last month he talked to the Virginia House of Burgesses about them forts the Frenchies are puttin' up on the south side of Lake Erie. Dinwiddie told the assembly the Crown wants 'em to take some tax money an' raise a militia. Well, the House was already up in arms about some fool taxes the king started slappin' on the colonies. The whole meetin' turned into such a ballyhoo over the new taxes, nothin' was done about raisin' a militia a'tall."

"That's it?" Nate was appalled.

The hunter cocked his head. "Far as the House is concerned. When Dinwiddie found out the Frenchies took Logstown, too, he—"

Bob's mouth gaped in dismay. "They took Venanga an' Logstown? Both?"

"'Fraid so. An now from what you say, they got Smith's."

"Aye." Nate let out a weary breath. "Guess they figgered on gettin' themselves one more before the hard winter sets in. What galls me is there ain't nobody doin' a blasted thing to stop 'em."

"That ain't entirely so." A slow grin widened Stuart's weathered face. "The governor dubbed some young surveyor named Washington a major an' sent him forth."

"Then Dinwiddie did raise a militia despite the House of Burgesses."

"Not exactly." The other hunter swapped grins with his partner. "He sent Washington with a letter, him an' a couple'a longhunters an' a interpreter. Now ain't that just a hoot! 'Monsieur Frenchie, would y'all please leave? We ain't got no militia, but we'd sure appreciate it if ya'd go.'" Both men howled.

Nate failed to see the humor in any of it and noted that Bob didn't either. "Well anyways, you boys know what you're walkin' into."

"That we do." Reynolds sobered. "That's why we're fixin' to turn south when we reach the west fork of the Monongahela. Goin' down Cherokee way. Winter furs won't be as plush, but we'll still have our scalps."

Nate nodded. "That fork was froze over when we crossed it."

"We ain't plannin' to go over it again. Figure we'll stay on this side. We best get a move on, too. Only got a couple more hours before dark."

Even with his dismissal, both hunters turned to Rose, looking much too pleased at the sight of her. They tipped their caps as Nate wrapped a proprietary arm around her.

"Been a real pleasure, ma'am."

Chapter 38

Y ou're back to lyin' again." Robert accused with a scowl.

Hiding her amusement, Rose busied herself with Jenny Ann, handing her a piece of meat to chew on.

Nate snorted in disgust. "Easier than goin' into the whole story, ain't it? Them two blabbermouths don't need to know Rose was a bondwoman."

"Ah. So now you're lyin' to me *and* yourself."

Leveling a glower on his partner, Nate snatched up the cradleboard. "You sure are gettin' fussy in your old age." He helped Rose into the straps. "Come on, let's get goin'. Time's a'wastin.'"

There wasn't much point in trying to start a conversation, considering the mood the two frontiersmen were in. Struggling to keep up with Nate, Rose tossed a backward glance at Star, who appeared to share her opinion as she and Bob lagged behind.

Out in front of everyone, Nate's fast pace only increased as time went by. Rose finally took hold of her shoulder straps to ease the cradleboard's weight and ran to catch up, latching on to his arm. "Are you trying to run off and leave us, or what?"

His mouth in a grim line, he slowed a bit but didn't look down at her as he normally did.

Something was definitely wrong. Recalling that he'd mentioned something about the two of them and the baby being together before the longhunters came along, she moistened her lips. "Nate, what you said before. . . I want you to know you had the wrong idea entirely."

He marched on, still not deigning to look at her, even once.

Rose felt a lump growing in her throat. "I would never use you and then callously cast you aside. I—"

"I know that." His eyes remained on the terrain ahead, but his demeanor eased a fraction. "It's just. . .I been takin' too much for granted. Once we get back, you'll see."

What did that mean? She wished she could look into his eyes, see his heart.

"I'm real rough around the edges, an' you talk an' write all refined-like. I have a hard time just figgerin' out how to spell even easy words."

"That may be true. But you know many other things—important things—that I don't have the slightest idea about."

"Mebbe. But they won't count for much where you come from."

"And my papa's skills wouldn't be worth much in the wilderness, either."

"It don't matter. I just been thinkin' fool thoughts about us. God ain't about to let me have a lady like you. You hear how I talk. I ain't never gonna get it right."

Before she could respond, he stretched out his stride again, leaving her in his wake.

Rose's spirit sank to her toes. Did the man actually think she was that shallow? That judgmental?

No, there was a whole lot more to it than that, and well she knew it. What had the housekeeper often asked Mariah when the girl fancied herself married to some rich Arabian prince? Oh yes. *A fish and a bird might fall in love, but where would they build their nest?*

And where would she and Nate build theirs?

The grueling pace Nate set that afternoon continued throughout the remainder of the day. Thankfully the trail stayed fairly level, with only an occasional iced-over brook to cross. Rose found the walking stick a welcome asset.

Finally they angled off the trail into a dense stand of firs that would provide a good windbreak and some shelter for the night.

Rose hoped Nate would be in a better frame of mind when he turned to speak to her. Alas, he didn't even make eye contact.

"I heard a gobbler back yonder. Tell Bob I'm goin' huntin'." With that, he strode away.

The resigned droop of his shoulders hit Rose hard, and tears stung the backs of her eyes. His attitude toward her wasn't exactly rude, but it was impersonal. Painfully impersonal. She couldn't decide whether to cry or scream.

Robert, who'd followed at a more leisurely pace with Shining Star, caught up to her. "Where'd Nate go?"

"Hunting."

"Must'a heard that gobbler." His tone remained nonchalant, as if nothing was amiss, but he flicked a glance up at the clouding sky. "Let's find a dry spot to spend the night. Looks like we could be in for some snow."

Star smiled at Rose and moved behind her to lift the cradleboard from her back. She propped the sleeping baby against a tree trunk. "Jenee oui-saw."

"Yes. She's been very oui-saw." Returning Star's smile, Rose again noticed how much the Indian girl reminded her of her youngest sister, Lily. How she wished the two of them could sit down and have a relaxed conversation over a cup of tea, the way she and Lily so often had done in their cozy kitchen. But Star's English was almost nonexistent, except for a few words she rarely used, so that was not to be. A deep sigh came from inside.

She could tell Robert wanted to question her about Nate, but she had no answers. Avoiding his inquisitive look, she blurted the first thing that came to her mind. "I shall look for dry firewood under the trees."

After that, Rose did whatever she could to stay occupied. While on her knees gathering needles for their beds later, she reached up in a fir branch to swipe away a cobweb. As she did, she saw Robert and his lady sitting together on a shared robe before the fire, his arm wrapped around Star as they snuggled within the confines of the other robe.

Looking closer, she saw that he was reading a scripture and then translating it. Star would listen intently, now and then asking a question. With the young maiden's sweet nature and her willingness to learn about the Lord, she and Robert would have no problem finding a place to build their nest. All one had to do was look at them to know they were God's choice for each other. Or were they? Nothing seemed clear anymore.

Off in the distance, the sharp report of a gunshot echoed through the trees.

Nate must have gotten his turkey. He'd be back any minute. Rose crawled out from under the tree and brushed needles from her hair as her heartbeat picked up.

Rose, Rose. . .my Rose of Sharon. Aching inside, Nate knew he'd only been fooling himself. No matter what she might say now, once they reached a town, she'd see what a rough cob he truly was. *Lord, help me to accept that she's way outta my reach. Help me to let her go, like a real gentleman.*

Releasing a pent-up breath, he reloaded his weapon. A snowflake landed on the musket barrel, followed by another on his hand. He looked up at the leaden sky as more flakes swirled around him. He'd better get back to camp before the storm let loose. Picking up the turkey he'd shot, he glanced around in the quickly fading light. From about a quarter mile away, the unmistakable glow from a campfire was like a beacon drawing him home.

About to head toward it, he detected a staccato of familiar padding sounds coming his way from farther up the trail. . .moccasined feet! The Senecas! All eight of them! They came to a sudden halt mere yards from where he stood.

Crouching low, Nate couldn't tell if the Indians had seen him. But what he saw made his heart stop. One of the trackers pointed wordlessly toward Bob's campfire. It had to be the same trackers who had been dogging them for a week.

Still panting from their run, the Indians poured powder into the flashpans of their muskets, preparing for an attack.

Confident that they didn't know he was there, Nate pulled the plug from his own powder horn and loaded his musket, knowing the sounds he made would only blend with theirs. Then he took careful aim at the one who appeared to be the leader.

He pulled the first trigger, then the second. The flash from the explosion blinded him momentarily, but he heard the man grunt, then groan. He'd hit his target.

Now he was one.

The first rifle fired at his flash.

He dodged to the side.

Whooping and yelling, the war party emptied their weapons. Musket balls whizzed past him, thudding into the ground.

Lord, let Bob hear all this and be warned. He crashed through the brush in a different direction, hoping to draw the Indians away from the camp. The women needed time to hide.

From the corner of his eye, Nate saw the fire's glow suddenly disappear. His friend had understood. He'd surely send the women to safety.

Father God, don't let 'em get Rose and the baby. Protect them!

Lacking a second to reload, he dropped his musket to free his hands and pulled out his hatchet and hunting knife as he sprinted on.

Half the Indians followed after him, splitting off from the group.

Knowing the rest of the Indians were headed for Rose and the others, Nate swerved in that direction.

A flash and an explosion echoed from camp.

A yell of pain pierced the air.

Bob had hit his mark, but he might not have time to reload before the Indians were on him.

The runners weren't far behind. Nate knew from the sound of their feet that they'd reach the camp about the same time he did. And even with two of them down, six still remained.

Too many for him and Bob.

Lord, hide the women so they won't find them. Only You can help them.

"I'm comin', Bob," he shouted into the growing darkness.

A flash and crack split the air, followed by another yelp.

"Got one more," Bob yelled back.

Guided by the spark of light from his friend's rifle, Nate charged into the small clearing just as the remaining Indians got there.

"Over here," Bob hollered, and Nate rushed to his side.

Holding his empty musket like a club, Bob stepped around to cover Nate's back with his.

The braves knew they had the upper hand. They circled and taunted, their fiendish voices mocking as they jabbed their muskets toward Nate and Bob in sport, then danced back. Finally one of them tired of the game and swung in earnest.

Bob blocked the blow with his rifle, while another wielded his at Nate.

He fended it off with his hatchet, but the musket barrel sliced across his thumb. He almost dropped the weapon. Behind him he heard the sound of steel meeting steel.

One of the Indians swung from Nate's other side with the butt end of his musket. Nate put up his knife arm to block it. Pain shot up to his shoulder. A few more well-placed blows and he'd go down. If only he hadn't discarded his musket back there. Rose—

"Lord," he bellowed, fending off a vicious jab, "take care of the women!"

"God be with them!" Bob hollered.

Two braves swung their muskets at Nate. He blocked a head blow. The other caught him behind the legs, taking him down. He had to get up.

A musket shot rang out.

A Seneca brave slammed heavily into Nate then slid to the ground beside him. Pushing the man off, he scrambled to his feet.

As the other braves turned toward the threat, one more shot found its mark. Another of them grabbed his belly and sank to his knees.

Two more reports from smaller weapons caught one in the throat. The other shot missed either of two braves who'd dropped into a crouch.

In one swift motion, Nate brought his hatchet down against one Indian's neck as Bob flipped his musket butt first and took a mighty swing at the last one's head.

Stillness filled the air.

The two friends glanced at one another in the near dark. All the enemy were down. But how? Who had fired those shots?

At that moment, longhunters Reynolds and Stuart emerged into the open. "Howdy, boys," Reynolds said nonchalantly. "Thought mebbe you could use some comp'ny."

Nate stared in shock, his mouth gaping.

"Better check an' see iffin' any of them redskins is playin' possum," Stuart suggested. "Wouldn't want no surprises, would ya?"

"No, we sure wouldn't." Recovering his senses, Nate uncovered the smoking ashes with his foot until he found some live embers. Then, grabbing long sticks off a pile, he jabbed them into the coals to set them afire for use as makeshift torches. "I counted eight of 'em when they stopped on the road."

The hunters and Bob reloaded their muskets.

After a head count of the war party's dead, they found that only one had escaped into the wilderness. Nate looked around for the women but couldn't spot them. "Wherever you women are, stay put," he yelled, then he turned to Bob. "You better stay here, just in case." Then he and the longhunters took the torches and started after the runaway's tracks.

"There's no way he's gonna be a threat." Nate rubbed a knot on his arm. "Look at that trail of blood he left behind."

Reynolds gave a sober nod. "Yeah. He'll bleed out soon enough." The threesome headed back to the camp as the light flurry turned into a steady snowfall.

Chapter 39

As he and the other men returned to the camp, Nate saw that Bob had dragged the corpses into the brush and had a blazing fire going. The women had also come out of hiding. Rounding a drooping fir tree, he could feel the warmth emanating from the flames. But it was the sight of Rose that really chased away winter's chill.

She turned around, and her blue eyes locked with his.

Nate felt his knees go rubbery. She'd come so close to being taken or killed. But God had sent the longhunters to save her. To save them all. His eyes smarted as he went to her.

She opened her arms to him. Wrapping her in his embrace, he drew her close, kissing her hair, her upturned face, never wanting to let her go.

Suddenly he swept a frantic glance around. "Where's Jenny?"

Rose reached up and cupped his face in her hands. "Right over there, propped against that boulder." She tipped her head in that direction.

Tugging her along with him, he strode over and picked up the cradleboard, holding it between them.

Jenny Ann grinned at him around a piece of slobbery jerked meat clutched in her fist, and Nate bent his head and kissed the baby's plump, rosy cheek. "God heard our prayers, little angel," he whispered hoarsely.

"He saved us all."

With a tremulous smile, Rose touched his face. "So He did. The Lord surely cares for His own." A slight frown drew her brows together, and she took a step back. "By the by, where's that turkey you went after? It would appear God sent us some company for supper."

Nate laughed and pulled her close again. "He sure did."

The enticing aroma of roast fowl permeated the air as Rose snuggled close to Nate. With Jenny on his lap, the man had yet to stop grinning, and the pair were a sight to behold. The little one gnawed on a bit of a wing he'd sliced off for her as everyone waited for the gobbler to cook through.

Across the fire, lovebirds Robert and Shining Star sat with their heads together, whispering back and forth in their own little world.

Mr. Reynolds turned the spit, his eager eyes willing the bird to finish so they could all delve into its juicy meat.

"Wish we had somethin' besides the bird to offer you boys," Nate said, watching him. "What made you turn back, anyway?"

Stuart shrugged a burly shoulder. "Luck. Pure luck. We just pulled off the trail so's we could unload the horses b'fore the storm cut loose." He peered up at the lightly flaking sky. "Thought fer sure it'd be snowin' a lot harder by now. Seems it's slowin' down."

"Anyway," Reynolds cut in, "we heared them Injuns a'runnin' up the trail an' knowed they was the ones ya tole us about." He caught a dripping from the turkey and licked his finger.

His partner nodded. "Who else'd be runnin', 'ceptin' if they was chasin' somethin' or bein' chased. So we pulled the animals down below the trail an' drew our muskets an' waited." He patted his brace of pistols. "Them redskins stopped when they seen our tracks, mutterin' amongst themselves whilst they caught their breath."

"Yeah." Reynolds smirked. "One kept pointin' our way. But they decided to keep goin'. Figger they was fixin' to come back after us once they took care of y'all."

Stuart's gaze centered on Rose. "Couldn't let them savages get at you purty little ladies."

As Nate stiffened beside her, Rose pressed her hand over his to make sure he remained calm.

"That wasn't luck, friends." Robert looked from one hunter to the other. "Even before we cried out to the Lord, He had help comin'. Ain't God good?"

Shining Star tugged at his sleeve.

"Oh yes." He smiled at Rose. "Star wants you to know she's gonna learn English as fast as she can. She wanted to tell you before not to be afraid, that ever'thing would be all right. She said. . ." The fire reflected against moisture in his eyes as he drew a ragged breath. "She knows He's her God, too, now, because He speaks her language, not just English." He lowered his dark eyes to Star and winked. "The Lord told my bride not to fear. Ain't that somethin'?"

The sight of the couple blurred behind tears of her own as Rose realized the full meaning of Robert's words. His bride. . . Nothing could prevent him from taking her to be his true wife now.

"Well, congratulations!" Obviously understanding his friend's comment, as well, Nate whacked his thigh with his palm.

The two longhunters exchanged uncomfortable glances. Stuart cleared his throat and stood up. "Me an' Reynolds better go unload our animals whilst that gobbler finishes up. Mebbe we can come up with somethin' to add to the meal, if'n you folks don't mind us stayin' the night."

A muscle worked in Nate's jaw as he set Jenny on the robe beside him.

"Of course we don't mind," Rose blurted before Nate could come up with an excuse for them to leave. "I can probably find some fairly dry needles for beds under that big tree yonder." She pointed to one a sufficient distance away.

"Why, thankee, ma'am." Tipping his cap, Stuart nodded to his pal and the two started back to the trail to collect their packhorses.

Once they were out of sight, Rose turned to Nate. "There's something you need to get straight, Nate Kinyon." She hiked her brows to emphasize the point as she looked deep into his eyes. "You were doing some real backtracking this afternoon. But if you think I'm going to release you from your marriage proposal, you can just forget it. I happen to be in love with you, and I'm holding you—"

His lips collided with hers, effectively silencing her with a breath-stopping kiss. She melted into it, wanting it to last forever.

But they'd forgotten about Robert. Across the fire from them, their chaperone gave a meaningful "harrumph."

Eventually Nate broke away from Rose and chuckled at his pal. "Quit worryin'. Soon as we get to a preacher-man, Rose and me are gonna marry up. Right and proper." He met her gaze, a mischievous glint in his eye. "Yessir, right and proper."

Those precious words rendered her momentarily speechless.

With Jenny snuggled inside the cradleboard on her lap, Rose watched the muscles in Nate's back stretching and tensing as he and Robert paddled downriver on the Potomac, dodging chunks of ice. After two days they would reach Nate's and Robert's childhood settlement, Conococheague, a name she still had problems pronouncing.

She flicked a despondent look at the masculine attire Nate had acquired for her at the horse trader's trading post in exchange for his hatchet. Though worn and oversized, the garments were better than her nightgown, to be sure, but Rose cringed at the thought of having to meet Nate's mother and his brother's family with men's clothing cinched about her waist.

She'd had the last laugh, however, when she'd presented herself in the frayed and stained outfit that swallowed any hint of her feminine figure. "If my proper English neighbors could see me now," she mused with a wry grimace.

Surprisingly, Nate's expression turned worshipful. "You've never looked more beautiful to me."

Emotion swelled within her at those tender words. How could she not love him? Unable to reach him now, since Shining Star occupied the bench ahead of her, Rose flipped the cradleboard around and planted a kiss on the baby's cheek instead. Jenny giggled and mashed into Rose with a sloppy kiss from her little wet mouth. It made Rose's heart contract. The darling wouldn't have many more chances to return her kisses once she was relinquished to her grandparents next spring. Rose refused to expose the child to any more winter weather.

Glancing again over the top of the cradleboard toward Nate, Rose noticed Shining Star's rigid posture. The Indian girl had been deadly silent since Robert had announced they'd be docking soon. Recalling how fearful she had been herself of going into a strange and unknown foreign world, she leaned forward and tapped Star's shoulder, motioning for her to turn around on the seat.

When the girl complied, her dark, doelike eyes held a wary look.

Rose placed a palm over Star's tightly clasped hands and smiled. "Not afraid. God is with us."

Shining Star pursed her lips together, and a tiny smile trembled forth as she gazed upward. "Not afraid."

"We're comin' in," Nate hollered over his shoulder. "Conococheague's dead ahead."

As Star stiffened, her eyes flaring wider, Rose gave the girl's clenched fists an encouraging squeeze. Then she pointed at Star and then herself. "You, me, together. Not afraid."

The Indian maiden smiled as she clutched Rose's free hand between both of hers and leaned forward. "You, me, Nate, my Bob."

Rose grinned. Shining Star and *her* Bob, and Rose with *her* Nate. Very soon now, she and Nate Kinyon would become husband and wife. Her heart nearly burst with joy.

⌁

Riding beside Rose on horses borrowed from the blacksmith, Nate chuckled to himself thinking of the surprise his family would have when he arrived with an almost-bride and a baby. He tightened his arm around wide-eyed Jenny, noting how her sweet smile drew attention from passersby. His gaze drifted to Rose, his love, wearing the tattered and smudged maroon cloak over her frontier attire and looking more beautiful to him than any woman he'd ever seen.

Nevertheless, she hadn't relaxed the tight set of her mouth as they neared his family's home on the muddy road. Nothing he'd told her about his kind, loving mother or his spry sister-in-law allayed her fears.

"We turn here." Reining his mount onto the less-traveled path through the woods, he looked over his shoulder at equally tense Shining Star, riding alongside Bob, and gave her a reassuring nod. "We're almost there."

"Wonderful." A flat smile accompanied Rose's comment.

There had to be a way to perk her up. He tipped his head. "Bob's place is just up the road."

Staring toward an upcoming clearing, she gave an aloof nod.

"Looks like Jonah cleared more land," Nate commented as they reached the edge of the still-bare trees. "He plants wheat and corn mostly, and some flax for spinnin'. Course, it's all plowed under now. Looks lots better come spring. He's got a couple half-growed boys to help out."

"How nice."

Nate could barely hear her soft answer. He saw her focus on the large cabin ahead with smoke curling up from its twin chimneys. No one was in sight, but two spotted dogs crawled from beneath the front steps and started barking, announcing their arrival.

"Halloo the house!" Nate hollered, adding to the ruckus.

Immediately the cabin door swung open and a pair of young redheaded boys ran out. James, the gawky twelve-year-old, gave a loud hoot. "It's Uncle Nate! An' Bob Bloom!"

Evan, his ten-year-old sibling, gawked, stretching his mass of freckles. "An' they brung women!"

That brought broad-shouldered Jonah into view. He emerged

carrying three-year-old Gracie, his golden-haired daughter. The last time Nate had seen her, she was a mere babe. And on Jonah's heels came his slim, reddish-blond wife, Margaret, along with their mother, who had aged noticeably in his absence. "Nate, my dear boy," she murmured, the care lines in her face softening with her smile. "High time you got back." She drew her shawl close about her thin form as she hurried toward him. Then her gaze landed on the cradleboard in front of him. "You got a babe, Nate? And I ain't even met yer wife!"

Nate lowered Jenny down to her. "This is Jenny Ann, Ma. An' she ain't my baby. Leastwise, not yet." He swung down and wrapped his mother and the baby in a big hug. "I'm sure glad to be home." He meant every word.

Stepping back from her, he turned to Rose, who hadn't attempted to dismount. He reached up and helped his reluctant love down then wrapped a protecting arm around her. "Ma, Jonah, Maggie, this here's Rose."

"How do you do," she managed as the rest of the family crowded close.

"Well, come inside outta the cold," Jonah said. "You all must be hungry." He looked up at Bob. "Why're you still sittin' up there? You come, too."

Bob shook his head. "I think mebbe me an' Shining Star oughta head down to my place." He slid a glance to her.

"Nonsense," Margaret cut in, her green eyes twinkling. "There ain't nothin' but mice an' spiders at that ol' place of yers. Come in an' warm up."

Bringing Rose with him, Nate reached over to Margaret and gave her a grateful hug. Unlike so many of their neighbors, his family had always made Bob welcome despite his Indian blood.

Margaret eased out of his embrace and arched her golden brows at Bob. "'Sides, if you don't come in, we won't know how many of Nate's tall tales to believe."

Everyone laughed as she yanked Nate's scruffy beard. It was then he

309

realized how much he'd missed the gal's quick tongue. He switched his attention to Bob and watched him help his lady to the ground.

Leading the way to the house, Jonah nodded to his sons. "James an' Evan, go see to the horses. An' rub 'em down good."

"Yes, Pa."

Ma, still holding Jenny, sidled over to Bob and tugged his shoulder till he bent his head for a peck on his cheek. "Well, now. I see you got yourself a woman, too. Purty li'l thing she is." She gave Shining Star a welcoming smile.

He drew Star close to his side. "This is my sweet bride."

"Seems you boys've been real busy." She turned to eye Nate and Rose. "I reckon you up an' married, too, an' without so much as lettin' yer ma know."

"That's not how it is, Ma. Rose is my betrothed. We—"

Her mouth gaped. "Oh." She glanced lovingly at wide-eyed Jenny then placed a sympathetic hand on Rose's shoulder. "Sorry about yer loss. You got a fine lookin' babe here." She made a silly face at Jenny Ann and earned a gap-toothed grin.

Despite the fact that Ma was mistaken in her assumption, her sympathetic gesture must have done the trick. Nate felt Rose relax against him as they walked up the porch steps.

Bob followed a step behind. "You don't know the half of it. Once we get our gals in out of the cold, *I'll* tell you all about it."

"Now that's what I like," Margaret gushed. "An eager tattler."

Nate stood with his brother and Bob at the potbellied stove, watching James and Evan, in their Sunday breeches, lighting every candle in every holly-decorated sconce in the simple church. Two days after arriving home, he and Bob were marrying their sweethearts. Two days that had lasted forever.

Fragrant pine boughs with trailing red ribbons adorned the ends of the dark, wooden pews. Breathing deeply of the evergreen scent, Nate couldn't help grinning. "Sure was nice of folks to decorate the church for our weddin.'"

Jonah chuckled. "It's for tomorrow's Christmas Eve service."

"Well, I'm getting' my Christmas present early."

"Sure hope Shining Star likes it." Bob let out a nervous breath. "Everything's so new to her. But we both wanted a proper church ceremony to give our marriage credence in the eyes of our neighbors an' to say our vows before God."

Nodding, Jonah gave Bob's shoulder a squeeze. "Even so, it's best we're just havin' the minister an' the family. That timid bride of yers would'a had a hard time with a passel of strangers gawkin' at her."

"Aye. An' with Rose an' Nate stayin' with us till spring, she'll have time for Rose to teach her the white way of doin' things. Mebbe my ma would've felt more welcome if she'd had somebody like Rose helpin' her."

Nate's heart swelled with the realization that others knew how special Rose was. He was the luckiest man alive. This was his wedding day, and his bride would be walking up the aisle to him any minute now. . .if those fussy women ever got here.

Jonah's brow furrowed. "I just can't figger out why a educated lady like Rose would wanna hook up with a rough-an'-tumble rover like my brother."

Nate was about to say something in his own defense when he heard the wagon roll up to the church. He quickly rubbed a smudge from his buckled shoe on the back of his other knee-length stocking.

"They're here!" James hollered at the top of his lungs.

Starting forward, Nate felt his brawny brother's hand staying him. "No you don't. I'll go help the women. You two go stand up front. You ain't allowed to see yer brides till they come traipsin' up the aisle."

Nate swapped a wry glance with Bob as Jonah and his carrottops hurried outside.

It seemed to take forever for the door to open again. But soon enough, it swung wide, and Jonah's dark-haired younger sons, Norman and Nathan, burst in with the exuberance possessed only by seven- and five-year-olds. Both were in their Sunday best, rumpled from play. "We're here!"

Little white-haired Pastor Reynolds, bespectacled and attired in somber black, followed the boys. He shook a bony finger at them. "You boys need to settle down and be quiet. Sit over there." He nodded to Nate and Bob as he joined them down front.

The waiting was getting to Nate. He swiped his damp palms down the fancy maroon frock coat he'd borrowed from his brother then grinned at Bob, who wore a gold-trimmed brown outfit he'd left at home and looked as anxious as Nate felt. "Sure are a couple'a dandies, ain't we?"

Bob, in a cravat of ruffles up to his chin, grunted and kept staring at the door.

Finally it opened again, admitting Ma and Margaret in their finery, carrying Jenny and three-year-old Gracie. Reaching the front pew, Ma handed the baby to Maggie then ambled up to Nate and Bob. She fussed with their frilly cravats and tugged down the backs of their frock coats. "There." She stood back and looked them both up and down. "You'll do." Turning around, she spotted James in the back of the room. "Tell the gals they can come in now. Then you an' Evan come sit with us."

Hand in hand with Shining Star, Rose stepped in, looking like a princess in a frilly lavender frock of Margaret's. A garland of holly wove through her upswept hair, while wisps of soft ringlets around her face added an exquisite fragile quality to her delicate features. Nate could hardly draw breath at her incredible beauty.

Beside her, Shining Star looked equally stunning in another of Margaret's dresses, this one in ivory taffeta with ecru lace, a combination that accented her tanned skin. A wreath of holly adorned her glossy black hair that hung straight to her waist.

Nate heard Bob's sharp intake of breath at the sight of his beloved, and he wondered how he and Bob could have gotten so lucky. *Thank You, Lord.*

But his brother was right. How could someone like Rose want to marry him? Was she coming to him merely out of gratitude? He had to know. Ignoring her solemn expression as she drew nearer, he shook his head. "Reverend, would you be kind enough to excuse us a minute?"

Grabbing Rose's hand, he all but dragged her to the back of the church, leaving behind a chorus of gasps. There he turned to her, positioning himself as a shield to hide her confusion from the family. He took her by the shoulders and looked deep into her eyes. "I'm givin' you one last chance to back out, Rose. You're much too fine a lady for a backwoods fella like me. You don't have to go through with this weddin'. I'll still take you anywhere you want to go, get you an' your sisters set up however you—"

She put a finger to his lips and stared up at him a moment. "Could it be that you're the one who's getting cold feet?"

He stood his ground. "Your last chance. Once we're married, that's it. I ain't ever lettin' you go."

"I'll hold you to that, my loose-footed frontiersman. I told you I love you, Nate Kinyon, and I do. More than I can ever express. So let's go get married."

A huge grin spread across his face. He hauled her into his arms and gave her the kind of kiss he'd wanted so long to give her.

"Nate. Nate." Jonah tapped his shoulder. "Don't you know nothin'? The kiss comes after, not before."

Nate gazed down at his Rose. "Yeah. After, too."

"And every day after that," Rose whispered, her eyes on him alone. "Every day after that."

Epilogue

Drinking in the fragile beauty of spring, Rose walked up the knoll that soon would be theirs. Nate trotted ahead with giggly Jenny Ann on his shoulders. Watching after them, Rose noticed that the snow was gone from all but the highest hills, and the meadows overflowed with wildflowers in a rainbow of hues.

"Come on, slowpoke." Nate motioned her forward. "Let's eat in the kitchen."

Smiling to herself, she grasped the food basket tighter and hurried to catch up. Today was finally warm enough to have a picnic. . .on the very spot where Nate would build their home. Robert had so wanted them to live nearby he'd deeded half his father's farm to Nate.

"Our kitchen'll have milled boards." Nate swung the toddler to the ground. "An' as many windows as you want. We'll paint the place any color you fancy."

Rose reveled in the joy in his eyes. Her husband had insisted on spending the savings his mother had socked away for him to build her a *proper* house, as he called it. "I'm partial to yellow, I think, with black shutters and a front porch. Yellow will always remind me of Jenny Ann after she goes to live with her grandparents." At the thought, some of her joy faded.

Nate tugged her close and kissed her cheek. "Today, sweetheart, Jenny's ours. And today me and our little angel are hungry. Ain't that right, firefly?"

The little curly-top looked up from where she squatted to pull at a violet.

"Lunch it is, then." Rose lowered the basket to the ground. "Where exactly did you say the kitchen would be?"

Before he answered, Nate spied their two friends coming up the road in the farm wagon and waved at them with both arms. "Here come Bob an' Star. Do we have enough to share with them?"

Rose laughed. "By all means. They shall be our first guests in our new home. Help me spread the cloth, sweetheart."

While Robert parked his wagon in front of the barn and started across the meadow with Shining Star, Rose got out the platter of fried chicken and the loaf of fresh-baked bread and set it on the tablecloth with the not-so-welcome help of Jenny Ann.

"You two are just in time." Nate gestured toward the food. "As Rose said, our first guests."

Happy and relaxed even after a trip to the settlement, Star smiled at Rose. With a toss of her long hair, she pulled a bunch of colorful ribbons from the pocket of her sage chambray skirt. "Ribbons. For you and me and Jenny."

"Wonderful." Appreciating the thoughtful gift as much as Star's advancement in learning English, she patted the spot beside her. "Sit down. I want to hear about your day."

Once everyone was busy eating, Nate turned to Bob. "Any word in town about what the French are up to these days? Now that the rivers are thawed good, we should be hearin' somethin'."

"Aye." Robert wiped his mouth on his napkin. "Remember that Washington fella what was headed to Logstown an' Venanga with them letters? You know, from Governor Dinwiddie, askin' the Frenchies to leave? Well, hear tell he managed to escape by the skin of his teeth—an' we know how that feels. Folks along the seaboard have made him a big hero. The governor's sendin' him up to Frederick County on the Virginia side of the Delaware to raise a militia. An' he sent Bill Trent, Washington's tracker, farther south to Augusta County to raise another one.'"

Noticing Nate's keen interest in the news made Rose uneasy, but she kept quiet, waiting to hear what he had to say.

"Augusta County. Ain't that down where the Shenandoah splits off? Sounds like the governor's finally takin' things serious."

"That ain't all." Robert smirked. "He sent letters to every other governor, lettin' 'em know his plans, an' letters to all the tribes to take up the hatchet against the French."

"Good." Nate gave a thoughtful nod. "Insist they take one side or the other, not desert us like the Shawnees did."

"Frederick County ain't but ten miles away, across the river. What say we go give them boys a hand?"

The thing Rose feared most Bob had put into words. She turned troubled eyes to Nate.

He pulled her into a hug. "It's all right, honey-pie. I ain't goin' nowheres till we have the house all built, the crops planted, an' a garden in, just like we talked about. An' not till after we see your sisters an'—" His gaze shifted to Jenny, sitting in the middle of the tablecloth, chewing on a crust of bread in her little yellow dress.

Rose knew what he'd left unsaid. *And till we take Jenny up north to her relatives.*

"Right." Bob cut a glance to Star. "The war ain't goin' away anytime soon. We can always join up later. Oh. Speakin' of Rose's sisters, I brung back letters. The post rider come through last week."

Letters! Rose could hardly wait for Robert to pull them out of his linsey-woolsey shirt.

"This one's for you, Nate." Robert handed the first to him. "An' Rose, these're for you."

She quickly scanned the outside to see who they were from. Two were from England! She hadn't heard from her father since she'd left Bath. The others were from her sisters. "Would you excuse me for a few minutes?" Without waiting for an answer, she strolled away from her friends and walked down the hill. She knew she'd cry and didn't want them to see her tears.

She opened her father's first, and her eyes swam at the greeting penned in his familiar hand: *Dearly beloved daughter.* Blinking to clear her vision, she breathed with relief as she read of arrangements he'd made with his debtors to pay off the remainder of his debt.

> *Do not worry. . . Your brothers and I are working hard to become solvent again. Then every pence will go toward retrieving my darling girls. I will not rest until I see each of you happily situated once more.*

His second missive brought even more hope:

> *I have sought out a solicitor who was able to retrieve thirty of the fifty brooches Lord Ridgeway absconded with. Once I sell them, I should have funds enough to send for you girls within the year, the good Lord willing. . . .*

Rose hugged the stationery to her breast. Perhaps she'd done the right thing for Papa and the family after all. She herself would not return to England, but hopefully Mariah and Lily would be able to go home. Next she unfolded Lily's letter:

> *Dearest Rose,*
>
>   *I must send my deepest congratulations on your marriage. It filled my heart with joy to hear that you are happy and have a life of your own with a loving husband. That is my dream, as well, as I suppose it is for most girls. Perhaps someday I will find similar happiness.*
>
>   *I miss you so much, Rose. I long for your visit this spring. I know I shall love your Nate. After all, how could I not love the brave hunter who has made my dear sister so happy? We shall*

*have so much to talk about. I shall count the days until I can hug
you to my heart. Until then, do take care, and keep me in your
prayers, as I keep you always in mine. . . .*

Rose's heart crimped. Sweet, priceless Lily. How grand it would be to
show off big, handsome Nate, the husband she never would have had she
stayed in England.

With a happy sigh, she unfolded Mariah's missive:

Dear Rose,

*I was glad to hear from you. I assumed I would have
wonderful news to relate by now, that Colin and I had pledged
our love for one another. I know he cares for me as I do him, but
alas, we get only the smallest snatches of time together, a mere
moment here and there.*

*If Papa ever forwards money as he promised me, I shall buy
back my papers and room with another family nearby. Then
Colin will be able to visit me without the watchful eye of his
mother. I am sure he will propose then. Of course, an elopement
would be ever so romantic, do you not agree?*

Mariah, Mariah. Rose shook her head. It was imperative to get to the
girl soon and have a serious talk with her, if it wasn't already too late. She
read on:

*Speaking of romantic, I could hardly believe that you, the ever-so-
serious older sister, actually got married. You and not me. Who
would ever believe that?*

Rose rolled her eyes. Would that girl ever grow up? As disturbing as
it had been to see Mariah sold to a plantation owner, at least she'd been
placed in the home of a virtuous matron. Rose shot a prayer of thanks
heavenward. When she and Nate reached the plantation, she'd thank the
woman profusely.

"Rose! Rose!"

Glancing up from Mariah's closing words, she saw Nate hurrying toward her with Jenny riding high in the crook of his arm. He sported a grin from ear to ear while tears streamed down his face.

"What is it?" Alarm clutched Rose's stomach. Nate never cried.

"You're not gonna believe this." He held out a letter in his free hand. "It's from Jenny's grandparents. Seems old Mr. Wright got caught in a blizzard an' got frostbite. His lungs ain't so good now. He an' the missus had to move in with their son, who's already got a bunch of young'uns, an' the wife's with child. Mr. Wright says they're not able to take in another mouth to feed. He says if we're willin', they'd be pleased to have papers drawed up so's we can keep Jenny. Can you believe it? Jenny's ours. Ours!"

It was too good to be true. "Let me see that letter." Snatching it from his fingers, Rose scanned the words. Tears of joy sprang to her eyes, and she grabbed her two loves in a big hug, smothering them with kisses.

Finally able to gain control enough to speak, she dried her face on her apron. "This has to be the crowning moment of my life. To think I get you *and* Jenny. God is marvelous!" She held up all the letters. "And everyone in my family is doing fine—except maybe Mariah. Gorgeous, willful Mariah."

"Don't worry about her." Nate wrapped Rose in his free arm and kissed the top of her head. "We'll be goin' to see her soon enough. An' if God can make everything turn out this good for us, I'm sure He can whip that sister of yours into shape, too."

Rose looked up into the hazel eyes she so loved and laughed. "Quite right. Our God can do anything." Taking Jenny Ann out of Nate's arm, she twirled the little girl around, making her giggle. Then, getting misty-eyed again, she gazed up at her beloved, stalwart husband. "God has given me more happiness than I ever dreamed possible. No one can ask for more than that." Raising to tiptoe, she planted a kiss on his lips, just knowing it would bring out that mischievous smile of his.

She could never get enough of that.

Discussion Questions

1. When a crisis struck her family, Rose took matters into her own hands, but she was never sure she made the right decision. Have you ever made a rash decision, hoping to solve a problem, and ended up making it worse? How did you deal with it?

2. When Rose and her sisters arrived in the colonies, they were sold on the auction block like slaves. What are the advantages of being a bondservant rather than a slave? Any disadvantages?

3. Instead of starting a new life in America with her sisters, Rose was carted off into the wilderness. Did life ever take you somewhere you never wanted to go? What were the unexpected blessings you experienced? What were the negatives? How did the experience change you?

4. Rose's faith was built on a strong foundation. Though she did experience doubt from time to time, she remained close to God. Do you have a particular passage or verse from Scripture that you cling to in times of trouble? Are you aware of God's presence in your daily life?

5. Rose had settled nicely into her circumstances when she was faced with a new challenge—an orphaned baby to care for. Soon after that, her owner died. It's said that God doesn't give people more than they can handle. What are your feelings about that statement?

6. Which character in Rose's Pledge did you most closely identify with? Why?

7. When the circumstances of your life seem to contradict God's promise to work all things together for good, are you able to keep trusting Him, or do you tend to lose heart? Are you still able to worship God?

8. What characteristics that Rose possessed attracted Nate? How do you feel about the "unequal yoke" the Bible talks about in 2 Corinthians 6:14?

9. Nate had known the gospel from his childhood but wandered away from it. What things opened his eyes to his need to renew his faith?

10. Rose and Nate found their happy ending. Do you believe God has a happy ending in store for you? On what do you base that conviction?

MARIAH'S QUEST

DAUGHTERS OF HARWOOD HOUSE
Book Two

DEDICATION

For their infinite patience, encouragement, and tireless support during
the writing of this story, we lovingly dedicate this book to our families.
May the Lord's richest blessings be always upon them.

ACKNOWLEDGMENTS

The authors gratefully acknowledge the generous assistance provided by:
Elaine McHale
Fairfax Regional Library
Fairfax, VA

Her help in gathering necessary period data and maps
and in sharing her knowledge of various settings
and prominent figures who played a part in colonial America's
fascinating history was most sincerely appreciated.

Special thanks to:
Delia Latham
Robin Tomlinson

Their excellent help in critiquing the manuscript along the way,
proofreading, and adding polish was truly valuable.
May God bless them both.

Chapter 1

Baltimore, Maryland, 1753

Gentlemen! As I promised, I've saved the choicest for last."

Zachariah Durning, captain of the *Seaford Lady*, resembled an overstuffed goose in his ill-fitting dress uniform and powdered wig as he addressed the crowd of buyers on the Baltimore dock. His gold buttons threatened to pop when he puffed out his chest.

Mariah Harwood's heart pounded with excitement. . .and a mixture of dread and anxiety. She and her two sisters were about to be auctioned off as if they were no more than horses or cattle. But to whom?

For the past seven weeks aboard the huge ocean vessel, Mariah had held fast to the dream that some rich and stunningly handsome colonist would sweep her up in his arms and take her on a great adventure. Yet, standing on display before this assemblage of tradesmen like a flag on a flagpole, she knew she'd most likely be purchased by some uncouth man and end up scrubbing floors in a mean wife's kitchen for the next four years. Four crucial years. By the time she served out her indenturement, she'd be an old maid with rough, red hands.

She could not let that happen. She *would* not. After all, bearing a strong resemblance to her late mother, had she not always been considered the beauty of the family with her violet-blue eyes and black curls? And had she not turned down all of three marriage proposals in the recent past? She grimaced. If only she'd known then of the dire financial straits that would so unexpectedly befall her family and shatter all hopes of snaring a wealthy suitor.

"These three young lasses have been schooled in all the social graces, as well as the art of fine cooking," Captain Durning hollered for all to hear. "They can also read and do sums. Any one of 'em would make an ideal lady's companion or children's governess."

"Put up the one in blue," a fat man with bushy side-whiskers hollered. A gap in his waistcoat revealed a missing button, and the fingernails on his pudgy hands were chipped and dirty. "I'll bid on her."

Mariah gazed down at the fancy taffeta gown she'd donned that morning and swallowed. *I'm the one wearing blue!* What a stupid, romantic fool she'd been to deliberately sell herself into servitude for the inane reason that her chances of making a profitable match here in the colonies were likely to be far better than they'd been back home in England.

The captain reached down and hauled Mariah up onto the auctioneer's platform. "I'll expect a starting bid of no less than twenty-five pounds for this one."

Her heart in her throat, Mariah scanned the crowd sweltering beneath the June sunshine. Surely there must be a few, far more pleasing bidders than the sloppy old man who'd spoken up, men of higher quality—and hopefully far more attractive to the eye.

"Captain Durning!" she heard her older sister, Rose, challenge in her no-nonsense tone. "You agreed to sell us as a family." Determination glinted in the expressive, azure eyes she leveled on the commander of the ship, her fists planted on her slender hips.

Hope sprang anew inside Mariah. As forthright as Rose was in that sensible, nut-brown gown, she'd put an end to this travesty. Surely she would. She'd always done her utmost to look after the family to the best of her ability, putting their welfare far above her own.

But Durning didn't even bother to acknowledge honey-haired Rose. "What do I hear for the first bid?"

"I'll give ye twenty pounds." The paunchy onlooker raised a finger high. "Not a pence more."

Gritting her teeth, Mariah resumed her desperate search for a more promising individual.

"Twenty-one," came a voice at the back of the gathering.

Mariah turned her attention in the direction of that rich voice and caught a glimpse of a younger gentleman astride a long-legged bay. Her pulse skipped a beat. There he was! Just like in her dreams. Tanned and raven haired, and attired in a loose shirt and fitted breeches tucked into tall boots, he locked his dark eyes with hers. Entranced and enthralled by the fine figure he made atop his mount, Mariah willed him to outbid any others. *Please. . .please. . .*

"Twenty-two," she heard on the fringes of her consciousness as she continued to stare at the man she prayed would rescue her.

His mouth quirked into a half grin. "Twenty-three."

Trying to contain her hopeful smile, Mariah nibbled her lip.

"Mister Durning!" Rose interrupted more sternly. "I shall be forced to call the authorities if you do not honor the agreement you made with our father." A frown marred her otherwise feminine features but somehow only added to a beauty that radiated from within.

Mariah felt her smile wilt at the edges. Would the young gentleman part with enough funds for her *and* her sisters? The starting bid asked for her alone was far more than the captain had paid their father for all three of them.

"We have no written contract, wench," Durning spat, his florid complexion darkening as he glared down at Rose. "I'll thank ye to keep yer mouth shut."

"And I'll thank you to honor your word as a gentleman, sir." Rose had never been one to give up easily.

Mariah glanced again at the handsome rider at the rear of the crowd. He'd pushed his tricornered hat back, exposing features so stunningly perfect as to have been fashioned by an accomplished sculptor. His grin widened as his gaze remained focused on her alone. Her smile regained its strength. Perhaps there was hope, after all.

Nevertheless, the confrontation between the captain and her older sister continued. "What we have, shrew, is yer name on a legal document that says I have the right to sell the three of ye to whomever I please." Durning puffed out his bulging chest again. "And if ye don't keep quiet, I'll have ye locked in the hold of me ship until I complete the rest of me business."

"Not before I summon the port authorities." Rose whirled around, her expression rife with purpose.

The last thing Mariah wanted was to be parted from her sisters. . .but she could ill afford to lose her ardent bidder, either.

"Good sirs." The captain nodded to some men in the front. "Lay hold of this baggage and hold her whilst I fetch my men."

The insufferable cur actually intends to lock poor Rose in the hold? Mariah felt her own anger coming to the fore. The man's insensitivity was not to be borne.

One of the onlookers laughed as he and another fellow grabbed Rose's arms. "Don't fret, Cap'n. We'll see the lass stays put."

Trying to wrench free, but to no avail, Rose turned her fury on the two ruffians. "And I'll see you and your manhandling cohorts brought up before the magistrate."

Outraged at the injustice of seeing her sister being treated so roughly and held against her will, Mariah started forward to aid her, but the captain caught her arm and held her fast.

Their youngest sister, Lily, flaxen-haired and delicately formed, edged next to Rose and tugged on her ruffled half sleeve. "Please, Rose. Don't say anything more. They'll take you away." At a tender fourteen, Lily was too young and innocent to lose the sister who had mothered her since she was three years of age. Shy by nature, a flush on her fair cheeks matched the pale pink of her gown and accented the sprinkling of freckles across the bridge of her pert nose.

Rose's taut body slumped in defeat as the fight left her.

Mariah swung her attention back to her dream man and sighed her gratitude. He was still there, beholding her.

"I'll bid thirty pounds on the beauty in the blue frock." He tipped his head slightly in her direction.

Thirty pounds! No one had to tell Mariah that was an exorbitant amount to pay for four years of service.

"Thirty-one," came another voice on the opposite side of the crowd. With every fiber of her being, she willed her hero to bid more.

His grin widening with confidence, the young man hooked his leg over the pommel of his saddle, a sure sign he was prepared to stay as long as it took to win the bid. "Forty."

A murmur swept the crowd.

Such a high bid! And all for her. Truly he was her knight of the realm.

A long pause ensued. When no further bid was forthcoming, the captain gave a decisive nod. "Sold! To the gentleman on the fine stallion."

The handsome rider gave a triumphant laugh and nudged his mount forward, weaving through the crowd until he reached the platform. He reached out to Mariah.

With a nervous giggle, she moved to the edge and allowed him to pull her and her voluminous skirts onto the bay steed. His arms encircled her, and the scent of his bay rum cologne blended with the smell from the baking houses that provided bread and rolls to seagoing vessels. The man smelled every bit as good as he looked.

But leave it to Rose to ruin the moment. Marching right up to the two of them, she snatched a handful of Mariah's blue taffeta hem. "Come down from there this instant."

"Miss Harwood does have a point." Captain Durning nodded.

Mariah's breath caught. Surely he hadn't changed his mind about the sale.

"Ye'll not be taking that lass anywhere until there's hard cash in me hand and ye put yer signature on the indenturement." With a smug look, Durning turned to Rose. "Everything proper and legal."

Her lips in a grim line as she glared at the captain, Rose yanked on Mariah's skirt again.

Mariah had no recourse but to offer her new owner an apologetic smile and permit him to lower her to the ground, which he did, but ever so slowly. He then dismounted and came to stand beside her, enveloping her hand in his. Mariah sensed from the dedication in his expression that he would have paid whatever amount of money it took to purchase her. It was a heady notion.

Then a rather unsettling and unwelcome thought intruded, bringing her back to earth. This powerfully built man, however handsome and charming he appeared, did happen to be a total stranger. Why had he bought her? What exactly were his plans for her? For all she knew, he could be an abuser of women. Or worse!

As she tried to absorb the fact that she had no idea why a complete stranger would offer good money to purchase her papers, she felt Rose latch on to her arm and tug her away to stand between her and Lily. Now that her hand was no longer tucked inside her new owner's, Mariah missed the comforting warmth his grasp had provided.

She glanced over her shoulder to find him standing directly behind her. His dark brown eyes gazed down on her with a sympathetic smile. This man was not someone to be feared. Surely he had stepped wondrously, magically right out of her dearest dreams. She allowed herself a moment to admire his manly features.

So caught up was she in the moment, she scarcely noticed when her baby sister Lily was put on the block for sale and stood with head bowed, trying to be invisible. Nor did she feel concern that Rose was again acting like a mother hen and causing a humiliating fuss, arguing with Captain Durning. As the two events made their way into her consciousness, however, Mariah decided to use them to her advantage. With Rose otherwise occupied, she turned once more toward her gentleman. She certainly didn't want him to entertain second thoughts about the exorbitant bid he'd made. But the captain's voice drew her back to the moment.

"Sold to the fine gentleman in the front."

Mariah searched the crowd to find the individual who'd bought Lily.

Appearing to be in his late twenties, and attired in coarse, homespun clothing, the man was no gentleman of wealth. With dark brown hair and eyes of soft blue, he did have a kind face, though, and a tall, lean build similar to their own father's. More important, Rose seemed pleased, and so did Lily. At least a modicum of the younger girl's trepidation seemed to have eased.

"Hie thyself up here, wench." A sour scowl accompanied the captain's command, and Rose's smile lost its luster as the two ruffians who'd stayed her earlier bumped past Mariah and hoisted Rose onto the platform with boisterous laughter.

With all her older sister's discordant protests, Mariah knew Rose had made a spectacle of herself. This became even more evident when guffaws and a round of applause resounded from several quarters. How mortifying!

She checked to see her owner's reaction but saw that he was pre-occupied with toying with the wispy plume of her bonnet.

He came alongside her, now that Rose no longer hovered, and took her hand in his with a gentlemanly bow. "Allow me to introduce myself. My name is Colin. Colin Barclay, of Barclay's Bay Plantation."

Mariah smiled and gave a sweeping curtsy. "Pleased to meet you. I'm Mariah Harwood, daughter of the finest goldsmith and jeweler in Bath, at your service." As the irony of her statement dawned on her, she flashed a wry grin. "Quite literally, it would seem."

"And I yours." Colin accented his grand gesture by lifting her hand and brushing it softly with his lips.

Remembering Rose, Mariah shot a guilty glance up at her.

Her older sister had other worries at the moment. She stood rigidly beside the captain as he raised his voice again.

"Now, if ye want a full day's labor for yer money, this spinster here's the one yer lookin' fer. The female's five and twenty. In her prime. She's run an entire household since she was thirteen. Raised her four siblings, including two brothers, and ye've seen how the lasses here turned out." The reprobate cocked a self-satisfied brow.

Rose looked utterly devastated. Mariah's heart went out to her. In reality, Rose had been far more to her and the rest of the family than Captain Durning had expounded. The very selling of herself into servitude had been a desperate measure she'd taken upon herself to save their father from debtor's prison. She had intended only to sell herself, but Mariah and Lily had volunteered to accompany her for their own personal reasons, no matter how altruistic they'd considered themselves. Young Lily hadn't wanted to be parted from the only mother she could remember. And as for herself, well. . . Mariah turned another admiring look back at her handsome new owner.

"The wench's sisters may have virtues enough," someone yelled, "but this one's got the tongue of a fishwife!"

Laughter at poor Rose's expense again rang out. These unfeeling men were making cruel sport of her. . .even if the last remark did happen to be funny. Mariah couldn't squelch the smile that twitched her lips.

And Rose saw it.

Chagrined, Mariah quickly covered her mouth with her free hand as warmth climbed her cheeks.

Durning quieted the crowd with a raised arm and continued. "The woman's only actin' the way of any mother hen worth its feathers. She's tryin' to keep her little chicks tucked beneath her wings. Of the three of 'em, she's by far the most experienced worker."

Mariah was glad that the captain, the real deceiver, finally defended Rose.

The haggling started up in earnest but was interspersed with paltry comments. Someone said her hands looked soft; another said she and her sisters' clothes looked too fine. "Mayhap the lasses are more used to givin' orders than takin' 'em," one finally suggested. Mariah rolled her eyes.

By this time, even Durning himself appeared weary of the process. He hiked his pretentious bulk up and scowled at the speaker. " 'Tis true, the Harwood sisters come from excellent stock on t'other side of the water. To see any of 'em put to work as simple scrubwomen would be a pure waste. This one in particular is accomplished at preparin' tasty foods. She can put every spice ever brought to the British Isles to proper use."

That remark accelerated the bidding to such a pace Mariah couldn't discern the source of each offer as they rose a pound at a time to nineteen.

Then from the rear came a piercing high voice. "Did ye say the lass is a good cook?"

"Aye."

"I'll gi' ye fifty pound fer her."

"Sold!"

Astounded murmurings swept through the gathering, and Mariah swung to see who'd offered such an unheard-of price without so much as a second's hesitation. Her mouth dropped open in shock.

The buyer climbing down from a loaded wagon was by no means a fine gentleman. His clothing and floppy hat looked soiled and disheveled. As his scuffed boots reached the decking and he turned to face forward, she saw that he was a squat older man who couldn't possibly have bathed in months. In a deplorably smudged and droopy ruffled shirt, he kneaded his frizzled beard and headed straight for the platform.

And straight for Rose.

Following the captain as he stepped down to meet the unkempt man, Lily rushed to Rose's side. "What are we to do, Rose? You cannot go with that nasty lout. He's horrid."

In complete agreement with Lily, Mariah drew close to her sisters. "We must not allow that disgusting creature to take you off to heaven knows where. I shall have Colin speak to Captain Durning on your behalf."

Despite her own unbelievable turn of fate, Rose's brows dipped into a frown at Mariah's words. "Colin is it? And I suppose *Colin* is already addressing you by your given name, as well."

Mariah's hackles went up. "Upon my word, Rose. This is not the time for such trivial nonsense." She whirled away to fetch her own stylish buyer.

Right on her heels, Rose caught up with her and wrapped a staying arm around her as they approached Colin Barclay. She spoke to him in her forceful tone. "Sir, before you sign my sister's papers, I'll thank you to relate exactly what duties will be expected of her in your employ."

What a crude thing to imply. Mariah felt her face grow hot with embarrassment. She lowered her gaze to the splintery planks of the dock. Embarrassed or not, she wanted to hear his answer, to set her own mind at rest.

"To be quite truthful, Miss Harwood," he said, his voice smooth and unperturbed, "I have no duties in mind for her whatsoever."

At his odd reply, Mariah peered up from beneath her bonnet's brim to see his relaxed and smiling face as he continued.

"But I assure you, my mother shall be most pleased at my finding someone of your sister's refined qualities to be her companion."

What a perfect response to Rose's impudent inquiry, Mariah mused, marveling inwardly.

Her older sister looked stunned. "You. . .you bought her for your mother?"

"Why, yes. Of course. Surely you didn't think me the sort to have something else in mind for the lass." He arched his brows in pure innocence.

Mariah had a hard time keeping her mirth to herself.

Rose, however, was unimpressed. "Then I'm sure you'll not mind pledging to see my dear, virtuous sister placed into your mother's watchcare before the sun sets this day. And you'll see to her religious instruction as well."

That was beyond rude. *"Rose."*

Colin placed a calming hand on Mariah's arm as he met Rose's eyes. "You have my most solemn word, miss."

Somewhat mollified, Rose withdrew a shard of lead and a scrap of paper from her pocket. "Might I ask where I might post my sisterly correspondence? I should hate to lose touch with one of the only two relatives I possess on this continent."

"Of course. Send it to Barclay's Bay Plantation."

Mariah swelled with pleasure as the conversation receded into the background. Colin Barclay must be the owner of one of those sprawling, prosperous farms she'd heard that so many of the British aristocracy had come to America to establish. Why, he could quite possibly be related to a lord, or even the king!

A sudden gasp from Rose interrupted her musings. *"A day's ride?"*

Letting out an impatient breath at having missed some pertinent details, Mariah suddenly recalled her older sister's impending dire fate.

She turned to Colin. "Pray, sir, forgive me, but I'm afraid my sister and I have a matter of much deeper concern. We must not allow that swarthy old man to take her away. Would you please speak to the captain? Implore him to withdraw those proceedings."

For the first time, Colin's expression turned grave. "My dear Mariah, the man bid fifty pounds."

"Yes, we're aware of that." She offered her most pleading smile. "However, if you would just try."

He gave a sad shake of his head. "I regret to say all closing bids are final. I do find it rather astounding, though, that one so unkempt should have that amount of ready cash on hand. One can only wonder how he came by such funds."

So nothing could be done. Mariah caught Rose's hand and gave it an empathetic squeeze. Still, she could not bear to think the worst, especially after exchanging addresses with her sisters and learning that correspondence to Rose could be sent to the Virginia and Ohio Company in Alexandria. From what Colin had told them, that was a town not far from his plantation. "We shall keep in close touch," she assured Rose. "Everything will be just fine." It would. It had to be.

Mariah's optimism prevailed as the moneys were paid and signatures recorded, as she again was lifted up to Colin on his finely bred horse, and as she waved a fond farewell to her two forlorn-looking sisters. Her spirits continued to stay high as she rode through Baltimore with Colin pointing out the many mercantiles and shops of what appeared to be a very prosperous city. Truly it proved to be far beyond her own expectations.

But once they passed by the last sprinking of buildings in the bright midmorning sunlight and she found herself enshrouded by eerie, shadowed woods and totally alone with this strange man, she came to her senses.

As glib as Colin Barclay—if that was even his true name—had been as he'd reassured Rose of his good intentions, Mariah could now imagine any lie might roll as sweetly and smoothly from this charmer's lips—this man who now held her captive within his arms.

Who was he? Where exactly was he taking her? And for what purpose?

Unable to imagine what uncertainties awaited her when they reached their destination, Mariah's fears raced ahead of her through the primeval forest in this unknown land.

Chapter 2

M ariah. . .that is a beautiful name."

They'd ridden through the dim woods in silence for a time. No sounds accompanied the steady *clop-clop* of the horse's hooves other than the rush of wind through the treetops and the trilling of birds, so Colin Barclay's richly modulated voice startled Mariah. He had a sort of lazy-sounding accent she found quite pleasant to the ear. She struggled to maintain a calm demeanor before answering. "So I've been told."

Neither spoke for another quiet span, until Mariah decided that conversing might help to dispel some of her unease, particularly if she selected the topic. "My father chose to call my other sisters by rather fanciful biblical names—Rose of Sharon and Lily of the Valley. But because I favored one of my late aunts, I was named after her."

"It suits you perfectly." His mouth was so close to her ear, she felt the warmth of his breath. "Mariah. . . Your name fairly floats on the breeze like a will-o'-the-wisp."

She answered cheerily, hoping to keep the moment light. "My, but aren't you the poetic one. Speaking of families—"

"I didn't know I was." His breath feathered across her ear again.

"Speaking of families," Mariah repeated evenly as she sat up straighter, "I've got two brothers at home in Bath. Have you any brothers or sisters?"

She heard him inhale, and the leather saddle creaked as he adjusted his position. "I'm the only surviving son. I do have three younger sisters, however. The youngest is eight, and the oldest is fifteen."

Mariah gave a small nod. "As you must have concluded from the speech that dreadful Captain Durning gave regarding the three of us, our mother went to be with the Lord more than a decade ago, rest her soul. Are both your parents still living?"

"Yes." A low chuckle rumbled from his chest. "They're both very much alive."

"Then you are truly blessed." With that third reference to her family's faith, Mariah hoped to quell any untoward plans Colin Barclay might have. Though she was by no means as ardent as Rose in her religious beliefs, Mariah did retain certain standards, and she knew her actions on the auction platform had stretched propriety more than a little.

Gazing forward, she noticed they were about to break out of the trees, into the safer light of day. She spotted a river just ahead of them on the wagon-rutted road and saw a ferry dock jutting out at the bottom of the bank. A light wind stirred shallow whitecaps here and there among the current. "Will we be crossing to the other side?"

"Aye, as a matter of fact, we will. We'll cross this river along with several others before we reach my place."

"So many?" Mariah frowned. Just how far away was this place of his? And would the daylight hold out until they reached their destination?

"Yes. Quite a few. We'll dismount for the ride over, give Paladin a chance to rest. It'll take us almost the entire day to reach the plantation at the leisurely pace we've been travelin'," he drawled. "Since we're ridin' double, I don't want to put too much on the boy." He leaned harder against Mariah to administer a pat to the bay's muscled dark brown neck. "He's bred for speed. I've won some pretty pennies with him."

"He certainly is a fine-looking animal." Mariah deftly tilted forward to keep at least the semblance of a proper distance between her and her owner. So the man was a gambler. How many other vices did he have?

As if taking her subtle hint, Colin straightened his posture. "Yes, we're quite proud of our stable."

We? Was the blighter married? He couldn't possibly be, could he? But then it was entirely feasible there may not be a mother, either. It might be advantageous to plan some sort of hasty escape, should one become necessary. He'd reported that Alexandria, where Rose was headed, was a short distance from his plantation. She might be able to seek a safe haven there with her older sister. In any case, Mariah knew she would need her luggage. "With such a distance to your plantation, do you think my trunks will arrive by wagon before the morrow?"

"Of course. I gave the driver a generous tip. He's probably not more than a mile or so behind us." He paused. "Speaking of those trunks—if the gowns they contain are even remotely as fashionable as the one you're wearin', you could have sold them and paid your own fare to Baltimore, thereby avoidin' an indenturement entirely. Not that I'm complainin' at all."

Picking up on the eager note in his tone, Mariah decided she'd be relieved when they were able to dismount so she could see his face and discern his true merit. She tried for a bright lilt when she spoke. "Surely you know a young gentlewoman could not possibly present herself in public without an adequate wardrobe." Then, recalling the way Rose had ravaged all their best frocks, she couldn't help a moment's grousing. "I do grieve, however, that my sister felt compelled to sell my two most elegant evening gowns."

"Hmm. If you don't mind my askin'," Colin said as they started down the bank, "what dire calamity befell your family that necessitated your having to sail across the ocean? I believe you said your father is a goldsmith and that you resided in a most fashionable resort, did you not?"

"Ah, yes. The calamity." Mariah shook her head, feeling her blood heat at the memory. "The cause was the untimely death of a rapscallion young nobleman. The young lord had purchased dozens of very expensive brooches on account for his many lady friends, for which my father was never reimbursed. After the scoundrel's death, his uppity skinflint uncle refused to honor his nephew's enormous debt. In turn, my father was not able to pay his."

"I see. Say no more for the moment," Colin spoke quietly as they reached the dock. "Ferry operators have the loosest tongues in the colonies."

As Colin swung down from the stallion, Mariah eyed the wiry ferrymen, one at the mule-drawn wheel and the other opening the front gate of the docked flatboat. She wished she could question them, learn from their lips who exactly her handsome owner was. But as he took his time lifting her down, then wrapped an arm about her waist before leading the horse onto the raft, she doubted she'd have the chance to question anyone.

Mariah had to admit that Colin Barclay had not lied about the distance, at least. They'd passed numerous plantations containing miles of rolling, cultivated farmland and several charming hamlets brimming with a veritable symphony of flowers that took her breath away with their brilliant hues. The colonists appeared every bit as industrious as the folks back home in Britain. She suppressed a weary sigh when Colin finally suggested they stop at a roadside inn to rest the horse and partake of a meal. The horse wasn't the only one who needed a rest. Hours of bumping her bottom against the hard leather saddle had taken its own toll. Would she be able to manage anything akin to a ladylike walk once her feet touched solid ground?

Colin reined their mount onto a gravel-lined drive that fronted a two-story fieldstone building with royal-blue shutters and double doors. A sign hanging from a signpost read KNIGHT'S REST INN. He swung down to the ground and reached up to assist Mariah. The weakness in her legs did make it difficult to stand, momentarily, and she more than appreciated the way he steadied her with a strong arm.

A freckle-faced lad came running from around the side of the inn, his floppy cloth cap almost tumbling from his copper hair with each footfall. "Mr. Barclay! Back already?" Then, spying Mariah, he slowed to a stop and gawked at her. "Oh. Uh. . .I better see to your horse."

Grinning, Colin flipped him a coin. "I'd appreciate that, Billy."

Even outside the structure, Mariah could detect a delicious mixture of food smells emanating from within, and her stomach came close to rumbling. Thank heaven it wouldn't be another moldy shipboard meal awaiting her here! And the boy had called Colin by name, so surely that had to be her owner's true identity. Mayhap everything else he'd told her would prove to be true, as well. Perhaps he actually did have a mother to whom he would deliver her.

As he opened one of the blue doors and escorted Mariah inside, she determined that by the time the meal was over, she'd learn whether or not he had a wife, or her name wasn't Mariah Harwood.

"Good day, Mr. Barclay." The exuberant greeting came from a flaxen-haired serving girl balancing a tray of soiled dishes against her shapely hip as Colin escorted Mariah across the inn's low-ceilinged common room. The girl's gaze then swung to the beauty on his arm, and her smile flattened.

The server had every reason to be envious, Colin conceded. Any woman who entered Mariah Harwood's sphere would place a distant second. Long lashes framed her stunning violet eyes under tapered brows, and beneath her straw bonnet, silky brown-black curls caressed her slender shoulders. He could hardly keep his eyes from focusing on the soft, rosebud lips that turned up at the corners. The English beauty was as much a champion as Paladin. "Where would you like us to sit, Peggy?"

Her attention returned to Colin, and she flopped her free hand in a casual gesture. "Anywheres. We ain't too busy this time of day. Will you be wantin' a meal?"

"Yes. And some cool cider, if you please."

The ruffle on her mobcap bobbed with her nod as she carted the soiled dishes to the kitchen.

Colin figured that if they chose to sit at one of the long wooden tables occupying the center of the room, some bloke might scoot in next to his lovely companion. Wanting to keep her all to himself, he seated Mariah at a small square table by a window, then took the opposite chair while she settled her skirts about her. Only a sprinkling of other patrons talked among themselves as they enjoyed their food. None seemed to pay Colin and Mariah any mind.

"I hope I don't reek of horse too much," Mariah commented, wrinkling her nose. "That serving girl, Peg, didn't seem too pleased with me."

Colin chuckled. "My dear Mariah! You are a star that outshines all other young maidens. I would imagine you'd be used to that sort of reaction by now."

The small ivory plume on her bonnet dipped as she gifted him with a coy tilt of her head. "La, but you do flatter me."

"Truth is not flattery."

"That may be so. However, my sister Rose never ceases to remind me that true beauty is not outward but comes from within."

He sat back and grinned. "Ah, yes. The valiant Rose. She makes quite the impression on one."

Mariah's tapered brows knitted closer as her expression filled with dismay. "Dear Rose. Having to go with that grimy oaf who bought her. I cannot believe she's bonded to someone like that awful man. I do hope she will fare all right."

Reaching across the table, Colin covered Mariah's smaller hand with his. "Don't fret. Your sister seems to be a stalwart sort. And I'm sure we saw that fellow at his worst. Since he works for a fur company, he most likely just arrived from the wilderness. Once he reaches home, his missus will no doubt make sure that he's scrubbed down good and proper."

"Oh, my." Mariah sighed with longing. "I've not had a real soak in a tub since we departed England." Twin spots of color suddenly sprang to life on her cheeks. She jerked her hand from beneath his and covered her mouth, her eyes wide with shock. "I cannot believe I uttered something so unseemly in the presence of a gentleman. Pray, do forget my rash words."

"Never fear, my dear Mariah," he said gently. "Unseemly or not, I'll see that you have your wish the moment we arrive at home."

His remark seemed to aid the return of her composure, as she visibly relaxed. "Bless you." She paused. "I certainly wouldn't want to cause your wife undue inconvenience."

Colin couldn't help but chuckle at her not-so-subtle attempt to gain personal information. "I have no wife, I'm sorry to say. . .nor even a betrothed, much to the dismay of my matchmaking mother."

He caught the barest hint of a smile playing with a corner of Mariah's rosy lips just as Peggy arrived. The serving girl bore a platter loaded with tall glasses of cider and plates heaping with shepherd's pie, along with generous chunks of crusty bread. Setting it down, she distributed the various items without meeting either of their eyes and quickly swung away, her serviceable indigo skirt flaring with her movements.

Mariah seemed oblivious to the girl as she immediately picked up her fork and speared a bit of meat. Obviously her ladyship wasn't too coy to reveal she was as hungry as he was. Suddenly, however, she stopped, her fork posed midair. "Do forgive me. I was so caught up in the delicious scent of real food after the sorry ship's fare we were forced to endure that I completely forgot my manners. You must think me a heathen, not waiting for you to bless our food."

She expected him to pray aloud? In this public place? A quick glance around revealed that the other customers didn't even know he and Mariah were there, but from the corner of his eye he could see Peggy observing them. Still, he couldn't allow this lovely Englishwoman to think a Virginia gentleman was any less a Christian than she. "Shall we bow our heads?" Even as he said the words, he felt heat climbing his neck. "Father in heaven, we thank You for this hearty meal. And thank You," he tacked on for good measure, "for Mariah Harwood's safe arrival to our shores. We know it had to be Your providence that brought me to the Baltimore wharf at the very moment she was most in need. In Jesus' name. Amen."

"Amen." After her echoing whisper, Mariah met his eyes, her own filled with questions. "May I ask what brought you to the docks so far from your home?" She sliced a bit of the pie's potato crust.

"Horses. I delivered a mare and her foal to a man about to embark by ship to Bermuda. I made certain the animals were safely aboard and then left. . .and that's when I saw you in your lovely blue gown and bonnet."

"I see." With a smile, she lifted her food to her mouth.

Colin slathered butter on a chunk of bread and took a bite, wondering how his father would take the news that forty pounds of the horse money had been spent to purchase a bond servant they didn't need. Then he realized his father was the least of his worries. The biggest challenge ahead was how to get Mariah into the house past his mother. A slow smirk tickled his lips. Of course, he could rent her a room across the river in Georgetown. Digging into his slice of shepherd's pie, he glanced up at the stunningly beautiful, but rather prim, young lady across from him. No. No matter how much she'd flirted with him from upon the auction block, she'd actually stiffened whenever he'd moved too close to her during their ride here. No doubt she'd balk at the very idea of being his mistress. . .delicious though the notion might be.

He had no other choice. He had to take her home with him to the plantation. Taking a sip of cider, he mulled over the story he'd concocted for Mariah's sister, how he'd bought her for his mother. The more he thought about it, the more he surmised that perhaps it was just the ticket.

"Mariah," he ventured after a few more thought-filled swallows of his drink, "I noticed when you signed your name to the bond that you had lovely penmanship. Did you, by chance, handle any business correspondence for your father?"

She blotted her lips on her napkin. "Why, yes. I did. And because of my handwriting, I also answered the various invitations our family received to social engagements."

Excellent. "And I'm sure you possess many other accomplishments, as well. The art of stitchery, perhaps."

A frown creased her smooth brow. "Stitchery. Such a tedious endeavor. I'll allow I can do it adequately, if I must, but I much prefer playing music for others to stitch by."

Good. Good. "You play an instrument, then."

"I play two, in fact. The flute and the harpsichord. I can also play the cello and violin a bit, if need be."

Even better!

"But alas, Rose sold my flute when she sold my prettiest frocks, as well as forfeited my dowry." Her lips thinned to an angry line; then with a sigh, she relaxed and mustered a weak smile. "No sense crying over spilt milk, as they say. I must learn to embrace whatever the Good Lord has in store for me."

Colin reached an empathetic hand across the table to cover hers again. "Be assured I will do all in my power to make your introduction to our fair land as enjoyable as possible." He had to admit it did sound good and was easy to say. But getting Mariah past his formidable mother and comfortably ensconced in their home would take far more effort and ingenuity. . .if it were even possible.

Chapter 3

Colin felt Mariah inhale deeply and knew she was about to speak.

"Since we took leave of Baltimore, we've passed through quite a few farms and plantations surrounded by forest, and a scant number of small villages. Is Alexandria merely another hamlet, or is it, perchance, a city?"

He reveled in her British accent and liked listening to her lyrical voice. . .almost as much as he enjoyed holding her within his arms. He only wished he'd been able to hold her close during the numerous ferry rides, particularly the last one, across the Potomac. They had arrived in Virginia at last. "Alexandria isn't a city like Baltimore, but it does boast a fine little string of shops. I'm afraid we won't be traveling into the town this evening, however. The crossroad just ahead runs alongside the river and edges our plantation."

"And how much farther do we still have to go?" she asked over her shoulder.

Colin sensed her weariness. A ride on horseback from the port of Baltimore was a challenging distance for even an experienced rider, and added to her ordeal on the auction block and the ensuing parting with her sisters; she'd had a long, trying day. "Less than an hour." He glanced at the sinking sun. "We should arrive home in time for supper. I'm honored to report that our cook happens to be one of the best in the county."

A slight tip of her head acknowledged the information.

Much of his uneasiness over having purchased Mariah had dispelled during the hours since leaving the roadside inn in Blandensburg. Now as they turned east onto the river road, he mentally tallied the reasons for his confidence. The young Englishwoman was a perfect fit for his family. Besides the excellence of her education, her every mannerism was grace itself. His sisters could learn a lot about being accomplished young ladies from Mariah. And best of all, she spoke with the cultured accent his mother continually tried to instill in the rest of the family.

He smiled to himself. Coming from a Boston merchant background, his mother considered the more relaxed drawl of a Virginian quite common. "*Quite common, indeed,*" she'd told them all hundreds of times. He and his pa strove to speak properly whenever they were in her presence. She was certain to appreciate having Mariah around.

Tilting his head a bit, he studied the delicate curve of Mariah's very tempting neck. Even if it weren't so tempting, four years' secretary and tutor service for a paltry forty pounds sterling was an astounding bargain. Besides, he was a grown man. He'd be twenty-five in a few months. High time he stopped allowing Mother to question his every decision.

"If I might ask, how do you plantation folk pass leisure time, living so far from a city?" Mariah asked, the musical lilt in her voice pleasuring him yet again.

Colin recognized that, as a stranger in a strange land, she needed to be put at ease. He gave a light chuckle. "You won't be bored, I can assure you. We have parties and afternoon teas and do almost everything our more sophisticated town dwellers do. If there happens to be an interesting play or musicale in one of the larger cities, we don't find the distance overly daunting. We go downriver to the port and catch one of the coastal packets that ply the waters between our cultural centers." For a moment he envisioned himself having this lovely Englishwoman on his arm wherever an activity might take them, a delightful possibility.

Mariah nodded, then straightened her spine. "There's a rider coming toward us. I think he's trying to get your attention."

Leaning to peer around her, Colin spied Dennis Tucker, his lifelong chum from the neighboring plantation, waving an arm. He groaned inwardly at the bad timing. With the young man's golden-boy looks and natural charm, the two of them were forever in competition when it came to the local belles, and Tuck would definitely be interested in Mariah.

As his friend rode up to intercept them, Colin raised a reluctant hand in acknowledgment. "I'd hoped to keep you to myself a bit longer," he said under his breath near Mariah's ear, "but. . ."

As expected, Dennis wasted no time in filling his hooded hazel eyes with the sight of the English beauty. "Thought you'd be in Baltimore a few more days, Colin." His lips quirked into a teasing grin. "I say. Looks like you spent your last farthing, too." With his focus still on Mariah, he reached up and removed the plantation hat from his sun-streaked blond hair. "Good afternoon, milady. Dennis Tucker at your service. And it appears you are in serious need."

"What do you mean by that?" Colin interjected before Mariah could respond to the interloper and instruct him in the art of proper introductions.

"It's obvious, isn't it?" A smirk added a glint to his eyes as he edged his mount closer. "For someone who set out with a wealth of horses the last time I saw him, you somehow managed to lose all but one. Why else would a damsel with the face of an angel be crowded onto Paladin with a man so unworthy of her undeniable beauty?"

Colin ground his teeth in irritation. "Tuck, allow me to introduce you to Miss Harwood, our houseguest. And now if you'll excuse us, we're in a bit of a hurry and must be on our way. You know how Eloise gets in a tizzy whenever a family member is late for supper."

Reaching for Mariah's hand, Dennis swept it up and brought it to his mouth. "Miss Harwood. The pleasure is all mine."

Colin reined his mount away, forcing his friend to release his hold.

"Till we meet again, miss," Dennis said with a gallant tip of his head. Replacing his hat, he shifted his gaze to Colin. "Before you rush off, I was wondering if you'd heard anything significant regarding that business up north—about those French soldiers heading down into the Ohio Valley. You'd think Governor Clinton in New York would assume his duty and do something to stop them." His attention drifted back to Mariah. "After all, we have our womenfolk to think of. . .especially our very loveliest ones."

Mariah swiveled toward Colin with a puzzled expression. "Are the French on the verge of an invasion? We had no word of this in England."

"It's nothing to trouble yourself about. Dennis is referring to some turmoil brewing hundreds of miles from here over trading rights with the Indian tribes."

She relaxed and turned forward again.

Dennis flashed a sheepish smile. "I must apologize, miss. I wouldn't dream of causing such a lovely lady a second's distress. In fact—"

"In fact," Colin interrupted, taking a firmer grip on Paladin's reins, "any more delay and we'll surely be late for supper. We must press on. No doubt you have an appointment to keep yourself, since you're headin' toward town."

"Indeed. I was on my way to the Pattersons' for dinner and cards. Lexie and Mary Ann invited me yesterday after church." He continued to ogle Mariah. "I'd venture to say they'd be pleased if you two would join us. You know the Pattersons always put on a generous spread."

"Another time, Tuck." Colin nudged his mount into motion. "We're expected at home."

"I'll drop by tomorrow, then, to hear the latest from Baltimore," his friend persisted.

Colin suppressed a groan and spurred Paladin to a faster pace.

⚯

The setting sun had turned the river into a glorious amber ribbon by the time the horse veered onto a rambling lane shaded by towering oak trees. Observing the sprawling fields on either side, Mariah studied the large, brownish-green leaves of the crop Colin had told her was tobacco. Until this moment, the only tobacco she'd seen had been in small pouches Papa had used to fill his pipe.

As her gaze drifted ahead, she saw a magnificent, two-story white house with black shutters, sitting like a jewel amid stately trees and gardens. Pristine round columns fronted a porch that extended across the anterior. Her heart swelled with joy. This beautifully situated mansion was to be her new home!

Colin had spoken only the truth. He had not lied about his name or where he lived. This incredibly handsome man truly was her Prince Charming. . .everything a girl could want. And he was attracted to *her*.

As the horse picked up its pace, obviously eager to reach the stable, Mariah couldn't help but smile. The animal was no more eager than she was.

"We're almost there," Colin announced, taking a firmer hold on the reins to keep Paladin from breaking into a trot. "I do hope my home pleases you."

"It does. Very much. It is breathtakingly lovely." But even as she uttered the words, a disturbing thought spoiled the moment. As an indentured servant, how much of the grace and comforts of this elegant home would she be permitted to enjoy? Thus far, Colin had treated her like an honored guest, not a bonded worker. *Dear Father in heaven*, she finally remembered to pray, *I quite forgot to place myself in Your care. Please make my dearest dream come true. Amen.* With a twinge of guilt, she imagined Rose would view such a prayer as a selfish request. But surely the Lord wanted good things for His children, didn't He?

Mariah filled her eyes with the splendor of the flower-bedecked fountain gracing the center of the circle drive as they neared the mansion.

On their approach, a young girl sprang up from one of the chairs on the veranda and ran through the open doorway. "Mother! Poppy! Come and look! Colin's back, and he's bringin' a woman with him!"

Behind Mariah, Colin emptied his lungs with a grunt. "That was Amy, our little snitch. I vow, she's worse than a town crier."

Before Mariah could respond, people started pouring out of the house. A tall, distinguished, bearded man and two girls—one who appeared about Lily's age and one a bit younger. The threesome stood staring in surprise from the edge of the porch.

Surprised, but not dismayed, Mariah hoped with bated breath.

Then a slender, gracefully elegant, and handsome woman attired in rich turquoise brocade stepped outside. Mariah knew immediately where Colin had inherited his good looks, from his raven hair to his dark brown eyes. Truly the woman would have been the belle of the ball in her younger years—the belle of *any* ball.

As the girl Colin called Amy came alongside her mother, Mariah realized that all three daughters had inherited their father's complexion. Each of them had varying shades of golden blond hair, while his held a smattering of silver among the strands.

"Colin, my dear," the woman said as she started down the wide gray steps, "we didn't expect you home for several more days." Her gaze then centered on Mariah, and she offered a decidedly practiced smile, more polite than warm.

The extra tension Mariah felt in Colin's arms as he assisted her to the ground added to her renewed trepidation. She hurriedly smoothed down her hopelessly wrinkled skirt. Undoubtedly it smelled of horse. She swallowed as Colin dismounted.

As the rest of the family continued to watch from atop the stairs, Mistress Barclay reached the landing and stepped toward Mariah with a hand outstretched in a gesture of greeting. "Welcome, my dear. This is a pleasant surprise."

Mariah curtsied the best she could, considering her wobbly, saddle-weary legs. "Thank you, madam. 'Tis my pleasure."

The older woman tilted her intricately coifed head in question. "I do not believe you are one of our local gentry, are you?"

"No, Mistress Barclay. I was born in Bath, England. I've only just arrived in the colonies."

"How delightful." Her smile widened. She turned to her family as they came to join them. "I should like you to meet my husband, Eldon. And these are our lovely daughters, Victoria, Heather, and our youngest, Amanda." Each of the girls bobbed a curtsy in turn.

"I'm very pleased to meet all of you," Mariah said, offering a smile.

"But everyone calls me Amy," the youngest drawled, crowding in front of the others.

"Or Brat," Victoria, the oldest, added, rolling her eyes.

As Amy pursed her lips and turned to retort, Mariah interceded. "Which do you prefer, Amy or Amanda?"

The youngster looked up at her. "The way it sounds when you say it, either would be real fine."

"*Really* fine," her mother corrected.

The girl flicked a swift, irritated glance in her mother's direction. "Either name is *splendidly* fine." She fluttered a hand in a theatrical flare.

Mariah had to admit the child was a bit of an imp.

Colin moved alongside her just then. "Mother, Father, I'd like to present Miss Mariah Harwood. She and her family are recent arrivals to our fair land."

"Harwood." Mistress Barclay turned to her husband. "My dear, I don't believe you've mentioned a new family in the neighborhood by that name."

Mariah moistened her lips, intending to clear up the misunderstanding, but an African slave stepped out of the front door just then. Her dark head, swathed in red calico, nodded to Colin's mother. "Mistress Barclay," she announced in a drawl more pronounced than Amy's, "suppa' is served."

"Thank you, Pansy. And we'll be needing two more place settings."

"Yessum." She switched her expressive dusky gaze to Colin. "Welcome home, Masta Colin. We wasn't 'spectin' y'all back so soon."

As the servant returned inside, Colin's father kneaded his trim Van Dyke beard and addressed him. "That's true, son. We weren't. Did the transfer go as planned?"

"Yes, sir."

"We'll have no business talk for now." Colin's mother threaded her arm through Mariah's and started for the steps. "I should like to get further acquainted with our lovely guest."

Mariah gulped in dismay. Guest! They had no idea she was actually purchased help. This would not do at all. "Mistress Barclay, I don't think I should—"

"Miss Harwood is concerned that she smells a touch horsey," Colin piped in, speaking over her.

His mother chuckled softly. "I'm afraid she'll find that's quite normal around here. We can, however, remedy the situation." Releasing her hold on Mariah, she turned back to her oldest daughter. "Victoria, dear, would you please show our guest upstairs so she can freshen up a bit? We'll delay dinner a few minutes. And Colin, you don't exactly smell like a rose, yourself."

He laughed and ushered Mariah and his sister inside.

Entering the marble-floored foyer and noting the exquisite crystal chandelier overhead as they approached a grand, graceful walnut staircase, Mariah turned and shot him a meaningful look. Wasn't he ever going to tell his family what she truly was? To her dismay, he and Victoria ignored her and exchanged casual comments while mounting the stairs.

As she reached the top landing, Mariah forgot everything except what lay before her eyes. These people were wealthy beyond all expectation. A delightful sitting area overlooked the tastefully appointed foyer below, where huge urns of fragrant summer flowers topped mahogany pedestals situated between gilt-framed family portraits. Her assessment of the splendor was interrupted as Colin took his leave and strode into one of the rooms down the hall.

"This way," Victoria said pleasantly and led her into a bedroom easily twice the size as the one Mariah and Lily had shared back home.

Mariah barely concealed her awe as she beheld the utterly feminine bedchamber obviously belonging to the two older sisters. Matching brass beds with frilly canopies, one done up in pale pink, the other in soft lavender, were separated by a carved washstand. A pair of armoires faced each other across the expanse of the room, dark spots against the floral wallpaper.

Victoria led her to the commode, bearing a hand-painted pitcher and bowl. Lace-edged white cloths for washing and drying hung on either side of a large oval looking glass. "I'll help you out of that gown so you can refresh yourself."

"Thank you." Mariah observed Colin's sister's reflection as the girl gently undid the lacing in the back of her gown. Such sweet features housed those enormous azure eyes. A yellow ribbon that matched her flounced day gown held thick golden curls off her face as she met Mariah's gaze in the glass.

"I must say, your gown is quite stylish," Victoria admitted. "Is it what they're wearing in England this season?"

Mariah nodded. "It's one of my newer frocks. But I'm afraid that for now a good brushing will have to disburse all the travel dust. My trunks won't arrive until later this evening."

"Not at all. You can wear something of mine—that is, if you don't mind wearing one not quite so up to date."

"How kind of you, Victoria. I'm sure whatever you loan me will do nicely."

Dipping one of the washing cloths into the bowl, Mariah squeezed out most of the water and placed the cool dampness to her throat.

"Do people really go to Bath just to take baths?" a childlike voice asked.

Mariah caught reflections of the two younger girls in the mirror. They had come in without her notice. She grinned at them, then continued her ablutions. "The baths are large indoor pools where a number of people can benefit from them all at one time. The waters come hot out of the ground and contain healing minerals that attract older folk with aching joints. In season, the city is filled with music and dramas, and young maidens stroll about with their friends, hoping to catch the eye of dashing young gentlemen who will then invite them to dance at the evening ball."

Heather, the middle daughter, scrunched up her face. "That sounds a bit silly, if you ask me." She flicked a strand of nearly straight blond hair out of her face.

"Well, I don't think it sounds silly at all," Victoria breathed, her beautiful eyes gleaming as she looked over Mariah's shoulder. "You children will understand when you're older, I'm sure."

Heather snorted. "You're scarcely two-and-a-half years older than me, you know."

"A very important two-and-a-half years," her older sister said, arching her brows. She began working on the corset that had been one of the causes of Mariah's discomfort that day. "Heather, would you fetch my lavender gown out of my armoire? I think that would look nice on Miss Harwood."

"You may call me Mariah, if you wish." She felt someone tug on her arm.

"Are all those people naked in the baths?" Amy wanted to know. Questions filled the blue eyes in her heart-shaped face.

Victoria and Heather both gasped, but Mariah burst out laughing. This was like being with sisters back at home in her own room. She swung around and gave Amy a hug. "No, little one. They wear bathing costumes. It's all perfectly respectable."

A thought came to her as she stepped out of the dress pooled at her feet. How delightful it would be if she were a real guest in this happy and wealthy home. . .or perhaps, someday in the future, the mistress. . . .

Colin washed, changed, and brushed his hair before rushing out of his room and down the hall, the envelope of money in his pocket. He needed to speak to his family before Mariah came down.

As he reached the stairs, he slowed. What exactly would he say? *Lord, please give me the right words. You know how much I want her to stay.* With a last glance at the room where the girls had taken Mariah, he descended the steps at a deliberately slow pace. If he did not appear calm, how could he expect his parents to be?

Voices drifted from the parlor, so he joined them there.

"You look much better," Mother said with a smile as she looked up from her embroidery. "I've been wondering, Colin, dear, where exactly it was that you met the lovely Miss Harwood. How did you happen to bring her home unannounced?" She set the needlework aside on the lamp table next to her Queen Anne chair.

Not even a moment's grace? He swallowed.

His father rose from the brocade couch. "Cora, my love, do allow us to take care of the horse business before you start the inquisition."

With a slight frown, she opened her mouth to protest, then sighed.

"As you wish. First business, then the inquisition."

"Did Lindsay try to get away with paying less than we agreed upon?" Father asked, as he and Colin strode past the massive unlit fireplace to an open window overlooking the flower garden.

Colin smiled. "He tried, but once he examined the animals, he stopped attempting to negotiate." Removing the envelope containing the contract and banknotes, he felt his heart pounding. "Pa, I'm afraid you'll find it forty pounds shy."

His father frowned. "But you said—"

Giving the older man's arm a squeeze, Colin edged him farther away from Mother.

Too late. She tossed aside the hooped material she'd resumed working on and came to her feet. "What did I just hear? Forty pounds is missing? What on earth have you been up to?"

Chapter 4

I'd appreciate it, Mother, if you didn't speak until I've finished," Colin requested with all the confidence he could muster. "I'm sure you'll appreciate what I have to say by the time you've heard the entire story. First, however, let's all sit down." Not wanting to earn a disapproving glare from her, he concentrated on using proper diction.

As they took seats, Colin noticed his father didn't appear quite as suspicious as his mother. But then, the older man had always been harder to read.

"To begin with, I had just finalized stabling the horses aboard ship when I happened to notice this lovely young woman in very fashionable blue standing on the city's auction block."

"An auction block!" From the look on Mother's face as she glanced out to the grand staircase, one would think he'd said Mariah had come straight off a prison ship.

He shook his head. "You must stop leaping to wrong conclusions. Miss Harwood's being there was actually quite heroic."

She tucked her chin in disbelief and opened her mouth to respond, but Father placed a hand over hers. "Cora, love, let's hear the lad out. I'm sure there's more to the story."

"Thank you." Colin gave his father a grateful nod. "As I was saying, there she stood with a ship's blubbery captain touting what a highly educated gentlewoman Mariah was, how she played several musical instruments. He also reported that she'd sacrificed her own opportunities to willingly accompany her sister—or rather, two sisters—here to the colonies."

"Aha!" Mother gasped. "So she and *two* sisters, no less, could actually be infamous criminals." A note of triumph rang in her voice.

"No, Mother. Wrong again." Colin fought to squelch his mounting irritation with her. "Miss Harwood's sister Rose learned that their father, Bath's finest goldsmith, would be put in debtor's prison because a young lord met an untimely death before he could pay a huge debt he owed the man. Therefore, Mr. Harwood was unable to meet his own expenses. Without consulting her father, Rose packed up most of their furnishings and sold them on the Bristol docks to satisfy her father's creditors. She even used her sisters' dowries. But she was unable to raise the full amount, so she contracted an indenturement with a ship's captain."

"A reputable father wouldn't allow such action," Pa interjected.

"I'm sure he wouldn't had he known of her intent. But it was too late. She'd already paid out the money. Upon learning of her deed, her two sisters were loathe to have her sail to this foreign land alone. Out of their love for her, they also contracted with the same captain. The crafty man made a solemn promise to sell them together, but upon arriving in Baltimore he reneged and sold them separately."

"I know the kind," his mother admitted. "Always profiting from others' misfortunes."

At that moment, their slave, Pansy, stopped at the doorway and rapped softly on the jamb. "Mistress, Eloise be wantin' to know how much longer y'all wants her to hold suppa?"

"Just a few minutes more," Mother answered, then turned back to Colin.

"Considering that these highly accomplished sisters were not the usual bond servants," Colin went on, "and considering our Miss Harwood's remarkable beauty, I was appalled to see a number of unsavory types intent on bidding for her. They made no attempt to disguise their vulgar reasons for wanting her contract. I simply couldn't allow her to fall into any of their despicable hands."

His father nodded and sat back with a knowing grin.

His mother, however, pursed her lips and huffed. "So, my gallant son, you had to charge right in and save the fair maiden. . .with your father's money. Just tell me, what possible use do we have for another servant? All our needs are already being met." One of her brows rose slightly higher. "Or can it be that, like those other men, you decided to buy her to meet some personal, might I add baser, need of your own?"

"Mother! I cannot believe you would think such a thing of me, much less speak those words aloud." He purposefully sat straighter. "To be quite honest, my thoughts were of you. You and the girls. Not only does Mariah have exquisite penmanship for writing letters and invitations, she's been educated in all that finishing school nonsense, and—"

"It's that finishing school nonsense," she inserted, elevating her chin, "that turns a clumsy girl into a marriageable wife and mother."

Colin realized with a measure of relief that she'd fallen right into his plan. *Splendid!* "Well, you and Pa are planning to send Victoria off to that ladies' academy in Williamsburg this fall, are you not? And at substantial expense, even though she doesn't want to go. Now you won't have to send her away. Mariah will be here for the next four years, long enough to turn all three girls into simpering, British-accented gentlewomen, and for a fraction of the cost you expected to lay out. Plus, she plays four instruments, and having just arrived from a fashionable resort city in England, you'll have the advantage over other ladies on the latest styles. Think about it."

She tapped an impatient finger on the armrest of her chair. "Well, I can see she's certainly made a believer out of you, at least." Mother's doubtful tone attested that she remained unconvinced.

What more does she want? Colin elaborated further. "I had the opportunity of meeting both her other sisters. In fact, the eldest one insisted we were not to neglect Mariah's religious instruction. She made me promise to deliver—as she so aptly put it—her 'virtuous sister' to you before nightfall."

That information put a grin on his mother's face. "You don't say." Releasing a sigh, she tipped her head to one side in thought. "Very well. I suppose we can give Mariah a try. I did not fail to notice, however, that you have already begun calling her by her given name. That's far too familiar for such a brief acquaintance, to be sure. And should I ever catch you two in any sort of dalliance, I promise you this: we will sell her at once."

By the time Mariah left Victoria's room with the other two girls in tow, she looked and felt much improved in a clean frock, with her hair restyled. Even with her corset laced so tightly she could scarcely breathe, she found the bodice more than a little snug, but the strategic placement of a lace handkerchief helped alleviate the problem. She knew the gown's lavender hue, her own favorite color, was quite flattering and brought out the hint of violet in her eyes.

In addition, the girls seemed delightfully eager to get to know her, though they continued to address her formally, as their mother wished. As they reached the top of the graceful staircase, Mariah hoped the dinner with their parents would go equally well.

Her confidence faded on the descent. Detecting a decided strain in the voices coming from what must be the parlor, she sensed that Colin had most likely told his parents about her. *Please, dear Lord, give me just this one perfect night.*

Halfway down, she saw her rescuer and his parents exit the room. Colin and Mr. Barclay smiled up at her. Mistress Barclay did not.

What exactly had he said to them? How she wished she could get him aside and ask. But of course, that would be impossible at the moment. She made a concerted effort not to falter as she continued down. "I do hope I haven't kept you all waiting overly long," she ventured cheerily.

"No. Not at all." Mr. Barclay inclined his head. "You look lovely, my dear." He turned back to his stony-faced wife and offered his arm. "Shall we go in to supper, Cora, my love?"

The girls trailed after their parents, three sunny blossoms in their blue, green, and yellow pastels.

Colin offered his arm to Mariah. "Everything is fine," he whispered, pulling her arm within his. "And Pa is right."

"About what?"

"You look lovely. Exceptionally so."

She relaxed a little. "Thank you, kind sir." Releasing a pent-up breath, she gazed up at her handsome knight of the realm. Once again, he'd made everything right. On the other hand, if everything was right, why was his mother not smiling?

The dining room, Mariah noticed upon entering, fit in perfectly with the other beautiful accoutrements in the mansion. White wainscoting lined the lower portion of the walls, with pale blue, flocked wallpaper above. A slightly smaller chandelier above the long, lace-covered table sent rainbow prisms dancing over the gleaming china and crystal goblets set before each place. Colin drew out one of the mahogany chairs in the center for Mariah and took a seat next to her.

Lively Amy scooted onto the chair on her other side, while her sisters took their places across from them.

On the edge of her vision, Mariah could see Colin's parents occupying the head and foot of the table. She casually adjusted her position just enough to avoid Mistress Barclay's brittle stare.

A half door swung open, and the maid, Pansy, entered the room. Attired in a serviceable black dress with a crisp white apron, she carried in a tureen of a delicious-smelling soup and began ladling it out.

Mariah's stomach crimped. She'd thought the fare at the roadside inn had smelled enticing, but this was pure heaven. Colin had not exaggerated about his family's excellent cook. She sighed as she waited for her soup. Hopefully, his mother would keep any unpleasantness she might have planned until after the meal.

Once Pansy had dished out Mariah's portion of the creamy chicken soup, Mariah was about to pluck up her soupspoon when she remembered her napkin. She unfolded it and placed it on her lap as a lady should.

It was that precise action that saved her further embarrassment, because before she could reach for her spoon again, Mr. Barclay cleared his throat. "Let us bow for prayer."

Of course. Mariah cringed. How easily she had forgotten her manners.

"Our Father in heaven, we do thank You for continually showering us with such bounty. I pray we never take Your blessings for granted. And Lord, I especially want to thank You for bringing Miss Harwood to our home to tutor our girls. Because of her, my precious daughters will not have to be sent away to school. I would miss them terribly. We pray this in the name of our Lord Jesus. Amen."

A definite stirring from across the table could be heard even before the man concluded his prayer. Mariah opened her eyes to see a grin dancing across Victoria's face. "Do you mean it, Poppy? I don't have to go to that awful school? Becky Sue absolutely hated it there. She was forever sharing horror stories about the dreadful headmistress."

"Yes, dear," her mother replied, "but what a marvelous improvement that school has made in Rebecca. She's so much more graceful and mannerly since enrolling there." She turned to Colin. "Wouldn't you agree, son?"

He drew his attention from Mariah and focused on his mother. "I can't say I noticed, myself."

"Me neither," Amy piped in. "She only acts stiff and snooty and ever so proper when old people are around. The rest of the time she's her regular old self."

Her sisters giggled along with her, making it all the harder for Mariah to keep a face as straight as their disapproving mother's.

The mistress shifted her sharp stare to Mariah. "Well, now that we'll have a tutor right here at home, I'll know from the start if we're getting our money's worth."

Would she ever. A woman with her sharp eye would never miss a thing. Just observing the elegant lady of the manor delicately fill her spoon and lift it to her mouth, Mariah had no doubt the woman would fit right in were she dining with royalty.

Carefully raising her own spoon to her lips, Mariah assured herself she'd do her best in the task of tutoring. She'd been an apt student herself.

No one had to tell her that catching a man of any consequence required diligent effort. And for now, as an educator, she'd surely be given a room in the manor and take her meals with the family—and Colin—every day. That certainly beat having to scrub floors as she'd feared she'd be forced to do as a bond servant. Yes. In her quest for Colin, she'd be diligent. Extremely diligent. After all, as her instructress, Miss Simkins, loved to remind her, Rose, and Lily, "*A man has no need to buy a cow if he can get the milk for free.*"

She stifled a smile. Things were working out quite well. If only Mistress Barclay would smile, even once.

Chapter 5

Colin exhaled a slow breath of relief when his mother finally relaxed enough to sip at her soup. The meal continued in silence for a short span, until the soup bowls were taken away and the main courses served.

Cutting into a slice of roast pork, Father looked up, his expression pensive. "Son, I was wondering if you'd heard anything of consequence regarding that business out in New York's backcountry." He forked the meat to his mouth.

The change of subject could not have come at a more opportune time. "Not much." Colin bit a chunk of his buttered bread and chewed it before elaborating. "The Six Nations are asking Governor Clinton to take action."

"The Iroquois tribes?" The older man left his fork suspended in the air. "What difference could it possibly make to them? No matter which nation sends traders in, they'll still be able to exchange their furs for trade goods."

"Perhaps." Colin cocked his head. "But they claim it's tearing their tribal alliances apart." He paused and took another bite.

"Likely they're just hoping to arrange a better deal, get more presents from the powers that be."

"I wouldn't be too sure of that." He toyed with the fresh collard greens on his dish. "According to the word floating around, it sounds a bit more serious. The main chiefs made agreements to trade exclusively with the British as long as our soldiers will ally with them against their enemies—the northern tribes who made treaties with the French. Seems some of the more remote Iroquois villages feel it's better to go with French strength and the northern tribes than to stick with English weakness." He speared a chunk of meat and rested his hand beside his plate while he spoke. "They're very aware of the French invasion into their territory. So rather than be overrun, they are aligning themselves with the French and the tribes that used to be their own sworn enemies."

"I see." His father reached for another slice of bread and tore it in half before buttering it. "Sounds like there's much more to the situation than I thought. If England wants to maintain that flourishing trade with the Indians, they'd better make a forceful showing of their own."

"Speaking of a flourishing trade," Colin said, glancing down at Mariah, "the man who purchased Miss Harwood's sister is in the fur business."

That got Mariah's attention. Eyes wide, she returned his gaze while reaching for her water goblet.

"The man made one astounding bid for her. Fifty pounds." He switched his focus to his father. "Fifty pounds, without the blink of an eye. It silenced the rest of the bidding at once. Perhaps we went into the wrong business, Pa."

The older man chuckled. "That may very well be. But don't forget, European fashions change every few years, and—"

"Every season, Papa," Victoria corrected airily.

He gave his daughter a fatherly smile. "Even if fur muffs and hats never go out of fashion, the frontier may one day be trapped out, just as our coastal counties are. And as your mother likes to remind us, ships and goods may sink, but our land will still be here. Right, Cora?" He tipped his head toward her.

She smiled in her superior way, but Pansy's arrival with a laden tea tray precluded a response. "Pansy, dear, I believe we'll have our tea and this evening's dessert in the parlor." She then turned to Mariah. "We had a harpsichord shipped from London a few months ago but as yet have not had the privilege of hearing it played well. I'm afraid too many years without an instrument have diminished my already limited skill. Perhaps you'd be so gracious as to treat us with a sampling more pleasing to the ear."

" 'Twould be my honor, Mistress Barclay."

Colin held his breath. His mother was testing Mariah's honesty. Was she truly accomplished in music, or had everything she'd said thus far been fabricated?

Moments later, escorting Mariah through the wide double doorway leading into the parlor, he didn't sense any trepidation in her. But his steps slowed as they drew near the large, intricate-looking instrument with dual keyboards.

She smiled up at him, then patted his hand before moving away to smooth her palm across the polished wood surface. Turning back to his mother, who had taken a seat nearby, she dipped her head. "May I?" Without waiting for an answer, she dropped onto the harpsichord's stool and adjusted her skirts around her. She poised her fingers above the keys, then looked up at the family. "It has been awhile for me, as well. But I shall do my best."

Colin cringed. That was not what he wanted to hear her say. Still, he remained near the instrument for support. Or possibly, her protection.

Mariah ran her fingers up and down the keyboards as if she knew what she was doing, then stopped and looked over her shoulder at the others.

What now?

"I must say, it has lovely tone and seems to be in tune."

"Yes," Mother replied. "I hired a man who came all the way from Philadelphia to set it to rights after it arrived."

"Philadelphia," Mariah breathed. "And how far away is that? I have yet to learn where the various cities in the colonies are located."

She was stalling. Colin had no doubt.

"He took a coastal packet," his mother answered. "I can't say how far it is overland."

"We have a map in our schoolroom," Amy piped in. "You can look at that and see."

Colin stopped breathing. That's right, a diversion. Probably just what Mariah was hoping for.

"I shall look forward to checking the map," Mariah said and rested her fingers on the keys again. Smiling, she began to play—beautifully play—a charming, lyrical tune unfamiliar to Colin.

He drew his first real breath since entering the parlor.

The family took their time enjoying their raspberries with coddled cream as a welcome evening breeze filtered through the lace curtains of the parlor's open windows.

"Miss Harwood?" Heather inquired in an airy voice.

"What is it, dear?" Mariah interrupted her slow perusal of the room's elegant furnishings and turned her attention to the quietest of Colin's three sisters.

"Would you please teach me to play the harpsichord like you do? I've never heard anything so beautiful in my life."

"Once you're older," Victoria cut in, "you'll hear even prettier music. Last winter at the Christmas ball, the Tuckers hired a string quartet. They played wonderfully well. It was quite. . .romantic." She closed her eyes with a dreamy smile.

Colin removed his arm from where it rested against the fireplace mantel, his movement drawing Mariah's gaze. "I agree with Heather. I've never heard our instrument played more beautifully."

"Why, thank you, Mr. Barclay," Mariah said lightly, making sure she used his formal name, since his mother was watching them both closely. She raised her teacup and turned back to the girls. "Actually, I think it would be lovely if we were to create our own musical ensemble as my sisters and I did. One or two of you might also want to lend your talents to the violin or cello, or possibly the flute."

Excitement brightened Heather's expressive blue eyes as she swung toward her parents. "Oh, Mother, could we?"

For the first time, Mariah glimpsed the elegant older woman's expression soften with a warm smile. "You'll have to ask your father, dear. Musical instruments tend to be quite costly."

"Papa?" Heather pleaded.

His demeanor also gentled as he smiled at his charming middle daughter. "Of course, Heather, my sweet. Since I'll be riding in to Alexandria tomorrow on tobacco business, I'll stop by the music seller's and see what I can find."

"Oh, thank you. Thank you." Leaping to her feet, she went to her father and gave him a big hug.

Never one to be outdone, Amy followed suit. "I want an instrument, too."

He laughed and included her in the embrace. Watching as he kissed the giggling girls, Mariah felt a pang of homesickness. Would she ever get another hug from her own papa? She hadn't begun to realize until now the full price of leaving her homeland.

"One for each of you," Mr. Barclay said, his gaze including Victoria in the group. He then peered over his daughters' heads. "Colin, I would appreciate your company on the morrow. It always helps to put forth a united front when dealing with buyers."

Colin shot a quick glance at Mariah before answering. "Of course. I'd like to challenge Quince Sherwood to a race, anyway. I think their filly Brighton Rose is ready for the test."

"I agree." His father gave a nod.

Colin will be gone all day tomorrow. Mariah's uneasiness returned with the realization that she'd be left alone here with his mother. For the entire day.

Outside, several plantation dogs began barking in chorus, adding to her distress.

Colin strode to the open window and looked out into the dark, then turned back to Mariah. "I forgot. That must be the wagon bringing your trunks."

"Trunks?" His mother put her teacup aside and came to her feet. "How many trunks does the girl have?"

"Three."

"So many?"

"Yes. Which room shall we put them in?"

The lady of the house paused no more than a second. "Put them in the room adjacent to Amy's."

Colin tucked his chin in disbelief and stared at her. "You're delegating Mariah—Miss Harwood—to the room with the brat?"

"Yes." She smiled quite triumphantly and sat back. Taking up her tea once again, she lifted the cup to her lips and took a sip. "It's the perfect place for her."

Something was different. Mariah came awake to an unaccustomed stillness. Raising her lashes, she realized she was no longer at sea in a rolling, creaking ocean vessel, sharing a cramped cabin with several others. She had her own private bedchamber. She sighed and stretched languorously.

No doubt this personal haven of hers was far more sequestered than Colin might have hoped. His very clever mother had placed her in a room that could only be reached by passing through Amy's. And Amy's door faced her parents' room, with naught but a small second-floor sitting area separating them.

So much for any untoward dalliances with the son and heir. If what Colin had said regarding his youngest sister proved to be true—that she was the family snitch—he would find a venture through the girl's room to reach Mariah's door much too intimidating. Yes, Mistress Barclay had been clever indeed.

Mistress Barclay!

Mariah sprang up to a sitting position. She was supposed to meet the woman downstairs first thing this morning. And just how *first thing* was it? Throwing back the covers, she padded over the braided rug to the window and moved aside a sheer curtain panel to check the angle of the sun.

It had barely risen. Mariah sighed with relief. In the fragile morning light, she gazed down to dew-kissed fields of leafy plants and on to a line of trees edging the distant river that already reflected the sky's growing brightness. Such a delightful change after weeks of viewing nothing but the vast expanse of the dark Atlantic, and before then, a city crowded with stone buildings and cottages that blocked the sight of the surrounding countryside.

How pleasant it would be to simply wander outside and stroll the grounds in the cool of the morning, but alas, that was not to be. Turning back, Mariah grimaced at the sight of three overflowing clothing trunks that occupied so much of the limited space in her small room. They would have to stay there. The room lacked a wardrobe for her use. Since it had once housed a slave nanny when Amy had been an infant, the room was nowhere near as fancy as the family bedchambers. It contained only one small chest of drawers, which also served as her commode, and a wall rack with three hooks. Dreadfully inadequate for storing the contents of her trunks. Nevertheless, walls painted a soft green kept it from feeling gloomy, as did cheerful, apple-green calico curtains and a colorful counterpane. Accommodations could have been much worse, to be sure.

Mariah poured water into her washbasin and made swift work of her morning toilette before rummaging through her things to find a no-nonsense, unembellished gown a tutoress might wear. Every one of her frocks sported an abundance of wrinkles, since she'd unfolded them last evening to show all her gowns to Victoria.

Discarding several that appeared too grand, she wished for the first time in her life that she'd had a measure of Rose's more sedate taste in clothing. Finally she chose a deep rose gown with front lacings. It would have to do. Besides, she could dress in it without assistance.

After struggling into her layers of clothing, she brushed out her hair, then snatched it up and twisted the thick curls into a rather severe bun.

Colin wasn't the person she needed to impress today. Remaining here depended entirely upon his suspicious mother.

La, how she wished Colin had been master of his own house.

Amy remained sound asleep as Mariah tiptoed through the young girl's large, pink-and-white bedroom and opened the outer door, hoping she'd risen before Mistress Barclay. Alas, the door across the sitting area stood wide open. Both of Colin's parents must already be downstairs. And since Colin planned to leave with his father for Alexandria shortly, he must likely be up and about himself.

The last thing Mariah wanted was to be abandoned by him on her first day in the household, but there was little hope of his changing his mind and staying behind. Naturally he'd want to live up to his responsibilities. Scooping up her skirts, she hurried to the staircase and descended, praying all the way down that some miracle would cause Colin to remain at home. *If not, Lord, please make Mistress Barclay decide to allow me to stay here for the duration of my indenturement.*

Just as she reached the bottom landing, the older woman strolled from the parlor into the foyer looking exceptionally regal, even in her dressing gown of pale-blue *peau de soie*, her dark hair in a long, loose braid down her back. "Mariah. Come with me to the dining room. We can discuss matters over breakfast." No smile softened the invitation.

Mariah tamped down her unease. At least Colin's mother planned to feed her. Not to be outdone by the matron, she straightened her own posture. After all, Colin would also be there.

He was not.

The long sideboard held a variety of foods and a tea service. Mariah noticed that some of the artfully arranged fare had already been removed. Obviously the men had enjoyed an early breakfast before leaving for their jaunt to the city.

Without a word, the mistress served herself, so Mariah did the same. Then the older woman took her place from the night before and motioned for Mariah to take a nearby seat. Once they were both settled and Mariah lifted her cup to her mouth, Mistress Barclay leveled a pointed stare at her. "Shall we ask the Lord's blessing?"

Humiliated yet again by her out-of-practice manners, Mariah closed her eyes for a brief second, then returned the delicate teacup to its saucer and bowed her head.

"Our most gracious Father," the woman began, "we thank You once more for Your wondrous bounty and ask Your blessing upon it. Amen." She then sat back and took up her own cup as she studied Mariah, causing her great uneasiness. Finally, she spoke. "I want you to know I am no fool."

Mariah cut a swift glance at her. How should one respond after such a comment?

A knowing smirk twitched a corner of the matron's lips. "I know exactly why my son bought your papers, so let us not dance around the issue. The fact is, you are here, and while you are part of this household, I shall be charitable and give you a trial period, though I have serious doubts that you will work out."

Making an effort to remain composed, Mariah swallowed and met her gaze. "Madam, I assure you, I shall put forth my very best effort to educate your daughters in all the graces. You will not be disappointed. And if the current quality of their penmanship is not a credit to this fine home now, I promise it will be shortly."

Mistress Barclay dismissed the remark with a wave of one hand. "Indeed. Well, that can be hired. What I'm more interested in is a marked improvement in their diction. I cannot abide the lazy sliding of words so common in this area. My girls must be able to mingle successfully with those of the Bay states as well as those of British society."

Confident that she had no lack of expertise in those elements, Mariah formulated an apt round of praise for her abilities, but the woman gave her no opportunity to utter a word in her defense.

"My husband and I are adamant that our daughters marry respected merchants or men of other successful enterprises. I myself would not be adverse to a man of the cloth, as long as he happens to be well placed."

"I see."

"No, I don't believe you do. City dwellers are more interested in monetary dowries than those which include land, and we do not plan to sacrifice even an acre of our property for the purpose of securing advantageous marriages for our daughters." She spread marmalade on a triangle of toasted bread and nibbled a corner of it.

"As mentioned in the conversation around the table last eve," Mariah inserted, "the land is here to stay. And lovely land it is, I must avow."

The older woman's expression hardened. "Let me be clear on this. My husband married me against his family's wishes. I brought no land to the family, you see, only the profit from a ship in my father's merchant fleet. After only a few years, the vessel sank in a storm. You, of course, do not possess even that much. I will not allow a marriage between you and Colin, no matter what. Not even should you turn up with child."

Mariah gasped, lurching to her feet.

Mistress Barclay caught her hand. "Do sit down again, my dear. I do apologize for being so. . .blunt. However, it is imperative that you understand how serious I am about this." She paused briefly. "Your main duty, while you are here, will of course be tutoring the girls in their lessons. You will have one day off each week. I think that should be Sunday—after you have attended services with us."

Under any other circumstance, Mariah would have left the table and stormed out the door. But where could she go? All her worldly belongings were upstairs, and by law the Barclays did own her services for the next four years. Four years. She drew a defeated breath and sank back down on her chair. "The girls' speech. I suppose if you want them to be accepted everywhere, they'll need to know at least a smattering of French. Have they had any instruction in that language?"

"No, they have not."

Mariah let out a humorless chuckle. "Then, it appears I have my work cut out for me."

Surprising Mariah, the stern matron smiled. "Perhaps you will turn out to be worth the money my son paid for you after all." Then the smile vanished. "But make no mistake. If you betray me in the slightest way, I will sell you to the first old wretch I see."

Chapter 6

Early morning light added translucent beauty to the verdant countryside on the way to Alexandria, sprinkling dewy diamonds over wildflowers and among the tall grasses dancing on the breeze. Riding beside his father's dapple gray stallion, Colin tried to compose in his mind the perfect words that would secure the older man's commitment to the cause. . .that of convincing Mother to retain Mariah's services for the next four years. He discarded idea after idea as weak and sought a better approach to the subject.

An unexpected laugh broke his concentration. He raised his gaze to the fair-haired man at his side, who shook his head, still chuckling. "You've certainly managed to make things challenging for our little Amy."

What a strange comment. Colin reined Paladin closer to his father's mount. "Whatever do you mean?"

"That lass you brought home." His shrewd blue eyes focused on Colin. "What could Amy possibly bring home that could top a new bond servant?"

Colin frowned. "I don't understand."

"You know as well as I do, son, that the little squirt makes it her life's ambition to try and outdo you, outrun you, outrace you on horseback, even outeat you—"

"Only if the food is somethin' she particularly likes," Colin inserted on a chuckle of his own. "But I do catch your meanin'. I hope Mother doesn't find out that the little imp jumped off the edge of the waterfall into the creek last week. It seems that Old Samuel, our horse groomer, told her I'd done it when I was her age."

His pa nodded thoughtfully as the two mounts plodded along. "I've always been careful not to let Amy get wind of all the critters you used to tote home, especially after the opossum she sneaked into the house last month. In its frenzy to escape, that varmint shredded one of the drapes in my study. Needless to say, your mother was in high dudgeon over that episode."

"Our little snitch does manage to get herself into piles of trouble, that's for sure." Grinning as a few of Amy's escapades came to mind, Colin felt his humor wane, and he turned serious. "The difference is, I did not bring Mariah home on a mere whim."

Pa shot him a look of disbelief—one that made Colin reiterate his position.

"Well, perhaps it was a whim at first. I'll readily admit it. But as she and I conversed during the journey home, I began to see what a perfect fit she is."

"You mean, *felt* her perfect fit, I daresay. Otherwise you would've done the logical thing and had her ride on the wagon with her luggage."

Colin cut him a sidelong glance. "If you were my age and that had been Mother, would you have consigned her to a tediously long, bumpy wagon ride?"

His father thought for a moment. "That's not a fair question. However, since you brought up the subject, I certainly would not have taken such liberties with a woman like your mother unless I'd planned to wed her— even if that Puritan blood of hers would have permitted such action." He eyed Colin. "May I ask if that is your intention for this young, penniless English maiden? This indentured servant you've thrust upon us?"

"Well, I—" A low-hanging branch necessitated Colin's having to duck beneath it, a most welcome diversion. He was nowhere near ready to answer his father's query. He watched a squirrel scamper up a tree as they passed by.

"I suggest you give the matter some serious thought, son. You know your mother will fight you tooth and nail, should that be the case. Even worse, she'll send the girl packing someplace where you'll never be able to find her. She's that determined for you to marry one of our local belles—hopefully, one with her own strict religious upbringing. Constance Montclaire, for example." A chuckle rumbled from his chest.

Colin had no doubt his father adored his mother, despite all her rigid New Englander ideas. And Colin would settle for no less than that kind of affection himself. "Constance may be Mother's choice, but she's not mine. I'd rather remain a bachelor all my days than marry without love."

Abruptly, Father reined his horse to a stop, prompting Colin to do the same. "You couldn't possibly be in love with Miss Harwood after just one day. The very idea would be absurd."

Pa had really put him on the spot. "Correct me if I'm wrong, but it seems I recall you telling us all that you fell in love with Mother the first time you laid eyes on her."

"That was different. She and I met at a Christmas ball in Baltimore. She'd come down from Boston to visit a cousin. Her very clothing attested to her family's wealth."

Not to be dissuaded, Colin pressed on. "I also considered Mariah's attire to be exquisite. She was elegance itself, not only in her appearance but her bearing, as well."

"Perhaps, my boy, but my lady was standing in the ballroom of a fine manse. Your young woman was perched on an auction block. Forgive me if I point out the obvious difference."

"I understand what you're saying, sir. All I ask is that you make certain Mother gives Mariah a fair chance to prove herself. If you'd met her sister Rose—she could have been Mother, the way she pinned me down with her questions and her insistence that Mariah continue her religious instruction."

"So she believes the girl still needs some instruction, then."

Colin let out a weary breath. "No. It wasn't like that at all. Rose Harwood was deeply worried about handing her sister over to a man she'd never met. She had no way of knowing my true character, my motives. She was concerned for her sister's welfare."

"No doubt." After a moment's pause, Father relaxed his tight lips and nudged his mount forward again. "Very well. You've made a good case. I'll do my best to corral your mother. We'll take it one day at a time. Let's just hope Miss Harwood doesn't say or do anything to make your mother determined to sell her to the first reasonable bidder before we get home."

Deriving encouragement from the older man's response, Colin breathed a bit easier. "Thank you. I'll appreciate having your help with Mother, sir. That's all I can ask." For a moment he was tempted to add that it was his name on the indenturement papers, not his mother's. Neither she nor his father could legally sign off on the documents. But Colin wasn't ready to offer any kind of ultimatum just yet, or draw a line in the sand over a lass he'd barely met. Still, at this very minute he wished Mariah was sitting on Paladin in front of him with that silly feather flopping in his face and that he was smelling the delicious, slightly briny *eau de Mariah*.

He exhaled a long breath and changed the subject. "How do you feel about posting a letter to your friend Yarnell Lewis in Williamsburg after Quince Sherwood and I set a date for a race? I heard his horse made a good showing last month in Charles Town."

⚊⚊⚊

Mariah spent most of the day in the schoolroom at the end of the upstairs hall, assessing the education her three charges had acquired and compiling a list of the various texts she would need in the months to come. Mistress Barclay popped in numerous times doing her own assessing—of Mariah. It was very unnerving, since the only time Mariah had done anything akin to teaching school was when she'd helped her younger siblings, Lily and Tommy, with their reading and sums before they set off to Master Gleason's classes.

Now, thank goodness, the school day was over. Mariah had scarcely announced that fact before Amy raced madly out of the house and down to the stables, her mother's reprimands trailing after her to no avail.

But most gratifying, the mistress of the house had seemed pleased by what she'd seen. She almost smiled when she entered the schoolroom as the other girls took their leave. "That seems to have gone well." She glanced down at Mariah's desk. "I assume that is a list of the supplies and books the girls will be needing."

"Yes, mistress." A slight pause. "However, there is one thing in particular that I need, if I may be so bold."

"And it is. . . ?"

"I've not had a bath since I set foot on that ship, only a few basins of seawater to freshen up with on occasion. If it is not too much trouble, would it be possible—"

The older woman blanched. "I have been remiss. I should have thought of that myself. I shall have Lizzie and Ivy see to it at once."

"Thank you most kindly."

An hour later, feeling more refreshed than she had in weeks, Mariah found herself in Victoria's room demonstrating a new hairstyle on Heather's smooth, golden tresses. "Watch, Victoria. The hair has to be brought up to the very top of her head, quite high, or it will begin to sag."

The fifteen-year-old stepped nearer for a better view as her sister sat at the dressing table, watching their reflection in the large oval mirror.

"Now, twist it round and round but not too tight," Mariah said, exaggerating her movements a bit so the procedure could easily be observed. "When it's all twisted, except for the last eight or ten inches—which I'll thread through to the center and curl—it must be secured with pins and a pretty comb. Like this."

"Even if Ah do all that, Ah vow it shan't look like yers," Victoria said in a slow drawl.

"*I* vow it shan't look like *yours*," Mariah echoed, more crisply.

Heather giggled. "You are as bad as Mother!"

"And I shall continue to be until the two of you start speaking like the proper young ladies you are." Suddenly feeling she sounded more like Rose than herself, Mariah drew a surprised breath before returning her attention to Heather's hair. "Once I have everything secure, I shall very carefully catch a few tendrils here and there to bring down in curls to tease the back of her neck. And of course, I'll do the same in front of her ears to soften the look around her lovely face."

"I don't have a lovely face." Heather spoke barely above a whisper and lowered her lashes.

Mariah reached out and lifted the girl's chin with the edge of her index finger. "Now, how can you possibly say such a thing? Take a good look at yourself—those gorgeous azure eyes, those rosebud lips, and exquisite cheekbones. In just a few years, they'll definitely be finer than mine—and finer than a lot of other girls' your age."

"Do you really think so?" The twelve-year-old met Mariah's gaze in the mirror.

"Absolutely. In fact, I daresay your father will have to hold the young men off with a brace of pistols—"

Heather giggled.

"Just as I'm sure he's doing for Victoria right now."

The humor in Victoria's face evaporated. "I hardly think so. The one person I wish would admire me still thinks of me as a little girl."

"I know who that is," Heather singsonged.

"Hush!" Her sister silenced her with a frown.

"It's Tuck. Don't try to deny it."

Mariah made a mental note of the information. Ah yes, the dashing young gentleman she and Colin had met on the road yesterday—the one on his way to visit another young lady.

Victoria averted her blushing face but managed an angry retort. "I said, hush! Or I'll tell about you know what."

With an exasperated sigh, Mariah rolled her eyes. "And I, for one, care very little how much you girls argue, as long as you do it with precise diction."

"I say bravo to that." Their mother swept into the room, already dressed for the supper hour. She looked more elegant than ever in a sapphire taffeta gown with a ruffle at the hem. The sleeves of her gown dripped with lace at the elbows.

"Miss Harwood is showing us how to create the latest hairstyles from England," Victoria blurted, obviously hoping to distract her mother from whatever she might have overheard.

The lady of the house moved closer and eyed Mariah's work. "Yes, that is quite nice, Heather. It makes you appear six months older, at least." A teasing smile tugged at her lips.

"Does she not?" Mariah piped in as she continued pinning. "Back home, my sister Lily and I spent hours and hours practicing hairstyles on each other."

"Oh?" Mistress Barclay arched her slender brows. "You did not have a maid who dressed you?"

Mariah could see no reason for anything other than the truth. Lies were too hard to keep track of. "No, ma'am. We had only a housekeeper. But anytime we needed help with some little thing, she was kind enough to assist us."

The older woman offered one of her polite yet humorless smiles. "Well, you might be happy to learn we have two upstairs maids and two downstairs, plus Eloise our cook, and of course, Benjamin, the butler."

"You are truly blessed." Mariah flashed an equally practiced smile, then turned to Victoria. "Would you please fetch the curling iron from the brazier?"

The three Barclays watched as Mariah deftly curled Heather's top locks and the scattering of tendrils, making them as springy as Victoria's natural curls with the aid of the heated iron. Heather bobbed her head back and forth, a huge grin displaying her perfect teeth. "I do look older, don't I? And not just by six months."

Mistress Barclay's smile softened. "Yes, my darling. You shall be the belle of the evening." She turned to Mariah. "Do instruct Lizzie on the latest styles. I'm having some neighborhood ladies over for tea in a few days, and it would be great fun to show off a bit."

"Of course. I'd be pleased to."

"Oh, and do hurry, girls. The men arrived home a few minutes ago, and Eloise will be serving supper promptly at seven." Mistress Barclay's normally pursed lips twitched into a tiny smile. "The cook declared, with a shake of that finger of hers, 'Ah don't wants no repeat o' las' night, neithah.' " That said, the lady of the manor turned and sashayed out of the room.

The girls bubbled into laughter, and Mariah joined in. She couldn't believe the perfect southern accent the mistress had mimicked, considering her dislike of a lazy drawl. The elegant lady of the house actually had a sense of humor.

The day had gone so much better than she'd believed possible this morning. Now Colin was back. Who knew what wonders the evening might hold?

"Victoria, do take Heather's place. And Heather, be a dear and set the curling iron to cool. Victoria's curls need very little help. We've got to hurry."

Chapter 7

Colin would have given his right arm to know how Mariah had fared with his mother during the day. Calling on every ounce of self-control he possessed, he somehow managed to effect an air of disinterest as he, Amy, and his parents waited in the parlor for the English beauty and his other sisters to come downstairs.

Mother let out a huff. "Amy, do stop fidgeting with your hair bow. It's quite annoying."

"It's too tight," the wiggle worm replied.

"That, young lady, is your fault. You should have returned from the stables sooner." She rose from the settee and walked behind her daughter's chair to retie the blue ribbon.

With his mother's attention diverted, Colin took the opportunity to step away from the mantel and move closer to the doorway, where he had a better view of the staircase.

"Eldon, dear, how did things go in town today? You didn't mention the results of your trip."

His father drew a deep breath, obviously enjoying the delectable aromas emanating from the dining room, where large, covered serving dishes of hot food lined the sideboard, awaiting the arrival of the family at the table. "Fine. It appears we'll be getting a good price for both the tobacco and the grain."

"Splendid. And you planned to go to the music seller's. Were you able to find any instruments for the girls while you were there?"

He opened his mouth to answer but closed it again as the rapid patter of footsteps sounded on the stairs. He stood from his chair and followed Colin out into the foyer.

Heather flew into their father's arms first, breathless with excitement. "Papa! Did you buy me a violin or a flute?"

"We'll talk about music over supper, my darling."

Victoria descended at a more sedate pace, followed by Mariah, who met Colin's gaze with a radiant smile.

She looked as pleased to see him as he was to see her. Attired in peach taffeta adorned with delicate lace, her hair drawn back in a cluster of dark curls, the young woman's incredible beauty never ceased to amaze and enthrall him. Returning her smile, he took several steps toward the stairs.

Suddenly her smile lost its luster as she darted a glance beyond him.

Colin didn't need to turn to know his mother had made an appearance. He saw it in Mariah's stilted expression. Sensing they were being watched, he veered slightly and reached a hand up to Victoria. "You look very pretty this evening, little sis."

She beamed. "Do you think so? Mariah fixed my hair. She says it's one of the latest styles the ladies in England are wearing."

"Papa!" Heather cut in, latching on to her father's arm. "Please. I can't wait. I need to know now."

He chuckled and drew her into a hug. "Of course, my sweet. I surrender. I bought an instrument for each of you." He gave her a peck on the cheek. "I was unable to find a flute, as you hoped, but the seller did have two violins and a cello. I hope that will please you."

"What do you say, Mariah?" Heather swiveled in her father's embrace and turned to her. "Will they do?"

A light laugh accompanied Mariah's nod. "I should say those

instruments will do very nicely, dear. Perhaps once you've mastered those, your father can see about adding a flute at some future date."

The older man shifted his attention to Mariah. "As a matter of fact, I've already done so. I asked Mr. Smith, the music seller, to inquire hither and yon for a flute. I'm confident one will turn up before long."

"Oh, Papa! You are wonderful!" Normally shy Heather threw her arms about him and gave him a big hug. "Where have you put our instruments? I must see them."

"Why, upstairs, of course. In the farthest reaches of the house."

"In the schoolroom?"

"Yes. The three of you can go up there and start screeching the bows across the strings to your heart's content. After supper." He softened the remark with a playful wink.

Watching the loving exchange, Colin's gaze once again gravitated to Mariah, and he wished he could give her a playful hug. . .or any kind of hug. In one short day she had brought new life into the household. How could anyone not see that and adore her as much as he did? Well, perhaps not quite so much, he amended, aware of his mother again. He turned to find her intense brown eyes narrowed and focused on him. He flashed his most charming smile. "How was your day, Mother, dear?"

"Productive." The curt answer gave indication that she would not be so easily swayed.

Colin was spared further placation of the lady of the house when the brass knocker banged against the entry door. The butler, Benjamin, appeared out of nowhere and opened it wide to allow the visitor to enter.

Pa stepped forward. "Why, Dennis Tucker. I must say, this is an odd time for you to come calling. To what do we owe this unexpected pleasure?"

Colin stared at the interloper who stood resplendent in a fine navy frock coat and gray breeches, his ruffled white shirt accenting his tanned complexion, and he rolled his eyes.

Dennis swept off his three-cornered hat and handed it to the butler. "Didn't Colin tell you to expect me?" His gaze roved the gathering, stopping on Mariah. He gave a polite bow of his head. "Miss Harwood.

Delightful to see you again." His gaze lingered briefly, then he returned his attention to the man of the house. "I didn't mean to intrude. Perhaps another time."

"Nonsense, my boy." Pa said. "You know you're always welcome here."

"Why, of course." Mother swept toward him. "You're most welcome. Amy, go tell Eloise there'll be one more for supper, and ask Pansy to set another place." She flicked a glance at Mariah and back to Tuck, a scheming glint in her eye. "We're delighted to have you join us. Shall we all go to supper?" Taking Father's arm, she strolled through the parlor toward the dining room.

Colin cringed at his mother's sugary sweet graciousness and turned on his heel to escort Mariah, but Tuck was already offering the young beauty his arm. It would have been gratifying to wipe that satisfied smirk off his pal's face, but Colin could not afford to make a scene, could not reveal the depth of the feelings he already had for Mariah. He'd never before been so drawn to a woman.

Fortunately, Victoria moved beside him and threaded her arm through his. Something about the soft light in her eyes and her sweet smile revealed that she understood.

He filled his lungs and manufactured a grin as he patted her hand before starting after the others. "Shall we?" He'd just been outflanked on two sides, but the battle for Mariah Harwood had barely begun.

This is not good. Strolling into the dining room on Dennis Tucker's arm, Mariah managed to govern her emotions admirably. There was no denying Mistress Barclay's pleasure in having someone other than Colin show interest in her, and it wouldn't hurt Colin to have a little competition to increase his regard. . .but one look at Victoria, and Mariah could see the girl's heartache. That was really not good. The last thing she wanted was for Victoria to decide she'd rather be sent away to school than stand by and watch her tutoress steal her secret love's affections. But what could be done? Mariah had no idea how to keep both mother and daughter happy when their desires were at such odds.

Her thoughts in a muddle as she allowed Tuck to seat her, Mariah decided avoidance of the whole drama might be the most prudent tactic. She turned to Heather, being seated on her other side by Tuck. "Heather, dear, have you given thought to which instrument you'd prefer to learn first, the violin or the cello?"

The girl looked at her in all innocence, unaware of the tension surrounding Mariah, and her face brightened. "May I try both of them before I decide?"

"Of course." Only wishing Victoria looked as happy as her sister, Mariah felt added despair as Tuck positioned himself so closely that his arm brushed hers.

Across the table from Heather, Amy leaned forward and addressed her father at the head. "Poppy, I wish you only bought two instruments. I can't abide stayin' inside all day every day. I'm already spendin' hours and hours practicin' readin' and writin' and cipherin', how to walk and how to talk. And now music, too?" The last phrase ended on a high-pitched whine.

"Please speak properly, child." Her mother wagged her head. "The study of music is for your own good, and you did request an instrument of your own. It's time you stopped spending so many hours down at the stables. Whenever you return to the house, you smell like an old horse blanket, for pity's sake."

"Oh, Mother."

Mariah surmised that if Amy had been standing, she'd have emphasized her last protest with a stomp of her foot. She made an attempt to smooth the child's ruffled feathers. "You know, Amy, I've heard so much about your stable of Thoroughbreds, but I've yet to see them. If you promise to work at your music studies, I'd be honored to have you introduce me to every horse on this farm."

Amy brightened a bit. "Can we do it tomorrow?"

"If your mother approves." Mariah tipped her head at Mistress Barclay.

The lady of the manor smiled slightly as she eyed her daughter. "Only if you apply yourself to music for at least one hour."

"A whole hour?" The child's shoulders sagged. Then, with a look of resolve she perked up. "Oh, very well. One hour at music and one hour showin' Miss Harwood the stables."

A chuckle rumbled from her father's chest. "Colin, my boy, perhaps you and I should take Amy along with us the next time we deal with the tobacco buyers. She drives a hard bargain."

Mariah chanced a quick glance at Colin and saw him looking at her with a satisfied grin, even as he answered his father. "As you wish. If anyone could wear those thieves down, it would be our little squirt, for sure."

Mulling over the thought of touring the stables with the youngster on the morrow, Mariah had little doubt that Colin would somehow manage to be there at the same time. How hard could it be to distract an eight-year-old so they could steal a little privacy? A few moments would be enough to whet his interest, while not so much time that his mother would be alerted. Yes. A few sweet stolen moments. . .

"Shall we bow our heads?" Mister Barclay offered a simple blessing, and directly after the *Amen*s, the tall African butler brought the first serving bowls to the table. Dressed in crisp black and white like the other house slaves, Benjamin moved quietly and efficiently without being obtrusive, as did Pansy and shy little Ivy as they assisted him.

Victoria was the first to start the conversation. She offered their guest a tentative smile. "Tuck, we're so happy to have our Miss Harwood here as our own private tutoress. Colin graciously bought—"

Though Mariah was impressed by the girl's diction as she spoke in the rather cultured accent she'd been practicing, the word *bought* hit a sour note. Mariah was grateful when Colin's voice overrode his sister's gentle tones.

"Yes, Tuck. I was extremely fortunate to find such an accomplished instructress for my sisters and hired her on the spot. Now Victoria—and hopefully the other girls—will never have to be sent away to school. They made no secret of their dislike of the idea."

For a split second, Mariah feared the mistress would finish what her daughter started by mentioning that she was actually here as an indentured servant. Then she realized it wouldn't be in her employer's best interest.

The woman wanted Tuck to think Mariah was a worthy conquest.

Apparently the young man did just that, as he tilted a dimpled cheek toward Mariah and smiled. "Beauty and education. What more could one ask?" A spark of humor lit his hazel eyes.

Remembering Victoria, Mariah shot a glance across to see if her jealous young charge would finish telling Dennis Tucker what she'd started saying a moment ago. But the girl was filling her plate as if nothing were amiss, which unnerved Mariah all the more. At any moment the lass so chose, she could blithely blurt out that Mariah was nothing but a bond slave—no matter how much she tried to pretend she wasn't.

A subject change was again in order. She turned to Colin. "Mr. Barclay, while you and your father were in Alexandria, were you successful in arranging the horse race you were hoping to schedule?"

He blotted his lips on his napkin and met her eyes. "Please call me Colin. Otherwise I'll think you're addressing my father. And yes, our friend Quince Sherwood is going to invite a few other horsemen he knows to participate. We thought it would be grand to make a festive day of it. Games, a picnic, that sort of thing."

Secretly reveling in the intensity of his gaze, Mariah had a fairly good idea what he meant by a *festive day*.

Tuck whacked his leg. "I say, old man, that sounds like great fun." He then tilted his head toward Mariah. "Miss Harwood, I'd be honored if you'd accompany me to the festivities."

Her spirits sank. Would this day never end? "Actually," she fibbed, "I promised the girls I'd accompany them to all social gatherings. Didn't I, Victoria?" She waited for what seemed forever for the lass to answer, hoping, hoping. . .

"Why, yes, she did." Victoria feigned a note of regret in her voice. "But, Tuck, you'd be most welcome to join us, of course." She offered him a bright smile.

Mariah stifled a sigh of relief.

"Now that that's settled," the lady of the house announced, "I suggest we finish our meal before it gets cold."

For the second time, Mariah felt utterly grateful to her mistress.

Perhaps she'd survive the evening after all. She relaxed and took another spoonful of her venison stew.

The conversation then centered on an upcoming wedding at a neighboring plantation, guests who were expected to attend, and the gala celebration afterward. Mariah gave it little attention, since she didn't know anyone mentioned. She was glad when Pansy brought in the dessert.

"Oh, I almost forgot," Tuck drawled.

Everyone looked up from their bowl of peach cobbler to him.

Mariah stiffened, wondering if she would be the topic yet again.

But the young man turned his attention to Colin. "I originally came by to find out if you'd learned anything new about that French force marching down toward the Ohio River. You didn't have a chance to elaborate when we met on the road yesterday."

Mariah breathed more easily. Men and politics. She only half listened as Colin related to his friend the same information he'd given his father the evening before.

Tuck shook his sandy head. "When I was at the Patterson Plantation last night, the men there were talkin' about it. If New York's governor doesn't raise a militia to stop 'em, Mr. Patterson says Governor Dinwiddie will. He said the Virginia Colony ain't about to hand over the Ohio Valley to the Frenchies. There's too much wealth in the fur trade. Patterson said Dinwiddie won't wait months for word to get to England and orders to come back. By then the French could have all the tribes bought off, and the whole territory would be lost to us."

Mr. Barclay shook his head, a worried expression drawing his brows together. "Let's just pray that Governor Clinton will send his Indian agent, that Johnson fellow from up in the Mohawk Valley, to meet with the tribes loyal to the Crown. From what I hear, he has great influence with them. He even married one of them. If he can keep the Indians from siding with the French, they'll just have to traipse on back to Canada again."

"Right." Colin nodded. "That'll probably be the end of it." He then glanced across the table at Mariah. "As Pa and I mentioned last night concerning your sister, there's nothing to worry about."

"It would be a sorry shame if nothing came of the affair." Tuck flashed a strange grin. "I, for one, would love a chance for some high adventure, ridin' off into the great unknown. Wouldn't you, old man?" He eyed Colin.

Mistress Barclay let out a weary breath. "Enough politics for one evening. We have a special treat for you this evening, Dennis. If Miss Harwood would favor us with a few pieces on the harpsichord. I think you will be pleasantly surprised."

Bravo! Mistress Barclay outmaneuvered everyone again and returned us to her agenda, pairing me with Dennis Tucker. Mariah squelched the snide thought. But one thing was certain. Quite the expert manipulator, the lady of the manor was a woman to be admired. . .and watched—closely watched.

Chapter 8

Colin looked at his timepiece. He'd been at the stables for more than an hour and was running out of things to check on. He gazed up at the big house. How much longer would Mariah hold class before she dismissed the girls?

Noticing the furtive glances between Old Samuel, the Negro horse groomer, and redheaded Geoffrey Scott, the trainer, Colin knew they were puzzled at his puttering around with nonessentials.

At last he spotted movement on the covered office porch, where bright afternoon light played over flouncy skirts. Mariah and Amy had finally come outside and would reach the stables in moments.

He turned to Geoff. "When my sister and Miss Harwood arrive here shortly, I'd appreciate bein' able to have some time alone with the tutor. See if you can come up with somethin' to divert Amy's attention elsewhere. You know the child's tendency to. . .exaggerate." Tattle was closer to the truth.

Geoff nodded with understanding and flicked his green eyes in the direction of the girls. "So that's the beautiful Miss Harwood the little gal's been telling us about, the bond servant you brought home from Baltimore."

Colin turned and saw that Mariah and Amy had already passed the rose garden. Even from this distance he was caught by the Englishwoman's matchless beauty. He switched his attention back to the horse trainer. "Yes. But she's not to be treated like a servant. I expect you to show her the utmost respect." Even as he spoke, he realized coming to her defense was becoming a habit.

Geoff eyed Colin straight on. "I would hope the lass will be treated with respect by one and all."

Knowing the trainer to be a zealous Presbyterian, Colin surmised the man's "one and all" referred to more than just the hired help. "That goes without saying. Miss Harwood is a real lady."

With the barest hint of a smile, Geoff glanced beyond him. "Then I'll trust you to be a true gentleman yourself."

"Of course." It appeared Colin would find no ally in the horse trainer. Added to that, he could hear lanky-framed Old Samuel chuckling as he mucked out the stall beside him. Ignoring the white-haired slave, Colin cleared his throat. "If you'll excuse me, I'll go fetch the young ladies."

This balmy afternoon was the first time Mariah had been outside the manse since her arrival at the plantation, and she was truly in awe of the beautiful grounds she could now observe close-up. The plants in the kitchen plot teemed with life, emitting a healthy freshness that blended with the sweet perfume from the rose garden, where blooms in varied hues stirred on the breeze. She breathed in the mixture of scents as she and Amy headed for the stables and pastures that lay downwind of the big house.

Mariah discovered the vast farm had buildings, sheds, and cabins enough to be its own small village. Beyond the structures, she could see a goodly number of slaves out in the fields, cutting leaves from the long rows of lush tobacco plants and stacking them in neat piles.

"Look, there's Colin." Amy pointed toward the stables and grabbed

Mariah by the hand. "He's there with Mister Scott and Old Samuel. You'll like both of 'em."

Being tugged along by the girl, Mariah had trouble dismissing the sight of so many African slaves laboring in the hot sun. As a bond servant, she had only a few more rights than those fieldworkers. Mistress Barclay had the legal entitlement to order her out in the fields alongside the slaves at any time, should she so choose.

"Blast!" Amy huffed. "Here comes that bossy brother of mine. Colin always has to butt in. I wanted to be the one to show you the stables myself."

"And you shall." Mariah gave the child's hand an encouraging squeeze. But she could no more hold back the smile already dancing across her lips at the sight of the strikingly handsome son and heir than she could stop the sun from shining.

"Go away, Colin." Amy folded her arms and pouted. "I'm going to show Miss Harwood the horses."

"As you wish, squirt." He grinned. "I won't say a word. . .except good afternoon to you lovely ladies."

"Such drivel," his sister groused, as if she'd just been insulted.

Colin stopped in front of them. "Why do you say that, little sis?"

"Because I'm not some simpering 'lovely lady.' That's why."

Still having problems containing her smile, Mariah patted Amy's shoulder. "Ah, but someday you'll be the belle of the county. Wait and see."

"Oh, pshaw!" She rolled her blue eyes. "I wish I was born a boy. I want to race horses like Colin. But nobody will let me ride anything but my stupid ol' pony."

Colin gave one of her braids a gentle tug. "I wouldn't call Patches stupid. He was my very best friend when I was your age."

"Hmph. And I bet they let you go out ridin' all by yourself, even when you were a lad. But they won't let me. I always have to wait around and wait around till somebody has time to go with me."

Mariah glanced at Colin, wondering how he would respond to that. The child seemed to be quite a handful no matter where she was.

He didn't bother to answer and changed the subject entirely. "So which horses are you going to introduce Mariah to?"

"All of them, of course." She flipped a braid behind her spindly shoulder. "I'll start with the ones in the paddocks, then show her the ones in the pastures."

Nodding, his gaze lingered for a second on Mariah. "Well, if you don't mind too much, I'd like to tag along. I promise to stay out of the way and let you do all the talking."

The child cut him a shrewd glance. "Oh, all right—even though I know you're only here so's you can be with Miss Harwood where Mother can't see the two of you."

Mariah had to fake a cough to keep from laughing out loud. Amy hadn't been fooled for a second.

Colin grunted, then gestured broadly, a grin lighting his eyes. "Well, now that we all know why we're here, lead the way, *mademoiselle*. After you. . ."

As the child immediately set out for the paddocks, Colin moved next to Mariah and reached for her hand.

She sidestepped him and clasped her fingers behind her back. "What are you doing? You'll get me sold out of here!" she hissed in a fierce whisper. "Your mother is probably watching us from a window this very second."

He released a weary breath and relented, and they walked on in companionable silence.

～～～

Having been guided through the well-ordered stables and out to pastures framed by tidy, white fences that stretched on forever, Mariah was impressed by the magnificent animals and surroundings. Why, this horse farm would equal that of any earl or viscount back in England. People in Britain had no idea how very prosperous the colonies had become. If only this plantation could belong to her and Colin one day. . . . She glanced up and locked gazes with him. If only. . .

Colin gave a meaningful lift of his brow. "I do believe our trainer is in the tack room." He turned to his sister. "Don't you think our lady should meet him, Amy?"

The child's expressive blue eyes sparkled with excitement. "And Ol' Samuel, our groom. They're lucky, Miss Harwood. They get to live out here by the horses." She snatched Mariah's hand. "This way."

They ambled to the far end of the stables and stepped through an open doorway into a spacious room that smelled of leather. Rope, harnesses, and bridles draped its sidewalls, and in the middle, a series of wooden sawhorses held gleaming saddles ready to be plunked atop horses at a moment's notice. At the end, a wiry, white man of medium build and a lanky Negro with frizzled white hair stood before a long workbench cutting leather strips.

"We're here!" Amy's proud announcement rang in the quiet.

The workers turned around, their tools still in their hands.

The slave's snowy head dipped politely.

Mariah gave an answering nod.

"This here's Miss Harwood, the bond slave I've been tellin' you about," Amy said.

Bond slave. Mariah seethed. The imp could have talked all day without uttering those words.

The other man lay aside his strange-looking knife and stepped forward, nodding a somber greeting. "How do you do, Miss Harwood. I'm Geoffrey Scott, the horse trainer." A multitude of freckles stood out against his fair skin as his lips slid into a smile, putting her more at ease.

"I'm very pleased to meet you. Both of you." Her gaze included the groom.

"Amy tells us you've come to turn our young girls into proper ladies." Mr. Scott's tone indicated a measure of disbelief as a teasing glint sparked in his green eyes.

Mariah laughed lightly and shot a glance to the child. "That is the goal."

He studied her without wavering. "Then I trust they'll be receiving spiritual instruction also. Along with Bible reading." His stern gaze moved to Colin.

"Why, yes. They will." Raising her chin a notch, Mariah attempted her own austere expression. "Grace and humility are vital attributes every individual must endeavor to seek."

Colin cleared his throat and directed his attention to the trainer. "I understand Patches has been off his feed for the last few days."

"What did you say?" Amy looked up at her brother, her eyes wide with worry. "Is he sick?"

Mariah wondered the same thing. Amy had proudly pointed out the adorable white Shetland pony with its large brown spots and commented on his gentle nature. He hadn't seemed to be ailing.

"Oh, there's probably nothing we need to be worried about." Mr. Scott patted Amy's blond head in assurance. "He might not be having a good day, is all." Something about the man's soothing tone confirmed Mariah's suspicion that the suggestion of a sudden malady was a ploy.

"Even so, you will check him for any odd swellings or carbuncles, won't you?" Colin asked.

The man cut another hard glare at him. "Aye. One can't be too cautious."

"Amy." Colin tipped his head at his sister. "Why don't you go with Geoff and help him. After all, Patches is your pony."

She swung a glance between him and Mariah and back, then clamped her teeth tight. "Oh, all right. I'll go check on Patches. For five minutes."

"Ten," Colin blurted.

"All right, but you'll owe me a lot for ten." Amy latched on to the trainer's hand and tossed a smirk over her shoulder. "Come on, Mr. Scott. Those two want to be alone." She rolled her eyes with the emphasis on the last word.

A chuckle rumbled from the redhead's chest. "Ten minutes, you say." Unhooking the chain of a pocket watch, he handed it to Amy. "I'll let you keep track of the time, little lady."

⁓

"Let's stroll outside, away from the smell of the stables, shall we?" Colin tucked Mariah's arm within the crook of his elbow and led her out the back entrance, out of sight from the house.

"As you wish, milord." But once in the open air, Mariah let out a nervous giggle that bubbled into laughter.

Colin found it infectious. Despite his irritation at his sister and the trainer, he echoed her merriment.

Still laughing, she made a wide gesture with her free hand, and he realized that a number of slaves and their overseer stood a short distance away, staring at them. His humor died. Was there no place on this blasted plantation where someone wasn't watching?

"I'm sorry, Mariah," he said, growing serious as he turned her to face him. "I've been hopin' for an opportunity to get you alone."

"I know." She took a handkerchief from her ruffled sleeve and dabbed at tears her laughter had caused. "Though 'tis very unwise, as you well know."

He drew her farther away from the building, away from the unwelcome stares. "I must confess, I had no idea Mother would do everything in her power to keep me from you. The way she's been guardin' that house, one would think she's on sentry duty."

"Quite." Mariah's sad smile crimped his heart.

Leaning closer, he searched her face. "I've been remembering the time we spent together on the road from Baltimore. It was rather enjoyable, and I've missed it. I'd hoped you had, as well."

"Of course I have," she murmured, gazing up at him with those gorgeous, alluring violet eyes. "I appreciated the way you pointed out various settlements and landmarks along the way. And I liked hearing about your family and your home. You were very kind to me."

His heart throbbed double time.

"Nevertheless, you must understand that your mother made her position deadly clear. She will not abide any dalliance between us." She averted her gaze. "Or participation in any other activities I'm too ashamed to mention. I am to remember my place."

"I'm so sorry. Mother can be a touch blunt at times. She's quite set in her ways." He attempted to draw Mariah closer.

She shook her head and backed away, looking in both directions, then warded off any further advances with a hand. "Please, Colin, we must not." Still gazing at him, her worried expression dissolved into one of tenderness. "But since we do have this short moment together—which is all that is allotted to us just now—I want you to know I think very, very highly of you. I do. But—"

"Say no more, my lady." He paused. "I believe I've come up with an idea. A plan, really." *Yes, a perfect plan.* Satisfied with its brilliance, he offered her a reassuring smile. "Just leave everything to me." He gestured for her to follow as he turned and started toward the stables again. "So, tell me, how did our little snitch's first music lesson go?"

Humor returned to Mariah's beautiful face as they headed back inside to collect Amy. "You really don't want to know."

Chapter 9

During the next two days, Colin's statement about having a plan kept Mariah wondering as she worked with his sisters on their school subjects and music lessons. She spent a good deal of time mulling over those mysterious words in her mind even as she demonstrated to the girls how to subtly draw attention while strolling about a room. She illustrated how to flirt with the eyes just enough to intrigue a man without being overly blatant, how to use the fan and parasol to spark interest, and how to *accidentally* allow a bit of ankle to show amid a flurry of skirts and petticoats. The two younger sisters quickly tired of that sort of playacting.

Victoria, however, was particularly eager to learn and did her best to mimic Mariah's movements as gracefully as possible. "Is this the way?" she would ask. "Please show me once more."

Mariah showered Tori's efforts with profuse praise while the other girls were absorbed in laboring over their sums. "I'm sure you shall have no difficulty capturing Dennis Tucker's affections. . .and we'll be sure to invite him to join us as often as you wish."

"Oh, I do hope he starts noticing me," the fifteen-year-old breathed on a sigh. "After all, I'm not a child anymore." She toyed with one of her honey-colored ringlets.

"That is true. However, your mother has set a lot of store by your marrying a prosperous merchant, you know." Mariah softened the reminder with a smile. "She does feel she has your best interests at heart. She wants you to have a successful future." *Just as I wish for myself.*

A dreamy glow filled Victoria's azure eyes. "Mother has a whole list of wants, I'm sure. And so have I." With a flutter of her long lashes, she snapped her parasol open and made a ladylike circuit of the room, bestowing condescending smiles and nods on her younger sisters as she passed.

Mariah couldn't help but smile at Victoria's determination.

A light tap sounded on the door, and Lizzie opened it and leaned her mobcapped head into the room, her smile bright against *café au lait* skin. "Tea is bein' served on the veranda, missy."

The words scarcely left the slave's mouth before books and parasols slammed shut and the three young ladies flew out of the room to the top-stair landing, where they came to a sudden stop, hiked their chins, and paraded down the steps at a more sedate pace, with Mariah trailing after them. A smiling Victoria hopped over the final two steps in front of Heather, as if she somehow expected her charming Tuck to come calling.

As the little group emerged from the front entrance to join the rest of the family out on the veranda, Mariah reveled in the welcome breeze wafting up from the river. Today was by far the warmest since her arrival. The heat compelled her to remove all but one thin petticoat beneath her dimity gown adorned with multihued pastel flowers. Its short sleeves allowed the breeze to cool her arms.

Colin and his parents already occupied some of the wicker chairs surrounding the cloth-covered table as Amy dashed to a vacant seat beside her mother. The two older girls and Mariah bobbed into quick curtsies. If anything, Mariah decided, this family tended toward too much formality.

"Be seated, girls." The mistress directed a cool smile at them. "The ice is melting in the limeade."

Mariah immediately headed for the prudent seat on the sharp-eyed woman's other side, noting the heavenly sight of moisture coursing down the glasses at each place setting in the heat of the day. Just as she was about to pull out the empty chair, Colin reached from close behind her and drew it back, then seated her. She did her best not to react to his nearness, even when his arm inadvertently brushed against hers, causing a delicious tingle.

"Do hurry up, everybody." Amy ogled the platter of small sandwiches, tea cakes, and sugared raspberries, her blue eyes wide.

"Oh my." Mariah turned to Mistress Barclay while Colin returned to his place across from her. "The drinks look especially delightful on such a warm afternoon." Even more delightful, Mariah would be able to slip an unnoticed glance at Colin on occasion from this vantage point. Hopefully he would also be discreet.

Over the persistent drone of cicadas proclaiming the arrival of sultry weather, Mr. Barclay offered a brief blessing for the food. The second he finished, Amy's hand snaked out and snatched a cucumber and watercress sandwich. The child always seemed quick and full of energy no matter the time or temperature.

Mariah's preference lay in the frosty drink. Enjoying the feel of the cool, slippery glass as she raised it to her lips, she took a long sip, letting the refreshing ice chips brush her lips.

Beside her, the lady of the house, slightly flushed from the heat, in a gown of ecru linen, took a draught from her limeade, then blotted her lips on her napkin. Across from the mistress, Mr. Barclay and Colin fared a bit better in thin white shirts with the top buttons open. Mariah turned her attention to the older man. "Sir, may I ask how you managed to supply this glorious ice in such hot weather?"

Setting down his drink, he flashed a friendly smile. "There's a nice little cove not far below the falls where the ice gets quite thick in the winter. We cut ice blocks there, wrap them in burlap, and cart them by wagon to our icehouse near the creek."

"Falls? I didn't know there was a waterfall nearby."

Colin entered the conversation. "It's not exactly nearby. It's a fair ride from here, actually. And it's not just a mere little fall but quite a spectacular series of cascades. Perhaps some day next week—after classes, of course—we could take a ride up to see them."

The mistress stiffened, but Amy all but jumped out of her seat. "Me, too! I love the falls."

"Of course, squirt. We wouldn't dream of going there without you." But her brother's lackluster tone belied his cheerful words.

"Can we go tomorrow? Please?"

"No." Her mother caught Amy's chin and turned it toward her. "Tomorrow is the Sabbath. And as you know, the Reverend Mr. Hopkins and his family will be here for Sunday dinner. Hannah Grace will want to visit with you."

"Oh, I forgot." The child slumped back in her chair, then popped forward again. "Then how about—"

"No, not Monday, either," Colin interjected. "I have to go into Alexandria to meet with Quince Sherwood about the horse race Saturday after next. Soon as I find out how many others will be competing, I must have the announcements printed up and pay a couple of lads to distribute them throughout the area. Once word gets around, folks from all over will show up with their picnic baskets and set up games for the children. And of course the tinkers will be there as well, hawking their so-called miracle remedies. Heaven forbid there should ever happen to be an affair where they fail to make the most of it."

Victoria set her partially eaten sandwich on her plate. "Oh, Mother. I simply must have a new summer frock made, and a matching parasol." She shot a merry glance at Mariah, obviously hoping to test her new attention-getting techniques on Tuck.

"You already have a selection of very nice gowns, dear," her mother reminded her.

"But not in the latest fashion." She looked at the mistress with a pleading expression. "I want a gown similar to Miss Harwood's. The dimity is ever so pretty. I'd be the envy of every girl in attendance. Please?" She scrunched up her face for added measure.

Mistress Barclay perused Mariah's frock as she nibbled a piece of tea cake in thought, her expression gradually losing its resolve. "Monday is not possible. I've invited the neighbor ladies for a light lunch that day, as you well know."

"But Mama, any later and there won't be time to have my dress properly made."

Appreciating Victoria's use of the more familial *Mama* in the same sentence with the word *properly*, Mariah realized the girl was no amateur at begging.

Her mother sighed, obviously growing weary of the topic. "Colin said he has quite a lot of business to take care of in Alexandria. Unless your father is able to go with you, you won't have a chaperone. Eldon?" She swept a questioning look at her husband.

"I'm afraid not." Mr. Barclay gave a slow shake of his head. "Cora, my love, Patterson and Clark will be here while their wives are lunching with you. We'll be occupied in my study."

She arched a brow. "Oh yes. . .you men and your private card games."

"Then Miss Harwood could come with me," Victoria quickly inserted. "In fact, I'd truly like her to come. She could assist me in selecting the perfect fabric and prettiest trims like the fashionable ladies in England are wearing."

Aha. So this must be the plan Colin had hinted at. Mariah reached for a slice of cake. This was getting interesting.

"What about me, Mother?" Heather jumped into the fray. "If Tori gets a new frock, I should have one, too."

Mercy me, a fly in the ointment.

An unexpected smile moved across Mistress Barclay's lips. "You're quite right. And Amy shall go as well. You shall all have new party frocks for the event." She plucked a raspberry from her plate and placed it in her mouth as she switched her attention to Mariah. "In fact, I would like you, Mariah, to have Mistress Henderson make you at least two new dresses. Plain ones. There's no need for you to walk about looking like a fashion plate while you're tutoring the girls." She paused, narrowing her dark brown eyes in added contemplation as she tapped her index finger against her bottom lip. "I think black would be too austere. Perhaps gray would be more suitable. Yes, gray will do admirably well. And have her send two mobcaps along. Those lovely curls need protection from the summer sun."

The cake turned to sawdust in Mariah's mouth. The message was clear.

Amy, however, folded her arms and pouted. "I don't wanna waste a whole day bein' fitted for no new day gown. I have enough dresses."

"*Being* fitted for *any* new day gown," Mariah heard herself blurt out, the tutor in her rising to the occasion despite the growing ache in her heart.

The child leveled a glare at her. "And *being* corrected all the way to town and back again, no doubt." She shook her head.

At that, a round of laughter erupted, lightening the moment. But Mariah couldn't help noticing Colin's deflated expression at having his plan go awry. Her heart went out to him. . .even though the sad turn of events was probably for the best. There was still time. Four years of time. Nothing had to work out just yet. She averted her gaze to the tall oaks lining the drive and watched the lush branches swaying on the summer wind, trying to envision herself looking bland as a turtledove.

Mistress Barclay's voice brought her back to the moment as she caught her daughter's hand in hers. "Amy, dear, how about this? Colin will take all of you girls with him when he leaves for Alexandria early Monday morning. By the time you've all been fitted for new gowns, your brother should have concluded his business affairs. Then you can return home for a quick lunch, after which you can all ride up to visit the falls and spend the rest of the afternoon there. Make a whole day of it. Wouldn't that be jolly fun?"

Amy's bottom lip made an appearance, and her forehead crinkled with a frown. "But why can't I just wait at home for the rest of them to get back from town? Why do I have to go there at all?"

"Because that is the only way I will permit you to go to the falls. That is my decision."

The child mulled the concept over in her mind then, accepting her fate, stood from her chair and flung her arms around her mother's neck.

"Oh well. At least I'll have a whole day with no lessons."

Mariah saw disturbed glances pass between Colin and Victoria, and she took another sip from her tall glass. Another of Colin's plans to get her alone may have been squashed. More's the pity. But it played right into Mariah's own scheme—keeping her desirable self always dangling before him but just out of reach. . .even if she would look a bit on the plain side most of the time. That little Amy surely did come in handy.

With any luck at all, years from now, when she and Colin were wed with children of their own, Mariah would be sure to thank both his ever-watchful mother and the snitch for the excellent maneuvers that would help two people in love get together. Properly.

No matter how many obstacles were thrown in the path.

Chapter 10

On her first Day of Rest in the new land, Mariah rode in a gleaming black landau carriage, a completely new experience for her. In this luxurious conveyance, she and the wealthy Barclay family could see and be seen by everyone they passed. She smiled on a wave of pleasure. Her pious sisters, Rose and Lily, must be keeping her in their daily prayers, because Providence had definitely smiled upon her.

The open carriage had room for only six passengers, so Colin sat up top with the immaculately dressed driver, who guided a matched set of beautiful white-stocking bays at a sedate pace. Facing the rear in the deeply cushioned leather seat with Victoria and Heather, Mariah sensed Colin's presence behind her on the box bench. . .so close. Yet with her parasol shading her, there was no way he could view her.

She'd chosen her prettiest gown for the occasion, tiered lavender silk accented with delicate snowy lace, and taken extra care styling her hair. The upstairs maids, Lizzie and Celie, had done wonders with the girls, and in their summer pastels, each one could pass for an exquisite doll, as could their elegant mother. Even the men—and Colin, in particular—

drew attention in their brocade waistcoats and vests and tall silk hats. Surely the assemblage looked like royalty as they rolled smartly along the graveled road in the cool of the morning.

Sitting across from her with his wife and Amy, Mr. Barclay tipped his head at Mariah. "You're most fortunate on your first Sabbath with us to have a formal church service to attend."

Her brows dipped in question. "I don't understand."

"Our Reverend Mr. Hopkins shepherds two other flocks in Truro Parish. He must travel to a different one each week. But because our prospering port is gaining in population, he hopes to remain in Alexandria permanently in the not too distant future."

"I see." The information came as a surprise. So this village they were heading to lacked a full-time minister. Obviously Colin had exaggerated the town's attributes.

The distinguished Barclay patriarch turned to his wife with an affectionate smile. "On the other Sundays, Cora selects scripture readings for us, and we have private family worship at home."

The mistress eyed Mariah. "If you'd care to, we should like you to choose the section to read sometime. Next week, perhaps. And jot down a few questions for us to discuss, as well. It's important for the girls not only to know the scriptures but to understand their meaning and purpose also, so it can be applied to life."

Me? Prepare a Bible lesson? Mariah hoped she didn't betray her shock. On the other hand, she'd sat through innumerable tiresome sermons throughout her life. Surely she could dredge a bit of one of them from the recesses of her mind. "As you wish." Would the woman never stop testing her?

Mr. Barclay, seemingly unaware of the undercurrent, chuckled. "You'll soon learn, child, that my lady was not raised in the less demanding Church of England. She's a Massachusetts Puritan, a Congregationalist. And a particular follower of the famous Reverend Jonathan Edwards."

Having never heard of the man, Mariah leaned forward. "I'm afraid I must admit I'm not familiar with the name."

"I'm sure you wouldn't have heard of him," Mistress Barclay said in her husband's stead. "He's one of New England's more impressive ministers. Through his preaching and writings, he's garnered quite a dedicated following in the colonies. They call themselves 'New Lights.'"

"New Lights." Mariah cocked her bonneted head back and forth beneath her parasol. "That does sound rather interesting." Hopefully that would placate the woman.

"I'm glad you feel that way." The mistress brightened. "Then I shall loan you a copy or two of his writings to study. And later we shall discuss them."

"I should like that, madam." Aware she'd just spoken an untruth on the Sabbath, of all days, Mariah deftly switched the topic. "Mr. Barclay, I've noticed how very lush the fields of tobacco appear. They're quite different from plantings in southern England. The other day, I watched as your workers cut leaves and stacked them with utmost care. Why is that?" She already knew the answer but wanted a diversion from the previous, less than welcome topic.

It did the trick. The rest of the drive to Alexandria, the plantation owner expounded at length about tobacco and the other crops and workings of his vast enterprise. On Mariah's either side, his daughters emitted occasional sighs of boredom. Once, however, as they passed a lane leading to a manse that appeared as large as the Barclays', Victoria jabbed her gently in the ribs. "Tuck's place," she whispered. Mariah surveyed the attractive grounds and smiled.

Soon homes and trades shops began to appear along the road. After passing a few cross streets, the driver guided the landau onto one just ahead. The street lacked any hint of prosperity, so Mariah couldn't help but wonder if the main part of the town spread in some other direction, especially when the red-spoked carriage pulled onto a dirt lot. Peering down the road, she decided it looked even less settled and turned quietly to Victoria. "Is this the center of Alexandria?"

The girl smiled and wagged her head, sending honey-gold ringlets dancing before and behind her slim shoulders. "Not at all. The market square is farther down the Royal Road, and there's also a lot of business down on the quay."

That news came as a relief, particularly when their carriage came to a stop beside two others equally grand. A quick glance of assessment revealed that, although the other carriages were pretentious, the church building itself was far from it. Only Mrs. Barclay's gift for veiled assaults kept Mariah from commenting on the meagerness of the simple clapboard structure.

She and the older girls waited politely for the elder Barclays and Amy to exit the vehicle. Then Mariah and the two budding maidens rose, filling the interior of the carriage with their bevy of ruffled skirts. Mariah waited for the girls to precede her, hoping that if Colin helped her last, he would naturally escort her into the chapel. After all, how much safer and more proper could she be in his company than while they were attending service in church?

"Milady." Looking up at her with an expectant grin dancing in his eyes, the handsome son and heir extended a gloved hand.

She tilted her parasol to shield her face from his parents' view, then gifted him with a slightly mischievous smile of her own.

As they strolled toward the entrance, Victoria slowed ahead of them and waited while Mariah and Colin came up beside her, then tipped her head slightly with a flick of the eyes toward the church.

Mariah shot a glance forward and saw Dennis Tucker on the top landing, watching them approach.

A tiny frown on Victoria's smooth brow reminded Mariah of the promise she'd made the previous evening, that should Tuck happen to be at church this morning, she would invite the young man to come on tomorrow's outing. The promise wouldn't exactly further her own pursuit of Colin, at least not at this moment. Nevertheless, a promise was a promise. She suppressed a huff of disappointment and thought of a way to snag the young man's attention.

Walking alongside Colin, Mariah came to an abrupt stop. "Oh, la. I've a stone in my slipper." She bent to remove the shoe, surmising that Colin would lean down to assist her. When he did, she whispered into his ear. "Your sister Victoria is quite smitten with Dennis. Ask him to join us tomorrow."

"But—" He frowned.

"Please. We need her allegiance." Straightening, she spoke in a louder voice. "There, the stone is out. Thank you, kind sir."

"You're most welcome." Though offered politely, the remark lacked his usual jovial grin. He did, however, give her a meaningful nod as he took her hand and placed it within his arm. "Shall we go greet my friend Tuck?"

<hr/>

The sun was high in the sky when the landau rolled to a stop at the rear of the Barclays' home.

"Hurry, girls." The mistress shooed her daughters out of the carriage with an impatient wave of her hand. "Go fetch the food and drink from the springhouse. And don't get yourselves dirty. The Reverend Hopkins and his family will be here shortly."

Watching her charges clamber to the ground without waiting for assistance, Mariah frowned, wondering why they were being asked to do servants' work.

Mistress Barclay directed her attention to Mariah. "We keep the Sabbath as best we can. Once our house slaves have completed their necessary morning duties, they are free to spend the rest of the day as they wish."

"How very gracious of you. If there's anything I can do to assist with the meal, I'm happy to do so." It never hurt to act helpful, even if Sunday was supposed to be her free day after service as well. Mariah waited for the older woman to precede her down to Colin's waiting hand.

"Thank you, child. But Reverend Hopkins assured me he and his good wife are quite interested in becoming better acquainted with you. I'd appreciate it if you'd entertain them until dinner is served."

Mariah halted on the bottom carriage step. Entertain the minister? Her? And be asked all sorts of questions?

Waiting below for her to step down, Colin took her hand and gave it an encouraging squeeze, then turned to his mother. "And of course there'll be no mention of the fact we hold Mariah's indenturement papers." He spoke with finality.

"Of course not, dear." She gave him a small smile, but there was no accompanying sparkle in the woman's eyes. She took her husband's arm and started toward the house.

Not today, anyway. Mariah stared after the haughty woman. She then gave Colin a half smile and mouthed her thanks as her foot reached the gravel drive.

"It's been some time since the good reverend and his wife honored us with a visit." He tucked Mariah's arm in his. "Let's wait on the veranda for their arrival."

His mother turned back. Her forced smile had vanished.

Mariah gulped. "Perhaps I should help your mother prepare a tray of cool drinks for our guests, this being such a warm day."

To her relief, the woman's smile returned. "Yes. I would appreciate that."

Now her son's congenial expression faded.

Mercy me, but this endeavoring to keep everybody happy is proving to be very trying, indeed.

To Colin's relief, the Hopkins family took longer than expected to arrive, so Mariah was spared the minister's inquisition before the meal. And when everyone finally sat down at the table, Colin and his eager sisters made certain the conversation focused on the upcoming race day, rather than on Mariah and how she happened to become part of the household. Still, from the blatant stares he'd caught from thin-as-a-rail and bespectacled Reverend Hopkins and his short, plump wife, Colin could tell the pair were desperate to question her.

After the meal of cold meats and crisp salad reached its conclusion, Colin, his father, and besieged Mariah accompanied the couple out on the veranda while Victoria and Heather remained inside to help their mother clear the table. Amy wasted no time at all in taking off for the stables with the minister's daughter, Hannah Grace, and her younger brother, Jamie. Colin knew the man of the cloth would suspend his curiosity no longer. . .nor would his wife.

"You were right. It is much cooler out here," Reverend Hopkins declared. Removing his somber ministerial frock coat, he hooked it over one of the cushioned wicker chairs, then seated his wife and took the empty chair next to her. "You folks have a fine home and plantation."

"Thank you." Father followed his guest's suit and gestured to Colin, and they both shed their heavy outerwear, then took seats on either side of Mariah. "We rather enjoy our life here."

"Miss Harwood." The thin-faced man swung his attention to her before she'd even settled her skirts about her. "My good wife tells me you hail from Bath, England."

"That is correct, sir."

"Marvelous. I attended college at Oxford and spent several holidays in your fair city. By the by, which church did you attend?"

Colin sat back in his chair, surprised how quickly the clergyman moved from small talk to the inquest.

Mariah appeared relaxed as she met the man's gaze. "All of my family are members of Vicar Nielson's congregation. Perhaps you yourself attended St. John's while visiting Bath."

"My, yes. A fine church that is. Handsome building, as well."

"Indeed. We've always enjoyed it." She hiked her chin a notch, adding to her air of dignity.

Mistress Hopkins pursed her full lips, plumping out the apple-dumpling cheeks beneath her salt-and-pepper upsweep. "How is it that you happened to take leave of such a popular resort to travel across the water for a position as tutoress?"

Leaning forward, Colin answered the nosy woman. "Miss Harwood came here to be close to family."

"You don't say." Nudging his spectacles a bit higher on his nose, the minister cut her a shrewd glance, then slid it to Colin. "What family might that be? Perhaps I'm acquainted with them, since I shepherd three separate flocks in the area."

"Her older sister is with an associate of the Virginia and Ohio Fur Company. I'll be inquiring after them on the morrow, when I conduct some business in town."

The minister's wife arched a skeptical brow. "With an associate, you say."

Colin was swiftly growing irritated with the presumptive biddy and fought to keep his tone even. "As Miss Harwood is in our employ, her sister is also respectably employed."

"But of course," the woman demurred. "There is no shame in honest labor."

No shame, but no honor either. Colin noted the woman's satisfied smirk. How dare she come here seeking fodder for Alexandria's gossip mill, when all one had to do was take one look at Mariah to realize she was a gentlewoman caught in an embarrassing but temporary circumstance.

His father finally entered the fray. "Miss Harwood comes to us as a highly qualified tutoress as well as a gifted musician. We are most fortunate to have her in our household, and our daughters have already benefited from her accomplishments." He turned to her. "Perhaps later we might impose upon you to entertain us on the harpsichord with a musical rendition or two."

She gave him a grateful smile.

"I'm sure that would be most enjoyable." The minister peered across the table again at Mariah. "Still, as tutoress, I would hope you are including spiritual matters in the Barclay girls' education, as well, child."

"Indeed I am, sir." Mariah tucked her chin. "This is, after all, a Christian home."

"That is true." The reverend nodded in thought. "I've had many a spirited conversation with the dear lady of the house, since she comes from the land of the Puritans." He clasped his hands together. "Speaking of spirited, might I ask your thoughts on this morning's sermon?"

Mariah cut Colin a disturbed glance. The two of them had spent far more time merely enjoying sitting side by side than they had in paying attention to the man's dry discourse. She straightened her posture. "I believe your sermon centered on Psalm 139, did it not?"

"Quite. And what insights did you glean from King David's words?"

Colin attempted to stall for a few minutes. "We were discussing that on the way home, weren't we? It seemed each of us hit on a different point."

Mariah smiled at him and returned her attention to the clergyman. "I always find myself caught up in the beautiful lyrical wording. 'If I take the wings of the morning, and dwell in the uttermost parts of the sea. . . .' I do believe someone has set those very words to music in one of the pieces I've played."

"Ah, yes. Beautiful." Reverend Hopkins then spoke with more conviction. "But the meaning behind the Psalm has far more passion. 'O Lord, thou hast searched me, and known me. Thou knowest my downsitting and mine uprising, thou understandest my thought afar off. Thou compassest my path and my lying down, and art acquainted with all my ways. For there is not a word in my tongue, but, lo, O Lord, thou knowest it altogether.'"

Colin suddenly felt a twinge of guilt for having been less than truthful with the minister. Still, Mariah needed his help. "That scripture truly is powerful. Very powerful. To become aware that we have such an all-knowing and all-seeing God, One who cares enough to take particular interest in each and every one of us, that is an extremely profound truth. Is that not what we were talking about earlier, Miss Harwood?"

"Why, yes." She gave his wrist a secret squeeze under the table. "And you worded it most succinctly. Don't you agree, Reverend Hopkins?" She offered a smile that included his good wife. "And I want to add that I thank our Good Lord every night for bringing me to such a God-fearing family."

Delighting in her words, her voice, Colin wove his fingers through hers. Tomorrow. Tomorrow they'd be leaving his mother's ever-watchful eyes behind and spending the entire day together. And despite the nuisance of tattletale Amy's presence, he'd find a way to be alone with Mariah.

By hook or by crook.

Chapter 11

Colin prided himself for acting the perfect gentleman on the carriage ride to and from Alexandria. Positioning Amy and Heather on either side of him, he made sure his youngest sister would have nothing to tattle to their mother about when they returned home for the noon meal. He didn't want to cause the slightest trouble that could spoil plans for their afternoon outing—the horseback ride to the Great Falls.

It had taken him awhile to get used to the idea that Victoria was infatuated with Dennis Tucker. When they stopped by his friend's plantation to pick Tuck up on their return trip, she found the perfect spot for him—next to her. On her opposite side, Mariah appeared somewhat dull in comparison to Tori. As if in deference to the girl, she had chosen a frock far less fancy to allow Victoria to shine. Even her severe hairstyle lacked its usual bounce, while Victoria's golden curls and flowing ribbons danced on the breeze and reflected shards of sunlight as she chatted with Dennis. Colin began to see her with new eyes. . .the way any young buck might do. He found the concept unsettling.

When they reached the house and went inside for lunch, Colin followed the others, chuckling to himself that the business of courting could get so complicated. However, if Dennis happened to be Victoria's choice, he would do his utmost as her big brother to help her in her quest. After all, she could do far worse. Although Tuck often tended toward being on the footloose side and out for a good time, deep down he would invariably make the responsible decision.

The servants had yet to bring in the food, but delectable smells drifted in from the kitchen, promising a tasty meal. After the small group entered the dining room and found chairs, Mother joined them and took her customary place at the end of the long table.

Colin addressed her as he seated Mariah next to him in one of the side chairs. "Where's Pa? I thought he'd be eating with us."

"Down at the stables. He wanted to be sure the afternoon outing would be enjoyable for everyone, so he's selecting some gentle mounts for the girls."

"How thoughtful." Colin was relieved that his father would be preoccupied for a time. He had something to say that the older man would likely not approve of.

His mother directed her gaze to Victoria. "Were you girls able to find pretty fabrics and trims for your new gowns?"

As his sister opened her mouth to reply, Colin winced and held up a finger. "Before you ladies start talking ribbons and lace and other fripperies, I have a comment to make."

Just as he hoped, all eyes riveted on him.

"I think it's high time, Mother, for you to pay more attention to how Victoria dresses. The frock she has on today makes her seem much too—" He narrowed his eyes and stared at her. "Too grown up."

Victoria gasped, her mouth gaping in speechless shock.

The other young people exchanged puzzled glances but remained silent.

His mother appeared far from pleased herself as she spoke through tight lips. "Whatever do you mean, son?"

Not at all put off by her demanding tone, he cocked his head back and forth and straightened his spine. "It's like this. From the moment we reached Alexandria, it seemed every man in town began gawking at Victoria. Anyone with half a brain could tell what was on their minds. Then after I dropped the girls off at the seamstress's shop, I barely got half a block away before that upstart, Eddie Rochester, came running up to me, wanting to know if he could come calling on her this evening."

Mother's eyes grew wide as she swallowed the bait. The Rochesters were the wealthiest merchants along the quay. "Are you referring to Gilbert Rochester's eldest son?"

Colin smirked. "Quite. The one who's always tearing about the countryside in that fancy phaeton of his, kicking up all kinds of dust. Needless to say, I wasted no time in setting him straight."

"What did you say to him?" His mother clutched the arms of her chair.

"The truth. That Tori's just a child. Too young to start receiving callers."

Victoria paled and shrank in her seat in embarrassment.

"Too young!" Sinking back in her chair, Mother shook her head, her eyes ablaze. "This is not to be borne, Colin. You are turning out to be even worse than your father. I refused to tolerate his interference regarding our daughters, and I shall not abide such actions on your part either. Your sister is not a child. She will turn sixteen in less than a month, and she's a beautiful, blossoming young woman. As soon as you've eaten, I expect you to ride straight back into town and inform Edward he's more than welcome to call on Victoria at any time."

Colin had the sinking feeling he'd overplayed his hand a fraction.

"But Mama!" Amy lurched to her feet. "He's takin' us to the falls this afternoon. You promised." Folding her arms, she plopped back down onto her chair, her bottom lip protruding.

"I'll go first thing in the morning." Colin gave his mother a placating nod. "If you're absolutely sure you want that Rochester whelp hanging around here."

"He is a bit pushy," Victoria admitted in a subdued voice. "He's been tryin' to catch my attention at church for some time now. I've just ignored him."

Tori must have caught on to his attempt to whet Tuck's interest by injecting a little competition, real or imagined. Colin breathed a little easier. With any luck at all, having her and his friend otherwise occupied would give him some time alone with Mariah, which was the whole point of the outing.

"Darling." Mother spoke to Victoria in a more soothing maternal tone. "That's what young men do whenever a young miss catches their fancy. You really should be flattered. That particular gentleman would be quite the catch for any girl. Now, enough of this sort of talk. It's time to eat." Picking up a silver bell near her plate, she rang it.

Colin saw Tuck slide a glance to Victoria. One that lingered, as if seeing her for the first time.

Mariah must have noticed as well. She nudged Colin's foot with hers.

And now the rest of the day awaited them.

Mariah doubted there had ever been a more glorious summer day. The dreadful heat of the Sabbath had gradually dissipated during the night, and a milder, flawless morning dawned. Now a little past midday, luscious, billowy clouds floated across the bluest of skies, and birds of every hue and voice gave tribute to nature's perfection as the small group plodded their way over the rolling, wooded terrain toward the Great Falls.

Walking their long-legged Thoroughbreds beneath a shady canopy of trees to rest them, Mariah looked at Colin and chuckled as Heather and Amy sprang up into their saddles and galloped ahead in the wake of two young fawns sprinting through the forest. "At last. 'Tis a full week since you and I have been able to speak freely without someone reporting on our every word."

"Only a week?" A wry half smile twitched his lips as he tugged on Paladin's lead and drew him alongside her horse. A cool breeze from the river below ruffled the full white sleeves of his blouse and toyed with a lock of his hatless hair. "Seems more like a month." His dark eyes drifted to Mariah's and took their sweet time there before he so much as blinked.

"Before my sisters come back, I do want to apologize for not apprising you of something you may not know."

She tipped her head in question.

"I am but an heir to my family's wealth, still awaiting my inheritance. But my father assures me it won't be the case much longer. He's promised to deed over a portion of our land to me when I turn five and twenty—which is a mere seven months hence. At that time I'll have my own income to do with as I wish—and my own home, should I choose to build one."

He made it sound as if it was important for her to know those things, as if she would somehow be a part of it. But seven months. That was a long time to wait when one was forced to live under the thumb of his domineering mother. Still, so be it. Seven months or—heaven forbid—seven years, Colin was a man who was more than worth the wait. She moistened her lips and peered up at him through her lashes. "If it is not too bold of me to ask, do you so choose to build a home of your own?"

He flashed a sheepish smile. "Actually, until a week ago I hadn't given the matter much thought. But now the possibility seems to be growing more enticing all the time." He reached for her hand, his gaze still roving her face. "Mariah, we've known each other for such a short while, you and I, yet from the first moment I saw you, I knew you were incredibly special, and that proves to be truer by the moment. You must know you're all I think about every day, all I dream about at night. I don't think it was by some bizarre twist of fate that we met. I believe you came into my life for a reason."

Hearing the words she had hardly allowed herself to dream about, Mariah could scarcely draw breath over the throbbing of her heart. She'd never seen such a depth of feeling in Colin's expression before, and she was thankful that Victoria and Dennis weren't near enough to witness it, since they were riding a ways behind them.

Or were they?

Suddenly aware she could not detect the sound of the couple talking or the clop of their horses, Mariah turned and looked back along the trail. They were nowhere to be seen.

Colin scowled. "I can't believe this. A few subtle nudges on my part, and my pal absconds with my sister." He swung up onto Paladin and wheeled him around.

Mariah reached a hand up to stay him. "Wait a moment, Colin. Surely they'll be coming into view any second. Don't embarrass Victoria unnecessarily. She's been mooning after Dennis Tucker for so long, and he's finally beginning to show interest—thanks to you."

His expression darkened. "Indeed. Well, there's interest, and then there's interest."

Unable to resist such a perfect moment, Mariah gave him a coy smile. "And which kind of interest do you have in me, if you don't mind my asking?"

"Both!" Ramming his heels into Paladin's flanks, he sped off in the direction they'd come.

Both. Exactly what she'd hoped with all her heart to hear. She let out a slow breath and climbed aboard her mount. If only she hadn't discovered Victoria was missing. Perhaps there might even have been a proposal of marriage, had the moment lasted a bit longer. If she had ever doubted before, those doubts had just been put to rest, even though she could not imagine how things could ever work out toward that end. Particularly with Mrs. Barclay to consider.

Watching after Colin, she saw him rein his horse to a halt. Beyond him Victoria and Tuck rode slowly into view, laughing and absorbed in each other, completely oblivious to the fact that the protector of Victoria's honor awaited them. How amazing that this man who wouldn't give his sister a few measly minutes alone with her new beau had done nothing this entire week but think up plans to get Mariah alone.

Once the big brother made certain the couple took note of his meaningful glower, he came back to join Mariah. He shook his head while matching Paladin's gait to that of her mount, and his demeanor lightened noticeably. "I was hoping to distract Amy, particularly when we reach the falls, since she loves to play in the water there. But now this." He lofted a hand in the air in a helpless gesture. "My little sister will be the least of my concerns. It's my oldest one I'll have to keep a close eye on."

Mariah slanted him a smile. "Surely you can trust your best friend to be a gentleman."

"You jest." Scoffing, he tossed a glance of disbelief over his shoulder.

Surmising that the young man could be trusted about as much as she could trust Colin, given the right opportunity, Mariah stifled a giggle. "Well, kind sir, you did say the falls are very beautiful. There'll be other times for us, I'm sure."

He didn't respond immediately, just plodded along, a thoughtful tilt to his dark head. "The day of the race." He nodded with finality and relapsed back into his drawl. "I'll make certain of it then. That mother of mine has been runnin' my life far too long already, whether she's had reason to do so or not. It's time I put an end to her meddlin.'"

Even though Mariah hoped with all her being that he spoke the truth, she couldn't ignore the twinge of uneasiness at the level of his determination. "You do remember her threat to sell me to some vile stranger," she murmured, as if voicing the thought aloud would bring the horrid prospect to reality.

A slow, smug grin moved across his lips. "Ah, but you forget one thing. Whose signature is on those papers?" He quirked a teasing brow. "Not hers. Mine."

Chapter 12

The next two weeks stretched on interminably. Mariah's thoughts insisted on reverting constantly to the horseback ride to the Great Falls. She'd come so close to securing a marriage proposal from Colin that afternoon. So close. But with him occupied in overseeing his sister's conduct during the remainder of the outing, there'd been no further mention of the possibility of a shared future for the two of them. Mariah now had no other recourse than to wait until the day of the upcoming race for another opportunity to be alone with him, and patience never had been her dominant virtue.

To be fair, Colin had tossed her a few meager crumbs of his affection now and then since their return—a private look, the occasional folding of her hand within his beneath the dining table. But sly little Amy managed to snag the chair between them most mealtimes, no doubt following her mother's instructions.

These days Colin and his father spent most of their hours out with the horses, since Mr. Barclay had decided to enter a second promising filly from their stables in the racing competition. Mariah filled the majority of her time with her teaching duties. Heather, the quiet middle daughter, showed amazing promise when it came to learning the violin, and Mariah truly enjoyed working with the talented young miss. Even if fate determined her stay here on the plantation to be cut short by marriage, she hoped to be permitted to keep helping Heather to master the instrument.

Increasingly, her dreams centered on taking her leave of this magnificent plantation and living with Colin in a fine home of their own. But since that all-important conversation on the way to the falls had been aborted, there hadn't been a single moment for them to be alone long enough to formulate any plans. Their very first day back, he'd been forced to make good on his lie to his mother by returning to Alexandria and convincing Edward Rochester he was welcome to come and call on Victoria. In turn, that young man's almost daily presence spurred Tuck to drop by most evenings as well.

Fanning herself while her charges composed essays regarding their jaunt to the falls, Mariah switched her attention out the small window, staring unseeing at a summer sky fragmented by the branches of a maple tree just outside.

Victoria obviously relished having wealthy and handsome young bachelors devoting endless evenings to showering her with attention. Mariah couldn't help but envy the girl as she watched from the sidelines, playing the harpsichord while Tori and the others danced and sang. Observing Colin coaxing shy Heather to dance with him did bring a smile, however. He was by far richer and better looking than either of the two young swains. He was sure to be a gentle father to his and Mariah's children. If. . .

She sighed and averted her focus to the music before her. The someday of her dreams could prove to be a long way off.

⁓

Race day arrived at last with a flurry of activity. Amid excited giggles and complaints, every hair on every head had to be in proper order, and every new garment had to accentuate the girls' slender bodies perfectly, especially Victoria's. "After all," Mistress Barclay had declared the day before, "we must all be at our best. We cannot look like paupers before our neighbors."

But no one looked forward to the day in Alexandria with more anticipation than Mariah as she floated down the stairs in her own most stylish summer gown. In daffodil lawn, its full skirt was drawn up on either side in a soft apron effect to reveal ruffled petticoats, and a broad sash of emerald satin formed a flowing bow in back. Around her neck she wore a delicate cameo on an emerald ribbon, a prized treasure that once belonged to her mother. She hoped to dazzle Colin enough today that she would become a betrothed woman before the sun set. Of course, the event would likely have to be kept secret until his inheritance had been secured, because under no circumstance—even considering her indenturement—would she go to his home or his bed without a proper certificate of marriage.

Her imaginings were interrupted when Amy bumped past her on the stairs. "Do hurry. Mama said I could bring Patches along with us. After the race and the picnic, she said I can ride around on him with the rest of the kids."

"I'm sure that will be—" Mariah stopped midsentence as Amy bolted away, the leather soles of the child's slippers echoing across the marble floor of the foyer and out the open door. *It'll be most enjoyable for Colin and me*, she added mentally with a wry smile. Having the youngster occupied was vital to the plan.

Reaching the bottom landing, Mariah strolled toward the entrance, her closed parasol tapping beside her like a stylish cane. *Dear Lord, I know You want what's best for me. . .and for my sisters*, she added for good measure. *Once I'm wed to Colin, I shall be able to buy their bond papers and perhaps even send Rose and Lily back to Papa in England. He'd like that, I'm sure. So whatever I must say or do today, I just know You'll agree will be for the best. Thank You.* Gratified that she'd remembered to pray, she stepped out into a glorious, dew-kissed morning.

The landau would be used again today. Jericho, the driver, stood resplendent in a crisp black uniform as he waited beside the open carriage door to assist everyone into the conveyance. Choosing a seat facing the rear so Mistress Barclay would be able to face forward, Mariah wagged her head and smiled at the sight of Amy. The child was turned to the rear and on her knees, facing her little spotted gelding.

"You get to come with us, Patch. We're gonna have so much fun!"

"You'd better turn around," Mariah urged the girl. "I hear your mother coming, and you're crushing that lovely new skirt."

Amy flipped around and smoothed her rose taffeta frock as her sisters preceded their mother out the door.

Heather, attired in ruffled peach, and Victoria in a soft blue the identical hue of her eyes, looked especially fetching as they approached the carriage. But though the new day gowns were lovely on the girls, nothing could compare to Victoria's breathless smile at having not only one beau but two!

Mariah squelched a smug smile. Today her parents would be there to chaperone their budding daughter. With any luck at all, the elder Barclays would be so busy watching Tori, they'd have no chance to oversee Colin and her. *Yes, Lord, this truly will be a wonderful day.*

Once the women were settled with their parasols safely stored and the driver had climbed up to his seat, the mistress cleared her throat. "Jericho, you may proceed now."

"Yes, Miss'tus." With a snap of Jericho's whip, the carriage lurched into motion.

"I wish Papa were here to see our new frocks," Heather lamented. "And my new parasol. It's ever so pretty."

"So do I, dear." Her mother looked across at Heather, who sat beside Mariah. "But you know he and your brother needed to take the horses into town yesterday so the animals would be completely rested for today's race."

"I know. But he's never seen me in anything this pretty. It makes me look grown up, does it not?"

Mistress Barclay offered a warm smile. "Yes. Ever so grown up. But your father always thinks you're beautiful, no matter what you wear."

Mariah couldn't keep from chiming in. "And I think that all of you look as marvelous as any stylish London family traveling to Bath on holiday."

"Do you really think so?" A faint pink tinge rose over Victoria's fine cheekbones as she reached up to touch the intricate cluster of curls Lizzie had fashioned for her.

"Absolutely. 'Tis an honor to be riding with you."

Her flattering words didn't seem to faze the lady of the family. Unsmiling, she swung her gaze to the passing countryside. "I do hope both horses fare well in the race today. Should that be the case, Eldon believes it would entice more of the gentry to buy locally, rather than import their Thoroughbreds from England."

Mariah gave her a polite nod. *Splendid! Another concern to keep the Barclays' time filled. Yes, this was going to be a very good day.*

"I never expected so many people!" Mariah turned in her seat to peer over her shoulder as the landau crunched along the graveled road toward Alexandria. Even with the town buildings some ways off, crowds already milled about, blocking the road. In the distance, canopies of different sizes and shapes edged a long, narrow clearing, and men stood at each one, buying and selling. Others hollered above the noise, hawking their wares. Oblivious to the melee, children darted among the throng, rolling hoops and skipping arm in arm.

Along each side of what Mariah surmised was the racecourse, colorful groups had already gathered in the shaded areas beneath the trees and laid out blankets and quilts for their picnics. All this for a simple horse race! She shook her head in wonder.

Amy suddenly sprang to her feet and leaned over the edge of the carriage. "I thought so! A parade of musicians is comin'! With two drummer boys in front!" She swung her attention to Mariah. "Please, can I play a drum instead of that ol' violin? I hate those screechy strings, and a drum would be so much more fun."

Mistress Barclay reached out and tugged her daughter back to her seat. "Do try to be a young lady, child. . .at least until we get situated. And no, you may not have a drum to pound on. Drums are for announcing special events or beating out a cadence for soldiers to march by, definitely not for making parlor music."

The girl slumped down with a morose expression and crossed her arms with a huff.

"We're so sorry." Mariah hoped her soothing tone would placate the little imp. " 'Tis just one of those small disappointments we young ladies must face because we were born as daughters and not sons. But as you get older, I'm sure you'll learn to appreciate all the things you'll get to do that boys cannot."

Amy's dangling foot gave an angry kick to the padded leather seat board. "You mean like spending hours and hours in front of a mirror having your hair yanked and pulled? Ha! I'd rather gig frogs."

Her sisters, on either side of Mariah, burst out laughing, and she could do no less.

Even the lady of the family lost some of her starch by chuckling behind her gloved hand. "Mercy me, Amy-child. You are the gray hairs on my head."

The slightly off-key assembly of drummers and fifers marched off the road and continued on until they reached the edge of the racecourse, where their piercing ruckus ceased.

Mariah smiled at Heather. "When your flute arrives—a proper flute, mind you—you'll learn to make the sweetest sort of music, not at all like that annoying noise."

The girl's expression turned dreamy. "Indeed. I once heard a street musician in Charles Town playing a flute. His music was ever so enchanting and sweet."

"Yes, dear, I'm sure it was." Mistress Barclay smiled and reached over to give her daughter an empathetic pat, then called up to the driver. "Jericho, turn off here and drive us to that sprawling oak down near the far end."

"Yes'm. Y'all sure ya wants to go that far away?"

"Quite. I prefer to be away from the dust and racket."

As he reined the matched team dutifully off the road and headed for the spot she'd indicated, the mistress gave Mariah a nod. "We'll actually be able to see the finish line much better from there."

Amy again hopped to her feet. "Look, here comes Colin and Tuck—and that Eddie Rochester of Tori's, of course."

Victoria craned around to see them, but Mariah caught her arm and shook her head. " 'Tis best not to act too eager."

"Somebody else is with them. He looks quite tall." Amy frowned and leaned out so far over the edge Mariah feared she might topple off. "I don't know who it is. Do you, Mama?"

The matron glanced in the direction of the approaching young men and gave a half smile. "I do believe it's that young Washington lad, George, if I'm not mistaken. So sad about his brother dying of smallpox. I heard he's inherited Mount Vernon."

"You don't say." Victoria's blue eyes grew brighter.

"Don't waste a second thought on him, daughter," her mother cajoled. "Little money came with the inheritance. I doubt he'll amount to much."

"Well, he sure sits a horse fine." Victoria maintained her interest as the men drew up alongside.

Dennis Tucker swept his tricornered hat off his sandy head in a grand gesture and beamed, centering his hazel-eyed gaze on Victoria. "Good morning, ladies. What a pleasure to see such a bounty of beauty in a single carriage."

Not to be outdone, lanky, freckle-faced Edward gave a wry smirk. "A veritable bouquet of Fairfax County's loveliest blossoms, to be sure."

"Why, thank you." Mistress Barclay tilted her head to one side, and the wispy plume on her summer bonnet dipped delicately with the motion.

Mariah took the opportunity to admire Colin, attired in black racing pants and tall boots, a full-sleeved white blouse, and a gray-striped vest. He looked incredibly handsome.

And he was filling his dark eyes with her, his look conveying all the desire for her she knew he kept hidden inside.

Lest his mother notice their locked gazes, Mariah smiled politely at him. "Mr. Barclay, I don't believe I've met your friend."

Colin blinked, then regained his composure. "Ah, yes. Quite right.

George Washington, I'd be pleased to introduce you to Miss Harwood. She's the tutoress to my sisters that Tuck mentioned. I believe you've met my family."

The serious-faced young man tipped his hat and gave a polite bow of his head. "How do you do, miss." He offered only the hint of a smile as his blue eyes took in the whole group. He nodded to Colin's mother. "Mistress Barclay. A pleasure to see you again."

"Are you racing today with the others?" Mariah asked, noting the well-muscled gray he rode.

"Yes, but only for the sport. My horse is more accustomed to climbing mountains than running about a track."

"Aye." Colin placed a hand on the young man's shoulder. "George has been appointed by the governor, no less, to survey the backcountry."

"My." Mariah studied the serious newcomer. "For one so young, I'm sure that must be quite an honor." Just as she'd suspected, opportunities in this new country truly did abound. She scanned the other riders. "I wish you all good luck. May the best horse win." *And may I win my prize as well—the one awaiting a few short hours from now.*

Nice going, dunderhead. Colin clenched his teeth so hard his jaw ached as he called himself every foul name he could think of. He'd had that race in the bag. But after being in the lead for nearly the entire time, a flash of yellow distracted him as Mariah cheered him on from the sidelines, and the horse on his flank sped on by over the finish line, along with one of the others. Colin came in third. Why did she have to choose that all-important moment to look so breathtakingly beautiful that he'd lost his focus and eased up on Paladin? Well, nothing could be done about it now. Time to join the family and pretend he still had an appetite.

Striding up to the green plaid blanket where Mariah was busy helping his mother set out food for the picnic lunch, he let his gaze linger on the English beauty. The yellow gown gracing her enticing form made her look like a delicate spring daffodil waiting to adorn someone's elegant table. It was a wonder that the other competitors in the race hadn't been distracted as he'd been.

At least Pa's filly, Queen's Lace, had been the victor. Colin couldn't help but smile. The poor young thing was so frightened by all the horses chasing her, she'd practically killed herself trying to get away from them.

But there was another filly Colin didn't plan to allow to get away. Not today. He eased down onto the wool blanket beside Mariah.

He sensed her awareness of him as she casually brushed a brown-black curl from her shoulder without acknowledging his presence.

"I couldn't be more proud of Queenie today," Father gushed as he sat down beside Mother. "I truly believe our Thoroughbred business will begin to pay for itself in the very near future."

"I do hope so, Eldon." She gave his arm a gentle squeeze. "This enterprise has been quite expensive. And we'll need a considerable amount of money in the next few years." She tipped her head meaningfully in Victoria's direction, where her daughter sat with a beau on either side.

Colin knew his mother referred to the cash money that would be required to pay for his three sisters' dowries once they were married off to merchant heirs like Edward Rochester. She was determined that Colin's own marriage would bring more land to the family. Mother was also resolute to see him wed to one of the local plantation belles. Preferably one from a neighboring farm, like prissy Constance Montclair.

Suddenly aware that his pa was pronouncing the blessing over the food, Colin bowed his head. He was so torn. The fact was, he did want to bring property to his family, just not at the expense of his happiness. And he'd never known such incredible joy as had been his good fortune since Mariah came into his life.

He swept her a sidelong glance. Her head was bowed in prayer, and parted curls revealed a tempting, slender neck. He let his eyes rove the alluring curve. A lot of men managed to have both: a proper marriage and a mistress on the side. They seemed to fare well. Why couldn't that work for him?

"Amen." His pa finished, bringing a swift end to Colin's musings. Before the man could tack on the encouragement to eat, everyone began helping themselves to the fried chicken and summer salad. Father just grinned. "Your mother and I have been invited to visit the Lawrences after we finish eating. Harold Lawrence expressed an interest in buying our young winner."

A pleased murmur made the rounds.

" 'Twould be my honor to attend Victoria while y'all are occupied with business," Tuck offered with fork in hand as he flaunted one of his charming grins.

Mother met his gaze. "That's most thoughtful of you, Dennis. I gladly leave Victoria and Heather in yours and Edward's care. My daughters are to remain together at all times."

Colin squelched a smug grin. He should've known she was much too astute to be fooled by Tuck. Inhaling deeply of Mariah's lemon verbena perfume, he took a healthy bite of his drumstick.

"Oh, and Colin." Mother dabbed her lips with a napkin. "Do see that Amy and her pony don't get into any mischief while we're discussing things with the Lawrences."

"Mama!" Bread crumbs flew from Amy's mouth as she lurched to her knees. "You said I could ride around with the other kids. You promised."

"And you may, darling." She bestowed an indulgent look on her daughter as she spoke in her calmly superior voice. "Your brother will just be there to see you don't get too exuberant."

Not this time I won't. Pretending not to be disturbed in the least, Colin took a sip of his lemonade. Today, the little snitch was as eager to be rid of him as he was of her. He tipped his head at his mother. "This has been a delectable spread, Mother. Truly superb, as always."

Chapter 13

Idly twirling her lacy parasol, Mariah stood in the shade of a hickory tree not far from the entrance of the livery barn. Colin had gone inside to saddle Amy's pony, and from the significant look he'd given her on his way past, she knew he had no intention of remaining in the child's company for long.

She glanced around while she waited, noting that the crowd had thinned a bit. Some folks had left for their homes, while many continued to lounge at their picnic spots under the trees. A number of people still browsed the wares of the peddlers, and others loitered in front of a nearby tavern. A few passing men had sent Mariah suggestive grins, but she pretended not to notice as she admired the scenery. There couldn't have been a more perfect summer day.

Just how long does it take to saddle a little horse? She tapped her foot impatiently in the grass for several seconds, then left the protection of the tree and started toward the open barn doors. In the darkened interior, she saw Colin talking seriously to Amy as the girl sat astride her pony. From his unflinching stance, Mariah could only guess at the instructions he was giving her, since he intended for his sister to go riding on her own without him.

"I promise! I promise!" Pouting her displeasure, Amy rammed her heels into Patches's sides, and the pony lurched forward into a trot, barely missing Colin's booted feet as it charged out of the barn and past Mariah. "See you later!" The girl's joyous shout trailed off as she bounced away, long blond waves whipping behind her.

Watching after her young charge, a sudden uneasiness gnawed at Mariah's conscience. Amy was, after all, only eight. A very reckless eight. Anything could happen to her.

Colin strode out into the light at last, and he, too, wore a dubious expression as he joined Mariah.

She continued to watch down the road until Amy brought her pony to a halt alongside three other youngsters on ponies; then she glanced up at Colin. "Do you think she'll be all right?"

He shrugged a shoulder, as if Amy were the least of his concerns. "The squirt's been riding since she was two. I'm sure she'll be fine." Turning his attention from his sister to her, he tucked Mariah's hand into the crook of his arm.

"I suppose you're right." She somehow managed a confident smile, assuring herself that nothing should distract her from her own goal this day.

"The air's still filled with dust from so many people milling about." Colin's voice was low and promising. "Why don't we leave all the hubbub behind and take a stroll in the woods behind the livery?"

"That sounds most refreshing." Mariah smiled demurely up at him and allowed him to guide her along the side of the paddocks. But she couldn't help fighting a giggle at his calling the cacophony of sounds here "hubbub." Had he ever been to Bristol on market day, he'd know what real noise was.

He continued to lead her away, out of the sight of curious eyes as they meandered toward the seclusion of the trees. "Did you enjoy the race?"

"Oh, yes," she teased, "particularly when you were willing to risk it just to acknowledge my presence."

He chuckled. "Not only did I risk the race, it was that mind-stealing beauty of yours that cost me the victory. I now understand how the face of Helen of Troy could sink a thousand ships. I'm sure she had nothin' on you."

Truly flattered, it was Mariah's turn to laugh lightly. "Are we women that dangerous, milord?"

"Indeed you are. I'm afraid I'm in jeopardy of losing not only my heart but my very soul to you." The mirth in his face vanished as his demeanor turned serious.

Mariah's heart skipped a beat. "Good sir, please don't think me so terribly dangerous. All I ask of you is your heart. Your soul I must leave to God."

He cocked a dark eyebrow as he continued to study her. "Are you quite sure of that? Because you've completely bewitched me."

Reaching up a tentative hand, Mariah palmed his cheek, lightly stubbled with a dark afternoon shadow. "I do believe 'tis quite the other way round." She tilted her chin and smiled into his compelling brown eyes. "You have been my greatest temptation from the moment I first caught sight of you."

A chuckle rumbled from deep in his chest. "And you think you didn't tempt me? As you must have deduced by now, my family had no need of a bond servant, yet I went so far as to part with my father's good money to purchase you."

"You did indeed." She continued to drink in his handsome face. "And that makes you my hero."

He didn't respond immediately but let his gaze envelop her as his smile faded and his other hand covered her fingers on his arm. "I want to be more than just a hero to you, my dear Mariah. Much more." Then, as if suddenly remembering where they were, he turned and checked over his shoulder.

Mariah did the same. She could see no one watching them. In a few more steps they reached the cloister of deep shade beneath boughs and tangled vines. She closed her eyes as a cool breeze ruffled the ferns and shade grasses, brushing gently across her face and neck. It was quiet in the woods, as if they'd entered another world, just the two of them.

Colin drew her to him and lowered his mouth to capture hers.

Stunned at first, she felt a thrill spiral through her being all the way down to her toes. His mouth was so seeking. . . .

After an eternal moment wrapped in his powerful embrace, feeling his heart throbbing along with hers, she regained her senses. Easing out of his arms, she thrust him away and raised trembling hands to ward him off. "Mr. Barclay!" It had not been prudent to let him take her so far from the safety of other people. This definitely was not how their private interlude was supposed to play out.

"I. . .don't understand." Stricken, he just stared at her, uncertainty clouding his face.

Whether his frown signified confusion or anger at her rebuff, Mariah could not tell. She only knew she needed to proceed with care. "Kind sir, if I gave you the impression that I was someone with whom you could dally, I beg your forgiveness most ardently. My feelings for you are honest, sincere. . .and quite pure." Spinning on her heel, she straightened the lace ruching on her bodice, hoping to dredge up a convincing tear or two.

"Mariah." His quiet voice was very near. "Forgive me. It's just that I. . ." He released a shuddering breath.

The sigh did it. Her eyes swam. She turned back to him and took his hands in hers, tears trembling on her lashes as she gazed up at him. "I know, Colin. Truly, I do. Pushing away from you was the hardest thing I've ever done in my life. My whole body is aquiver from your touch. But I cannot help but believe 'twould be best if you do as your mother wanted from the start."

"What are you saying?"

"You must sell me off. Otherwise, I fear you'll be the ruin of me. Rose, Lily, my Papa. . . I could never bring such awful shame to my family. I just couldn't."

Gazing deeply into her eyes as his hands tightened around hers, he hiked his chin. "And you shan't." With his thumb, he wiped the pearl of moisture that had finally started its journey down her cheek. "No more tears, my love. The very moment my father signs over the southwest section to me as he promised, I'll announce our intention to marry." He pulled her close again, ever so gently, and lifted her chin with the edge of his finger. "If that's agreeable to you, of course."

"You would marry me? Are you sure? You know I come with no dowry." She gazed longingly into his eyes, vitally needing this binding commitment from him. "I'm certain that once my father has recouped his losses, he'll take it upon himself to send me something. I fear 'twould only be money, however, nothing compared to the land your mother expects you to bring to your family when you marry."

He grunted in disgust. "Mother. She's much too ambitious for her own good. Your love and your sweetness are all the dowry I shall ever desire, Mariah. I just regret that we must keep our betrothal a secret until January, and that you must continue on under her thumb until then."

Mariah gave an insignificant shrug. "She isn't so bad, truly she isn't. She merely wants the best for her family, as would any mother. I pray I will love my children as deeply as she does hers."

"Children." A slow smile spread across his lips. "I suspect you'll be the most beautiful mother who ever lived, and I hope someday we'll have daughters who look exactly like you."

"And sons," she said lightly, "who look just like you." In a burst of enthusiasm, she wrapped her arms around his neck. "Oh, Colin, dearest Colin, this is the happiest day of my life."

Unable to contain his own happiness, Colin laughed as he caught Mariah's luscious form to him and swung her around. He wanted to shout to the world that this beautiful creature had agreed to be his, his forever.

She laughed, too, throwing her head back in joy. "Yes, yes, I'll marry you."

"Let's go tell everyone! I cannot keep this to myself." Setting her down and tucking her against his side, he started back toward the clearing. Then he slowed and turned to her. "That is what I'd like to do. But we can't, of course. I know that all too well." He cupped her soft face in his hands and absorbed its stunning beauty. "January seems an eternity away. It will be difficult to keep my distance from you and act as if nothing has changed between us."

"I know. We shall have to keep ourselves incredibly busy until then." She offered him a saucy grin. "Have I told you what a wonderful talent Heather has for music? I do believe she'll be playing duets with me in no time at all. Would it not be wonderful if she could play at our wedding?" Her violet eyes glowed as she spoke, adding even more to her allure. "Yes, that's what I'll do. I'll spend my lonely hours working with Heather until she has mastered the violin. Have you a favorite piece you'd like me to teach her for the ceremony, perchance?"

Absorbed in her voice, Colin felt it was all the music he would ever need.

"Do you?" She stared up at him questioningly.

He smiled, realizing she expected a response of some sort. "Anything that pleases you will please me."

Mariah tilted her flirty face up to him, a teasing glint in her eyes. "I shall remind you of that years from now when you're being obstinate."

"Years from now. I like the sound of that." Taking her hand in his, he began walking again, matching his stride to hers as he cast a glance around. "Why can't it be spring? I would love to pick a huge bouquet of wildflowers for you as a remembrance of this day."

She reached over with her free hand and gave his elbow a squeeze. "I need no token to remember this lovely day. Not as long as you keep looking at me the way you are right now."

Colin raised her hand to his mouth and pressed a kiss to it as he stared longingly at her tender lips.

"But I do think we ought to get back and check on Amy, don't you?"

Realizing Mariah must have read the desire in his gaze, Colin began walking again. "Quite right. The squirt can get into trouble faster than a pair of barn kittens at milking time."

Emerging into the slanting afternoon light behind the livery, Mariah opened her parasol against the sun's bright rays and moved a few respectable steps away from him. "I do hope no one has missed us."

He scoffed. "I can't think of anyone who would."

The words were scarcely out of his mouth when a high, shrill voice called out his name.

Mariah stiffened with fear. "Who could that be? I pray 'tis not your mother."

"Of course it isn't." He'd spoken with more confidence than he actually felt. As he picked up the pace, growing apprehension pricked at him. "They're visiting the Lawrences, remember? Dickering over the price of the filly."

When they rounded the front of the barn, Colin spied Heather and Victoria searching the road into Alexandria and waved his arm at them. "We're over here, girls!"

Both spun around and picked up their skirts as they ran to him.

"Where are Tuck and Edward?" Mariah asked, scanning the area and seeing neither young man.

Panting from the run, Heather flashed a sly grin. "Hiding out, no doubt."

Colin, however, tensed, his rage rising. "Where are those bounders? They were supposed to stay with you."

"I'd forget about them if I were you," Victoria announced, looking from him to Mariah and back. "Mother's not in high dudgeon over those two. She wants you. Now."

Chapter 14

Amy stood with her parents and the Widow Doolittle in front of the woman's cottage on the far end of town. Frantic and on the verge of tears, the child wrenched free of Mother and ran toward Colin and Mariah as they approached. "Tell Mama it wasn't me! Tell her it was Henry Jay and Walter that did it. Not me."

Taking stock of the dour expressions on the faces of his parents and the widow as Amy flew toward him, Colin let out an exasperated huff. How long had the girl been on her own? Ten, fifteen minutes? More? This was not good.

The adults stood stock-still, glaring, their scowls aimed right at him.

He caught Amy by the shoulders as she barreled into him. "What's going on?"

"Henry Jay and Walter," Amy sputtered, out of breath. "They rode their horses straight through Mistress Doolittle's vegetable garden. But I didn't. I was careful and rode around it. Cross my heart and hope to die." She turned her beseeching eyes up to Mariah. "You believe me, don't you?"

Mariah reached out and brushed a strand of hair from Amy's sweaty face and tucked it behind her ear. "Yes, sweetheart, I do. You must try to calm down while we see to the matter. Surely there'll be some compensation that will satisfy the woman."

Watching Mariah as she settled Amy down with such tenderness, Colin's love for her doubled. She would be—

He glanced down the road and cringed at his parents' heated glowers. Picking Amy up, he trudged toward them with dread, knowing that in all likelihood their anger would be directed entirely at him. They would never think of being short with their youngest child. He had, after all, been ordered to keep an eye on her.

His mother's discerning gaze oscillated between him and Mariah.

Beside him, Mariah's steps grew hesitant. Just as well. She shouldn't be the one to catch the brunt of Mother's rage. Pausing, Colin glanced down at her and saw that her face had lost all color. "My dear Mariah, you'd best go and stay with Tori and Heather. They're under that old oak tree watching. From afar." He pointed in their direction. "I shouldn't be long."

"Are you quite sure?" she whispered.

"Of course. And here." He set Amy down. "Take her with you. I'll handle this."

Mariah clutched his hand. "Do be careful." Her eyes were clouded with fright, making her appear so vulnerable it cinched his heart.

"Don't worry." Starting back toward his parents, he drew a steadying breath and let it all out in a whoosh. "Time I became a man and stood up for myself." Though muttered to himself, the words bolstered him.

He barely reached the somber threesome before his mother opened her mouth in preparation for one of her tirades. Giving her no chance to lay into him, he spoke out from several steps away. "I understand there's been quite a disturbance here." He offered the tiny, birdlike widow his most sympathetic smile. "Having boys galloping roughshod through your garden, churning up your neat plants, must have been most frightening, to say nothing of the cost."

The little lady's thin lips gaped open. "Indeed. And—"

Colin cut in, overriding her. "Even though my sister did not happen to be one of the children who destroyed your vegetables, I was the one who gave her permission to ride with those boys, so I feel partly responsible for the destruction. More than partly, to be honest." It never hurt to add a little something for effect. "That is why for the remainder of the growing season I shall personally see that you have fresh vegetables every week for your table. Enough for preserving for your winter stores, as well."

During that pronouncement, he felt his parents' stares of displeasure boring into him as he attempted to smooth the widow's ruffled feathers. And the woman herself had yet to look mollified.

He reached into the pocket of his vest and withdrew several coins. "For all your trouble, Mistress Doolittle. Please allow me to put a smile on that handsome face of yours." He placed the money in her palm. "I want you to stroll right down to Miss Raeford's millinery this minute and buy yourself the fanciest bonnet she has in her shop."

A wary smile did tremble on her lips as the taut lines in her weathered face softened. "Mercy, Mr. Barclay, I couldn't be takin' your money."

"Nonsense." He closed her bony fingers over the coins. "I'll expect to see you sporting that new bonnet at church next Sabbath. By the by," he added casually, "while you're gone, would you mind if my parents and I step into your parlor for a moment? We have some private business to discuss."

"I don't mind a'tall." Her smile remaining in place, she turned to his mother. "You an' yer mister make yerselfs right to home, Mistress Barclay."

It seemed no easy task, but Mother finally pulled her glare off Colin and pasted on an answering smile for the Widow Doolittle. Colin wondered if the little woman realized it was as starched as a Sunday collar. "Thank you." With a significant look at his father, Mother turned and marched up the stone pathway to the older woman's porch steps.

Pa elbowed Colin in the ribs as they followed her. "Try to make your mother happy," he whispered. "If she's not happy, I surely won't be."

What about my happiness? It took considerable restraint not to shout the question, but Colin knew better than to voice it aloud.

Once inside the cramped little home Widow Doolittle occupied,

Colin noticed how worn the upholstery was on the settee, how dreary and faded the furnishings all appeared. "Before we start, do you think we could see about having the poor woman's furniture refurbished? This place is little more than a hovel. Surely someone of her age and all alone deserves better."

Mother's head snapped around. "What?" Then she glanced at her surroundings, her gaze falling on the frayed cushions. "Yes. That's quite thoughtful of you, Colin." Her soft tone turned hard. "However, it won't lessen the fact that you broke our agreement."

"I beg to differ." He hiked his chin. "Not once did I actually say I'd stay with Amy while she went riding with the other children. I was afoot, if you recall. How could I be expected to keep up with a trotting pony?"

"Don't play the fool with me. And don't think for one moment that I'm unaware of things that go on behind my back." Her slitted eyes flashed fire as she stepped closer. "I made the conditions for Mariah remaining in our service abundantly clear from the start. Yet the first chance you get, you choose to defy me and break our agreement."

"Your agreement. Your dictate." Colin hurled the words back at her with equal force.

She stiffened, arching a brow. "And my consequences. This very day I shall find some other fool willing to buy Miss Harwood's papers. It shouldn't be too difficult. I saw more than a few men ogling her today."

Colin held his ground. "And just how do you intend to sell someone you do not own? It's my signature on her papers, not yours. Legally I'm the person in charge of her fate." He stepped within a foot of her, satisfied that he'd played his trump card.

To his dismay, she did not budge. "That may very well be. But I'm sure the wench is not worth the cost of your home and inheritance. For all we know, your oh-so-proper tutoress could be a common thief or even a—a prostitute."

At the urge to push that vile accusation back down her throat, Colin stepped away and inhaled a calming breath. She was his mother, he reminded himself, and deserved his respect. He swallowed and took another tack. "Mother, you and Pa married for love. You told me that yourself more than once, and I know the two of you have been happy together all these years. How could you want less for me, your son? Or even poor, moonstruck Tori. She's wildly infatuated with Tuck. But he's from a mere plantation, and you will do your utmost to prevent her from marrying him because it won't fit in with your own selfish plans. She'll be kept from her happiness, too."

"Pshaw." His mother fluttered a hand, as if the news was of no significance. "Victoria's just a silly child. She has no idea what she wants. And you, Colin. Do you think that generations from now, your grandchildren will be gratified to know that our land was parceled off for the sake of your sister's puppy love? Or worse, that you would give up everything for some nameless, penniless pretty face—though I seriously doubt she'd marry you if you were the penniless one."

"Now that's quite enough!" Fists balled with fury, Colin turned away before he did something he would regret. "For all I care, you can take my inheritance and—"

His father caught his arm. "Stop! Both of you. Stop makin' ultimatums you may later regret." Having bellowed the order without bothering to conceal the light Virginia drawl he knew his wife detested, he lowered his voice and continued. "Son, you and your mother both need time to consider the ramifications of what you're saying." He wrapped one arm around Colin and the other around Mother. "I have a better idea. Let me tell you about it."

Both solemn faces swung their gazes to him in silence, neither ready to give an inch.

He spoke calmly and precisely, gazing from one of them to the other. "The meeting with Harold Lawrence didn't go quite as well as I'd hoped. The offer he made for Queen's Lace was less than fair, so I didn't accept it. We all know that filly's worth considerably more than he was willing to pay. So I've formulated a plan that might rectify the situation."

Regarding the confidence in his father's face, Colin held his breath, waiting to hear what the patriarch was about to say.

"Here's my thought. I propose that you, Colin, take Queenie and

Paladin on a packet north to Philadelphia and New York, then on to Boston. Set up races in those cities to show both of them off. They're the best in our stables. See if you can garner better offers for our Thoroughbreds."

That sounded feasible. . .

"Then, after they're sold, I want you to take that money and sail to England."

Colin's heart slammed to a stop. *He can't be serious!*

"Go to a few of the best horse farms in Britain and purchase a good stud. We'll need to introduce some new blood in our line to stay ahead of the competition here."

"But—that'll take months." Having finally found his voice, Colin tucked his chin. How could he consider going away, being parted from Mariah for some indefinite period—especially now that they had grown beyond mere attraction and wanted to share a future together?

His father nodded, gravely serious. "That's the point, son. I suspect you believe you have feelings for Miss Harwood. One would have to be blind not to see the sparks that fly whenever you two are in close proximity to each other. If those feelings truly are serious, the time apart will make that clear."

So speechless he could hardly think straight, Colin mulled his pa's idea over in his mind. It wasn't anything like he'd hoped or expected to hear. But the more he thought about it, the more he realized that perhaps his father was right. The plan would calm the waters for now. It would also guarantee Mariah's safe harbor until he returned—and to ensure that safety, he would take her papers along with him. Unwelcome or not, Pa's suggestion just might turn out to be the best for all of them right now. He glanced over at his mother.

"If I actually agree to this and sail to England, I'll travel to Bath while I'm in the country and bring proof that Mariah is who she says she is. You'll see she's been telling the truth." He then turned to his father. "And while I'm gone, I expect Mariah to be treated with Christian charity."

"You have my word." Pa gave a nod.

"And yours, Mother?"

She didn't respond for several seconds. Finally she inhaled a deep breath and slowly released the air. "She shall be treated with Christian charity."

Her reluctant promise put Colin only partially at ease. He could only hope that "Christian charity" meant the same thing to her as it did to him.

Chapter 15

Colin shook his head in amazement at the unbelievable agreement he'd just made with his father. Leave here, leave Mariah, for who knew how many months? Yet, all things considered, he couldn't get past the logic that it really was the best course to take. And the sooner he left, the sooner he'd return.

Still in the widow's shabby parlor, he darted a thoughtful look at his father. "Well, if I'm going to do this, I suppose there's no time like the present. Since both horses are already in town, I see no reason to take them all the way back to the plantation. The day is only partially spent. I'll go down to the quay and book passage on the next northbound packet." He kept his tone even and businesslike to prevent Mother from interfering or interrupting.

His father nodded. "There should be at least two packets at the docks as we speak. They brought people in for the race. I believe at least one of them is set to embark tomorrow at first light."

"Good. Then if Mother would be kind enough to pack some of my things," he went on without looking at her, "you can have them sent to me this evening, along with whatever traveling funds you expect I'll need. I'll secure a room at the inn and handle the boarding of the horses for the night." He paused, hating to delve into the next subject. "I do have one personal request, though, Pa." He leveled a serious gaze at him. "I'd like you to send Mariah's papers to me along with my luggage. I put them inside last year's ledger for safekeeping."

"Of course. I'll take care of everything."

A small sound came from his mother, one Colin surmised heralded her disapproval. But neither she nor her granite expression said a word. She did, however, glance toward the door, indicating her wish to leave this place.

Since he could say or do nothing at this point to win her approval, he sought his father once more. "I'd like a few moments alone with Mariah before y'all leave town. I need to assure her she'll continue on as tutoress for the girls and that she'll be treated with the respect and kindness due her position while I'm away." Turning on his heel, he headed for the entry before his mother could issue a protest.

At the door he stopped and turned back. "Perhaps while I'm speaking with Mariah, the two of you could go and see about having Mistress Doolittle's furniture re-covered."

Mother merely stared in her steady, aloof way, but Pa nodded in assent. "Of course. Otherwise we might forget."

"Also, I promised to make certain she's kept in vegetables. Since I won't be around to see to that, I'd appreciate it if you would make those arrangements also." That said, he opened the door and stepped out.

"There, Cora, my dear," he overheard his father say in a soothing voice. "You see? He's still the same thoughtful son he always was."

Colin paused, listening for his mother's response.

"Hmph. He was until that hussy stole his senses," she snapped, her stubborn anger as strong as ever.

Disappointed, he closed the door quietly after himself and crossed the small porch to the steps, wondering if the decision to leave immediately—or at all—really was for the best.

Waiting in the shade of the sprawling oak tree with Colin's three sisters, Mariah did her best not to appear anxious, though she would have given anything to know what was going on inside the little clapboard house. Tuck and Edward had come to join her and the girls now that Mistress Barclay was no longer in sight, and sitting on either side of Victoria in the shade, they kept Tori enthralled with their tales of derring-do. Amy had climbed onto a low-hanging branch and perched there with her legs dangling as she kept vigil on the widow's cottage, watching for the rest of her family to emerge.

Heather gravitated to Mariah's side. "Is this flute not the grandest thing ever?" She held out the shiny silver instrument her father had picked up in town and presented to her a short while before Colin met up with her parents.

"Yes, dear. It's lovely. But you'd better keep it in its case so it won't get dusty from the breeze, don't you think?" She gave the girl an encouraging smile.

"I want to try it first. Then I'll put it away." Holding it to her lips, she blew into the tiny hole, trying unsuccessfully to make a pure sound—or any sound at all. She scrunched up her face. "How do you make it work, Miss Harwood? Please show me."

At the moment, with her fate being warred over by the girl's family, giving a flute lesson was the last thing on Mariah's mind. Nevertheless, she took the long, thin tube from Heather and did her best to look happy to do so. "This is how you hold it." Showing her the proper angle, she placed her fingers along the keys. " 'Tis important to hold the flute parallel to your lips so you can blow into the headjoint, like this." She demonstrated the process, raising her fingers up and down on the keys to make a trilling sound.

"Oh, that is so pretty, like the sound of a robin's song." Heather's blue eyes glowed with anticipation. "I cannot wait until I can make pretty music."

"You will, in no time at all, if you practice faithfully. I promise. Now, come here." Gesturing for the twelve-year-old to come and try again, she placed the flute in the girl's hands and positioned her fingers just so on the proper stops and her left thumb on the lever. Then, lifting Heather's elbows, she helped her to hold the flute snugly against her mouth. "Now flatten your lips and blow."

As the girl followed her instructions, Mariah turned the flute slightly to catch the air just right, and a pure tone emerged.

"I did it! I actually did it!" A grin spread from ear to ear, making Heather's eyes sparkle. She thrust the instrument to Mariah. "Please play something for us, Miss Harwood. I want to hear how it should sound."

Mariah gaped at her. "Here? Now?" She glanced around, her gaze landing on the widow's cottage. *Whatever would Mistress Barclay think of my playing a flute in public?*

"Yes, miss. Please do." Tuck came up from behind them, followed by the others, who all nodded in agreement.

"Mercy me. I hardly think it would be ladylike to make a spectacle of myself."

"We'll all crowd around you then." Heather motioned to the small group for them to form a ring around Mariah. "No one will be able to see who's playing."

"Oh, very well." Mariah sighed as the young people circled around her. Being careful to stand where she could peek past Tori's two suitors and keep the gate of the widow's house in sight, she hesitantly accepted the flute from Heather. If Mistress Barclay appeared, she'd stop playing immediately.

Lifting the instrument to her lips, she played a familiar lilting tune.

Tuck grinned with recognition and started singing the lyrics to "Greensleeves," and one by one, the others joined in. Except for Amy. The child kept craning her neck to look up the street. Suddenly her mouth popped open and her eyes grew wide. "It's Colin."

Glancing beyond Victoria's beaus, Mariah saw the child's brother striding swiftly toward them.

He was not smiling.

A sickening feeling churned her insides. She lowered the flute and handed it to Heather. "Please excuse me." Breathless, she shoved past the young men and headed, heart pounding, toward Colin.

They met in the middle of the street. Mariah searched his face, trying to discern what might have taken place, but he took her arm without speaking and turned her toward the racecourse, where the family's landau remained parked in the shade of a tree.

Had his parents convinced him to retract his proposal? "What is it, Colin?"

He hurried her along. "We need a little more privacy."

Footsteps sounded from behind as little Amy caught up with them, her face pale with panic. "Am I in big trouble, Colin? What are they gonna do to me?"

He stopped and knelt before his sister and took her by the shoulders. "Everything's fine, squirt. Nobody's mad at you. Just go back to your sisters, will you? I need to speak to Miss Harwood alone." A light nudge sent her on her way.

Mariah's blood seemed to drain away, and a chill ran through her. It must be worse than she thought. They must be going to sell her off. What would become of her then?

Once she and Colin reached the tree sheltering the carriage, he stopped. With a tight smile, he took her hands in his.

Seeing no real hope in his expression, she could wait no longer to hear her fate. "What is it? Do tell me."

He cocked his head. "Nothing has changed between us, my love. You and I will marry, with or without my family's blessing."

Sensing a *but* coming, Mariah held her breath.

"But I'm afraid it won't be for a while. Something *has* changed, and that centers around where I'm going to be for the next few months."

Colin was to be sent away? Frowning in confusion, Mariah waited for him to explain.

"To appease my mother and to further our Thoroughbred enterprise, my father has requested that I travel to several cities here in the colonies. Afterward, I must take a quick trip. . .to England."

She nearly choked. "Quick trip, you say! When it takes six weeks to sail to England and six back? You'll be gone for ages!"

Catching her hands again in his, Colin smiled gently. "I meant that

I don't plan to spend more than a few days in Britain at most. I'm going solely to purchase a new stud for breeding purposes."

"But. . .England." An unexpected bout of homesickness swamped her. To think that Colin would be sailing to her homeland, and she would remain behind made unbidden tears sting her eyes. Still, the thought came to her that there might be a personal benefit to his crossing the ocean. "Perhaps you could visit my family, see how they're faring— should you travel anywhere near Bath, of course."

"I intend to do just that, sweetheart. I plan to book passage on the ship heading for the Bristol port. I hear there's a fine horse farm between there and Bath. It will be my honor to call on your father while I'm in the area."

"Oh, I'm sure Papa will be glad to meet you, to have news of my sisters and me and know that we arrived here safe and well. I should have already posted a letter to him. And to my sisters, really. I've been so busy I just haven't. . ." Realizing she was babbling, her vision of him blurred behind a sheen of moisture. "Oh, Colin, whatever will I do without you?" Only sheer determination and unwillingness to make the situation harder for him kept her from bursting into tears.

He lifted her hands to his mouth and brushed his lips across her fingers. "You'll concentrate on the fact that I'm coming back as soon as I possibly can. I was able to extract a solemn promise from my mother that you will be treated properly in my absence."

A lump formed in Mariah's throat. "She knows we're betrothed?"

He offered a sheepish smile. "I didn't exactly say the words. I reckoned it would make living here harder for you if I wasn't around. But I know she suspects we have feelings for each other. So I've decided to take your bond papers with me. She can't do anything without them. You'll be all right until I come back. I promise."

Despite her own sadness, he looked so concerned that Mariah mustered a smile and reached up to brush aside a lock of dark hair that had fallen across his furrowed brow. "Well, we'll have to make the most of it, somehow. I don't want you to worry about me in the least. As long as I know I have your love, I vow I shall do all that is in my power to gain your mother's goodwill."

He grinned, crinkling the corners of his eyes. "My sweet Mariah, you are far more than a man could ever dream of. I feel incredibly fortunate that you came into my life. But alas, it is my sad duty to bid you farewell now. I must hasten down to the quay to book passage for the morrow. I shan't be returning home with you this eve."

Her mouth dropped open in dismay. "You won't? Not even for a night?" Gripped by panic, she clutched at his vest, as if by holding on to him she could make him stay.

With a look of intense longing, he gave a somber shake of the head. "It's for the best, my love. I can't bear the thought of a long good-bye. It would only cause both of us more pain." Gently he removed her hands and kissed them. Then he looked deep into her eyes and pressed the softest of kisses to her trembling lips. "I must go now." Releasing his hold, he turned on his heel. "Don't forget: I love you, Mariah. I'll come back as soon as I can."

Mariah was utterly devastated as she watched her handsome betrothed walk away, leaving her behind to an uncertain fate. He'd made so many promises this day, even declared his love. But now he was leaving her for a raft of exciting cities—cities filled with beautiful women. He'd fallen so quickly for her beauty. Might he be as easily captivated by someone else? A woman with wealth and breeding who'd be acceptable to his family? Or even worse, would he be tempted by a whole flock of young, unattached maidens and forget her entirely? A small cloud drifted across the sun just then, dimming its bright light. Mariah felt as if it had drifted across her heart, blocking the only security she'd known since her arrival at the Barclay plantation.

Then a truly frightening thought twisted her insides. What of Mistress Barclay? The woman was so adamantly opposed to a union between her son and a bond servant. What clever form would her retribution take?

Chapter 16

On the ride home from Alexandria, Mariah studiously avoided looking at Colin's parents. The couple sat in pregnant silence on the opposite seat of the carriage, and both wore churlish expressions. Next to them, Victoria kept turning around to cast longing glances back toward town, obviously disappointed that she'd had to leave her two beaus so soon. Her dream-filled eyes gave no clue as to which young man she actually preferred. Mariah suspected that the sudden attention being showered upon her by both Dennis and Edward was too heady an experience for Tori not to take full advantage of it. She was, after all, barely on the brink of womanhood.

Lost in her thoughts, she felt Amy's small hand search through the mass of ruffled skirts to find hers. The child held tight, a tremor revealing her trepidation that her parents' wrath would soon crash down on her. But Mariah had no doubt who the real target would be. Herself. And there was nowhere to run to escape her fate.

Thank Providence for Heather, sweet Heather. Thrilled with her new flute and completely oblivious to the tension in the air, the girl wore a bright smile as if this day had been the finest of her entire life. She removed the instrument from its case and held it reverently in her hands. "Show me again where to put my fingers, Miss Harwood." She gazed expectantly up at Mariah.

Wishing the twelve-year-old had not drawn the unwelcome attention to her, Mariah did not dare a glance across to the elder Barclays but drew a nervous breath and took the silver tube from Heather. "Like this." She raised it and positioned each of her fingers slowly and deliberately on the proper keys, one at a time, and held them for Heather to study. Then, forcing a small smile, she handed the instrument back.

Heather did her best to do as she'd been shown and nearly got it right. "Splendid. You've almost got it." More than aware the Barclays were watching, she struggled to ignore the pair as she gently adjusted Heather's little finger. She spoke as quietly as possible over the creaking and crunching of the landau as it rolled along. "Practice lifting up from each key one at a time until the movement feels natural."

Glad for the chance to divert her attention away from the older couple for a bit, she watched Heather work on her fingering. But when the girl raised the flute to her lips and took a breath, Mariah quickly stayed her with a hand. "I think 'twould be best if you just practice moving your fingers. We'll work on tones at home."

Mistress Barclay broke the stilted silence. "Yes, daughter. I cannot abide unnecessary noise. I have a beastly headache."

Knowing the woman's last comment was directed at her, Mariah cringed as a dreadful sense of foreboding chilled her whole being. *This is what Colin had left me to: his vengeful mother. How could someone who had avowed his deep love forsake me like this?*

For several days after their arrival at home, Mariah was ill at ease, waiting for Colin's mother to lash out at her, pile on extra chores, deprive her of privileges, or administer some form of punishment. But to her utter amazement, Mistress Barclay's veiled innuendo on the homeward ride from Alexandria never amounted to anything. As the next couple of weeks passed, the woman seemed quite relaxed, and though not overtly friendly toward Mariah, she acted as if nothing were amiss. At first Mariah thought the woman's courteous attitude was the result of her own extra efforts to be especially helpful and polite. It finally dawned on her that with Colin separated from her, there was nothing for his mother to find fault with.

She continued her duties as tutoress, instructing the girls in academics and all the female arts, plus giving them their music lessons. Of course, she often found herself obligated to ride with Amy as bribery for practicing the violin. Though Mariah begrudged the time spent riding horseback, she discovered that chasing after Colin's youngest sister was helping her to become a rather accomplished horsewoman. He would surely be surprised to discover her new skill when he returned. If he returned.

But no matter how busy her daytime hours were, the solitary nights were hard to endure, when she was alone in her tiny room and thoughts of Colin held free rein in her mind. She missed him so and wished desperately that he would send word to let her know she was still in his thoughts, especially since she'd heard that the most stylish young ladies in the colonies resided in Philadelphia and New York. He'd given his father three pounds to give to Mariah for pin money, and though she appreciated his thoughtfulness and generosity, she would have much preferred a letter from him.

To her knowledge, no correspondence had arrived for his parents either, unless Mistress Barclay had kept silent about hearing from her son and had seen to it that any missive to Mariah was destroyed. The woman did seem to have a certain smugness in her demeanor. Mariah wondered if his mother was still concocting secret plans that would keep Colin from returning to the plantation for a very long time.

—————

Pleasant weather and calm seas had enabled the coastal packet to make good time as it carried Colin and his horses around the peninsula and up to Philadelphia. Aware that all types of business was conducted on the wharves, he was gratified by the considerable interest Paladin and Queen's Lace drew during their boarding in Alexandria and disembarking at the "red brick city." No sooner had he brought them down the gangplank, when two wealthy Philadelphia merchants approached him and agreed to arrange a horse race to take place within the month.

Colin spent the following three weeks ensconced in a nicely appointed guest room in the elegant brick manse of his uncle Matthew Lewis, a prominent lawyer. The bed with its jewel-toned coverlet was more comfortable than his bed at the plantation, and the rich furnishings were the best money could buy, but it wasn't like home.

Uncle Matt and Aunt Harriet loved to give and attend all kinds of dinners and extravagant events, and this evening the family was invited to a summer party at the home of one of Uncle Matthew's colleagues. Colin would have preferred another quiet evening to himself but knew it would be impolite to expect his relatives to go to the affair without him. Even if he begged off, they'd want an explanation, and he wasn't ready to provide any personal details.

Buttoning his burgundy silk waistcoat, he moved to the wooden mirror stand and checked his reflection in the long, oval looking glass to make sure his attire had been pressed neatly and fit well. He let out a deep, slow breath. Nothing fit as well as Mariah did when she was on his arm. How empty his days seemed now that he could no longer see her stunning face, hear her lyrical voice. The past weeks seemed an eternity, and time still stretched out before him like an unending road.

A knock sounded on the door, and his cousin Paul barged in without waiting for an invitation. Tall and slim, at twenty-six he retained a boyishness about him that glinted in his smoke-colored eyes and lopsided grin. "Do hurry, old man. We're going to be late. I want to get my bid in for as many minuets as possible with Evangeline O'Hara. Eve's sure to be the prettiest girl there."

"Is that right?" Colin made an effort to sound interested.

"Rather. So do me a favor and don't turn on your charms around her. You have my blessing when it comes to any of the other belles. Just leave Evangeline to me." He leaned to peer into the looking glass and ran fingers through his already neat light brown hair.

Colin gave him a pat on the shoulder and lapsed into the drawl he was trying hard to overcome. "Fear not, cousin-mine. My romancin' days have come to an end. I've already found the one girl for me. She happens to be the most beautiful woman in the entire world."

"Surely not." Paul guffawed. "How would you even know that until you've seen them all?"

The words were like cold water splashed in Colin's face. He had to admit Paul was right. There must be any number of young misses as delectable as Mariah—ones with sufficient wealth to satisfy even his mother. Was his attraction to the English lass merely because she was the always-tempting forbidden fruit? He cut a speculative glance up at his cousin. "You make a good point, old chap. What are we waiting for? Let's go and see what the fair city of Philadelphia has to offer."

Six weeks. Six long weeks, and still no word from Colin. Was he alive or dead? Had she the slightest idea where to write, Mariah would have gladly put quill to paper if only to let him know what a thoughtless, cavalier blackguard he was. He wouldn't have had to extol his undying love for her in a letter were he concerned his mother might read it. But surely he could send a word or two—anything to let Mariah know he still thought about her.

Such morose, frustrating thoughts assailed her as she and Victoria stood on the veranda watching the girl's two beaus riding up the lane. In anticipation of the late afternoon ride, Tori had donned a gown of delicate blue lawn that accented the hue of her eyes. Mariah, on the other hand, continued to play down her own appearance by wearing her dull teacher's gray and capturing her curls in a tight bun. She didn't want to draw attention from the young belle.

Amy was already down at the stables. She'd hiked her skirts and sprinted to tell Old Samuel to saddle their mounts the moment Tuck and Edward came into view. She never missed an opportunity to go riding, whether her young presence was welcome or not. But then, her mother considered the child as suitable a chaperone as Mariah, probably even more so.

Peering again down the tree-shaded lane, Mariah cast a more assessing gander at the young men. It would only take her a little cunning look here, a bit of flattery there, to whisk one of them away from Victoria. Like Colin, Tuck was heir to his plantation, not the head of the household. . .not as promising as Mariah would like, while Edward was the son of a wealthy merchant and often bragged about his family's eight cargo ships. As Mistress Barclay said, ships could sink, taking with them an abundance of goods. But a rich family like the Rochesters could easily replace a lost vessel. Were Mariah to be presented to Edward's parents properly, without mention of that bothersome bond, she just might be accepted by the family. . . .

Beside her, Victoria raised her arm in a jaunty wave. Then, completely dismissing everything Mariah had taught her, she bounded down the steps and out to the curved drive to greet her callers before they even reined their mounts to a stop.

Mariah rolled her eyes and glided out with practiced grace to meet the men. Sorely tempted to pick one of them, she figured it might be best to concentrate on Edward, since he wasn't such a close friend of Colin and his family.

However, as both suitors dismounted in haste, vying to be the first to reach Victoria, the girl's happy laughter tore through Mariah. Tempting as it might be to lure one of the young men away, she knew she couldn't do it. Tori had been such a shy, lovesick lass when Mariah first arrived. It would be unbearable to watch her crawl back into that sad state again—especially after so many hours had been spent teaching her the art of courtship.

"Good afternoon." She offered a polite nod as she reached the lively threesome. "Amy and I will be tagging along on today's ride, but we shouldn't bother you."

Tuck flashed his usual flirty grin. "Rest assured, your company never bothers us."

"Nevertheless—" She slanted an assuring look to Tori as they started for the stables. "I shall spend the greater portion of the ride chasing after our adventurous Amy, in all likelihood, so I'll trust that Victoria will be safe with you two."

Edward's freckled hand went to his chest. "But of course. I, for one, wouldn't dream of allowing the smallest mishap to befall the lovely lass."

"Splendid." Mariah lengthened her steps to go ahead of the others. Suddenly she realized she was turning into Rose, her responsible older sister. *The spinster.*

Shocked by the idea, Mariah scoffed inwardly. Why, had she not just finished writing out a number of invitations to a horse and phaeton race the family planned to host on the first Saturday in September? Surely there would be an abundance of young men there to participate in the event. Before that day was over, she might possibly find another suitor for herself. One Mistress Barclay would approve of—and perhaps even help her to secure!

Mariah glanced over her shoulder at Amy, who lagged behind. The child always dawdled when coming home after a run on her horse, but then, the girl was permitted to straddle her pony rather than sit on a rib-jouncing sidesaddle. Mariah frowned at her. "Do hurry!"

The eight-year-old gave a sullen shrug and heeled Patches into a trot to catch up.

Victoria and her beaus had returned to the stables a good ten minutes ago. Mariah knew if she and Amy didn't make haste, there wouldn't be time enough for them to wash off the horse smell and change for supper.

"There's Mr. Scott." Reining her pony alongside Mariah's Thorough-bred mare, Amy shouted and waved at him. "We're comin', Mr. Scott."

Helping Samuel rub down the horse Victoria had ridden, the trainer paused and waved back, and Mariah suddenly wondered if the man had a wife. No one had ever mentioned one.

She maneuvered her mount closer to Amy's as they rode along the path between two plowed-under tobacco fields. "I'm curious. Mr. Scott has never said anything about having a wife living here. Does he have one, perchance?"

"Huh-uh. I think he had one, but she died or somethin'. If he wanted one, though, he could get one real easy."

"Why do you say that?"

" 'Cuz I heard some of the widows at church talkin' about what a good catch he'd be, what with him makin' so much money, and all."

"What do you mean?"

Amy cut her a flippant look. "Oh, that's right. You wasn't here last spring when ol' Mr. Dumfries came ridin' in here big as you please. He offered Mr. Scott twice what Poppy was payin' him to come work for him. Mr. Scott's the best horse trainer in the whole blamed colony. Maybe even all the colonies."

How interesting. "I see. Offered so much money, I'm surprised he didn't take the position."

"He prob'ly would'a, but I ran up to the house and told Poppy what was goin' on. He came down an' offered Mr. Scott the same money if he'd stay here."

"La, he must be a highly valued man." Mariah nudged her mare forward again, viewing the redheaded trainer through more enlightened eyes.

As they approached the stables, Mr. Scott laid aside the curry brush he'd been using and strode over to help Mariah dismount. When he reached up to her, she offered her brightest smile as she came down into his arms. "Thank you," she gushed in her most pleasant voice. "I do hope we haven't kept you and Samuel from your meals."

"Not at all. Pansy doesn't bring our meals until after the family has been served."

"Oh, I didn't know that." It dawned on her that she knew very little about the workings of the plantation because she spent the bulk of her days in the upstairs schoolroom. "Speaking of supper, Amy, dear, run to the house and wash up, and I'll be along shortly."

Mr. Scott moved to the mare's neck and patted it as he gathered the reins.

"She's a fine riding horse, is she not?" Mariah ventured. "But watching the gentle way you work with all the stock, getting them to do your bidding, 'tis no wonder."

His green eyes swerved from the animal to her. "That's the trick, young lady. Firm but gentle handling, and a lot of patience, of course."

For a split second, she thought the man was going to smile. And though he did not, she kept hers from faltering. "I know just what you mean. Amy, too, needs lots and lots of patience, plus a firm but gentle hand."

He gazed after the girl as she ran toward the house, and his eyes crinkled at the corners as a slight grin softened his guileless features. Mariah wouldn't have described him as handsome, exactly, with that long face and slightly mocking mouth. Yet there seemed a compelling quality about him and an honesty not to be overlooked. "She's a corker, all right." His smile faded as he turned back to Mariah. "You're a teacher, Miss Harwood. What did you think of the sermon on 1 Peter chapter 3 last Sunday?"

"Oh, that." Mariah's smile evaporated. "Obviously some husband must have lodged a complaint about his wife."

The normally serious-mannered man burst out with a belly laugh. "Actually I was referring to the promise the passage contained: 'For the eyes of the Lord are over the righteous, and his ears are open unto their prayers.'"

A rush of warmth rose over her cheeks. "Mercy me. I mostly remembered the part where wives aren't supposed to dress pretty but let their inner beauty shine out. Oh, and let us not forget the part about being in subjection to their husbands." She grimaced.

Mr. Scott's lips broadened into a cordial smile, and a spark of humor in his eye added a certain degree of appeal that changed her mind about his not being handsome. "You must not have heard the command where the husband is to give honor to his wife and treat her gently because she's the weaker vessel, and how they're heirs together in the grace of life."

"I'm afraid I missed that part. The third chapter of 1 Peter, you say? I shall read it again this eve before I retire." She took a step backward. "I'd best go now and make sure Amy doesn't get into any more mischief before supper."

He chuckled. "Good luck."

On her way up the path to the manse, Mariah couldn't dismiss the trainer from her mind. Was he in his own quiet way hinting that he desired her? Perhaps even wanted her for his wife? If not, why had he brought up that business about husbands and wives being heirs together in. . .what was it? Oh yes, heirs together in the grace of life.

Curious to see if he was watching her walk away, she glanced back toward the stable. He was gone.

Just as well, she told herself. But still. . .

Chapter 17

Asoft September breeze stirred the lace underpanels on the open windows, and the sweet scent of late-blooming roses from the garden floated across the dining room.

"How sad," Amy mused, loading a huge amount of scrambled egg onto her fork. "Colin won't be here to race his phaeton. Poppy will have to drive it, and he drives as slow as a turtle. We'll lose for sure." Shoving the egg into her mouth, she spewed out another whining complaint from around the food. "And it's our race."

"Amy, really!" Victoria shook her head in disgust. "You managed to splatter egg all over the tablecloth."

Witnessing the exchange between the sisters at the dining table, Mariah hid her grin behind her napkin. The little imp was forever being taken to task for one thing or another. But nothing could dampen Mariah's spirits this day. After all, she'd lived the greater part of her life at the resort of Bath, where public balls or plays were scheduled for almost every evening during the season. Compared to her existence back home, life on a plantation in the colonies was decidedly more dull. Except today.

Today every family of consequence within twenty miles would be coming for the races. A dinner would follow, and later in the evening, a ball. The kitchen slaves had been cooking and baking for days, filling the house with marvelous, mouthwatering aromas. The Barclays had even hired a string quartet from Baltimore to perform throughout the afternoon and evening. It was certain to be a lively event.

On a shopping excursion into Alexandria with the womenfolk, Mariah had purchased an exquisite silk lace fan from France to go with her violet satin evening gown, and she had every intention of using that fan to its best flirting advantage. Smiling to herself, she picked up her cup of tea and took a sip. After all, it was Colin's fault for not having deigned to write a single line to her since his departure weeks ago. In essence, he himself had abandoned her to her fate.

"Mariah?"

Glad that the mistress had given the girls permission to use her Christian name at last, she met Heather's eyes across the table. "Yes?"

"Mother said me and Tori could play that piece you taught us durin' the dinner hour. I do hope we don't make any mistakes."

"*Tori and I*, dear." All this harping on drawls and proper grammar. Would it ever make a difference? "You've played that number flawlessly several times. Just pretend I'm the only one listening to you, and you'll both be fine."

Victoria released a sigh. "I do hope you're right. I don't want to make a fool of myself in front of Tuck. Or anyone else, for that matter, but especially Tuck."

As Mariah had suspected, Victoria was more interested in Dennis Tucker than she was in the merchant's son. If the mistress of the household knew that for certain, she surely wouldn't be happy. But considering the number of guests due to arrive today, perhaps Tori's interest would shift to someone entirely different. At her age, anything was possible, and the strawberry-pink gown of ruffled lawn she'd be wearing this evening would set off her feminine assets to perfection. A whole raft of young men might be drawn to her side.

Mariah swept a glance over her three charges as she forked the remaining egg on her plate. "We'd better finish eating so we can go upstairs and dress for the day. People will likely begin to arrive within the hour."

Amy tucked her chin and peered at Mariah through her silky lashes. "You must know if I get prettied up this early, I'll just be all dirty and mussed up by noon."

As if she'd been hovering out of sight eavesdropping on their conversation, Mistress Barclay chose that moment to amble in from the butlery. "I beg to differ, young lady. You won't be getting dirty at all, because I absolutely forbid you to go anywhere near the stables today. You'll act like a proper young lady and remain either inside the house or out on the lawn until race time, conducting yourself accordingly."

"But Mama." The child sank back against her chair with a miserable groan.

Her mother maintained her meaningful glare. "No buts. I already have more trouble than I can handle today. Speaking of which—" She switched her attention to Mariah. "I've been told that Lizzie, Celie, and Pansy woke up this morning, of all mornings, covered with red spots. From what Benjamin says, slaves from the Murray plantation just up the road have come down with the measles, and it would appear they have spread the malady to our people. I've told my husband time and again to stop allowing our slaves to mix with that Murray bunch on Saturday nights. His people appear less than well cared for, you know. But Eldon refuses to stop our slaves from mingling."

"Mercy me." Mariah wagged her head. "Measles. And today of all days. How unfortunate." She bit into her buttered biscuit.

"Quite. Needless to say, I cannot expose our guests to disease. The slaves will remain far from the premises until they recover. Some of our overnight guests will be bringing their personal servants with them, but there's no time this morning to train any of our field hands to help with serving the food. Besides the scheduled dinner for forty-five we'll be hosting, refreshments will be served during the ball afterward." A slight pause, and she let the cannon ball fly. "I'm sorry, but the duty must fall upon you, Mariah. I've no other recourse. You're simply going to have to help Eloise and Benjamin. I believe Ivy has not yet shown evidence of the illness, so unless she suddenly acquires the rash, she'll be able to assist as well."

Gasping, Mariah choked on her biscuit and started to cough.

The mistress shrugged a shoulder. "It can't be helped." That said, she took her leave.

Mariah glanced wildly around at the girls and saw that their mouths were also gaping. Surely this was just a nightmare. Yes, that's what it was. Any minute now she'd wake up.

Dressed in one of Pansy's extra uniforms—in hideous black—Mariah clenched her teeth together so hard her jaw felt like it would disintegrate. Her back ached, her feet ached, and she most likely reeked of kitchen grease and lye soap. Having been unable to snatch more than a minute here and there throughout the endless day to rest, she could barely keep her tears from breaking through the floodgates in back of her eyes and exploding forth in a torrent. This was to have been the most special of days. She should be flitting among the throng of visitors in a glamorous violet gown, fluttering the lacy fan demurely at dozens of handsome bachelors and catching their interest.

Instead, she'd been relegated to household slave, all but invisible in the shapeless black uniform and white apron. With a little more force than necessary, she plunked a heavy food tray on one of the three side tables now lining a wall in the dining room and removed a bowl of cut fruit and a platter of assorted cold meats and cheeses, setting them onto one of the remaining tables. If these fine people only knew that she, Mariah Harwood—lately arrived from the glorious resort of Bath, England, and now secretly betrothed to the son and heir of this very plantation—had been tripping about serving refreshments on the lawn all afternoon for everyone to gawk at! It was utterly humiliating and not to be borne.

Some guests, a number of them people she'd met at church and in the town shops, began gathering on the terrace just beyond the open glass-paned doors, chatting and laughing and enjoying themselves.

Savagely, she rubbed telltale moisture from her eyes, then rammed a stray strand of hair into the ruffled mobcap—*mobcap!*—Mistress Barclay insisted would keep most of the kitchen odors and smoke from seeping into her curls. She peered down at the latest white apron she'd put on over Pansy's uniform less than an hour ago. Already there were splatters here and there.

Dejected, she let out a huff. What difference did it make? Any of it? She'd never be considered worthy by any of these people ever again. She picked up the empty tray and started back toward the kitchen.

The patter of rapid footsteps came from the front of the house as Amy ran to her side. "Mariah, can I help?"

Mariah's eyes rounded as she beheld the youngest member of the household, golden ringlets straggling, hair ribbon askew, face and hands smeared with dirt, and several inches of her skirt pulled loose from the bodice. "What in heaven's name happened to you? Look at your hair. Your skirt. You look horrid!"

"Oh, this." Amy smirked, tugging at the gaping section. "It wasn't my fault, I promise. It was that Henry Jay again." Her lips pressed together in anger. "I was winnin' the footrace, and he just couldn't stand losin' to a girl. He jerked me back by my skirt, and I fell on the ground, and he fell on top of me."

"Amy, Amy. . ." Mariah just looked at her. "Supper will be served in just a few minutes. You cannot appear at the table in this frightful condition. Run upstairs as fast as you can and get presentable."

"But Lizzie's sick. There's nobody to fix my hair."

"Perhaps Victoria or Heather may still be up there. Tell them I said to do something with it. They're both getting quite good at fancying each other up."

"Tori always pulls my hair, and it hurts." The child's lower lip poked forward.

Mariah would have none of it. "Go! Now!" She pointed toward the staircase. "Catch your sister before she comes down. I not only want you to look as pretty as the other girls, I want you to look prettier. Do you understand? Now, off with you!"

"Yes, Mother!" With a toss of her wayward curls, the imp marched straight up the stairs with nary a backward glance.

Despite her weariness, Mariah couldn't restrain a smile as she watched after the disaster-prone child and shook her head.

"Thank you." Mistress Barclay stood in the butlery doorway. "For reprimanding Amy and sending her up for repairs." Then the bane of Mariah's hope strolled past her with her superior grace and rounded the long dining table as she headed for the terrace.

Mariah would gladly have chased after her and throttled her, only she was far too tired to do so.

The older woman whirled around.

For a moment Mariah feared that Cora Barclay had read her murderous thoughts.

The mistress tilted her head and met her gaze. "I know this has been a very hard and trying day for you." No emotion colored her features as she spoke the kind-sounding words. But having uttered them, she simply turned back again and walked out the door to join her guests.

"*Thank you, Mariah, for putting aside your fanciful dreams for the day and lowering yourself to be a doormat,*" Mariah muttered bitterly under her breath, her hands on her hips. "*I can never repay you for the great sacrifice you made for me.*" Hmph. A crumb of gratitude might have been nice. . . .

Then a more terrible thought surfaced. Even if Colin did still harbor the hope to marry her, would he honor their betrothal after he learned how she had been shamed this day before everyone he knew?

Once the morbid mental assaults started, others rushed in upon them. Colin's mother had been entirely too pleasant since her son had been forced to leave. Had this been her plan all along? The moment the devious woman had been waiting for to destroy her once and for all? Mistress Barclay, the ever-so-righteous Christian?

And what of those allegedly sick servants? Did they truly have the measles?

One way or another, Mariah planned to find out.

Mariah blinked awake, then closed her eyes against a bright ray of sunshine. *Sunshine!* She must have overslept. It had to be close to noon!

Throwing off her sheet, Mariah sprang to her feet. . .and groaned. Her legs were stiff, her back hurt, and her shoulders and arms ached from carrying so many heavy trays yesterday. She'd never labored so hard in her life. And poor Eloise! Mariah had never seen the plump, older slave looking so worn out as she'd been by the time all the dishes from the party had been washed and put away. Young Ivy had helped a little, at first. But she was a mere slip of a thing, and by midday she began to feel ill and took to her bed, leaving the bulk of the responsibilities to Eloise and Mariah.

Further remembrance of the day before brought a rush of humiliation that weighted down Mariah's chest. She'd never be able to dismiss the memory of staring eyes, the sneering remarks whispered behind fans. How would she ever rise above the shame? She most certainly wouldn't, not in this neighborhood, around those guests.

Oh no! We still have houseguests! Limping over to her washstand, she wondered why she hadn't been awakened and summoned to the kitchen. After pouring the contents of the pitcher into the bowl, she snatched a washcloth from its hook and placed it into the water.

The door swung open. "You're awake. Finally." Dressed for the day, Amy came skipping in. "Mama said not to bother you till you woke up. Heather got up a little while ago, but Tori's still sleeping. She stayed up till the very end, so Mama says."

Mariah squeezed moisture from the washing cloth and pressed it to her face, then turned to the girl. "Why was I not to be awakened? Surely Eloise wasn't expected to handle breakfast all by herself."

Amy shrugged a shoulder. "Tuck sent over two of their servants first thing this morning. They're down in the kitchen now, helpin' out."

"Thank heavens." With a sigh of relief, Mariah replaced the cloth on its hook and hobbled to her bed to lie down again.

"Oh, I almost forgot." Amy whirled around and dashed to her

adjoining bedchamber then returned just as swiftly. "Here." She held out a piece of correspondence. "Storekeeper Gladdings must've brought mail with him when he delivered supplies yesterday. Nobody noticed it layin' on the—"

Mariah didn't hear any more of Amy's ramblings. At last! A missive from Colin! She snatched the letter from the child and tore open the wax seal. Unfolding the paper, she scanned quickly to the bottom to check the signature.

Her heart sank. It was from Rose.

"Who's it from?" Coming closer, Amy angled her head, trying to peek at it.

Mariah took a second to control her disappointment. " 'Tis from my sister Rose."

"The one who got took away by the smelly man?"

She gave a weary nod.

"Read it to me, please. I never get mail."

"Very well." Feeling a headache coming on, Mariah patted the spot next to her on the bed. "But afterward you must promise to go and occupy yourself elsewhere for a few hours. I'd like to get a little more sleep." *And perhaps have a good cry.*

Only half paying attention to the written words herself, Mariah read the rather vague missive from Rose aloud, before shooing Amy out. Then she lay down on the feather pillow and reread it more slowly. She felt a niggle of guilt for not having given either Rose or Lily much thought since her arrival at the plantation, but she drew comfort from learning about her older sister's situation. It was hard to imagine Rose living in some remote village with few amenities, but hearing that her employer had turned out to be a kind man after all was welcome news.

Mariah wished she could say the same about Mistress Barclay. Suddenly filled with righteous ire, she eased to her feet, completed her toilette, and donned a gray linen dress. Then she went into the schoolroom to answer her sister's letter. Rose would be shocked to hear just how badly she was abused here at the Barclays'.

As she put quill to paper, she paused. She had no qualms about telling Rose all about Mistress Barclay's mistreatment of her, but she'd refrain from saying anything unkind about Colin—at least until she knew for certain that he'd abandoned her. She wouldn't mention the secret betrothal or write that he planned to visit Papa in England, either. She wasn't sure he'd keep his word and actually visit the family in Bath. It would be terrible to end up having to eat her words. Yesterday she'd eaten about as much humble pie as she cared to eat. *Ever.*

Salutations Rose. She began her response with as much dignity as she could muster. *I was quite surprised to hear from you. . . .*

Chapter 18

The weak February dawn offered only pale light as a cold, damp breeze blew wisps of morning mist about. Mariah snuggled deeper into her woolen wrapper as she stood by the carriage to bid the Barclays farewell. She had mixed feelings about choosing to stay behind, but after her day of servanthood at the gala held by the family on race day, there was no way she could face attending a Valentine's Day wedding in Baltimore with some of the same people. More's the pity. She might have met some rich gentleman there who wouldn't learn of her circumstance until she'd completely bewitched him. But on the other hand, with the Barclays away, she'd have an entire week of freedom. . .freedom to set another plan in motion, even if it did happen to be somewhat less appealing than her original one.

It piqued her that Colin had never written. How was she to know if he even intended to come back?

Victoria leaned out the window of the now hooded landau and touched Mariah on the shoulder. "I wish I didn't have to go. I'd rather stay here with you."

Knowing that Tori reveled in having three attentive young men dropping by to visit her several times a week now, it came as no surprise that the girl disliked having to leave her beaus behind. She took Victoria's outstretched hand and gave it a squeeze. "Dearest, think of all the other young gentlemen you would disappoint if you didn't go to Baltimore."

"What gentlemen?" Tori's face clouded over. "I don't know a soul there."

"You will, sweetheart, trust me. And you shall have the most marvelous time if you just allow yourself to do so. Besides, think of how you would disappoint your cousin if you failed to arrive, particularly since you agreed to be her maid of honor."

"You're right." Withdrawing her gloved hand from Mariah's grasp, she settled back against the leather cushion once again, only slightly mollified.

Out the back opening, Mistress Barclay mouthed a thank-you to Mariah as her husband tapped his metal-knobbed cane on the frame of the carriage bonnet, signaling their driver to start the team.

The landau lunged away down the lane, with young hands reaching out from both sides, waving good-bye. Mariah found herself a bit bereft already. The girls had truly captured her heart. The big house would seem empty without them.

With a sigh, she turned to glance down at the stables. Mr. Scott would be out working one horse or another soon. Perhaps she'd meander down there. After all, she had only a week to entice the redhead's affections enough that he'd purchase her bond. Still, she shouldn't be too pushy, look too desperate. He had to be the one to make the advances. Or at least *think* that.

She would take her time. She turned back to the house, intending to dress in an appealing, but not overly adorned, gown, and fashion her hair in a simpler, refined style. It would make her appear older and more serious. Perhaps she'd even look up a verse or two from the Bible to discuss, giving her a purpose he'd appreciate for her going down there. She smiled. Yes, that's what she'd do. After all, being married to a respected man like him would restore her own respectability. . .and with any luck at all, he might even turn out to be a pleasant husband. And generous, as well.

But as she mounted the steps to the manse, beguiling thoughts of Colin—handsome, charming Colin—slowed her down. Could she truly settle for Geoffrey Scott after him?

Mariah paused on the top step and gazed longingly down the lane. The trees were barren now, like her dreams, and reached uselessly up at the uncertain sky as if pleading for warmth. Surely Colin would return within the month, and remote as it seemed at this moment, he might still intend to marry her. But in case he'd changed his mind, she needed to have another plan in place, because she certainly would not remain in that house if he cast her aside like an old horse blanket.

Just then her stomach rumbled, reminding her that she hadn't awakened early enough to join the family at breakfast. She headed for the dining room, where the warm glow from wall sconces helped chase away the dreariness of the day.

Eloise and Lizzie looked up on her approach as they began removing trays of food from the sideboard.

Mariah held up a hand. "Just a moment, please. Let me fill a plate before you take everything away."

"Sho' 'nough, missy." The older slave handed her a clean plate. "Ah reckoned y'all already ate."

"I'm sorry, no. I've been out bidding the Barclays farewell. By the by, since it'll just be me here this week, I'll take my meals in the kitchen with you all. No sense going to extra fuss for one person. That is, if you don't mind."

Eloise smiled her apple-dumpling smile, white teeth bright against her dark brown skin. "Ah be hopin' you say dat. Dat ways we all can get us a li'l holiday."

Mariah returned her smile and gave sweet Lizzie a nod. "Yes, a Valentine's Day present for us while the family's away."

Sitting down at the table with her plate of food, Mariah realized she'd included herself with the slaves. Not a good way to be thinking if she wanted to better herself. But as she watched Eloise carry out a heavily laden tray, she couldn't help but sympathize with the older woman. She knew firsthand how hard slaves worked, ever since she'd been forced to help out for a day.

A couple of hours later, Mariah put a warm shawl around her shoulders and made her way to the stables, having found a scripture verse and put it to memory. She hoped to launch a spirited—and hopefully prolonged—discussion with Mr. Scott. Small puffs of her breath crystallized in the damp air, and she knew the chilly temperature would add a touch of color to her cheeks. She opened the door and stepped inside.

The sound of tapping drifted from the lamplit tack room, where she found the trainer working alone, hammering a metal brad into a halter.

"Good morning," she called out cheerily, appreciating the warmth coming from a round black stove.

Startled, he turned. "Oh, it's you, miss. I thought you would've left with the family."

She shook her head. "No. I no longer feel comfortable accompanying them to social events."

His sympathetic nod indicated that he understood. "Did you want me to saddle a horse for you?"

"No, thank you." She made an effort to convey a touch of sadness in her smile. "It's just a treat to be able to take a walk whenever I choose to. Normally my hours are all planned out for me ahead of time."

"I thought you enjoyed your work." Averting his gaze, he picked up the small hammer again. "I've noticed quite a nice change in the girls. Heather, especially, has blossomed since you've been here."

"Hasn't she, though?" Mariah moved a few steps closer. "That little dear has a true gift for music, and it's helping her to overcome her shyness. However, I do wish tutoring the girls had been my choice and not a duty pressed on me because of that awful bond."

He glanced up at her, his expression serious, and spoke quietly. "Have a seat." He indicated a nearby stool as he pulled another out from under the workbench for himself. The lamplight cast a golden glow over his coppery hair with his movements.

An invitation to sit down. . .a definite bit of progress.

"A scripture comes to mind that you might find helpful." He reached for a worn black book lying on the end of the workbench.

Mariah squelched a sigh and the impulse to roll her eyes. If the worst came to pass, could she really put up with a man who preached at her day after day? Watching him leaf through the pages, she recalled that both Papa and Rose had often quoted scripture, yet she hadn't loved them any less for it. She propped up a smile and tried to appear interested.

"Ah yes, here it is." He glanced up at her then returned his attention to the passage before him. "In the sixth chapter of Ephesians. 'Servants, be obedient to them that are your masters according to the flesh, with fear and trembling, in singleness of your heart, as unto Christ; not with eyeservice, as menpleasers; but as the servants of Christ, doing the will of God from the heart.' And let me see. . ." He tilted the Bible closer to the light. "Yes, here it is. 'Knowing that whatsoever good thing any man doeth, the same shall he receive of the Lord, whether he be bond or free.' So you see, in the end, being bond or free matters very little. Most people have to labor at something all their lives, be they master, servant, or slave. We simply must set our hearts and minds on pleasing the Lord, since He gives us so many blessings."

Mariah focused on his compelling green eyes. "Now that I see things through that perspective, I feel so much better." Surely that response would please the man. For goodness' sake, all one had to do was look at the ragged field slaves living here to see that nothing they had could possibly begin to compare with the Barclays' wealth. She needed to take control of the conversation. "Speaking of scriptures, I have—"

Mr. Scott got up rather rudely and crossed to the door, opening it to a rush of cold air. "A roan?" He shook his head. "His father will not be pleased with that one."

His father?

Mariah sprang to her feet and flew to the doorway.

A horse and rider trotted toward them on the lane.

The rider snatched off his three-cornered hat and waved it back and forth.

Colin! He'd come back at last! But remembering how she'd been humiliated while he'd been away, and considering that he'd never bothered to write, Mariah doubted he would still want to marry her.

Then another sudden realization caused all the breath to leave her lungs and make her knees go weak. The two of them would be in the house together.

Alone.

For a whole week.

"Mariah!" Colin knew she probably couldn't hear him over the distance separating them, but he waved his hat in a wide arc and heeled Russet Knight into a gallop. No woman he'd seen in all his travels had remotely sparked his interest, not when he had the most beautiful one in the world waiting for him.

Nearing the stables, he noticed that her welcoming smile wilted, then disappeared as her lips parted and she took some backward steps.

Her reaction baffled Colin. Throughout his absence, all he'd dreamed of was leaping off his horse, taking Mariah into his arms, and kissing her—her face, her eyes, her mouth. Why did she appear stunned? He reined in directly in front of her and Geoffrey Scott and dismounted.

The trainer moved close to the animal. "I assume you know your father's not going to be happy that you brought back a roan." He ran his hands down the stallion's foreleg.

"He'll change his mind when he sees Russet Knight run. The horse will sire some great champions." Colin's eyes gravitated to Mariah. Why was she standing so far away? They were betrothed, were they not?

Geoffrey continued to study the animal, then gave an assenting nod. "He does have fine lines; I'll say that."

Would the man never stop talking about the blasted horse? Reluctantly, Colin shifted his attention back to the trainer. "He'll look even better once he's had a few days' exercise. He's just spent the last seven weeks aboard ship." He looked again at Mariah, who stood frozen in place, then at Scott, and his suspicions came to the fore. The two of them had just been together—unchaparoned—for how long? "How've you been, my love?"

Her attempt at a smile fell flat. "Fine. And I assume you met with success in your venture. We didn't expect you to return for several more weeks." She flicked a glance toward the mansion.

"I was successful, yes, and in as short a time as possible. I bypassed the trip to Boston." He paused, eyeing Mariah. "Isn't it a rather odd time of day to be visiting the stables?"

Geoffrey Scott stood and straightened his posture. "I assure you, Colin, nothing is amiss here. Miss Harwood merely came here to ask me a theological question." He turned his attention to her. "You hardly had time enough to voice it. But never mind. You can ask me another time. Colin's back." With what appeared to be a genuine grin, he slapped Colin on the shoulder blades. "Glad to have you home again."

Somewhat relieved to have the matter concerning Mariah and the trainer cleared up, Colin cut a glance to her, still puzzled that she seemed so standoffish. He'd find out why once they had some privacy. Offering his elbow, he tucked her arm in his. "Geoff, would you mind seeing to the horse?"

"Of course. It'll give Red and me a chance to get acquainted."

Leading Mariah away from the stable, Colin started up the pathway toward the house. Strange that the rest of the family hadn't noticed his return. He guided her toward the gazebo so they could speak privately before going inside. He needed some answers.

⸺

"Why are we going to the gazebo, Colin?" Mariah felt fully aware of his suspicions about her and Mr. Scott, and since they were entirely correct, she wondered what she could say in her defense. There were no slaves out working in the dreary weather, but she didn't want to take a chance on one of them overhearing the conversation and bandying it hither and yon. She pulled her shawl closer. " 'Tis quite cold out here. Shouldn't we—"

He continued walking. "I want a moment alone with you before we go inside."

She huffed out a vapory breath. She might as well tell him, he'd find out in a few minutes anyway. "Your family is not at home. They left this morning for a wedding at the Spencers'. Your cousin Susan is getting married."

"You don't say." His dark eyes gravitated to the house as a slow smile spread from ear to ear. He changed direction so quickly, Mariah nearly lost her balance.

" 'Tis true. And I can see your reaction to the situation is far different from mine. What will people say when they learn we've spent the week by ourselves in the house, with none of your family around?"

"Is that why you haven't given me a proper greeting?" His steps never slowed.

"Colin. You're not taking this seriously."

He cut her a half smile. "You are so wrong, my dear Mariah. I can't imagine a more perfect homecoming. Do stop balking, or I won't tell you about my visit with your family."

He had actually gone to Bath, just as he'd promised! He must still want to marry her! Exuberant beyond words, she pulled free. "Race you to the house!" Hiking her skirts, she sprinted away.

With a burst of laughter, he started after her. He reached her just as she got to the porch steps and caught her around the waist, twirling her around.

Mariah squealed with delight and threw her arms around him as he scooped her up into his arms and bounded up the steps. Once inside, he lowered her to the tiled floor, all humor gone from his eyes.

His ardent gaze drew her to him, and he captured her lips in a breathtakingly sweet kiss she never wanted to end. Her heart sang. Colin had come back to her, and he really and truly was hers.

"Ahem." A heartbeat of silence. *"Ahem!"*

Mariah dragged her lips from Colin's, and they both turned to see Eloise glaring at them, her fists planted on her wide hips.

"Why, Mammy Eloise," Colin gushed. "You're a sight for sore eyes." He tucked Mariah close to his side and tugged her along as he went to wrap his other arm around the slave's generous girth. He gave her a peck on the cheek. "I missed you and your delicious meals so much. By any chance, have you got a little somethin' to tide me over until mealtime?"

Not cracking a smile, she arched her scant brows. "I does iff 'n you unwraps yo'self from dat chil'."

Colin laughed and stepped a small pace away from Mariah. "I was just showin' her how much I missed her—missed all of you."

Staring hard at him, Eloise smirked. "Well, now dat we got da happy homecomin' outta da way, keep yo hands to yo'self."

He held up the guilty culprits without erasing his grin. "Now can I have somethin' to eat?"

"Go set yo'self down in da dinin' room. Ah'll bring y'all out somethin' directly."

The cook's interruption had brought both disappointment and relief to Mariah. She'd truly enjoyed being so thoroughly kissed. Her lips still tingled, wanting more. "May I have a cup of tea, as well?" she called after the slave.

Colin seated Mariah near the head of the table and bent to tickle her neck with the brush of his lips, sending yet another delicious chill through her. Then he sighed and took his father's chair. He took her hand and raised it to his mouth, kissing her palm.

Her heart drummed a staccato beat. It was so good to have her Colin back. She leaned closer to him.

"I've missed you so much," he murmured, his gaze holding hers. "You were all I thought about all the time I was away."

"And I you," she managed to whisper. "I was so worried you'd find someone more appealing."

"That's not possible." He cupped her face in his hand. "You are everything I—"

"Masta Colin! I said keep yo' hands to yo'self." Eloise paused in the doorway.

Chuckling, he straightened. "Yes, ma'am."

Mariah giggled behind her hand and turned to the cook as the woman neared the table. "From now on, we promise to be good."

"I don't know, Mammy." Colin wagged his head soberly. "That's gonna be a hard promise to keep."

The cook slammed a tray down between them, rattling the dishes. "Jes' don't yo forget who be da mammy aroun' here." She placed the food pointedly before him, then set out a cup for each of them. She stared him squarely in the eye. "Ah will be back. . .with da tea."

As the slave stormed out with a huff, Colin tilted his head at Mariah. "You'll have to excuse her. She's been motherin' me for as long as I can remember."

"You don't need to explain. I personally know what a fine woman she is. Why, if it hadn't been for her, I don't know how I would have—" Realizing she'd said too much already, Mariah clamped her lips together.

His grin disappeared. "What do you mean?"

Inhaling a shuddering breath, she released it in a whoosh of air. "I hadn't planned to go into that just yet. We were having such a lovely time. But I suppose you'll find out soon enough."

He leaned back in his chair with a frown while Mariah spoke in a rush.

"The house slaves came down with the measles the day of the phaeton races, so I was pressed into service. I had to help Eloise prepare and serve food and refreshments to the guests throughout that day. Thank goodness your friend Tuck sent two of their slaves over to relieve me the next morning."

Colin's expression turned granite hard. "Mother was responsible for this. She deliberately humiliated you."

Reaching for his fisted hand, Mariah smoothed her palm over it. "What's done is done, dearest. My question for you is, since all your neighbors and business associates saw me in that shameful position, is it possible you would still want to marry me?"

A muscle worked in his jaw as he gazed steadily at her. "So that's why you didn't accompany the family to Baltimore. Mother saw to it that you were no longer considered fit for gentle society."

He now fully understood the extent of the damage his devious mother had done. Mariah held her breath.

He reached over and caressed her cheek with the backs of his fingers as his demeanor softened, then took a brighter turn. "Perhaps Mother did me a favor without knowing it. She single-handedly kept all my competition away while I was gone."

Mariah relaxed and leaned into his comforting touch. "You were gone such a long time. But if you missed me so much, why did you not write to me?"

"Write!" He hiked a brow. "You knew where I was going and what I was doing. There was nothing to report until I went to see your father. And by that time, I knew I'd beat any post home."

"Papa! You did go to see him!" Mariah swept up from her seat and planted a kiss on his cheek.

Colin caught her to him with an eager laugh.

Mariah realized her mistake. Eloise would return with the tea at any second. She eased away and retook her seat.

It took several seconds for him to glance from her to the chicken and dumplings on his plate. Finally he picked up his fork and took a sample.

"How did Papa look?"

Swallowing his mouthful, he nodded. "Fine. He sends his love to you and your sisters. I found him most welcoming and liked him at once. That younger brother of yours, though, is a corker. He'd make a good match for our little Amy. He managed to wheedle a pony out of me."

"Surely not!"

"It's quite true." Colin chuckled. "I almost felt like I was home again. And the little beast did make a fine Christmas gift for him."

"A gift for the rascal, and not even a Christmas greeting to me?"

Colin's humor died. "I'm so sorry. That was terribly thoughtless of me." A guilty smile curved his lips, and he changed the subject. "By the way, I was able to persuade your father to seek a barrister's assistance regarding that financial problem. Both he and your father were hesitant to take an influential aristocrat to court, but I convinced them it was quite proper to do so."

Tears pooled in Mariah's eyes, clouding her view of this man who had come to the rescue yet again. "You truly are the most wonderful man," she choked out.

He took her hand in his once more. "And I have an entire *uninterrupted week* to show you just how wonderful I can be."

Chapter 19

Y ou know, the more I think about it, the more I have to admit you're right, sweetheart." Colin forked the last bit of his remaining dumpling into his mouth and washed it down with a gulp of tea as he and Mariah sat at the table.

Mariah tried unsuccessfully to read his expression as she set down her own cup. "About what?"

"We will need to be very discreet, not only after my parents return from Baltimore, but during this week, as well. Perhaps *especially* during this week. Our people here are loyal to a fault, but they also love to gossip. Word of our relationship could easily get back to my father and mother. I'll speak to Eloise and Geoffrey and ask them not to mention any of my lustful intentions toward you they happened to witness."

"Lustful intentions?" Mariah didn't like the sound of that at all. No wedding band graced her finger as yet, and she was not about to allow Colin liberties to which he was only entitled by marriage.

Colin chuckled and angled his head at her. "My lustful intention is to marry you, my dear Mariah. . .if you'll still have me, of course."

A huge smile curved her lips. "Yes! Oh, yes." Supremely grateful to hear him say those all-important words she'd longed so to hear, she reached over to give his arm a squeeze, but he warded her off with a raised hand.

"In that case—" He reached into his breast pocket and withdrew something in his closed hand. With a tentative smile, he opened his fingers to display an exquisite ring. "Your father assured me this would fit. Shall we try it?"

Mariah's heart tripped over itself at the sight of a beautiful amethyst surrounded by tiny diamonds. "You bought it from Papa?" Her eyes roved Colin's wondrous face as she nibbled her lower lip and held out her left hand.

"I did." Light from the wall sconces sparkled over the cut gems as he slipped it on her finger. "He wanted to give it to me without cost, since it was for you, but I insisted on paying. And look. He knows you well. It fits perfectly." He raised her hand to admire it more closely. "I chose this one because it reminded me of those incredible violet eyes of yours."

Mariah blinked back happy tears. "Oh, Colin, 'tis ever so lovely. I couldn't have asked for anything more beautiful."

"I'm so glad you like it." His lips spread into a satisfied smile. Then he grew serious. "Of course, you know that once the family returns, we'll need to keep the ring out of sight until I secure the land I've been promised. Only a few days more, my darling. I'll request it as soon as they get home from the wedding. The anniversary of my birth came and went while I was aboard ship. So I am now of age to take ownership."

Still admiring her ring of promise, Mariah raised her gaze to his and offered a melancholy smile. "Your birthday. Another celebration we weren't able to share."

"Don't worry, my love." Colin cupped her chin with his palm. "We'll have a lifetime of events to celebrate together."

"I hope you're right." Despite his brave words, Mariah couldn't prevent doubts from creeping in. "What if your father will only sign the land over to you if you agree not to wed me? Surely you know your mother especially will fight you on this. As her husband, he will have to give in to keep the peace."

He shrugged a shoulder. "They can protest all they want to. But after being separated from you for these unbearably long months, I'll not allow them to stop us from marrying. After all, I'm not without a few assets of my own. Last spring, Tuck and I both bought land between the ridges to the west of here. Do you remember that tall young gentleman I introduced you to at the race in Alexandria?"

"George Washington, I believe?"

"Right. Well, he's been working as a surveyor for the colony, measuring and marking off parcels of virgin land along the distant branches of the Potomac. The land out there is cheap, and George has been purchasing choice parcels for himself out of his earnings. He recommended some fine pieces of land for us to buy. I bought a picturesque little valley that has the South Fork of the Potomac running through it."

"La, your own valley." Mariah tried to insert some enthusiasm into her response, but as wonderful as that sounded on the surface, the thought of living so far from any sort of society was daunting. What about the Indians? Weren't they a concern?

Colin puffed out his chest, obviously proud of his investment. "Our land spreads between the Blue Ridge and Allegheny Mountains. Tuck and I canoed upstream to see our parcels last May. We traveled for miles past the last settlement. Can you imagine? We're the first people ever to hold title to that valley. If all goes well here, I'll take you there to see it next summer. Maybe sooner. Barclay Valley."

The place was so remote Colin could name the valley after himself! Mariah knew she wasn't anything like Rose. She'd never grow accustomed to living in such an isolated spot. She had a hard time concentrating on what he was saying as he continued on with enthusiasm.

"Don't look dismayed, my dear Mariah. It's an easy float downriver anytime we have a desire to visit the family. Also, I may not have mentioned this before, but I happen to own three fine brood mares of my own, plus their foals. All we would need is a good stud to start our own horse farm, if need be. So you see, darling girl, nothing shall keep us apart."

He rose from the table. "Come with me to the library. I'll show you on the map exactly where our land is—yours and mine."

"Yes," she managed as he pulled back her chair. "I'd love to see it." It was probably rather silly of her to conjure up all those stupid fears. As long as she was with Colin, he would continue to take care of her as he always had.

Surely he would.

As Colin opened one of the double doors to the library for Mariah, a loud pounding rattled the front door. Who could be calling at this time of the morning? None of the plantation workers used the front entrance.

He turned and crossed the foyer. While grasping the door handle, he heard Benjamin coming from the butlery. "It's all right, Benjamin. I'll get it."

"Yessuh." With a bow of his snowy head, the African flashed a friendly smile. "Glad to see y'all finally made it home, Masta Colin. We sho' did miss you."

"I missed all of you, too." Interrupted once more by the second round of knocks, he opened the door.

Dennis Tucker leaned a hand against the doorjamb, breathing hard. At the bottom of the steps, his mount also blew puffs of air and pranced nervously, its reins dangling loose on the ground.

Colin frowned. "Tuck! What's the big rush? Is your place on fire?"

"No." He panted, trying to catch his breath. "But I've come on urgent business. My kid brother saw you ride past our place awhile ago, but he didn't mention it right away, or I'd have intercepted you before you made it all the way home."

Colin glanced around at Mariah, who stood listening to the exchange with a puzzled expression. Exhaling, he stepped back to let Tuck in. "So what's got you all afire?"

"You haven't heard, then." He swept off his hat but held it in his hands.

"Heard what?"

"We're goin' to war!" His eyes flared wide with excitement.

Mariah gasped and hastened to join them. She pushed past Colin and faced Tuck, her hands on her hips. "Whatever are you talking about? At war with whom? You've been calling on Victoria at least three times every week, and I never heard one word from your mouth about any conflict."

"There's a very good reason for that," he shot back, hiking his chin. "Womenfolk always get hysterical anytime the word *war* is mentioned. Trouble's been brewin' for some time."

She pressed her lips together and released a breath. "That's absurd. If there was the least bit of danger, Mr. Barclay would never have blithely ridden off to a wedding in Baltimore."

Colin couldn't help but grin at her spunk. He looked from her to his friend. "She does have a point."

With a wary eye on Mariah, Tuck switched his attention to Colin. "I need to speak to you alone. Shall we adjourn to your father's library?" Without waiting for an answer, he strode across to the door Colin had opened moments before.

Colin turned to Mariah and took her by the shoulders. "Sweetheart, I'll be just a few minutes, I promise. And I also promise to tell you everything we discuss. So please go into the parlor and wait for me. I won't be long. You and I have plenty of our own business to take care of later." With a meaningful smile, he swung on his heel and followed his friend into the library, closing the door behind them. "So, what's this all about?"

Tuck met his curious gaze straight on. "Governor Dinwiddie received word back from England to call our militias to arms. He sent William Trent, an Ohio Valley trader, to Augusta County to lead their militia. He also sent George Washington upriver to Fredrick City to bring fifty men back with him to Alexandria for training and to be equipped. Dinwiddie instructed them to travel to the upper forks of the Ohio to build a fort."

Colin tucked his chin. "While it's still snowing? That hardly makes sense."

"This is serious, Colin. The French have to be stopped before they send more men down from Canada in the spring. George and the men from Fredrick City rode past our place just two days ago on their way to Alexandria. George told me that if you and I want to make sure the French are stopped before they turn their greedy eyes toward the backcountry where we bought property, we need to get ourselves down there to join him. We do happen to be part of the local militia, you know."

"But I only just got home. I haven't even unpacked."

"All the better. I spent all of yesterday convincin' Father it was my duty to go. I'm packed and was just waitin' for some food to be cooked for the journey. So don't worry about food. I'll share mine with you."

Colin was still trying to process the information Dennis had related. "But I—"

"What's the hesitation, Colin? With your family away, you won't have to waste your time arguin' with them."

"That's true, but still—"

Tuck barely paused as he rushed on. "By the way, Washington is already a hero. The whole colony is talkin' about him. Dinwiddie dispatched him to one of those Indian villages the French had taken over—one with an English trading post—to ask them politely to leave. I thought that was a foolhardy mission, myself, and it turns out George barely escaped with his life. He and his guide ended up comin' back across the mountains in winter *on foot*, with only scant supplies. Of course he's chompin' at the bit to get back there, this time with force."

Shaking his head, Colin kneaded his chin. "I know we're both signed on with the militia, but this is too sudden."

"Oh, and by the by," Tuck interrupted over his objections again. "Our friend George is now in command. He's been made a lieutenant colonel. I'm sure we can distinguish ourselves every bit as well as he has, if not better. How does Colonel Tucker or Colonel Barclay sound to you?"

"Fine. Fine. But as it happens, I have some rather urgent business here at home that needs to be taken care of."

Tuck rolled his eyes and let out a huff of breath. "Look, Colin, old man. Your family is gone for at least a week, if not more. I'm sure that once we ride into the Ohio Valley, we'll run those interlopers right off. We'll be back in no time at all. Even if we hadn't bought land on the frontier, it's still our duty to go. Our militia has been ordered to Alexandria."

Trying to dispel the tightness in his chest, Colin breathed out a troubled breath and gave a reluctant nod. "You're right. It is our duty." But why did it have to be now? Why, when everything he'd spent endless months longing for was within his grasp?

He glanced toward the door. How would he explain this to Mariah?

Chapter 20

After agreeing to meet Tuck at his plantation in an hour, Colin quietly closed the door behind his friend. He needed a moment or two—or better still, a day or two—to formulate words that would pacify Mariah.

That was not to be.

The library door swung open within seconds. "I saw Tuck charge down the steps to his horse and—" Mariah stopped speaking and crossed the room, her intent gaze searching Colin's expression. "I don't relish the look on your face. What did Dennis say that has you so upset?"

Colin exhaled a slow breath, still trying to gather his thoughts. "Let's go into the parlor, my love." He gestured for her to precede him.

She didn't move. She stood regarding him with a puzzled frown. "Whatever for? You were going to show me the location of the land you purchased."

"Forgive me, but that will have to wait. An urgent matter has arisen. Please. . ." He motioned again toward the door. From her confused demeanor, he knew this was not going to be easy.

With some hesitation, she finally turned and did as bidden. Once in the parlor she took a seat on the damask settee and sat with her hands in her lap.

Colin gave fleeting consideration to taking a chair as far from her as possible but summoned his courage and sat beside her. He took her hands in his.

"Well?" Her dark curls graced her shoulder as she tipped her head in question.

"There's no easy way to say this."

"To say what?"

"I. . .I'm afraid I must leave again."

"Leave!" Her slender brows dipped toward each other. "When?"

Colin swallowed. "Now. Our local militia has been ordered to report to Alexandria at once."

"What are you saying, Colin? Surely they can't mean you. You're not a soldier. You're a plantation owner. A horse breeder."

Hating the look of pain in her eyes, he stroked his thumbs across the backs of her small hands. "This isn't England, sweetheart. Here in Virginia we don't have a standing army. Able-bodied men normally meet every month or so for drills. And when trouble arises, we're obligated to serve."

"But—" Mariah averted her gaze for a heartbeat, then returned it to him. "If what you're saying is true, why would your father go off to Baltimore as if nothing were amiss?"

"The orders were issued only a few days ago. With me away in England, he probably saw no reason to alarm all of you, especially since the trouble with the French is on the other side of the mountains. But even at that distance it's still in Virginia's territory and therefore must be defended."

"But if no one knows you've returned. . ." She gave a little shrug, a pleading look of hope.

"People do know. I disembarked at Alexandria. Folks saw me when I rode through town. I'm honor bound to go. It's my duty."

"Honor bound!" With a gasp, Mariah tore her hands from his. "What about your honor to me? You made promises to me, too. Not ten minutes ago you assured me we'd be married. Soon! Yet now you say you're going to ride off for who knows how long, leaving me here to languish again, and still as an indentured servant."

"Mariah, my love, the important thing is that you'll be here under my family's protection till I return. I don't believe this venture will take us more than a month or two to put to rights. Once we arrive in force, the French are sure to hightail it back up to Canada. The Indians in the area are loyal to us. They've been quite happy trading with the Ohio and Virginia Company for several years now. They'll side with us. You've nothing to fear."

"The Ohio and Virginia Company." She drew her lips inward in thought then relaxed them. "My sister is with one of their traders, is she not? Do you think Rose could be in danger?"

Colin cocked his head. "I seriously doubt she would've been taken into Indian Territory." He took her hands in his again. "It would be unseemly to take a gentlewoman into such a primitive area."

"But you don't know that for certain, do you? If you must go to join the militia at Alexandria, I beg you to find out exactly where Rose is. She was bought by that man Eustice. . .Eustice something. Smith, I believe it was. Eustice Smith. Please, Colin, would you do that for me?"

He smiled. "First thing, my love. I'll go to their headquarters again before I report for duty. Surely they know where she is by now."

At the despair evident in her expression, Colin drew her to him and held her close. "I'm so sorry. I love you so very, very much. Leaving you—even the thought of it—is like tearing my heart out."

"Mine, too," she murmured against his neck, her lips soft and moist.

He raised her beautiful sad face up and took possession of those luscious lips in a deep, wrenching kiss. How would he ever make himself walk out that door? But reality brought him back to earth. One thing that could never be bought was a man's honor. He had to go.

Mariah paced the parlor floor, pausing every few minutes to look out the windows. Rain again. Would it never stop? It seemed the sky was weeping the tears she no longer possessed.

Two dreary, drizzly weeks had passed since the Barclays and Colin had left her in this big empty house alone. The family was to have been back in a week, but the foul weather must have delayed them. And Colin. . . Mr. Scott had expressed doubts that the militia would leave for the wilderness until the worst of the mountain snows had subsided. Small comfort, since wherever Colin was, he'd be out marching and drilling in this horrid weather. He could come down with lung fever and die. She shied away from the dreadful thought, unable to imagine an existence without him. At the same time, a tiny, shameful part of her worried on her own account. With Colin gone, her indenturement papers would belong to his parents, would they not? What would become of her then?

A gradual lessening of the heavy skies caused the room to lighten a bit, and Mariah moved to the window. Shafts of sunlight slanted through the clouds in the west. The storm must be coming to an end at last. She smiled. Perhaps she'd ride into Alexandria and check on Colin, make sure he was still in good health. He might have been able to learn something of Rose's whereabouts. Surely the rain would stop by the time she had a horse saddled. And she'd take some of Eloise's tastiest cooking along for him, as well.

Colin would be thrilled to see her; she was certain of that. She reached into the lace tucker in her bodice for the proof of his love and drew out the ring she wore hidden on a chain around her neck in case his family returned unexpectedly.

Turning from the window, she caught sight of a rider on the edge of her vision coming up the lane. Colin? *Please let it be him.* Perhaps he'd decided not to go with the militia after all. She tucked her ring back out of sight again.

But as the rider neared, she could tell it was someone else. With his hat pulled low against the rain, she couldn't make out the man's face. Dread cinched her heart. Was he the bearer of bad news?

She didn't wait for him to come to the door but snatched her cloak from the hall peg and tossed it about her shoulders as she hurried outside and down the steps. Before he even dismounted, she questioned him. "Have you come bearing news?"

"Actually, I have." He gave a nod. "I've some mail from Colin."

"You've seen him?" Hope sprang anew inside her being.

"Aye, at the militia encampment south of Alexandria. He's there with my son."

Suddenly Mariah remembered her manners. "La, please forgive me. Would you care to come inside out of the rain and have something warm to drink? You look drenched."

"That I am, miss." Swinging down to the ground, he shook rain from his slicker before following her up to the veranda. "I don't believe we've been introduced. I'm Albert Tucker, Dennis's father."

Now that she took a closer look, Mariah remembered seeing him at the gala on race day. Though considerably more heavy than his son, he did share the same hazel eyes and a smile reminiscent of Tuck's. "So pleased to meet you, sir. I'm Mariah Harwood, tutoress to Colin's sisters."

"Yes, I reckoned that. Dennis has often spoken kindly of you and how your tutorage has benefited the girls." He followed her inside.

"We find your son a very entertaining young gentleman," Mariah said, taking his rain slicker. "Do have a seat in the parlor. I'll go tell the cook we'll be needing refreshments."

Moments later, she found Mr. Tucker comfortably settled in a wing chair near the fire. He looked up with a smile as she approached. "Actually, I've come with several pieces of correspondence. Colin asked me to collect all the Barclay mail." He drew the items from an inside pocket of his frock coat.

"How kind of you." Mariah accepted the proffered missives and laid them on the side table, then took a seat across from him. Despite being intensely curious about the letters, she forced herself to give full attention to the visitor. "I assume Colin and Dennis are both well. I've been sorely tempted to ride into the city and check on them myself."

Mr. Tucker chuckled, then broke into full-blown laughter as he rested his hands on the full girth bulging at the buttons of his coat.

Mariah smiled politely while she waited for his humor to subside.

As his laughter died away, he wiped away some tears and took a shuddering breath. "My apologies, miss. It's just that every time I think of my son sloggin' through the mud, marchin' back and forth, back and forth, I can't help but laugh. He expected to be ridin' off on his trusty steed like some modern-day Lancelot to right all wrongs. It never dawned on him that in carryin' out his noble cause he might get dirty." He chuckled lightly again, then stifled it. "But the boy'll learn. My hope is that he'll come back a man ready to take up his responsibilities."

Mariah mulled over his words. "Did they, perchance, give you any idea of how long they'll be gone?"

"I'm afraid the boys don't know much at this point. But from what I gathered from a merchant friend of mine, most of the supplies the militia's been waitin' for have come in. I imagine they'll be leavin' soon."

"How long do you suppose they'll be out there?" Fearing the answer, she held her breath.

"That's hard to tell. Depends on how deeply entrenched the French have got themselves."

Mariah's spirits sank. "Are you saying they might be gone more than a month or two?" That was the amount of time Colin had figured the trouble would last.

He shrugged his shoulders and grimaced. "Don't be gettin' yourself all worked up, missy. The French are a long way down from Canada, and with a force of at least a thousand strung out for a couple hundred miles, that puts 'em a fair distance from their supplies. They should be runnin' out about now. It shouldn't take much to send 'em packin'."

Much as Mariah would have liked to believe that, doubts assailed her. "But wouldn't the Indians give them—"

Mr. Tucker wagged his graying head, his leather-bound queue brushing across his back. "We've got trade agreements with most of the Indians. They won't help the French. Now, stop your frettin'. And tell little Tori not to worry either. Worry causes lines in pretty faces."

Mariah detested being treated like a brainless twit. Nevertheless, she smiled while waiting for Pansy to bring in the tea tray. The sooner the man was served, the sooner he'd leave, and she'd be able to read the letter from Colin.

Another long, uncertain week crept by after reading Colin's disturbing note. According to him, Rose truly was deep in Indian country, but doing fine. . .or so the fur company proprietors had assured Colin, who considered the information further reason to remain with the militia. He vowed to rescue her sister if she was in danger. Mariah let out a weary sigh. Dear, brave Colin. Ever the hero.

Detecting a sound from outside, she rose from picking out a nonsensical tune on the harpsichord and meandered to the front window, where she spied the family's landau coming up the lane! "Thank heavens!" She slapped her hands together.

Then reality returned, and she wasn't sure whether to be glad or distressed. Having been in Baltimore these past weeks, they wouldn't know that Colin had come and gone. . .along with Victoria's Dennis Tucker. Possibly even Edward Rochester and the Fairchild lad who'd been coming to call. Hopefully someone along the road had informed the family of the trouble with the French so she wouldn't have to be the bearer of the unwelcome news.

She headed for the foyer to retrieve her cloak.

Benjamin came from the kitchen just then, wearing a happy grin. "Ah hears da carriage a-comin'. It's about time. We been lonesome aroun' here."

Always amazed at how much the slaves liked their masters— despite being owned by them—Mariah recalled that Geoffrey Scott had informed her that these slaves were Christians. Free in Christ, at least. She supposed that did take a measure of the sting away from being in bondage.

The tall African swung the door wide and stepped out to greet the arriving family and assist the women.

Mariah decided she could do no less.

Amy emerged first out the carriage door. "Mariah! We're home!"

She couldn't help laughing. "And so you are."

Victoria stepped down next. "Has my brother gotten home yet? Has Tuck come by asking for me? Or maybe Steven Fairchild?" She cast a furtive glance back at her mother, as if the third young man's name had been added to appease the woman.

Dread engulfed Mariah. The family knew nothing about the events taking place in the territory. "Let's get inside out of the cold, and I'll relay the latest happenings. First I'll go and tell Eloise you've come home."

"Yes, do that." Assisted by the butler, Mistress Barclay stepped gracefully down from the carriage. "If possible, we'd like an early supper. It's been a long and tiring day. Tell Eloise nothing special. Whatever's handy will do."

"Oh, and welcome home," Mariah remembered to say. "We've missed you." As she ran up the steps, she realized she actually meant those words. She truly had missed them—all of them—even the regal lady of the manor.

By the time she and Lizzie returned with a tea tray and a platter of small tea cakes and cookies, they found the weary family lounging in the parlor while Benjamin and the driver carted the luggage into the foyer. There was no sense of alarm among the group, so obviously Benjamin hadn't mentioned anything about Colin while she'd been in the kitchen.

Lizzie set the tea tray on the table and quietly took her leave. Mariah placed the cookies and cakes alongside. "Shall I pour?"

"Yes, please do." The mistress fanned herself with a handkerchief. "It's been a long, bumpy ride."

"Has there been word as yet from Colin?" Mr. Barclay sat down next to his wife. "Since we were delayed so long in Baltimore, we surmised he'd be here by now to greet us."

Just about to take her seat near the tea service, Mariah opted to remain standing. "Your son did, in fact, return home, sir. Three weeks ago. However, I'm sorry to report he was summoned to report for militia duty that same day."

"You're not serious!" His dark brows hiked high.

Mariah nodded. "Mr. Scott rode into Alexandria yesterday to check on them, and he was told the militia left for the Ohio Valley the previous day."

"They did what?" Teacups rattled on the tray as Colin's mother lunged forward. "Are you telling us that Colin left with the militia?"

"I'm afraid so, madam. He said he was duty bound to go with the militia and rout the French out of Virginia's western territory."

Mistress Barclay swung to her husband, a frantic expression contorting her face. "Eldon, you must go and fetch him home. He could get killed."

"Colin's gonna get killed?" Amy sprang to her feet.

Her mother turned toward the girls. "Go upstairs and change for dinner. At once."

"But Mama!" Victoria protested.

"Now." The mistress flicked a hand toward the door. "We'll talk later, after we've heard all the details and have sorted them out."

Watching the trio as they obeyed their mother, Mariah wished with every fiber of her being that she was going with them.

"Eldon, you must do something." Twisting her handkerchief into a tight, untidy knot, Mistress Barclay swung her troubled gaze back to him.

"There's nothing to be done, Cora, my dear. Colin has been on the militia roster since he turned sixteen. Surely you know that."

"But it never meant anything," she countered. "Just a bunch of young men strutting around the parade ground. Not leaving home and going off to start a war."

He let out an exasperated breath. "Well, it means something now, I'm afraid. We've heard the reports about the French moving into English territory. It was only a matter of time until something had to be done about it. Call the girls back, and let's have our tea. Mariah, would you pour now?"

"Surely, sir." The worst was over. Emitting a tiny whoosh of relief, Mariah sat down and picked up the teapot.

Suddenly Colin's mother shot a glare her way. "Why didn't you stop him?" She grabbed Mariah's hand. "You're such a clever girl, and he's so taken with you. I'm sure you could have used your feminine wiles to stop him from leaving."

Stung by the woman's vile insinuation, Mariah barely managed to set the hot china pot down before dropping it. "I tried, Mistress Barclay. I begged him not to go. Truly I did. But he insisted he had to go, that he was obligated. He would not be dissuaded."

The woman came to her feet and loomed over Mariah, her face

twisted, her hand raised, poised for a resounding slap. "You could have stopped him. You know you could have. If he gets killed it will be on your head. On your head! I want you out of my sight. Now!" She jabbed a manicured finger toward the door.

Chapter 21

Mariah's stomach roiled. She stared at the supper Pansy sent up to her room that evening after Cora Barclay's callous outburst. To think that after being so happy to have the family back home at last, she had been treated with such viciousness by her mistress. The woman had all but snarled as she berated Mariah for not preventing Colin from reporting to the militia. Why, a person would think she'd encouraged him to leave, when in truth, she'd begged him to stay.

Even more disturbing, his mother actually insinuated that Mariah should have used her womanly charms to induce him to remain at home—to sacrifice her greatest asset, her innocence. Highly unchristian of Mistress Barclay, indeed. Mariah grimaced.

Neither had the tirade been characteristic of the woman. Because of the grand hopes she held for her son, she had not been thrilled by an outsider's sudden presence in the household. Nevertheless, the mistress had heretofore treated Mariah with courtesy during her stay. She'd never been mean-spirited. Leaving the tray of food untouched, Mariah changed into her night shift and climbed into bed, even though she knew she'd face a restless night with little sleep.

Rising early the next morning, Mariah tiptoed through Amy's room without disturbing the sleeping child. Steeling herself to face her mistress—hopefully without an audience—she descended quietly. But inside she wondered if she was to be tossed out into the cold with no place to go until Colin returned.

At the bottom landing, she ran her fingers across her hidden amethyst ring. Perhaps if worse came to worse, and she was left to fend for herself, she might be able to sell a day gown or two to tide her over for a while. She still had more than two pounds sterling in her possession. Only as a last resort would she consider selling the beautiful ring.

She scarcely noticed the heat from the blazing fire while she traversed the parlor on her way to confront Colin's mother. The slight clatter of china drifted to her ears from the dining room. Upon entering, she saw to her dismay that both elder Barclays sat at breakfast.

Mr. Barclay stood to his feet at once, wiping his mouth with his napkin. "Good morning, child. I'd love to stay and chat, but alas, I have a full day ahead of me after having been gone so long." Then, coward that he was, he made a hasty retreat before Mariah had the presence of mind to answer.

She held her breath and flicked a swift glance at his wife.

"Do fill your plate and come sit down. I have something to say." The woman's tone was suspiciously pleasant, but Mariah wasn't sure if she'd caught a hint of warmth in those sable eyes.

About what? Mariah was sorely tempted to rail at her. *That shrewish mouth of yours?* But she refused to allow herself to act in a manner as unladylike as the uppity woman had displayed last night.

Despite not having eaten the previous evening, Mariah had little appetite. She chose a small serving of fruit and a buttered biscuit, then poured some tea and carried the items to the table, making certain an empty chair separated her from Mistress Barclay. She made a point of folding her hands and bowing her head in silent prayer. *Father in heaven, help me to swallow down this food, and help me not to let her get the best of me. In Jesus' name. Amen.* She raised her head.

Colin's mother set down her teacup. "Mariah, dear, I am. . .dreadfully sorry for my outburst yesterday. It was thoughtless and cruel. I should never have uttered such unkind words. I was overtired from our journey and not prepared to hear that we'd missed our son's arrival and departure. Nevertheless, I should not have taken it out on you. I hope you can find it in your heart to forgive me."

Realizing her mouth had fallen open, Mariah closed it and raised her tea to her lips, hoping to block some of her surprise.

The mistress continued. "Colin has always been extremely stubborn when he believes he's right. And as his father reminded me repeatedly, our son truly was obligated to report for duty." She smiled and reached across the space between them, catching Mariah's hand. "I beg you to forgive me for my ghastly behavior. . .please."

Something about the way her ladyship looked at her combined with that tender touch of her hand brought sudden moisture to Mariah's eyes. Until this moment she hadn't realized how starved she'd been for a bit of motherly affection. "I—I—" Her throat closed up as she fought against an emotional display. But try as she might, she was powerless to stop the unexpected rush of tears. "I'm—Excuse me," she blubbered between gasps as she blindly lurched up from her seat. "I—"

Mistress Barclay got up just as quickly. Coming to her side she drew Mariah close and patted her back. "No, dear. I'm the sorry one. I've been so obsessed with the notion of you spoiling my plans for my son, I haven't considered you and all you've gone through since leaving your home in England." She leaned back slightly and brushed aside a lock of hair from Mariah's face. "You truly are a beautiful and talented young lady, and from now on, I plan to make more of an effort to see that you're treated as such."

Desperately trying to get her embarrassing sobs under control, Mariah couldn't believe what she was hearing. Had Colin's mother implied she would champion her? Inhaling a ragged breath, she stepped back, wiping her eyes as she attempted a grateful smile. "I'm better now. I don't know what came over me." With a small, self-conscious shrug, she returned to her seat, and the mistress did the same.

A quiet moment passed while Mariah fortified herself with a sip of tea. Setting down her cup, she met the older woman's eyes. "Colin told me he was able to visit Bath while he was in England, and he brought me news of my family. I suppose it made me a bit lonesome for them, and a little homesick. I miss their gestures of affection. When you took my hand, I—" Another wave of feeling swamped her, and she drew another breath and fought off a new onslaught of tears. "Anyway, Colin accompanied my father to see a barrister about recovering the large sum he's owed. He feels quite confident that Papa will be reimbursed."

"I'm very pleased for you and your family." Though spoken kindly, some of the warmth was missing from Mistress Barclay's expression. "Colin went to call on your father, you say."

Mariah sensed that the woman's suspicions had again been aroused. "He did it as a favor for my sisters and me. I asked him to check on the welfare of my family if he happened to travel in the vicinity. My father was so very distressed when we departed last spring, I feared for his health."

The mistress gave a thoughtful nod. "Of course, that son of ours would do no less, I'm sure." She paused and her smile returned. "Speaking of being distressed, I suppose Dennis Tucker also went off with the militia."

"Yes, madam, he did. In fact, he's the one who came for Colin after Colin had barely arrived."

"Well, I can't say I'm sad that Dennis won't be around to turn Victoria's head for a while. Perhaps Edward will have a better chance now of charming her. Or did he report, as well?"

"I'm afraid that's something I do not know. But Victoria will likely be upset, regardless. She's so enjoyed all the attention the young men have paid her these past months." Mariah nibbled a bit of her biscuit.

"She has, hasn't she?" The woman's lips slid into an easy motherly grin as she took another sip from her cup. "My sweet baby girl is growing up. And Mariah, dear, I must not forget you. You've been doing such a wonderful job tutoring her and our other daughters also. Even Amy is beginning to act like a proper girl on occasion."

Mariah had to smile. "Thank you. Those girls are such dears that—"

"That's it!" Mistress Barclay clapped her hands together. "I have a wonderful idea. You deserve a special treat. And since our young men have traipsed off on their grand adventure, we should go on an adventure of our own. We'll take a coastal packet down to Williamsburg to see a play or two. That's sure to give Victoria something to think about other than her beaus. Besides—" She quirked a brow. "They have the most marvelous shops there."

Mariah was astounded that Colin's mother could act so nonchalant today after her violent reaction the previous evening. "But. . .shouldn't we wait here for news from the militia?"

Cora Barclay sent her a motherly look. "Not to worry, my dear. Eldon has assured me that the men won't even attempt to contact the French until after the spring thaw. For now they shall merely be getting into position and fortifying things. We've plenty of time."

My, how her fortune had changed since she arose this morning. Mariah glanced at her plate and noticed how much more appealing the food looked. She realized she was ravenously hungry. She picked up her spoon and dipped into the fruit. "Victoria has told me that Williamsburg is a lovely, genteel city. I would be thrilled to go on this little adventure with you."

From the deck railing of the coastal packet, Mariah gazed ashore at the busy wharf with its large warehouses and beyond to the higher ground that housed the sprawling settlement of Williamsburg. She turned to offer Mistress Barclay and the two older girls an excited grin. They'd arrived at last.

Though they'd all been eager to embark on the jaunt to the capital, three long weeks of bad weather had delayed their departure—stormy weeks that Colin had likely spent traveling into the backcountry. But as his mother had remarked often enough, her son had made the choice himself to go with the militia in the winter. Perhaps a bit of hardship would bring him home all the sooner. At least she could hope for that.

Refusing to dwell on the fact that Colin had once again left her to fend for herself, Mariah returned her attention to the activity on the waterfront, watching the burly dockworkers loading and unloading cargo from various vessels in the port.

Victoria moved up beside her mother as the gangplank was lowered to the dock. "Why can't we visit a few shops and show Mariah around town before we go to the Everards' house? You and Mistress Everard will spend hours and hours catching up on the latest happenings while we're forced to entertain those little girls of hers. That will be as tiresome as having Amy along, especially when Heather, Mariah, and I could be truly enjoying ourselves strolling about the shops."

Ambling toward the ship's gate, the older woman shot her daughter a stern glower. "And just what would my friend Diana think when our luggage arrived without us? I wouldn't think of being so rude, and neither should you. Besides, I've been wanting to see her and Thomas's new home since they moved in."

Heather, on her other side, spoke up. "You're absolutely right, Mama. I can't wait to surprise Francis and Martha with how well I've learned to play the flute and violin in a mere nine months."

Nine months! Had it really been that long? Following behind the threesome, Mariah sighed. Nine months since she'd come to live with the Barclays, and she had yet to wed Colin. The better part of a year as a bond servant, and she could see no end in sight. Yet her sister who'd been sent deep into the wilderness had managed not only to return to civilization a free woman, but marry. *Rose, married!* Mariah couldn't help but fight tears every time she recalled her sister's words in the letter that had arrived last week. Her rather plain, spinster sister had wed before *she*—the beauty of the family. And all because Colin cared more about promoting his honor than he cared about her.

Victoria slowed to join Mariah as her mother and sister strolled down the gangplank. She leaned close. "It's been two whole months since Tuck and Edward left to train with the militia, too," she murmured softly, then raised her voice to a normal level. "One thing is certain. If I happen to meet some handsome gentlemen who desire to spend time in my company, I shall not discourage them. In fact, I'd welcome thoughtful young men who refrain from leaving their ladies behind so they can go off to shoot at Frenchmen. What a useless pursuit."

Mariah had to smile. Perhaps Tori had the right idea. In this port no one knew Mariah was a bond servant. How tempting it would be to allow her own gaze to wander a little. Just then, a breeze off the water toyed with her light cloak. As she gathered the edges together, her hand brushed over the amethyst hidden on the chain beneath her lace tucker, proof of Colin's offer of marriage. She might not have the ring on her finger yet, but Colin was a far more desirable catch than that poor, woodsy frontiersman Rose had wed. Mayhap it would be best to wait a little longer. After all, he did happen to be the proverbial bird in the hand, if he'd only stop flying off all the time.

"Bolts of fabric from Paris!" a hawker shouted, dodging a loaded wagon and team rumbling across the wharf toward the business district. "Unloaded today! See them at the millinery shop!"

"Did you hear that, Mama?" Victoria all but ran down the gangplank. "Paris fabrics!"

Tucking her chin and elevating her brows, her mother caught hold of Tori's arm and drew her alongside. "Do remember you're a lady, Victoria. As soon as I hire a conveyance to take us, along with Lizzie and our luggage to the Everards', we shall be the gracious guests I know we can be. There will be ample time for shopping later."

"And lots of time to go to the theater, too." Heather's blue eyes sparkled.

Mariah understood the girl's reasoning. Musicians would be there to accompany the players. Just thinking about the possibilities ahead, her own excitement stirred. Why should she not enjoy herself while she visited the city with this wealthy family? Although she'd lived in Bath as a tradesman's daughter, most of the glamour and excitement of the resort had been reserved for members of the aristocracy. Here in Williamsburg with the Barclays, she could move in the best circles of the fledgling society—as long as no one found out she was a servant. For this week, at least, she truly belonged in the family. She threaded her arm through Victoria's as they approached a carriage for hire.

A gentle breeze stirred through trees just beginning to bud and leaf out on this gloriously mild day of April's second week. Overhead, in a sky of brilliant blue, puffy clouds floated lazily across the broad expanse. As the aged horse pulling the carriage clopped along Williamsburg's wide, packed-clay streets, Mariah turned her head this way and that, admiring the town's neat weatherboard houses with their broad-based chimneys. Many larger residences were made of brick and sat amid formal gardens that soon would burst forth in full glory. Surely that would be a sight to behold. Already the season's first brave flowers peeked out of the dark ground here and there, bobbing their bright yellow, white, and purple heads.

Beside her, Victoria sat in speechless anticipation, ogling every display window in the array of shops they passed. It would be hard to keep up with the girl once Mistress Barclay turned her loose. Smiling to herself, Mariah filled her lungs with the fresh breath of spring. This truly would be a grand adventure.

Chapter 22

Who'd have thought George Washington would have the audacity to order the military to travel in this miserable weather?" Tuck shook his head, and rain dripped from all three corners of his cocked hat. "It's takin' weeks."

Riding beside his friend as they headed for the Wills Creek Station, the first in a string of trading posts stretching all the way to the Ohio Valley, Colin chuckled and tugged his heavy wool cape closer. "Just be glad we're not walkin' in this muck like most of the other boys." He glanced back at the nearly three hundred men trudging up a trail heavily wooded on either side. Two loaded wagons lumbered slowly along, spitting mud at the grim-faced militiamen slogging along behind. A small herd of cattle churned through at the rear.

At least they were moving. Several times on the trip, the teams of horses had been unable to pull the wagons up a steep hill, and the men had to unload the crates and sacks and lug the supplies up through the slick mire themselves. With heavy rain and sleet hindering their progress, the group was making very poor time in reaching a post less than 150 miles from Alexandria.

Colin looked ahead, where George Washington rode at the front of the column. George expected his men to arrive at the trading post within the hour and rest there for a few days. Thank heaven.

Tuck edged his chestnut mount closer to Colin's and muttered a comment he'd made at least half a dozen times already. "The French enjoy their creature comforts far too much to be out in this freezing mess, you know." He exhaled a frosty breath. "I don't think George should've been put in charge of this expedition. He's too young, and we both know it."

Colin gave a nonchalant shrug. "Perhaps. But he does have some experience, at least. He's been comin' out here for the last three or four years surveyin'. If nothin' else, he knows the area. We don't. He also knows where the French are. He's even parlayed with 'em."

"And let us not forget," Tuck grumbled, "he's a particular friend of Lord Fairfax—"

"Who has Governor Dinwiddie's ear." Colin checked to make sure the men behind them weren't eavesdropping, then turned forward again.

"So." Tuck swiped a droplet off his nose. "He gets to decide that the rest of us catch our death out here in the elements. I should've stayed home. With everybody else gone, I would've had a clear field with lovely little Tori."

Colin narrowed his gaze. "No, you wouldn't. You wouldn't be alone with her. I'd be there to keep an eye on you."

"Ha! Like your mother watched you when you were sniffin' around your Mariah?"

My Mariah. So easily Colin's mind filled with thoughts of his English beauty, recalling the expressive violet eyes that stole his breath, the sound of her soothing voice. . . .

Tuck snorted. "You're far worse than me, old man. When it comes to a winsome belle, you end up talkin' out of both sides of your mouth."

"You're right." Colin couldn't help the sappy grin that quirked his lips. "But then, you were no better when it came to your older sister Trudie, as I recall."

Tuck's laugh met a swift end as he stopped and stared toward the front of the line.

A rider approached.

"I wonder who that could be." Colin heeled his mottled gray horse, Storm, forward and veered around the few rows of militia separating him from the front.

Tuck followed suit.

The burly rider reached Washington at the same time Colin and Tuck did. Soaked and muddy as his panting horse, he rendered a sloppy salute. "Sir, thank God you've come. The last of our men are just now stragglin' into Wills Creek Station."

"What men?" Washington's pocked face was stone rigid. "I was told the British regulars wouldn't arrive for another week or so."

"I don't know nothin' about that, sir. I'm with Lieutenant Trent. We was overrun by the French."

"I assume you're speaking of William Trent, are you not?" Frowning, George guided his mount closer to the newcomer.

"Yessir, I am. But he wasn't there when they come upon us. The first lieutenant left to get more supplies. Ensign Ward was in charge."

"And you say the French attacked you. Where was that, exactly?"

The man shook his head. "They *didn't* attack us, exactly. They come from upriver. Hundreds of 'em, in bateaux and canoes. And they brung cannons. I counted eighteen, myself. They had 'em all lined up, pointin' right at us."

Colin exchanged glances with Tuck. The French weren't holed up taking it easy during the winter weather after all. They'd gone down an ice-cluttered river, ready for battle. With cannons, no less. Definitely not good news.

"Sir," the bearded messenger continued, "there was only forty-one of us, an' our fort weren't near finished. Anyways, them Frenchies told us they wouldn't do us no harm iffen we'd leave and never come back. So you see, sir, we didn't have no choice."

Appearing to mull the information over briefly, Washington nodded with a calmness that surprised Colin. "Has Lieutenant Trent rejoined you?"

"Yessir. We met up on the trail. A good thing, too, 'cause we was gettin' a mite hungry, us bein' short of food, an' all."

Washington gave him another polite nod. "Well, thank you for informing me of the situation. Ride on back and inform your superiors we will be there shortly."

As the hefty militiaman snapped a salute and rode away, George turned to Colin, looking every inch the confident leader. "The French have taken the fort Lieutenant Trent was building where the Allegheny from the north and the Monongahela from the south join and become the Ohio River." He frowned and shook his head. "It's the most strategic location on the frontier. Whoever controls that spot controls all the waterways. It's vital that we take it back."

~~~

"Thomas Everard is a gentleman of standing here in Williamsburg," Mrs. Barclay remarked as the carriage drew up before a wood-framed townhome somewhat more modest, but no less charming, than some of the elegant mansions they'd passed. "He's the clerk of the General Court, you know."

Captivated momentarily by the sight of the Governor's Palace sitting like a jewel at the northern end of the broad street, Mariah nodded politely and returned her attention to the gable-roofed dwelling kitty-corner to it where they'd be staying during their visit. In all likelihood, it would contain furnishings as fine as any possessed by the Barclay family and their other affluent friends. She followed the family up the brick walkway to the front door, while Lizzie remained with the luggage.

The fashionably attired matron of the house rushed forth the moment the servant ushered the party inside. Tall and slender of bearing, she looked to be several years younger than Mistress Barclay. "Cora, Cora. I am so glad you've arrived. I've been on tenterhooks awaiting your visit ever since I received your letter."

As the women gushed their greetings to each other, Mariah's eyes drank in the richness of the central hall with its wainscoting and a fine staircase with elaborately turned balusters and sweeping handrails. The step brackets were richly ornamented with intricate carvings. Large urns positioned on cherrywood pedestals overflowed with fresh flowers emitting a heady fragrance into the air.

"Why, you're as beautiful as ever, I vow," Mistress Everard breathed. "And this can't be little Victoria, all grown up and so pretty." She released Mistress Barclay and took Tori's hands then reached for Heather. "And you, my dear, must have grown at least five inches since last we saw you."

"I can play the flute and violin now, too." Heather never missed an opportunity to mention her new talent.

"Oh my." The mistress placed a hand to her bosom. "How wonderful. You must play something for us later."

Just as the woman was about to turn to Mariah, what sounded like a herd of horses on the floor above came galloping toward the staircase. Down came two young girls, ruffles and lace billowing and bouncing, their sausage curls flying out. "Amy! Heather!" one of them called.

"Girls! Do calm yourselves!" A bit flustered, their mother turned back to her guests with a puzzled expression on her exquisite features. "Where is our darling Amy? I don't see her."

"I'm afraid Amy wasn't up to traveling aboard the packet, Diana," Mistress Barclay explained. "She's been having trouble with an upset stomach of late."

Mariah darted a glance to Tori and Heather to make sure they didn't blurt out the truth—that their little sister would rather sleep out in the stable with the horses than go shopping and attend plays, much less put up with what she considered silly, giggly, little girls.

The lady of the house shook her elegantly coifed head, her shining dark curls reflecting light from wall sconces. "How unfortunate. Francis and Martha were so looking forward to seeing her."

The joy on the faces of the young sisters wilted, and the older one, who appeared about seven, let out a whine. "Amy's not here? But I drew her a really pretty picture."

Her mother cupped her chin. "Darling, I'm sure Victoria and Heather would love to see your picture."

The youngest one, possibly five years of age, piped up. "Mine, too."

"Of course, sweetheart." Mistress Everard turned to the Barclay girls. "Would you mind going upstairs with my daughters? They've been working on a surprise for you girls since we received word you were coming."

"Of course not." Victoria's enthusiastic tone did not match her frozen smile as she cut a sidelong glance at her sister. "We'd love to, wouldn't we, Heather?" Snatching her sister's hand, she headed for the staircase and trailed up the steps after the giggling youngsters.

As the noisy group took their leave, the mistress turned back to Mariah. "And who is this attractive young lady you've brought with you, Cora?"

"La, forgive me, Diana. I should have introduced you." Mistress Barclay smiled at Mariah. "She's our private tutoress. We wanted someone a touch more educated and sophisticated for our girls than was offered at Miss Bridgestone's Academy. I'm most pleased to introduce Miss Mariah Harwood, from Bath, England. She's not only a wonderful instructress in all the womanly arts, but she's also an accomplished musician—much to our Heather's delight."

"Oh my." The young matron dropped into a quick curtsy. "I'm so pleased to meet you."

Mariah returned the curtsy. "And I you." If she didn't know better, she'd think wealthy Mistress Barclay was putting on airs for the wife of a clerk, bestowing such lavish compliments. But from the look of this fine home, especially in this colony, it was natural that a man in the governor's employ would be held in high esteem. Now, it seemed, so was she—so long as there was no mention of her being a bondwoman. Mariah highly doubted her mistress would divulge that. A smile tickled the corners of her lips.

"Oh dear, do forgive my lack of manners. Please join me in the parlor for refreshments." The hostess swept a graceful hand toward an open doorway, then turned to the uniformed slave who had let them in. "Gladden, would you see that tea is served right away?"

As they ambled into another front room with paneled wainscoting, Mistress Everard came to Mariah's side. "I've always longed to visit

England. My husband is from London, and he's promised to take me there one day. And I do so want to visit Bath while we're there. But before I ask you a thousand questions, I must catch my dear Cora up on the latest." She turned to her. "Cora, you are simply not going to believe this. . . ."

If Mariah had been acquainted with any of the individuals mentioned in an animated stream of who did this, who went where, and with whom, perhaps listening to the two matrons seated together on a burgundy-and-ivory-striped settee wouldn't have been so tedious. She'd all but memorized the delicate porcelain figurines on the walnut mantel, the gold-framed mirror above, and the red window hangings that appeared to be some sort of rich wool.

A sudden burst of flute playing came from the stairwell, evidence that the luggage must have been taken to the upper floor. But the music ceased as suddenly as it began, as if a door had opened and then closed. Then hurried footsteps came down the stairs and tapped across the floor of the great hall. Perhaps the women would stop their infernal gossiping as if Mariah weren't even there.

Victoria swept through the parlor entrance. "Excuse me, Mother, but you absolutely must let me go to the shops to find another pair of gloves. The ones that go with my sapphire evening gown are not among my things."

Her mother sent her a condescending look. "Dearest girl, I'm sure you're mistaken. You took such great pains in laying out all your accessories."

"I know." Her expression turned woeful. "I can't imagine how I forgot them. Please, Mama. I simply cannot wear mismatched gloves."

Since she'd seen Tori place those gloves into her trunk, Mariah knew the girl was not being truthful. But she wasn't about to say anything that would cause strife between herself and the sister of her betrothed.

Mistress Barclay drew a deep breath. "You are quite certain you didn't bring them?"

"Yes. I looked and looked."

"But we've only just arrived, dear. Diana and I are having such a nice chat."

"No need to interrupt your visit. Mariah could go with me." Victoria swung a hopeful glance to where Mariah sat across from the matrons. "You wouldn't mind terribly, would you?"

"No, not at all." She rose. "A walk would be refreshing after that long journey aboard ship."

Her mother swung a slightly suspicious glance between the two of them. "Very well. But be back in plenty of time to dress for dinner. We shouldn't want to look shoddy for the secretary to the governor, now, should we?"

"Of course not, Mother." Tori reached for Mariah's hand.

"Do you have enough money with you?"

"Yes, Mother. Thank you." She tugged Mariah toward the entrance.

"That girl," Mariah overheard the mistress comment as Victoria ushered her to the front door. "She may think she's matured, but she acts the silly, thoughtless child at times."

Moonstruck would be more like it, Mariah reasoned as she accompanied Tori out into the lovely spring afternoon.

They set a fast pace in the direction of Market Square.

"Thank you for rescuing me."

Victoria laughed. "Rescuing both of us. What with Heather's shrill flute playing and the little girls' screaming, I just had to get out of there." She caught Mariah's hand and slowed her pace as she leaned close. "Look ahead. Two handsome young men are peering into that apothecary window." Straightening her shoulders, she toyed with a curl dangling by her ear and hiked her chin as if she planned to ignore them.

Mariah knew it was merely a ploy to get their attention. She'd taught Tori that trick herself.

And of course it worked. Before the two of them reached the finely attired young men, they'd turned to stare.

The bolder of the two, slim, with light brown hair and eyes, grinned and tipped his cocked hat as he stepped into Victoria's path. "Good afternoon, lovely ladies. Or should I say, the loveliest young maidens ever to grace our fair city."

Completely disregarding all that Mariah had taught her, Tori giggled and extended a hand. "Why, what a gallant thing to say."

"But quite true." The other young man, lanky and somewhat taller, with russet hair and green eyes, bowed before Mariah and reached for her hand.

"Excuse me. I don't believe we've been properly introduced." Though said as a proper chaperone should, her smile betrayed her good intentions.

The first fellow, still holding Victoria's hand, spoke up. "If you two are attending the play tomorrow evening, I'm sure I can arrange a proper introduction then. In the meantime, for convenience's sake, I'm Willard Dunn, son of Dr. Arliss Dunn, physician to our honorable governor. And my friend is Ronnie—"

"Ronald Sedley," his pal corrected, puffing out his chest. "My father is in shipping, out of Yorktown."

"How lovely." Victoria practically meowed. "I'm afraid our family merely farms and raises Thoroughbred horses. I'm Victoria Barclay, of Barclay Bay Plantation, near Alexandria. Perhaps you've heard of it? Oh, and this is our Mariah."

The words *plantation* and *Thoroughbred* seemed to impress them.

As both men again bowed, Mariah realized that Victoria had included her in the family. She decided not to correct her. "We're very pleased to meet you, but we really must be on our way. We have some purchases to make for the play tomorrow evening." She withdrew her hand as the pair continued to stare. "We'll be most pleased for a proper introduction then." She took Victoria's arm and prodded her onward.

The girl glanced back and waved. "Tomorrow eve. . ."

After they'd gotten far enough away, Tori turned to her. "Why did you do that? They were so handsome and—"

"I agree. However, we know nothing about them, and a small bit of encouragement is sufficient until we do."

"But they just told us—"

"And everything they said could have been lies. That is why a proper introduction is always vital. They know it just as well as we do."

"Fine!" With a huff, Tori jerked her arm free. "Well, what I do know is that those attentive gentlemen saw no need to go riding out into the wilderness, leaving me with nothing to do but twiddle my thumbs."

The last words struck hard. Mariah hadn't been twiddling her thumbs for a mere few weeks. Colin had been gone for months, only to return for less than an hour before he was off again.

"I'm gonna flirt with every good-lookin' bachelor I see while we're here," Victoria drawled as she increased the pace. "Mayhap I'll find a beau or two willin' to come visit me at the plantation. Isn't Mother always wantin' me to marry a merchant's son? Well, I just might give that Mr. Sedley some extra attention."

The girl was proving to be quite headstrong. Thank goodness, Mistress Barclay would accompany them to the play. Mariah changed the subject. "There's that millinery shop the hawker at the wharf said had a shipment of fabrics. They might have gloves as well." She pointed to a tidy wooden building just ahead that held a display of feminine accessories in its window.

"You know very well that I don't need gloves."

"True. But we'd better not return without some. I, for one, wish to remain in your mother's good graces."

Never had she uttered truer words. Mistress Barclay could very well become her mother-in-law before the end of summer. And though Mariah had never been known for her patience, she had to remain true to Colin while she awaited his return. *Please, Lord, bring Colin home soon.*

Mariah wasn't sure how much longer her patience would stay her. Those obviously prosperous young men were entirely too tempting.

Chapter 23

Rubbing the stubble on his face, Colin promised himself he would shave in the morning. He wagged his head with a smile. If his mother could only see how lax he'd become with his grooming. He'd managed but a quick wash before supper with nothing more than a small piece of soap. Considering he still wore the same clothing he'd had on when they slogged through all the mud on their way here, no less than a full bath and a change of attire would make him feel human again.

Colin rose from where he'd stooped at the upper end of a small brook that sliced through the large, oval-shaped meadow. He could easily see why the Indians had named it Great Meadows. A gentle evening breeze feathered across his face as he left the small spring behind, reminding him how grateful he was that the weather had finally turned warm. Starting toward the large ring of campfires and makeshift tents, he viewed the setting sun as it crowned the surrounding pines with gold. Not a single dreary cloud in sight.

He calculated that it must be sometime past the middle of May. Surely by now, Mariah had received the letter he'd left at Wills Creek

Station. It would have been sent out with the first dispatch rider going back to civilization. As so many times before, Colin was overwhelmed once again with a deep yearning. *Mariah. My beautiful Mariah. We've had so little time together. So little. . .*

He heaved a woeful sigh as he passed by the herd of horses, hobbled and quietly grazing. Finding Storm among them, he was pleased that the Thoroughbred he'd ridden from home had managed the rigors of the rugged wilderness so well, especially since the mottled gray was a more delicately boned breed of horse. But then, Paladin, whom he'd sold on his trip, had more than proved the breed's stamina that marvelous day Colin had held Mariah close all the way home from Baltimore—the day he'd fallen hopelessly, helplessly in love. Even after all this time, echoes of her delightful, sparkling laughter rang in his memory. How he wished he could hear it now, on this waning, lonely evening. He missed her so much, his insides ached.

A number of the horses jerked their heads up from the grass. Ears flicking, the herd turned their necks in the direction of the dark woods to the west. Several cows just beyond them mooed low.

Closing his hand around his revolver and drawing the weapon from its holster, Colin tried to peer past the animals. He wheeled to face the camp and raised the firearm high, waving it back and forth until he caught the attention of several of the men.

His heart pounded as he crouched and moved swiftly toward the animals, his only cover in this open space. Waiting and listening, he hoped the other men had remembered to prime their flashpans, then breathed easier, recalling that everyone kept their weapons loaded and ready since Trent's men had met them at Wills Creek Station.

No unusual sound came to his ears, but several of the horses remained alert and uneasy. Something—or someone—was out there. Bear, mountain cat. . .or the French?

Movement in the deep shadows produced an Indian wearing only a loincloth and leather leggings that reached halfway up his thighs. A musket dangled from his hand as, glistening with sweat and breathing heavily, he jogged past the horses.

A minute passed. Then two. No other Indians appeared. Not ready to trust that the man was alone, Colin remained hidden, his gun propped on the back of a sturdy quarter horse and aimed in the direction from which the Indian had come. When no other sounds came from the woods, Colin noticed the horses grazed placidly once again. He glanced back at the encampment and spotted the Indian walking with Washington toward the colonel's tent. Obviously the ruddy man had come with a message.

Colin holstered his pistol and ran across the field for the tent, his curiosity piqued. Was the news good? Or bad?

Approaching the command tent, he noticed a number of enlisted militia milling about outside. Obviously they were as curious as he to learn why the Indian brave had arrived with such haste. Upon entering the sailcloth enclosure, Colin saw that Tuck and the other officers had all gathered inside. The Indian stood next to the colonel.

Washington spied Colin and addressed him in his usual formal manner. "Lieutenant Barclay. Thank you for your vigilance."

Colin nodded acknowledgment of the compliment, though he was more interested in what the Indian had come to report.

"Gentlemen." Washington swept a glance around at the officers. "Our visitor comes from our good ally, the great Chief Monakaduto of the Seneca people. Some of you might know him as Half King. I shall allow his messenger to speak the words of Chief Monakaduto."

He then nodded to the sinewy brown-skinned man. Fully armed with a knife and hatchet tucked in belted and beaded sheaths, the Indian held his musket like a staff. His head was shaved except for a braided hank of top hair adorned with beads similar to the numerous ones decorating his moccasins, an armband, and earrings. The man made a striking picture.

"I come from great Chief Monakaduto," he spoke in halting English. "He say French warriors come. They come quiet like the fox. This many." He spread his fingers and thrust them forth three times, then held up four fingers. Thirty-four. "Chief Monakaduto say you come. Chief and Seneca warriors take you. Make war on enemy."

Dennis Tucker gave a huff under his breath. "Thirty-four. That ain't so many. Surely they don't plan on takin' on all of us."

Washington pierced him with a withering glare. "Most likely they've been sent to spy on us, discover the size of our force and what weaponry we have."

Compared to the strength of the French force that took the fort from Trent's men, Colin knew their militia made up a rather pitiful adversary. However, they were supposed to be joined any day by a Colonel Fry, with a regiment of regular British soldiers and a few pieces of field artillery. So far there'd been no word from them.

"It's vital we intercept this party before they reach our camp." Washington swept a gaze over his officers. "Each of you pick ten of your best men to accompany me. Captain Trent, I'm putting you in charge here while I'm gone."

Trent, a seasoned frontiersman, grunted. "You sure, Colonel?"

"Yes. You'll know what to do."

Colin considered that oblique statement a touch ominous, but he also knew Trent would take extra care after having lost the Ohio River fort to the French.

"Barclay." Washington turned his pockmarked face to Colin, his eyes serious. "You shall come with me as my second-in-command."

The men who would accompany Washington had a bite to eat and gathered their supplies, but it wasn't until after ten that night that they left camp. Colin noted with disgust that not a star was visible. Heavy clouds again blanketed the sky, casting the party into thick darkness that grew even blacker as they entered the woods behind the Indian guide. Not a single torch would be permitted this night.

The Seneca, who called himself something like Sequahee, set a fast pace, forcing the men to jog in order to keep up with him on a trace so narrow and overgrown they had to travel single file in silence, with no torches, and no mounts for the officers.

Running behind Washington, Colin noticed within minutes that the men in back of him had begun to slow. He paused to let his winded friend Tuck catch up, then whispered to him. "Keep up. Pass it on." Then breaking into a full run to rejoin Washington and the Indian, Colin sent a prayer heavenward that the others would do the same. *While I'm at it, Lord, keep us all safe. And if it's Your will, give us a swift victory.*

He tried to ignore the cutting straps of his jostling pack and the burning in his chest, along with the aching of his feet. The best way to do that was to allow his mind to fly home to Mariah. He was running headlong into danger for the first time. He could get killed. What would happen to her if he wasn't there to protect her? He and the bond papers in his breast pocket had been all that kept his mother from selling the girl into some other man's hands. If he died, the document, along with his other belongings, would be returned to his parents.

The thought distressed him. He should have signed off on the papers before he left, freeing Mariah. If he survived this engagement with the French, he would take care of that matter as soon as he got back to ink and quill at Great Meadows. He would dispatch the papers to her by the first courier.

A stickery branch caught the sleeve of his woolen frock coat. Without slowing, he gave a quick jerk to free himself, then resumed devising his plan. He'd send a letter along, informing Mariah she needn't tell Mother she was free. She should stay within the family's protection until he returned.

If he returned.

His chest tightened as a sharp pain gripped his side. But he refused to stop until George did. He couldn't let the younger man beat him.

About the time Colin was ready to give up, long-legged Washington stumbled to a halt, completely out of breath.

Colin nearly ran into his barely visible leader in the moonless night. Clutching his sides, he bent slightly until his own breathing slowed.

"That brave—is still—running." Washington gasped, gulping air between words.

"I know." Colin shook his head in wonder as the man behind him bumped into him. "But he's not loaded down as we are."

Others caught up, panting hard. Tuck and some of the others coughed. "Take two minutes to rest," Washington ordered. "Pass the word down the line that I'll be setting a slower pace."

Colin's relief was short lived. The new pace might have been slower than the Indian's, but with Washington's ground-covering stride, their tall commander was still hard to keep up with except when the trail narrowed so that he had to stop and feel around, searching for the path. Worse, as the hours passed in pitch darkness, up and down hills, crossing streams, Colin sensed the men lagging farther and farther behind.

Panting, he trotted up to Washington and tapped him on the shoulder. "Sir, I think we need to stop," he whispered. "Take a head count."

"They've fallen behind?" the commander's quiet tone matched his own. "I believe so."

After waiting for several minutes, the count was still seven short.

Washington straightened his broad shoulders and spoke only loud enough for them to hear in the still night. "Men, we can wait no longer. We'll pick up the stragglers on the way back—if they haven't already returned to camp."

Shrouded in heavy rain clouds, the fragile hint of dawn was making an effort to illuminate the forest floor when Colin spotted more light up ahead. A clearing. As he drew closer, he noticed a longhouse with wickiups circled around it. A couple of cook fires already blazed. They'd arrived!

A village dog sensed their presence and began barking, and others joined in, announcing the arrival of the militia.

Washington paused before emerging from the line of trees and turned back to the trailing men. "Straighten yourselves. Look smart as we march in."

Beyond exhaustion, Colin couldn't help but grin as he pulled off his hat and tucked any stray hairs back into his queue before replacing it squarely on his head. George Washington truly was a most seriously proper gentleman.

Seneca warriors poured out of their dwellings, hatchets and rifles in hand.

Although Colin was so tired he wanted nothing more than to fall to the ground and sleep for a week, he knew he had to appear fit, show no fear to the villagers as well as be an example for his own men.

From an immense longhouse in the village emerged an Indian in his prime, perhaps forty years of age, powerful looking and heavily adorned with beads and feathers. Already tall, his elaborately quilled headpiece gave him an extra foot in height. Small wonder he was called Half King.

Washington flashed a broad smile and walked immediately to the Indian, his arm outstretched. Grasping the tribal leader's hand with both of his, he gave a hearty shake. "Great Chief Monakaduto, I bring you greetings from Governor Dinwiddie."

Half King stared stony faced for a moment. "Wash-ton." Then gradually, his expression transformed into an enthusiastic grin. "Welcome." Spreading wide a tattooed arm, he invited the commander into his council house.

George turned to Colin. "Have the men partake of their victuals now. We will be leaving shortly."

"Yes, sir." Although Colin would rather have questioned his superior's judgment, he heeled around to the weary company of militiamen. A portending drop of rain pelted his nose. With a sigh, he met Tuck's bleary eyes and slowly shook his head. What sort of fighting force could these sagging, bedraggled men possibly make?

Chapter 24

Mariah smiled to herself as she filled her plate with scrambled eggs, biscuits, bacon, and sliced peaches at the dining-room sideboard. She hadn't been in such a cheerful mood since Colin proposed marriage and presented her with the lovely ring—those few precious moments before he abruptly deserted her yet again. Now she had a letter from him resting this very moment in the pocket of her skirt—and he'd written not to his family but to her personally, which absolutely proved his commitment to her.

Mr. Barclay had ridden in from Alexandria last night, just as the women were about to retire, and he had brought two letters with him. One for Mariah and the other to his wife from her friend Diana in Williamsburg. As Mariah blithely returned to her bedchamber with her own unopened missive, she felt Mistress Barclay's vexed stare following her every step.

Thinking back on the grand moment, Mariah turned with her plate for the open doorway to the terrace. Now that the days had grown pleasantly warm, the family breakfasted outside in the open air, already perfumed with the scent of flowers. She found the elder Barclays and Heather seated at the round terrace table.

The lady of the house looked up and smiled as Mariah approached, but her eyes held no warm spark. "Good morning, dear. I trust you slept well."

"I did, thank you." Knowing the woman itched to know the contents of Colin's letter imbued Mariah with a new sense of power as she took a chair and breathed in the balmy breeze wafting from the river. " 'Tis such a lovely morning, is it not? The tobacco fields are quickly becoming quite lush and green."

Heather turned a questioning expression to her. "So, Mariah, what did my brother have to say in your letter? Is he on his way home—or will he be coming soon?"

Before Mariah had a chance to respond, Amy charged out of the doorway, her full plate tilting precariously in her small hand. "Don't even ask. She wouldn't read it to me last night. She said it could wait till morning, but I don't see why."

"Be careful you don't spill your porridge, brat." Following after her youngest sister, Victoria rolled her eyes.

Their mother leveled them both with a glare as they took seats. "Don't be impolite, child. It's most discourteous to pry into someone's private correspondence."

"Why, 'tisn't prying at all." Mariah, enjoying the moment to the fullest, favored them all with her sweetest smile. "I merely thought 'twould be more expedient if I read Colin's letter to everyone at once. In fact, I've brought it with me." She derived a measure of gratification from knowing he'd had foresight enough not to include anything of an intimate nature in it.

"Splendid." Mr. Barclay gestured to his two daughters. "Settle down, girls. After I give the blessing, Mariah can read her letter to us, if she so wishes."

What a dear man. Colin was a lot like him. Mariah bowed her head. She heard little of the man's prayer, however, as her thoughts returned to his son. Colin was by far more handsome than any of the fine gentlemen she'd met in Williamsburg—and much more of a stalwart hero. How sad that at this very moment he was somewhere in the wilds, risking life and limb for his family, his colony, and most particularly, for *his Mariah*, as he called her. She forced her attention back to his father's prayer.

"And Father," he continued, "we pray that You will find it in Your will to bring our son safely home to us. Soon."

"Amen." Having blurted the word out unintentionally, Mariah felt warmth tinting her cheeks. But Colin had left in mid-February, after all, and it was now the end of May. They all were anxious for his return.

"Yes. Amen." Mr. Barclay's voice contained a smile.

Amy spoke up immediately. "Read the letter now. Please."

Enjoying the experience of being the belle of the moment, for a change, Mariah grinned and withdrew the folded paper from her pocket. Slowly she spread it and lifted it up, aware that every eye around the table focused on her. "The letter is dated April twenty-first."

"That's over a month old!" The mistress frowned.

"Yes, it is. He writes: *'My dearest Mariah, I miss you and my family very much. When I left I had hoped to be home again long before now, but alas, that was not to be. When we arrived at Wills Creek Station, we were met by militiamen under Lieutenant Trent. They had been sent ahead of us to build a fort on the Ohio River, our destination. A large force of Frenchmen came from upriver and took it from them. We are now awaiting a regiment of regulars to join us.'*"

"What are regulars?" Amy scrunched up her face.

"British soldiers, my dear," her father explained.

"Surely that cannot be all he wrote. Do continue," Mistress Barclay urged.

Mariah returned her gaze to the lines penned by Colin's hand. " *'We will proceed to Great Meadows in Indian Territory and wait for them there before engaging the enemy. Pray for the rain to stop. Tell my family I miss them all. Most sincerely yours, C. Barclay.'* "

Before anyone could speak, she held up a finger. "He added a postscript: *'Tuck sends Tori his most ardent regards.'* "

Pinkening delicately, Victoria lowered her lashes and tried to contain her smile. It quickly wilted into a pout. "Tuck should've written a letter to me himself."

Heather sent her a sidelong glance tinged with a teasing grin. "Especially now that Tori's learned the truth about those other ardent admirers of hers in Williamsburg."

"What's this about?" Mr. Barclay looked from one of them to the other.

His wife shook her head. "Nothing at all, Eldon. Really. Diana Everard wrote a snippet of news about two young men who'd demonstrated an interest in Victoria while we were in their city. It's not of import."

Not to be put off, the older man narrowed his eyes. "What sort of demonstrating, if I might ask?" He pierced his oldest daughter with a speculative look.

Mariah hid her smile behind her napkin. The man was ever the devoted husband and father. Rather like her own papa, to be truthful. The thought was oddly comforting.

"It's nothing to fret about, dear." The mistress fluttered a hand. "Diana reported that Dr. Dunn's son, Willard, would inherit very little because his father is quite lax in collecting payment for his services. And the other young man's father—whom the lad alleged was in shipping— merely owns a ropewalk in Yorktown."

"What's a ropewalk?" Amy tipped her head to one side.

Her mother gave the child's hand a pat. "It's a place where men braid long strands of hemp into thick ropes for the ships."

"Well, it would appear then," Heather piped in, her sly grin broadening, "that Ronald Sedley's father truly is in shipping. Just not the very profitable merchant kind." She snickered at her little jab.

With a withering sneer at her sister, Victoria pursed her lips. "It means little to me. Neither of them was even a fraction as handsome or charming as Tuck, anyway."

"Or Edward Rochester," her mother added. "The son of the richest merchant in Alexandria is not to be discounted." She glanced around the table. "I vow, that's quite enough talking. Your food is getting cold. I'm sure Mariah wishes to finish with your lessons before the day grows uncomfortably warm."

Mr. Barclay drained the remainder of his tea and set down his cup. "I'm more concerned by the storm clouds hovering over the mountains, myself. I hope it doesn't rain too hard. The tobacco leaves are at such a delicate stage just now."

"Oh, la." Leaving her chair, his wife stepped to the rear edge of the terrace and peered past the house to the west. She turned back with a frown. "At this very moment, our Colin must be in a miserable downpour." Returning to her chair, she took the hand of a daughter on either side of her. "Everyone join hands. Our Father in heaven, I fervently pray that our son has a dry place to wait out the storm."

"And if not," Mariah added, "please enfold him within Your merciful warmth and comfort."

Colin released a disappointed whoosh of air. He'd hoped Washington's meeting with Chief Monakaduto would last a bit longer so he and the other men could rest from the fast-paced trek to Great Meadows. But less than half an hour found them on their way again, with the Seneca chief and two of his braves leading the way. Thankfully, these Indians set a slower pace than Monakaduto's messenger had last night.

As the misty rain turned to sprinkles, Colin restrapped his haversack inside his cloak, then stepped to the side of the elusive mountain path and whispered to each passing man. "Protect your powder. Keep it dry."

Every face held a grim expression, and Colin detected undisguised fear in more than a few eyes. This would be the first time any of them except Washington had ever faced a deadly enemy, and they were heading straight for the heavily armed French encampment.

The sprinkles turned to rain that fell straight and hard despite the thick forest growth. Large dollops pelted Colin's hat and frock coat and began to soak through to his skin. In no time at all, he was sure he couldn't have been more drenched if he'd gone swimming. His boots slipped and slid along on muddy, dead leaves as he stumbled over roots and stones on the trail.

Tuck moved up beside him, his tricorn drooping pitifully, his sword all but dragging on the ground. "If I survive this campaign," he muttered through chattering teeth, "and if I ever show up at your door askin' you to come play soldier again, you have my permission to shoot me. Right there on the spot."

Colin laughed aloud, the sound blasting into quiet broken only by the rush of falling rain. As Washington glanced back at him with a scowl, Colin slapped a gloved hand over his mouth.

Tuck immediately fell into line behind him.

Washington turned and raised a hand, halting the militia. He strode to Colin, swiping water from the leather haversack that held his paper cartridges as he walked.

Colin swallowed, fully expecting the leader to reprimand him in front of the men.

"Lieutenant Barclay," the colonel said quietly, "send an order down the line to fix bayonets. I doubt our weapons will fire in this rain."

Fix bayonets? A niggle of fear chilled Colin's blood. Hand-to-hand combat. As an officer, he'd been issued a pistol and a sword and had practice-fought alongside the enlisted men with their swordlike musket attachments. But the thought of actually slashing and stabbing other human beings had never seemed quite real. Until now. He steeled himself to sound confident before giving the order.

About a quarter of an hour later, Monakaduto stopped and pointed ahead.

The downpour had lessened to light sprinkles again. Without that cover of rain, Colin suddenly felt vulnerable.

Washington gestured for Colin and Tuck to join him and the chief. Silently, pistols drawn, they moved forward from tree to tree. Praying all the while that the powder was still dry, Colin peered ahead. He could make out some men huddled beneath an outcropping of boulders in a stone cliff.

Washington motioned for them to ease back. Ever so carefully, lest they be spotted, they backed away until they reached their party.

"Order the men to spread out in a semicircle," Washington said under his breath. "Have them move into firing position and await my order to fire. Lieutenant Barclay, take half the men to the right. Tucker, take yours to the left. Caution them against making any noise. With the element of surprise, a quick victory shall be ours. May the Lord keep and protect us."

As Colin positioned his men along the line, he felt compelled to whisper the leader's plea to each of them. "May the Lord keep and protect you." He knew this could very well be the last morning any of them might see.

Taking his own position behind a tree, Colin aimed his pistol at one of the French soldiers crowded within the shallow cave. The thought of ending that unsuspecting man's life disturbed him mightily, though he knew he had a duty to carry out. The safety of their own encampment at Great Meadows depended on it.

Suddenly Washington sprang into the open and gave a shout. "Fire!"

Colin squeezed his pistol's trigger and fired, but he heard only a dozen or so of the other weapons discharge.

An instant later, Washington shouted through the swirling gunsmoke. "Charge!" Then their commander raced forth, his sword in one hand, a pistol in the other.

Colin could do no less. Only a few sporadic shots came from the French, whose powder had become as damp as the militia's.

All was frenzy and fury, shouts and screams as Colin and the others swarmed the French, slicing and slashing in a violent rage.

Reason caught hold of Colin when a Frenchman tossed his knife to the ground, raised his hands high, and shouted something in his language. The man was surrendering!

About to slice down the fellow's shoulder, Colin stayed his arm. Heaving for breath, he looked around and saw that the rest of the enemy still standing had done the same.

The battle was over.

Surveying the area, he saw blood splattered all around him, on him, and on his sword. Nine Frenchmen lay dead. A wounded enemy soldier sat propped against a rock trying to staunch the flow of blood from his side. Others, bleeding from various areas of the body, remained on their feet. Assessing the scene, the realization that he'd been a part of that carnage sank like a rock inside Colin.

Chief Monakaduto let out an ear-piercing scream of victory as he thrust a bloodied scalp high into the air.

Horrified and sickened by the gruesome sight, Colin knew he must not show his revulsion. He strode stiffly over to where a granite-faced

Washington stood and forced himself to appear as calm as his commander while they watched the three Indians scalp the rest of the dead. His stomach roiled as he cut a glance at the prisoners. The stark fright clouding their eyes was palpable, as if they feared the possibility of suffering the same horrendous fate.

Once the last dead man had been scalped, Monakaduto stepped across a body with the unfortunate victim's scalp dangling from his hand. "Ensign Jumonville." He thrust the bloody thing toward Washington.

To Colin's amazement, Washington calmly took the offering and met the chief's eyes as he spoke. "This is a great honor that the great warrior chief of the Seneca gives me. You and your people will always be welcome in our camp, and we will help you in whatever way we can. This scalp that you have given to me I now give back into your care and ask that it now be carried to the Delawares who, I am told, have begun to cling to the French. Tell them this will soon be the fate of all Frenchmen in this territory."

The chief gladly accepted the return of the trophy.

Colin realized as never before why George Washington had been chosen to lead this expedition. Not only did he know the landscape and the customs of the local tribes, but with his straight posture and imposing height, the quiet young officer naturally commanded respect. He unquestionably had earned Colin's.

Indeed, Washington had grown into a true leader. And having survived this first bloody battle under the commander, Colin vowed he'd gladly follow Colonel Washington anywhere the man led.

Chapter 25

Mariah opened the window of the mansion's second-floor classroom to take advantage of the breeze, then turned to her students. "During this hour, girls, you may write invitations to as many of your friends as you wish to invite. However," she hurried to add in the face of the young ladies' excitement, "only those that have been scribed with the best of penmanship will you be allowed to hand out at church on the Sabbath."

Seated at her writing desk, Amy crossed her arms and stuck out her bottom lip. "That's not fair. I can't write as good as those two." She darted glances at both of her older sisters.

Mariah moved to the young girl's side and placed a reassuring hand on her thin shoulder. "I'll be judging each of you according to your age, and that is fair."

"Well, I think planning a quoits tournament is stupid and sounds medieval." With a disapproving wrinkle of her nose, Heather dipped her quill into her inkwell. "Especially if we're going to have other games as well, like graces and shuttlecock."

Victoria paused in her writing. "Really, Heather. The lads consider graces to be a silly girls' game and a shuttlecock tournament simply doesn't have a dignified ring to it. We have to include quoits."

Recalling similar foolish tiffs she and her own sisters had endured back in England, Mariah slowly shook her head. "Whatever you write, just make your strokes graceful and—"

A voice from the doorway interrupted her. "Missy Harwood."

Mariah turned to the downstairs maid. "Yes, Pansy. What is it?"

"Y'all has visitahs down in de parlor. Mist'ess Barclay says fo' y'all to come right quick."

Visitors! Mariah startled. Who would possibly be calling on her? Had Colin returned at long last? Glad that she'd donned her lavender muslin day gown rather than drab gray this morning, she reached up to see that the combs adorning the sides of her hair remained in place. "Who is it, pray?"

But her words failed to reach Pansy, who had already left for the servants' staircase.

All three girls laid aside their quills and sprang from their desks, curiosity lighting their expressions.

Tori started toward the doorway. "Mayhap Colin and Tuck are back!"

"Or someone's brought the viola Papa ordered," Heather suggested brightly.

"Well, whoever it is, I'm gonna be first to find out." With that, Amy bolted past them all.

"Wait! Stop!" Mariah almost had to holler to slow them down.

Thankfully, they complied seconds before they reached the grand staircase.

Mariah elevated a brow as she joined them. "We shall proceed to the parlor in a ladylike manner, as our guests—and your mother—would expect."

She had to remind them again halfway down. "Slowly, girls. Slowly." Finally, maintaining a calm appearance, they all strolled into the room.

A tall, magnificent-looking stranger turned toward them as they entered. He held a towheaded girl-child propped on his arm, and stepping from behind him, Rose—blessed Rose!—flew to Mariah, her arms outstretched.

Rendered momentarily speechless, Mariah barely managed a gasp as she grabbed hold of her sister and held on tight. Unexpected tears flooded her eyes.

After a long, hard hug, Rose eased back. "Let me have a look at you, dearest."

Not quite ready to relinquish the sister she'd missed more than she realized, Mariah dabbed at the moisture blurring her vision with one hand while clutching Rose's with the other.

Rose smiled and angled her head in assessment. "I must say, you're looking quite well. The Lord has truly answered my prayers. And Mistress Barclay tells me you've done wonders with her daughters."

Mistress Barclay! Peering past her sister, Mariah noticed the lady of the house, dressed to perfection as always, in emerald-striped dimity. She sat before a tea service, waiting for them all to join her. Mariah latched on to her manners and turned to the girls. "Rose, I'd like you to meet my charges. Victoria, Heather, and Amanda." She indicated each with a nod of her head.

The girls curtsied, bright smiles accenting their appealing charm.

"Can we stay?" Amy nibbled her lower lip, her eyes wide with hope.

"Yes, my dears." Her mother gestured toward chairs dotted about the spacious room. "If you sit quietly."

Mariah watched after them, then returned her attention to the tall, muscular man holding the toddler. The embroidered brocade frock coat he wore looked oddly out of place on his manly frame. A strip of leather held his dark, wavy hair in a queue.

"Mercy." Rose laughed lightly. "I was so thrilled to see you, my manners took flight. Mariah, dear, this is my handsome husband, Nathaniel Kinyon and our sweet baby, Jenny Ann."

"Your baby?" Mariah's mouth gaped for a second. "Oh. Your husband is a widower, then."

"Not at all." Rose bestowed a loving glance and gentle smile on her dear ones. "Jenny is our adopted child. Her parents died rather tragically, and her grandparents were ill prepared to care for her. They blessed Nate and me with that honor. We praise the Dear Lord for His goodness."

"She's very pretty, isn't she?" Having spoken her thoughts aloud, Victoria blushed.

Amy took advantage of the moment. "And her hair is so curly. It's almost white. Like an angel's halo."

Mistress Barclay sent them a remember-to-be-quiet look. "My sentiments exactly. But be mindful of your manners."

"Yes, Mama," they chorused.

Amy quickly scooted back in her chair and folded her hands like the little lady her mother wished she would become.

Still drinking in the sight of honey-haired Rose in her fashionable day gown of copper taffeta, Mariah barely caught Mistress Barclay's movement on the edge of her vision as the older woman reached across the small table.

"Mr. Kinyon, from whence do you hail?" The mistress handed him a cup and saucer.

He met her gaze and spoke, his voice low and somewhat commanding. "I'd say as the crow flies, madam, about eighty miles from here. Comin' downriver as we did, though, you could purt' near double that."

"Yes. Thank you." Rose accepted her proffered tea. "Even in one of those swift canoes we spent three days on the water—except, of course, whenever we had to portage around some rapids. But all in all, we had a safe, pleasant trip. And then to be greeted so graciously here by the lady of the manor. . ." She favored Mistress Barclay with a sweet smile.

"I could do no less for our Mariah. She's been an invaluable help to us." The woman paused. "You must stay with us a few days. We've plenty of room."

"Oh, yes, Rose. Please do." Mariah searched her sister's blue-gray eyes. " 'Tis so marvelous to see you, and you must tell me everything. This is your final destination, I hope, or must you travel on?"

Rose tilted her head. "Actually, we had planned to travel up the Susquehanna River to visit Lily after we leave here. But we heard a bit of news in Georgetown last eve and. . ." She turned sad eyes to her husband.

He cleared his throat. "I'd planned on waitin' to join up with the militia till after Rose had a chance to visit both her sisters. But I hear tell things is startin' to get hot again betwixt us an' them Frenchies. So, soon as I take my li'l family back home, me an' my partner'll be headin' out to join up with the other boys."

"What do you mean, exactly, by 'getting hot'?" Mariah clenched her hands together in her lap. "Colin and Tuck are with Colonel Washington even as we speak."

"Colin is my son," the mistress explained. "Dennis Tucker is his friend from a neighboring plantation. Do tell us what it is you've heard."

Gently bouncing Jenny on his knee, Mr. Kinyon eased back against the Queen Anne chair that looked far too inadequate for his large frame. He'd drained the tea in one gulp, and the delicate china cup he held all but disappeared within his calloused hands as he set it on the lamp table beside him. "Well, it seems Washington an' some of his boys surprised a party of Frenchies a few days ago. What they didn't kill, they took prisoner. It's only natural that the French'll retaliate first chance they get."

"What about our men?" Mariah swallowed her angst. "Were any of them killed?"

"From what I hear, only one of our boys passed on to glory. A couple others got a scrape here an' there."

"The name," Mariah choked out. "Do you know the name of the deceased?"

He shrugged a massive shoulder. "Don't say as I rightly recall. But he was from up along the Shenandoah, I know that. You folks prob'ly wouldn't know him."

Mariah added her relieved sigh to that of the mistress and the girls.

The older woman leaned forward. "Nonetheless, we shall add his grieving family to our daily prayers. And I thank the Lord my son is safe. For now, at least." She paused again, then continued. "Mr. Kinyon, Mariah informs me you are an experienced frontiersman. I'd be most grateful if you would keep a watchful eye on my son when you join the militia. I fear he can be a touch reckless at times."

"My brother Colin's the bravest—" Amy slapped a hand over her mouth and cut a worried glance in her mother's direction.

Rose's husband shot the child a quirky grin, then looked back at the hostess. "I'd be glad to, ma'am. Colin Barclay. I'll look him up."

"Thank you. Lieutenant Colin Barclay." She gave him a grateful smile.

He tipped his head politely. "Me an' my wife want to thank you for takin' such good, watchful care of our Mariah. I know Rose'll sleep a whole lot easier now that she's met you."

Having spent a good deal of the visit looking from him to Rose and back, Mariah had to admit that for such a commoner, the frontiersman was incredibly charming and handsome. Still, she had a difficult time reconciling the thought of marriage between him and her sister. They seemed so at odds, so different, from totally different worlds. How on earth had prim and proper Rose ever attracted a rover like him?

As Mistress Barclay passed around plates of tea cakes, Mariah swept a reassessing look at Rose. Her older sister's experience in the wilds of this fledgling country had softened and polished her like a priceless gem and brought out an inner beauty that glowed from her eyes. Hair the color of warm honey and fastened in a cluster of long, silky curls secured at the crown, sparkled in the filtered light streaming through the tall windows. And her fine, copper day gown complemented her coloring and adorned her willowy frame perfectly. At long last, Rose had blossomed.

Amy, sitting straight and holding her cup just so, directed a question to her mother in a quiet voice. "Mama, may I say something?"

No one could refuse the sweet voice. "Yes, darling. You may."

"I think Mr. Kinyon is gonna get as bored as me sitting here with all the women talking. May I please take him to the stables and show him our beautiful horses?"

"I'd be glad to hold the baby," Victoria offered.

"Sounds good to me." He smiled at the girls. "Hear tell you got a fine-lookin' string." He relinquished Jenny to Tori's willing attention and took Amy's hand.

"Thank you, child," Mistress Barclay said, then met his jovial hazel eyes. "My husband, Eldon, should be home in an hour or so, and I know he'll enjoy getting to know you. In the meantime, however, I am absolutely dying to learn how a gentlewoman such as your lovely wife survived so beautifully the adventure of being taken deep into Indian country."

"I'll leave the tellin' of that to her." Chuckling, he escorted his little guide outside.

"Yes. Do tell us about it." Heather's eyes sparkled as she leaned forward in eager anticipation.

Mariah was equally interested in hearing about her sister's new life. After the frontiersman left the room, she also knew Rose would be able to talk more openly about what sort of husband she had married.

Then her heart jolted. Out in the stables Mr. Kinyon would meet Geoffrey Scott. Of course, with Mr. Scott's consuming interest in the Bible, he could easily bring up the fact that Mariah had taken quite an interest in things spiritual. In turn, Mr. Kinyon might share with the trainer all kinds of tidbits Rose had told him about her proud, now spiritual and headstrong sister. And heaven forbid, if Geoffrey Scott should mention all the time she'd spent trying to endear herself to him on the off chance that Colin didn't return. That would be dreadful. Dreadful indeed, since the frontiersman would be joining her betrothed soon.

"Mariah." Rose touched her arm and peered closely at her. "Is something amiss?"

Trying to slough off her fears, Mariah propped up a smile. "Of course not. Do tell us your experiences since we parted in Baltimore—and how it was you came to acquire that darling little girl."

For the next half hour, it seemed Rose spared no details as she regaled the Barclay ladies with a lightly humorous version of her wilderness experiences. Mariah's respect for her older sister rose several notches as she slowly shook her head in admiration. "Well, that husband of yours should return from the stables shortly. While we wait, I should like to show you our lovely gardens."

Rose smiled. "Why, that would be marvelous."

"May I go along?" Heather asked, her eyes on Tori, who gently steered the toddler clear of any mischief in a room full of "pretties."

Mistress Barclay intervened. "I think the two sisters would like a moment alone, dear. They've much to catch up on, I'm sure."

Surprised at the older woman's thoughtfulness, Mariah stood to her feet. "Then if you will excuse us. . ." She gestured to Rose, and the two took their leave.

Outside, Rose linked elbows with Mariah as they strolled amid the lush display of flowers and trimmed hedges in the waning afternoon sun. "I believe I've done quite enough talking this day. I'd like to hear how the Lord has taken such wondrous care of you, and how you have fared in this new land. You seem to have a rather comfortable relationship with these plantation owners."

Mariah hardly knew where to begin. "It wasn't always so, I must confess." Beginning with her arrival and the initial cool reception, she condensed the past months as best she could as she brought Rose up to date. "And now they treat me as one of the family, almost."

Rose searched her face. "Is there any hope of your actually becoming one of the family? I remember you made some rather reckless statements in your letters."

It was no use trying to hide anything from that astute gaze. Mariah reached into her lace tucker and drew out the amethyst ring. "Colin has asked me to marry him, but we feel it's best to keep it a secret for now. He assures me the family will come around, in time. First he must return from serving in the militia. I pray he comes to no harm." She tucked the ring back out of sight.

Rose nodded. "Little sister, surely you're aware that secrets have a way of coming home to roost. Nevertheless, I shall join my prayers with yours, dearest. If the two of you truly love each other, I'm sure the Lord will work out His perfect will for you both."

Approaching footsteps drifted to their ears, and they looked up to see Nate and Amy coming hand in hand.

A proud smile lit Amy's eyes. "He loves the horses. We're hungry now. I think it's time to go inside and ask when supper'll be ready."

Mariah smiled and fell into step with the others, but a persistent concern plagued her mind. *Had Geoffrey Scott and Mr. Kinyon been too forthcoming with one another?*

Chapter 26

As Colin and Tuck led their horses on the second return trek to Great Meadows in the last three weeks, Tuck emitted a labored rush of breath. "This June has to be the worst month of my life, bar none."

"Quite." Too weary to laugh, Colin raised an arm and wiped sweat from his brow on his grimy shirtsleeve. "We'd have to go a far stretch to come up with a worse one."

Tuck grimaced. "Unfortunately, next month will probably be a match, if we survive, what with every Frenchman in the territory and every Indian from up north on their way to kill us."

"It's gonna get interestin', that's for sure. If nothin' else, I hope it at least stays dry." Colin couldn't help wondering if the Indians accompanying the militia would stick with them or disappear into the night, the way the Delawares had a week ago. Fortunately, Chief Monakaduto had remained loyal. He and a Seneca squaw chief, Queen Alequippa, had added forty warriors to the ranks—far fewer than Washington had expected to join after the resounding victory over the French the militia had experienced in May. But as beneficial as it was to have additional warriors, the fact that they brought their families with them rapidly exhausted the food supplies. For the past several days, this motley army had nothing but fresh beef to eat.

The horses were in even worse shape. Without a daily ration of grain, the mountain grass was not sufficient to sustain them, and they were deteriorating by the day. That necessitated leaving the supply wagons behind at the Ohio Company's Redstone Storehouse—empty though it was. With the animals too weak to bear any sort of burden, the militiamen were forced to haul the remainder of the equipment on their backs. Watching them struggle against the weight of the swivel cannons and their trunk-thick posts, Colin couldn't help but feel sorry for them—especially since the regular soldiers Captain McKay had brought up from South Carolina were exempted from that duty.

Behind him, Storm stumbled on the uneven trail. Colin glanced back at the Thoroughbred as it plodded along, sagging and dirty, its head drooping low. He gave the animal's muscled neck an encouraging pat as he thought of the emergency stores left at Great Meadows, where a small garrison of militia guarded prisoners that had been captured. Hopefully sufficient grain would be available there to restore the herd.

Colin cast a disparaging look ahead at McKay's scarlet-clad soldiers and ground his teeth. The king's officer refused to order his redcoats to do any physical labor unless they received extra pay, and Washington had no extra resources. So the British soldiers packed none of the equipment, nor had they lifted a pick, shovel, or axe to dig defensive trenches, build fortifications, or help cut trees when the trail needed widening for passage of the wagons.

Morale in the Virginia militia sagged, and the men were on the verge of forgetting about the conflict with the French and taking on McKay and his regulars instead. At the root of the dissention was the fact that Captain McKay insisted he outranked Lieutenant Colonel Washington because he was older and his commission came from the king, not a colonial governor.

A disgusted huff from Tuck interrupted Colin's murderous thoughts. "Know what Sergeant Emmons said this mornin'?"

"No. What?"

"He said if the Frenchies do find us, they'll have nothin' to shoot at but movin' targets, 'cause we ain't done nothin' but move hither and yon since we left Alexandria."

Colin grunted. "He might have a point. This is the third time we're headed for Great Meadows, after all. But remember, one of those treks was taken just to separate us from McKay's men."

"And here we all are, back together again." Tuck scoffed. "Beat's everything, huh?"

"All I've got to say is that high-and-mighty McKay better start takin' our situation seriously. According to Chief Monakaduto's scouts, the French have added great numbers to their ranks, along with the hundreds of Indians they already had with them."

"A pity these redcoats have never seen the way Indians fight." Tuck gave an exaggerated shudder. "If they had, they'd all be totin' and diggin' for all they're worth. They'd have trenches dug clear down to China."

Colin and Tuck trudged on in silence, punctuated now and then by a weary huff or a disbelieving shake of the head as they backtracked over terrain they'd covered before.

An hour later, the blessed sight of Great Meadows finally came into view. Banks created by knee-deep trenches that had been dug a few weeks ago now surrounded the encampment. Colin knew those fortifications would have to be greatly beefed up if they had any hope of surviving the imminent assault.

As they started across the swaying grasses, two men came riding out to meet their column. They headed straight for Washington and McKay at the front.

Colin nudged Tuck. "Might as well go find out what they have to report." He forced his bone-weary legs into a faster pace to pass the column of redcoats.

Tuck panted as he caught up. "Wouldn't it be marvelous if they came with orders sendin' us back to Alexandria?"

Colin didn't bother to respond to that far-fetched notion.

As the riders reached the commanders, one of them, a tall man in frontier attire, dismounted with a leather pouch in his hand. "I have a dispatch for Colonel Washington. From Governor Dinwiddie."

Washington took the pouch, his astute eyes never wavering from the man. "You aren't one of our regular dispatch riders." He shifted his gaze toward the one still mounted, including him in the assertion.

"Nay, we're not. Me an' my partner was on our way out here to see if we could help out, when we run across your man at Wills Creek."

"Sicker'n a dog, he was," his pal inserted.

Studying the pair, Colin noted that one of them had dark complexion and black hair, indicating the possibility of Indian blood. His own suspicions rose. Were they really who they said they were?

Lieutenant Trent, a former trader with the Virginia and Ohio Company, strode to the front, his head cocked as he peered at the newcomers. "Kinyon? That you?" A huge grin broadened his bewhiskered face.

"Aye. Me an' Black Horse Bob. We figgered you boys might need an extra hand."

"You thought right." The trader grasped the frontiersman's hand.

"Do you know these men, Trent?" Washington asked.

"I surely do. The Frenchies chased this pair outta their Muskingum store down on the Ohio last fall."

Washington broke into a rare smile and extended a hand. "I recall hearing about that. Was it true that you brought a white woman and a babe out with you?"

Shaking the commander's hand, Kinyon nodded. "Aye. We did. The gal's my sweet bonny wife now."

Forgetting his lower rank, Tuck edged forward. "What's in the dispatch, sir?"

"Yes." Captain McKay gave an arrogant tilt of his head. "It might be of consequence to us all."

"Of course." Washington's smile vanished. Opening the flap, he pulled out the stamped document and broke the wax seal. Unfolding it, he quickly scanned the paper, then looked up. "Considering our present circumstance, this is of little consequence."

"Well, what does it say?" McKay demanded.

Washington handed him the paper. "Governor Dinwiddie writes to commend all the men who were part of our last encounter with the French."

"You forgot to add the rest." McKay's face reddened with rage. "You've been promoted to full colonel."

The commander replied with equal force. "As I said, it's of little consequence at the moment." Retaking the paper, he folded and pocketed it.

"I brought two other letters with me." Kinyon withdrew them from the neck of his belted hunting shirt.

All eyes shifted toward him in the growing tension.

"A coupl'a letters for a Lieutenant Barclay." He scanned the group.

Colin's heart skipped a beat. *Mariah!*

"Letters!" Tuck piped in as Colin reached out his grimy hand toward Mr. Kinyon. "Are there any others?"

"No, 'fraid not." The frontiersman's negative shake of the head generated a number of grumbles from the gathering. He offered the onlookers a half smile as he handed Colin the two missives. "The Barclays asked me to deliver these when my wife an' I visited 'em a few weeks back."

"Thank you." Assessing the man and his Indian-looking friend, Colin wondered how this man and his woman happened to call at the plantation. They weren't the typical sort of visitors his family entertained.

"Give the order to march." Washington's command reminded Colin that the militia still had a number of rods to go before reaching the encampment—rods to cover before he'd find a private place to open his mail. The letters would have to wait.

The company hefted their gear and set out once again. Unfortunately, however, the instant they reached their destination, Washington called everyone to attention before they had chance enough for even a brief rest. "Men, we have not a second to waste. All those not tending the stock or preparing food, grab axes and shovels. We must start constructing a fort immediately." He eyed Captain McKay pointedly, as if challenging the man to order his regulars to help.

When McKay grudgingly acquiesced, Colin wasn't certain if he'd done so because the newly awarded full colonel had ordered the work or because the need was so dire.

While the various work parties began chopping down young trees, stripping off branches, and cutting pointed poles to size, Colin set his men to digging holes for the upright fort poles. During the frenzy of hard labor, the Indians inside the camp merely watched the action and talked among themselves. Not a good sign.

Colin noticed that Kinyon and his partner weren't among the slackers. Both took their turn digging holes beside Colin's already exhausted men. Curious about the frontiersman, Colin strode down the line to where the man worked, shirtless and sweating as he swung a pick. When Kinyon moved back to make way for a fellow with a shovel, Colin handed him a flask of water.

Smiling his thanks, the frontiersman raised the vessel and took a sizable gulp, then handed it back.

"Would you mind stepping aside with me for a moment?"

"Glad to." The big man handed off the pick and strode several feet away with Colin.

"You say you and your wife visited our plantation. Might I ask why?"

A deep chuckle rumbled from Kinyon's chest. "Kinda figgered that'd spark your interest. My wife is your betrothed's sister."

Colin blanched. "You know about our betrothal?" *Stupid question. Of course Mariah would tell her sister.* "Does my family know as well?"

He shook his head. "Mariah thinks it's your place to tell your kin. But my Rose was plumb pleased to see how well your folks are takin' care of her sister. She was more concerned for Mariah's—shall we say, welfare—than her little sister Lily's."

Colin had to laugh, remembering his encounter with prim and proper Rose Harwood. "I've no doubt of that. She wasn't too thrilled to see her sister ride off with a total stranger, one who was wholly attracted to Mariah's beauty. Would you believe she made me vow to deliver Mariah to my mother before the sun set, and also to see to her religious instruction?"

It was Kinyon's turn to laugh. "Sounds just like my Rose. She wouldn't have a lick to do with the likes of me till after I rededicated myself to the Lord." He turned serious. "I'm glad of that now. If not for God's protection, we never would'a escaped them Frenchies an' their Indian trackers." He nodded toward the gathering. "Speakin' of Indians, them Senecas ain't lookin' none too happy over there."

Colin followed his gaze. "I agree. Maybe they'd have been in a better frame of mind if they hadn't brought their families along. I wouldn't want to have mine here right now."

Kinyon glanced around and gave a wry grimace. "I'm startin' to wonder why I came. I don't see how we'll ever stand off the number of French and Indians that're marchin' this way."

"I'm sure Washington will have a dispatcher ride out for reinforcements. Our job will be to hold 'em off till then."

"Hmph. I sure hope you're right." Kinyon helped himself to the flask again and took another swallow before returning it. "Better get back to work. Rose wouldn't appreciate me losin' all this purty hair."

Having witnessed a few gory scalpings, Colin ambled over to another worker and handed him the flask. "Take a breather. I'll take over for a while."

The long afternoon dragged on. Not until a couple of hours after dark did Colin finally find a chance to retire to his tent and read his letters by wavering lantern light—with Tuck staring from a cot opposite him, desperate for word from Tori.

"I'll read the one from my father to you first." Colin smirked. "I'll not be readin' the one from Mariah out loud."

"But what if she—"

"If she says somethin' about Victoria, I'll let you know." He broke the seal and opened the first one:

My dear son,
    I trust all is going well with you and the militia. I have heard disturbing news about the number of Frenchmen coming down from Canada. If at any time you wish to relinquish your

commission and come home, I am certain I can pay another to
take your place. In the meantime, be extremely careful. Your
mother, especially, is most worried.

> *The girls send their love, as does Mariah and all our people.*
>
> *Your loving father*

Post Script: Tori is nagging at me to send Dennis her warmest regards.

Tuck reached for the letter. "Did she send Rochester her 'warmest regards,' too?"

"See for yourself." Colin relinquished the missive, hoping it would hold his friend's attention long enough for him to read the one from Mariah. He quickly broke the seal and spread the letter to catch the light from the hanging lantern:

My dear, dear Colin,

> *I miss you so. I pray each night that the Lord will send you*
> *back to me soon. We are all so worried about you. Your mother*
> *is convinced you will come down with some dreaded disease*
> *even before the Indians have a chance to kill you. I try to be more*
> *optimistic, because I know what a valiant hero you are. I am sure*
> *God would not take someone as worthy as you. Do come back to*
> *me soon.*

> *With my deepest, dearest regards,*
>
> *Your Mariah*

His heart contracting, Colin smiled. *My Mariah.* How he wished he was with her at this moment, inhaling the fragrance that was hers alone, devouring the sight of her beauty, tasting those luscious lips. . . . Folding the treasured missive, he tucked it inside his shirt, next to his heart, then stretched his weary body out on the canvas cot and closed his eyes.

"Well, did she say anything about Victoria?"

"No." Utterly spent, Colin let out a deep breath. "Blow out the light and get some sleep."

But for Colin, sleep refused to come. The thought that he might not return to Mariah kept him awake. An army ten—maybe twenty times their number was marching toward them, intent on taking their lives. He and everyone else here could be dead within the next few days.

Dead. . .and he had yet to make peace with his Maker.

Listening for Tuck's breathing to even out in slumber, Colin slipped off his cot and sank to his knees.

Father in heaven, "hallowed be Thy name. Thy kingdom come, Thy will be done on earth as it is in heaven. Give us this day our daily bread—"

Yes, Father, the cook says we have only enough flour and meal for one more day, and we've already done without for days. The men won't have the strength to finish the fort if we don't receive more food.

And Lord, forgive me anyone I've trespassed upon. I cannot think of anyone lately, unless it's my parents. You know I proposed marriage to Mariah without their approval. But You also know their disapproval was only because of her lack of a dowry. Aren't we supposed to be storing our treasure in heaven?

He shifted his weight from one knee to the other. *All right. I guess I'm trying to justify my dishonoring of my parents with a lie by omission. Now, where did I leave off? Oh yes, there's a huge enemy army heading this way to trespass all over us. I know You want me to forgive them, but I'd much rather have them change their mind and go back to Canada. I'd sure appreciate You putting them in the mind to do that.*

What comes next? "Lead us not into temptation." Well, Father, You know I have no access to that at the moment. But delivering us from evil is uppermost right now. Please deliver us, and I promise from this day forth I shall always pray for Your guidance first, instead of jumping into things like a stupid fool. And if You bless me and Mariah with children, I'll teach them to honor You and follow You all the days of their lives. Bless and keep all of us who are here at Fort Necessity, as George Washington dubbed this pathetic, half-finished place. And please give the commander the wisdom he needs to bring us through.

I ask this in the precious name of our Lord Jesus. For Thine is the kingdom and the power and the glory forever. Amen.

Rising from his knees, Colin lay down again on his cot, and for the first time in months, a restful sense of peace washed over him. Moisture filled his eyes. God had heard his prayer.

Chapter 27

Bone weary, Colin felt as if every muscle in his body protested as he strained to assist a couple of his men struggling to heft a heavy log with a swivel cannon mounted on it. "Easy. . .easy. . ." He grunted as they positioned the unwieldy weapon over the gaping hole that would hold it steady, then dropped the post in with a thud. Colin straightened and stretched his back. What on earth was he still doing here? Monakaduto and the Indians had sneaked out three nights ago, leaving the depleted ranks to fend for themselves. He should have deserted last night as so many of the smarter militia had done.

Small wonder they'd all cut out. He glanced behind him to the pitiful fortification they'd managed to build. Spindly spikes a mere seven feet tall surrounded their tents and the tiny hut where their meager stock of powder and other supplies were stored. If they had enough black powder for even two shots at each of the French and Indians in the force coming against them, Colin would be mightily surprised. And if the gunpowder stayed dry once the rain started up, it would be nothing less than a miracle.

He turned to a pair of young men nearby. "Bring out your cannonballs and fixin's. Then you two stay out here to man the swivel. The scouts say the enemy will be here within the hour."

"Just us two out here in the meadow, sir?" Private Walker's Adam's apple bobbed as he cast a timorous look back at the stockade.

The lad had every right to be afraid. Colin clapped him on the shoulder, hoping to instill a measure of courage. "For now it'll be you and the other artillery men. When the time comes, the rest of us'll join you."

As Colin turned to go and check the progress of the other eight swivel cannons being put into position, he spotted Nate Kinyon coming toward him from the fort, so he moved out of earshot of the two privates.

The frontiersman glared up at the ominous clouds in the sky and wagged his head as he reached Colin. "Man, I sure wish you would'a snuck out with them other boys last night. You're gonna be mighty hard to protect once the shootin' starts."

"If I'd have done that, I wouldn't be much of an officer and a gentleman, would I?"

"No, I reckon not. But leastways you'd'a been alive to see tomorrow come."

Colin shot a quick glance back at the privates to make sure they hadn't heard Kinyon's words. "If you think it's that bad, why are you still here?"

"Two reasons. First, I made a promise to that purty li'l gal of yours that I'd look out for you, an' second, the thought of them Frenchies comin' down here from Canada thinkin' they can run us all out sticks in my craw." He slammed a beefy fist into his palm. "Them Yorkers gotta know the French went down right past their back door. And what about Connecticut an' Pennsylvania? Where are their militias, I'd like to know."

Colin grimaced. "Governor Dinwiddie sent messages out to all the colonies and to our allied tribes. They were all informed of this threat." He released a ragged breath. "So we're it. That is, what's left of us. Almost a hundred men lit out during the night. Guess they figured they'd follow the Indians' example of three nights ago."

"Well, you can't blame Monakaduto and his bunch for takin' off. The chief tried to talk Washington into takin' a stand on top of a hill, 'stead of down here in the open. But even if we'd done that, the chief still wouldn't have hung around and risked his women an' young'uns. We're way too outnumbered." He paused. "Speakin' of young'uns, Rose's little sister is somewhere up off the Susequehanna. I'm hopin' if we thin Frenchy's ranks out enough, they won't head up thataway. One of the Senecas told me the French are low on powder and supplies, too."

Recalling Mariah's younger sister, Colin nodded. "As I recall, Lily's owner didn't pay all that much for her papers. I should've thought to send money enough to satisfy him and gotten her out of there months ago." He peered back over his shoulder at the makeshift circle of pointed poles. "If by some miracle I make it out of here, I'll do just that."

"Meanwhile, we'd best concentrate on the Twenty-third Psalm, that my Rose is fond of quotin'. 'Yea, though I walk through the valley of the shadow of death. . .' "

Colin glanced out to the dark, shadowy woods that appeared even more sinister under heavy clouds ready to burst at any moment. "David must have had a place like this in mind when he wrote that Psalm, that's for sure."

Kinyon chuckled. "He also wrote, 'I will fear no evil: for thou art with me.' "

Meeting his gaze, Colin forced as much of a smile as he could muster. "Thanks for the reminder, friend. I'll pass that on to the men." He extended a hand to Kinyon. "It's been good getting to know you. I'd best get back to my men now."

"I'll walk along with you."

Bloodcurdling screeches and howling war cries erupted from the far end of the meadow!

Colin wheeled toward the sound.

Painted Indians emerged from the forest!

Adding to the sinister sound of their frightful yowling, the Indians began firing their muskets sporadically. Out of range, the balls fell short of the artillery pieces positioned to fire in that direction.

Colin raced to the nearest swivel cannon. "Don't fire until they're within range!"

Militiamen streamed out of the stockade and formed a firing line, with Washington in front. They waited for the enemy to advance.

They did not. Instead, the Indians began dancing, waving their rifles and hatchets and screaming their blood-chilling cries.

Then firing burst forth from the trees bracketing the long meadow. Rather than marching out into the open field and facing the militia like gentlemen, the French had set up positions on the wooded hills barely fifty yards from the stockade and launched an attack from there.

Ammunition rained down from both directions in a deadly crossfire.

"Retreat to the stockade!" Washington hollered amid the deafening racket and flying musket balls.

Colin turned—

⸺

Another hot and humid day like yesterday. Mariah had promised the girls she'd finish with their lessons early and take Amy riding before noon. Sipping a gloriously cooling, iced lemon drink on the veranda, she waited for her young charge to bring the horses up from the stable. As much as possible, Mariah had avoided going down there since Rose and Nate left last month. She didn't want to deal with the penetrating looks Geoffrey Scott had been giving her since then.

Not wanting to be noticed, she glanced out of the corner of her eye toward the stables, where Mr. Scott stood talking to Amy as Old Samuel saddled the horses. Was the trainer questioning the child about her? Wanting to know if Mariah said her prayers at night? Asking what she taught the girls in their Bible lessons?

She cringed at the thought, recalling a conversation she'd had with Mr. Scott two days after Rose and Nate took their leave:

"I'd appreciate your opinion," he'd said. "When our Lord says we're to pray always, what sort of things do you think we should pray for?"

"To keep us and those we love safe, of course." Mariah answered quickly, blithely, considering Colin was in a dangerous situation in the wilderness.

"Yes, but what else should our prayers concern?"

She was quite confident in her answer. "At the moment, there couldn't *be anything of more concern than Colin's safety."*

"Indeed." With a narrow-eyed perusal of her, he smirked and turned his back.

Mariah's confidence collapsed as he strode away. For once in her life, she wished she'd have been more like Rose and interested in spiritual matters so she could provide wise answers to his questions.

That evening, in her quest to learn the answer the trainer sought, Mariah asked equally religious Mistress Barclay the same question.

"That's a very good question," the older woman said. "Let's both study the scriptures on prayer, and we can discuss them next Sunday."

That had not turned out well at all. Although much of prayer was supposed to be for the welfare of other Christians, the mistress found three verses in the epistle of James and made them memory verses for the family. They were most disturbing:

"Ye ask, and receive not, because ye ask amiss, that ye may consume it upon your lusts." Mistress Barclay considered just about everything Mariah secretly prayed for lust. But then, the woman had everything—she could afford to do as the next verse she wanted memorized said: "Humble yourselves in the sight of the Lord, and he shall lift you up."

The mistress saved the worst for last: "For that ye ought to say, If the Lord will, we shall live, and do this, or that."

Mariah gave a huff. Surely the Lord didn't expect everyone to wait for God to tell them every move to make every single moment. Besides, it seemed only natural for folks to pray for their desires—wasn't there a verse somewhere in the Psalms to that effect? Otherwise there would be nothing to pray about but the poor and needy.

The unsettling memory was terminated as Amy started up the rise astride her pony and leading the other mount. Mariah smiled with relief. A ride along the river road would be most welcome about now. Placing her glass on a side table, she started for the steps.

Galloping hoofbeats thundered toward them from the other end of the lane. At this time of day?

She whirled around and entered the house. "A rider is coming! Fast!" she called out.

Questioning voices and footsteps came from various rooms.

As Mariah returned outside and flew down the steps, the man skidded his mount to a halt in front.

"Why the hurry?" Mr. Barclay asked from the top landing.

"The militia's comin'." Panting and out of breath, he continued. "Comin' down the river road. Your boy was with the militia, wasn't he?"

"Aye, that he was." With that, Colin's father came down the steps two at a time.

Mariah's heart leaped. Her hands flew to her face. Colin was finally coming home!

Mistress Barclay lifted her skirts and started down with the girls. "Did you see our son, my good man?"

"No, ma'am. One looks pretty much like all the rest, they're so ragged and dirty and unshaven. Well, I'm off. Folks down the road'll be wantin' to know." Reining his horse around, he galloped away again as fast as he'd come.

"Hooray!" Amy clapped her hands. "Colin's comin' home!"

Mr. Barclay snatched the reins of the second horse from Amy's hand and leaped into the saddle. Without a word, he charged down the road, with Amy chasing him on her pony.

Wishing she'd thought of the horse first, Mariah ran a few steps after the pair, then stopped to watch. She felt Victoria move alongside her.

"They will let Colin leave the others and come home now, won't they?"

"I certainly hope so, dear." Her mother, coming up behind, wrapped both Mariah and Victoria in a hug. "Praise the Lord! They're back. Our Colin is finally coming home."

The day grew ever warmer and stickier as Mariah and the others moved up to the veranda to wait. No one spoke as they stood in tense silence, straining their eyes for a glimpse of their returning hero.

Mariah could scarcely breathe. The rest of her life depended on whether or not Colin still wanted to marry her. If, heaven forbid, he'd been—no, she refused to allow that thought to go further.

Mistress Barclay sank onto a veranda chair, but within seconds rose again to her feet, watching with the others the far end of the lane.

Watching.

Waiting.

Mariah considered running down to the river road but knew how foolish that would be in this beastly heat. She'd be all damp and drippy.

Where were they? What was taking so long?

Pansy brought a tray of cool drinks without being asked. Remembering the one she'd left on a table moments ago, Mariah picked up her glass and took a gulp. Tension made it hard to swallow.

The great clock in the entry hall bonged twelve times. She'd come out to go riding at half past eleven. Mr. Barclay and Amy had ridden away over half an hour ago.

Heather broke the long silence. "Do you think we'll recognize Colin? I've never seen him with a beard."

No one answered. More minutes ticked away.

At long last, two horses and a pony turned onto the tree-shaded lane. They were coming!

Mariah inhaled a nervous breath and took a sip of her now-warm lemonade.

One rider broke into a gallop, racing toward them.

Mariah's heart kept pace with every hoofbeat as she and the others hurried down the steps. Staring ahead more closely, she slowed. Halted. The man's beard was golden brown, not black. It was Dennis Tucker. Where was Colin? Icy fear clutched her insides.

"Tuck!" Victoria gasped, breathless, and ran to him.

He reined to a swift halt before her and leaped from his mount, grabbing her up and swinging her around.

They blocked Mariah's view. She moved past them, still staring into the distance.

As the other, slower-moving horses neared, she saw that Mr. Barclay's mount bore two people. Amy plodded along at her father's side.

"Thank You, dear Lord," Mistress Barclay whispered as she came up beside Mariah.

Amy suddenly kicked her pony's flanks into a gallop and sped ahead of the other horse, straight to her mother. Tears streamed down her face as she collapsed into the older woman's arms. "He's b–blind," she sobbed. "Colin's blind."

Blind!

From far away, Mariah heard a gasp, and realized it was hers. Colin couldn't be blind. He just couldn't be. She'd prayed. They'd *all* prayed for his safe return. Her reasons may have been a bit selfish, but his family's weren't. How could God do this to him, to her?

Yet there he was, hanging on behind his father, hatless, a dingy white bandage wrapped around his head, shrouding his eyes. As they came closer, Mariah saw an angry red scar slashed down his temple. They came to a stop in front of her. Colin's hair was pulled back in a dull, limp queue, his clothes torn and filthy. Worst of all was the look of defeat where there should have been a smile. Did he even know where he was?

Words were coming at her. Mistress Barclay grabbed her arm and gave it a shake. "Did you hear me, Mariah? I said run into the house and order a bath for Colin."

"Y–yes. Of course," she choked out.

Colin's head turned toward her.

"And food for you, Colin." She forced a brightness she didn't feel into her tone. "I know you must be famished for Eloise's good cooking."

Glad for the chance to escape, she grasped her skirts and raced up the steps, her mind a stunned whirl of confusion. Not all blindness was permanent, she reasoned. But as she reached the butlery door, a shocking thought surfaced. What if Colin's *was*? What good would her beauty— her primary asset—be then? It would mean nothing at all to him—if he even remembered her. Men with head injuries were often left addled thereafter.

She entered the butlery, her thoughts still in turmoil. Even if he still possessed a competent mind, what would life be like married to a blind man, waiting on him, leading him around wherever they went? Could she deal with a challenge like that? For that matter, could he? It wasn't fair. This should not have happened.

A sudden surge of anger overtook her. Colin had no one to blame but himself. He should never have left here in the first place. Was that blasted honor of his worth his sight?

Worth her hopes?

Chapter 28

Entering the kitchen, Mariah found Eloise wringing her hands and muttering under her breath as she paced back and forth. "My po' boy. My po' boy."

Pansy sat at the worktable blindly peeling a turnip while tears coursed down her face.

The sight of the slaves' anguish nearly made Mariah break down, too, but she had to stay in control. She drew a calming breath. "This situation is most disturbing for us all. But we must try to be as brave as I know he was."

"Does y'all know somethin' 'bout Mastah Colin dat we don't?" Pansy swiped at her dark eyes with the edge of her work apron.

Aware that the maid had misunderstood, Mariah shook her head. "I simply know that Colin is incapable of doing anything that's not heroic. Eloise, would you please fix a plate of food for him right away, and start heating water for a bath?" Without waiting for a response, she started to leave, then turned back. "Oh, I forgot. Dennis Tucker is here. I'm sure he'd appreciate something to eat as well."

Walking back through the butlery, Mariah had another thought. If the militia was returning, where was Rose's husband? He'd promised to keep Colin safe, but obviously he hadn't done that. He was probably too ashamed to show his face here.

Voices drifted toward her when she opened the door to the foyer. Gripped again by a sudden urge to cry, she pulled the door almost closed, leaving only a crack to peek through.

With his head still swathed in bandages, Colin came through the front door, supported on either side by his parents. Was he so addled that it took both of them to guide him?

The girls and Tuck streamed into the house just behind Colin, and though Victoria still clung to Tuck, her worried gaze never left her brother. Nor did anyone else's.

Colin shrugged out of his parents' grasp and reached for the cloth covering his eyes, lowering it.

Although Mariah's first instinct was to turn away, she forced herself to leave the protection of the door and move closer to see how much damage had been done to his wonderful face. To her surprise, his eyes looked as velvety brown as ever. Only his black beard and the red scar slashing his temple marred his appearance. Perhaps he wasn't blind after all! *Please, God, don't let him be blind.*

"Sunlight hurts my eyes," Colin said, the first words Mariah had heard him utter. And they were sane words!

"Then you can see, darling!" Joy filled Mistress Barclay's expression as she took his hand.

"No, Mother. Only light and shadows."

"But it's something, at least. Perhaps it will improve with time."

He released a weary breath. "The physician who examined me at Fredrick Town said if I hadn't started improvin' by now, he doubts I'll get much better." The statement came out in a flat tone, as if he spoke of nothing more important than the weather.

Mariah felt tears forming. She blinked them away.

Looking every bit as devastated as Mariah felt, Colin's mother reached out a hand and gently touched his face.

He flinched.

"Whatever future lies before us, my darling, the Good Lord will see us through," the mistress murmured. "We're just so thrilled to have you home again."

"Thank you, Mother. But right now, would you mind just seein' me to my room? I'm really quite tired." His monotone words betrayed no more emotion than his face.

Mariah bit the inside corner of her lips. He hadn't once asked for her. Was the old Colin gone? Forever?

Sorrow filled her as she watched Colin's parents assisting him up the stairs. The fear she'd most dreaded turned into a reality. Her Colin was gone. When the others gravitated to the parlor, she followed, not knowing what else to do.

The girls, talking all at once, hurled questions at Dennis Tucker.

"How did Colin get hurt?"

"Do you think he'll get better?"

Tuck held up his hands. "Whoa. Sit down, and I'll tell you what happened."

Mariah, as desperately curious as the sisters, sought the nearest chair and sank onto it.

Dennis remained standing.

"Sit, please." Victoria scooted over on the settee and patted the cushion beside her.

"No, I'm far too dirty." He inhaled a deep breath as his gaze turned to Mariah.

She wondered if Colin had told his friend about their secret betrothal. Unsure, she lowered her gaze to her hands, not wanting him to see her pain. She slowly raised her lashes as he began to speak.

"Colin was outside the stockade helpin' his men set up some swivel cannons when the French attacked us. Out in the open like he was, he didn't have a chance. Nate Kinyon was also out there. As soon as Colin fell, Nate hoisted him up and hauled him back inside the stockade. A musket ball caught him in the leg, but that didn't stop him. Colin owes his life to that brave frontiersman."

"Then Nate did the best he could," Mariah said in a near whisper.

"Quite. And you should be grateful that Colin was unconscious for the next three days. He missed our shameful surrender of Fort Necessity and the Great Meadows. Our militia was far too outnumbered. From what I heard, there's not another live Englishman on the other side of the mountain now." Tuck's expression turned brittle, the muscles in his jaw twitching. "All because none of the other governors would lift a finger to help."

"How awful." Tori sprang to her feet and went to him. "But you're home now, safe and sound. Surely the other colonies will understand the seriousness of the French invasion after learning about this latest atrocity."

The tension left Dennis' shoulders as he took her hands in his and smiled. "I hope so, sweetheart. I certainly hope so."

"I'm surprised Nate Kinyon didn't accompany you here, Dennis," Mariah interjected. "Was he too badly injured?"

"No, miss. The musket shot grazed his leg, but the wound was patched up afterward. Nate was with us most of the way back, but he lives upstream from here. When we reached his settlement, he went on home to his Rose."

Benjamin leaned his black face into the doorway. "Mistah Tucker, we gots some food for you in da dinin' room."

"Sounds great. Thank you. I could use a quick bite, then I must be off. My folks will think I'm dead if the militia passes by our place and I'm not with 'em."

With the three sisters clustered around Dennis, the foursome left the parlor for the dining room.

Mariah chose another direction. Desperate for a few minutes alone, she ambled outside and down the veranda steps, heading for the gazebo.

As she reached the corner of the manse and the charming white-latticed structure came into view, the floodgates behind her eyes finally broke. Hardly able to see for the tears, she picked up her skirts and ran past the hedged garden to the octagonal summer building where she wouldn't be heard. Sobbing openly, she raced up the steps and into the gazebo's shade, where she gave full vent to her sorrow.

She covered her mouth with both hands and slumped down to a bench as heart-wrenching wails from deep inside shook her being. Her beautiful man, the one who had always gazed at her with such worshipful eyes, her Colin who had traveled to Bath to help her father with his financial plight. . .Colin who brought back a ring as proof of his troth, who said he loved her, wanted to marry her. . . That man was. . .was her one true love. She knew that now. It wasn't his wealth she wanted, it wasn't his fine position in life. It was the man himself. She vowed she would do whatever it took, how ever long it took, to be with him, to take care of him, to love him.

Why had she never realized how deep her feelings for Colin had grown? Yet he hadn't asked for her, hadn't so much as spoken her name. Why hadn't he? Did he even remember her? All her scheming and planning had caught up with her, just as Rose predicted, and now Colin was quite possibly lost to her forever. Oh, how it hurt to love him still.

After a time, Mariah's sobs died away, and she pondered who Colin was now, how much he must have changed. What would it be like to suddenly become blind? She couldn't imagine being deprived of sight. Not being able to see everything that now lay before her eyes—this lovely home, its furnishings, the gardens, her clothes, the sight of Colin's teasing grin. A lifetime of darkness lay ahead of him now. Surely blindness must be akin to being buried alive.

She emitted a shuddering sigh. Even if he did remember her, Colin couldn't possibly still be the man who had asked her to marry him. No. His days of coming to her rescue were over, and he'd always been too much the knight in shining armor to allow her to come to his aid.

Tears again threatened. Angrily she shook them away. She must think of herself now.

She glanced down toward the stables. Geoffrey Scott was at this moment leading two horses toward a pasture gate—the two she and Amy had planned to ride earlier today. The trainer was perhaps a decade older than she, but rather handsome in a quiet sort of way. Narrowing her eyes as she studied him, Mariah shuddered. No. She could never wed Geoffrey, knowing Colin was so close, wanting to be with him, wanting him to look at her as he used to. The very thought of him never seeing her again made her heart ache.

Nothing was left to her but to write to Rose and Nate and ask them to pay off her indenturement, since Papa would eventually reimburse them. Then she'd go and live with them until she learned to stop loving Colin, how ever long that would take.

But then what? Rose and her husband lived in the woods outside a primitive settlement. What chance for any kind of an advantageous marriage would she find there?

Mariah let out a long, slow breath and glanced across the fields where the slaves were carrying the last of the tobacco leaves to the drying sheds. Summer would be over soon. Winter—dreary winter—would soon be upon them. For Colin it had already arrived. How would they all survive such sorrow?

One of Rose's favorite sayings drifted to mind: *Take care of today, and leave tomorrow's worries with the Lord.*

Of course. She'd been running headlong ahead of herself. Again. She would leave tomorrow to the Lord. Rising to her feet, Mariah tugged a handkerchief from her skirt pocket and dabbed away the remains of her tears. What was needed right now was to get through the rest of this woeful day. And the first order of business was to get some cold water to splash on her face. Crying made her look simply dreadful.

Mariah's eyes weren't the only ones swollen and red that evening at supper. Even Mr. Barclay's face showed signs that he, too, had wept. Attempting to give a brief blessing over the food, his voice broke when he mentioned Colin's name. And that made Mariah want to start bawling again.

No one else spoke either, except to ask occasionally for the pitcher of lemonade to be passed. The fried chicken on their plates grew cold as everyone just pushed it around in silence. Now and then someone would flick a glance toward the staircase and the upper floor, where Colin had asked to be left alone to rest. He had yet to speak to her, Mariah, his betrothed.

Finally Mistress Barclay rose from the table. "Shall we adjourn to the parlor? I'd appreciate it, Mariah, if you'd play the harpsichord for us this evening. Something soft and soothing, if you will."

"Yes. Something soothing." Mariah nodded, almost afraid to meet the older woman's gaze and see the anguish that his mother's heart had to feel.

But the lady of the manor wasn't looking at her. She stared past Mariah out the terrace doors, tears welling in her eyes.

Mariah breathed deeply to keep her own from spilling forth.

Never before had an evening been so quiet. No one spoke as they sat absorbed in their own thoughts, tears quietly flowing as Mariah played soothing pieces by Bach and Haydn. Thankfully having memorized them, she had no need to read the music through her tears.

Amy stood to her feet before the sky had darkened enough for stars to appear. "I'm tired. I'm goin' to bed." That from a child who possessed boundless energy?

Soon after, Victoria also got up. "It's been a long day." As she passed Heather, her sister followed.

Mariah continued to play, hoping the elder Barclays would also retire. She wanted nothing more than for this dreadful day to end. But the pair sat motionless, appearing oblivious to the music.

Detecting footsteps padding across the foyer toward the parlor, Mariah looked up from the keys and dabbed her wet eyes on her sleeve.

Lizzie, who'd been asked to sit outside Colin's door in case he needed anything, stood in the doorway. "Ma'am? Mastah Colin, he askin' for Missy Harwood to come."

Mariah's pulse began to throb in her aching head. Her hands froze on the keys. Colin wanted to see her! He had remembered her after all! Noting that his parents' gazes were now riveted on her, she hoped they weren't angry that he'd sent for her instead of them.

"If you'll excuse me," she managed to croak. She rose on shaky legs and started for the foyer.

"Give him our love," Mistress Barclay murmured after her.

"Yes, do that." Her husband put an arm about his wife and hugged her close.

Mariah didn't remember ascending the grand staircase, but reaching Colin's chamber, she entered and closed the door behind her. The room lay in darkness, devoid of a single lamp's glow. But faint light came from the open balcony doors, where she saw slight movement. "Colin?"

"I'm outside." He spoke in the same emotionless tone she'd heard earlier. "Come join me. It's cooler out here."

She found his shadowy figure in a chair with an iced drink jingling in his hand—the only other sound besides those of the crickets, tree toads, and other night creatures. Colin smelled of the pleasant spiced soap Eloise always made.

"Have a seat." He gestured in no particular direction.

"Thank you." Swallowing against a lump forming in her throat, Mariah settled her skirts about her on a cushioned, scrolled-iron chair nearby and forced a cheerful note into her voice. "You're right. 'Tis quite a bit cooler out here."

"How are my parents faring?"

His quiet question was hard to answer. What should she say? Realizing he'd asked her because he wanted the truth, she spoke in all candor. "They sent their love. And I do believe I can tell you that everyone is—is—"

He raised a hand. "No need to say more." He inhaled a breath, audible since only a small table separated the two of them. "When I woke up and discovered I couldn't see, I found it hard to accept, myself."

Mariah turned toward him. "Oh, dearest Colin, how dreadful for you." She wished she could see his face clearly, make out his expression.

"Nate Kinyon and his partner, Black Horse Bob, were there," he cut in as if she hadn't spoken. "They helped me past the worst part. Quoted lots of scripture, gave me long talks about how much worse things could be and the fine life I still have ahead of me." He gave a small huff. "Speakin' of Nate, he's truly an exceptional man. Your sister is fortunate to have him for a husband."

"Yes. When they were here, they seemed very. . ." She almost said, *very much in love,* but changed her mind. "Very well suited."

"Rose must be quite the woman, then. You should've heard the way he went on about her."

Mariah felt the same twinge of jealousy she'd always felt as a child when her aunt and uncle or their clergyman would go on and on about what a treasure Papa had in Rose. She inhaled a cleansing breath. "I'm sure Nate would praise her. Rose is a woman of great virtue."

For the first time, Colin turned toward her. "I'm glad to hear you say that." Reaching to the small table at his side, he plucked something rectangular from it and held it out to her.

Mariah grasped it and saw it was a folded document.

"Your indenturement papers. I've signed your release."

He was giving her back her freedom?

"But—"

"Dearest Mariah, I've had weeks to think about this. A beautiful woman such as yourself needs a man who will appreciate being able to feast his eyes on that loveliness every day the two of you spend together. Needless to say, I no longer have that ability."

Her heart stopped. "You're rescinding your marriage proposal?"

"It's the only gentlemanly thing to do. I don't want you to be saddled with a blind man for the rest of your life. And I'm certain your father would agree with me."

"But. . .but. . .I love you, Colin. Truly I do."

"I thank you for that. It's wonderful to hear. It really is. But I'm no longer the same man you fell in love with. And I don't want to be that poor blind fellow his long-suffering wife has to lead around. I'll make arrangements for an escort for you to your sister's in the morning. I'd also like you to take a nice colt and two fillies with you as a thank-you to Nate for saving my life, such as it is."

"No." How dare he make this decision without her?

"They'll follow along quite nicely, I'm sure."

"Who will?"

"The horses. They won't be much trouble. I'll have Geoff choose some with good temperaments."

"That isn't what I meant. I'm not leaving."

"Mariah, my dear, weren't you listening? There's nothing here for you anymore."

She sprang to her feet. "You are here! You are not nothing!" Clutching her hands together to calm herself, she lowered her voice. "This has been a very long day. We can speak again in the morning."

"My decision won't change."

Mariah whirled away. "And neither will mine."

Chapter 29

Mariah awoke in the pale pink light of dawn with new resolve. She'd lain awake for a good hour or more during the night, her mind vacillating from one emotion to another until she formulated a plan, a foolproof plan to make Colin want her to stay.

With a determined smile, she rose quietly, not wanting to awaken Amy in the next room. She made her bed and took care of her morning toilette, dressing quickly. Her appearance was no longer of importance to Colin.

But something else did matter to him. If he was so taken by Nate's mere description of Rose, Mariah merely had to do and say exactly the kinds of things her sister would. There'd be nothing to it. Hadn't she watched long-suffering Rose her whole life? Always doing for others, quoting the appropriate scripture for any occasion—at her?

Well, perhaps she wouldn't be quite as long-suffering as Rose. Her older sister had a penchant for taking self-sacrifice to such an extreme that, had she not ended up the lone white woman in Indian Territory, she surely would have continued her dull journey into a life of spinsterhood.

Chuckling to herself, Mariah thought back on the scripture she'd read to the girls a few days before: *"Put on the whole armor of God."*

Suddenly she remembered her betrothal ring. Removing it from its chain, she slipped the amethyst onto the correct finger, and held out her hand to admire its rich beauty. Then, after a passing glance at her sensible hairstyle, she turned on her heel and headed for the door. Convinced she was fully armored, she marched out ready for battle, but catching sight of Amy in slumber, she quieted her steps. War was far better waged without that child's impetuous mouth getting in the way.

No sign of life came from the older girls' room as Mariah tiptoed down the hall. Good. Going into a man's private chamber at this hour simply was not done. Pausing at Colin's door, she decided against rapping, since even that light sound might be heard. She walked in quite brazenly and closed the door behind her without a sound.

But Colin wasn't in his walnut four-poster bed. She scanned the masculine room with its sturdy furnishings and multihued coverlet only to discover it empty. Had he perchance stayed outside on the balcony all night?

Crossing the room, she checked to see if he was outside, and when he was not, she surmised he must have gone downstairs ahead of her. She hurried out, hoping to catch him alone, before either of his parents awakened.

She was too late. As she entered the parlor, the drone of male voices drifted from the dining room. Passing through the doorway separating the two rooms, she spotted Colin and his father at the far end of the long table, talking in subdued voices, half-eaten plates of food on the table before them.

Mariah paused, taking a moment to compose herself. She also took that moment to gaze on her beloved's strong profile. With the angry scar out of view and his face now clean-shaven, a person happening upon the scene would never guess he was a tragic figure who'd suffered a grievous wound in battle.

Those interminable tears threatened again, but she willed them away and resumed a resolute pace. The last thing Colin wanted or needed was her pity.

"Good morning," she singsonged, striding into the room. "Anything especially tasty for breakfast today?"

Both men abruptly turned toward her.

"Good morning." Mr. Barclay's cheerful tone matched her own. She wondered if his good humor was as false as hers.

Colin spoke in the same flat manner he'd adopted since his return. "Glad to hear you're up before the others. Fill your plate and join us."

"Thank you. I'll do that." Mariah didn't realize how hungry she was until the delectable aroma of fresh biscuits and gravy, cold ham, and spiced apples in cream wafted to her nostrils. She selected portions of each and poured herself a cup of tea before taking her place across from Colin. "You look quite rested, Colin." Raising her cup to her lips, she took a sip.

"I slept well. And you?"

"Thank you, yes." She placed her napkin on her lap and straightened her shoulders. She could play the polite conversation game as well as he. Maybe better. "I enjoy rising early before the business of the day is upon us. I shall be testing the girls on their French lessons this week." She turned to his father. "By the way, Mr. Barclay, did you not say you had some letters you wanted me to write for you today?"

"Yes, I did. But—"

"What my father means," Colin interrupted, "is that there's no need for you to spend time on correspondence. You'll be busy packing for your trip on the morrow."

"I'm sorry," she said in a sugary-sweet voice, "you must have misunderstood me last evening. I've no plans of going anywhere."

He spoke more forcefully. "It's already been decided."

At least he was showing more life. But unfortunately for him, he had no idea what he was up against. Mariah directed her attention to his father and held out her left hand, allowing the amethyst to catch the light from the sconces and reflect its full violet radiance amid the sparkling diamonds circling it. "I don't believe you've seen the betrothal ring Colin gave me. Is it not just the prettiest thing?"

The older man's shocked expression rivaled his son's.

"*Mariah.*" Colin shook his head. "You know—"

"What's that?" Mistress Barclay had entered the room unnoticed. "Did I hear correctly? You're betrothed to Mariah, Colin?"

Mariah spoke before he had a chance to respond. "Why, yes, Mistress Barclay." She lifted her hand to display the ring. "Colin bought this from Papa when he was in England and asked my father for my hand in marriage."

"That was before this happened," Colin grated through clenched teeth. He pounded the table with his fist, and scooting back his chair, lunged to his feet. "I've since given Mariah her indenturement papers, and I was arrangin' with Father for her transportation to her sister's when she. . .she. . ."

"I what?" Mariah shot up from her seat and planted her fists on her hips, wishing she were a foot taller as she eyed him, even though such an advantage would have been useless.

Both his hands had balled into fists as well, and she was very glad a large table separated them. Then slowly he unclenched his hands and turned toward his father. "Will you please handle the matter we discussed? I'm goin' to my room. Benjamin!" he called out. "I need you!"

"But, darling," his mother pleaded as the slave rushed in from the butlery.

"Let him go, Cora." Mr. Barclay met her gaze. "You can speak with him later."

As Mariah watched Colin leave on the African's arm, the enormity of what she'd just said and done began to dawn on her. Had it been not more than ten minutes ago she'd promised herself she would act just like Rose? Mortified, she dropped down to her seat again and picked up her teacup, wishing it made a larger shield. Her pulse throbbed in her throat so intently she feared it must be visible.

Mistress Barclay lowered her elegant self to the chair her son had just vacated and arched her brows. "What, may I ask, have I missed here this morning?"

"Quite a bit, my dear." Her husband tipped his head in amazement. "Your son and our tutoress were having a rather heated disagreement about her future. Seems they have differing views on how and where she should spend it." A most unexpected grin slid into place.

Speechless, Mariah could only stare.

The lady of the house hadn't been struck dumb, however. She leveled her gaze on Mariah. "You say you and our son are betrothed?"

Mariah breathed deeply, trying to still her pounding heart. "Yes, madam. Since February, when Colin returned from England."

The woman's glare hardened. "Why is it we are just now hearing about it?"

"Colin felt it would be best to wait until his return from duty with the militia. He thought it would be only a matter of weeks. But. . ." She gave a helpless shrug and raised her cup to her lips, swallowing a gulp of mint tea.

"Engaged all this time. And now that he's been blinded, you've suddenly lost interest, is that it? He's no longer worthy of your—"

Mr. Barclay interrupted. "You've got it backward, Cora." He reached for his wife's hand and enclosed it in his. "It's Colin who wants her to go."

"Oh." The mistress settled back in her chair and gazed across at Mariah, her dark eyes now soft with sympathy. "My son wishes to break off the engagement."

"Yes." Feeling emotion welling in her again, Mariah struggled to maintain her composure. "He thinks that just because he's blind I should stop loving him and find someone else. Well, I'm sorry, but I can't do that. I love him dearly, and I don't know how to stop loving him. I don't care about his blindness." Despite her best efforts, those blasted tears started again. Clutching at her napkin, she sprang from the table to escape before they noticed. "Please, excuse me."

"Wait!" Mistress Barclay also came to her feet. Circling the table, she approached Mariah and drew her into her arms.

Overcome by the unexpected tenderness when Colin's mother hugged her close and hard, Mariah's tears poured out in earnest. Sobbing uncontrollably, she melted into the older woman's comforting embrace.

Her tears stemmed from a mixture of joy and sadness, made even more intense when Colin's father came to join them and enfolded them both in his strong arms. For several moments, they wept together.

Finally, Mr. Barclay broke away and wiped his nose on his handkerchief. He spoke with emotions still quite raw. "Enough of this, ladies. God will help us all through this hard time, I'm sure. Colin included. Meanwhile, Cora, my love, dish yourself some breakfast, and the three of us will discuss the dilemma while we eat." He glanced warmly down at Mariah. "I've come to think of you as my daughter, Mariah, as part of our family, and your desire to stand by our son despite all that's happened means more to me than you will ever know."

Mariah stood in the doorway of the classroom, watching the girls ambling listlessly toward her for their morning lessons. She flashed a broad smile. "Good day, girls. I've a bit of news that might cheer you up."

Amy's expression brightened as she passed by on her way to her desk. "We can skip our lessons today?"

Mariah sent her a surely-you're-not-serious smirk. "I'm afraid not."

All three grumbled and took their places, obviously still weighted down by last night's gloom.

Reaching to close the door, Mariah spied Mr. Barclay at the top of the staircase at the other end of the long hall. He headed straight for Colin's room.

Her pulse picked up the pace. She backed into the schoolroom out of the man's view. How would Colin take his parents' decision concerning her? If only she could get the girls settled quickly and concentrating on their French verbs, she might be able to saunter down that way and overhear Colin's reaction.

She turned toward her unsmiling charges as they sat with their hands politely folded on their desks. "I know I promised to test you on your French first thing—"

"Promised?" Victoria scoffed, pursing her lips. "More like threatened."

"Yes, well, I'm aware that all our minds were too unsettled yesterday, so I've decided to give you some extra time to study." *While I sneak down to Colin's door and press my ear against it.*

Heather looked up, her azure eyes sad and troubled. "Oh, Mariah, havin' Colin come home blind is like havin' him come home dead."

It made no sense to correct the thirteen-year-old for dropping her Gs. This was not the time for a grammar lesson. The devastation felt by Colin's sisters was more than evident. Mariah crossed to Heather's desk and lifted the girl's chin. "That's simply not true, sweetheart. If you'd heard Colin bellowing his head off at breakfast this morning, you'd know he's nowhere near dead. He's very much alive."

Amy scrunched up her face. "Was he mad because Storm wasn't with him? He loves that horse almost as much as I do Patches. Almost as much as I love Storm. Did Colin say what happened to him?"

"I'm afraid not, dear." Mariah shrugged a shoulder. "The matter of his horse never came up. In fact, considering the mood your brother's in at the moment, I would suggest you wait a few days before mentioning the animal's whereabouts."

"But what if he got left behind someplace to starve?" Amy's chair screeched as she sprang from her seat. "He might be hurt. What if Storm's blind, too?"

Mariah moved to her and placed a hand on the child's shoulder, gently easing her back down to her seat. "Sweetheart, I'm sure nothing like that has happened. Most likely, another militiaman was riding him, since Colin wasn't well enough to be on horseback. Storm is probably stabled in Alexandria as we speak, waiting for someone to go and retrieve him."

"I'll do it. He knows me." Amy started to get up again.

Losing her patience, Mariah stopped her with a firm glare. "No one is going anywhere until after you've finished your lessons. I suggest you begin studying." She glanced at the other two sisters. "All of you."

It seemed to take forever for them to delve into their French vocabulary. But once they all were preoccupied and mouthing the verbs they'd been working on, Mariah knew she could leave. "I'll be right back, girls. I forgot something in my room."

It was the perfect excuse, really. If she happened by chance to overhear something along the way, no one could accuse her of eavesdropping. In fact, she'd keep to her side of the hall, in the event that Mr. Barclay—

or worse, Colin—should come out. Her stay in this house was quite conditional, after all. Everything she did for the next few days, at least, must appear above reproach. Then why was she out here now, with nothing but snooping on her mind?

Ignoring the twinge of conscience, she stopped directly across from Colin's room and craned her ear toward his door. Not a sound could be heard. Perhaps a step or two closer—

The chamber door swung inward! Mr. Barclay stood in the opening.

Mariah cringed at her bad timing. Surely the man could see her heart pounding beneath her bodice.

He stared at her briefly, then closed the door quietly behind himself. "Aren't you supposed to be with the girls?"

She prayed that the sudden warmth at her collar wouldn't rise to heat her cheeks. "Why yes. I just stepped out to retrieve a book from my room." Gratified that her response had come without hesitation, she breathed easier. "So, if you'll excuse me, I don't like to leave the girls unattended for long." She swept past him and headed for the door she shared with Amy. However, against her better judgement, she couldn't prevent herself from turning back. "Is all well with Colin?"

"As well as can be expected." No smile accompanied the statement. He strode past her and down the stairs, leaving her to speculate.

In case he paused on the steps for any reason, she continued on through Amy's room and into her own to fetch whatever book was most handy. But she wondered all the while what Colin's father had told him and how Colin had taken the news.

Mariah recalled that after breakfast, Mr. Barclay had decided to have Geoffrey Scott deliver the young horses Colin had mentioned to Nate— without Mariah. The decision thrilled her, even though that would give the trainer yet another encounter with Nate Kinyon. For whatever reason, Mr. Scott had been quite distant since his last conversation with her brother-in-law.

She let out a calming breath. The Barclays had decided to allow her to continue on as before, at least until the weather cooled. The mistress felt there was no need to make hasty decisions in such sweltering heat.

Mariah had the impression that Colin's mother was on her side, though the older lady never actually said the words. In all likelihood, there were very few local belles who would consider marriage to a blind man, no matter how rich and handsome he might be. Thank goodness for that. Given Colin's state of mind, Mariah wouldn't put it past him to propose to some other maiden just to rid himself of her.

But one truth remained. He loved her every bit as deeply as she loved him. He'd proved it to her over and over.

As she searched through the stack of books on the small stand beside her bed, the amethyst ring caught on the edge of one of the spines. She paused and let her gaze linger on the violet gem in its exquisite setting.

A smile played across her lips.

She'd do it. The more allies she had, the better. Scooping up the top book, she hurried back to the classroom.

Chapter 30

Returning to the classroom, Mariah assured herself she wouldn't be doing anything that should prick her conscience. Besides, this was nothing like trying to eavesdrop. Assured of her pure motives, she sauntered over to Victoria's desk and leaned down, placing her left hand strategically across the girl's French text. "Do you need any help with pronunciation?" Slowly she swept her hand across the page.

"No, I'm— Oh! What a beautiful ring." Tori caught Mariah's hand. "I've never seen you wear this before. What kind of stone is it?" Raising her lashes, she gazed up at Mariah, her sky-blue eyes wide, curious.

"Let me see." Heather rose and left her seat, with Amy traipsing after her as they came to look.

Amy leaned down to peer more closely. "Is it real?"

Mariah shrugged a shoulder. "I certainly hope so. Colin bought it for me when he visited my father. It's an amethyst."

"If it's from your poppy, it has to be real." Amy gave a confident nod.

Having returned her attention to the lovely ring, Victoria looked up again at Mariah. "But Colin returned home from England months ago.

Did he just now give it to you?"

"Actually, no. He gave it to me just before he left for the militia." Mariah's heart began to beat harder. "But since he had to go away again in haste after asking me to marry him"—all three girls gasped—"he suggested that we wait to tell your family until he came back home. So I've been wearing it on a chain around my neck."

"Oh, how romantic," Heather breathed, dreamy eyed.

Tori gazed down at the amethyst again, then at Mariah. "And Tuck was so happy to see me, I just know he'll propose soon, too." She twisted a finger around a golden curl near her ear.

About to remind the young lady that her mother would likely refuse her consent, Mariah chose not to burst Tori's bubble. She needed the three girls to be happy about her betrothal to their brother so they might help to further the cause.

"Hurrah!" Amy threw her arms about Mariah's waist. "I'm so happy! You're gonna be my big sister, and you won't ever have to leave us again." Abruptly letting go, she flew toward the door.

"Wait! Where are you going?" Mariah called after her.

The child didn't even slow down as she vaulted out the door. "To see Colin!"

"No! Wait!"

But her words had no effect. By the time Mariah reached the hall, Amy was charging into her brother's room.

Mariah dashed madly after her. What in the world had she been thinking? She should have thought things through before divulging news of her betrothal to that impulsive imp.

She hesitated only a second at Colin's open door, determined to catch Amy before she said anything. But stopping that girl was akin to stopping a waterfall.

Already the child's boundless energy had her jumping up and down in the middle of her brother's quarters. "I just heard the news!"

Mariah's heart sank. Too late. She closed her eyes.

"Why didn't you tell us?" Amy stopped and turned around, searching the room. "Where are you, Colin?"

Thank You, Lord. Mariah clutched her chest and tried to catch her breath. Colin wasn't in his room. She moved forward to collect his sister.

The door to the balcony swung open, and Colin came inside. "Is that you, Amy?"

Mariah halted in her tracks. She didn't want him to know she was there.

Amy had no such concern. "Yes. It's me. I'm real happy for you."

He tucked his chin and frowned. "Happy that I'm blind? Why would you be happy about that?"

"No, silly. I'm sad about that. I'm happy you're gonna marry Mariah."

Wincing, Mariah softly back-stepped toward the door. She had to get out of there.

But Amy gushed on with nary a breath. "That's the bestest thing I heard since. . .since you gave Patches to me. Isn't that so, Mariah?"

Mariah's heart stopped as she froze in place. She felt like a trapped rabbit and wanted nothing more than to escape and run.

His features hardening to granite, Colin raised his chin. "So my betrothed is here in the room with us."

"Uh-huh." Amy turned and pointed. "Right over there by the door."

A hole, Mariah thought. If only there was a rabbit hole to drop into. Still, she knew she had to stand firm. Too much was at stake. "I'm sorry Amy burst in on you unannounced, Colin. I know you asked to be left alone today. I'll take her back to the classroom." She took a step forward.

"No!" Amy stomped her foot and crossed her arms. "I want to talk to Colin. I want to tell him about me and Patches and all the things we did while he was away."

"Come, dear." Mariah tugged on the child's arm.

But Amy jerked free and turned a beseeching look up at her brother. "Colin, you were gone such a long time. Too long. Me and the horses missed you somethin' awful."

"Amy. . ." His demeanor softened a bit as he moved cautiously toward a wing chair to his right and ran a hand down its side, as if assuring himself it was positioned properly. Then he eased himself down to the cushioned seat. "I missed you a lot, too, squirt."

Hearing a gentleness in his tone that hadn't been there since his return, Mariah felt a ray of hope. Until he spoke again.

"Come give your brother a big hug, then run along. I'd like a private word with Mariah."

Amy glanced from him to Mariah and back and shrugged her thin shoulders. "Oh, sure." She ran into his open arms. After a sweet moment or two, she eased from his embrace and stepped back. "I reckon now you to want to hug and kiss and all that stuff, huh?"

He gave a small grunt and lightly swatted her bottom to hurry her on her way. "Somethin' like that. Oh, and Amy, please close the door on your way out."

She giggled and ran to do his bidding.

As the door slammed behind Amy, Mariah felt like a condemned person with a noose around her neck, waiting for the trapdoor to collapse.

Colin released a slow breath. "Seems you've been mighty busy this morning, haven't you?"

She cringed at the clipped syllables.

"Mighty busy." He wagged his head, a droll smirk tightening his mouth.

Moistening her dry lips, she shrugged a shoulder. "The girls noticed my ring." It was a lame excuse, and she knew it. For a second she had the impression that Colin could see, the way his glower bored into her.

He did not respond, just rubbed a hand across his chin.

Lowering her gaze from what she reminded herself was an unseeing stare, she noticed that both of her hands clutched handfuls of her skirt, crushing the muslin fabric. She tried for a casual tone. "Well, I really should get back to your sisters."

"Not so fast." He paused momentarily, as if gathering his thoughts. "Obviously I did not make myself clear when we spoke last night, so I'll repeat what I said. There will be no wedding, no matter how many members of my family you rally. Your brother-in-law told me you'd always been considered the clever one among your siblings, and I see you've proven him right."

Chagrined by the statement, Mariah did her best to sound appalled.

"The man has scarcely set eyes on me. He knows nothing about me."

Colin tipped his head. "It doesn't really matter." He stretched his long legs out before him and relaxed against the chair. "My decision wouldn't be any different if you were the queen of kindness itself. But if you will leave my home without any further protest, I'll give you a choice. If you don't wish to go live with your sister, I'll pay your passage back to England and give you a goodly sum to jingle in your purse, besides."

Mariah's hackles rose with each word. She could not believe he thought so little of her. Nevertheless, she composed herself and spoke evenly. "I understand that, at the moment, you believe your world has come to an end. But as time goes by, you'll come to realize life hasn't really changed so very much. And when that time comes, and you regain your senses, I plan to be here."

"My senses?" He scoffed. "All of them? Except, of course, for that particularly crucial one. . .my sight."

Mariah regretted her bad choice of words. She sought another tack. Oh yes, Rose. Say what Rose would say. "I can see I've upset you again. For that I am truly sorry." At a loss to say more, she backed toward the door, until her fingers grasped the handle. "I really must return to the girls. Perhaps we can talk again later."

"Wait!"

But Mariah whirled out the door and closed it behind her, ignoring his voice. She hurried away as fast as she could.

That had not gone well at all. She had to stop trying to manipulate the situation. If only she'd remembered her decision to act like her older sister before allowing herself to become so vexed. After all, when had anyone ever railed so vehemently at Rose—except for the night she informed the family she'd sold most of their prized possessions out from under them.

Slowing as she neared the schoolroom door, Mariah paused. The single reason the family had yelled at Rose was because, for once, she'd uncharacteristically taken matters into her own hands. She'd done the sort of rash thing Mariah might have done under those circumstances.

A grimace flattened Mariah's lips. Possibly she wouldn't have been quite as self-sacrificing as Rose had been, even selling herself. But for now, this situation required self-sacrifice. Colin needed that.

From now on, she'd stop trying to be clever, as Colin had so rudely put it. She would step inside Rose's very skin, martyr herself for the cause of Colin's ultimate happiness.

And hers.

Hearing the door to his chamber close and Mariah's footsteps receding down the hall, Colin closed his eyes in disgust. Some homecoming. He'd been positive that Mariah would gladly accept her release. Apparently, he'd underestimated her greed.

This added torment was more than anyone should have to endure. After weeks of travel in a bumpy wagon, listening hour after hour to the groans of other wounded men, he couldn't wait to leave the terrible defeat behind and return to familiar surroundings.

The defeat. The surrender. His only saving grace was that he'd been unconscious when Washington signed the surrender document and hadn't had to witness that humiliation. From the reports he'd heard, a heavy rain had started after he'd been shot and never ceased through the night. Because of their too hasty efforts to construct the fort, the gunpowder had little protection from the elements, and only a few able soldiers remained after the first barrage to fend off the surrounding horde of French and Indians. The situation had been hopeless from the start.

Nate said it was only by the grace of God that the French commander had even offered the militia the opportunity to surrender, and only then because one of his Indian scouts had reported hearing marching drums coming from the east.

Even now, Colin couldn't hold back a sarcastic chuckle. As if any of the other colonies would have come to their assistance. Knowing that their fellow English colonies refused to lift a finger to prevent the French from taking over their territories was indeed bitter medicine to swallow.

With a ragged sigh, he rose from the chair. Hands outstretched, he made his way to the bedstead, then edged around it to the night table for a drink of water. Soon, he vowed, he'd have this room memorized, then the rest of the house, and even down to the stables. He was determined not to stumble around much longer.

Finding the glass, Colin lifted it and took several swallows, enjoying the sensation of the cool liquid coursing down his throat. Somehow, with God's help, he'd survive being blind. His thirst sated, he set down the glass and sank onto the bed he could feel behind his legs. Yes, somehow he'd eke out a life for himself—just not the one he'd expected.

At that deflating thought, he lay back on the pillows and tried to blot from his mind the well-laid plans he'd always had for himself.

Sleep. He needed more sleep.

But as he lay there in the unending darkness, his anger refused to let go. Anger at the French, the heedless colonial governors, and a fate that would change a man's life forever. But mostly he was angry at that arrogant, selfish Englishwoman, Mariah Harwood.

Why had he never noticed her true nature before? In reality, the two of them had spent very little actual time together. Mostly he'd just thought about her, created in his mind the woman he believed her to be. . .and for no other reason than her beauty. She was the most beautiful, most alluring woman he'd ever seen in his life. The siren who lured sailors to their deaths on a jagged reef. The Delilah to his Samson. She was a liar.

Only after he told her to leave did she say she loved him. Not when it would have meant something, like the last time he'd feasted his eyes on her and held her in his arms and asked her to marry him. He might have believed her then.

But not now.

From what Nate Kinyon had told him, Mariah had not come to America with Rose out of a desire to help her sister or the rest of her family. She had come with all her superior ways with but one goal in mind—to catch a rich husband. And the mere fact that her catch ended up blind would not stand in the way of a fortune hunter like her. He frowned. Mother had seen through her from the very start. Oh, how he wished he'd listened to her.

A niggling thought crept in, and his gaze gravitated naturally toward the faint light streaming from the balcony's open door. If Mother had seen through Mariah to her devious, selfish nature, why had she so readily agreed with Father this morning to allow the pretender to stay?

Chapter 31

As time ticked slowly by, Colin found it difficult to get any much-needed rest. In his mind he could still hear the rush of heavy rains and recall slogging through the mud with the militia. The clatter of chopping trees for the fort echoed in his head, along with the roar of artillery and the sharp report of musket fire. And he could hear cries of the wounded, mournful and heartrending. The sounds never seemed to end. Perhaps in time, with any luck at all, they would.

But the darkness would be his lot forever. He might as well get used to it.

When he heard the girls leave their classrooom and go downstairs for the noon meal, he rose from his bed and began counting off steps to various spots in his room. Six steps to the balcony door, four steps from there to the wing chair, two more to the bed, five to the door to the hallway. With each successful journey around the chamber, his confidence lifted, and so did his mood. He wasn't even perturbed when he heard rapid running in the hall. It was to be expected in a house filled with lively sisters.

His door flew open.

"Colin!"

Glad to hear Amy's voice, he smiled. "Come sit down, little sis. Tell me all that's been happening. Is the horse from England faring well?"

"Oh, yes," she gushed. She hugged him, then flopped onto a matching chair, the scent of outdoors clinging to her like a shawl. "By the time Poppy even noticed him, Russet Knight was racing up the lane so fast Poppy didn't care what color he was." She paused for breath. "I couldn't wait any longer. I came to find out where Storm is, since he didn't come home with you. If he's someplace close, like Alexandria, I wanna go get him back."

Colin kneaded his chin. "I'd forgotten all about Storm. Thank you, squirt, for reminding me. Poor fellow, he's had a hard time of it. I'm sure he must be stabled somewhere near where the militia disbanded. Tell Pa to send someone after him."

"I will. And I'll tell Poppy you want me to go, too. Storm will be so glad to see me an' Patches. He's prob'ly real lonesome. I hope somebody took good care of him."

Colin chuckled as he heard her fling herself off the chair and dash away. He could just imagine the glee on her expressive face as she ran. The kid would turn herself into a horse if she could.

Settling back with a smile, he wondered if Amy would ever outgrow her fixation for horses. Being so much younger than her two sisters and never having been allowed to mix with the slave children, she'd had no one to play with except the horses. . .and him. Bless her heart, she was the only family member who didn't pussyfoot around him since he'd come home.

He stood and counted his way to the door. Time to start learning how many paces there were to the stairs.

On his third trip to the staircase and back, he heard someone coming up the servants' staircase. Probably Benjamin bringing his tray of food. He'd wait just inside his room and hold the door open for the slave.

But the footsteps didn't sound heavy like the butler's. They sounded light. Feminine. Had Mariah volunteered to bring his meal, hoping to get another chance at him? His lips flattened into a grim line.

"Why, thank you, dear," his mother said as she passed him. "I was wondering how I'd manage that. Where should I put your dinner?"

He sighed with relief and closed the door then turned toward her voice. "The table between the chairs will be fine."

"Let me help you to the chair."

"It's not necessary, Mother. I know where it is." He moved cautiously toward it and sat down.

"Oh. How wonderful. Your sight is improving after all. I've been—"

He shook his head. "No, it hasn't. But if you'd please have a seat for a moment, I have something to say."

"So do I, dear." Her skirts swished softly as she seated herself. "That's why I brought your meal myself. I wanted to talk to you."

"About what?"

"A few minutes ago, one of the Tucker family servants came with a message saying they'd like to drop by after supper. Of course, I sent a return invitation that they join us for our meal. From the way Dennis was hugging Victoria yesterday, I fear he intends to offer for her, and you know how I feel about that. I absolutely refuse to give up one acre of our land, and your father knows that all too well. I figure with the Tuckers at our supper table, we'll have the advantage. Particularly if you are present."

Having remained quiet out of respect as she prattled on, the anger building inside him boiled over. "With the poor blind son present, you mean."

She gasped. "Not at all. I meant no such thing. I just felt that having another adult on our side would help the cause."

"Let me get this straight. You still consider Tori as property to be bargained over—unlike me. Now that I'm damaged, you'll gladly pass me off to a lowly bond servant." He sniffed in disdain.

His mother took a sharp intake of breath. "Why, what an outrageous thing to say."

"I agree." But he didn't soften his tone.

"Concerning Victoria, she's a young, impressionable girl who will fall in and out of love probably a dozen times between now and next year. And yes, I'd prefer she marry advantageously. It's what I've always desired for all our children."

"Yet you don't think it an advantage for her to live close by, where she could still be part of our lives, and we could visit her whenever we please."

She didn't respond for a second. "That *is* a lovely sentiment, however—"

"But you don't mind sending her away to some far-off port city, while you invite a scheming bond servant to be your new daughter. Is that right?"

He heard her sink back in the chair. "My. You are being vicious today. But considering your recent trauma, I shall make allowance for that and let it pass." Her hand covered his.

He flinched and pulled away from her touch.

"Colin, dear," she began evenly, in her most patient tone. "I have spent many hours in prayer since your return. Many hours. And when I saw Mariah collapse into heart-wrenching tears after you so rudely rejected her, I had not the slightest doubt those tears were real. Her heart was shattered. I know she loves you very deeply."

Colin gave an inaudible huff but let her continue.

"Now, as for her being a schemer, I can only say that her service to us and her care for the girls has been above reproach and far outweighs any amount of money you paid for her. My only regret is that I was forced to order her to take on the duties of a kitchen maid when we were shorthanded the day of the race. For quite a spell after that humiliation, she was hesitant to join us whenever we had visitors."

He considered that information before answering. "If what you say is even remotely true, it's all the more reason she should leave this house. Being married to a blind man is decidedly not advantageous for such a talented and comely lass. She could do far better."

A weary sigh issued from his mother. "Son, I'm afraid you don't know the first thing about love: true, God-given love between a man and a woman, the selfless kind than overcomes any obstacle and endures regardless of adversity." The rustle of her skirts indicated she'd risen. "I apologize if I've upset you. I take into account that your feelings are all topsy-turvy right now. As for Mariah, we can discuss her another time.

But for this evening, I expect you to be a gentleman and, if nothing else, help entertain our guests. After all, Dennis is your best friend."

He felt the breeze from her wake as she started for the door.

"I'll send Benjamin up later to help you select your clothing." Without further word, she left, her light footsteps fading as she went down the hall.

"Hmph." Colin snorted, knowing that if he didn't join the party she'd probably bring every last one of those guests right up to his room. And the last thing he needed was to have this last small piece of sanctuary totally overrun.

Sanctuary. . .where people sought safety in the Middle Ages.

Sanctuary. . .

His mind drifted to England, a land of green hedgerows and charming hamlets. He recalled the magnificent cathedrals he'd seen there: cool, quiet places where one could almost feel the presence of God. He'd felt that same quiet peace the last night before Fort Necessity was attacked, when he'd knelt down to pray right after he'd made God a promise.

How quickly he'd forgotten.

A ragged breath came from deep inside, and his shoulders slumped. "Forgive me, Father. I know I was growling at Mother, when all she wants is what's best for us—even if she does happen to be wrong. From now on, Lord, I'll try to pray first before opening my big mouth. Please keep reminding me to do that. And please give me the calm to be the gentleman Mother wants this evening."

He wanted to add something about Mariah but didn't know where to begin.

*

"Shh!" Mariah put a finger to her lips as she and Victoria passed Colin's door on their way to the girls' room just beyond. "He might be asleep." And she certainly wasn't up to facing another bout with him at the moment. Reaching Tori's chamber, she ushered the girl inside.

A giggle bubbled forth from Victoria, who'd been flighty since hearing her beloved would be coming to supper. "I just know Tuck is gonna ask

Papa for my hand, so I must look absolutely perfect." She twirled happily in a swirl of sprigged muslin skirts as she danced toward the dressing table. Tugging the ribbon holding back her curls, she carelessly tossed it away, then lifted her golden tresses to the top of her head and arched her brows as she bent to gaze at her likeness in the looking glass. "You simply have to make me look spectacular, Mariah. Please."

Mariah couldn't help a light laugh. "Not too spectacular. You don't want to appear obvious, do you? How about perfectly pretty, instead?"

Victoria pursed her lips, and her blue eyes sparkled with joy. "I suppose perfectly pretty will do." Scooping her skirt to one side, she dropped down onto the dressing table stool. But her smile wilted as Mariah stepped up behind her and picked up the brush. "No matter how many times I've told Mother I love Tuck, I know she doesn't believe me. He's not the son of a wealthy merchant, you know. She's sure to try and stop us."

Mariah's first instinct was to urge Tori to get her father alone and extract a promise from him to say yes to a match between her and the young man from the next plantation. Mr. Barclay had such a soft heart when it came to his girls.

But what would Rose say? The twinge of conscience clanged into her thoughts as surely as if Rose were present. "I think we should pray about it, sweetheart."

Victoria's eyes popped wide, as if that was the last thing she'd expected to come from Mariah's mouth.

Nevertheless, Mariah persisted. "Let's bow our heads, shall we?" She waited for Tori to follow suit. "Dear heavenly Father, we know that You love us, and because You do, You gave us the commandment to honor our parents. Sometimes that is really hard to do. But we know that our parents also love us and want what's best for us."

Tori interrupted. "But, Lord, You said in Corinthians that it's better to marry than to burn, and I burn with love for Tuck."

That was too much for Mariah. She sputtered into laughter, and Victoria joined in. After a few moments, Mariah regained control and purpose. She wrapped her arms around her sweet charge and gave her a squeeze, then bowed her head once more. "Yes, Father, You certainly know Victoria's wish in the matter. We ask that You please soften Mistress Barclay's heart concerning Tori's deepest desire."

And Colin's, concerning my own. . . She released a pent-up sigh.

Chapter 32

After the butler helped him into clothing appropriate for the evening, Colin relaxed in his room. Or tried to relax. For the past two hours there'd been a steady cacophony of giggles, loud thumps, and slamming doors and drawers in the next chamber. The racket coming from Victoria's room seemed to have no end.

"From all the commotion, you'd think they were preparing for a coronation," he muttered. But then, for all he knew, that sort of nonsense went on all the time in the female world. He'd never before been confined to his room long enough to overhear the way his sisters conducted themselves when preparing for company. Truth was, the womenfolk in the family always emerged from their cocoons looking quite beautiful. . . especially Mariah. He called forth a vision of her in lavender ruffles that complemented her ebony curls and incredible eyes, then dismissed it with a scowl.

Someone rapped on his door and opened it.

"Mastah Colin, yo' folks wants you to go greet de guests now. I's to take y'all down."

"Thanks, Benjamin." Colin nodded and made a point of not hesitating as he crossed the room. "Don't take me down at such a slow pace that I look helpless."

"No, sah. We'll high-step it all de way."

Grinning at the mental image that conjured up, Colin took the butler's arm. "Have the Tuckers arrived yet?"

"Dey was jest turnin' on our lane when I come up fo' y'all."

"Good. Then I should reach the foyer before they knock."

"Dat's what de Missus say."

Colin grunted. For all her fine words, it appeared Mother didn't want him to be an embarrassment any more than he did himself.

As they started down the stairs, doors opened and closed behind him with a flurry of female whispers and the rapid patter of approaching slippers. The girls—and most likely Mariah—were coming in all their glory. They called out greetings as they raced past him.

"Hi, Colin."

"Love you, Colin."

Then he heard much more sedate footsteps. "Good evening, Mr. Barclay." Mariah matched her steps with his and the butler's as they continued down the wide staircase. "You look quite dashing this evening."

Colin reminded himself to be polite. Still, he didn't want her to attach herself to him. The Tuckers would be at the door any second. "Thank you. Your perfume smells nice."

His mother's voice drifted from the foyer as she instructed the girls to quiet down.

The brass door knocker tapped.

Colin's spirits sank. He had yet to reach the marble floor. How many steps remained to the bottom landing before the guests were admitted inside?

Mariah threaded her arm through his. "Benjamin, you may go answer the door. I'll allow Colin to escort me the rest of the way."

"Yes'm."

Before Colin could protest, the butler hurried away, leaving him at Mariah's mercy. He heard the door open.

"Last step," Mariah said softly. She moved with him toward the cluster of happy voices.

"Good evening, everyone," Dennis's mother gushed. "It was so nice of you to invite us. And Colin, it's great to see you up and about."

Mr. Tucker stepped closer and squeezed Colin's shoulder, speaking in his booming voice. "I second that, son."

"Yes, old man," Tuck piped in. "You're a far sight better lookin' than you were when we dragged you back here."

Colin nodded and smiled toward each voice. "We're glad you could come."

"And Mariah." Tuck spoke from right in front of her and Colin. "You look marvelous this evening."

"Thank you."

"I'm sure you look dashing as well, Tuck," Colin chided, "if Tori's sugary welcome was any indication."

"Colin! Please!" his sister gasped.

Mariah gave a quick yank to his sleeve.

"Only teasing, sis."

Mother finally came to the rescue. "Helen, Drew, it's such a warm evening I thought we might be more comfortable out on the terrace. Shall we?"

"Sounds delightful, Cora, my dear," Father said, taking charge.

"Heather?" Colin heard Tuck say, and he knew his friend would be escorting both sisters outside.

Colin grimaced, wishing he'd spoken sooner himself so he could walk with someone instead of scheming Mariah. "Amy?"

Mariah turned him to follow the others and spoke in a whisper. "Amy had supper earlier. Your mother thought it best, considering her, shall we say, indelicate way with words."

He emitted a low chuckle. "I'll bet she did."

"It's wonderful to see you in such high spirits, Colin," Dennis's mother said, walking ahead of him and Mariah. "You always were such a brave boy."

The pity in her tone made Colin want to retch.

Mariah, however, tightened her hold. "I understand that your son was also quite brave, Mistress Tucker. Victoria said he, too, was wounded."

"He was?" Her voice shook. "Dennis. Is it true? You were shot? Why didn't you tell me? You might've been killed."

Tuck quickly put her at ease. "A musket ball merely grazed my shoulder, Mom, that's all. Nothing to get upset about. It was all but healed by the time I got home."

As the woman questioned her son further, Colin felt compelled to express his appreciation to Mariah for steering the attention away from him. He leaned close to her scented warmth. "Thank you."

"No need."

A waft of cooler air brushed his face. They'd reached their destination, and he hadn't made a single misstep. He had Mariah to thank for that, too.

The chairs scraping around the table ceased quickly as everyone found seats. Colin managed to hold out Mariah's chair for her before taking his own. Her perfume so sweetened the air around him, he wondered if she'd applied the entire bottle.

Footsteps from behind preceded the aroma of roast pork, mashed potatoes, spiced applesauce, and collard greens, as the servants carried platters of food to the table and dished out portions to everyone. Colin appreciated having something besides perfume to inhale.

At the head of the group, Father eased his chair back and stood to offer the blessing. "Our most gracious heavenly Father, we thank You for this opportunity to fellowship with dear friends and enjoy the bounty You so faithfully provide. We ask Your blessing upon our food and our conversation. And we are most grateful for Your mercy in bringing our sons home to us again. May You watch over the colony of Virginia and the other colonies during this time of trial. Amen."

At least he didn't mention my personal trial. I'm thankful for that small mercy. Other sounds drifted to Colin's ears—the snapping of napkins to be placed on laps, the tap of forks against plates. He hoped he could manage the task of eating without looking foolish. While Mistress Tucker began expounding on Mother's lovely garden, Colin edged his fingers up from his lap to feel for his napkin.

Mariah's hand covered his and guided it to the cloth beneath his fork, then quickly slid her fingers away.

"Oh, yes," Mother said. "The star of jasmine cuttings I ordered last spring have done beautifully. Already they are climbing the railings and have such a sweet, heady, scent. Especially at eventide."

While everyone delved into the food, Colin nibbled on a buttered roll he'd felt on his plate.

Mariah cleared her throat. "Mistress Barclay, the pork is so deliciously tender, it falls apart at the touch of a fork."

Already having detected the meat from its aroma, Colin knew Mariah was trying to provide information for his benefit, and he appreciated her thoughtfulness. He managed to spear a piece of it and forked it to his lips.

"Why, thank you, dear. We are fortunate to have Eloise's skills. She's always been a wonderful cook."

"I agree, Cora," Tuck's mother said. "One of these days, I'd be most grateful if you'd send her over to teach our cook how to make those wonderful, flaky pastries she does so well. Hettie has never been able to master them."

Mother gave a throaty laugh. "I can send her, but I doubt she'll give up her secret recipes. They were passed down to her by a French Creole cook at her prior owner's."

"Speaking of the French," Father cut in, "when my daughter and I rode to Alexandria to retrieve Colin's horse this afternoon, I picked up a newspaper from Philadelphia. The publisher, a man named Benjamin Franklin, wrote a very interesting piece stating that if the colonies don't start cooperating with each other soon, the French could very easily concentrate their efforts, and with the help of their Indian allies, they could pick us off one by one."

"A pity he didn't write that before our valiant boys were forced to go to battle with too few men and insufficient supplies," Mr. Tucker said on a wry note. He set down his glass with a click.

"At least we Virginians put forth an effort," Tuck boasted. "And now, at long last, the House of Burgesses has agreed to spend twenty thousand pounds toward the cause."

Father chuckled. "Yes. And they finally got Governor Dinwiddie to sign it, including the rider abolishing that gold pistole fee on land patents. From what I heard, Dinwiddie was livid when he saw that proposed—again."

"Well," Mr. Tucker replied. "I, for one, am glad the rider was included. Gold is much too hard to come by in the colonies as it is, without shipping it over to England to fill their coffers."

"Getting back to that newspaper article," Father said, "there's a very-to-the-point picture in it. One of a snake being cut into several pieces, with the name of a colony on each section. Below it read, 'Join or Die.' Very apropos, wouldn't you say?"

Mother coughed lightly into her napkin. "I think discussing such a topic at the dinner table is definitely not apropos. Would you gentlemen mind saving this conversation for after our meal?"

"Quite right, Cora, my love. Till later, gentlemen."

Colin could almost see him raising his lemonade in a salute and tipping his head.

"Speaking of later," Mr. Tucker chimed in, "I have a bit of business I'd like to discuss with you and your son after supper."

Detecting an almost imperceptible titter from Victoria, Colin surmised she would be the topic. But why did his and Tuck's parents want him involved?

"I see." A curt note tinged Mother's voice. "Well, Eloise has made some delightful apple dumplings for our dessert. After we've had a chance to enjoy them, Helen and the rest of us ladies shall wait for you menfolk in the parlor. I do hope you won't be overlong. The girls have some lovely entertainment planned." She rang a silver bell to call for dessert.

Colin picked up his fork and made another stab at his plate. He still had some food to take care of. All in all, though, this promised to be a lively evening.

"Would you gentlemen care for a cigar?" Colin's father closed the library door for privacy.

"Don't mind if I do," Mr. Tucker responded.

Colin heard the humidor being opened and smelled the rich aroma of tobacco.

"I selected the best leaves myself," his father said, his inflection proud.

Not eager to handle something with one end on fire, Colin gave a negative wave of his hand. "Not just now, Pa."

"None for me either," Tuck said.

Colin stifled a smirk at the uncharacteristic hint of nervousness in his friend's voice. No doubt Tuck's palms were sweating, as well.

"Then let us be seated." Father spoke pleasantly. "We might as well be comfortable while we discuss our business."

Tuck took hold of Colin's arm and turned him a bit. "Come sit with me on the settee, old man." The slight tremble in his fingers on Colin's sleeve was more than evident. Obviously he needed moral support.

As they settled back against the damask upholstery, faint music drifted from the parlor across the way. Colin detected only the harpsichord and flute and figured Tori was too overwrought to play her violin. He figured she'd perched on whatever chair had the best view of the library doors.

Mr. Tucker cleared his throat. "I'm sure it's no surprise why we're here this evening. Our son Dennis has expressed a desire to wed your daughter Victoria. I've been told the only impediment to a marriage between the pair is the matter of a dowry acceptable to us both. Is that correct?"

Seated beside Colin, Tuck nudged Colin's shoe with his.

"Yes, that is true," Father answered. "Cora and I—well, the whole family, to be entirely correct—think very highly of Dennis. He more than proved his worth by not shirkin' his duty last winter."

No one spoke for a few seconds. Colin had expected his father to say more, to state the dowry he and Mother, especially, were willing to send with Tori—unless he was waiting to hear Mr. Tucker's proposal first.

Mr. Tucker shifted in his seat. "Since you and I both agree our farmland is worth far more than a mere sack of coin that is easily squandered, Dennis and I have come up with a simple solution. If Colin would concede to deed over his property on the South Fork of the Potomac, it would in no way diminish your fields. You could reimburse Colin the price of that land, plus a small profit, of course."

Caught off guard by the suggestion, Colin suddenly realized why the Tuckers had wanted him present. He hoped his expression hadn't betrayed the disappointment that sank in his heart like a rock. Not only had his own dreams been tied to that parcel, but it hurt to think they knew he'd never bc able to fulfill those dreams now.

Obviously his father noticed his lack of response. "Tuck, what do you propose to bring to the marriage?"

"M–me? I. . .uh—"

Mr. Tucker cut in. "Eldon, you know Dennis is sole heir to all our properties."

"Quite. But I'd like to hear what his plans happen to be for my daughter."

"Plans?" Tuck finally managed. "I plan to love her and cherish her, sir. And the moment you agree to our marriage, I plan to start building a cottage for us." He turned slightly in his seat. "A cozy little honeymoon cottage near where the brook comes out of the woods in the west section. Our own private place."

The more his friend rattled on, so full of dreams for Tori and himself, the more dejected Colin became. If he hadn't lost his sight, he might've been discussing his marriage to Mariah this evening.

Father interrupted his thoughts. "Well. That would please Victoria, I'm sure. But as to the South Fork parcel, that is not my decision. It's for my son to decide."

Hoping to hide his melancholy, Colin sat up straighter and raised his chin. He forced himself to speak in a normal tone. "It sounds like a reasonable solution to me."

In a flash, Tuck grabbed him and hugged him, thumping him on the back. "Thank you, my friend. Thank you." He sprang to his feet. "I must go tell Tori."

"If you happen to see Benjamin in the foyer," Colin called after him, "tell him I need to speak to him." He lumbered to his feet and turned in the direction of his father. "I'm rather tired now. Would you give the ladies my regrets?"

Chapter 33

Mariah could scarcely concentrate on the classical pieces she'd chosen to play for the dinner guests. Though she rendered each one flawlessly, her attention remained focused across the way, her angst easily as keen as Victoria's. The girl sat forward in her chair, her gaze fixed on the library doors.

Hoping against hope that by some miracle Colin's desire to marry her would be rekindled as he listened to his friend's plea for Tori's hand, Mariah released a ragged sigh. Surely he'd noticed what an asset she'd been to him this evening. What an asset she would always be.

The library door swung open, and Mariah's fingers accidentally struck the wrong keys. Fortunately, no one seemed to notice as Dennis rushed across the hall to the parlor, grinning from ear to ear.

Mariah couldn't help smiling herself when Victoria jumped to her feet and flew into the young man's open arms.

Mistress Barclay, however, didn't appear so thrilled. The woman's grim expression revealed the realization that her lifelong plans for her daughter had been thwarted.

But Dennis Tucker's mother rushed to the couple and embraced them both. "Praise be! I have a new daughter."

"And I have a new brother!" Heather laughed and joined the celebrants.

Tuck drew Tori close to his side and strode to her mother, who remained seated and unsmiling. "I hope you will be happy for us. It won't be necessary for you to give up any of your land holdings."

She tilted her perfectly coiffed head. "I don't understand. Your father is willing to accept money instead?"

"Not exactly." He gave her a smug smile and hugged Victoria. "Colin has agreed to deed his land on the South Fork to me, and in turn, your husband will compensate him."

Stunned by that news, Mariah rose from the harpsichord stool. "Are you referring to the parcels you and he bought in the backcountry?" The land Colin had promised to take her to see.

"That's right." He turned back to Mistress Barclay.

Her demeanor changed to one of approval as she stood to her feet and took their hands in hers. "Why, what a perfect solution. I'd never have thought of it."

Tuck shrugged a shoulder. "Well, the property is in question at the moment because of the French. But I'm willing to gamble that the colonies will come together soon and push the French forces back to Canada, where they belong."

"I'm. . .so pleased for you." Mariah somehow managed weak congratulations as she started for the doorway. She could no longer bear to be around Victoria and Tuck and their overflowing joy.

Mr. Barclay and Colin emerged from the library at that moment. "I'll return shortly," the older man called over his shoulder as he and his son started up the staircase.

Mariah's spirits sank even further. So Colin also felt the need to escape. Obviously he didn't want to be near her after having just forfeited the land he promised would be theirs alone.

She clenched her teeth as rage overtook her despair, then composed herself and turned to the happy couple with a forced smile. "I'm truly thrilled for you both. But I'm afraid I have a bit of a headache, so if you'll please excuse me. . ." She hurried out of the parlor, almost crashing into Dennis's father as he came to join the lovebirds. "Forgive me," she blurted but kept going.

On her way up the stairs, she met Mr. Barclay descending, a huge grin broadening his mustache. She breezed past him with a polite nod.

Her anger continued to build. At the top landing, Mariah glared at Colin's door. It was high time she gave him a piece of her mind. Marching straight for his room, she reached for the handle. But her hand froze before touching the metal. Were she to barge in and start yelling at him, she'd end up crying. And the last thing she wanted to do was bawl in front of him over this latest all-too-evident rejection of her. She'd already been humiliated beyond belief.

Blinking back stinging tears, she continued on to her and Amy's door, only then remembering that the child was in the room. Her shoulders sagged. Taking a deep breath to fortify herself, she walked in.

Amy tossed a stuffed horse aside and jumped up from her bed. "Well? What did Poppy say?"

"He's agreed to allow them to marry." Surprised at her own flat tone, Mariah propped up a faint smile.

"Oh, goody. Tuck is always so much fun."

"Indeed. Why don't you go downstairs and congratulate them?"

The words had scarcely left her mouth before Amy charged out of the room and down the hall.

Thank goodness. Some peace at last. Without so much as a backward look, Mariah crossed to her chamber and the blessed darkness within, closing the door behind her. Hot tears streamed down her cheeks before she was halfway to her bed.

Her foot tangled in a carelessly discarded garment, and she stumbled to her knees, catching herself at the edge of the bed. She sobbed even harder. All was lost now.

Sagging against the mattress, her head drooped as she gave vent to her grief. Then she peered up through blurry eyes. "Why did this have to happen, Father? What have I done that was so bad You'd allow things to turn out this wrong? I haven't flirted with any of the men who come here—even though You know they stared at me. Nor did I go after those young swains in Williamsburg who were oh, so willing. I've been trying to be good like Rose." She searched the darkness. "Are You even there, Lord?"

Utterly bereft, Mariah collapsed in her sorrow. It was true. God didn't care about her at all.

From somewhere deep inside, Mariah sensed a voice telling her to open her Bible at the bookmark.

The bookmark. Where had Mistress Barclay left off last Sunday and instructed her to continue with the girls? She couldn't remember. Colin had come home then, and she'd simply forgotten the passage they'd been discussing.

Pulling herself up from the floor, she drew a handkerchief from her skirt pocket to wipe her eyes and nose, then lit her lamp. She rummaged through her stack of books till she found the leather-bound volume.

The protruding bookmark caught her eye, and she admired the delicate flowers Rose had embroidered all around its edges when she'd fashioned it as a Christmas gift years ago. *Oh, Rose, if only you were here with me to hold me and love me. I'm so alone.*

Dabbing at a new onslaught of tears, Mariah sank onto her bed and opened the Bible. A tiny smile tugged at the corners of her lips when it opened to the preachy book of James. Her gaze immediately was drawn to a verse in the fourth chapter:

"Humble yourselves in the sight of the Lord, and he shall lift you up."

"It always comes back to that, doesn't it, Father? Seems I'm always praying for what I want, working and trying to that end. And it always falls apart. I give up." A new river of tears flowed like rain on a windowpane. *I give up.* She'd never felt so defeated in her life. *Dear God, You say You want us to come humbly to You. Well then, here I am. This miserable mess I've made of my life and myself is Yours if You want it. From now on, whatever You want me to do or say or be, I'll obey You. From this day forth I'm Yours to do with as You wish.*

An indescribable warmth began to flow through her being, filling her, fuller and fuller, until there was no room left for pain. All pain, all angst, all her sorrow miraculously evaporated like dew in the sunshine.

God did love her after all. He loved her so much that He was hugging her from the inside out, making her new.

She picked up the Bible to read again. She wanted to know more. So much more. She flipped to the Gospel of John. Rose always said that was a good place to start.

———

Mariah didn't have the slightest concept of how long she'd been reading her Bible when the outer door burst open, and excited chatter and laughter spilled in as three giggly girls returned.

Without knocking, a glowing Victoria whirled into Mariah's chamber, followed by her sisters. "Isn't this the most marvelous day there ever was?" Flinging her arms wide, she closed her dreamy eyes and twirled in a circle.

"Yes, dear." Amazingly, Mariah meant it from the heart. "A most marvelous day, indeed."

The threesome sprawled onto Mariah's bed, all talking at once.

"Wait!" Laughing, she laid aside the Bible. "One at a time, please."

Victoria grinned. "Me first. After all, it's my wedding day we're talking about." She snagged Mariah's hand and held it to her bosom. "And you must, you absolutely must, come with me to the dressmaker to help me choose the loveliest satin and lace. My bridal gown must be the most perfect gown ever, the envy of every girl in the colony."

"Tell Mariah how Tuck talked Mama into having the wedding in just two months." Heather jabbed her sister with an elbow. "He really, really wants to marry Tori."

Mariah's mouth gaped. "Two months! That's an awfully short time to plan a wedding."

"Actually," Victoria said, "it'll be in ten weeks. That's when the leaves should start displaying their beautiful fall colors. Can't you just picture the guests coming up our lane with the trees all ablaze? And what do you think about weaving autumn branches into a wedding arbor?"

Not to be outdone, Heather inserted her intentions. "Of course, I'll be playing something airy on the flute to go with the wind rustling through the leaves. It'll be perfect."

Heather is turning into quite the romantic, Mariah thought with a smile.

Amy rose to her knees. "And Mama said I could go with Poppy to deliver invitations to all the neighbors."

"Oh, yes." Victoria tousled her kid sister's hair. "Those to Mother's family in Boston will have to go out in the post right away. Wouldn't it be wonderful if some of our relatives came from such a distance? Just for my wedding?"

Laughter bubbled out of Mariah as she drew Tori into a hug. "Yes, sweet girl. It would be wonderful. And you're quite right. This is a most marvelous day."

Chapter 34

Colin seethed as incessant plans for Victoria's wedding bombarded him from all directions at the breakfast table. Was there nothing else of worth in the world to discuss? The sole reason he'd come downstairs to eat with the family was to prove to them and himself that he could maneuver his way to the dining room without help. Now he regretted his stupidity.

"Mariah," Tori gushed, "what would you think of a rich brown chiffon threaded with gold? With my golden hair and the vibrant autumn leaves, brown would be truly stunning. Can't you just imagine?"

Mother spoke up. "Darling, we have such a short time to plan. There's no time for ordering special fabrics. I'm afraid you'll have to choose from the materials Mistress Henderson has available in her shop."

"Quite right." Mariah's teacup clinked against the saucer as she set it down. "I noticed some lovely silks from India when last we were there. But rest assured, Tuck is so eager to make you his bride, your gown won't matter. He won't see anything beyond the love in your eyes."

Pa harrumphed. "He's a bit too eager, if you ask me."

At this, all the women broke into laughter.

Et tu, Mariah? Colin grimaced and let out a disgusted breath. One would think she'd at least have the decency not to flaunt her lack of sorrow over their broken engagement in front of him.

As if oblivious to his displeasure, Mother and the girls continued parrying wedding ideas back and forth. Beside him, Mariah reached over and squeezed his hand.

He snatched it away and felt around for his fork. Picking it up, he shoveled food into his mouth, no longer caring how much fell to the table or dropped on his clothes. He just wanted to get out of there as soon as possible.

After a few quick bites—each one punctuated by a feminine titter or high-pitched shriek—he shoved back his chair and got up.

"Colin, dear," his mother said, "must you leave us so soon?"

He turned for the doorway and mentally tallied the eight paces it would take to get him there. "I have a headache."

"Another one? How dreadful. Eldon, perhaps you should ride for the doctor this morning. I'm sure he must have some powders that could help."

Colin shook his head. "It's not that kind of headache." He made a point of striding in the direction he fervently hoped would take him out of the room and not into a wall. After he managed to pass safely through the opening dividing the dining and parlor rooms, he heard Mariah's cheerful voice.

"Ladies, I think perhaps we should temper our exuberance whenever Colin is present so we don't upset him. Don't you agree, Mistress Barclay?"

He paused to hear his mother's answer. "Yes. We were quite thoughtless, carrying on so. We should be more considerate."

Hmph. First insensitivity, and now pity? That enraged Colin all the more. He thrust a foot forward, only to realize he'd lost count and had no idea where he was. He had to resort to feeling his way the remainder of the distance to the foyer. After a few false starts, he finally felt the marble tiles beneath his shoe. Far enough. "Benjamin!"

The door to the butlery opened. "Yessuh?"

"Would you accompany me to my room? I'd like to speak to you."

"Yessuh." The African came to his side and clamped a big hand around Colin's elbow.

Colin began to relax as they walked toward the staircase, and some of his ire subsided. But not all. "Please inform Eloise I'll be taking all my meals in my room for the time being."

He felt a slight stiffening in Benjamin's touch. "But suh, the missus won't be happy 'bout dat."

"That may be, but things aren't always to our liking, are they?"

"No suh. Dat, fo' sure, is de truth."

Detecting an underlying sadness in the butler's voice, Colin realized that he, too, had just been insensitive. His blindness had cost him a good deal of his freedom, but Benjamin had never known any freedom, not from the day he was born. He gentled his tone. "Benjamin, you've been such a faithful servant my whole life, and I want you to know I appreciate it. If there is ever anything you want or need, don't hesitate to ask."

Thank goodness for Amy, Colin thought as the two of them headed down toward the stable—even if she did walk him into walls and ruts from time to time. But he was getting a bit better at navigating with the help of a cane. He just wished it was a few inches longer.

With all the preparations for the upcoming wedding, the past several days had been to his advantage. Everyone in the household was so busy rushing about, they'd pretty much left him to his own devices. After all, heaven forbid if a wedding were to take place when a speck of dust remained in the house, or a stray leaf should fall upon the perfect lawn.

His shin banged into something hard. "Oww!"

"Oops. Sorry." Amy squeezed his hand. "I didn't steer you over enough to pass the water trough."

He exhaled a disgruntled breath and reached down to rub the knot he could already feel forming.

"Amy, you always need to let Colin know what's ahead of him," Geoff reminded her.

Colin raised his chin in greeting. "I heard you were back from delivering the horses to the Kinyons." That was the main reason he'd come to the stable in the first place. He was eager to hear about the trip.

"Aye." The trainer took Colin's other elbow. "How about a cup of tea? We have a lot of catching up to do. And Amy, why don't you go help Old Samuel? I believe he's currying your pony right now."

On their way to the tack room, Colin inhaled the familiar, welcoming smells of leather and oils and smiled in appreciation.

Geoff guided him to a seat, then poured tea into two mugs and sat nearby. He immediately began rattling off details about the mares that had foaled recently, which horses had been sold, and the racing times of the three fastest ones. "By the way, I took a good look at Storm this morning. He should muscle up again within the next few weeks. I don't know yet if he'll ever be as fast as he was before. Looks like he took a real beating during the time you were involved with the militia."

Colin gave him a droll smile. "He's just lucky we got back before he was served up for dinner. Our food supply was down to nothin' by the time we reached the first settlement and could buy enough grain and meal to see us the rest of the way. But Storm has already proved himself. He'll make a great stud." Which brought him to the real reason he'd come to the stable. "How was your visit with the Kinyons?"

He heard Geoff stretch his legs out in front of him. "They were surprised and thrilled when I delivered the horses, but Nate Kinyon said you didn't owe him anything. He only accepted them because you were so bent on rewarding him."

"He's right." Colin nodded. "I was. It's important to me for Nate and Rose to have them." He paused. "What about his wife? What did you think of Rose?" He took another sip of tea.

"Hmm. I'd have to say she doesn't have Miss Harwood's striking beauty, but she's comely enough. Her kind of beauty comes from inside. A God-given goodness, you might say. It's hard not to look at her and admire her."

Colin cocked his head to one side. "I'm sure you're right. And to think I could've bid on her that day, instead of a—"

"Aye." Geoff took a last gulp of tea and set down his mug. "But Kinyon mentioned that his wife believed her sister had grown up a lot since she's been here with your family, considering she was a rather fickle, feckless girl in her younger days."

"More of an opportunist, I'd say," Colin said wryly. "Nevertheless, Mariah was actually quite put out when I ended our betrothal." For some reason, it was important that people knew it was he, not Mariah, who ended the engagement.

"I'd imagine it must be hard having her in the house with you now. You might consider solving that problem by giving her her freedom."

Colin grunted. "That's been done."

"You don't say. Then why is she still here?"

A smirk played across Colin's mouth. "I believe she thinks she'll eventually wear me down. But that's not gonna happen."

Geoffrey didn't respond right away. Colin could hear him toying with the empty cup. "Now that you mention it, I don't mind telling you I've had my own doubts about her sincerity. While you were away in England, she would glide herself down here in those expensive clothes of hers, asking me all manner of theological questions. But once you returned so eager to see her, she never again came flattering me with her sweet smile to ask my learned opinion about some Bible passage."

This information concerning his devious wench niggled at Colin, but he refused to be affected by it. After all, hadn't he made some promises to the Lord, of late? "I'd be interested in some friendly theological debates myself. I'll hog-tie Amy to keep her put long enough for her to read some scripture to me. What book would you suggest we start with?"

"Colin? You in there?" Tuck's voice floated toward him from outside.

"Yes. Come on in." He noticed the glow from the doorway darken with a shadowy specter as his friend entered the tack room.

"I brought Duchess." A furry head slid onto Colin's knee.

Having already detected the characteristic panting of the friendly dog, Colin scratched the collie behind her ears. "How ya doin', old girl?"

"Have a seat," Geoff offered.

"Thanks." The other end of the bench complained as Tuck sat down. "Mom an' me was laughin' last night about the way Duchess used to herd my little brother Sam away from the outside fires, horses an' carriages when he was little. That dog's always been a great natural herder. And the thought came to us she might be a sight better than Amy at walkin' with you, Col. You could keep Duchess on a short leash, right beside you."

Colin arched his brows, considering the offer. "It's worth a try. You sure you don't mind loanin' her to me?"

Tuck responded with a chuckle. "She'd probably be happy to escape Sammy. The kid's gettin' too big to ride her anymore, but he keeps tryin' anyway."

"Hi, Tuck. Hi, Duchess," Amy said out of the blue. Colin hadn't even heard her come in. "I heard what y'all were just talkin' about."

That didn't surprise Colin. She never missed anything—except telling him about that water trough, of course. His shin still throbbed.

"You mean about Sammy tryin' to ride the dog?" Tuck asked.

"Uh-huh. And I got a splendid idea. How about we swap my pony for Duchess?"

Colin tucked his chin. Were all girls fickle? "I thought you loved Patches."

"I do. I love him a whole lot. He's been the bestest. But I'm growin' up, and it's time I had a real horse, not just a pony."

All three men chuckled at the bodacious imp.

"So you think you're big enough now for a Thoroughbred, is that right?" Colin turned toward Geoffrey. "What do you think, Mr. Scott? Is Miss Amanda ready for a real horse?"

"Hmm. What one did you have in mind, missy?"

"Russet Knight."

Colin almost choked. "He's the fastest one in the stable. You'll start on Snowflake."

"*Snowflake!*" Amy moaned. "She's slow as molasses."

Tuck entered the mix. "Plenty fast enough for an eight-year-old."

"*Eight!* I'll have you know I'm nine and a half."

"Eight, nine, or ten," Colin said, "it's the pony or the mare. Take your choice."

She released a snort of defeat. "Oh, all right. Snowflake."

"And one more thing, little sis. Don't be in such a hurry to grow up. We'd all miss havin' you around. A lot." *Especially me*, Colin added silently. She'd brought the only little sparks of happiness he'd had in his life.

Chapter 35

U sing her very best penmanship as she wrote out wedding invitations, Mariah found it almost impossible to concentrate on the task. An hour ago, Colin, Amy, and that exceptionally intelligent dog had passed right by her on their way out to the stables. She couldn't help glancing up from the table on the terrace every so often and gazing toward the barn, but they were nowhere in sight.

She chided herself for being concerned. Far better to pay attention to the costly paper Mistress Barclay had been hesitant to risk at the hands of her daughters. Surely her fingers would stay steady long enough to pen this one last note.

The mistress and the two older girls would be home soon from yet another gown fitting. Then, thank heavens, they'd all sit down and help address the invitations. How could one family have so many acquaintances?

Mariah smiled, remembering how Amy had chattered incessantly about the morrow, when she and her father would ride into Alexandria with invitations needing to be sent out on north- and south-bound coastal packets. Then they would deliver the remainder personally to all their local friends. That would be the highlight of the entire affair for the girl. The child had spoken of little else for days. And most important, she'd sit proudly astride her new Thoroughbred, a handsome chestnut with a white star centered between its huge brown eyes.

As Mariah sprinkled silver dust on the last invitation to dry it, she caught movement on the edge of her vision. Colin and his sister were leaving the paddocks behind and heading toward the manse. Amazingly, instead of holding on to Colin, Amy was skipping backward ahead of him.

His whole demeanor had improved dramatically since the collie's arrival a couple of weeks ago. Colin now walked with assurance, appearing as tall and confident as when she'd first met him. He no longer squinted in the sunlight and had regained most of the weight lost during the militia's weeks of privation. Of course, the fancy cane he used added additional flair.

Duchess wagged her long, furry tail against Colin's leg as they walked, no doubt shedding hairs on his breeches. Though Mistress Barclay had allowed the animal to stay inside the house, she'd frown whenever she spied a hair on her son or the furniture. She kept the maids busy searching for each and every strand or tuft of rust-colored fur—even though the dog had been bathed twice and brushed daily since its arrival.

As Colin and Amy neared, Mariah's gaze lingered on his strong, handsome face. She rarely saw him for more than a few seconds here and there since he took his meals in his room and declined to spend evenings in the parlor with the family. As much as she longed to be near him, she suspected he stayed away because of her. She had finally reached the conclusion that for this family's peace and happiness to be restored, she would have to leave. And she would, once Victoria was married and on her way.

Besides, Rose was in the family way now, with her first baby due to be born in December. Mariah didn't want to miss the blessed event. Her hand moved to the letter in her pocket as it often had since she received the gladsome news yesterday.

Duchess started barking.

Looking to see what had drawn the dog's attention, Mariah spotted the Barclay landau coming up the lane. A second carriage followed.

The family was not expecting guests. Mariah stood for a better view. "Oh, dear." She recognized Mistress Engleside and her two rowdy sons, whose towheads bobbed up and down with the vehicle's movement.

Amy, however, let out an exuberant yelp and ran to meet her young friends. No doubt the boys' feet wouldn't hit the ground more than two seconds before the scuffling and chasing around would start.

Mariah glanced back to Colin. Though his sister had deserted him, his steps hadn't faltered. Still, perhaps she should go to him, in case he needed assistance navigating through the carriages and people. She doubted he'd appreciate help, especially from her, but she descended the veranda steps anyway as everyone converged amid happy chatter and the high-pitched greetings of the children.

Colin and Duchess halted just short of the first conveyance. "Good afternoon to you all," he said. "If you'll please excuse me, I was about to retire to my room."

"Colin, dear," his mother called after him, but he didn't turn back.

Mariah watched in amazement as he quickly found the steps with his cane and mounted them. He and the dog disappeared inside the house. She bit back her disappointment that he'd passed right by her again as if she didn't exist.

"Oh, blast!" Amy latched on to Mariah's arm as the chattering womenfolk started toward the house. "Would you do me a favor, Mariah? Please, please, please?"

Mariah eyed her. "What have you gotten yourself into now?" The boys, appearing none too clean, crowded close.

Amy tossed her blond head. "It's nothin' like that. I promised Colin I'd read to him as soon as we got back. And now I can't. I have company."

"But you know he doesn't want anyone but you to read to him."

The child fluttered a hand as if that was of little import. "Oh, he's not nearly so grumpy anymore, and you read so much better than me." She bobbed up to her tiptoes with a pleading look. "We're readin' some real interestin' stuff right now. Even Colin couldn't answer some of my questions."

"You don't say. And what were you reading?" Mariah stalled, warring against her desire to be near her beloved for a few minutes.

"About the apostle Philip and some man called a eunuch. Colin tried to 'splain somethin' about bulls and oxen, but I thought it was a *man* Philip was baptizin'. Maybe you can figure it out and let me know later. Will you do it? Please, please?"

"Very well." Mariah knew she shouldn't have agreed. *But, Lord, is it terribly selfish of me to want to be near him, speak with him, this one last time?*

"Thank you! Thank you!" Amy grabbed Mariah in a hug, then hitched up her skirts and took off for the stables with the boys.

Returning inside, Mariah cast a furtive glance at the staircase Colin had ascended moments before, and uncertainty slithered through her. He'd be most displeased. But perhaps after she let him know she'd be leaving they could have a pleasant chat. . . .

She took a deep breath, then bypassed the stairs and headed for the butlery door. She'd stop at the kitchen for a tray of refreshments, to give him time to get settled and allow her heart to stop its infernal pounding.

Duchess, lying at Colin's feet, gave a throaty bark as the chamber door opened.

He smirked. "I reckoned you'd run off to play with those other brats, Amy."

A moment of silence.

"It's not Amy. She asked me to come read to you in her place."

"Mariah." The woman never missed a chance. "That won't be necessary."

She moved closer. "Truly. 'Twould be my pleasure."

Colin inhaled, recognizing the fragrance that was hers alone. Why did she always have to smell so good? And why did her voice have to sound smooth and rich as warm honey?

"I brought some refreshments." Coming entirely too close, she placed the tray on the table.

He gave a resigned sigh. If she was going to insist on staying in this house with the blessing of every other member of the family, he might as well get used to it—for all the good it would do her. "As you wish."

He heard her fussing around, placing items on the table and removing the tray. "Eloise sent up a bit of her iced peach tea and some spice scones."

"Please thank her for me."

"I'll do that. Is it all right if I give Duchess a scone?"

"I reckon." He could tell from the rustle of skirts that she'd taken her seat, and he surmised she was probably wearing that shiny emerald gown that complemented her coloring so well. Strange how much stronger sounds and smells affected him now that he could no longer see.

"I have to tell you," Mariah said, "how much reading for you has improved Amy's reading skills."

He nodded. "She does seem to be getting better. She still needs to spell out big words, though."

Mariah gave a light laugh. "I still remember the first time I saw her. You were so right; she is a handful. But such a fun, happy one."

Chuckling, Colin found himself beginning to relax. "She's a corker, that's for sure." Perhaps things wouldn't go so badly, after all. He reached out a cautious hand and found the frosty glass.

"Where's your Bible?"

"On the bureau."

She swished quietly away. Even the sound of her soft steps enticed him. He couldn't help but remember her alluring curves. . .and those incredible violet-blue eyes. Too late he realized her being here was not such a good idea. He was on the verge of telling her so, when she spoke.

"I received the most wonderful news yesterday. Rose, my sister, is with child. She's due to give birth in December. So I thought I'd take a riverboat up there after the wedding and spend some time with her. If you don't mind."

If I don't mind? Was she joking? He'd been trying to rid himself of her since he returned—unless this was some kind of ploy to get him to beg her to stay. "You're free to come and go as you please. Give your sister and Nate my best wishes and sincere prayers for their child's safe entrance into the world."

A heartbeat's silence preceded her next words as she returned from fetching the book. "I will gladly do that." She settled into her chair again and opened the Bible. "Now, did you finish with Philip and the Ethiopian eunuch that Amy found of such interest?"

Colin couldn't stop his grin. "Absolutely. We're definitely finished with that."

"Then I'll begin with Acts, chapter nine: 'And Saul, yet breathing out threatenings and slaughter against the disciples of the Lord, went unto the high priest, and desired of him letters to Damascus to the synagogues, that if he found any of this way, whether they were men or women, he might bring them bound unto Jerusalem.' "

Even if the words were full of strife, the lilting music of Mariah's voice melted pleasurably into his ear. Colin took a sip of his cool drink and eased back to listen.

" 'And as he journeyed, he came near Damascus: and suddenly there shined round about him a light from heaven: and he fell to the earth, and heard a voice saying unto him, Saul, Saul, why persecutest thou me?

" 'And he said, Who art thou, Lord? And the Lord said, I am Jesus whom thou persecutest: it is hard for thee to kick against the pricks.

" 'And he trembling and astonished said, Lord, what wilt thou have me to do? And the Lord said unto him, Arise, and go into the city, and it shall be told thee what thou must do.

" 'And the men which journeyed with him stood speechless, hearing a voice, but seeing no man. And Saul arose from the earth; and when his eyes were opened, he saw no man: but they led him by the hand, and brought him into Damascus.' "

Blind! How dare she toy with him! Colin sprang to his feet. "That is not where we left off."

"I'm afraid it is." Sadness cloaked her gentle words.

He didn't want to believe her, yet there was a ring of truth in her voice.

"Chapter eight ends with, 'The eunuch saw him no more: and he went on his way rejoicing. But Philip—' "

"Right. I remember." Colin lowered himself with care, hoping he hadn't moved away from his chair. He despised looking helpless. Once in his seat, he silently thanked the Lord. "Read on. Let's get the blasted section over with."

"As you wish. 'And he was three days without sight, and neither did eat nor drink.' "

"That was me." He spoke in a flat tone. "They told me I'd been unconscious for three days. And when I woke up, I was blind."

"I can't imagine how you must have felt."

"Yes, well, go on. I'll have a word or two with Geoff later about picking this chapter."

She let out a hushed breath and continued. " 'And there was a certain disciple at Damascus, named Ananias; and to him said the Lord in a vision, Ananias. And he said, Behold, I am here, Lord. And the Lord said unto him, Arise, and go into the street which is called Straight, and enquire in the house of Judas for one called Saul, of Tarsus: for, behold, he prayeth, and hath seen in a vision a man named Ananias coming in, and putting his hand on him, that he might receive his sight.

" 'Then Ananias answered, Lord, I have heard by many of this man, how much evil he hath done to thy saints at Jerusalem: And here he hath authority from the chief priests to bind all that call on thy name.

" 'But the Lord said unto him, Go thy way: for he is a chosen vessel unto me, to bear my name before the Gentiles, and kings, and the children of Israel: For I will shew him how great things he must suffer for my name's sake.

" 'And Ana—Ana—' " Mariah's voice had grown increasingly hoarse. She stopped reading and drew a ragged breath.

Colin knew she'd started weeping, feeling sorry for him. It had been hard enough to endure hearing the passage without her pity. "Finish or leave," he said, not bothering to mellow his tone.

He could tell from her raspy breathing and sniffling that she was trying to regain control. If she didn't manage to recover her composure soon, she'd have him tearing up, too. He broke into the silence. "Unlike Paul, I was not given back my sight, but the Lord has made me see myself for the cocky, vain peacock I was."

"And me, as well." Emotion still clouded her words. "You saw me for the vain, selfish princess I was. What I didn't see in your eyes and hear in your voice, the Lord showed me. And believe me when I say it has not been pretty to look at—or live with. I've had to face what a hedonist I've always been, seeking my own pleasure, my own desires. It's been—a. . . hard lesson." Her voice broke.

Please don't cry. Didn't she know the sound of her weeping wounded him to the core?

She drew a deep breath. "But one lesson I shall never forget." She paused abruptly. "I'm sorry, but I don't think I can. . ." She gulped in more air. "I really must go."

"Wait." Without thinking, he reached across and snagged ahold of her skirt before she could rise. "I need to say something. To thank you, actually. I know it was rude of me to tell you to leave me alone. But you've been more than gracious about doing as I asked."

"No need to thank me. It was merely my feeble attempt to stop being so selfish and. . ." She swallowed. "So grasping."

"Grasping?" He frowned.

"Quite. You were right to cast me aside. Once you were unable to see the outer person, you beheld the ugliness that dwelled within me. You saw the real me, and I repelled you."

He tipped his head. "If that's what you thought, why did you stay?"

"I don't know. I just couldn't make myself leave. But I'm trying, Colin. Truly I am. If I can convince myself I'm merely going to Rose's for a short visit, I might actually go. And then, God willing, perhaps I'll find the fortitude to make myself stay there."

He considered her words, knowing how hard it must have been for her to be so openly honest with him. "Surely by now, Mariah, you have some idea of what life would be like married to a blind man."

She scoffed. "Perhaps if you'd stumble around more and act like a blind man, that would help. But oh, no. You must go around looking and acting more like my valiant hero every blasted day."

He felt her bump against the table and knew she'd gotten to her feet.

"So I really do need to leave this place now, or I'll never—"

Thrusting himself up, he reached for her and drew her into his arms, his heart throbbing in his chest. "Never what?" he managed to whisper as her scented warmth stole all other thought.

"Never stop loving you." Her trembling palm cupped his cheek.

He could not discount the sincerity in her voice, any more than he could ignore the love he still held for her. Maybe she still had flaws. Maybe they both did, but obviously the Lord was working in both their hearts. The last thread of his resistance unraveled. "My sweet, beautiful love. I have one more request. Please don't stay away for long." He lowered his head, and his yearning mouth found hers.

Chapter 36

"Thank goodness the rain last evening was light." Mariah threaded her arm through Colin's as they strolled out of their favorite place—the gazebo, where within its shadows, she always allowed him to kiss her. Her lips still tingled from his last kiss. "All our lovely autumn leaves might have come down."

Colin chuckled. "They wouldn't dare. Mother wouldn't allow it."

"I hope it stays nice for the wedding, day after tomorrow." She paused. "Oh, there's a dip coming up ahead."

"How many times do I have to tell you? I don't need your help unless I'm about to walk off a cliff or something equally hazardous."

"Well, I'm talking about a muddy bog from the rain. So you go right ahead and wade through it then. But I'm planning to walk around it." She started to pull away.

He caught her hand and tucked it back into place. "I do believe you're always gonna be a handful, my love."

"Only because you insist on being difficult over my slightest suggestions." She veered them to one side of the mushy spot on the lawn.

"You've been saving me over and over since the moment we met."

"Ah, yes, that was quite the moment—you standing up there all gorgeous in royal blue. I'm amazed I didn't have to bid a whole lot more than I did." He tipped his head and softened his voice. "Mmm, you smell good. Let's go back to the gazebo. I want to kiss that beautiful face some more."

"Certainly not." Mariah dodged as he tried to nuzzle her neck. "I'm sure half the plantation saw us as it is. Likely the only thing keeping your mother from taking a leisurely stroll out to the gazebo is the fact she's too busy keeping Tuck's hands off Victoria to wonder what you and I are up to."

He gave her waist a squeeze. "Well, she'll only wonder for two more days."

"Mmm. I can hardly believe we're actually going to be husband and wife."

"Aye. Then no one can say anything when I want to kiss you." He lowered his head to capture her mouth.

"Colin." She leaned away. He was getting much too eager. Time to change the subject. "It was sweet of Tori to allow us to share her day. The Lord has truly been with us, having you come to the auction at just the right moment, then bringing us together again at the right moment. His timing is perfect. I thank God every day that your mother and my sister never stopped praying for us."

He nodded in thought. "I'm really glad Rose and Nate are coming to our wedding. I'd like to get to know them both better."

They passed the arbor with its leafy branches already wound into a lovely arch where the double ceremony would take place. Mariah drew a tremulous breath. "I am so looking forward to seeing Rose. I hope the trip downriver isn't too strenuous for her, being with child. And I hope Mr. Scott reached Lily in time for her to come also. You did say it wouldn't take more than two weeks if he rode straight through. Of course, there would've been the matter of persuading her employer to let Mr. Scott buy back her papers."

"Leave your worries with the Lord. If possible, she'll get here on time."

"But we've only two more days—"

"I know, love." He stopped and took her face in his hands. "Two days, and I can finally have you all to myself."

"Me and your other girl, Duchess," she teased.

"I probably won't be needin' her for a while. She can spend more time with Amy."

Mariah turned. "Speaking of your sister, she's riding here fast, with the dog chasing after her. Oh, dear. She just galloped up on the lawn. Your mother will be furious."

Amy brought Snowflake to a turf-kicking halt. "Guess what!"

"You're in trouble again?" Colin grinned toward her voice. "You'd best get that horse off the lawn. You know every blade must be perfectly in order for the wedding."

The girl grimaced at him from her perch in the saddle. "In a minute. Guess what! Mariah's sister and husband and little one are walking up from the landing this very minute! And Rose is lookin' kinda fat. You know what that means."

Rose is here! Forgetting decorum, Mariah rose to tiptoe, wrapped her arms about Colin's neck, and kissed him right on the mouth while Amy gushed on.

"And Poppy took the carriage into town to meet the coastal packet. People are all startin' to come. Even Aunt Hester, all the way from Boston."

Laughing, Colin tightened his hold, keeping Mariah close. "Aye, squirt, they are. Now take that horse back to the stable. Quick!"

"And put on something pretty," Mariah added. "Maybe that'll make up for the trampled grass."

"Oh, all right." Pouting, Amy nudged the Thoroughbred into motion, and off she went.

Colin gave a playful tug to one of Mariah's curls. "Shall we go meet your family?"

⁓

Colin wished he could actually view the joyous reunion as Mariah left his side to administer hugs one by one. But the laughter in their voices spoke volumes as greetings were batted back and forth. He was especially glad Nate was here.

"And of course you all remember Colin," Mariah said brightly. "Except for this little angel." She caught Colin's arm and stepped close again. "Darling, I'd like you to meet Jenny Ann."

Plump, damp fingers reached from Mariah's embrace and touched his face. He caught the tiny hand and nuzzled the little one's palm. She giggled.

"Jenny has the blondest hair you ever did see," Mariah supplied for him, "and huge blue eyes, clear as the sky. Isn't she the friendliest little thing?"

Detecting an undeniable odor wafting up to his nose, Colin smirked. "I believe little Jenny has brought an extra present with her—that might need attending."

"Quite right." Mariah stepped back from him. "Rose, why don't you and I take her and go freshen up a bit while the men get reacquainted?"

"Sounds wonderful." Rose's voice drifted back to Colin as the women started away. "I'd like to put my feet up for a while, too, if you don't mind."

"Nate, why don't we go sit on the veranda?" Colin turned in the direction of the women's departing footsteps. "Would you like tea or something stronger?"

"Tea'll do fine." Nate came alongside. "First, though, where should I put our luggage? Womenfolk sure do need a passel of stuff with 'em."

Colin laughed. "They certainly do. Just set the bags down by the front door, and I'll have Benjamin tote 'em up to your room."

"I must say, you sure look a sight better'n when I last saw you."

Colin's cane tapped the first step. "Quite. But then we were all a dirty, smelly bunch." His foot found the riser, and he started up. "By the way, how's that leg of yours comin' along?"

"It weren't much to holler about. The ball went clean through, an' I've got most of the strength back. I figger another month or so. . . ."

Someone hurried out the door and came toward them. "I heard you got here, Kinyon," Tuck said. "How've you been?"

"Good. Great to see you again."

"Tuck," Colin interrupted, "give Pansy a holler, would you? Have her bring us out a tea tray."

Once the men took seats around the table, Colin spoke. "So, Nate.

Did you get all your crops harvested? You were plannin' to paint your house, too, as I recall. I don't remember the color."

"Yellow. And once Rose saw the color of your front door, she wanted ours the same. I had to do a whole lot of mixin' before I got it just the right shade of dark blue, too." He sniffed. "Women always make a lot of work for a man. You two positive you wanna get hitched?"

Colin and Tuck both laughed. Then Colin cocked his head. "Considerin' my infirmity, I believe I'll get out of most of it. But Tuck, here, is already jumpin' through hoops. He's got men buildin' a honeymoon cottage as we speak. Ain't that right?"

"It was my idea," Tuck said in a defensive tone.

"Right." Colin smirked. "And what colors is she havin' you paint every room and every door?"

Nate guffawed. "Yeah. What shade of pink does she want in the bedroom?"

"Carry on, you two," Tuck said. "It doesn't matter what color the walls are after the lamps are snuffed. Speakin' of that, Colin, have you and Mariah decided whether or not you're goin' with us to Philadelphia for the honeymoon? We could have a lot of fun together."

Colin nodded. "We'll come on one condition. I want plenty—and I do mean plenty—of time alone with my wife."

"Trust me, old man," Tuck snickered. "That won't be a problem."

At that, they all burst out laughing.

The door opened, and footsteps approached. "I brung the tea, Mastah Colin. I be pourin' it fo' y'all." Pansy set the tray on the table and served the men before returning to the house.

His mind still lingering on enticing thoughts of the honeymoon ahead, Colin took a drink of the fragrant tea.

"Either of you heard anything new about them Frenchies takin' over the Ohio Valley?" Nate asked. "We're so far upriver, we're always the last to get any news."

"I drove into Alexandria for some bricks yesterday." Tuck's enthusiastic reply turned Colin's head toward him. "That's all anyone at the brickyard was talkin' about. They can't wait for next spring to take up arms and run those blighters clear back to France."

"What about England?" Nate probed. "Dinwiddie heard from the king yet?"

Colin chimed in. "No. But if nothin' else lights a fire under the British, the fact that the fur companies won't have any new pelts to ship next spring sure will. Added to last year's huge loss, that's a tidy amount of profit they won't be countin'."

"There was mention of somethin' else," Tuck said. "The governor of New York has called for a meeting with the Mohawks and any other Iroquois tribes that'll come."

Nate scoffed. "I doubt many chiefs'll show up. Most of 'em have gone over to the French. They're loyal to whoever brings in the trade goods." He crunched into a cookie and talked around it. "The Iroquois in the Mohawk Valley only listen to one white man—a large landowner up that way by the name of William Johnson. He learned their language an' knows what pleases 'em an' what sets 'em off. Even got hisself an Indian wife an' made a pile of money off tradin' with 'em. Problem is, the governor thought Johnson was gettin' too big for his britches an' fired him from the job of Indian agent. The Indians have refused to parlay ever since."

"This is not a time for personal squabbles," Colin mused. "Or pretty soon the French will have bought the loyalty of every Indian on both sides of the Appalachians."

Nate broke in again. "From what Tuck just said, I'm sure that New York governor's had enough pressure brought to bear that he's rehired Johnson. That must've stuck in his craw. But right now he needs to be concerned about the folks livin' out on the fringes. Folks like Rose's sister Lily."

"I'm quite sure we'll have Lily here with us very soon," Colin informed him. "I sent my horse trainer—you met him when he delivered those horses—"

"Aye. Fine fella, that Scott. And thank you again. What with the fur trade gone, those mares' foals will bring in a nice bit of extra jingle— enough to keep the women happy, at least. But what were you sayin' about Lily?"

"Six weeks ago, Geoffrey Scott left here for her place up off the Susquehanna. He took enough money with him to free her and get her back here. We're hopin' they make it in time for the weddings."

"Right." Tuck clamped a hand on Colin's shoulder. "Our weddings. Two more days, old man. Two more days."

Chapter 37

Returning from her own little haven, curling iron in hand, Mariah paused at the door to the older girls' chamber she and Amy now shared because of all the overnight guests. It was almost noon, and the room overflowed with life and laughter and females still in their dressing gowns. The upstairs maid, Lizzie, was assisting the Barclays and Rose in beautifying heads of hair for this afternoon's weddings.

"Tori, stop elbowing me!" Heather, sharing the bench in front of the looking glass with her sister, held up a palm full of hairpins for their mother.

"Then move over," Tori demanded. "I'm the one getting married today, you know. Ouch! Lizzie, you're pulling my hair."

"Den be still, missy, or you's gonna get burnt wi' dis hot iron."

Taking her curler to the brazier to heat it, Mariah smiled as she watched Rose attempting to catch all of wiggly Amy's hair up with a ribbon. How many times in past years had she watched Rose fixing Lily's hair in that same style. Now here she was, fussing over this restless imp with that same limitless patience. It was as if the Harwood sisters had never left home. Almost. If only Lily had arrived in time for the wedding. . .

"There, Heather. All finished." Mistress Barclay's own coif reflected the latest fashion as she turned to Mariah. "Come, dear, it's your turn."

Warmth for her new mother-in-law filled Mariah. Smiling at the older woman, she made her way to the dressing table. Mere months ago she couldn't have imagined Colin's mother approving of her, much less insisting on styling her hair for her wedding.

Mother Barclay gently brushed out the length. "Don't you find it interesting that you look more like me than any of my own daughters? Both of us with dark hair and identical complexions. Now when someone asks if you're mine, I can say, 'Yes, she's my oldest.' " Still holding the brush, she wrapped her arms around Mariah and gave her a hug. "Thank you for giving Colin back his smile. He had me quite concerned."

A sheen of moisture filled Mariah's eyes as she glanced at the older woman's reflection. "And I should like to thank you for being you. You kept me safe even when I wasn't certain I wanted you to."

Tears gathered in Mother Barclay's eyes, also.

"Oh, now, none of that," Rose cajoled from across the room as she tied a pink bow in Amy's tresses. "Red eyes will surely detract from all this finery."

Mariah and Colin's mother both dabbed at their eyes and joined the others in laughter.

A quick knock sounded at the door, and Pansy brought in a tray of food. "Eloise figgered y'all wouldn't be comin' down to eat, so we's bringin' it to y'all."

A person bearing a second tray came behind the maid, and as Pansy moved to the side, there with the widest grin stood Lily!

"Oh, Lily! You came!" Mariah leaped up and flew to her. Mother Barclay quickly whisked the tray out of the way as Mariah and Rose smothered their baby sister in kisses and hugs.

Mariah finally tore herself away enough to introduce the girl to the others in the room.

"I feel as if I already know all of you." Lily's face beamed. "Mr. Scott told me all about you on the trip here."

"We've heard much about you, too," Mother Barclay said. "However, I did expect you to be somewhat younger."

"You do look older," Mariah agreed, assessing the golden waves pinned high atop her sister's head. Loose tendrils framed her heart-shaped face. "Didn't the Waldons treat you well?"

"Of course they did." Lily gave her another hug. "They're fine, Christian people. I couldn't have asked for a kinder family."

Mariah touched Lily's shoulder. "Lily, why don't you come with Rose and me to my room for a few minutes so we can catch up while the others continue getting ready. We've a couple of hours before the ceremony."

"Indeed." Lily's gray eyes widened. "I had to thread my way through hordes of people down on the lawn. There must be at least a hundred guests milling about."

"Two hundred would be more like it," Victoria corrected as Lizzie put the finishing touches to her cluster of silky curls. "Isn't it exciting?"

"It surely is, and I'm so happy to be one of them," Lily answered over her shoulder as her sisters escorted her out the door.

Once the three young women were in Mariah's room across the hall, Mariah flipped her mass of loose black curls out of her eyes and pulled Lily down on the bed with her. "We've missed you so."

"I know just what you mean," she said. "I didn't know how I longed for you until I actually saw you. And you, too, Rose. You positively glow. Marriage and motherhood certainly agree with you."

Rose eased herself down onto the coverlet with a smile. "I must say, Mistress Barclay is correct. You've grown up a lot this past year."

Lily gave a light laugh. "I had to if I was going to emulate you. I had three young children and a baby to care for, not to mention a household to run."

Mariah shot her a questioning look. "So Mistress Waldon's health has not improved overmuch?"

"Some days she's better, but alas, those good days are getting farther and farther apart."

Rose gave an empathetic nod. "I don't understand why Mr. Waldon moved so far away from family and learned physicians."

"Actually, it was his wife, Susan, who insisted on the move," Lily told her. "They had already purchased the land, and John had spent weeks at a time away from the family building the house and barn and getting their first crop planted. Susan refused to let her capricious illness interfere with their plans. They'd already waited until the baby's birth, then months of useless doctor visits. She didn't want to wait any longer. She's quite the courageous lady."

"Still," Rose said with a shrug, "their going seems foolhardy. How long has she been ill?"

"Her joints began swelling a few weeks after the birth of baby David. And the fevers and rashes come and go. The physicians in Baltimore didn't know what to make of it. Mostly they wanted to apply leeches." Lily grimaced. "Susan didn't feel she had enough blood as it is, without those slimy creatures draining any more."

"I see." Rose caught Lily's hand and patted it. "Small wonder you appear so much older. You've had three children under eight, a baby, and a sick woman to look after. Thank heaven that's behind you now that you've come to us. Mariah and I both want you, so now your toughest decision will be whether to remain in this beautiful mansion with Mariah, or come to my more humble but very loving home and live with Nate and me."

Lily gently drew her hand from Rose's and stood, facing both sisters. "Those are both lovely, tempting offers, but—" She reached into the drawstring purse dangling from her waistband. "Mariah, please return these funds to Colin for me." She handed over a wad of banknotes.

"But—I don't understand." Mariah stared at the money, then gazed up at Lily.

"That's the money Colin sent to buy my papers. I refused to let Mr. Scott approach the Waldons about it. My place is there, with them."

"But, dearest," Rose protested. "With that amount of money, surely Mr. Waldon could easily hire someone else. Someone older, more experienced. . ."

"But not someone who cares for them as I do. I almost think of the children as my own. Rose, Mariah—" She reached for their hands.

"When Mr. Scott arrived with the offer to purchase my bond, I followed Rose's example. I got down on my knees and prayed until I was sure of the Lord's will for me. So when we left to come here, I made certain my return trip was already arranged."

"No!" Mariah sprang to her feet. "I've heard the men talking. By next spring the English are going to go to war with the French in earnest—and you live in a much too vulnerable area."

"Nate agrees," Rose said. "Why, our Jenny's mother and father both died at the hands of Indians who raided their farm not far from where you live."

Lily rolled her eyes. "Really, Rose. Those people lived at the very edge of civilization, west of the Susquehanna River. We have a blacksmith, a carpenter, a harnes maker, a metal worker, and even a pastor, of sorts."

"What about a fort, in case of attack?" Mariah challenged.

"Well, we don't have an actual fort of our own, as yet, but the men are planning to build one. The men of the cove go to Harris's Ferry once a month to train for the militia, just as they do everywhere else. And a group of Moravians has lived among the tribe to the north of us for years, and the Indians at Shamokin have all pledged their loyalty."

"I don't care about any of that." Mariah crossed her arms. "I want you with us. I'm sure Colin would gladly send two servants to replace you. Surely the Waldons would be better served that way than by a mere slip of a girl."

Lily met Mariah's concerned gaze. "As I said, I'm convinced that the Lord wants me there, and there I shall stay until He wishes me to go elsewhere."

"Oh, Lily," Mariah moaned as she drew her baby sister into a hug. "If the Lord truly wants you there, then I will try my hardest to be happy for you—even if I will still worry about you."

Rose grunted and shifted her unwieldy body off the bed. "Speaking of happy, we won't have a very happy groom if we don't finish getting you ready."

"Quite right!" Mariah pulled them both into another embrace. " 'Tis my wedding day!"

"Time to go, honey." Mariah gave a gentle push to Amy's back.

The child looked darling in a frilly taffeta gown of rose, a pink bow in her pale blond hair. She stepped out the front entrance on her hopefully graceful and slow parade down the veranda steps, past the many seated guests, to the wedding arbor just out of sight. From a basket on her arm, she scattered yellow and burgundy leaves along the path.

Lovely airy music drifted from Heather's flute up near the front as she provided accompaniment for her sisters along their way.

Victoria had a stranglehold on Mariah's hand. "I'm so nervous." Her face paled despite the touch of rouge on her cheeks. "Mayhap Mother was right. She said I was too young to get married."

Mariah smiled. "Darling, you'll do just fine, I promise. Dennis is probably shaking in his boots, too. Oh, that's your cue." She adjusted the stylish hat over the girl's golden tresses. "Start walking—and don't forget your bouquet by the door. And remember to take small steps."

Letting out a shaky breath, Tori reached for her nosegay of red roses, her hand visibly trembling. Then she put a slippered foot out the door and began her slow walk toward the arbor. Mariah watched after her, noting how fragile she looked in an exquisite gown of white lace. The full skirt trailed behind her with each hesitant step. She made a beautiful bride. She was young, that was true. But her whole life lay before her, waiting to be experienced with the young man of her dreams. And they would grow old together.

Recognizing her own musical cue, Mariah glanced at herself in the credenza mirror. She'd donned the taffeta gown she'd worn the day she first met Colin, and though it was elegant in its own way, it would by no means upstage Tori's. Besides, to Colin she'd always be the girl in the royal-blue gown, and this way, he would at least see her in his mind. She caught up her bouquet of white roses, then floated out the door and down the steps. The day was lovely—mild, with a mere whisper of a breeze, and fluffy white clouds scattered across a cerulean-blue sky.

Colin was so right when he said his mother wouldn't allow it to rain.

Her lips lifted at the thought, and the smile grew as she spied Rose seated near the front with Nate and Lily. Nate bounced an enthralled Jenny Ann on his knee. Immediately across from them were Mariah's new in-laws. They were all family now. *Father God, I am so richly blessed. . .thank You.*

Her gaze traveled to the colorful arbor where Victoria now stood gazing worshipfully up at a grinning Tuck, handsome in dove gray, then on to the black-robed minister. But she'd saved the best for last. Her eyes found God's precious gift to her.

Colin stood resplendent in an embroidered satin frock coat of *café au lait*, with black velvet breeches and white stockings. A ruffled cravat rested just below his chin. His unseeing dark brown eyes appeared full of joy as they searched out the sound of her footsteps.

Realizing she'd hurried her pace to reach him, she slowed it again to match the tempo of Heather's music.

At long last, she reached his side. When she took his hand, Colin smiled and folded hers within the crook of his elbow—always her protecting hero. He bent close, and his breath feathered her curls as he whispered in her ear. "I've been waiting here forever, my beautiful bride. What took you so long?"

"I guess I had a lot of growing up to do," she whispered back. "But I'm here now—and forevermore." And they turned to face the minister.

"Dearly beloved," the Reverend Mr. Hopkins began, "we are gathered here, in the presence of God and this company, to witness the joining of this man and this woman"—he nodded toward Dennis and Victoria—"and this man and this woman"—his head turned slightly to include Colin and Mariah—"in holy matrimony."

Mariah raised her lashes and gazed up at Colin. His melted-chocolate eyes were so soft with love, she almost felt he could see her. Her heart crimped with bittersweet joy, and she sent a silent prayer aloft. *Forgive me, Lord, for spending so much of my life in a quest for wealth above all else, when You were waiting to show me that the abiding love of a wonderful man is the true treasure beyond price.*

Discussion Questions

1. Mariah journeyed to the colonies with her sisters, but her motivation for the trip was completely self-serving. What factors in her life may have turned her focus inward rather than outward? Does she remind you of anyone you know?

2. Despite the advantage of having been raised in a Christian home all her life, Mariah's faith was shallow and only on the surface. Do you think God answers prayers that come from a selfish heart? Do you believe God really hears *all* of your prayers? If so, why?

3. Colin's mother was a thorn in Mariah's side, and she never really could relax around Cora Barclay. Have there been people in your life who required you to have an extra measure of grace? How did that turn around for you?

4. What kinds of things from Mariah's past actually helped her in her relationship with the Barclay family? What lessons in your past turned out to be valuable in your present life, and why?

5. Colin was attracted to Mariah from the moment he laid eyes on her. Does physical attraction alone make for a lasting relationship? What other things should a person consider? What is the most important requirement for a Christian in choosing a life partner?

6. Colin had also grown up in a strong spiritual environment, yet he rarely gave much thought to God until he found himself in a tough spot. Why do you suppose people so often wait for something bad to happen before they realize their need for the Lord? Do you think a person can run out of chances?

7. Was there a particular character in *Mariah's Quest* that you identified with? Why?

8. Mariah wasn't *all* bad. What were some of the characteristics in her life that were actually redeeming graces?

9. While Colin was off with the militia, Mariah and his family prayed daily for his protection and safety. Yet he received a permanent injury that changed his whole life. Why do you think God allows bad things to happen to good people? What "good" came out of Colin's blindness for Colin and Mariah?

10. When the future looked dark for Mariah and Colin, they found the peace that only comes from a heart that is completely surrendered to God. With their faith renewed, do you think they could have found happiness even if they hadn't been reunited? Is there a scriptural truth for that?

11. God sometimes works in roundabout ways to bring His purposes to pass. Why do you suppose that is? Can you pinpoint one of those mysterious miracles in your own life?

12. Mariah and Colin found their happy ending with each other. But that doesn't happen for everyone. How can we truly be sure God knows best?

LILY'S PLIGHT

DAUGHTERS OF HARWOOD HOUSE
Book Three

Acknowledgments

The authors gratefully acknowledge
the generous assistance provided by:

Nathaniel Thomas MLS
Reading Public Library
Reading, Pennsylvania

Sarah Annibali
Lebanon Public Library
Lebanon, Pennsylvania

These individuals helped us gather necessary period data
and shared their extensive knowledge of various settings
used in this story. To you we express our sincere appreciation.

Special thanks to:

Delia Latham
Robin Tomlinson

Your tireless critiquing of our work in progress,
together with suggestions and comments along the way,
were an immense help. May the Lord bless you both.

Dedication

This book is lovingly dedicated to our Lord and Savior, Jesus Christ,
who blessed this magnificent nation from its founding, and to our
families, whose love and support makes our writing possible.

Chapter 1

April 1757

Urgent barking pierced the breezy solitude of the April afternoon.

Dropping corn seed into the freshly plowed trench, Lily Harwood sprang to her full height and whirled toward the sound, her heart pounding. *Please don't let it be Indians.*

Duke, the Waldons' big shaggy dog, stood poised at the edge of the porch, his huge brown eyes fixed on the path leading through the woods behind the squat four-room log cabin to the wagon road. A growl rumbled from his chest, and he barked in the direction of the forest—a kaleidoscope of spring greens and pine so thick the sunlight barely penetrated the foliage to dapple the mossy, fern-covered ground.

Lily slung the strapped seed bag to one side and pulled out the pistol weighting down the pocket of her work apron. She shrugged at the Waldon boys guiding the horse and plow. "A neighbor, most likely." Nevertheless, she positioned herself behind the workhorse.

Eleven-year-old Matthew laid their long musket across Smokey's back, its flintlock cocked and ready, while Luke, nine years old, capped the horn of black powder dangling from the gray gelding's harness.

Lily drew a nervous breath. In the three years since the invasion from the north, no French or hostile Indians had raided farmsteads along Beaver Creek. But other families a mere twenty miles away had been brutally murdered or carried off captive. One could never be too cautious in this area of Pennsylvania.

Still barking, Duke leaped from the porch and headed toward the path.

Motion at the log dwelling caught Lily's attention as towheaded Davy, the family's irresistible four-year-old bundle of energy, bolted out the door with his sister Emma hot on his heels. The redheaded girl latched on to her little brother's collar and yanked him back inside.

Matt wagged his head, muttering under his breath. "The kid's been told a hundred times not to come outside when the dog's barkin' like that."

Dragging her gaze from the path along the far side of the house, Lily glanced at her brave young helpers, both of whom had unruly hair the same light brown as their father. Freckle-faced Luke had a white-knuckled grip on his hunting knife as he peered beneath the horse's neck, while Matt stared through the sites of the musket, his finger steady on the trigger. Lily's heart crimped as she studied the lanky boy. Matt had a lot of his father in him. . .the same speculative blue eyes, the same heart-wrenching smile. Both lads looked older than their years. With their father away with the militia, they'd been forced to grow up fast.

"Remember, you only have one shot," she reminded Matt. "Don't shoot unless you absolutely must."

A grimace tweaked the older boy's mouth as he cut a shrewd glance her way.

His brother gave a huff. "Wish *I* had a gun 'stead o' just a dumb knife. I can shoot good as *he* can."

Lily slanted him a half smile. "I wish you did, too." Even more, she wished the cabin wasn't blocking her view of the path.

Suddenly Duke's barking ceased. Tail wagging, he loped up the path out of sight.

He must recognize whoever is coming. Releasing a pent-up sigh, she nodded to the boys, and they left the protection of the gelding to cut across the plowed field and greet the visitor.

A familiar figure came into view with Duke jumping playfully on him. Lily's heart stilled. " 'Tis your father!" Her whole being warmed with relief and joy.

But the boys had already sprinted toward him, kicking up clods of dirt in their wake. "Pa! Pa!"

The cabin door slammed open. Out flew Emma and Davy, screaming their delight. All four children crashed into their papa and were swamped in a huge hug, laughing at once as the dog yipped and leaped in circles around them.

John has come home again. Drinking in the glorious reunion from some distance away, Lily feasted her eyes on the man of the house, tall and muscular in the sturdy clothing he wore for military duty. Her heart contracted. If only she could run to him and be pulled into those strong arms, too. . .feel safe and warm and deeply loved, have those penetrating blue eyes filling her with delicious shivers. But knowing it could never be stole the joy of the moment. She was not his wife. His beloved Susan, of delicate health and quiet manner, waited inside.

Just then, John looked across the field to Lily. He flashed a grand smile and raised a hand in a wave.

For one heartbeat she held his gaze. Then she forced an answering smile and wave and turned before her longing eyes betrayed her. She trudged to the horse to unhitch the gelding from the plow. The Waldons would be too excited over John's safe return to plant more seed today. As she led Smokey back to the stable, she watched the happy family go inside the cabin. . .to Susan. Without a doubt the sweet, bedridden woman of the house had heard the joyous racket and knew that her John had come home. Had his wife strength enough, she'd have run outside with their children to welcome her husband home with the same loving fervor as they had.

Closing her eyes against an ache of sadness as she entered the rough-hewn stable, Lily felt her neck and shoulders sag. She rested her cheek against Smokey's warmth. "Father, I'm in dire need of an extra measure of grace—and a *proper* love for each member of the Waldon family."

So many times over the past year she had prayed that same prayer. So many times she'd endured the same gnawing ache of hollow hope.

A rumbling neigh from the gelding reminded her she had yet to remove his harness.

Lily patted his muscled neck. "Yes, my mighty steed. You have needs that must be met, too." Filling her lungs with a deep breath laced with a hefty blend of animals and hay, she reached for a buckle and unfastened it as an ironic thought surfaced.

She could be released from her own bonds almost as easily. She only needed to contact her sister, and Mariah's generous husband would dispatch a man at once with money to buy her freedom and escort her away from the constant threat of Indian attack, away from the tiresome care of an invalid and her children, away from looking after this frontier farmstead. She could return to her family's loving bosom that quickly. The offer had been waiting for her acceptance for the past three years.

But how could she leave? She'd been a mere fourteen years of age when John Waldon had purchased her indenturement papers nearly four years ago and brought her to this cove. In that time she'd set the house to rights, harvested many a crop, and raised these children. Little Davy was but a babe in arms when she'd first arrived. As much as she struggled against feeling entitled, Lily couldn't help thinking the children and this farm belonged as much to her as they did to Susan. More, in fact. Hadn't she earned it all?

And John. . .

Her vision blurred behind hot tears. Angrily she sniffed and swiped them away as she hefted the heavy halter collar and hooked it onto the wall. All her life she'd been taught that coveting was a gross sin, and here she was, coveting Susan's family yet again. "Forgive me, Father. You know I struggle against these feelings whenever John gets leave from Fort Henry. I cannot seem to help myself."

How strange that when he was away she managed splendidly. She loved Susan Waldon like a beloved sister. Throughout the woman's lingering illness, Susan was so appreciative and long-suffering, who could fail to love her? *She needs me here desperately. Yet I betray her kindness and trust whenever John walks in the door.* A twinge of guilt snaked up Lily's spine, and she closed her eyes. *Please, please, dear Lord. Take this vile, sinful desire from me. Or find a way for me to leave this place without hurting them. Or me.*

John reveled in the sound of the children's voices, their laughter, their hugs, though those very hugs were making it nearly impossible to crowd through the doorway into the bedroom. He ached to see his dear Susan. The gaggle of youngsters, all talking at once, burst past the doorjamb as one.

His wife's faint voice penetrated the bedlam. "Welcome home, my love."

John's heart lurched at the sight that met his eyes. Susan sat propped up in bed, the colorful quilt surrounding her in marked contrast to the pallor of her skin. Had her cheeks been so sunken the last time he'd gotten furlough? Had there been dark circles underscoring those once vivid blue-green eyes? She looked so thin against the puffy pillows. Had she stopped eating entirely? His beautiful redheaded bride was a mere ghost of herself. But the sweet smile. . .that was all his beloved Susan.

Davy broke free of his siblings. "Mama! Look who's here!" His words vibrated loud as he ran to her bed and flung himself against it.

She winced as if the sudden jolt caused pain, but her smile never wavered. "Yes. I see." She reached out a frail hand to the child. "Your papa is home. . . . My Johnny."

Her use of his childhood name reminded him that he'd loved her since he was ten years old and the two of them were studying catechism at their local Anglican church. He gently pried himself free of the children and moved toward her. "Kids, would you mind leaving your mama and me alone for a few minutes?"

Davy's lips protruded in a pout. "But you just—"

Emma grabbed her little brother's arm and pulled him to the door. "Mama needs a hug from Papa, too. Without us crowding in."

John gazed after his seven-year-old daughter. The only one of the children who had a fair complexion and hair the same glorious shade of red as Susan's sounded so grown-up.

As the boys elbowed and shoved their way out of the room, Emma lagged behind long enough to bestow a treasured smile as she closed the door behind them, a long copper braid falling forward with her movement. She'd been as young as Davy when John had first signed on with the militia, and she was growing up so quickly. The children were all changing so between his leaves from the fort. He released a ragged breath.

"It's so good to have you home," Susan whispered.

"Oh, yes." He gazed lovingly at her. "I've missed you more than I can say." Easing down beside her, he carefully drew her into his arms, but instead of the comforting softness of her womanly curves, he felt the fragility of her frame in his embrace. The unthinkable could no longer be denied. Barring an outright miracle from God, if something wasn't done soon, she would die. "Oh, Susie-girl, my brave sweetheart," he murmured against hair once shiny and silky, now limp and dull. To think she'd given up the comforts of a privileged life to elope with him when he was not yet twenty. If only he could provide some of those childhood comforts for her now.

And he would!

"You've been gone too long." Her breathy whisper held little strength.

He drew her closer and kissed her temple. "I'm glad I'm here now, to hold you." One way or the other, he'd convince her to go to her family in Philadelphia. She must know it was vital for her to go. A physician there might know more about her life-draining malady than the doctors who'd examined her before they left Baltimore. This time he'd compel her to go—escort her himself, if he had to. If he was late returning to duty at Fort Henry, Captain Busse would understand.

Easing his hold on her, John looked into her eyes. "Sweetheart, we've—"

The door banged open. Pint-sized Davy burst into the room and stopped short of the bed, a frown scrunching his freckled nose. "Ain't you through huggin' yet?"

John couldn't help laughing as he gently settled Susan back against her pillows. He reached for the boy. "Come here, my boy. It'll be a long time before I'm through hugging any of you."

Lily dried her hands at the washstand by the cabin door. It would look suspicious if she stayed out in the stable any longer. Besides, John would most likely be hungry. She plastered on a welcoming smile and strode inside.

The family sat clustered around the finely crafted dining table that John, a journeyman furniture maker, had made the first year Lily came to live with them in Beaver Cove. Before the war. Davy perched on his father's lap, his wiggly hands ever in motion, and Susan sat wrapped and pillowed in the rocking chair at the warm end near the hearth.

John and Susan both wore happy smiles as they looked Lily's way.

"Come in. Come sit with us." John patted the vacant chair at the table.

"How about I get you something to eat and drink first? You must be hungry." She forced a brightness into her demeanor as she moved past the table to the fireplace. "We've beans and carrots left over from nooning."

He spoke around Davy's head. "Sounds mighty good. I haven't eaten since we left Harris's Ferry this morning."

"We?" Across from his father, Matt leaned forward. "Did the other fellas from Beaver Cove come home, too?"

"That they did. All five of us. We floated down the Susquehanna from Henry's Fort yesterday, then this morning we borrowed a canoe and paddled up the Swatara as far as Beaver Creek. Our stream was running too fast, so we walked in from there."

Davy swiveled toward him. "Did ya see any Injuns out there?"

More than interested in the answer, Lily straightened from stirring the coals under the suspended bean pot and turned.

John's jovial expression had vanished. "No, Son. Has there been sign of them in the cove?"

"Uh-huh. Last Sunday." Luke's eyes twinkled. "Micky MacBride said Pete Dunlap saw moccasin tracks in the woods behind the Bakers' old place."

"You don't say." John's worried brow matched Lily's alarm.

Matt jabbed his brother in the ribs. "Don't listen to him, Pa. Pete likes to stir things up, is all. He prob'ly was nowhere near that far upstream."

Somewhat relieved, Lily poked life into the glowing embers beneath the water kettle. "I'm sure Matt's right. Even so, we tie Duke to the porch post at night so he can't go chasing off after some raccoon."

Luke nodded. "That way Duke can warn us before any Injuns can sneak up an' shoot arrows at him. They do that, ya know, to keep dogs from warnin' folks."

Susan's plaintive voice cut in. "Boys. Please." She drew a labored breath. "Enough unpleasantness. Let's be happy your father is home—and the rest of our fine militiamen."

Poor, helpless Susan. It must be hard to be brave when one is in too much pain even to walk. Lily had watched the young woman getting weaker with each passing month, while she herself seemed powerless to do anything about it.

John leaned over and kissed his wife's cheek. "Since there hasn't been any trace of the French or Indians around the fort, Captain Busse released half the militia to come home and get our crops in. He gave us two weeks. When we return, he'll let the others go."

"Only two weeks?" Susan asked the question Lily wanted to ask. "When will this horror ever end?"

As Lily poured steaming water into the teapot, John moved closer to Susan and wrapped an arm around her. "I can't say, my love. But rather than take this time to plant, I plan to see you and the children on your way to Philadelphia. You'll all be much safer with your family, and you'll finally be under the care of a much more learned doctor."

"But we'd never see you then." Susan's voice became stronger than Lily had heard in weeks. "It's quite safe here. Truly. Folks are only a gunshot away." She swung her gaze to Lily. "Tell John how we celebrate Sundays now."

"Of course." Lily smiled and set the teapot on the table. "But first, Emma, would you please get your papa a cup and fork while I dish up his food?" Considering the fragile rein she had on her emotions, the last thing Lily wanted to do was look at John while she spoke. "The other families along the creek road have been coming here for church services for a while now. No one wants to travel more than a mile or so, since spring is so rainy."

"Roads get slick as snot after a good rain," Luke piped in.

"Slick as snot," Davy echoed, flashing a baby-toothed grin up to his father.

"*Davy.*" Frowning, Emma beat Lily to the reprimand. "You know you're not supposed to say that. And neither are you." Hands on her hips, she glared at Luke.

Lily saw John rub a hand across his mouth, but his laughing eyes couldn't hide his mirth. She continued explaining the Sabbath happenings. "We push the furniture back and set up benches. Grandfather MacBride reads from the Bible—"

"An' we sing lots an' lots of songs." Davy gave an emphatic nod. "Then we all eat till our bellies pooch out, an' I get to go out an' wrestle with Charlie an' Joseph."

After Lily set a plate heaped with beans, carrots, and bread, John picked up a fork and wolfed down a couple of bites. "That does sound like fun, and real nice for you, Susie-love." He bestowed another adoring look on his wife. "But I still want you to go to Philadelphia. There has to be a doctor there who can help you."

She shook her head. "Please, darling, don't waste this wonderful home-coming on that subject. We're all here together. Let's enjoy the moment."

"I agree. You need to eat." Lily poured John a cup of tea and met his gaze. "You're much too thin, and I've only two weeks to put some weight back on you." The words were out of her mouth before she could stop them, and her face flamed with embarrassment. She knew she should have said *we have,* not *I have.* She really must be more careful.

Chapter 2

We hoped you'd come home a few times during the winter months, John. The endless days from Christmas until now have seemed like forever."

John swallowed his mouthful of hearty spiced beans and smiled at Susan. "I know, my love. It felt like that for me also, but Captain Busse believed the French were planning a surprise attack. Turned out he'd been given false information by our Shamokin Village Indian allies. There's always more rumors and waiting than action."

"Thank the Lord for that," Lily remarked from the hearth.

John glanced up at her, surprised when she immediately averted her gaze. Odd. "It does get tiresome languishing at the fort. But you're right. We're most grateful to the Lord."

"Amen." Little Emma's affirmation was rife with feeling.

"Yes. Amen." John grinned. It felt wonderful to be home. Only why was Lily acting so shy? Perhaps she was hesitant to remind him that her indenturement would come to an end in two months. The quiet English girl had fit in so well here and been such an invaluable help to them all, he couldn't imagine what the family would do without her.

While the children chatted on about the happenings at the cove since Christmas, John tried to concentrate on his delicious, home-cooked meal. But with the troubling sound of Susan's raspy breathing beside him, he could not deny that with Lily's imminent departure approaching, it was more vital than ever to convince his wife to go to her family in Philadelphia.

His gaze meandered once again to Lily as she stirred the coals and added another log to the dwindling fire. Nothing remained of the frightened, wide-eyed waif of a bond servant who'd trembled uncertainly on the auction block in Baltimore years ago. That wisp of a girl had blossomed into an engaging young woman, her wheat-gold hair a shining halo braided about her head. The Lord had given this family a priceless gift in her. In truth, John had a few misgivings about Lily in the beginning. But she'd turned out to be quite the capable young woman. . .nursemaid to his wife, almost-mother to his children, excellent housekeeper, and willing farmhand. Hard to believe that in a mere two months the law would require him to give the winsome, golden-haired angel two pounds cash money and supplies enough to see her safely back to her sisters.

She turned her face up to his then, and for an instant he was lost in the luminous depths of her gray eyes as a flush of pink swept her delicate cheekbones.

John gathered his errant thoughts and swallowed. Two pounds. How could he spare that sum? Since being called to militia duty, he'd been unable to practice his furniture-making trade, and with his long absences, the farm barely produced enough to keep the family and livestock fed. Philadelphia was the only answer.

"Papa, you're not listening." Emma tugged his linsey-woolsey sleeve. "I said—"

"Forgive me, honey. I was enjoying being here so much my ears couldn't keep up." He reached past Davy and gave her a hug.

She shrunk away a bit, and her nose scrunched up. "You need a bath, Papa. Bad."

He could only chuckle.

"Emma!" Lily gasped. "I daresay that was hardly polite. But I'd imagine your father would appreciate a nice warm soak. I'll start heating extra water." She snatched up the water bucket and emptied it into the kettle. "Matt, would you and Luke mind taking the bucket and milk pail out to the well and filling them with water?"

"Yes, ma'am." Both boys scooted back their chairs and hastened to do her bidding.

"Lily's been such a blessing," Susan said in her thready voice. "I don't know what we'd do without her."

John released a pent-up breath and studiously avoided glancing at the lass again. How would he tell his wife their lovely helper would be gone in two months? His family simply had to leave this place—even if Susan still dreaded facing her domineering father after all these years.

Up in the loft, John tucked Davy in for the night. "Time for your prayers, boys."

The little scamp looked completely innocent as he gazed up, his blue eyes shining. "We won't have to ask Jesus to keep you safe tonight, 'cause you're here with us."

"That's right. Not tonight." John bent and kissed the child's forehead.

As his sons murmured their private pleas to the Lord, John recalled how close he'd come to losing his life the previous November when he'd been shot through his calf muscle—an injury his family knew nothing about, but one that still ached whenever it rained. He thought back on the morning when he and several of his buddies were chasing after a raiding party up the Tulpehocken Path. They hadn't seen any sign of the group since.

Although the French and their allied Indians were gone for now, John knew they'd be back, and soon. What was to stop them, as long as James Ambercrombie was commanding the English forces? Upon the newly arrived general's first and only encounter with the enemy, the pathetic excuse for a leader had set a new standard for incompetence by causing the senseless slaughter of many of his own soldiers.

John thanked God that he was stationed at Fort Henry with Captain Busse instead of with the army at Lake Champlain. Had King George dispatched an even halfway capable commander, the French would've been pushed back across the Great Lakes long ago and taken their Indian allies with them.

Now the French would be even more emboldened.

And Beaver Cove was in more danger of attack than ever before.

At the hearth, Lily stirred the huge footed pot containing the cubed potatoes and smoked ham she was preparing for tomorrow's Sabbath meal. Then, unhooking a potholder, she plucked the pressing iron from the hot metal plate sitting among more fiery coals and brought it to the worktable to iron John's finely woven white shirt for the morning church meeting. She wanted him to look his best. Smoothing a hand over the material, Lily lost herself in the memory of the smile he'd given her earlier this evening when thanking her for preparing his bath, and her heart ached with longing.

"Why are you cooking and ironing at this late hour?"

Something inside her went completely still as John descended the loft ladder. She did her best to sound casual as she spoke in low tones. "I'm cooking for tomorrow, the Sabbath." The realization struck her then that with the rest of the household now abed, the two of them were in the common room. . .*alone.*

He seemed unaware of her discomfort. "Sunday. I'd lost track of the days." Having reached the bottom, he started toward her, the chiseled lines of his face relaxing into an amiable smile.

Lily's inward struggle made her hands tremble, and she gripped the iron harder. She'd never found it hard to converse with John before. He'd been as much a friend as he was the owner of her papers. It was not his fault that her traitorous feelings had grown beyond her control. *Say something. Don't make him suspicious.* She drew a shaky breath. "We womenfolk find it easier if each of us prepares one large dish to share with everyone. And of course you'll need freshly pressed clothing, since folks wear their finest to service."

John walked past her and plucked a cup from a shelf, pouring himself a steaming cup of tea from the pot left near the fire. "You've grown up to be a very responsible young woman, Lily."

Did he have to stay so close? She put more effort into ironing.

"I doubt your sister Rose would've been so eager to help me purchase your papers if she'd known you'd end up in a remote settlement like this, where an Indian attack could happen without warning. I'm even more surprised that after your other sister married a man of wealth, she wasn't able to convince her husband to buy your papers from me." He eased down in the dining chair nearest her. "You probably don't know I thank God every day that she didn't."

Lily didn't know how to respond. To think John actually thanked God for her, thought of her every day, just as she did him! Of course, his thoughts were undoubtedly far more *proper*, she chided herself. How would his opinion of her change if he learned that Mariah's letters never failed to remind her of Colin's offer to retrieve her—or worse yet, if John discovered the depth of her yearning for him?

She filled her lungs once more and reined in her dangerous thoughts while she adjusted the fabric. Then, picking up the iron, she changed to a safer subject. "The older boys have been very good about searching the surrounding woods for signs of danger." At his appreciative nod, she continued. "While Matt and Luke were out the other day, Matt shot a buck near the creek. The boys came back for the horse to haul the buck home. Without so much as calling me to help, they managed to string up the stag and dress it out. I knew they wanted to surprise me, so I didn't let them catch me peeking out the window."

John tipped his head in thought. "And I found the three of you out planting when I arrived. You've done a great job with them, Lily. I especially appreciate your tender care of Susan."

The intrusion of his wife's name squelched the rush of tenderness

Lily felt for John. Reminding herself yet again that he was a man known for his kind words to everyone and that she had no reason to feel slighted, she forced a light note into her tone. "Well in truth, Davy can be quite the handful from time to time. But I do love watching our little Emma trying to act the grown-up young lady."

John sighed, drawing her attention to him as a wistful flash of regret creased his forehead. "I'm missing so many of their growing-up years. I know I'll never get them back."

"Perhaps. But you are putting your life at risk patrolling along the Susquehanna River. Every day you and the rest of the militiamen put yourselves between the war parties and us. That's worth a lot."

He gave a noncommittal shrug. "Sorry to say, the war's not going well at the moment. And Susan has gotten so much worse. . . . Even I can see that. I must demand this time that all of you leave here for Philadelphia."

His words troubled Lily. She shook out his still-warm shirt and draped it over a chairback as his resonant voice went on.

"If you could have the family's clothing packed by Monday morning, I'd be able to travel with you—at least as far as the mouth of the Susquehanna. I'll sign off on your bond papers, so once you get my dear ones to Susan's family, you'll be free to travel on to your sister's."

So John had also thought about her indenturement contract nearing its conclusion. She replaced the iron on its heating plate on the hearth and turned to face him. "If you're worried about me leaving before the war ends, pray be at rest. I assure you I would never abandon Susan and the children. I love them far too much."

His deep blue eyes slanted downward as a grateful grin spread across his features. "I never for a moment thought you'd abandon them. In fact, I'd planned to pay extra for your irreplaceable service to my family until the war ends. Even after that, if you're not opposed to remaining with us. But now with Susan having grown so much worse, I fear her only hope is that her father will hire the best physicians his money can afford. There's no other recourse."

Lily had to be honest with him as she met his gaze with an unwavering one of her own. "Perhaps had we gone, as you urged her, last fall, things would be different now. But I'm afraid leaving here at the moment is no longer possible. Surely you can see that."

He didn't respond right away. Lowering his head, he rubbed a hand over his face, then looked up with a kind of desperation he'd never before shown. "Her need to be under the care of a competent doctor is so urgent now. I won't accept her argument any longer, that she always wants to be here when I get leave."

"John." Lily spoke frankly, despite knowing her words would inflict unbearable pain. "I doubt Susan would survive as much as the wagon ride to the Swatara. Even if she could, there's the matter of days she'd have to spend on a damp keelboat afterward and then the trip from the mouth of the river on to Philadelphia. I understand it's at least fifty miles overland to the city, or a weeklong voyage around the Chesapeake peninsula. Such a journey in her fragile condition is out of the question. It's been three months since she's been able to endure even the brief wagon ride to the MacBrides' for church. I'm grateful everyone loves her so much they're willing to crowd in here every week so she can be part of the service."

"So am I, Lily-girl. So am I." John's attempt at a smile was a pitiful failure. He remained silent for so long, Lily was loath to intrude on his thoughts. Finally he spoke again. "I still have to believe there's a way to make this happen. I'll speak to the men tomorrow to see what can be done."

At a loss as to how to answer such blind faith, Lily turned back to the fire to check the potatoes. Susan's worst fear had now become hers. If they were all sent to Philadelphia, she'd be expected to travel on afterward to Mariah's. She would never see John again.

Chapter 3

With a mixture of pride and sadness, John helped his sons bring in boards for the neighbors to sit on during the Sabbath service. The boys had grown up so much since he'd been in the militia. Already Matt sported muscles in his upper arms, and farm chores were broadening his hands. Even his expression had a mature seriousness about it, and eyes once alight with a youthful tendency to mischief now radiated a kind of sadness in their blue depths. Would Luke also be forced to relinquish his childhood so quickly?

"That keg needs to be a couple of feet closer to the wall, Pa," his younger son commented as he hefted one end of a long board.

John grinned and complied. Today the boys were directing him, not the other way around. As they set up this last bench, he tried to envision six fairly large families occupying the eight rows facing the hearth. "Has another family moved away while I was gone?"

Matt straightened. "No. Only the Thorntons and Bakers left the cove. Everyone else is still around."

"You sure there'll be enough room for them all? Last time I counted there were forty-seven folks hereabouts."

Lily's airy, feminine voice rang out. "That was before our two new babies. We now have forty-nine."

John turned to her. He almost didn't recognize the willowy young woman standing in the doorway of the room she shared with Emma. Instead of her everyday homespun, she'd donned one of the better gowns she'd brought from England, altered now to fit her slender, womanly curves. In a shiny fabric of cornflower blue, with lace adorning the neck and dripping from elbow-length sleeves, the gown projected a delicate tinge of blue to her gray eyes. With her wheat-gold locks swept back and up into a cluster of ringlets, she looked exceptionally fetching.

"The Randalls normally listen from up in the loft." Lily glided gracefully toward the hearth and looked about, as if approving the placement of the benches.

John let out a slow breath when Matt's voice drew his attention away from their bond servant. "That's why we swung our beds crossways and moved 'em closer to the railing."

He flicked a glance up to see that the three cots now made one long bench.

Lily moved to the wooden board below the window. "Of course, with five extra men here, we'll all need to sit much closer than we usually do." She began shelving the breakfast dishes that had been left to air dry. "Mayhap we can set some of the wiggly tots like Davy on our laps."

"I'm not takin' him." Luke smirked.

Chuckling, John ruffled the boy's unruly brown locks, noting they could use a little more slicking down. "Don't worry. I'll hold the squirt."

"Good." Luke raked his hair with his fingers, trying to restore the limited order. "With you sittin' with us, maybe Robby Randall won't try to crowd in so's he can sit by Lily." He rolled his blue eyes in disgust.

Matt snickered. "Can you believe it? With old Mr. Randall off with the militia, Robby thinks he's man enough to come sniffin' around her."

Glancing over at the subject of the conversation, John caught a new flush of color pinkening the back of her slender neck. He cleared his throat and changed the subject. "What about the meal after the service? How do we set up for that?" Even as he spoke, he wondered if an English maiden with Lily's obvious beauty and refinement could be interested in a country lad a year or so younger than herself. But then, all the young men her age and older were in the militia. Even if they weren't. . .

Luke's voice cut into his musing. "Soon as the service is over, us menfolk roll in a couple a barrels to hold up some of the boards and make a long table outta them and the kitchen table. Once the ladies set out the food, us kids fill our plates and eat first so we'll have more time to go out and play."

"Yeah." Matt harrumphed. "But it galls me that Judy an' Anna MacBride an' the Randall twins got so uppity they think they're too old for the rest of us. They eat with the adults now." He gave a sarcastic shake of his head.

John managed not to reveal his surprise that Matty was already noticing the feminine sex. The lad truly was growing up. "How old are those gals? I've lost track."

"Judy's fourteen, Anna's almost thirteen, and Gracie and Patience just turned twelve."

"And actin' prim and proper as cats," Luke piped in, his freckles spreading apart with his grin. "Swishin' their skirts around like they was as old as Cissy Dunlap or Lily."

"Twelve." John did his best to maintain a straight face. "Matt, you turned eleven yourself on your last birthday, as I recall. Well, all I can say is neither of you is just *acting* older. You're *being* older. I'm proud of you both."

His boys stood a bit taller.

John couldn't help noticing that Lily wore an affectionate smile also. Her eyes sparkled with mirth as her gaze drifted to his, sharing the moment. Then her smile vanished like dew in the morning sun as she turned away and busied herself with the dishes again.

Why the sudden change? John couldn't think of anything he'd said to offend her since he'd arrived home. Or was she still embarrassed about the Robby situation? Women were difficult to figure out. He cut a glance to his sons. "Boys, with so many folks riding in, we'd best go out and fill the watering trough."

Puffy clouds scudded across the morning sky as the crunching of wagon wheels and clomping of farm horses announced the arrival of Beaver Cove's residents for the Sabbath service, the women in their very best homespun, the men spruced up with slicked-back hair and worn, but clean, attire. After trickling inside and milling about with greetings and chatter, the older folks took seats on the benches John and the boys had lugged in, while the youngest kids scrambled up the ladder to the loft.

Sandwiched between the older Waldon boys, Lily could scarcely breathe. John sat at the end next to Susan's rocking chair, with Davy on his lap and Emma snuggled close. Matt urged two of his friends to fill in the last two spaces to his right, preventing Robby Randall and younger brother Donald from monopolizing Lily. She appreciated that small distraction. John looked entirely too handsome in his burgundy frock coat and ruffled cravat, though the outfit did show wear. She didn't dare allow her gaze to linger on him.

She glanced ahead to the other families chatting happily with their neighbors. During this last period of duty, none of the valley's men had been killed, as Willard Thornton had been last year, or wounded, like Calvin Patterson two years ago. Cal's wife, Nancy, appreciated having her husband home, but his shattered knee was the heavy price paid for that privilege. Lily sneaked a glance over at John and thanked the Lord for protecting him.

"Ahem. Time to start this service." Ian MacBride, or Grampa Mac as the children called him, moved to the front of the hearth, his callused hand raised for silence. The oldest resident of the cove, at six feet he was also the tallest, and sinewy, but his grave demeanor belied a merry heart. Lacking an ordained minister within a thirty-mile radius of Beaver Creek, the grizzle-haired man with bushy whiskers had become their spiritual leader of sorts.

Lily had found the casual arrangement a touch strange at first, having grown up in Bath, England, with its magnificent cathedral, but she'd come to treasure the man's unschooled wisdom and looked forward to his scripture reading and related comments. His slight Scottish accent with its rolling *r*'s fell pleasantly on her ears.

People were still exchanging greetings with the returning soldiers, so Elder MacBride swept a slow glance around, gathering the attention of each individual in the simple log dwelling. "I ken we're all pleased to have our men back home with us again—even for just two weeks—so let's bow our heads and give thanks to the Lord for this blessed time. Father God, we thank and praise Ye for keepin' our soldiers safe and healthy despite the smallpox that ravaged the forces up in New York. Ye ken how much we missed our men, Lord. Not just because we love 'em, but with 'em bein' farmers, Ye ken the land needs 'em too. We trust Ye to see that we all have food on our tables and that the roof dunna' leak till this war ends. And if 'tis Thy will, Lord, we ask for peace to return to Pennsylvania and the other colonies. We ask this in the name of Thy Son. Amen."

Quiet *amen*s and nodding heads expressed the agreement of the gathering.

"Now," he continued, "let's stand and sing 'Praise God from Whom All Blessings Flow.' "

Lily saw John retain hold of Susan's slim hand while he stood with Davy in his other arm, and her heart ached. Susan needed her husband desperately. But heaven help her, so did Lily. Unable to endure their display of affection, she lowered her lashes.

While the rafters vibrated with song, Lily had something else to fill her mind. She basked in everyone's exuberance, enjoying the richness of extra male voices among the crowd.

Two hymns later, Elder MacBride hooked his wire-rimmed spectacles over his bulbous nose and opened his frayed Bible, a cue for everyone to sit again. "Before getting back to Ephesians chapter five, I'd like to read a few verses from Psalm 101 as a fittin' preamble for our passage. 'I will sing of mercy and judgment: unto thee, O Lord, will I sing. I will behave myself wisely in a perfect way. . . . I will set no wicked thing before mine eyes.' " Then he bowed his head. "Our Father in heaven, we offer our thanks for the Word Ye gave us for our instruction. Amen."

"I will behave myself wisely. . . . I will set no wicked thing before mine eyes." Lily shifted in her seat. Had Mr. MacBride seen the longing for John Waldon in her gaze? She looked for a sign in the Scot's expression that would expose her sin but saw none as his huge, veined hands leafed through his Bible. She shot a furtive glance past the children to John, then Susan.

Both sat placidly, paying rapt attention to the older man. Lily berated herself for her foolish fancies.

" 'Be ye therefore followers of God, as dear children; and walk in love, as Christ also hath loved us, and hath given himself for us an offering and a sacrifice to God for a sweetsmelling savour. But fornication, and all uncleanness, or covetousness, let it not be once named among you, as becometh saints. . . .' "

His voice droned on, but Lily heard nothing past those words. She knew her thoughts were unclean and covetous, just as he said. Sitting motionless between the two unsuspecting boys, she felt dirty, unworthy even to be in this house, much less a good friend of all present. Her heart contracted in abject despair.

Eventually the elder's book slammed shut, snapping Lily's attention once again to the front.

"And may our Lord bless the readin' of His holy Word."

The statement was scarcely out of the man's mouth before Emma, Davy, and the other youngsters made a mad dash outside. While everyone else clambered to their feet and began moving benches aside and constructing the long dining table in the center of the room, Lily shook off her morose mood. The Sabbath was always a gladsome day when everyone looked forward to a hearty dinner and fine fellowship. She refused to let her silly dreams steal her cheerfulness. Somehow God would help her get over the folly of untoward thoughts and forbidden longings.

As she moved out of the way to stand beside Susan's rocking chair, Matt followed her. "I s'pose you noticed Jackson Dunlap swiveling around time and again to gawk at you." A note of sarcasm colored his tone.

"Why, no. I was concentrating on Mr. MacBride's reading."

He scoffed. "Well, you better watch yourself. He's probably gonna try to get you alone the first chance he gets. He's nothin' but a rough ol' cob, even if he does think he's some kind a war hero, irresistible to females."

"Yeah. Watch him." Luke echoed his brother's advice.

Lily found her charges' protective behavior charming and gave them an affirmative nod. "I'll keep that in mind."

Luke touched her arm as she turned away. "Frank ain't no better. Watch out for him, too."

From the corner of her eye, Lily saw John come to a stop a few feet away as he watched the menfolk bustling about. Hopefully he hadn't overheard his sons' comments.

She turned to Matt and Luke. "I think your father might need assistance in helping the other men."

Just then, Susan reached up and touched Lily's hand.

Lily's heart sank. Surely the mistress had perceived her guilt during the elder's reading. She looked down at the ailing young woman, expecting to see censure in her expression.

Instead of reproach, a sweet smile rested on Susan's lips. "My little men are jealous. They don't want some strapping young fellow to whisk you away from us."

"So 'twould seem."

"Nor would I, dear Lily. I couldn't bear to lose you."

Contemplating the remark, Lily returned Susan's smile and excused herself to help the other ladies. For all their sakes, she hoped she could conjure up warm feelings for at least one of the stocky Dunlap brothers. She glanced out the open doorway, where Frank and Jackson huffed with effort as they wrestled a barrel up the steps, grinning at one another in triumph. With dark brown hair and hooded brown eyes, both had matured considerably over the past three years. Though neither bore any obvious battle wounds, the ravages of war showed on their faces and in their eyes, just as it did in John's. No doubt they'd welcome the loving affection of a gentle maiden.

The trouble was neither young man held the least appeal for her.

The only one her heart cried out for was John.

Releasing a tortured breath, she sent another desperate prayer aloft. Surely God would keep her strong. His ways were perfect. If it was His will that she leave this family and go to live with Mariah two months hence, it would be the best for all concerned.

So why did that conviction lack even the slightest comfort? Her unwitting gaze slid to John Waldon, smiling tenderly down on his wife as he gently kneaded her shoulders, and Lily's heart ached so, she pressed a hand to her breast to stop the pain.

Chapter 4

Not since Christmas had John felt as sated as he did after the delicious meal prepared by the ladies of the settlement.

When he and the other men meandered outside afterward, he noticed his best friend, Bob Randall, patting his slight paunch. A family man of medium height, with three sons and five daughters ranging in age from seventeen to nine months, Bob had sable hair; close-set hazel eyes; and a short, dark beard. John chuckled when the man emitted a loud belch. The group paused a moment to watch the youngsters, exuberant in their play as they raced along the wagon road with their hoops and sticks. Then, heading away from the melee of screams and shouts, they strolled off the porch.

Ian MacBride nodded in the direction of the furrowed Waldon land. "I see yer boys got most of your fields plowed up this week."

"Right. Them and our girl, Lily. When I came in yesterday, she was out there ankle-deep in mud helping them."

"That little miss has been worth her weight in gold," rail-thin Cal Patterson remarked as he limped along from a shot-up knee he'd gotten during a militia conflict. With sandy blond hair and light brown eyes, the father of five had two sons and three daughters. "It's a wonder how she's kept your place goin' whilst you been away. Susan, sickly as she is, has nothin' but praise for the lass." His grin gave prominence to his protruding chin.

Expecting the overeager Dunlap boys to join in the praises regarding Lily, John glanced over his shoulder. But they and a few other young lads remained behind on the porch, peeking in on her and the other girls helping the womenfolk with the dishes. John scowled.

The men halted between a cart and wagon, and a few propped a foot on a hitch or a wheel spoke while they visited.

Richard Shaw, John's closest neighbor, and the only landholder younger than he, straddled the long hitch of the cart and leaned against the front boards, pulling out a small pack of tobacco to fill his pipe. "I shore do love Sabbath dinners. 'Specially when the women serve that dried apple pie. Not that I'd allow to mention it, but my Ruthie ain't the best cook in the world." Blue eyes twinkled beneath his wavy brown hair as a sheepish smile plumped out his ruddy cheeks. His relaxed stance compressed his medium frame and height a bit.

"What with five bairns under eight, one bein' a wee newborn," MacBride commented on a wry note, "I doubt yer good wife has much time for pie makin.'"

Richard warded off the Scot's words with his pipe and a grin. "Like I said, I ain't gonna mention it."

The other men chuckled, and stocky, barrel-chested Toby Dunlap removed his own tobacco pouch from a vest pocket. His deep-set eyes seemed a darker brown against balding gray hair. His family consisted of a daughter and three sons, two of whom were nearly grown.

John glanced around. "Speaking of not riling the womenfolk, while we're here, we need to talk about building a blockhouse. As Pat and Bob know, I had my mind set on taking my family down to Philadelphia during this furlough. But with Susan having deteriorated to such a low point, I fear taking such a risk."

Ian MacBride's son Patrick gave John's arm an empathetic squeeze. "I don't relish sayin', there's quite a change from the last time we was home. You have the sympathies of every man here, friend." A good, steady family man like his father, Patrick was also a fine militiaman. Lean and tall, he had the same commanding presence as the older man, and shared the same penetrating blue eyes. He'd provided Ian with two grandsons and three granddaughters.

"Ye have our nightly prayers, as well," Ian added. "From what Pat told me about how the English commanders are bunglin' their campaigns up in New York, I'm with ye. It might be wise to start takin' extra precautions. That wee line of defense you fellas have along the Susquehanna may not be sufficient this year. We dunna' want to walk off and leave everything you all have worked for. A blockhouse is a bonny solution. A solid place to hole up, if ever we need to."

"Since we're located pretty much in the middle of the settlement—and with Susan to consider—I'd like to build it over there, across the creek." John pointed down between the springhouse and the smokehouse, where several years earlier he'd built a footbridge using a broad, sturdy log that had fallen across a narrow spot of the flowing water. His neighbors from that side of the creek had used it to cross this morning, leaving their rigs on the other side.

Bob Randall kneaded his bearded chin, his hazel eyes narrowing in thought. "That would be the most likely spot. There's plenty of timber close by, and we could stock it with barrels of water, firewood, and a store of cornmeal and lard. That way, folks could stay inside till help could get there."

"We need to stock extra black powder along with the other provisions," Toby Dunlap said. "We could start buildin' tomorrow, while we have this good weather, since you boys are expectin' to leave within a fortnight."

John checked the sky. Recent rains had left the land spongy, but that would prove no hardship. "I figure we could all plant during the morning hours and spend the afternoons here this week felling trees and cleaning off the branches. Then early Saturday morning we could start raising the blockhouse. That okay with everyone?"

A collective nod made the rounds.

"It would help Ruthie be a far sight less jumpy at night." Richard swung a glance at the others. "Even though the Shamokin Village Indians have stayed loyal so far, the ones from up north prob'ly know the location of every settlement along the Swatara. They've already done their worst at the more isolated farms, especially those just below Blue Mountain."

"True. Quite true." Cal Patterson spoke on a droll note. "The redskins aren't even usin' the river. They sneak down their warrior paths. With the Bakers and Thorntons pullin' out last summer, makin' our place the last farmstead up Beaver Creek, and with that old Indian path bein' no more'n a couple miles north of us, Nancy's about to jump outta her skin every time she hears a bird call, sure it's an Indian."

Aware that the two men who'd spoken of their wives' fears weren't serving in the militia, but here at home to protect their families, John glanced back toward his cabin. No one was around to protect *his* family— or his brave Lily. Yet the delicately bred British maiden who'd lived her early years in comfort had not once voiced her fears to him. Despite the lack of protection she had every right to take for granted, she'd learned to thrive here in this rugged wilderness. In fact, she herself was all the protection his family had. She and two half-grown boys.

A smile played over his lips at the recollection of her standing out in the field yesterday with a pistol aimed at him as he emerged from the forest. Small wonder the Dunlap boys were eyeing her speculatively, the bond servant who lacked even the smallest dowry. They'd probably come around every day now to make sure she was as capable as she was soothing to the eye.

Strange, how he'd never fully noticed the incredible beauty she'd become.

"It's all settled then." Bob Randall whacked his broad-brimmed hat against his thigh, emitting a puff of dust. "Tomorrow afternoon the lot of us'll be here with our axes."

John again eyed the young bachelors lounging about on the porch of his cabin. Bob's son Robby had turned seventeen, and apparently shared

Jackson and Frank Dunlap's interest in Lily. Even now the three elbowed one another in playful rivalry to have best access to the window. Robby, with his open, honest face and manner, possessed a kind of magnetism that attracted girls, especially with that curly hair of his. . .and he'd still be here after the burly brothers returned to militia duties.

Lily stifled a yawn as she detected the rumble of an approaching wagon the following Saturday. *Oh my. They're here already—and so early.* She'd risen before dawn each morning that week to bake extra cornbread for the neighbor men hard at work felling trees. The added chore, along with cooking, washing clothes, helping plant, and seeing to the needs of her mistress, had taken its toll.

John had assured her she needn't help Matt and Luke in the fields. But Lily knew he had few precious days here, and the sooner the workers were finished each afternoon, the more time he'd have to spend with his wife. She would make every effort to see that the couple had as much time together as possible.

Today would be different, however. All the residents of Beaver Cove would come to lend a hand, and no one would leave until the structure was finished. It would be a long day.

Davy gave a high-pitched holler. "Joey's here!" Leaping down from the chair he'd stood on to peer out the window, he bolted for the door and flung it open, dashing outside to join his playmate.

"Hey, wait for me!" Emma followed in her brother's wake, coppery braids flying.

"Shut the door!" Lily's command came too late. With a resigned sigh, she ceased stirring the pot of beans simmering above the coals and went to close out the crisp morning air before the warmth of the house escaped. The cold always bothered Susan.

The arriving wagon brought the MacBrides. As it rounded the house to park in the open area between the cabin and the corncrib, Lily released a breath of relief. She dreaded having to deal with the persistent Dunlap brothers through yet another tiresome day. Or worse yet, poor lovesick Robby. The Randall lad had managed to stay in close proximity to her all week long, no matter how hard Jackson or Frank tried to crowd him out—when they weren't vying with each other for the same reason. Were it not for the fact that John would also have to depart for Fort Henry when the burly pair took their leave, she'd wish they were already gone. It was a struggle to remain polite and calm while being ogled whenever she stepped outside. The duo's dark, hooded eyes were far too penetrating.

Forgive me, Lord, for complaining. I know the day will take care of itself. Right now, Susan awaits my attention.

After fluffing the pillows in the rocking chair kept near the hearth, Lily headed for Susan's bedchamber at the cabin's far end. When she entered the room, her heart caught at the sight of the almost undetectable rise her mistress's gaunt form made beneath the blankets, but she smiled and spoke cheerily. "Emma and Davy are thrilled that all the children will be here today."

"So I heard." A slight smile accompanied Susan's murmur.

" 'Twould be quite nice if you could come out into the front room and visit with the ladies for a while."

"I'd like that."

"I'll call John, so you won't have to walk so far."

"No, please. I know he believes he helps when he carries me, but it's really quite…painful. I don't want him to know. He worries so about me."

Lily's brows drew together in sympathy. "Oh, dear. I'm sorry. I should have realized that. Well, from now on, we shall try to outsmart him." Helping Susan up to a sitting position, she gently drew the young woman's legs off the bed and put on her slippers. "Ready?"

"I think so." The statement sounded less than certain.

Slowly and cautiously, Lily brought her mistress to her feet and steadied her until Susan could support most of her own slight weight. They then made the tedious, shaky journey to the rocker. Once Susan was comfortably seated, Lily noticed beads of perspiration forming on her mistress's brow and knew her efforts had been enormously taxing.

Again came the ominous reminder that Susan Waldon was losing her battle against the mysterious ailment that had sapped her strength. She ate like a bird at mealtime and drank very little. She requested the bedpan only twice a day now. Over the years, Susan had grown so dear to Lily that the two of them were almost as close as sisters, and the thought of losing such a sweet friend was hard to bear.

"I hate to be such a bother."

Lily let out a ragged breath as she adjusted the pillows around her mistress and tucked a light quilt about her legs. "I do wish you wouldn't keep saying that. 'Tis my joy to help you. Truly it is." Threading a few loose strands of hair back into Susan's night braid, she bent to kiss her cheek. "There. Now you look quite lovely."

Susan touched Lily's hand. "Thank you, my darling girl."

Giving her friend's hand an answering pat, Lily felt a sharp twinge of guilt slice through her like a knife. She drew a pained breath and straightened. *Susan would be far less generous with her compliments if she knew the battle that raged every day inside the heart of her bondwoman.* Hating herself for being such a Judas to a helpless invalid, she turned toward the hearth.

Susan caught a fold of Lily's skirt before she could step away. "I fear I won't be able to stay out here for long today. It tires me so."

With a nod of understanding, Lily met her hollow, blue-green gaze. "Once you've greeted everyone, I shall help you back to your bed. But should you feel a need to go sooner, just raise your hand. I'll be at your side at once."

"You're far too good to me."

Movement outside the window caught Lily's attention as a familiar ruffled mobcap bobbed into view. "Oh, here comes Grandma Margaret, and I'm sure Pat's wife, Agnes, is with her as well. They're always such a comfort." Looking back at Susan, she noted the fine lines of suffering already crimping her forehead. "After things settle down, I'll send Grandma in to talk to you. I want you to be completely honest with her. She might know of a special tonic that could help you."

Please, dear Lord, let Maggie know something—anything—that can be done for Susan. There must be something else I could be doing or could have done. Please don't let her die. If she were to pass on while John is away with the militia, how would I cope? How would he? How would the children? What would become of us all?

Chapter 5

F ood's on! Time to wash up!"

Hearing Lily's airy voice, John turned and saw her on the footbridge, a gentle breeze feathering a wisp of golden hair about her head and curling the hem of her long apron. He drank in the delectable picture.

"Great. I'm starved." Curly haired Robby dropped his end of the log he and John were toting to the blockhouse, and it hit the ground with a hand-jarring thud before John could let go. He shook his head as the lad sprinted toward the cabin, with the Dunlap swains right behind him, all trying to be first to catch up to the lass. Lily was of marriageable age, and John conceded it was to her advantage to be sought after. But the realization depressed him. She deserved better than any of these jackanapes. He felt a strong need to protect her from ill-suited young bumpkins.

As the other neighbors ceased working and started toward the cabin, Bob Randall came alongside John, and they headed for the log bridge. "That boy of mine ain't one bit happy to have those Dunlaps back. I reminded him they'll be goin' with us when we leave, an' Robby says he'll bide his time till they're gone."

John gave a nonchalant shrug.

"He's carvin' a real fine figurine to give Lily. He wants to make a good impression on her."

Squelching a smirk, John responded in a flat tone. "She's very kindhearted. I'm sure she'll appreciate his effort." There was no need to elaborate, but he couldn't help himself. "She was accustomed to expert craftsmanship at her home in England."

His friend's expression dimmed. "Oh yeah. I forgot about that."

Chagrined, John clapped him on the shoulder. "Hey, don't listen to me. I know she'll be pleased. She brought next to nothing with her when she came to live with us. How could she not appreciate a thoughtful gift?"

A brief silence followed, and John felt the need to amend further. "Since Robby's interested in working with wood, he might consider apprenticing with me after the war. . .when you don't need him, that is."

Bob grinned. "Mighty kind of you, John. He'll be glad for the offer. 'Specially if Lily's still on the place."

No doubt. Suspecting his friend was trying to sweeten his son's bid for the girl, John felt a touch of rancor inside. He tamped it down with a civil answer as they stepped off the bridge. "Her term of service will be up in two months, you know."

"I figured as much."

"She promised to stay on with us until the war is over, though. After that, she'll probably go live with her sister. You remember, the one who married that wealthy plantation owner back in Alexandria."

He nodded. "But there's nothin' to keep her from changin' her mind between now and then, is there? Everyone knows she's been a pure blessin' to your family, and folks around here would sure miss her sweet ways."

Not nearly as much as I would. It was all John could do to keep from shouting the thought as he and his friend stepped over a protruding root. But he knew better than to voice it. She was a mere bond servant, but she'd become much more since joining the household. She was a real part of the family, and he couldn't imagine how empty the house would seem were she not around. "Yes, and so would we—especially Susan. She'd be lost without Lily. They've grown incredibly close."

At the mention of his wife's name, guilt wrapped cold fingers around John's conscience as they neared the blend of aromas from the food-laden table. He tipped his head at Bob. "Tell the others to start eating without me. I haven't looked in on Susie all morning. Think I'll go spend some time with her." But even as he said the words, his unwitting gaze gravitated to the gentle gift that was Lily. He saw her cast a despairing look over her shoulder at the eager young bucks drooling over her as she entered the house.

A table for the noon meal had been set outside near the cabin because of the mild day. The instant Grampa Mac uttered the *amen* over the platters of roast venison, fried chicken, and fresh-baked bread that had been spread before the workers, Matt gave a shout. "Lily! Over here!"

She only half-heard him as she emerged from the house with a pewter pitcher of spring water. Her attention centered on John coming straight toward her, his expression unreadable. A tentative smile trembled on her lips.

He flashed a half smile as he paused on the steps. "Lily, my dear. You're my true blessing."

His tone had been quiet, casual, as if he'd said something as unstudied as "pass the butter." But *his dear? His true blessing?* She had no idea what to make of such comments.

"Lily!"

"Coming, Matty." Still staring in puzzlement after the boy's father, she collected herself and hurried to the long table where Matt and Luke sat proud and tall with the men after having worked alongside them all morning.

"Here you are." Filling the older lad's glass, she gave him a teasing smile, then did the same for Luke before moving to their friend Sam.

"Don't forget me, Miss Lily." Jackson Dunlap flashed a devilish grin from the far end of the table, a glint in his brown eyes.

Lily was grateful most of the neighbors were too busy devouring their food to notice his impropriety. "After I take care of this end." She managed not to gloat when the young man's grin lost luster. He'd been most persistent this week, cornering her with brazen stares while offering flimsy excuses for crossing the creek and coming to the cabin time and again.

But then, being twenty-two, the oldest bachelor in the valley, it was probably natural for Jackson to feel desperate. Three years of militia duty had cost him his chance to seek out marriageable young maidens from the other settlements along Swatara Creek. Lily kept that in mind as she ignored his advances.

Just then, Ian's wife, tall, bony Margaret MacBride, approached the table with another platter of chicken, the ruffled cap hiding her braided gray coronet bobbing with each step. The woman's faded blue eyes never missed a thing. Lily was relieved for Maggie's presence as she neared the Dunlap brothers, whose shameless leering made her feel undressed. She steeled her features against that discomfiting awareness and reached past Jackson to retrieve his glass, actually detecting heat radiating from him.

When she replaced the glass, his callused hand clamped over hers.

She jerked hers away in reflex, knocking over his drink. Water spilled everywhere.

"Dunlap! That'll do." John's demanding censure came from the porch.

Lily and Jackson both swung their attention to him.

"You about through there?"

"No, sir, not quite." A tiny smirk tweaked the young man's mouth as he turned back to his plate and picked up his fork, swapping a snicker with his brother as he shoveled in a chunk of venison.

Lily surmised John had been watching from the doorway, and her spirit felt lighter as she refilled Jackson's drink. John's proprietary tone made it clear that he disapproved of Jackson Dunlap's pawing. She especially liked his thinking she was *dear* and calling her *his* blessing. Not Jackson's. Never Jackson's.

Nine o'clock arrived, and tiny stars speckled the night sky as the men finished chinking the new blockhouse in the glow of lantern light. The evening had gradually cooled, with crickets and tree toads trilling in chorus.

Stretching a kink in his back at the rear of the newly completed structure, John felt as old as Ian. It had been a long, grueling week, plowing and planting till two each afternoon, then felling, stripping, and sizing trees until dark. Today had been the hardest, hoisting the ungainly logs into place, then laying the upper floor, and finally constructing the roof. Every bone in his body ached in protest when he bent to pick up a lamp in each hand.

"Pa!" Frank Dunlap's voice retained an unbelievable measure of energy as the nineteen-year-old called out to his father. "Get your fiddle and strike up a tune. I'll fetch the gals."

"Hold on there, laddie." Ian MacBride's gravelly voice threw a damper on the suggestion. "It's too late for a frolic tonight. The wee ones are all tuckered out, and I dunna' mind sayin' that includes me."

"Same here, Ian. Same here," several neighbors echoed with weary finality. A murmur of assent flowed through the group.

Donny Randall let out a huff. "But Grampa Mac. That's why we worked hard to finish up. Besides, Cissy and Judy both promised me a dance." His voice cracked on the last word, and he jammed his hands into his trouser pockets.

His father grunted. "No, Son, the reason we worked so hard was to make sure our loved ones will be safe while we men are away."

"But that's not fair," older brother Robby chimed in.

The other lads, frowning in mutinous agreement, grumbled their displeasure. The shadows cast by the scattered lanterns exaggerated their woebegone expressions.

Not to be dissuaded, MacBride raised a calming hand. "Tell ye what. After Sunday service tomorrow, and after our Sabbath meal, we'll have a wee bit of music to celebrate this occasion. What d'ye say?"

"You mean that?" A note of doubt colored Jackson's tone.

The elder's whiskers flared with his broad smile. "I dunna' reckon the Lord'll mind a little singin' and dancin'. Folks in Bible days danced with joy to the Lord from time to time, ye ken. So as long as you lads keep in mind it is the Sabbath, we'll do our celebratin' on the morrow."

Jackson jabbed his brother in the ribs and muttered under his breath. "The old goat can dance *his* way, and I'll dance *mine*. . .holdin' on to my sweet Lily."

Standing close enough to the pair to overhear the comment—and even to knock those two woodsy heads together—John clenched his fingers around the lantern handles to restrain himself. Lily came to the cove as a penniless bond servant, and he should be thrilled she was so popular, but elation over that prospect eluded him. He did have prior claim, after all. And Susan, of course. *Please, dear Lord, help me to be happy for her. . . . You know I'm not.*

~~~

After the last wagon headed off into the crisp night, John trudged across the porch and into the house. The warmth from the hearth burned his face, reminding him he hadn't been inside since visiting with Susan at noon. A small lamp and the fireplace illuminated the main room, and a quick glance about revealed it was empty except for Lily.

She sat at the hearth end of the dining table, elbows propped on its surface, her hands circling a cup. She looked up and shook her head. "You look as exhausted as the boys did when they came in. Come sit by the fire. I'll get you a cup of tea. How about some of Nancy's sweet ginger biscuits to go with it?"

"Sounds wonderful." Grasping the tails of his outerwear to lift the garment over his head, he paused, watching her go for the refreshments. A sudden wave of grief swamped him. Blinking hard against a stinging in his eyes, he turned away and stripped off his coarsely woven overshirt. A few short days and he'd leave home again. He'd sorely miss having someone care enough to wait up for him after a grueling day, offering him tea and a little sympathy. . .like sweet, lovely Lily.

He hooked the warm shirt on a spike by the door and took a calming breath before striding to a chair near the hearth. It scraped the plank floor as he tugged it out and dropped onto the seat across from hers.

"The boys didn't even have to be told to go to bed tonight," she said, bringing over his cup and a small plate of cookies. "They hardly managed a good-night before clumping up the ladder to their beds. I doubt they had enough energy to change into their nightshirts."

John watched her move gracefully around to the other side of the table and retake her seat. "They worked as hard as the rest of us. I was very proud of them." Realizing he was still gazing at her, he averted his attention to his tea and brought the steaming cup to his mouth.

"This has been a good day. So much got accomplished." Though she'd spoken quietly, her voice sounded years older than it had when she'd first come to live with them, shy and sad at being parted from her sisters. She picked up her own cup. "Being from a prosperous resort city established since Roman days, I'm always amazed at how very different these little wilderness settlements are."

Was that her way of hinting she wanted to return to England as soon as she could? John set down his mug. "I reckon they are."

She gave a nod. "The full-time residents of Bath are mostly inn-keepers and established tradesmen, you know, everyone trying to better themselves financially and socially, never wanting the taint of failure to touch them."

"It's no different in Philadelphia and Baltimore, when it comes right down to it."

"Perhaps. But here in the wilderness, folks are concerned about each other and work together helping one another out. If the people of Bath had been half as caring about the welfare of their neighbors, Papa wouldn't have felt compelled to hide the fact he'd been cheated out of a huge sum of money. People would have come to our aid and donated enough funds to pay his creditors until Papa could recoup his losses. Folks around here truly live by the Bible principle to love your neighbor as yourself." Her gaze gravitated to the ceiling. "We hold our church services in this simple abode, yet I feel closer to God here than I ever did in that magnificently ornate cathedral in Bath."

She was happy here. John relaxed and gave an offhanded shrug. "It's a wonderful place to live. . .even without all the shops you womenfolk love so much." A teasing smile tugged at his lips.

Lily chuckled. "Now, I wouldn't go so far as to say that."

Laughter bubbled up inside John, but it died as he noticed how beautifully the firelight played across her blond hair. How. . .

Coughing came from the bedroom—his and Susan's. Assaulted by guilt, he frowned and cocked an ear toward the sound.

"I spoke to Eva Shepard and Grandma Margaret about her condition today," Lily said, drawing his attention back to her. "I told them Susan eats hardly anything. Eva suggested that rather than only offering food at mealtimes, I should bring her a little something once every hour and encourage her to take a few bites. And Maggie said Susan should drink water or tea along with it. I do think that might help. I don't know why I never thought of doing so myself."

John released a slow breath. "Mayhap because you have so many other burdens. And now one more is added."

Meeting his gaze, Lily offered him a weary smile. "You forget I have the children. Sweet little Emma has taken it upon herself to brush Susan's hair every morning, and she is careful to be really gentle with her strokes. She also picks wildflowers for her." She paused in thought. "Even Davy loves to help me with his mama. He's really a tenderhearted little boy."

"Right. When he's not yelling and stomping his feet in here like a buffalo."

Her smile broadened. "He surely is the life of the house. One cannot deny that."

And you're the heart. John barely caught himself from blurting the thought aloud. How could he be thinking such a thing when his beloved wife lay at death's door? He picked up his cup and drained the last of his tea. "Well, I'd best get to bed myself. The neighbors will be back again in the morning." *Along with that randy pair, Jackson and Frank Dunlap.*

Chapter 6

Lily paused on the footbridge for a solitary moment. After the Sabbath meal, most of the other young people had hurried across to the blockhouse for its inaugural frolic. As heavy footfalls coming up behind jarred the log beneath her, Lily's spirits sank. There was no mistaking those Dunlaps.

Purposely not turning to greet them, she held on to her cheerful attitude while taking measure of the tall, square, newly completed structure. The bottom floor had only one entrance and no windows. The top half of the upper floor, however, was open all the way around, creating a roofed watchtower. "It's hard to believe you men finished that in such a short time."

"We had to." Frank craned his neck around her. "So you an' me could dance the first reel together." A rakish spark lit his dark eyes.

"Quite right. You did ask before the others." She deliberately took lively steps away from him.

"Don't forget, I get the second," Jackson reminded from behind his brother.

"And Robby is third, and Donald fourth." Though she'd spoken lightly, she thought of the younger girls and turned to face the pair. " 'Tis important to me that when you dance with the other lasses you really and truly enjoy their company. I'd hate for you to hurt any of their feelings."

"That's what I love about you." Jackson grinned. "You always think about others before yourself."

"And I love your smiling ways." Frank was not to be outdone.

Lily looked from one to the other and back. "Thank you both for your flattering comments, but we'd better hurry. I hear your father's fiddle striking up a tune."

Descending the steps cut from the large end of the log, Lily was impressed by Jackson's surprisingly mature compliment, that he considered her character rather than her appearance. Perhaps her preoccupation elsewhere had blinded her to his attributes. After all, he was part of the military, and that required a certain sense of responsibility. He likely possessed other fine qualities, as well, if given a chance. This afternoon she'd study each of her suitors with a less biased eye.

Ignoring the steps as they followed her, the brothers leaped off the log. Each grabbed one of her arms, tucking it within his.

Jackson gave her arm a squeeze. "I'm glad John's not comin'. A body'd think he was your big brother, the way he watches over you."

Lily glanced back across the creek to the house, where on the porch with the older folks, John sat next to Susan, exactly where he should be. His wife needed him so, and his visit was nearing an end. Their time together was precious. Turning forward, she warded off a swell of disappointment by trying to recall Jackson's compliment, but the words he'd said eluded her. Despite her best efforts to the contrary, thoughts of John stole them away.

Tears blurred Lily's vision as she folded the last small loaf of bread in cheesecloth and placed it in the top of John's knapsack, above the items she'd packed the previous evening. Two week's leave had passed too quickly, and any moment now, John would emerge from the bedroom, from his last good-bye with Susan.

He was leaving. How ever would she cope? Or Susan or the children? She had to cope. They all would. Blotting the moisture from her eyes with the hem of her apron, she drew a steadying breath.

The first blush of dawn glimmered in peach-hued glory through the trees. Soon he'd be on his way. She sank onto her dining chair and poured herself another cup of strong tea as she stared at the knapsack slumped on the table. He had to realize how desperately ill Susan was, yet he was determined to report back to military duties. How could he be so callous?

A creak sounded behind her. The door at the parlor end opened, casting John in a silhouette as he stepped out of the bedroom and closed the door.

Her chest tightening, Lily came to her feet.

He crossed the room, and the flicker from the hearth fire mirrored in his clear, blue eyes as he met her gaze. Stopping directly before her, he spoke quietly. "She finally agreed."

"To what?" Surely he hadn't convinced his wife to attempt the trip to Philadelphia!

"To let us write to her father and have him send a physician here. She knows she's not strong enough to travel. The man can easily afford to send the best. . .if he will."

Elated, Lily caught his arm. "Oh, John. What a splendid idea." Then coming to her senses, she removed her hand, lest he think her forward.

He didn't seem to notice her discomfort. "Susan probably told you he wrote a letter to her soon after we eloped, saying he'd disowned her. It caused her no end of grief."

"Yes. I find it hard to believe a father could be so heartless. She can barely speak of him without tears filling her eyes. It's been a great sadness."

"Has it ever. Over the years, I've tried to convince her he'd written those words in the heat of the moment and that if he knew of her illness, he'd want her to get well again."

"Indeed. 'Tis only right."

He nodded in thought, then tipped his head. "Well, my dear girl, I'm afraid I must be on my way. If you wouldn't mind, I'd appreciate it if you would pen the letter while I saddle Smokey. I'll take the missive as far as the mouth of the Swatara and give it to someone to take downriver from there. Hopefully, Mr. Gilford will receive it within a week or so."

"Y–you're taking the horse?" Their only horse. . .

A gentle smile softened his features. "Only as far as the MacBrides'. Young Michael promised to ride him back later this morning."

Somewhat relieved at the news, Lily watched John toss on his heavy hunting shirt and walk out of the cabin. How silly she'd been to panic over an animal. It was John's departure that warranted all her angst. She would hold herself together until he actually bid her farewell and took his leave. She would get through this. After all, the man was her best friend's husband. He must never know of the improper desires of her heart. The last person who deserved to be hurt was Susan, her dearest friend in the world.

After collecting the writing materials, she could hardly concentrate on the correct words to say in her plea to Susan's father. John's departure kept intruding. She forced herself to use her finest penmanship, which did help.

Too soon his footsteps sounded on the steps, and he blew in on a rush of cold morning air.

Lily folded the hopefully sincere request then dripped wax from a nearby candle to seal it. Rising, she held it out to John. "I did my best to explain her condition and the *urgency* of her need." She hoped her emphasis on the word *urgency* would give John further pause about leaving. Surely he realized his wife's very life was draining away. How ever could he go?

"Thank you, Lily-girl. I've no doubt about that." He slipped the letter into his haversack and hooked one arm through its strap. Blinking sudden moisture from his eyes, he swallowed hard. Then he took a step closer and reached out a hand to cup her face. "Please, dear Lily, don't look so frightened. Cal Patterson and Toby Dunlap have promised to scout the Indian path every day. If they see anything suspicious, they'll fire warning shots. Don't forget to answer with a shot of your own. Then immediately reload and—"

She covered his hand with hers. "I know. You've taught me well. And get Susan to the blockhouse as soon as possible."

"Right." His eyes searched hers for an eternal moment. Then, unexpectedly, John drew her close and wrapped his arms around her. Crushing her against himself, he buried his face in her hair. "You don't know how wretched I feel having to leave you here with all this."

She felt the whisper of his breath ruffle a few stray hairs. Pressing closer, she clasped her arms about him, not daring to breathe, not daring to hope. . . .

Then, just as suddenly, he released her and averted his gaze. "Forgive me. . . . I must go." Snatching his rifle from above the door, he hurried out, leaving her bereft of his comforting warmth.

Oh, how she had reveled in that brief embrace, feeling the strong beat of his heart, inhaling the woodsy scent that was his alone, feeling for an instant that her dreams might—

Reality tore away that wayward hope. Awash in a wave of tears, Lily ran blindly to the door and flung it wide for one last glimpse of him, no longer caring if John saw her cry.

But he was already mounted and riding away.

⌐———

Reaching the MacBride farmyard at the break of dawn, John spied his friend Patrick stepping off the porch of his darkened house.

"It's started."

The dreaded news gripped John as he dismounted. "Where? When?"

"A few weeks ago, up New York way. Fifteen hundred—maybe upwards of two thousand—French and Indians attacked Fort William Henry at Lake Champlain."

The concept of an attack of that magnitude was harrowing.

Patrick caught Smokey's reins and wrapped them around a fence rail. "They outnumbered the men at William Henry at least five to one." He eyed John. "Don't look so down in the mouth. It seems when the French sent Major Eyre an order to surrender, the post commander responded that he and his men would defend the fort to the last man."

"Good for him. Who wants to be taken prisoner and handed over to be tortured by bloodthirsty Indians?"

"You can't guess what happened next." Unaccountably, Patrick cracked a grin. "The French burned all the outbuildings and the fleet of sloops and whaleboats, then turned around and went back home." He clamped a hand on John's shoulder. "Can you believe it?"

John tucked his chin in disbelief. "Who told you that?"

"Ham Lister, from up the Swatara, near Fort Lebanon. He stopped here for the night yester's eve on his way home."

"Well, if what he said is true, it sounds like the French have been taking lessons in fumbling from General Ambercrombie."

Patrick hooted. "That's just what I told Lister last night."

At his friend's grin, John felt his own smile break forth. "Who knows? There may be hope for us yet."

"Ain't that what we been prayin' for?"

"Quite." John shifted his stance. "By the way, speaking of praying, I have a letter in my knapsack to post, and it needs to be well received. It's going downriver to Susan's father, asking him to send her the most learned physician in Philadelphia."

Patrick hiked a brow in understanding. "Didn't you tell me her pa had a successful brickmakin' business?"

"Right. Her family is quite prosperous." He began untying his bedroll from behind the horse's saddle. "The problem is that all of Susie's life, her father and older brother dictated her every move. And for her to marry a mere furniture-maker's apprentice was out of the question. I have to say, though, since having children of my own and knowing the powerful love I have for each one, I can't help but believe Mr. Gilford must still care for his daughter. . .enough to send a good doctor."

"What father wouldn't?" Patrick tipped his head toward John's belongings. "Put your stuff on the step with mine till the others get here."

"Will do." After setting down his gear, John spoke in all candor. "You know, if it hadn't been for Susie agreeing to have me send that letter, I doubt I could've walked out the door this morning. She's so weak. Almost helpless. It's the worst possible time for me to go away. . .only it can't be helped." He grimaced. His leaving had been imperative. Even discounting the prospect of being charged with desertion, a more important reason remained.

Lily.

Somewhere along the way, she'd become far more than just a bond servant. . .more than a young sister. . .more than a friend. He loved Susan with his whole heart, and nothing would ever change that. But he could not deny he had developed feelings for Lily, also. Feelings he had no right to have. No matter how hard he prayed for strength, one look into those pleading gray eyes of hers, and he'd caught her to him, held her close, felt her soft body pressed against his. Even now, the very breath he drew retained her warm scent. Coward that he was, he positively could not remain at home any longer. *The Bible does instruct us to flee from temptation. . .and that's what I'm doing.*

Pat's voice cut into his thoughts. "Here come those Duncans, right on time. If anybody was goin' to be draggin' his feet this mornin', I figured it'd be Jackson. That boy's sure sweet on your Lily."

My Lily. The memory of Jackson putting his hands on her infuriated John, but he restrained himself from blurting something malicious. Until now he'd always liked the lad. Time to start treating him with his due respect again. Jackson might not be educated, but he was a hard worker. Even with bullets flying all around them, he'd proved to be worth his salt as a soldier. Only last year, when John had been shot, it was Jackson who'd helped him back to the fort. He owed the kid.

All the same, John didn't want to be fielding questions about Lily. Especially not now. "I'll take my belongings to the canoe. By the time we float down past the mouth of Beaver Creek, Bob'll be there waiting."

Gathering spring greens along the creek, Lily glanced at Emma, noting how the little girl favored Susan, with her huge blue-green eyes, delicate cheekbones, and heart-shaped face. The child somehow seemed older than she'd been herself at that age. "You truly are a big help, do you know that?"

The little redhead smiled. "I like to help, 'specially on a nice day like this."

"Me, too." But Lily couldn't help observing Emma's overly fair complexion. The child spent far too much time inside, sitting with her mother.

Emma glanced over Lily's shoulder and let out a disgusted huff. "Aww, here comes that pest."

Lily followed her helper's gaze, to see Davy running pell-mell down the bank. She gasped when he tripped and tumbled to the bottom in a shower of gravel. But undaunted by the new dirt ground into his breeches, he sprang to his feet. "What'cha doin'? Playin' in the water?"

"No, dummy. We're pickin' greens for Mama's soup." His sister flared her apron wide, displaying her bounty.

"I wanna help." He grabbed up a bunch of water grass. "See? Green!" He held up the straggle of blades with a muddy hand.

Lily responded before Emma could deride her brother again. "Why, thank you, Davy. But we're looking for special green leaves." She held out a ruffled leaf from her apron's collection. "See if you can find others like—"

Duke's barking echoed from the barnyard. Sharp. Ominous.

"Somebody's comin'!" Davy sprang like a jack-in-the-box to his feet.

Lily caught him by his shirttail before he could bolt and spoke in her no-nonsense tone. "Wait here. And be quiet. I'll go see what's wrong." The approaching supper hour was an odd time for anyone to pay a visit. Leaving the children behind, she climbed the bank and searched toward the house, where the dog remained on alert, still barking toward the wagon trail.

Matt and Luke charged out of the stable, with Matt sprinkling black powder in his musket's flashpan as he ran.

When the dog's barking became even more shrill and steady, Lily stopped and pulled out her tin of gunpowder to ready her own weapon. He'd have quieted by now if it were a neighbor approaching. Reluctant to expose herself, she sidled up against the corncrib and peered around it, while the boys sprang up the cabin steps and waited in the porch's late afternoon shadow.

The sound of several horses pricked her ears.

Fear trickled down Lily's spine. John had been gone less than three weeks. He wouldn't be coming back so soon—unless a war party was headed this way. Uneasiness spread through her.

Four mounted riders trotted up alongside the cabin and reined in, facing the front. Two wore the familiar attire of frontiersmen, and two had on tailored suits. From her position, Lily couldn't make out their faces.

She saw her brave Matt step out of the shadow, his weapon crooked in his arm, but not aimed, letting the newcomers know he was armed. "Afternoon." His brother moved to his side.

One of the frontiersmen hiked his chin. "Afternoon, lad. This the Waldon place?"

"It is."

"Thank the good Lord." One of the better-dressed men began to dismount, and the others did the same.

Deciding they seemed genuine and posed no threat, Lily moved into view, her worry escalating as she walked toward the group. "Have you brought bad news? Has something happened to John?"

As one, they turned to her. "No, miss." A distinguished, older man of medium height, with fading auburn hair and a thin mustache, tipped his hat. "Actually, we fully expected him to be here."

"I'm afraid he's not. May I be of service?"

"Allow me to introduce myself. I'm Brandon Gilford. Susan Waldon's father."

Susan's father? Lily couldn't believe her ears. He'd come! "Is the gentleman with you a physician?"

Mr. Gilford's companion, equally well dressed but more thickly built, bowed slightly. "Dr. Harold Shelby, at your service, miss."

"Praise God!" Rushing forward, she threw her arms about Mr. Gilford's neck. "Thank you! I prayed you'd come."

Clearing his throat, the man gently extracted her arms. But his mouth spread into a jovial smile. "I'd prefer it if you'd turn that pistol the other way."

"Oh. Of course." As Lily blushed in embarrassment, Matt and Luke jumped off the porch and shook hands with the visitors.

The two little ones came running out of the trees, with Davy in the lead. "How do. How do," the towhead called out on the way. "I'm Davy. What's your name?"

Lily snagged him before he slammed into the men. "Mr. Gilford, I'd like you to meet your youngest grandson, David. Right behind him is our sweet Emma, and I believe Matthew and Luke have already introduced themselves. Children, this is your grandfather."

"You mean like Grampa Mac?" Davy scrunched up his nose.

"No." Matt came to his brother's side. "This is our real grandpa. Mama's papa. He's brought a doctor to help her get better."

Mr. Gilford's smile vanished, and lines of worry furrowed his brow as he met Lily's gaze. "How is my daughter, Miss—"

Lily blanched. "Oh. Forgive me. I'm Lily Harwood. Your son-in-law hired me to take care of Susan."

He gave a nod. "The letter I received merely stated that she had a prolonged ailment which Baltimore physicians could not diagnose and that she was in dire need."

Lily endeavored to convey the situation without using words that might overly alarm the younger children. "Suffice it to say her health is most tenuous. Do come in, gentlemen. Matt and Luke, would you please see to the horses?"

As the group started inside, Davy latched on to Mr. Gilford's hand. "I like grampas."

"And I love grandsons, my boy." He chuckled.

Watching the exchange, Lily's relief was so palpable at knowing the men had come to help, she wanted to cry, but there was no time for tears. Four guests had just arrived for supper.

She only wished it could be a more joyous occasion.

Chapter 7

This is our house." Davy puffed out his chest, jabbering with boyish pride as he led his grandfather and the other guest inside. "Our pa built it. And we have the bestest table in the whole cove. Pa made it before he went off to kill Injuns."

Preceding Lily into the cabin, Mr. Gilford shot a frown back at her.

Obviously the man had no idea that John had gone away. Afraid of what he might say, Lily squeezed Emma's hand. "Sweetheart, our guests must be awfully thirsty after their trip. Would you please run down to the springhouse for the pitcher of buttermilk?"

The child opened her mouth as if to protest, then closed it. "Yes, ma'am." She turned with a swirl of her muslin skirt and raced down the steps in an obvious rush to get back before she missed too much.

"And Davy, go out to the cellar and get four more big carrots—so we can fix supper for our company." The explanation squelched the imp's inclination to balk. With his lower lip protruding, he scampered off.

Lily gestured toward the parlor. "Do have a seat, gentlemen." Having heard from Susan about her father's finely appointed mansion, she couldn't help casting an assessing look around the simple room with its sturdy, pillowed chairs—all John and Susan's handiwork. The only embellishments were a pair of framed proverbs Susan had embroidered in her better days and hung on the walls. Even the window curtains had faded over time and showed wear. Surely a prosperous city dweller would find the abode crude indeed. But that could not be helped. Either the man would approve of his daughter's circumstances or he would not. Nothing could be done about it.

Despite her misgivings, Lily saw only deep concern on the gentleman's face as he paused in the middle of the long room. "May I see my daughter?"

"I'll take you to her, sir." But as she neared Susan's chamber, she added a warning whisper. "Please prepare yourself. Susan is extremely thin and frail. Very weak."

His golden brows shelved over his eyes in concern. "Just take me to her, Miss Harwood."

Lily hoped that after all the years that had passed, the man didn't still harbor anger toward her dear friend. "This way, please."

Reaching the bedroom door, he rushed past Lily and strode in, then stopped so suddenly, she nearly bumped into him.

"I thought I heard visitors." Lying in bed, Susan had expended the effort to sound cheery as she attempted to raise her head. "Lily, dear, would you help me sit up?"

Lily sidestepped Mr. Gilford and hurried to the bedside. Plucking an extra pillow from a nearby chair, she reached under Susan's shoulder and brought her up with very little assistance from her mistress.

Mr. Gilford, lingering near the doorway, released an audible breath and spoke in a hoarse murmur. "Susan, it's your papa. I'm here, honeybee." With a watery smile, he crossed to the bed.

"Papa? Is it really you?" Reality gave Susan's voice strength. "Papa!" She stretched out her hands to him.

With a moan, the loving father knelt beside his daughter's bed and drew her gently into his embrace, and the two wept in each other's arms.

Lily's eyes flooded at the joyous reunion she'd hardly dared hope to see. The good Lord had brought the man here, had provided a father and a daughter with a chance to erase silent years that had separated them, before it was too late. Knowing she was no longer needed, Lily slipped quietly from the bedchamber, swiping away her tears with both hands.

"Miss?" The doctor looked up as Lily closed the door behind her. "May I speak with you?" Seated in the parlor with the two bearded frontiersmen, who looked ill at ease dressed in heavy garb in the warm room, he stood to his feet. He smoothed his brocade waistcoat over the curve of his belly.

"Of course, Dr. Shelby." She sniffed, trying to regain her composure. "Please join me near the hearth, if you would. I need to check the stew." She was loath to speak of Susan's personal ailments in front of the backwoods strangers. Reaching the fireplace, she unhooked her big wooden spoon and potholder and lifted the lid from the footed kettle, giving the mixture a few stirs.

The physician stopped beside her. "Miss Harwood, the letter you wrote to Mr. Gilford was quite vague. Would you describe in detail the nature of your mistress's ailment?"

Gathering her thoughts, Lily replaced the spoon and moved past him to take a seat at the table.

He did as well, never taking his eyes from her. "Is the invalid contagious?"

Elevating her brows, Lily stared into his wide-set eyes. "No, sir. When I first entered into service for the Waldons, Mr. Gilford's daughter had recently given birth to Davy. Her joints had started to swell, causing her a good deal of pain. The physician in Baltimore suspected it was some sort of rheumatism and gave her a tonic, along with salves he felt might help. They did not."

He pursed his lips. "So. Might I ask why the Waldons left Baltimore for this remote settlement if she was unwell?" The man glanced around the rustic room, his disdain more than obvious.

Offended by his superior attitude, Lily felt her hackles rise. "They'd already purchased the land here, and since the doctor didn't know anything else to do for Susan, she insisted they not alter their plans to move here and put down their roots. Sometime later, when a skin rash developed, her husband wrote to the physician for advice."

"What was the doctor's name? Perhaps I know of him."

"A Dr. Whetsler, I believe."

He nodded. "Yes. He's considered competent enough."

"Indeed. Well, he suggested the rash might be due to something she ate. He sent more salve, which helped somewhat. After that, Susan had good days and bad as the swelling and rashes would come and go. . . up until this year, that is. Now it's as if her condition has moved deeper inside her. We've become very concerned about her breathing of late. . . and her heart."

She leaned closer and lowered her voice. "And I don't think Susan is"—hesitant to speak of such private matters, Lily searched for more delicate words—"expelling her fluids as she should."

Dr. Shelby rubbed a hand across his stubbly jaw. "I was afraid of this. So, I might add, was her father."

"What do you mean?"

"Some years ago, an older aunt of Susan's suffered from the same ailment. And its onset also came after the birth of a child."

At his words, relief surged through Lily. "Oh. Thank heavens. Then you'll know what can be done for my mistress. That's splendid."

His expression did not waver. He wagged his head and sighed. "I'm afraid it's quite the opposite, child. I tried every remedy possible. The good woman continued to waste away and finally passed on, leaving all my colleagues in Philadelphia and Boston as baffled as I was."

Alarm tightened Lily's throat. "Surely there's still hope for Susan! There must be something you can try. Some way to alleviate her condition."

"The most advice I can offer at this point is to keep Mrs. Waldon as comfortable as possible, until. . . ."

Having her hopes dashed at her feet, Lily's heart plummeted. She jumped up. "That's it? There's nothing to be done? I refuse to accept that."

Angry now, her breaths came out fast and hard as she crossed her arms in despair.

"What's happening?" Davy charged into the cabin, clutching carrots in his hand. "Are you gonna do somethin' without me?"

Schooling her features, Lily composed herself and knelt down to his level. "No, dear. We won't do a single thing without you. Thank you for fetching the carrots for our stew." She took them and stood up.

A flash of movement out the window revealed Emma coming, soft-footed and cautious as she toted the big, heavy pitcher of buttermilk.

Suddenly the dire news the doctor had uttered filled Lily with new horror. Her knees went weak, and she caught hold of the chairback. *Dear Emmy. Would the sweet child one day suffer the same terrible fate as her mother?*

Mr. Gilford spent nearly every waking moment of the next two heartrending days with his daughter. His presence lifted Susan's spirits so there seemed a slight improvement in her condition. Her smiles came more easily, and Lily often heard light laughter drifting from the bedchamber where Susan visited with her father.

But the time had come for the party to leave for Philadelphia once again. Passing by the room, Lily caught sight of Mr. Gilford sitting on the edge of Susan's bed, rocking her in his arms and kissing her. Their tearful farewell brought a lump to Lily's throat. She feared it would be their last time together.

The man's voice was husky with emotion as he murmured in his daughter's ear. "The moment I get home, honeybee, I'll make arrangements to bring your mother to visit you. It'll take awhile longer to get here next time, though, since we'll have to travel upriver."

"I know, Papa. Mama could never abide riding horseback." Susan brushed at her tears with a trembling hand. "Thank you for. . .being my papa again. I missed you so."

He buried his face in her hair and clasped her tight. "I can't believe I let my foolish pride come between us. It was unpardonable. I shall never forgive myself." Finally he eased away and stood to his feet, emitting a ragged breath as he gazed down at the wasted form of his once-healthy child. "I love you, my darling daughter," he mumbled hoarsely and rushed from the room.

Lily barely got out of his way as he stumbled toward the front door, his fists rubbing his eyes. Running after him, she nearly collided with him when he stopped short.

He swiveled on his heel, his eyes red and puffy. "I loathe having to leave my darling girl here. It's not safe." He'd expressed the sentiment several times since his arrival. "If only she could. . ."

Lily placed an empathetic hand on his arm. "I know, sir. If only."

"The French are on the move down from Lake Ontario again, you know. And with a very large force."

"Yes, so you've mentioned before. And if you're aware of that, I'm certain the commanders of our northern forts are, as well. I pray they'll be better prepared this year."

Mr. Gilford scoffed. "They would if they'd put brave fighters like our Rogers' Rangers in charge. But no—the king sends us cowards from England to lead our men. What a waste." His eyes narrowed. "John Waldon should never have abandoned my daughter here to face this danger alone. That mortician's whelp has no business—"

Lily squeezed his arm and frowned. "Please sir, do lower your voice."

He glanced toward Susan's room and drew a futile breath.

"Mr. Gilford, when John's militia was called to service, Susan was suffering only from swollen joints. And though he desperately wants to be here now, you know he would be charged with desertion were he to leave his post."

"Yes. Well. We'll see about that. The man should be here. His superior is Captain Busse, I believe you said. Rest assured, I'll be paying Governor Denny a visit as soon as I reach Philadelphia. I am not without influence, I assure you."

"In that case, I shall pray for your success. All of us would appreciate having John home where he belongs. Susan needs him now, most desperately."

His pale brows flattened as his demeanor eased, and he touched the side of her face, bringing to Lily's mind the remembrance of John's parting touch. "You are an incredibly brave lass, Lily Harwood. My daughter cannot say enough good things about you. I'd like to thank you personally for taking such wonderful care of my Susan and the children." He paused. "Speaking of the children. . ." Turning, he opened the door and strode outside.

A few yards beyond the porch, the youngsters stood waiting with Dr. Shelby and the frontiersmen. The three men sat astride their mounts. Mr. Gilford approached the group but spoke to his grandchildren. "Dear ones, my offer still stands. Any of you who would like to come with me and see where we live, I'd be more than happy to take you along. Emma?" He moved closer to the little girl. "Your Grandmother Gilford would dearly love to meet you, to see how much you look like your mama did when she was your age."

Emma shyly met his gaze. "I thought you said you were going to bring her here."

"That's true. I did say that."

"Then thank you, Grampa, but I can see her then. My mama needs me here."

"Wait!" Davy shoved between his sister and the older man. "I changed my mind. I want to go to Phila—Phila—def. I'm a good rider, you'll see. I won't fall off. I wanna go." Excitement laced his expression. "But I hafta be back for supper. Lily's makin' apple pandowdy just for me."

Mr. Gilford knelt down before the child. "I'm afraid you'd have to skip supper if you came with us, Davy. It takes three days to get to Philadelphia on horseback."

"Nights, too?" He took a step back. "I guess I shouldn't go so far. Mama and Lily'd miss me too much."

"Yes, lad." His grandfather sighed. "I suppose they would." He turned to the older boys and extended a hand to them in a firm grasp. "You're the men of the house while your father is away. I'm counting on you to take care of my dear ones." Then, looking back at Lily with a sad wag of his head, he mounted his horse, and the group rode away.

The wall clock in Captain Busse's office ticked off seconds as the man sat back in his chair, his fingers steepled over his stomach. "Look here, Waldon. If I were to allow everyone leave who says he has someone who needs him at home, there wouldn't be a—" Waving a hand uselessly in the air, he shook his head. "You know what I mean."

John tipped his head, hoping. "But sir, Bob Randall and Pat MacBride can verify what I'm saying. My wife is failing fast. I fear she won't be with us much longer." It galled him to have to beg for something that, under normal circumstances, would be a given. But he had to try.

"Might I remind you that you told me your wife was ailing over a year ago, and she hasn't passed on yet."

Rage boiled up inside John. The man was not only devoid of sensitivity, he was inferring John was a liar.

At John's stony silence, Busse came to his feet behind his desk. "I apologize, Corporal Waldon. That was a horrible thing to say. Truth is, since I was ordered to send half our men north to Fort Augusta, I simply can't spare a man. The folks in the settlements south of here are depending on us—including your own family." He shrugged. "I'm sorry. I can't give you leave."

A knock sounded on the office door.

"Come in." Busse hiked his chin at John. "That'll be all."

The orderly saluted the commander as he passed John in the doorway. "Governor Denny just rode in with a party of men, sir."

"Reinforcements?" The leader's tone held an optimistic note.

John felt renewed hope himself. Maybe he'd be given leave yet.

"Sorry, sir. Merely an escort."

Despite his disappointment, John couldn't help feeling impressed that the governor himself had come here. Had the war ended? Had he come all the way from Philadelphia to announce it personally?

Glancing out the headquarters' door John spotted a distinguished-looking man who must be the governor out on the porch, facing rapidly gathering militiamen. Obviously they, too, knew there had to be an important reason for someone in such a high position to visit this remote fort.

"Men." The gentleman in his fine attire raised a hand for order. "First of all, I wish to thank each and every one of you for your service. If not for your sacrifice, we, the citizens of Pennsylvania, would not be able to rest at night. Therefore it is vital that when your year is up, you re-enlist."

Groans of outrage came from every quarter as the enlisted men swapped dark glowers.

Flicking travel dust from his frock coat, the governor shifted his stance. "Men, our very colony is at stake. I entreat you to write to your friends and neighbors. Ask them to come and join you in this fight."

A shout came from the ranks. "What friends? What neighbors? Every settler that can be spared's already here."

Governor Denny gave a grave nod. "Then we must dig deeper. Sacrifice more to save our colony. The situation is quite dire. Last year the burning and pillaging came within thirty miles of Philadelphia."

"Then how about you give this speech to all them city fellas sleepin' safe an' sound in Philadelphia?" came from the back of the gathering. "We ain't seen hide nor hair of none of them hereabouts."

Bob Randall chimed in from the side. "And while you're at it, send back our men who got sent up to Fort Augusta. We're spread thinner than skimmed milk here. And we got a lot a territory that needs coverin' betwixt us an' the other forts."

"Hear! Hear!" shouted others in chorus.

The governor raised his hand for silence. "Again, I thank you all. I shall speak to you more formally once I've had a chance to confer with your commander." With that, he heeled around and headed for the doorway John occupied.

John quickly stepped aside, glad the men had spoken their minds.

He joined Bob as the crowd began to disperse. "In November, when my enlistment is up, it'll take a whole lot more to get me to sign up again than some glad-hander showing up with lots of words, but without a single company of reinforcements."

"*Reinforcements!*" Behind Bob, militiaman Fred Stuart snorted. "I overheard one of the governor's escorts admit that even New York Indian Agent William Johnson can't rally his Mohawks to fight for us anymore—and you know how they love bloodying those tomahawks of theirs."

"That doesn't sound good." Bob huffed. "I heard they think of him as one of their war chiefs. Isn't Johnson married to one of their Indian princesses?"

"I say we all just walk on outta here right now," Stuart muttered. "Go collect our families and traipse on down to Philadelphia and sit down on our behinds, like them fine city folks are doin.'"

Bob sniffed in disdain. "If we did that, the Frenchies would move in and burn up everything we spent all this time breakin' our backs over."

John nodded in sad agreement. "We hoped to give our children a future they'd never have if we hadn't come out here." He sighed. "Being away from my family for months on end, it's hard sometimes to remember why I'm here." He turned to Bob. "Busse turned down my request for leave. Again."

His friend clapped him on the shoulder with a commiserating wince. "Sorry. I figured he would."

"But. . .Susan's dying, Bob. I can feel it right here." He pressed a fist to his chest. "She's dying, and I'm not there. Duty or no duty, I'd never be able to live with myself if I couldn't be with her at. . .the end." He all but choked on the last word.

Chapter 8

"Susan. . .Susan. . . Please speak to me." Leaning over the bed, Lily gently shook her friend's arm. A wave of grief washed over her like a flood. There was no denying the end was near. Susan's breathing during the night had become so labored Lily had been unable to sleep. She'd gotten up several times to check on her. Now, finding no response except that horrid rasping, Lily could only send desperate pleas heavenward, praying for strength. . .praying for her friend to live one more day. . .praying that John would come to be with his wife in her final moments. Susan deserved that much. So did he.

Scuffing and banging came from the main room as the children readied the house for the Sabbath gathering. *They don't even realize it may be their mother's last day, Lord.* A heaviness pressed on her chest, making it hard to breathe. Should she tell them before the service, or spare them? *What should I do?*

Stepping out of the bedchamber, she quietly closed the door. A quick glance revealed the older boys setting up the benches.

"Hurry up, Lily." Matt plunked his end of the board down atop a keg.

"You're not dressed for church. Folks'll be comin' any minute."

Afraid to open her mouth for fear her throat would close around the dreadful news, Lily schooled her expression to remain composed and acknowledged him with a nod. She spied Emma across the way, trying to tame Davy's cowlick with a comb as the imp squirmed beneath his sister's hand. The children were so happy, so busy. How could she steal their joy by telling them about their mother now? She propped up a smile. "Your mama doesn't feel up to joining us for the service this morning. I think it's best if we don't disturb her. We'll let her rest."

Walking into the bedroom she shared with Emma, grief gave way to anger. How could she concentrate on something so trivial as dressing? John should be here. He'd seen his wife's condition before he'd gone off almost three months ago. He had to know Susan would only continue to grow weaker. Lily had sent word relating the situation not two weeks past. Surely it had reached him.

And what of Susan's parents? Mr. Gilford had promised to return posthaste with his wife, yet where were they? Five weeks allowed them more than sufficient time to return by river. Their daughter and her children had been waiting for them, watching for them, for the past fortnight.

Dear, sweet Susan. She'd suffered more than a body should endure. How it hurt to see the pain in her eyes, and in the children's, as she grew steadily more fragile and helpless. If her parents ever did arrive, it would likely be too late.

Weary from too little sleep and already sticky from the July heat, Lily slipped into the bare minimum of petticoats and tossed on the first gown she touched. Whipping her hair up into a simple knot, she jammed enough pins in to hold it in place, hoping the dark circles under her eyes would keep Robby Randall from being such a pest today. She had no patience for his constant hovering.

She sighed and turned away from the mirror. The last thing she felt like doing was taking part in a Sabbath meeting. She swept her eyes toward the ceiling. *Father God, please fill me with Your love and charity. And please, tamp down the rage building inside me. Susan so needs Your touch now. I don't know how to pray for her. She's in Your hands. Please be merciful. . . . She's suffered for such a long time.* Drawing a calming breath only reminded her of her dear friend's constant struggle for air. Life was so unfair to the poor, abandoned wife.

Adult voices drifted from the other side of her door as neighbors began to arrive. Straightening her shoulders, Lily manufactured as much of a smile as she could and went out to greet them. Why, oh why, did this have to be the Sabbath?

"There you are, Miss Lily." Ian MacBride bobbed his white head in greeting as he strode toward her between two rows of benches. He flicked a thumb in the direction of the door. "The others are still outside, tryin' to keep cool."

"'Tis rather close this morning, is it not?" Lily flattened her lips.

The elder held out a thick, folded paper to her. "A fella goin' upstream dropped this letter off with yer name on. From that Mr. Gilford, looks like."

She elevated a brow in scorn. "A letter? Fancy excuses, more likely." Her eyes swam as she looked up at him. "Even as we speak, their daughter is in there dying, and her father sends a useless letter."

Moved by the news, the Scot wheeled around and bolted for the door.

Men. Lily glared after him. *All they ever want to do is escape.*

"Maggie, lass," Ian called. "Come inside, would ye? I need to speak with ye."

His wife appeared at once, as if she guessed something was amiss. Lines of concern deepened in her long, thin face as her astute, azure eyes beneath the ruffled cap looked right at Lily. "Oh, no. Has Susan passed? The children don't seem out of sorts."

"No. She's still with us. . .unless she stopped breathing while I was dressing." Unwilling to let the couple see how truly desperate she felt, Lily averted her gaze to the plank floor.

Margaret MacBride gave a commiserating squeeze to Lily's shoulder as she and her husband crossed to the sickroom.

Lily trailed behind them, feeling a pang of remorse for having misjudged them both. The older woman's presence always brought comfort, and Lily more than appreciated her patient concern, her motherly advice.

"Merciful heavens," Margaret murmured as she caught sight of Susan, gasping open-mouthed for every breath. She sank down onto the bedside chair and took Susan's limp hand. "How long has the dear child been like this?" She swung a questioning glance to Lily.

"I first heard her shortly after I retired last eve."

Margaret shook her head and met her husband's eyes. He bowed his head in prayer.

Outside, shouts erupted, aggravating Lily even more.

Ian parted the curtain to peer outside, but the window faced the opposite direction. "More folks comin', I 'spect."

His wife looked up at him. "Go ask them to be a bit more quiet, dear. Let them know this dear child isn't up to joinin' us at service, that I'll be sittin' with her. Oh, and when Eva gets here, send her in, would you?"

"I'll go wait for her." He left the sickroom in haste.

Lily felt a new rush of bitterness as he deserted them. . .one more fault she'd have to confess to the Lord along with having misjudged him earlier.

Margaret reached out with a bony hand and patted Lily's arm. "Don't you be frettin', child. Me an' Eva, we'll be stayin' here with you till our Susan passes."

"Oh, thank you." Crumbling with relief that Toby Dunlap's sweet mother-in-law would also join them in the vigil, Lily clutched onto the bedpost, her eyes brimming with tears. "You have no idea how much I'll appreciate having you both here. It's been. . .so hard."

"Don't I know it." Margaret picked up a cloth from the nightstand and gently blotted Susan's damp brow. "I been where you are more'n once in my life."

Yet again, Lily was grateful to be living among these kind people. When her own mother passed away, not one neighbor had come to lend a shred of assistance or comfort to her sister or their father except the physician. Rose had been barely thirteen at the time, and everything had fallen to her and Papa. With four younger siblings to care for and a household to run, small wonder Rose had grown into such a strong person. Lily had admired her older sister all of her life and hoped one day to emulate her.

If only Rose were here now...especially when the time came to break the sad news to the children. She always managed to say just the right thing.

"The young'uns don't know how bad their mama is, do they?"

Lily shook her head. "I didn't want them to see her like this. I just..."

"I understand." Margaret gazed down once more at Susan, her eyes soft. "You might consider sendin' Emma and Davy off to spend the night with their little friends."

"Yes, that would be best. I particularly wouldn't want sweet little Emma to see her mother's final struggle. 'Twould be something she'd carry in her memory the rest of her life. 'Tis best they remember her smiling, even in her illness." Lily paused, considering how to relate her next comment. "The doctor said there's a possibility that Emma might be stricken with this same affliction in years to come. Susan's aunt also died of it."

"Mercy me." Margaret kneaded her forehead. "What a frightful thought. Speakin' of that Philadelphia doctor, are you ever going to break the seal on the letter from Susan's pa?"

Lily glanced down to see the missive crumpled in her fist. "I forgot about it." She slid a nail beneath the edge and broke the wax seal, then unfolded the paper and read it aloud.

My dear Miss Harwood,

I cannot express the pain it causes me to be sending you this message instead of coming there personally with my wife. When I reached home, I rode to the stable to see to the needs of my horse before entering the house. I missed the quarantine sign posted on the front door. Our house servant has contracted the smallpox, and no one who enters may leave until the notice has been removed. My wife and I considered sneaking away under the cover of night. But then we thought better of it. We would never forgive ourselves were we to bring the pox to you all. We shall come as soon as we are free. Please convey this and our deepest love to our most treasured daughter and her children.

Your humble servant,
Frederick Gilford

"Now the commander at the fort will *have to* allow John to come home. You'll see." Margaret smiled, but her confidence waned after a glance at Susan. "For all the good it'll do our dear saint here."

Lily's vexation brought heat to her face.

"Our Pat sent us a message a few days back."

"You don't say." The realization that the post was getting through, just not to *her,* made Lily clench her teeth. She hadn't received a word from John in weeks.

The older woman droned on, oblivious to Lily's anger. "Mail's been real slow comin' from the fort. But Pat's been sent south to the fort at Harris's Ferry, and he found somebody comin' our way. He wrote that with the threat of them blasted Frenchies, river traffic upstream of the ferry has purty much stopped altogether."

"And?" Lily wasn't interested in excuses.

"Pat's surprised John hasn't up and deserted. John *is* that worried about his dear Susan. But the captain ain't givin' nobody leave. I was gonna tell Susan that today an' let her know her husband's itchin' to get to her."

"He should have deserted." Lily no longer tried to conceal her bitterness.

Margaret offered a droll smile. "If he did that, honey, they'd just come an' get him, lock him up for Lord only knows how long. They could even hang him."

In her heart, Lily knew that was true. John was not a heartless lout, but a loving, caring husband and father who loved his family deeply. He'd have moved heaven and earth for the opportunity to come home to them had it been possible. Her anguish spilled over into self-pity, and a wrenching sob burst from deep inside. Clapping a hand over her mouth, she swung away from Maggie.

In an instant, the older woman rose and drew Lily into her comforting arms. "I know, child, I know. It's been powerful hard for you here alone. But we're here with you now."

A Sabbath service, somewhat subdued, went on without a hitch, though spiritual leader MacBride did cut it short out of respect for Susan. No one made mention of the inevitable, yet folks seemed to sense the unspoken fate looming over the household, and the adults were considerate enough to keep their voices quiet.

That did not extend to the children. Lily detected Davy's squeal above the racket of the other children as they played blind man's bluff outside after the meal. Glancing out a small loft window, she saw little Harry Shaw spinning blindfolded Davy round and round amid peals of laughter.

Emma stood in the circle with the other children, but she wasn't laughing along with them. Her eyes remained focused on the house. Despite everyone's efforts to act as if this Sabbath was the same as all the others, Lily's little darling sensed something was terribly wrong with her mother. Never before had she and her brothers been barred from Susan's room for so long a time.

Emma, especially, needed to be away from here, and so did Davy. Lily knew it was imperative for the little ones to leave for at least a day or two. She stuffed the last article of Davy's clothing into a pillowcase and climbed down the loft ladder. Then, collecting a second pillowcase holding Emma's things, she ambled out the door.

The sound of splintering wood caught her attention. The older boys were occupied with throwing hatchets and knives at the bull's-eye painted on the side of John's abandoned carpentry shop.

She paused for a moment, studying Matt and Luke, both of whom wore grim expressions. Her explanation that their mother was sleeping and shouldn't be disturbed could not fool two such bright lads. They knew the truth. Lily felt their eyes on her as she passed by the adults speaking in hushed voices around the outdoor table.

"Lily, child." Ian MacBride, seated at the head, crooked a finger at her.

She turned back to him, hoping he wasn't expecting another report on Susan.

A kind sparkle lit his watery eyes. "Cal, here, has volunteered to ride to the fort and fetch John as soon as he gets his family home. The commander's sure to let John come now."

Having had her hopes dashed too many times already, Lily barely restrained herself from spewing her mounting exasperation. Somehow she managed to utter something trite but acceptable. "That would be a kindness." Then before she could blurt anything further, she turned on her heel and continued on to her young charges.

She waited until Davy had tagged one of the other teasing, dodging children and gleefully ripped off his blindfold before stepping up to her little towhead. "I've a most splendid surprise for you, Davy."

"For me?" His eyes rounded with delight.

"Yes. You're going to go play at Joey's house today."

"I am?" He swung his gaze to his five-year-old MacBride friend. "Hear that, Joey?"

"And his mama said you could even sleep in his bed with him tonight. Is that not marvelous?"

Davy grabbed hold of Joseph and the pair jumped up and down together. Then he stopped, his grin turning to a frown. "You mean I can stay all night? Till morning?"

Lily knelt before him. "Yes, for this one special night. Your mama and I want you to have lots and lots of fun. And just so you won't get lonely"— she opened his pillowcase and drew out his stuffed lamb that had been his sleeping partner since babyhood—"Wooly is going with you."

The boy's mouth dropped open. "Wooly! You get to go, too!" He snatched the stuffed animal from Lily's grasp and caught Joey's hand.

"Let's go climb in your wagon right now!"

From behind, Lily felt tugging on her skirt. She turned around to her Emmy.

Tears filled the little girl's blue-green eyes as she stared despondently at the second pillowcase. "You're sendin' me away, too, aren't you?"

Lily tugged the child into her arms and cradled her head. "I'm so very sorry, sweetheart. It's best."

"My mama's dyin', isn't she?"

Lily couldn't bring herself to lie to the child. "I'm afraid so."

"Doesn't she want to see me?"

"I'm sure she would, if only she were able, honey." She blotted Emma's tears with her apron. "But she can't now. She's no longer awake. I'm thinking the Lord wants to take her away gently while she's asleep."

"Up to heaven, where she won't hurt anymore." Emma's chin began to tremble as new tears spilled over her lashes and down her fair cheeks.

Lily's heart crimped with an ache beyond words. "Yes, darling, where she won't hurt anymore."

"Will the angels brush her hair for her so she looks pretty? And bring her flowers?"

A soft smile tugged at Lily's lips even as her own eyes swam. "I'm sure they will. They'll take special care of her because she's been sick such a long time. And the Lord will take care of all of us, too. But right now, it's best if you go visiting."

Emma released a shuddering breath. "All right. I'll go. But if mama wakes up again, tell her I love her. I want her to know that."

"I'll surely tell her for you."

"Am I goin' with the MacBrides, too?"

"No. I thought you'd rather stay at the Pattersons' with Mary. Her father is going to ride to Fort Henry to fetch your papa home."

"He is?" A glimmer of hope glistened in Emma's moist eyes. "I'll tell Mr. Patterson to hurry 'cause it's real important." Resigned to her fate, the child took the pillowcase of belongings from Lily and started for the Pattersons' cart.

Already missing her little ones, Lily turned to see that everyone had climbed aboard their wagons. This Sabbath that had seemed so interminably long had ended earlier than usual. It couldn't be past two. Watching the families leave, she mustered a smile and waved at Davy as the wagon wheels crunched over the trail.

The last wagon had barely disappeared into the trees when Matt and Luke approached her, their demeanors gloomy and despondent. "Where do you want us to start digging?" Matt asked in a dull voice.

"What?"

"Mama's grave."

Her little men stared at her, their arms akimbo, ready to do what needed to be done. Lily reached out and pulled their unwieldy bodies close. "Your mother is still alive, but she's no longer conscious. Grandma Margaret and Eva Shepard are sitting with her. I'll let you know when it's time."

"We want to start on it now," Luke said, his voice wavering.

His brother nodded. "We don't want no one else doin' it."

Lily looked from one to the other, seeing their determination, knowing their need to be doing something—anything. She realized their being outside, working through their feelings of helplessness was far better than waiting in the house. She could hardly face going back inside herself and breathed a silent prayer of thankfulness that Margaret and Eva had stayed behind to wait with her.

"Well, I believe your mama was partial to that pretty little knoll behind the pasture, where the first spring flowers always bloom. I think that would be a fine spot."

With a solemn nod, the lads walked, shoulders sagging, to the shed where the tools were stored.

Lily watched after them, feeling their despondency. *Please, dear God, bring John home quickly. Not for me, but for the children. They need him now.*

Yet even as she prayed, she couldn't keep from desperately needing him herself.

Chapter 9

Susan never regained consciousness. Approaching the midnight hour, she drew one last, gurgling gasp, and her soul took flight. The features so recently pinched with suffering relaxed, and an almost-smile settled over her lips. The death watch had finally, mercifully, come to an end.

Silver-haired Eva Shepard's generous bosom rose and fell as her faded blue eyes darted from Lily to Margaret; then she got up from her chair and drew the sheet over Susan's face.

Lily's own heart seemed to stop as she swallowed a huge lump in her throat and stared at the still form beneath the quilt.

With a sigh, Margaret reached out and touched her arm. "Go fetch the family Bible, child. You need to write down the date of her passing."

"Oh. Of course." Walking out into the cabin's darkened main room, Lily lit a table lamp, then collected a quill and ink jar and brought them to the dining table. The Bible still lay open to 1 Corinthians, where she'd been reading earlier. She flipped to the beginning of the volume, to the page where family records were listed.

Scanning down the contents, she sank onto the nearest chair. The facts of the Waldons' life together were all there—their births, the date of their marriage, the day each child had been born. Now Lily would make this unhappy recording. She dipped the quill into the ink and tried to steady her hand as she wrote: *Susan Gilford Waldon died on Sunday, the tenth day of July, 1757.*

Finished scribing the words, she closed her eyes against stinging tears. Dear, sweet Susan had died at such a young age. She'd lived a scant thirty-one years, five months, and two days, far too many of which had been spent under unspeakable suffering. It was so unfair. So senseless.

Lily blew on the wet ink. *Oh, Lord, please don't let this cup of suffering visit our little Emmy, too. . . . I beg of You.*

Closing the Bible, she glanced up at the loft, where the boys lay sleeping. Tomorrow morning would be soon enough to tell them about their loss.

By the time the sun passed its zenith, much had been accomplished. Ian MacBride had come by shortly after dawn to check on Susan's condition. Upon hearing the sad news, he rode across the creek and asked Richard Shaw to build a coffin; then he rode on to inform the rest of the families in the cove. Because of the hot, sultry weather, he scheduled the funeral service for the following evening, figuring that if Cal Patterson didn't run into trouble, he'd be back with John by tomorrow afternoon.

John. . .here. . .tomorrow. Try as she might, Lily couldn't keep the thought out of her mind. How would he deal with having missed his wife's final moments?

Washing the dishes after the noon meal, she noticed that the pounding of hammers in the workshop had become sporadic. She looked across to the squat building. Mr. Shaw and the boys must be almost finished with their task. The boys. As before, they wanted to keep busy away from the house while Lily helped the older women prepare their mother's body for burial.

The dog started barking, and a different sort of pounding drifted her way now—but not from the shop. She pushed the window open wider. Hoofbeats. Someone was coming. Fast. Wiping her hands on her apron, she hurried out the open door. It couldn't possibly be John coming so soon.

She reached the edge of the porch just as the rider rounded the building. *Ian MacBride.* The older man's mount skidded to a stop before her, lathered and panting hard.

Ian swung a frantic glance about. "Richard! Where's Richard?"

"In the shop."

Having heard the commotion, Mr. Shaw, Matt, and Luke exited the building with weapons in hand and approached Ian with questioning frowns.

"Matt!" Ian ordered. "Ride over to the Shaws' and on to my place. Tell the women to bring the children here to the blockhouse while we're gone. You, too, Lily. Richard, mount up. We've no time to spare!"

Lily's heartbeat quickened. Something was amiss. "Where are you going?"

Even as Mr. Shaw bolted for the hitching rail and his horse, Lily leaped from the porch and captured Ian's mount's bridle. "What's happened?"

His wife echoed Lily's question from the porch. "Yes, Ian. What's wrong? Are we bein' attacked? We need to know."

"We didn't hear no warnin' shots," frizzy-haired Eva piped in as she came alongside Margaret.

"There weren't any." Ian stared at them momentarily, then dismounted. He stepped up to Lily and took her by the shoulders, his demeanor grave.

A dreadful foreboding tightened her chest. Whatever the trouble was, it couldn't be good.

The old man's eyes softened as he gazed down at her. "Now, I dunna' want ye to be frettin', lass. There was only three of 'em, near as we could tell."

"Three of whom?" Lily felt her panic rising.

"We're thinkin' Indians. They was most likely sent ahead to scout out the cove. When Mary and Emma dinna' come back from takin' leftovers to the springhouse, Nancy sent her Henry to fetch them. He come runnin' back alone, just as I rode in."

Lily clutched his arms. "Are you telling me Indians took Emma and Mary?"

He gave a guilty shrug. "Dunna' be worryin'. They're afoot and canna' have much of a lead. That's why I dinna shoot off a warnin'. Dinna want 'em knowin' we was onto 'em so quick."

"Quick!" Lily all but spat. "Why on earth did you ride all the way back here?"

"I come for Richard. With most our men gone, there's only me, Toby, and Richard. Robby'll come with us, but he's young." Ian swung up into his saddle. "That's why we want you womenfolk to go the blockhouse, just in case."

Eva fisted her plump hands on her hips and leveled a stern glare. "You're sayin' they might be usin' this to pull you men away from the cove."

Before he offered a response, Lily saw that Mr. Shaw had mounted and started toward them, but in his own good-natured time. She whacked Ian's horse on the rump. "Go! Now! Both of you. Get those little girls back!" Her knees almost gave way as she imagined her sweet angel in peril.

As the pair galloped off, Matt and Luke raced out of the stable, dragging unsaddled Smokey by the reins. "The Indians have Emma?" Matt yelled. "Luke, run in and get the musket."

His brother sprinted for the house.

"No!" Lily shouted. "You were given another important job. Go tell Ruthie and Agnes. Now. And hurry back. Bring Davy with you."

"Wait, Matt," Luke called from the porch. "I'm goin', too."

The older lad held up a hand, taking charge as he scrambled up on the big-footed farm horse. "You're needed here. Help Lily carry food and supplies to the blockhouse." Ramming his heels into the horse's flanks, he galloped toward the creek and the Shaw place a quarter mile away.

As Lily watched Matt ride confidently away, past the springhouse and beyond, the possibility of what could happen to poor little Emma flooded her mind. . .the tortures. . .the unspeakable horrors. Her little girl was so young, so tender.

'Tis my fault. I was the one who insisted she go to the Pattersons'.

Only the night before, Lily had pleaded with God for Emma. Surely the Lord would not answer her prayer in such a cruel, heartless way!

She started for the porch steps, but her shaking legs would not cooperate. She collapsed onto the bottom one, all pretense of control gone. Burying her face in her hands, she convulsed into wracking sobs. How much could a person bear? Susan lay dead in the house, and Emma— *"Emma!"*

John readjusted the knapsack strap gouging his shoulder and trudged with his scouting party through the gates of the stone fort. Weary after having searched the far side of the river as far as the Tuscarora Indian Path for the past three days, he was gratified there'd been no sign of the French. He shrugged off his gear and leaned his musket against the inside wall, then strode toward headquarters to report. As he walked, he pulled a rag from his belt to wipe the sweat and grime from his face.

"Waldon! Wait up!" Pat MacBride cut across the parade ground toward him.

John paused long enough for his neighbor to fall into step with him.

"How'd it go out there?" Pat asked.

"We didn't see a sign of danger. What about the Juniata Path? Spot anything suspicious along there?"

"Nope, nary a thing. Who knows? Maybe the French are gettin' stopped by our boys up north."

"Or better yet, pushed all the way back to Canada. Wouldn't that be great?" Swiping again at his damp forehead, John hiked a brow. "Any dispatch riders come in from up New York way while we were out?"

Pat wagged his head. "Just one checkin' in from Fort Augusta. Here it is already July, an' we're still just hangin' around, waitin'."

"Yeah." John clenched his teeth as he and his friend neared head-quarters. He could've been to Beaver Cove and back half-a-dozen times by now, spent time with Susan and the rest of the family, checked on how Lily was coping with things. . . .

"Rider comin'!" The shout came from the south watchtower.

Captain Busse and his orderly stepped outside headquarters and focused their attention on the gate. Then the commander spotted John and came down the steps. "Corporal Waldon. See any movement between the river and the Tuscarora Path?"

Stiffening his posture, John saluted his superior. "No, sir. Not a sign."

The captain grunted and returned his attention to the gate as the rapid thud of hoofbeats grew nearer.

John also turned toward the sound as a rider came through the gate.

Slowing his mount to a walk, the newcomer whipped off his hat.

Cal! Recognizing his neighbor, John wondered if the man had decided to reenlist even with his bad knee.

Cal rode straight for headquarters and reined in, but without bothering to greet the captain, he lowered his gaze to John. "Thank the good Lord you're here an' not out on patrol."

Dread gripped John. Only one thing could have brought his friend here right now. *Susan.*

"I rode hard to get here, John. Your wife took a turn for the worse." He moistened his lips and averted his eyes to the ground. "She's been real bad. I hate to say this, but it wouldn't surprise me none if she already passed on."

Before John could process the information, Busse stepped around him. "You're Private Patterson, aren't you?"

A frown drew his bushy eyebrows together. "I was, sir."

"Which way did you come, perchance?"

Hearing their voices as if from far away, John gaped at the commander's audacity to butt in where he wasn't wanted. Still, stunned by the dire news Cal had delivered, he stood silently by while his friend answered.

"I cut across from Beaver Cove to the Susquehanna, an' took the trace north from there."

"Did you see any sign of the French? Any scouting parties?"

"Just some of your men, sir."

Having had quite enough of Busse's questions, John spoke up forcefully. "*Captain*. Permission to speak, *sir*."

The commander reluctantly shifted his gaze. "Permission granted."

"I'm sure you heard Patterson's news. I must go home. If not for my wife," he railed bitterly, "I have four young children there and must see to their welfare."

The captain had the grace to look a bit guilty as he inhaled a deep breath and shifted his stance. "I...uh...am sorry about your wife, Waldon. Go see to your family. I'll give you five days to take care of things. Take extra mounts so you'll get there faster. But go home by the Tulpehocken Path and watch for Indian sign along the way."

John couldn't believe the man's gall—expecting him to take time to scout on the way home to his dying wife!

Busse edged closer to John and spoke for his ears only. "A large war party has been sighted north of Fort Augusta. Godspeed."

The frogs and insects along the creek kept up a steady racket punctuated by the occasional hoot of an owl. This long night refused to end. Too stressed to sleep, Lily shared sentinel duty on the top floor of the blockhouse with Cal's grief-stricken wife. Nancy Patterson, known as the cove's most fervent worrier, idly twisted a strand of her light blond hair within an inch of its life as she and Lily slowly, silently circled opposite sides of the perimeter, staring beyond the moonlit clearing into the inky blackness of the woods. As they watched and waited, they prayed fervently, ceaselessly, for the men to return with their girls...their little girls who'd been dragged off, frightened, helpless in the foul hands of savages.

"Think they'll be all right?" Nancy's whisper barely broke the silence as she turned her swollen blue eyes to Lily.

I don't know! How could I know? Lily wanted to wail. But she forced herself to remain calm, recalling how her sister Rose might answer a senseless question. "We must trust the Lord," she finally murmured. "Little ones are very precious to Him. I'm sure He'll send angels to protect them. We have to believe that."

"I know. I do. But it shore is a hard thing." Nancy drew a ragged breath and turned her attention outward once again, her slender profile gilded by moonlight.

It was a hard thing for Lily, too. She'd had no words of comfort for the boys, especially Davy. She wondered if she truly had the kind of faith it took to trust God's providence when it came to someone she loved so dearly. Her faith had done precious little for Susan Waldon. Even now the young woman's ravaged body lay inside the cabin, waiting its final commitment to the earth. At least she would never know her little daughter had been captured and perhaps—

Unable to finish the unthinkable possibility, Lily struggled against feeling resentment against Nancy for allowing the little girls to go down to that creek alone. She should have kept them inside, safe. The Patterson farmstead was the farthest one upstream. Nancy had to know her place was the most vulnerable to attack. Why hadn't she worried about that when it mattered?

The bouts of anger inevitably gave way to self-condemnation. Lily knew she should have had the foresight to send Emma home with the Shaws to play with their Lizzie. But the Shaws lived no more than a quarter mile away, and she feared Emma might take the notion to run home if she were that close.

Utterly spent, Lily sighed. It was no one's fault. . . . It was everyone's fault. *Why on earth are any of us still here? We should have left a year and a half ago.*

Coming again to the side of the structure facing her farm, Lily paused as she'd done every circuit since climbing the ladder from the windowless room below. The cabin's outline was barely discernable through the growth along the creek. And over there, Susan lay in her room in the inky darkness, still in death, all alone.

Would this night never end?

Steps sounded on the ladder. Lily moved to the hatch to assist the person up onto the deck.

"Sure is stuffy down there." Patrick's wife, short, plump Agnes MacBride, took in a deep breath. "Thank goodness, the children are all finally sleepin' sound." She tipped her auburn head as her small hazel eyes met Lily's gaze.

"Even Davy?" Lily asked.

"Aye. He's sleepin' betwixt his brothers."

Nancy came to join them. "What about mine?" Worry drew her golden eyebrows into a V above her pert nose.

"Your boys was real good about playin' with li'l Sally till she drifted off."

A sudden twinge of envy gripped Lily. Even if Mary were never found, Nancy would still have baby Sally to love and cuddle. Emma was the only little girl Lily had. The only one. She ground her teeth and glanced up-creek again. "Where are those men? Ian said the Indians didn't have much of a lead. *Where are they? What's taking them so long?*"

Chapter 10

The afternoon dragged on as John and Cal Patterson rode their mounts along the Blue Mountain trail. As if sensing John's heaviness of heart, his friend refrained from needless chatter. But inside, rage and resentment toward a commander who would order them to go miles out of their way at such a pressing time all but consumed John. Only prayer helped him to get beyond the anger.

Oh, God, if my precious Susie is to be taken away from me, please let her passing be a gentle one. She's been so patient in her suffering, so brave, with thoughts only of me, of the children, and Lily. She told me she didn't want us to be angry or sad, but to dwell on the happy times. He swallowed, and his shoulders slumped. *How I wish there could have been more of the joyous times. She deserved a happy life, but I failed her. Lord, be close to our little ones. Help them to accept Your will quietly and go on as their mother would have wanted. She was so proud of them all.*

John had to admit that Busse hadn't been completely heartless. The man had provided two extra horses for the trip, making it possible for him and Cal to reach Beaver Cove in the same amount of time the more direct route would have taken with only two mounts. A pity the river had too many twists and turns for a swift canoe trip.

His thoughts drifted again to Susan, and he recalled a beautiful bride in filmy lace, her red-gold curls a glorious tumble beneath a crown of field daisies, her turquoise eyes alight with hope. She'd been so filled with dreams. He hoped she'd seen some of them fulfilled along the way. She'd made a wonderful mother, doting on each baby yet never allowing the older children to feel slighted. *Oh, Susie-girl. How can I face life without you?* He bowed his head once more in prayer.

When darkness descended on the already shadowy forest, they plodded cautiously onward, not chancing the lighting of torches to illuminate the trail, but relying on the horses to carry them along the centuries-old Indian path. According to the captain, the enemy had been spotted a few miles to the north. They could easily be closer.

After several hours, they came to a small clearing bathed in the subtle light of the moon.

Calvin moved alongside John and muttered the first words he'd said in quite a spell. "The horses should get some rest."

John nodded and veered off into the grassy meadow where their mounts could graze while the two of them caught whatever sleep they could. While they unsaddled, hobbled, and rubbed down the horses, he longed to question his friend about Susan, the children, and Lily. But voices carried easily on the night air.

After laying their saddles beneath the outer edge of a tree's low-slung branches, they crawled inside the shadowed haven and rolled out their bedding.

A few yards away John's horse nickered.

Then Cal's.

John grabbed his musket and lunged forward, snatching his powder horn loose. Cal followed suit, and they uncorked their black powder, pouring a smidgen of the grainy substance into their flashpans. John marveled that his neighbor's stiff leg hadn't slowed him down a bit.

Up the wooded trail, a horse returned the greeting of the hobbled mounts, and a lone rider came out of the trees at a slow gait.

John rose to his knees. Shoulders tense, he raised his musket and took aim, cocking an ear for sounds of others approaching. Hearing none, he spoke just loud enough to be heard. "Who goes there?"

The rider jerked on his reins. "Robby Randall, from Beaver Cove."

"Fool kid," Cal muttered. "What are you doin' all the way out here, ridin' through the night?" He accepted John's help to get up.

"That you, Mr. Patterson?" Robby asked.

"Aye."

"Thank the good Lord." The lad kneed his mount toward them.

John met him halfway across the clearing. "What are you doing this far north all by yourself in the middle of the night?"

"I'm headin' for Fort Henry."

Puzzled, John shook his head. "Why would you come this way? Are you being chased?"

"Nope."

"Don't tell me the cove was attacked!" Cal piped in.

"Nope. If you two'll stop askin' questions, I'll tell you. Me an' the other men are after Injuns what took our little girls. We think there's only three of 'em, but they'll prob'ly meet up with others, so Grampa Mac sent me to get help."

"Which of your sisters did the varmints steal?" Cal asked, his voice deadly quiet.

"None of mine." The lad hesitated, then looked down at Calvin. "I'm real sorry, Mr. Patterson, but your little Mary was one of 'em."

Cal gasped and grabbed hold of John, his fingers biting into John's flesh. "My Mary. They took my Mary."

"She ain't the only one." Robby turned to John. "They took Emma, too."

The news punched into John like a fist. "That can't be. We live more than a mile downriver from the Pattersons, past several other farms."

" 'Fraid it's true. Lily sent Emma to stay with the Pattersons for the night. She, uh, didn't want her there, watchin'. . .you know. . .your wife takin' her last breaths."

His legs starting to give way, John leaned hard on his musket for support. "Susan's dead, and my baby girl's been carried off." He could hardly choke out the words.

Cal's big hand clamped on to John's shoulder and shook it. "We gotta saddle up. Go after 'em."

The urgency in his friend's voice jerked John into action. He glanced at Robby as he wheeled toward the spot where he'd left his gear. "How far back did you leave the others?"

"A couple a hours back. It's been real hard, you know, the redskins on foot, cuttin' through thickets an' up rocky cliffs. We had to get off our horses an' drag 'em after us lots of times. Once the Injuns hit this trail, we thought we'd have 'em for sure. But they must'a got wind of us, 'cause they cut off into the woods again, headin' north. That's why Grampa Mac sent me to get help. When I left 'em, they was tryin' to track them sneaky savages by torchlight."

Calvin yanked Robby's sleeve. "You sure they still got our girls?"

"Last I seen. The girls ain't got no shoes on."

Slinging his saddle onto the back of the nearest horse, John prayed out loud. "I don't even know what to say, Lord. Those heathen savages are dragging our frightened little barefooted girls through brambles and thorny bushes and across roots and rocks, cutting their feet all up." He stopped as a more terrifying thought chilled his blood. "If they haven't already slit their little throats and cast them aside. Please help them, Father. Send Your angels to be with my Emma; be with Mary. Keep them safe. Please, God, it would be more than I could bear to lose my wife and my daughter on the same day."

Lily jerked awake as a shaft of light hit her eyes. Sitting up, she realized she was in the windowless blockhouse, and the beam came from the square opening in the ceiling. All the horror came rushing back. "Emma!"

She scrambled to her feet. The day must be half gone. Surely the men would've been back by now if they'd rescued her darling and Mary.

Her insides tightened around the unthinkable. *What if none of them return?*

No! She would not dwell on that unspeakable possibility. The men would find the girls and bring them both home, safe and sound.

Looking around, she realized she was alone in the bottom floor of the blockhouse, with its crude dirt floor. Where was everyone? They couldn't all be up above, or she'd hear them. Climbing the ladder rungs, she reached the opening and searched the deck.

Bob Randall's petite wife, Edith, stood on one side, frowning as she idly twisted an errant mousy brown curl around a finger. Hearing Lily, she flashed a worried smile. Her son Robby had ridden out with the men. "Did you get any sleep?" she asked in her quiet way, concern softening her light brown eyes.

Lily only grimaced.

"Nancy woke up about half an hour ago. The two of you shouldn't have taken the entire night watch. You should'a woke me an' Ruthie up."

"We couldn't sleep. Where is everyone?"

"Down there." Edith nodded below. "They're havin' a picnic outside. We told them not to get too noisy."

Joining her neighbor at the rail, Lily gazed down on the scene. It looked so pastoral with everyone gathered on several quilts in the shade of the structure. The women chatted, and the little ones giggled as they ate from wooden trenchers or tin plates. Her little Davy, being his usual busy self, was using his spoon to sword fight with his friend Joey.

Nancy, however, stood off by herself, looking northward, anguish frozen on her face.

Knowing exactly how her neighbor felt, Lily focused across at the cabin. Susan's body still lay over there. . .a day and a half in this relentless summer heat. Something must be done. Now. Today.

Exiting the building, she walked around to its shady east side.

"Lily, girl." Margaret waved her over. "Come and have something to eat, child. Sit with us a spell."

Even though she hadn't eaten since the night before last, Lily had no appetite. She did force herself to swallow a few bites before Davy came running, full of questions.

"Did my mama really go to heaven, like Socks? Where's Emmy? When's she comin' back?" He dropped down on his knees before her.

Before Lily could answer, Matt plucked his little brother up and whisked him away. His own expression hard-set, he carried the child up to the watchtower.

Luke, fighting tears, ran after them.

Not having dealt with her own grief as yet, Lily would have liked nothing more than to collapse and weep until she had no tears left. But she knew if she gave in, she would never stop crying. Better to remain strong for the children. There'd be time enough for sorrow in days to come. She turned back to her meal, picking up the only thing that looked remotely appealing, a cup of tea. As she took a swallow of the hot liquid, she glanced around at the other women. Their expressions were not so much sympathetic as they were wrought with tension. They knew any of the other children could have been taken as easily as Mary and Emma. Any of their homes could have been burned to the ground and the residents massacred by the savages, as had happened at other settlements.

Every woman here had a loved one away, either at Fort Henry, manning a line of defense, or out tracking the kidnapping Indians. Not a wife among them could be certain her husband would come home alive.

But. . .they were men. Not two helpless little girls.

Lily caught herself before she sank into that pit of despair. Her fears would have to wait. There was something more immediate to tend to. She swept a glance up to the fifteen-year-old Randall lad. "Donald, I need you, Sammy, Jimmy, and Pete to come with me back to the house."

All eyes turned to her.

"Why?" Jimmy Patterson's youthful face contorted with puzzlement, then smoothed out again. "Sure 'nough, Lily. Whatever needs doin', we'll help you with it."

All the lads were having to take up their manhood too soon. When would this madness come to an end? She set down her empty cup and rose to her feet. "Shall we go?"

"We lay this dear young woman's body to rest," Grandma Margaret droned in a sympathetic tone, her back to the grave as she faced Lily and the other women and children clustered in a semicircle about her. Rays from the slanting sun filtered through the trees on the knoll, casting long shadows over the scene. "And we thank Thee, Lord, that our Susan is free of her pain and suffering and is now basking in the light of Thy glory. We ask Thee to comfort each of her children and fill them with the assurance that they are loved as much as ever."

She paused and centered her attention on Lily, who stood with Davy tucked against her to keep him still as the older boys flanked her, all huddled together. Then she resumed speaking, this time with force. "And Father, we beseech Thee to bring our precious baby girls home safe and sound. . .our girls and our men."

"Amen" resounded from every woman and child in the circle.

"Most gracious God," Margaret continued, her tone gentle once more, "we look forward to the day when we will see Susan again in heaven, see her wonderful smile, hear her sweet laugh. We express our deepest thanks that our sister is now at peace in Thy loving arms. We praise and worship Thee for Thy goodness and care, and we beseech Thee most fervently to keep little Emma and Mary safe, in the name of our blessed Lord Jesus. Amen."

As everyone looked up at the close of the prayer, Margaret turned to the grave. "We commit the body of Susan Gilford Waldon to the earth from whence it came, to await the glorious day when we will all be raised to meet our blessed Jesus in the sky. Ashes to ashes. . .dust to dust." She reached for the shovel in the waiting pile of dirt and emptied its contents atop the wooden casket.

Lily's heart thudded at the hollow sound of clods falling atop the few little wildflowers the children had picked and laid along the lid. She'd thought she'd be ready to face this moment, but the depth of emptiness that filled her stole her very breath.

The older woman handed the shovel to Matt.

He stared at it, then turned his swollen, red-rimmed eyes up to Lily.

She gave him a nod, barely holding back her own tears as he filled the shovel and emptied it in the grave, then handed the tool past her and Davy to Luke.

The nine-year-old wiped his sleeve across his eyes and followed suit, but as he attempted to hand the shovel on to the next person, Davy jerked free. "Me, too. Mama needs my dirt, too."

Reluctantly, Lily nodded her assent, hoping the child understood enough to carry out the task with respect.

The tyke jammed his foot down on the iron edge of the shovel's scoop, and with his hands halfway down the handle, he brought up the dirt and let it trickle into the grave. He looked up at the sky with a triumphant smile. "See, Mama? I help real good." Then the little big man handed the shovel to Lily. "Your turn."

Despite her sadness, Lily's heart swelled with joy. Davy understood. He knew his mother wasn't lying in that grave, but in heaven with God. She drew a steadying breath and added her own shovelful of earth.

Moments later, as the others took turns filling in the grave, Agnes MacBride moved alongside and wrapped an arm around her. "I'm sure John would've been here by now, if he could've."

Lily barely managed a nod as her fury at the fort's commander flared again. And though she knew it was irrational, her anger at John resurfaced. And at Mr. Gilford. Most of all, she condemned herself for sending Emma to the Patterson farm. She'd known Calvin was leaving to go fetch John home, that no man would be on the place to guard the family.

She glanced across the gathering to where Nancy Patterson had been standing with her toddler.

Nancy was gone.

Turning on her heel, Lily spotted her. Carrying little Sally, her neighbor had left the wooded knoll and started across the footbridge on her way back to the blockhouse. No doubt Nancy would climb up to the watchtower and continue searching the forest beyond—not for Indians, but for the return of the men. . .her Cal and John. She'd be watching even more intently for those who'd gone after their girls.

It would be dark soon. The little ones had already been out there one night. *Please, dear God, bring our children home to us. Please.*

"Lily."

She pulled her gaze back to the knoll, to Matt. "Yes?"

"Me an' the rest of the boys are gonna tend to the animals."

Lily glanced toward the pasture, filled now with the extra livestock brought in from the other farms.

"You women need to take the young'uns back to the blockhouse while we're gone."

"Quite right." She laid a palm alongside his smooth cheek, tipping her head as she let her eyes roam her young man's face. "I hadn't noticed. You're almost as tall as I am now."

Matt gave her hand a squeeze. "I know." A half-smile tweaked his mouth. "Better go along."

Lily turned away before he could see the tears she could no longer restrain. Matt. Matt, who'd been only seven when she first arrived to look after the children, was now looking after her.

Chapter 11

The late afternoon breeze feathered over the clearing, ruffling the edge of Lily's muslin gown and toying with her hair. She caught a wisp that blew into her eyes and tucked it behind her ear as Davy's chatter broke into her thoughts.

"When folks die, people bury 'em real deep."

"Is that right?" She did her best to sound interested.

"Uh-huh. That's so dogs and wolves can't dig 'em up." He looked down at the mound of earth Lily, Agnes, and Ruth were patting with the flat of their shovels to smooth out the grave. "I wish Mama wasn't so deep, though. I miss her a lot."

Agnes stopped to wipe perspiration dripping into her eyes. "When your pa gets home, he can make your mama a fine-lookin' cross, what with all them nice tools he's got an' all."

"Maybe he'll let me help." The little boy puffed out his chest. "I'm good at helpin'. Mr. Pat-a-son went to bring Pa home, didn't he, Lily?" His huge blue eyes sparkled. "When's he gonna get here?"

Agnes answered for her. "We're not sure, little man. Soon, we hope."

Just then a wild, piercing shriek came from the blockhouse beyond the trees. Lily froze. *Indians?*

Musket fire erupted from the upper floor.

Duke and the other families' dogs took up a cacophony of growls and yapping.

Alarmed, Lily glanced about her. Half the people were scattered hither and yon. She and the two neighbor women—and Davy—were still here on the wooded knoll. The older boys were off tending livestock. Not one of her own was at the blockhouse!

Answering shots blasted from farther away, followed by a scream from the log structure.

Snatching Davy's hand, Lily reached for the pistol she'd tucked in the crutch of a nearby maple tree.

Beside her, Ruth clutched the handle of her shovel in a white-knuckled grip, visibly shaking. *"Oh, Lord, we're gonna die!"*

Agnes, musket now in hand, rushed to Ruthie and gave her a sound slap across her sallow face. "No time for hysterics, gal." She then snagged the young woman's hand and pulled her down behind a tree. "Stay put."

Lily dragged Davy along as she ran to a break in the trees. She could see riders—not Indians, at least—coming down the trail on the other side of the creek, but she couldn't make them out in the lengthening shadows.

When the horsemen emerged out of the woods and into the clearing, Lily released the breath she'd been holding. "It's our men!" Racing off the knoll, dodging trees and brush, she headed for the creek. *Please, Lord, let Emma be with them. Bring her back to us.*

Matt, Luke, and the older boys reached the fallen log first and let out a gleeful hoot. "They're back!"

Davy jerked free and sprinted for the footbridge ahead of Lily. His little legs working hard, he scrambled across with her on his heels. Lily desperately needed to see the riders clearly.

Ahead of her, the boys veered to the right as they reached the clearing. Lily followed. Panting for breath, she stopped, her eyes widening at the sight before her. Two little girls—*Praise be to God!*—Emma! Her little one rode double behind one of the men.

A cry tore from deep inside as Lily bolted straight for the approaching horse, her eyes filled with one small person. "Emma!"

Leaning out to peer around her rescuer, Emma reached out a hand to her. "Lily!" Then she burst into tears.

Reaching her, Lily pulled her darling off the still-moving horse. A tearful Emma collapsed into her waiting arms, then clung so hard, Lily could scarcely draw breath. She smothered the little girl with kisses. Emmy, her precious child, was home again.

Lily breathed a wordless prayer of thankfulness as she hugged the filthy little angel to her breast. Emma's braids had come loose, and her pretty red hair was dull and matted. Scratches and bruises covered her arms and legs, her neck bore definite rope burns, and one little eye was black and swollen. Lily's heart wrenched as her own eyes brimmed with tears. "Oh, my darling Emmy." She drew her close again.

Matt, Luke, and Davy crowded around them, crooning sympathetically as they reached out, needing to touch their sister. "Glad to have you back, Sissy." Then Davy's voice rang out above the rest. "Pa!"

John? Lily followed the child's gaze, and her heart skipped a beat. John was home! She'd been so absorbed in the joy of Emma's return, she hadn't noticed her rescuer! And at his weary smile, all the anger she'd harbored during his absence evaporated.

As John beheld the joyous, tearful reunion of his daughter and Lily, he easily identified with the lass's emotion when she tugged Emma off the horse. He'd felt the same way the moment he'd had his daughter safe in his arms. Fully aware that Indians wouldn't hesitate to murder little captives if they got wind of an impending attack, he, Calvin, and Robby had approached the camp with stealth. They waited long after dark, after the children had been cruelly bound to trees and the three young braves finally fell asleep, before they unsheathed their hunting knives and made their move.

The sleeping girls never heard the gruesome deed, but woke to two elated fathers who swiftly cut away their bonds and smothered them in hugs before whisking them away. Having Emma in his arms once more had been the most joyful, yet painful, moment of John's life. He knew exactly how relieved Lily felt to have the child back.

When Lily looked up and saw him, her lips parted and she stared for a brief heartbeat. Then she gave a cry of joy and rushed with Emma right past the boys and into his waiting arms.

He enveloped them both, near tears himself, as the boys charged over and grabbed on. Davy jumped up and down. "Up! Up! I want up, too!"

Reaching down, John lifted the little tyke into the embrace, immediately finding himself in a stranglehold around his neck as his son peppered him with kisses.

"Hey, ever'body!" Davy hollered. "My papa's back!"

His son's words brought John up short. The captain had given him a mere five days, and he'd used a costly chunk of that to rescue Emma. How could he possibly desert them all again the day after tomorrow?

John trudged up the hill alone. The sultry gust of evening air rustled the leaves and carried the scent of fresh dirt—dirt covering his long-suffering wife's final resting place. With heavy heart, he picked up a clod and crushed it in his hand, watching it dribble through his fingers, just as Susan's life had. It was so senseless. A soft-spoken woman, she'd never had an unkind word for anyone. She shouldn't have had to endure that debilitating ailment.

According to Cal, she'd been in a coma even before he left for the fort, so there was little hope John could have reached her before she drew her last breath. If only Busse had allowed him to come home weeks ago, when he'd begged for leave. His and Susan's marriage had been a good one. They'd loved each other since they were the same age as Matt and Luke, and it crushed him to think how brief her time on earth had been. How would he live with the knowledge he hadn't been with her at the end, holding her hand?

He should have pestered Captain Busse ceaselessly until the man let him go. . . . But the truth was a small part of him abhorred the idea of watching the love of his life take her final breath.

No. I left that to Lily and the children.

John sank to his knees. "I'm sorry, Susie-girl. So sorry I'm such a coward."

"Papa!"

Davy's cry brought John to his feet. He swung around to see his little boy scampering up the rise.

"Son." He shook his head in exasperation. "I told everybody I wanted a few minutes alone with your mother."

"That's why I had to come." Davy huffed, out of breath. "I runned as fast as I could."

The statement made no sense. John knelt before the boy. "Davy—"

"Mama 'splained it to me. So's I wouldn't worry."

"What are you talking about? What exactly did she tell you?"

"She said the body she was wearin' wasn't no good no more, that it hurt all the time. So she was goin' up to heaven to get a new one. She said Jesus would give her a brand new one up there. Lots better than this one. An' she said she'll be right there waitin' for us. Soon as my body don't work no more, she's gonna make sure I get the bestest new one they got in all of heaven." He stretched his arms apart to add emphasis.

Even with his heavy heart, John felt the twitch of a smile. "Did Mama really tell you that? The last part, I mean."

"Well"—Davy scrunched up his face—"not a'zackly. But that's what she meant. I know it." He studied his feet for a second, then looked up again. "Mama always told me she loves me better than anything. So you'll see. She'll get me the best one they got."

John did smile then. He pulled his little scamp into a hug.

Davy eased back enough to look straight at him. "So anyway, you don't need to be frettin' about Lily's red eyes or Matt's or Luke's. They was just cryin' because they was scared them mean Injuns was hurtin' our Emmy. An' they was right about that, huh? She gots bad marks all over." Easing out of John's grasp, he raised a clenched fist. "If I ever see them bad Injuns, they'll be sorry."

Reaching out, John took hold of his son's little fist and peeled back the fingers. "The Indians who took Emma are already sorry for what they did, Son." He tousled the towhead's hair. He knew he should say the righteous words: *forgive them as we would want to be forgiven, leave the vengeance to the Lord.* But even though they lay dead, he still hadn't been able to forgive them himself. Maybe in time, once his little girl's scratches and bruises healed. . . . He released a ragged breath.

Rising to his feet, he took Davy's hand. "Well, my little man, if your mama's not here, I reckon there's no sense in us hanging around, is there?" He started toward the cabin.

"Nope." His son skipped along at his side. "But it sure will be differ'nt, not havin' her to take care of no more."

"I know what you mean." John cast a backward glance at the sad-looking grave, strewn with a fading rainbow of wilted flowers. His childhood sweetheart, too fragile to live on earth any longer, had gone on without him.

"Oh no! Ever'body's leavin'!" Davy wrenched free of John's hand and bolted across the meadow. "Don't go! I still wanna play!"

But the neighbors never slowed. John knew it was natural for them to load up and return to their homes. There'd been no evidence of a war party in the area, merely the three scouts who'd taken the children. And those varmints would never report to their chiefs again. Still, a very real threat remained. Captain Busse had relayed the sighting of an approaching force, and no one could be certain whether they'd come south or follow the trail east along Blue Mountain and continue down through the "Hole" and on toward Reading. Would they descend on a larger town this time?

Regardless, it was too dangerous for his family to remain at Beaver Cove without him any longer. He'd see them on their way before he left for the fort. His beloved Susan was gone—to get her new body. John couldn't help smiling when he thought about Davy's remark.

He climbed through the pasture fence just in time to see the last wagon heading out, carting with it a lamb, a calf, crates of chickens, and children. Worn-out Ian MacBride, slumped in his saddle, herded the larger livestock behind. Chasing after Indians for two days had taken a lot of starch out of the old fellow. But thank God, he and the others had never given up. John would be indebted to them for the rest of his life.

He scanned his farmstead, the piece of land where he'd invested all his hopes and dreams for himself and his children, the place he'd built with his own hands. Now it may have been for naught: the cabin he'd planned to expand one day into a bigger, nicer home filled with fine furnishings he fashioned himself; the stable already roomy enough to house six large animals; the corncrib; his workshop; and the springhouse, smokehouse, and sheds. He'd practically broken his back digging the cellar. Then there were the fields and orchard, the fencing—all in jeopardy. If everything were burned out, would he have the heart to start over?

He exhaled a harsh breath. Tonight he'd put aside his worries and enjoy his family. His time with them would be much too short.

Watching his dear ones waving to the MacBrides from the porch, he noticed that Emmy had on a fresh dress. Lily must have bathed her and tended her wounds and now had his daughter tucked close to her side. If ever he'd doubted the love the British girl had for his children, he never would again. She certainly was God's blessing to them all.

He increased his pace to reach them, then slowed a bit as he noticed Eva Shepard, Toby's mother-in-law, standing with them. Why hadn't the woman gone home with her family? What possible reason could she have for remaining behind?

Of course. *Lily.*

Could the woman possibly have seen the way he'd looked at the lass the last time he was home? A familiar twinge of guilt waylaid him. Surely he'd managed to hide that forbidden yearning.

Or was it the way he'd drawn Lily close to him today, held on to her. When he'd been bestowing kisses on all the children, had he inadvertently kissed her, too? He might have. He wasn't sure. He'd been so happy to see them all.

One thing was certain. From the way Eva was eyeing him, her arms crossed as he approached, she wasn't here merely to help out. She was here to chaperone Lily.

Chapter 12

Lily listened through the open kitchen window while her family washed up for breakfast. Their laughter and good-natured banter was a welcome change from the heavy sadness that had enveloped the household since last spring, when John had gone off with the militia and Susan's health had waned. Now that the man of the house was back, the light chatter fell on her ears like music from the cathedral choir at Bath. But even though the family was acting as if nothing had happened, Lily knew that soon enough the finality of their loss would sink in, and they'd all be forced to face their grief.

Silver-haired Eva came up behind her. "This'll be a fine homecomin' breakfast."

"So I'm hoping." Reluctantly, Lily left the window. "Thank you for making the blackberry syrup. Everyone will love it on the flapjacks."

"Aye, lass. We'll have us a good stick-to-the-ribs meal." She brushed flecks of loose flour from her generous bosom. "Then later, I think you an' me need to have a little talk."

"Oh? Did I forget to do something?" Lily thought she'd taken care of everything concerning Susan's burial the day before.

The older woman wagged her mobcapped head with a smile. "Nothin' to fret about. Right now, I'm so hungry I could eat a horse."

"So sorry, then." Quirking a teasing smile, Lily picked up the platter of sliced salt pork and took it to the table. "You'll have to settle for a hog."

Eva chuckled.

Still, Lily couldn't help wondering what her neighbor had on her mind. She hoped the woman hadn't caught her gazing in an unseemly way at John at supper last night, especially after having put so much effort into not looking at him. But she could not have related the joy Mr. Gilford's visit had brought Susan, or the letter the man had posted to them, without looking in his direction.

Unless. . .Eva wanted to lecture her about that telling moment when she'd first glimpsed John and literally thrown herself at him. She hadn't made the slightest attempt not to appear inordinately glad to see him. Oh, mercy.

"Mmm. Can I have more syrup?" Fork clutched in his fist and wearing as much of the sticky sweet as he'd eaten, Davy besought Lily.

Luke cocked a grin and pointed his own smeared finger. "Just let him wipe his flapjack down his shirt."

"Oh, give the boy all he wants," Eva said, positioned a generous distance away from the messy pair.

Lily wasn't quite so invulnerable, seated next to Davy. On her other side, Emma sat in silence, toying with the food on her plate. The child had hardly uttered a word since her return. Whenever she wasn't glued to Lily or her pa, she huddled curled up in a corner or under the table, often crying without a sound. Lily mourned for the child, wondering—but dreading to know—what unspeakable abuse she'd endured. She eased away from the little girl enough to pour more syrup on Davy's already soggy flapjack.

At the end of the table, John set down his fork. "Now that we're about finished. . ."

Lily shot him a glance. The happy expression he'd worn when the family gathered for breakfast had turned serious. Did he, like Eva Shepard, have something to say she didn't want to hear?

The jovial banter between the older boys ceased as Matt and Luke slid wary glances at their father.

Wiping his mouth on his napkin, John laid the cloth down and cleared his throat. "First of all, I'd like to thank you ladies for this wonderful breakfast—the best I've had since last I was home."

Lily smiled but remained quiet.

Eva, however, stood and began clearing the table. "Shucks, John. It's a special day. Your family wants to celebrate your homecomin.'"

"Yes. Well, speaking of that, there's something you all need to know. I was given only a few days' leave. As much as I hate to say it, I'm duty-bound to start back to the fort. . .tomorrow."

Davy's fork clattered to his plate. "Papa! No! It's not fair."

His brothers grimaced and exchanged incredulous looks.

Emma's little hand slowly moved across Lily's lap and found hers.

Lily swallowed the lump forming in her throat and fought back tears already trembling on her lashes. John's children had suffered the loss of their mother only three days past. They needed him more than ever before. How could he leave them again so soon? What sort of love could be so cruel?

As if oblivious to the sullen mood that descended on the room like a smothering blanket, John continued. "After much consideration, I've come to a decision, Lily. I want you to pack everyone's clothing today while the boys and I drive our stock over to the MacBrides'. Then first thing tomorrow morning, I'll take you all down to the Swatara and hire a canoe. I'm sure Matt and Luke will be able to handle paddling it as far as the Susquehanna. Then you're to secure passage on a keelboat the rest of the way."

"The rest of the way?" Lily's voice emerged in a hoarse whisper. It was finally happening. He was dismissing her. "But—"

He held up a hand. "Please, let me finish."

With an aching heart, she pressed her lips together.

"I know you promised to stay and look after the children until I return for good. But in the light of Susan's passing and the current potential for an Indian attack, I won't hold you to that any longer. You told me Mr. Gilford has expressed a desire for his grandchildren to come and stay with him, so that's what they'll do. I have every confidence the man will see to their needs, but I'd be pleased if you'd consent to remain with them—at least until they're settled and comfortable. Once this ugly business with the French is over, I'll reimburse you generously. You have my word."

No one spoke for an instant.

"I ain't leavin' here." Matt slapped the table, rattling the utensils. "Mama always said our future was on this land. We don't have nothin' back in Philadelphia. I'm not goin' off an' leavin' the corn an' beans an' the sorghum we planted for somebody else to harvest."

"Me neither." Luke sat up straighter.

Lily had never heard them defy their father before. Shocked, she swung her attention to John.

"I understand how you feel, boys," he said evenly. "But I need to know you're all safe. It's as simple as that."

"Hmph. We'd like to know *you're* safe, too, Pa," Matt retorted. "But that ain't stoppin' you from goin' back to that blasted fort, is it."

John slowly shook his head. "You know I have no choice."

"Well, neither do *we*. Luke an' me have to stay here. Keep the place goin.'"

His younger sibling nodded in assent.

Lily marveled that the two had become a force of one. More amazing, they'd rarely had an argument during the past year and truly had worked hard on the place. In the ensuing silence, she turned again to gauge their father's reaction.

Eva finally chimed in from the side. "You know, John, if the boys stay here, me 'n Maggie'll check in on 'em from time to time. So will the other neighbors, I'm sure."

John looked over at her. "So you folks are all planning to stay? Even knowing there's a war party coming down out of New York and heading this way?"

"That's right." She hiked her chin, blue eyes flashing. "Like your lad said, we done worked too hard to just cut out an' run. 'Sides, you militia boys are up there ready to stop 'em, ain't 'cha?"

He gave a conceding nod. "We'll do our best." Returning his focus to his sons, he stared at them a few seconds, then huffed out a breath. "Very well. Against my better judgment, I'll agree to let you stay here. . .if Ian MacBride will consent to accompany Lily and the little ones on the canoe trip as far as the mouth of the Susquehanna." He turned to her, his eyes pleading. "Would you be willing to go with my children? I'd do it myself, except I have extra horses I'm obliged to return to the fort."

Lily felt battered little Emma's hand still clinging to hers. She couldn't bear the thought of parting with the sweet angel again so soon, nor could she subject her to the possibility of being recaptured by savages. She filled her lungs with a shaky breath and moistened her lips. "Emma would be much safer in Philadelphia, that is true, and so would Davy. Their grandfather Gilford appeared to be a kind, loving man. I'm sure he'd be elated to house them until it's safe to come home. No doubt the quarantine has been lifted by now. I agree to take them. But"—she added force to her words—"then I'll return here and look after Matt and Luke. I'll not leave them by themselves with no one to cook or wash for them and see they get their lessons."

"No. That is out of the question." John tightened his lips.

He truly meant to send her away. Her heart sank with a sickening thud.

"You'd be alone on the river then. It's far too risky."

Lily strengthened her case. "I'm sure Mr. Gilford would provide an escort for my return. Perhaps the frontiersmen who guided him here to the farm. I'd prefer coming back overland anyway. 'Tis much faster than a slow, cumbersome journey upstream."

"Lily. . ." John looked from her to Eva Shepard and back. "Once you deliver the children and remember how wonderful it is to feel safe again, you may decide not to return to Beaver Cove."

"Oh, I'll be back. You can be certain of that." She gently disengaged Emma's hand and picked up the milk pitcher. "Would anyone care for more?"

"Me. Me." Davy squirmed in his chair. "We haveta hurry up and eat, Lily. We hafta pack my stuff. I'm gonna get to go on a boat all the way to Phila—Phila—"

"Delphia," Emma whispered, the first word she'd spoken in hours. But a tear spilled over her swollen eye and trickled down her cheek.

Lily filled Davy's glass half full, then set down the pitcher and wrapped her arm around Emma. If no one else needed a safe haven, this baby girl had to leave here to feel safe again. . .no matter how empty the house would be without her.

She raised her lashes and met John's gaze, seeing there a tender look that said he was aware of her concern, that he shared it as well. Then he averted his eyes, increasing the awkward silence filled with words unspoken. It was like her heart was being winched.

What might he have said to her if Eva Shepard wasn't hovering nearby? She didn't dare allow her imaginings to drift in that dangerous direction. But at least the forthcoming trip would eliminate the need for the older woman to lecture her.

Lily could hardly bear to think back on John's emotional farewell to his two older sons when she and the little ones had waited with their luggage to begin their journey. Even now, soaking in warm, silky luxury in a tub filled with sudsy water at a travelers' inn, she could still envision him barely managing to contain his tears. Matt and Luke had tried so hard to be brave and manly, promising to work hard and keep the place in order as the threesome hugged and kissed, administering awkward thumps on each other's backs.

Downstairs, a hotel maid was looking after Emma and Davy in the front parlor of Stevenson's Tavern while the pair watched travelers ride by on the post road between Baltimore and Philadelphia. The sights enthralled Davy, who had rarely seen a stranger before embarking on the trip downriver. He couldn't wait until tomorrow when the three of them would board another vehicle—not so fancy as one of the stylish carriages that made the little fellow's eyes widen like saucers, but a stage wagon. Lily herself felt a niggle of excitement about going to a city she understood to be even larger than Baltimore.

If only something would put a smile on Emmy's face.

A pity there hadn't been time to stitch some proper clothing for the children before they left, instead of their plain homespun. Lily could have salvaged enough material from one of her fine gowns or an old waistcoat of John's. She glanced down the lace front of the day gown she'd laid out to wear when she and the children would go for supper. Thank goodness she hadn't grown any taller since sailing across the sea from England or grown overly buxom. Mayhap she wouldn't be too out of fashion.

Out of fashion! A laugh bubbled out of her. To think being fashionable had been one of her greatest concerns before coming to the colonies. Such a foolish, naive lass she'd been then. At Beaver Cove she'd hesitated about wearing her lovely gowns, since most of her neighbors usually wore homespun garments. But a tiny part of her wondered if John would think she looked pretty tonight, had he come with them.

Dear, considerate John. Here she was soaking in a tub, anticipating supper in the public room, while he was stuck at a primitive fort that lacked even the simplest of comforts.

John. . . She recalled his expression of relief when Ian and young Michael both volunteered to canoe with her and the children down to the Susquehanna and see them aboard a flatboat. He had given each child a hug, a kiss, and a promise to come for them in November, when his enlistment was up. A wailing Emma clung so tightly to her pa it had taken the combined efforts of Lily and the MacBrides to peel her away. Only Davy bubbled with joyous anticipation.

Without attempting to unravel the tangled feelings the bittersweet memory gave her, Lily relaxed in the water up to her neck. One would expect she'd be quite good at good-byes by now, after being ripped away from her own father, two sisters, her dearest friend—and John— numerous times. She would survive this parting, too. She forced herself to concentrate on the present. It had been a lifetime since she'd bathed in water she didn't have to haul in and heat. Basking in the privilege, she smiled as a whiff from the briny Chesapeake Bay teased her nose.

In her deepest heart, Lily wished John had rendered the same kind of farewell to her as he had to Davy and Emma. His handsome features relaxed when he turned to her, and his eyes softened. An ocean of words they might have said, had they been alone, lay between them. Lily knew he still loved Susan, and she accepted it because it was only right. But still, there was that invisible cord of shared heartache, shared longings, that bound them together. No use trying to deny it.

But gentleman that he was, he only enclosed her hand in his much larger one and spoke words that still echoed in her heart. "My dear Lily, once you reach civilization and the children are settled, you may very well realize all you've been missing. You're a beautiful young woman, you know, and your sisters must be concerned for your safety. I'm certain they'd endeavor to see you pleasantly situated in an advantageous marriage. I, too, care very much what happens to you, and desire—" He glanced away, then took a breath and continued, his voice husky. "I'm already so utterly in your debt I shall think no less of you should you choose to travel on to the Barclay Plantation in Virginia. You are so very deserving."

"As I told you before—"

He touched a finger to her lips, stopping her words. "Please, lass, do what's best for you." Sweeping her up into his arms, he waded into the water and set her down in the canoe. "May God always keep you in the palm of His hand."

Despite the MacBrides' presence, Lily would have liked him to kiss her good-bye. He did not. But something in his gaze told her he had to leave right then, or he never would.

"Godspeed, my dear ones," he breathed.

Blowing soap bubbles away from her mouth, Lily struggled to contain stinging tears as she recalled John's compliment. *You're a beautiful young woman.* She let the memory linger at the edges of her mind, drawing from it what little comfort she could.

Just then, Davy, with his typical exuberance, burst into the room.

She'd forgotten to bolt the door! Lily gasped and grabbed a towel from the stack on the nearby chair, slapping it over her.

"Lily! Quick!" The imp flew past her to the window. "The biggest horses you ever saw!" Glancing over his shoulder, he widened his eyes. "Oops! I forgot. You're takin' a bath."

She arched an eyebrow and gave him a stern look. "Quite right. Now be a gentleman and go back out. And close the door behind you."

"But, Lily." He turned again to the window. "They're giant horses, and they're pullin' a giant wagon. You gotta see."

She let out an exasperated breath. "Emma wanted to bathe next. But since you're here, I suppose you—"

"Huh? No!" He backed toward the door. "I haf ta go back downstairs now. I'll go get Emmy."

As he made his escape, Lily pressed a hand over her mouth to muffle her laughter. There was no faster way to get rid of that scamp than to mention a bath. She only hoped Emma would relax enough to enjoy her time in the tub. Lifting the sopping towel out of the water, Lily wrung it out and draped it over the back of the chair to dry.

Most of Emma's bruises were fading away, and now that the journey had taken them far from danger, Lily hoped her darling's fears would fade as well. The child had sat close and still on the boat trip, but her eyes constantly scanned the wooded shorelines, as if expecting a painted savage to leap out of the forest and snatch her out of the canoe. *Dear Father in heaven, please relieve those fears. Replace them with Your love. Help her to feel safe again.*

By the time Lily rose from the tub, dried off, and donned fresh undergarments, Emma had slipped into the room, her black eye now a sickly yellow.

"I hear you and your brother have been having fun watching the travelers pass by." She dropped her day gown over her head and threaded her arms through the elbow-length sleeves.

"We shouldn't a come here." The little girl's voice sounded thin, trembly. "Nobody has a musket or pistol or nothin'. Indians could sneak in here an' grab anybody they want."

Dismayed, Lily settled the gown over her petticoats and snugged the front lacings a bit as she sat down on the bed. She held out her arms to the wisp of a girl.

Emma moved into them, calming immediately.

Lily raised Emma's dainty chin with the edge of her forefinger. "Sweetheart, there's a very good reason why no one is carrying a weapon. There's no need. We're several days away from the nearest Indian."

"But they could come down the river, like we did, real easy. Pa said they came all the way down from New York, and that's far."

Drawing her closer, Lily hugged her tight. "Listen carefully, Emmy. Thousands and thousands of people live here along the seacoast. They have entire armories filled with guns and cannons if they ever have need of them, and the Indians know that. Believe me when I say you are completely safe here. No Indian will ever, ever take you away from us again."

Emma's little arms moved up to wrap Lily's neck, her nose all but touching Lily's as she peered deep into her eyes. "Promise?"

"Promise." Lily smiled gently. "Remember how, back at home, I always took the pistol when I went very far from the house?"

She nodded.

"Well, I'm far, far from our house now, and I didn't even bother to bring it. That's how sure I am that we're safe. Now, how about running down to the kitchen and asking them to bring your bathwater upstairs. Oh, and see if you can find out what they'll be serving for supper this eve." She eased out of Emma's grasp. "Just think, Emmy. Supper without us having to cook it or clean up afterward. Won't that be marvelous?"

A hint of a smile tickled the little girl's mouth, the first Lily had glimpsed since the ordeal. "Really and truly? We just get up and walk away? We don't clear the table or nothin'?"

"Really and truly. Today you and I are young ladies of leisure."

"Hm. Ladies of leisure." Her smile broadening, she scampered away.

Watching after her, Lily knew her little angel would soon be Davy's rather serious, bossy older sister again. *Thank You, Father.*

The closing door emitted a whiff of baking bread. . .bread someone else had made for their pleasure. Breathing in the aroma, Lily wondered if mayhap the niceties of civilization would prove to be too tempting to resist, after all. What really awaited her back in Beaver Cove? Could she—or John—ever betray Susan's memory? He'd all but ordered her not to return. Yet there'd been something in the low timbre of his voice, the tender touch of his hand, the way he'd scooped her up and gently deposited her in the canoe. And that yearning look. . .

Or was it all merely her overactive imagination?

Still, he had said she was beautiful.

Stop it, you silly goose! Lily lurched to her feet and grabbed for her day gown's ties, tightening them so hard she was almost afraid to breathe. *The poor man's wife just died.*

Chapter 13

Is this Grandpa's house?" Holding on to Lily's hand, Davy stared wide-eyed at the gambrel-roofed brick dwelling with its generous dormers and large Palladian window above the columned portico. Black shutters adorned the first-floor windows, and manicured shrubs bracketed the entrance. "It's as big as the tavern where we stayed last night."

" 'Tis the home the gentleman at the corner indicated." Lily's body ached from the long, bumpy stage ride to Philadelphia, and her feet hurt from the hour they'd spent walking the cobblestone streets searching for the Gilford residence. But the lovely garden enclosed by a wrought-iron fence was a refreshing sight to her eyes. Taking advantage of the chance to drink in the lavish array of pastel roses, she filled her nostrils with their heady perfume.

Emma squeezed Lily's other hand and pointed. "Look at the door. It's blue and as shiny as glass."

"Yes, it is." Of far more import, no quarantine sign remained posted. "Come along." Letting go of the little girl's hand, she unlatched the scroll-worked gate. John had not exaggerated when he said Susan's father ran a very prosperous enterprise. This substantial home was proof. It wasn't as breathtakingly grand as Mariah's mansion, but it was a far cry from the cabins at Beaver Cove.

As they neared the porch steps, both children began to lag behind.

Lily paused. "There's nothing to fear. Remember what a nice man your grandfather is? How much he loved your mama? He loves the two of you just as much."

A worried look crimped Emma's face. "But what if Davy breaks something?"

The imp had the grace to look guilty.

Lily fought a smile. "Let's just hope he doesn't." Taking him by the shoulders, she gave him a warning glare. "No one is happy when something special is broken, but that doesn't stop people from loving each other. Let's do our best to mind our manners and be especially careful. Now, come along." She started up the neatly painted steps, and her charges followed.

As they approached the door with its brass lion's head knocker, Emma tugged on Lily's skirt. "Look how clean the porch is. Maybe we should take off our shoes."

"Yeah. My feet hurt." Davy stooped down.

Lily pulled him back up. "You need to keep them on." The children hadn't worn shoes since early spring, and likely their feet hurt even more than hers. She reached for the knocker and rapped twice.

"Oh, let me!" Davy jumped up, trying to reach it.

"If no one answers our first summons, I'll pick you up and let you knock again, how's that?"

He shrugged. After a few seconds, he stretched his arms up to her. "Now?"

As Lily reached down for him, the door opened. An unsmiling, middle-aged woman wearing a mobcap, starched white apron, and black service dress swept a glance of appraisal over Lily and the children. One eyebrow arched. "If you're looking for a handout, you need to go around to the kitchen." She started to close the door.

Lily quickly stepped within the portal. "We've come to see Mr. Gilford. These are his grandchildren."

The woman eyed them more critically. "They aren't any grandchildren I've ever seen."

"That's 'cause we live in Beaver Cove," Davy announced.

A visible change came over the servant's demeanor. She quickly stepped back to allow them entry. "The master and mistress are upstairs dressing for supper. If you would kindly wait in the parlor. . ." She gestured toward an archway to the right of the tastefully appointed entry. But rushing up the wide staircase, she glanced back with that same expression of doubt.

Again, Lily wished she'd had time and funds to have had the children properly clothed. Far worse, she dreaded having to be the one to bear the sad news of Susan's passing.

Walking into the parlor, Lily noted that the furnishings would have been respectable even in a cosmopolitan city like Bath. Susan's father had done remarkably well for himself in his trade. Her gaze assessed the sapphire velvet drapes with sheer underpanels; the upholstered settee with its matching Queen Anne chairs, done in satiny stripes of blue and silver; and lamp tables in dark wood. The same rich wood capped the fireplace with a mantel that held porcelain figurines and an intricately carved clock.

"Wow." Standing openmouthed with her brother in the archway, Emma grabbed Davy's hand. "Don't touch anything. Come with me." She led him to the settee and perched gingerly on the edge, tugging him onto the seat beside her.

The blessed sight of Emmy becoming her old self again, mothering Davy, almost brought tears to Lily's eyes. She smiled and crossed to one of the companion chairs. But before she could sit down, she heard a door bang open on the upper floor. Rapid footsteps descended the staircase.

"Where are they?" Auburn-haired Mr. Gilford rushed into the room and went straight for the children, his thin mustache spreading wide with his smile. "Emma. Davy." He gathered them into his arms and kissed each in turn. Then he turned to Lily, and his joyful expression fell as the reason for her presence dawned on him.

She nodded gravely. "I'm so very sorry, sir."

A surge of grief brought moisture to his eyes, and he rubbed a hand down his face.

Lily waited for him to regain his composure before uttering the words she'd prepared ahead of time. "I want you to know our dear Susan's passing was made so much more peaceful because of your visit. She spoke of little else afterward, and some of her last words expressed how happy she'd been to see you again. She loved you very much."

It took a brief span before he could respond as he tried to come to terms with his daughter's loss. Then he drew a fortifying breath. "But for that blasted quarantine, her mother would have been able to visit her as well," he muttered, still holding the little ones. "The city official came only yesterday to remove it. I went immediately to the stage office and purchased our fares to the Susquehanna. Olivia and I would have set out for Beaver Cove in the morning."

Lily stepped closer to the stricken man and laid an empathetic hand on his sleeve. "I can only imagine how hard the waiting was for you both."

He nodded and hugged the children close again.

"I realize our coming was not announced, sir, but you had offered to have Emma and Davy come visit. . . ."

"Absolutely." His enthusiasm returned. "Thank you for bringing them to us. It will mean so much to their grandmother." With the children still clinging, he wheeled around and strode out to the entry. "Olivia!" he shouted up the stairwell. "Forget your state of dress! Come down at once. I have a wonderful surprise!"

Lily had thought she'd been pampered at the travelers' inn merely because she'd been able to bathe in a real tub. But for three days after she and the children arrived at their grandparents' home, they'd been treated to a whirlwind of luxuries. Mistress Gilford proved to be a tireless shopper, scouring the bookseller's for picture books, the toy shop for playthings, and arranging for her seamstress to provide wardrobes for her grandbabies and Lily. And once the older couple learned of Emma's ordeal, they both lavished extra love on her.

"Look what Grandma bought me, Lily." Lying in bed next to Emma, Davy pointed to a stool in the corner of the nursery, where an assortment of lead soldiers stood in a row. "I have this many." He held up all his fingers. "And Grandpa said if I go straight to sleep, he'll help me build them a fort tomorrow, just like Papa's."

Lily gave him a pleased smile.

"The one on the littler horse. . .that's Captain Busse. I'm gonna make Papa the general. The general's the captain's boss. That way, Papa can come home anytime he wants."

"Aren't you the clever lad." Lily tapped his nose with her finger.

On his other side, Emma propped herself up on an elbow. "Grandma's seamstress is making a dress just like mine for my new dolly."

"That's marvelous, sweetheart." Lily shifted her gaze to the porcelain doll that lay on the pillow on Emma's far side. "You couldn't ask for more generous or kinder grandparents." Had they been otherwise, she'd never be able to leave her little ones in their care. "I hope you remembered to thank them."

"We did," they said in unison.

"Good. Now it's time to say your prayers."

"Me first." Always wanting to be first at everything, Davy pressed his palms together and bowed his head. "Dear heavenly Father, thank You for the food, for the soft feather bed, for my new clothes, an' for my new whip-an'-top an' the bag of marbles. But most of all, for my lead soldiers. Amen."

Emma tucked her chin and glared at him, then looked at Lily with a long-suffering shake of the head. "I'll do it right. Dear heavenly Father, thank You for taking care of us even when we think You can't. . . ."

Lily's heart melted over Emma's having to learn such a hard lesson at such a tender age.

"Thank You for Grandma and Grandpa and all the pretty things they bought us. Bless everybody here and back home in Beaver Cove. And please keep Papa safe till he comes to get us. *In Jesus' name,*" she added with emphasis as she peered at Davy. "Amen."

"Well done." Leaning across the bed, Lily kissed each of them again. "Sweet dreams. See you in the morning." Then, after blowing out the bedside lamp, she left the room and headed downstairs to have supper with the adults. She wished the little ones were coming with her, but she'd been reminded that in polite society, children were fed and put to bed before the evening meal was served. How unfortunate that folks would allow stiff rules to deprive them of some of life's most precious times. She had so enjoyed meals with the family all together—even if they could get loud and rather messy on occasion.

Reaching the bottom landing, she heard voices coming from the dining room and recalled that the Gilfords' eldest son and his wife had been invited to dine with them. Lily stopped before the gilt-framed mirror to check for any out-of-place curls or a twisted tucker. Assessing herself in her lovely new gown of ruffled ivory dimity, she decided if not for her work-hardened hands and newly tanned face, she'd have looked quite presentable. No bonnet had been able to shield her from the reflection coming off that mile-wide river.

Well, nothing could be done about that now. She plastered on a pleasant smile and glided toward the dining room, just as she'd been taught by her sisters so long ago, to meet the older brother Susan had often talked about with fondness.

A tempting array of delicious aromas greeted her as she entered. The sideboard displayed a wider variety of items than it had the two previous evenings.

At the head of the table, Susan's father rose, and his son, a man of equal height, but less breadth, did as well. He, too, had a mustache, and bore a marked resemblance to his sire. "Lily, dear, I'd like you to meet Warren and his lovely wife, Veronica."

As Warren nodded politely, the overhead candlelight cast a warm glow on his auburn hair, a few shades richer than his father's. Beside him, his sable-haired wife also nodded as he reclaimed his chair. Their gazes lingered a touch overlong as they took the measure of Lily.

"I'm pleased to meet you," Lily breathed as Mr. Gilford drew out the chair next to his and seated her. She settled her skirts around her.

At the foot of the table, Mistress Gilford, looking regal in an emerald satin gown, her salt-and-pepper hair in an elegant upsweep, plucked a silver bell from beside her and rang for service.

The younger Gilford mistress leaned forward, her ice-blue eyes cool as they focused on Lily. "Mother Olivia tells me you're from Bath, England, that you're the daughter of a jeweler." She blinked as she elevated her little pointed chin.

Lily caught the hint of skepticism in the woman's voice. "That is correct."

"Your family must have had an enormous reversal of fortune for you to be sold into bondage." She took a dainty sip from her water goblet, looking quite pleased with herself.

"Veronica." Mistress Gilford silenced her daughter-in-law with an arch of the brow.

" 'Tis quite all right," Lily replied. "I don't mind answering." She leveled a languid gaze at the impertinent young woman. "My father did not sell me. After he'd been swindled by an unscrupulous aristocrat, my eldest sister took it upon herself to pay our father's debtors by selling our furniture as well as herself to a sea captain sailing for America. Though my father did all he could to cancel the contract, he was not successful. I did not want my sister to undertake such a journey alone, so I convinced him to allow me to sign on as well. Unfortunately, and contrary to the sea captain's promise, we were separated and bonded to different individuals after we disembarked the ship. For some time now, another sister and my father have both offered to buy back my papers. But with Susan's poor health to consider, I could not find it in my heart to leave her or the children."

"I see." Veronica Gilford's comment still sounded dubious as a maid set a plate of food before her.

Lily retained her syrupy sweet tone. "Fact of the matter is, my term of indenturement ended weeks ago. When I leave here, I must decide whether to return to Beaver Cove to look after the older Waldon boys or travel on to my sister's, as Susan's husband urged. He fears for my safety as he does that of all his children. My sister, by the by, is wed to Colin Barclay, of Barclay Bay Plantation in Virginia. Perhaps you've heard of it. They are reputed to grow some of the finest quality tobacco in the colonies. Lovely mansion, and such restful grounds. I attended my sister's wedding there not three years ago."

"You traveled while you were still indentured to the Waldons?" Veronica gave a snide half smile.

"Quite right." By now everyone had been served. Lily felt compelled to direct her next words to Susan's mother. "Your daughter always treated me as if I were her little sister, a beloved member of the family. We became the very best of friends. I shall miss her sorely."

"That would be so like her." Sadness filled Mistress Gilford's eyes, and she lowered her lashes. "My greatest regret is that I was unable to be at her side when she needed me most."

Lily wished she'd have been seated near enough to the older woman to comfort her, but she had to rely on spoken words. "Susan understood. Truly. She asked me to send you her deepest love." Lily hadn't the heart to tell them their letter regarding the quarantine had arrived too late.

Thankfully, Mr. Gilford changed the subject. "Shall we bow our heads?"

As he led the family in prayer over the meal, Lily emitted a silent breath of relief. How very much she missed the simple, genuine folk of Beaver Cove.

Chapter 14

R iders comin'!"

Standing in the long, slow line of militiamen waiting in the dusty compound for another tasteless supper of beans and cornbread, John glanced up to the watchtower, where the announcement had initiated.

"Sure hope they're bringin' better food," someone behind him muttered.

"I hope they're bringin' good news," Patrick MacBride said.

A sarcastic chuckle issued from the back of the line. "Like the war's over."

Pat nudged John. "We could use some news like that about now."

Within moments, a pair of frontiersmen rode into the fort and reined their mounts straight for headquarters. Neither wore a smile.

John spotted Captain Busse buttoning his red jacket as he came out of his office. Still resentful of the officer, the sight of him filled John with rage. His eyes narrowed and his fingers dug into his wooden trencher.

Stepping closer, Pat squeezed his shoulder. "You need to get past that, John."

"I've tried, believe me. I just can't. Every time I see the man I'm reminded that I wasn't there for my wife in her last hours because of him."

"Perhaps the Lord thought it more important for you to leave here at the perfect moment to save your daughter," Pat said quietly. "Ever think of that?"

John slid him a glare. "Yeah. The last time you mentioned it. But had I been home, Emma probably wouldn't have gone to the Pattersons' in the first place."

"Then again. . ." Pat shrugged. "She might have. You can't keep tryin' to second-guess what might have happened. You need to ask the Lord to help you forgive. That's the only way you're gonna find peace." A gap opened in the line, and Pat moved forward, then turned back to John. "Pray about it."

Pray about it. If only it were that easy. John gave a bitter smirk. "Right now, the only thing I can think about is my boys. Matt and Luke are at home. *Alone.* Matt had a birthday this week. He's only twelve. Just a kid."

"Aye."

"Another birthday I missed. And as much as I appreciate Lily and want her to be there for the boys, that may not happen. If she gives any serious thought to herself, she'll go to her sister's place in Virginia where she'll be safe—and looked after, for a change. She's carried far more responsibilities than any lass should have to bear, and for a family that isn't even hers."

Reaching the serving table, John held out his trencher. After the unappetizing fare was plunked onto it, he and Pat found an empty wall to lean against.

As he sat down with the stone wall cooling his back, the last rays of sunshine gilded the fort with golden light, reminding John of Lily the morning they parted. He'd never forget the pain in her face as she floated away in the canoe. The early morning sun glistened on the tears in her eyes. The memory made it hard for him to breathe whenever he thought of it. Of her. He was a first-class heel. His wife was barely cold in the grave, and he couldn't stop thinking about Lily. What he really needed to pray about was for God to forgive his untoward thoughts.

"And we ask Your blessin' on our food an' the rest of the evenin', as well."

Becoming conscious of his friend's voice, John added his own silent plea. *Dear Lord, do what You will with me, but please don't allow my children or Lily to suffer because of my unwillingness to forgive Captain Busse—or for my unholy thoughts about her.*

While Mr. Gilford, at the head of the table, offered a blessing for the food, Lily sent her own unspoken prayer heavenward. *Father, for almost a fortnight, I've asked for Your guidance but have received no answer. Where would You have me go? Should I stay here with the little ones, go on to Mariah's, or return to Beaver Cove? I need an answer. Please.*

She knew such a prayer was presumptuous, but what else could she do? There was no one to advise her, and she didn't dare base her decision on her desire to see John again. That would be terribly wrong.

Becoming aware of the scrape of soupspoons on china, Lily raised her head, realizing that the others had started to eat.

Veronica Gilford's cool gaze focused on her as the haughty woman daintily lifted a spoon to her mouth.

Lily moistened her lips. Warren's wife had been hostile from the moment Lily had entered the dining room. And though Lily had received an invitation from the elder Gilfords to stay on as the children's governess, now that she'd met Susan's older brother and his wife, she had no intention of subjecting herself to further snobbish treatment. When she'd visited the Barclay plantation, Mariah's in-laws had treated her like family. Despite knowing she was a bond servant, they'd bestowed their love upon her.

Warren's voice brought her out of her reverie. "Father, you'll never believe what I heard at the newspaper office today."

"Oh?" His father blotted his mouth on his napkin.

"I'm beginning to wonder if it's wise to trust these so-called generals the Crown sends over from England. They haven't the foggiest idea how to wage war in America."

"Get to the point, Warren. What happened?"

Yes, Lily urged silently. *Are John or his boys in danger?*

Warren gave a droll huff. "Remember that huge army that gathered in New York, heading up to Lake Champlain under General Ambercrombie? They were to retake Fort Ticonderoga and the lake."

Lily relaxed. He wasn't talking about Pennsylvania.

"There he was," the younger man continued, "with all those men and all those cannons, going against a fort reported to be undermanned. And after dragging those fool cannons across that long distance to batter down the stone walls, he was so stupid he didn't wait for them to be brought from the rear. Instead, Ambercrombie ordered a frontal assault. Sent thousands of foot soldiers—mostly New Hampshire militiamen— with nothing but muskets to charge a stone fortification with a battery of cannons pointed at them."

Mr. Gilford leaned forward, his hands gripping the table edge. "What was the idiot thinking?"

Warren's voice took on a bitter note. "After eighteen hundred colonial men were senselessly slaughtered, not British regulars, mind you, the general panicked and ordered a hasty retreat, leaving those unused cannons behind."

Stunned, Lily stared in disbelief. *Eighteen hundred men.* Thank the Lord John was stationed farther south, under the general command of a more sensible officer, Colonel Weiser, who was in charge of the string of forts in Pennsylvania. If such mishandling were to continue, all the backcountry could be lost to the French. No wonder John had been so adamant about her and the children leaving. Perhaps this was God's answer. She should travel on to Mariah's.

"Warren, darling," Veronica said, slightly agitated. "You must have a talk with Warren Junior. Before we left home"—she switched her attention to her mother-in-law—"I overheard him tell his friend Willy he's going to run off to join the militia the day he turns fifteen."

"Oh, la," Mistress Gilford commiserated.

Lily remembered that Warren and his wife had two lads older than Matt and Luke.

Veronica returned her attention to her husband. "I'll not have any sons of mine slaughtered over some backwoods territorial nonsense."

"Yes, dear. We've already discussed this at length." Warren switched his gaze to Lily. "We were disappointed you hadn't brought Susan's older sons with you. I'd like to have met my nephews."

She angled her head and shrugged. "They refused to come, and it was hard for their father to argue with them so soon after. . ." She chose not to mention the recent death. "Both Susan and John always impressed upon the boys that their future was there on the land."

"Nonsense." Mr. Gilford shook his head. "We could easily bring them into our business."

Warren flashed a stern glance at his father before turning again to Lily with a benign smile. "Yes. I'm certain we could find work for them at the brickyard, stacking and loading. Perhaps making deliveries."

Lily fully understood the young man's look of disapproval. Warren's sons were in line to inherit the business, and he didn't want them to have any competition. His wife, of course, would be of the same mind. No wayward sister's offspring would get in the way of *their* children's inheritance.

Matthew and Luke, young as they were, had been right to remain on their land. Hopefully, General Ambercrombie would soon be replaced by a more competent commander, and the farmstead she and the Waldons had worked so hard to develop would once again be secure. Instead of a lifetime of stacking someone else's bricks, the boys would one day be making beautiful furniture with their father, furniture to grace all the homes that would be sprinkled throughout the Susquehanna and Swatara Valleys in years to come.

The Lord's direction suddenly became crystal clear, and a peace flowed through her. She would go back to Beaver Cove. If she didn't, Matt and Luke might find staying at the farm too difficult, too lonely.

They might give up and come to Philadelphia only to labor in some lowly position for their uncle.

Her boys needed her there to cook and wash, to help bring in the harvest. And for their future, they needed her to give them their schooling. Her own future would have to wait.

~~~

"Peaches should be ripening at my place about now." With a sigh, John picked up his pewter cup and washed down the last of his cornbread with weak tea. The thought of the plump, sweet fruit on his tongue caused him to yearn for juicy peaches smothered in rich cream and honey. He hadn't enjoyed such a delicious treat in ages.

"Aye." Pat shifted his weight against the stone wall. "My ma makes mouth-waterin' peach pie. What I'd give for a hunk of that now."

"Or maybe I'd have them sliced thin over a sweet biscuit. Lily makes biscuits lighter than air." John closed his eyes, envisioning the delectable golden brown scones hot from the dutch oven.

Abruptly, Pat elbowed him and motioned with his head. "Looks like we got company. Them two long hunters that rode in a couple a minutes ago are comin' straight for us."

John groaned and turned his attention toward the approaching frontiersmen. Surely Captain Busse wasn't sending him and Pat out roving again! They'd just come in from scouting this afternoon.

Blast it all! The woodsy pair didn't veer off anywhere but stopped right in front of him and Pat.

"One of you happen to be John Waldon?" The larger of the two, a strapping figure with dark brown hair beneath a coonskin cap, nodded in greeting. Merry hazel eyes flicked from John to Pat and back.

Already harboring considerable anger toward Busse, John didn't bother to get up. He responded in a flat tone. "That's me."

The man dismounted and stretched out a hand. "Well now. I'm plumb pleased to finally meet up with you, man. Nate Kinyon, husband to Rose Harwood."

"You don't say!" Breaking into a grin, John put down his trencher and grasped Kinyon's huge hand. "Glad to meet you—and to know you've still got your hair."

A chuckle rumbled from the man's chest. "Same here."

Belatedly, John remembered his manners. "Pat, I'd like you to meet Lily's brother-in-law. He lives to the south of us, along the Potomac River."

They exchanged nods, and Kinyon gestured toward his companion, whose darker complexion and almost black eyes hinted at possible Indian heritage. "This here's my partner, Bob Bloom."

The man swung down from his tall black horse.

At the conclusion of greetings, handshakes, and light banter, Pat left the group to fetch food for the visitors.

John met Nate's gaze. "So, how are Rose and your little ones?"

The smile evaporated from Kinyon's face. "Sorry to say, Bob an' me ain't seen our families since the thaw."

His partner spoke up. "An' if a serious offensive ain't mounted against Fort Duquesne soon, I ain't gonna be signin' on again, neither."

"I feel the same way," John agreed. "I can't believe nothing's been done about that French fort. The Indians attacking the Pennsylvania frontier come from there."

"Down along the Potomac and Maryland's backcountry, too," Kinyon supplied. "The French are givin' 'em presents hand over fist to keep 'em fightin' us."

"So I heard." John wagged his head. "They've been ravaging west of the Susquehanna for more than two years now. Not so much our side, though. I thank God every day I settled to the east. I expect you've heard what happened to the folks over near Fort Granville last year."

"Aye." Bob Bloom flipped a long braid over his shoulder. "The best the governor of Maryland has managed is to build a fort a bit west of our farm. They finally finished it this year."

"Your people do know not to surrender, right?" John asked.

Kinyon's expression turned grave. "Sure hope so. Better a quick death than one at the hands of them Shawnee, with them bone-chillin' torturous habits of theirs."

"I thought you boys were with the Virginia militia."

"We are, but we live on the Maryland side of the river."

"What brings you to our neighborhood?"

"Me an' Bob come across the tracks of a sizable war party headin' this way, so we followed 'em. Before they got to the Susquehanna, though, they turned north. We figgered they was gonna cross somewheres above Fort Augusta, so we cut across to give fair warnin' to you folks here before headin' up to Augusta. We suspected they'd try to bypass that fort an' go east along Blue Mountain, then sneak down through the Swatara Hole, where the creek cuts through. Raise havoc down the Schuylkill River."

"You two must be the ones who brought the news by a couple weeks back."

"Aye." Kinyon nodded. "But we got to Augusta too late. Instead of stayin' together, the Indians split up into smaller parties an' headed in different directions. Folks in Berks County got attacked. That ain't far from Reading."

"We heard about that." Pat walked up with trenchers of food for the longhunters. "They say that last week Indians caught some children outside at one of them German settlements an' hacked 'em to death." He handed the men the victuals, then dropped down beside them with a troubled frown.

"At another place," John added, "families staying at one house while their men were out picking fruit were set upon by Indians. The women put up a fight, but before their men could get to them, three of the children were carried off."

"Speakin' of kids bein' snatched away," Pat piped in, "same thing happened to John's Emma an' another little girl from Beaver Cove. But thank the good Lord, the men were able to catch up to them red devils an' get their daughters back."

Nate paused in eating, and his dark brows rose in alarm. "Your Emma? What about Lily an' the rest of your family?"

Even though he'd surmised the subject would eventually turn to his family, it was still difficult for John to speak about them. He exhaled a breath. "Emma had gone to our neighbors, the Pattersons, to spend the night at their place when some Indian braves grabbed her. I was on my way home for my wife's funeral when we crossed paths with men going after Emmy and the Patterson girl. Thankfully, the Lord led us to them before the little ones were hurt too bad."

A sympathetic tone softened Kinyon's boisterous voice. "God was with you for sure. I'm glad you was able to find Emma in time. But. . .you say your wife passed on? I'm right sorry to hear that. I know you've had a run of bad luck. Lily's letters to Rose never failed to mention Mistress Waldon's sufferin'." He bit off a chunk of bread.

John could only manage a nod. "At my urging, Lily took Emma and Davy to my wife's family in Philadelphia. She had it in mind to return to the place to stay with my older boys, but considering the danger, I told her that once the youngsters were settled, she should travel on to her sister Mariah's. She'll most certainly be safe there."

"Aye." The hint of a smile tweaked Nate's lips. "That'll save Rose a pile of frettin'. But ain't those boys of yours a mite young to stay on the place alone? They should'a gone to Philly, too."

John shrugged. "Matt's twelve now, and Luke will turn ten next month. But you're right. Even though Pat and I have fine, caring neighbors and have built us a solid blockhouse, it would've eased my mind considerably if my sons had gone with Lily. The thing is, if I forced them to leave, they threatened to jump out of the canoe and go right back."

Pat laughed. "Knowin' those two, they would'a done it, too."

"They'd put a lot of hard work and sweat into our farm," John elaborated with a mixture of pride and angst. "They refused to leave their harvest there to rot. Those boys of mine have been working the place like men ever since I've been in the militia."

"Sounds like you got kids a man can be proud of," Bob Bloom inserted with a knowing nod. "Hope mine grow up to be just like 'em. May the good Lord look after 'em an' keep 'em safe till you get back home."

Having finished his meal, Nate set the trencher on the ground. "I'd say from the letters Lily wrote to my Rose, she'll make some farmer a real fine wife."

"That she will." The begrudging statement sank in John's heart like a stone.

" 'Course, she could end up weddin' a plantation heir, like Mariah did." Then a wary grimace colored Nate's demeanor. "Considerin' the passel of Injuns roamin' this area, a trip through the wilderness back to your place would be mighty risky at this point. I'm purely glad to know Lily's out of harm's way."

And likely out of my life forever. John's chest banded painfully at the thought.

Chapter 15

Lily's eyes sprang open. Again.

Her anticipation—or more accurately, anxiety—had interrupted her sleep several times throughout the night. This morning she was scheduled to leave for home on horseback. She glanced out the open window, where the beginnings of dawn had barely started lifting the curtain of night.

Tossing back the sheet, she left the dreamy comfort of the feather bed and padded across the woven-thrush summer carpeting to look outside. A faint glow silhouetted the brick dwelling across the street. She'd never get back to sleep now. She might as well get dressed.

Feeling around in the darkness for the flint-striker on her nightstand, Lily found it and lit the wick of her bedside lamp. Her gaze immediately fell upon the letters she'd written to her sisters before retiring last eve. They had yet to be sealed. Reaching in the drawer for a piece of candle, she paused and opened the message she'd penned to Rose. She read over her explanation for returning to Beaver Cove instead of going on to the Barclays in Virginia:

*No doubt Mariah will feel I should give thought to my future,
now that my time of indenturement has ended. But I cannot.
Not yet. You, dearest Rose, have always been my example, and I
have always admired your integrity. You sacrificed your marrying
years to stay at home and take care of us. Then, here in America,
the Lord brought a marvelous and loving husband into your life
and blessed you with sweet little ones. I do long to see how they
have grown, but I cannot, until I know my own dear charges are
all safe and sound. I truly believe the Lord is sending me back to
look after the boys. I join you in constant, fervent prayer that the
Lord will return your husband to you just as I pray for John and
our other brave Beaver Cove men.*

With a sigh, Lily skipped over the rest and folded the heavy paper before putting flame to the candle and allowing a dollop of wax to drip on the outer edge and create a seal. She then stacked the missive atop the letter to Mariah.

Even as she lifted her night rail over her head, she lacked the absolute certainty that returning to the farm was God's leading. Part of her felt assured that she'd made the right decision, but the other part of her questioned whether the choice to go was merely her own willful desire. She wished the Lord would speak audibly to her as He had to Moses and Samuel in the Bible.

She dropped to her knees and spoke softly. "Father, if I'm not supposed to go back to Beaver Cove, please create a circumstance that will prevent me from making that mistake. I truly desire Your will, and not my own. But if I am to go, please, give the Gilfords the kind of tender love for Emma and Davy the children desperately need. I know I've asked this before, but"— she shrugged—"perhaps I should ask You to give me peace about leaving them here. I shall miss them terribly. And I needn't mention how nervous I am about riding a horse on such a long trip. You know my experience has been limited to short jaunts on my brother Tommy's pony in England and our gentle workhorse at the farmstead."

Lily paused and raised her gaze heavenward. "One more thing, Father. . . the men who will be escorting me are not the ones who accompanied Mr. Gilford. He says they come highly recommended, but still, a lone miss traveling with two total strangers. . ."

Huffing out a worried breath, Lily came to her feet. Surely the Lord was weary of hearing those same requests over and over. Time to get dressed.

Why, oh why, had she given in to her weakness? Lily knew she should have slipped out before the children woke up. But no, she'd had to have a last hug and kiss from each of them before departing. Now two whining, teary-eyed darlings tore at her heart as they begged her not to go.

"Please stay with us. . .please." Still in nightclothes and barefoot, Emma and Davy trailed Lily down the stairs and out the door. They stayed on her heels all the way to the gate.

Lily slid an apologetic glance to Mr. Gilford, who waited in the street with the two longhunters he'd hired to escort her. Beside them, three mounts and a packhorse raised tiny bursts of dust as their hooves pawed the cobblestone street in impatience.

Emma latched on to Lily's hand, tugging her backward. "Matt and Luke are bigger. They told you and Papa they could take care of themselves."

"I'm big, too." Davy pouted, his lower lip protruding. "I wanna go with you." He yanked on her dark gray skirt and elevated his voice to neighborhood pitch. "I wanna ride the horsies!"

"No, silly!" His sister jerked him away. "I want her to stay here with us, where it's safe."

Lily knelt and drew the little girl close, smoothing down her rumpled hair. "Matt and Luke can do the farm work well, but they don't know how to cook or do women's work. They've surely got the kitchen in a horrid mess by now."

"I—wanna—go!" Davy threw himself at Lily and clutched her shoulders, nearly toppling her.

She managed to disentangle him and tugged him around to the front to include him in the embrace. "There's a fine cook here, sweetie, and servants. And you have your grandma and grandpa to look after you and give you lots of hugs and kisses and read you stories until it's safe for you to come home. We'll all be together again soon. I promise."

The towhead squirmed free. "I ain't scared a no Injuns. I'll get a sword like my lead soldiers, an' stab 'em an' cut their heads off."

Rendered speechless by his tirade, Lily breathed with relief as Susan's father stepped in and scooped the boy up. "Davy, my boy, I do believe you need a few sword-fighting lessons first before you go charging off to fight, don't you think? How about you and I make us some practice swords? I've got just the right pieces of wood in my workshop." With a wink at Lily, he toted the diverted little fellow away.

Emma, however, clung all the tighter. "Please don't leave me. . . . Please. . ."

Lily's heart cinched as she kissed her darling's little red head. "Sweetheart, you know I have to go. And the only reason I feel it's right for me to leave is because I know you and Davy will be safe and loved here." She gently removed Emma's arms from around her and stood to her feet. "You know I'd rather stay here with you. But your other brothers also need someone to look after them and keep *them* safe."

Steeling herself against the tears rolling down Emma's fair, freckled cheeks, she strode to a long-legged dun and took the reins from the hand of one of the silent frontiersmen. His frizzy red beard hitched up on one side as he smirked at his hook-nosed partner. Neither hunter looked happy, and Lily wondered whether their displeasure stemmed from dissatisfaction over the price they'd agreed upon, their distaste at having a woman along on an arduous journey, or worse—concern about the Indians reportedly raiding farmsteads in Berks County.

She had concerns of her own—especially since she'd never ridden sidesaddle. Before she could voice any doubts, however, the red-bearded man rolled his hooded eyes to the sky and grunted as he hoisted her up onto the contraption.

Hooking a leg around the tall pommel, Lily had second and third thoughts about her decision to set off into the wilderness with the swarthy, rumpled pair. Nevertheless, she determined not to let it show. She would conquer this fear. She would.

Gazing down from that lofty height, her eyes misted at the sight of the shattered little girl sitting on the hard stones, arms about her drawn-up knees, weeping as she rocked to and fro.

"I love you, sweet Emmy," Lily somehow choked out. "We'll come back for you as soon as it's safe. Now go back in the house. There's a good dear." Without waiting for the men to mount, she clucked her tongue, starting the horse down the street before they could see her tears. Emma was still emotionally fragile, but right now, Matt and Luke needed her more.

Plodding along after the shaggy duo, Lily ground her teeth in vexation. The rawboned guides rode with their jaws hard-set, not even talking to each other as they led the way out of Philadelphia. All they'd done since setting eyes on her was look her up and down with ill-concealed disdain and then ignore her as if she didn't exist. She could only surmise that the two considered her a soft, silly female who had not the slightest inkling of what she was getting herself into. On the other hand, she decided as she emitted a spiritless breath, she *was* riding sidesaddle in a fashionable riding costume of summer wool trimmed with emerald velvet and a matching hat with a feathery plume. Perhaps they needed no further reason for their opinion.

The city buildings and mansions gradually gave way as the road led out of town toward Reading, and passing the last dwelling, Lily decided to make an attempt to dispel some of the men's misconceptions. She guided her docile mare up between them. "I don't believe we've introduced ourselves. I'm Lily Harwood, from Beaver Cove."

They both grunted and continued to stare straight ahead.

She tried again. "How might I address you gentlemen?"

The red-bearded one, obviously the spokesman, emptied his lungs and turned to her. "The name's Hap Reynolds. That there's Virgil Stewart." He indicated his cohort with a crook of his thumb.

"Mr. Reynolds and Mr. Stewart." She offered a polite smile to one, then the other. "I'm pleased to make your acquaintance."

"We don't much cotton to that *mister* stuff. Call us Reynolds an' Stewart, or Hap an' Virge. Yer choice."

She gave a hesitant nod, not quite ready to comply with such familiarity as first names. "Reynolds and Stewart, then. Well, could you give me some idea of how long it will take us to reach Beaver Cove overland?"

"Depends." The frizzled beard hitched again as Reynolds smirked at his buddy.

"On what?" It appeared she would have to drag information out of him a word at a time. She struggled for patience.

"The weather, the cricks, an' streams."

"An' the Lenape." Hook-nosed Stewart snickered. He flashed a gap-toothed grin at his pal and nudged his broad-brimmed hat a fraction higher.

Lily had no idea what a Lenape happened to be. "Is that a lake or a mountain?"

Reynolds chuckled at her naïveté. "Not *what*, missy. *Who.* They're the Injuns you folks insist on callin' the Delaware, after that river."

Despite the heat of the day, Lily felt a cold shiver. The Delaware and Shawnee tribes had been attacking from Fort Duquesne with the French. "Have there been more massacres between Reading on the Schuylkill and the Susquehanna?"

He shrugged. "Couldn't say. We just come south from the council meetin' Indian Agent Johnson in New York called. The man's doin his best to keep the friendlier tribes fightin' with us. Considerin' the mess them Brit generals is makin' of things, our allied Injuns is becomin' real standoffish."

A low chuckle rumbled from Stewart.

Lily did not consider that information particularly humorous. "I presume, then, that you're also rather reluctant scouts for the British. Is that correct?"

"More or less." Reynolds cocked his head. "We git our orders from the governor of Pennsylvania."

"I see. Then what Mr. Gilford told me is quite true. He must be a personal friend of the esteemed gentleman to be able to acquire your services."

"Don't know about that. But I never shy away from makin' a little extra coin on the side."

"Oh?" Lily wondered what sum Susan's father had paid them.

"Aye. The governor's sendin' us out to check on Fort Augusta, an' yer kinda' on our way."

"I was told it will take us two days to get to Reading."

Reynolds grunted with a nod.

"An' that's the last feather tick you'll be sleepin' on." The grin Virgil Stewart slanted her way made Lily uneasy. "Sure ya wouldn't rather take a nice easy riverboat trip up the Susquehanna?"

She refused to be scared off by his words—or his leer. "That would be nice, Mr. Stewart, but I cannot spare the time. Mr. Gilford's young grandsons are all alone on our farm." She paused. "Speaking of which, I noticed there's no extra musket for my use. Perhaps when we get to Reading you might help me purchase one that shoots true."

Four bushy eyebrows rose high as the scraggly pair eyed her with dubious expressions. Then Reynolds spoke up. "Those're awful big an' loud, missy. Ya sure ya want one?"

He seemed to enjoy having fun at her expense. Lily leveled a glare at him. "I will also require a horn of black powder. Enough so I can make a sufficient supply of cartridges before we start into the wilderness. It always helps to be prepared, would you not agree?"

Neither longhunter uttered another disparaging remark after that. She might be dressed like a simpering lady, but she refused to be treated like one. Still, she knew she'd be quite sore after riding on this silly female contraption all day. In all likelihood, tomorrow would find it difficult for her to walk. "By the by." She addressed Mr. Reynolds. "I should like to trade this useless sidesaddle for a regular one as soon as possible."

At that, the two sour-faced guides burst into a belly laugh.

"My pleasure." Reynolds's beard widened with his grin. "A good sensible saddle."

Lily surmised she'd finally earned a bit of respect in their eyes, but she still hadn't appreciated that suggestive leer from Virgil Stewart. She changed the subject. "I know the wilderness is vast, but is either of you acquainted, perchance, with Nate Kinyon?"

"Kinyon! That backwoods scalawag?" Reynolds tucked his scruffy chin. "We crossed paths now and ag'in, back when trappin' an' tradin' didn't guarantee a scalpin'. Once Virge 'n' me helped him out when he was in a tight spot with them heathens, too."

The news cheered Lily considerably. "Nate is my sister's husband. Mayhap you've met her as well, out along the Ohio. Rose Harwood."

Hap Reynolds whacked his knee and turned to his buddy. "Well, I'll be hornswaggled. This here gal's sister to that bondwoman ol' Eustice Smith took back to his tradin' post, rest his ornery soul." He switched his attention to Lily. "How's that purty Rose doin'—her an' that li'l orphaned babe she was a'motherin'?"

Lily smiled. "She and Nate married. They now live along the Potomac, where Nate and Black Horse Bob have adjoining farms, and are doing splendidly, as far as I know."

"Well, li'l missy." Reynolds nodded. "Since yer kin to Nate an' that li'l Rosie gal, Virge an' me'll be takin' extra care to git you home safe."

"I'd be most grateful for that." She relaxed a few degrees. "You two are a true godsend."

Virgil Stewart snorted through his nose, parting his droopy mustache. "I ain't never been called that b'fore."

But noting the pair's rather embarrassed, closed-mouthed grins, Lily knew she'd now be in good hands. She sent up a silent prayer of thanks to the Lord.

Chapter 16

Throughout the hard day's ride out of Reading along the Tulpehocken Creek Trail, the lanky guides spoke scant words to one another, and only then in whispers. Fearing a possible Indian attack, Lily spent so much time peering into the dense brush and trees crowding the path on either side that her head began to throb.

At last they reached a sheltered spot along the trail where they could camp for the night. But as wary as she'd felt earlier that day, matters worsened after a cold supper of jerked beef and biscuits when the men started drinking something that smelled suspiciously like rum. Fortunately neither of them had eyed her suggestively, but her fears doubled nonetheless. The confidence she'd felt three days ago after bringing Nate Kinyon's name into the conversation dwindled, and for the first time since departing from Philadelphia, she worried about her safety with these supposed protectors. Despite her exhaustion, she remained awake under her oiled canvas tarp until long after she heard snoring coming from both hunters.

Lily felt a smidgen of relief the following morning when the men appeared to have no lingering effects from their drinking, but it took her a number of steps after rising for her legs to lose their stiffness. She wished they could build a fire, since the glow would not be easily seen in the dense forest. But the guides chose not to.

Stewart handed her a biscuit from a grubby canvas sack and whispered into her ear. "The smell of smoke's a dead giveaway if any hostiles is about."

Hostiles! In close proximity? The fact that the man resorted to whispering increased her fears. Lily washed down the hard biscuit with cold water, trying not to compare the limited fare with the sumptuous breakfasts she had enjoyed at the Gilford house.

She untied the tarp shelter and folded it, noting that the covering was damp from sprinkles during the night. Her belongings and gear, however, remained dry. She encouraged herself with the reminder that God was with her. Recalling some of the experiences her sister Rose had laughingly related about her life in the wilds, Lily had to admit the Lord had definitely kept His hand on her sister through far worse circumstances than these. Rose was convinced that God always looked after those who belonged to Him. Lily focused on that thought.

She grabbed up the mare's bridle and blanket and strode through the trees to where the hobbled dun had wandered. She slipped the bridle over the horse's ears.

Hap Stewart came alongside and spoke again in that worrisome, soft rumble he'd used earlier. "After a spell, we'll be leavin' the crick trail and cuttin' south toward Fort Lebanon. We should git there sometime after high noon. We could stay there for the night, if ya like."

Lily continued to work, readying her mount for another day of travel. "Thank you, no. I'd rather keep going. I need to get home to the boys." More than a fortnight had passed since she'd left John and his sons, and she had no idea if any of them was still safe. There seemed no end of things to fret about, and she could only trust the Lord to look after them. *Please, Father, look after us all. Take this gnawing worry from me. Help me to feel Your peace.*

They broke camp and traveled onward. After a few hours, whenever they happened to break out of a stand of woods, they came upon cleared fields and farmsteads dotting the gentle hills and vales. Lily was especially heartened by the distant sight of a man driving a hay wagon. . .the first person she'd seen since leaving Reading yesterday morn.

Ahead of her, Reynolds nudged his chestnut gelding into a faster gait, and Lily and Stewart followed with the packhorse.

The wagon driver tipped his head politely when he reached them. *"Guten tag."* Obviously one of the German settlers who purchased land in the backcountry along with the English-speaking people, he drew his sturdy farm team to a halt.

Hap Reynolds touched his hat brim. "Folks hereabouts have any trouble with Injuns lately?"

The farmer rattled off something in German, then with a curt nod, slapped the reins over his team's backs and rumbled by with no more than a quick glance.

Lily had heard the Germans kept to themselves for the most part, though Indians attacked their settlements as often as they did those of the English. She looked over at Reynolds. "Did you understand anything he said?"

"No. We'll come up on the fort purty soon. If anybody knows anything, the militiamen posted there will."

The prediction proved to be true. But as Lily rode with her escorts into a large clearing a short time later, the fort's appearance came as a disappointment. In the center, a stockade of sharpened poles surrounded a blockhouse similar to the one her neighbors had built at Beaver Cove. In comparison to how John had described Fort Henry, this fortification was far less substantial. Fort Henry was built of stone. Still, riding toward the gates, she felt a sense of relief. Unlike their own blockhouse, this one housed militia, at least.

Glancing about, she saw several uniformed men out in the meadow, digging a trench. Another, just outside the gate, worked with a colt on a rope. Short and stocky, with the beginnings of light stubble emphasizing a pronounced underbite, he raised a hand to stop them, then strode in their direction, bringing the young horse along. "Where'd you folks come from? See any sign of a war party?"

Reynolds reined in. "Nope. We're comin' from Reading."

"Along the Tulpehocken Creek?"

"Aye."

The man shook his head. "A farmer and his wife were killed and scalped up that way four days ago."

"What about to the west?" Virgil Stewart asked. "Hear tell of any trouble out thataway?"

The soldier shrugged. "Can't say for sure. Whoever's still left between here and the Susquehanna ain't travelin' much. Leastwise, not in this direction. Some of our men are out rovin' that way now."

"No word a'tall? That don't sound good." Reynolds met his pal's gaze then turned to Lily. "Ya sure ya wouldn't rather stay here where it's safe, lass?"

"Are you and Stewart going on?"

"Aye. But we got orders."

"Well, so have I." The Lord did want her to keep going, didn't He?

⌁

The afternoon waned as the trail grew perceptively more narrow. Lily again rode single file between Reynolds and Stewart, while the packhorse brought up the rear. They'd passed the last cutoff to a farmstead a quarter hour ago, and an uneasy feeling began gnawing at her. She tried to fix her mind on more pleasant subjects.

When a cool breeze found its way through the thick undergrowth, Lily gladly turned her damp, sticky face into it, recalling the glorious, lavender-scented bath she'd had at the travelers' inn. The first thing she'd do when she reached home was fill the tub with tepid water and soak away her tired muscles.

"Hold up!" Stewart's order came from behind. . .and not in a whisper.

Hap Reynolds whipped his horse around and eased past Lily to reach his partner.

Lily's heart pounded as a strong, acrid smell assaulted her nostrils. Smoke. She searched forward through the tree growth to where thick clouds of smoke billowed upward—much more than would issue from a chimney.

"Stay here with the gal." Without another word, Reynolds circled his pal and the packhorse. Within seconds the dense forest swallowed him up.

"Might as well rest the horses," Stewart muttered, dismounting.

Grateful for the chance to rest her backside as well, Lily swung to the ground. When she saw Virgil Stewart pull his musket from its scabbard, she did the same and stepped back into the brush. The two of them stood on alert, waiting, listening, expecting Hap Reynolds to return with news. Minutes stretched like hours, but peering up at the sky, Lily saw that the sun had moved very little.

The clatter of fast-moving hoofbeats announced Reynolds's return back up the forest trail. He pulled hard on the reins, bringing his panting, lathered horse to a stop. "Got there too late. The man an' his wife are dead." He grimaced and wagged his head. "Them murderin' savages took off on foot with what looked like the tracks of two young'uns. No more'n four or five years old, I'd say."

Davy's age. Lily gulped past a lump in her throat.

"They must'a just left. The corpses was still warm an' seepin'." He shot a look to his partner. "Hand off that packhorse to the gal, Virge. We can catch 'em easy a'fore it gets too dark."

Lily's blood turned cold. They were leaving her here? Alone?

Stewart untied the packhorse from his saddle. "How many is there, ya 'spect?"

"Four, near as I could figger." He turned to Lily. "Take them horses off the trail far 'nough so's you can't be seen. Unload 'em best ya can."

Her insides trembling, she wanted to beg them to stay with her. But. . . little ones. How could they not try to save innocent children?

"If we ain't back by mornin', head on into the Palmyra settlement. It's only a couple a miles ahead." He pointed in the direction they'd been traveling.

Lily had no choice but to tamp down her panic and tug her dun and the packhorse between two matted spreads of berry bushes.

The longhunters snatched up fallen fir limbs and brushed over her tracks, then mounted and rode farther down the trail a short distance before cutting off on the other side.

Watching after them through the branches of her haven, Lily appreciated their having taken that small precaution on her behalf. She did her best to ignore her fear and stripped the gear and supplies from both animals then hobbled them. In all likelihood, the men wouldn't return for hours. She decided it might be prudent to find a safer, more secluded spot to hide, some distance away from the horses. No matter how well hidden the animals were from the trail, they could easily give away her position by making rustling noises or whinnying.

After filling her pockets with hard buns and dried meat, she slung a blanket over her shoulders and strapped on her water flask, cartridge pouch, and powder horn. Then, hefting the tall, awkward musket to one shoulder, she plucked a fallen fir branch from nearby and began the painstaking job of wiping clean any footprints she'd made backing away from the horses.

By the time she came upon a hemlock with low-hanging limbs skirting the ground, her whole body ached from trying to keep the musket aloft while sweeping away the traces of her presence. She swished debris back across the bared earth and stretched to loosen the kinks from her spine. With a backward glance in the fading light, she was fairly sure she'd left no readable sign.

She hunkered down into a crawl and backed herself and the six-foot-long weapon beneath the limbs, brushing away the last of the evidence. When she bumped into the tree trunk, a nervous giggle erupted. She slapped a grimy hand over her mouth to stifle the sound. If Mistress Gilford could see her now. The woman had been so adamant that she have just the perfect bonnet to go with her fancy riding costume. . .and here she sat in dirty homespun on old, dusty pine needles with cobwebs in her hair.

Her mirth vanished when the reason she'd been left here hit her full force. Two people lay dead among the ashes of their home, and their little ones had been kidnapped. What horrors had those dear children witnessed before the savages hauled them away? *Dear Lord, look after those babies. Take care of them. They must be so frightened, like my sweet Emmy was. And please bring Mr. Reynolds and Mr. Stewart back safely. I cannot imagine traveling on without them.*

Hours dragged by. Lily had long since eaten from the food in her pockets and watched darkness descend until she could no longer see her hand before her face. She'd never felt so alone in her life. Where were her guides?

A distant gunshot echoed through the woods. And another. Three more followed in close succession. The frontiersmen had only a single-shot weapon apiece. Had they been wounded? Killed?

Please, dear God, don't leave me out here alone. . . .

Chapter 17

Something crawled across her nose. Lily groggily brushed it away and opened her eyes. *A spider!* She lurched up, fully awake, banging her head on the branch right above her. Dust rained down, probably bringing more of the hairy pests with it. Scurrying out from under her shelter, she dusted herself off, head and body, shuddering all the time.

Rays of sunshine peeked down through the canopy of forest leaves from a rather high angle. Lily realized that after catching only fitful snatches of sleep during the night and waking at every noise, she had finally fallen into a deep slumber.

But. . .she glanced around. The men. They never came back.

She reached cautiously beneath a pine limb for the musket and its fixings, then started moving slowly, silently through the thicket toward the spot where she'd hobbled the horses. After only a few steps, she caught a whiff of smoke. Her guides would not have lit a fire. Renewed panic surged through her. No. She must not give in to fear. She had to stay calm. There might be a farmstead nearby.

The breeze appeared to be blowing from the other direction this morning and could have carried the smell from the Palmyra settlement. But like yesterday's smoke, this was far too strong and heavy to be from a mere fireplace.

Lily stepped gingerly out into a tiny clearing and glanced overhead. Billows of thick smoke crawled toward her from not very far away.

What should she do? Yestereve, a farmstead to the east of her had burned to the ground. Now one from the west had met the same fate. For all she knew, Indians might have passed right by her on the trail during the night. Another shudder rocked her being.

A few yards off to the side, a sudden fluttering of feathers almost stopped her heart as a covey of ground birds took flight. What—or who— had flushed them out?

A horse neighed in the distance. Then another. Lily prayed it was the longhunters returning. She stopped and cocked an ear, waiting for an answering neigh from the men's mounts.

None came.

Backing toward the fir tree again, she used her free hand to brush away her footprints until she and the weapon were again within its shelter. The single shot from her musket would do little good.

Seconds passed. Having heard nothing else, Lily felt foolish, huddled here with the spiders. She used the rifle to move a branch aside.

The rumble of low voices came from where she'd left the horses. Hopefully Reynolds and Stewart had come back for her. But. . .on foot? She hadn't heard hoofbeats.

Lily strained to gain sight of her guides, but with all the trees and underbrush she'd put between herself and the animals, it was impossible to see anything. The frontiersmen would have no idea where she was. Surely they'd call out to her. She waited. . .and waited.

When she detected the snap of twigs and the clomp of horse hooves, Lily surmised that the animals were being led back onto the trail. Surely the longhunters wouldn't go off and leave her.

But what if the pair assumed she'd gone on to Palmyra? After all, she'd carefully covered her tracks.

Unless these were Indians. . .the ones who'd set the farms ablaze!

Slowly, noiselessly, she crawled from beneath the branches. Keeping below the undergrowth, she inched toward the small meadow and raised her head for a peek.

No one was there.

She could still hear sounds coming from the direction they'd taken, so she rose cautiously to her feet. A dire realization came to her. Whoever it was had crossed the trail and headed north!

Sprinting to the place where she'd left the mare and the packhorse, she stopped and checked the ground. A multitude of footprints met her gaze—too many to have been made by Reynolds and Stewart. And all of them were from moccasins!

Overwhelmed at how close the Indians had been to her, Lily's knees began to give way. Only the support provided by her musket kept her from sinking to the ground. As strength slowly flowed back into her, she inhaled another strong breath of smoky air. *She* might be safe for the moment, but what about the folks who lived in that house? Had they been warned? She didn't recall hearing any gunshots. *I pray, Lord, that they got safely away before the savages got to their farm.*

And what about children! Had any more been captured? Mr. Reynolds had told her that Indians sometimes stole youngsters to hold for ransom. Lily scanned the footprints more closely, looking for small ones. When she found none, she nearly cried with relief. But what if she had? What could she have done? She'd never felt more helpless in her life. *Dear Father, please tell me what to do, which way to go. I have no idea.*

No matter how much she dreaded it, she knew she had to go to the burning farm. Someone there might still be alive and in desperate need of help.

About half a mile to the west of her haven, Lily came upon a clearing where an assortment of buildings smoldered. During her trek through the woods, she'd hoped and prayed neighbors in the vicinity would have seen the smoke and hastened to help. But to her great disappointment, no horse or wagon team sat parked in the barnyard. No one had come.

Taking full measure of the scene, Lily realized the farm lacked even its own wagon, nor was there any livestock in the pens. The family must have fled after spotting smoke issuing from the neighboring farm.

She stared forlornly at the smoking ruins, knowing the same could happen to the Waldon farmstead. Even if this family had not suffered the vicious attack, they'd lost their home and all their worldly goods. It was almost September. Many of the crops were already harvested and would have been stored to see them through the long winter. It was a huge loss.

Whatever had possessed her to leave Matthew and Luke alone at the farm? She should have insisted that John hog-tie his sons and toss them into the canoe. Filled with renewed urgency, she purposed to get to the boys before the Indians did. She would get them safely out of there.

But another chilling thought gave her pause. John had said the Palmyra settlements lay no more than ten miles south of Beaver Cove—and the Indians were even now cutting through the woods and heading in that direction!

Dear God, I beg of You. Keep my boys safe until I get to them.

Shoving the musket through a tangle of thorny bushes, Lily would have given anything to feel safe enough to travel on the trail, but she had no idea where the small raiding party was headed. They could have changed direction. Worse, they could be a part of a larger group sent by the French to ravage the countryside.

By staying close to the trail, she'd reach whatever fortification might exist at the Palmyra settlement. There she hoped to find someone to guide her across the hills to the Swatara Creek and Beaver Cove.

The ever-present stench of smoke lacing the air gradually diminished as she distanced herself from the burning farm, but the smell grew powerful again a short time later. Perhaps the wind had shifted. Wiping her grimy finger on a fold of her skirt, she licked it and held it aloft. The wind had not changed. Another place up ahead of her must have been set ablaze.

Lily felt utterly defeated. Tears stung her eyes and blurred her vision. Savagely she swiped them away, loathing her weakness. She would not give up. She would head north on her own. She had no other choice.

Checking her pockets, she found she still had a hard biscuit and two pieces of dried beef. She'd save it for supper. And if she didn't get back to the cove before dark, she'd survive one more night in the woods. She'd done it before. At least it was still summer. Thank heaven for that.

She filled her lungs with air. Turning toward the trail, she listened for several seconds, then crossed it, brushing away her footprints as she went. She was now on the north side—the same side taken by the Indians who stole her horses. And the same side as the last burning farm.

Determined to keep her eyes and ears alert, she dodged through the thick forest growth, keeping the source of light filtering through the trees to her right. She didn't know if she would reach the Swatara above or below Beaver Creek, but she'd worry about that detail once she came to the river.

The sun had risen high in the sky by the time Lily hiked down a rocky gully and into a small glen with an inviting spring. She stopped to fill her water flask and take a short rest. The small pool edged by water grass and a few reeds looked enticingly cool. As she filled the drinking container, she took a precious moment to enjoy the commonplace sounds of birds twittering overhead. A squirrel chattering as it watched her from a tree branch made her smile.

Once she'd corked the flask, she splashed water over her face to clean off the accumulation of perspiration and dust. It felt incredibly refreshing. She realized her feet needed attention as well and quickly stripped off her shoes and stockings, then sat down on a mossy boulder and lowered her ankles into the cool pond.

Eyes closed, she reveled in this small luxury as her feet began to lose their pain, only to be replaced by the aching of her shoulders and arms from lugging the heavy musket and using the awkward weapon to clear the way before her. She'd gotten so little sleep, it was hard to resist the temptation to take a nap in the cool grass.

That would have to wait for another day. With a sigh, she pulled one of the pieces of meat from her skirt pocket and bit into it.

A twig snapped behind her!

Chills shot through Lily as she whirled toward the sound.

No more than twenty feet away, a stag stared at her through some ferns. Vastly relieved, she sighed. She'd invaded his watering hole. But how easily it could have been savages. Chiding herself for having become careless, she stuffed the dried meat back into her pocket and raised her feet out of the water. She patted them dry with her skirt and replaced her footwear.

Suddenly the deer bounded away through the trees and the squirrel above stopped chattering. The sound of breaking twigs and slapping brush made its way down into the gully. Something big was coming!

Grabbing her musket, Lily dove off the rock and into a stand of ferns among the trees. Would a bear sniff her out? She certainly smelled ripe enough. It took only seconds to realize the noise was not being made by a large animal, but by men moving swiftly as they splashed through the small brook below her and up the other side of the hill.

She cautiously raised her head enough to have a look. Through the smattering of tree trunks, she spied several nearly naked Indian braves. One pulled the packhorse still loaded with the food and blankets and other necessities that would have provided sustenance for her homeward journey. She ducked back down immediately, her heart pounding. Likely the raiding party had done its worst and was now heading northeastward, toward the Swatara Hole, where the creek cut through Blue Mountain to the north.

Lily hoped they were the only raiders in the area. She'd wait here a little longer, then travel on.

When she again set out for home, the close call gave wings to her feet. But before an hour passed, heavy clouds rolled in, and the sky darkened. The faint scent of rain carried on the breeze. Without the sun to guide her she could no longer be sure which way north lay. Didn't moss grow on the north side of trees? She searched about but couldn't see moss anywhere.

Then she remembered something John had once told her. The Swatara Creek was the watershed all the little brooks and streams of the area fed into. All she had to do was follow any one of them, and she'd eventually come to the creek. *Thank You, dear Lord. You truly are looking after me.*

Feeling more encouraged than she had all day, Lily walked down a slope that led to a tiny streamlet. If she followed it and hurried, she might reach Swatara Creek before the rain let loose.

She did not. Not more than an hour or two later, the clouds opened up and great dollops of water splashed down onto the tree leaves, dripping off branches. Lily desperately yearned to go on, but she loathed getting drenched with night approaching. She looked around for the nearest big tree with thick branches and huddled against its trunk, tucking her legs and damp hem as close as she could.

Daylight faded without the rain slowing down, and morose thoughts filled Lily's mind. Here she sat under a tree again, this time wet from head to toe. Shivers wracked her body. What if she never made it home? What if she were captured and hacked to death, or mauled and eaten by some wild animal? No one would ever know what became of her. The little ones, Davy and Emma. How would they fare if they lost both their "mothers" in the same month? And the boys. They could be under attack at this very minute. *John, your children need you to come home. I need you.* She hugged herself all the tighter. *I need you so desperately to hold me close, to tell me everything will be all right.*

Sloshing and crunching sounds coming across the debris and fallen leaves overpowered the sounds of rain.

Lily snatched up her musket. Had someone come across her tracks? Had she been followed?

Chapter 18

T hat's my boy yonder!" A big grin splashed across Patrick's face.

John followed his friend's gaze and saw young Michael MacBride on the opposite side of the Swatara, waving his arms and jumping up and down.

With a gleeful shout, the lad swung around and ran back to the house, likely to fetch his grandfather so the raft could be brought across the water.

John was relieved to see the MacBride farmstead still standing. Several militia rovers had reported recent attacks on homes a few miles away on the outskirts of the Palmyra settlement. After he and Pat passed a particularly gruesome scene where all the buildings lay in ashes and bodies had been left to rot after being hacked and scalped, they were glad to hear that remaining families in the area had sought shelter within the stockade. John and Pat were frantic to get home and check on their own dear ones.

Even with Nate Kinyon and Black Horse Bob tracking for them, it seemed John and his roving party had only been chasing ghosts. The

Delaware war party sneaked past the Swatara Fort in the Hole, then split up and split again. For the past three days, John's group, along with Nate and Bob Bloom, had tracked one small band of raiders. But just when they thought they were closing in on the savages, the trail vanished in a stream. The Indians had sent off a packhorse to throw the searchers off track. John's group found the decoy but never discerned the point where the war party had emerged from the water.

The loose packhorse was minus all goods except tied-on haversacks. John figured its owner must be lying dead somewhere. The gravity of the situation compelled their leader, Sergeant Forbes, to allow Nate and the Beaver Creek men to travel on to their cove, while Bob and others continued the search for the war party.

John ground his teeth. If Fort Duquesne wasn't taken from the French soon, vicious raids could go on forever—and Beaver Cove would inevitably be targeted. Sloughing off his frustration, he dredged up a grin at the cheerful greetings from the other side of the broad creek as Ian MacBride and his grandson hauled the raft they had rigged with a ferry rope over to fetch them.

Jackson Dunlap moved to John's side, a sullen glower darkening his brown eyes. "Sure wish you didn't send Lily away." The stocky young man had voiced that comment at least a dozen times over the past weeks. "Me an' Frank's enlistments is up the first of September. Near as I can reckon, that was yesterday. We won't be goin' back. Neither of us."

"So you've said." John kept his eye on the raft.

"An' like I tol' ya, I was plannin' on takin' her to wife now that she ain't bound to you no more."

John nodded a response. He'd already explained his reasoning to the persistent upstart till he was blue in the face.

Jackson droned on. "Soon as I see my folks, I'm headin' on out to fetch that li'l gal back here. Her sister lives on one of them tobacco farms on the Potomac, don't she?"

John cut a glance to Nate Kinyon. Being a backwoodsman himself, Nate didn't seem to have a problem with this jackanapes courting Lily.

But John did, and he detested being trapped in this same conversation with Jackson yet again. "Her sister lives on a *very prosperous plantation*." He hoped the emphasis on the Barclays' prosperity would dampen the guy's enthusiasm a bit.

It didn't.

"Aw, that don't matter none to Lily. I heard her say a dozen times she placed more value on friends she has here than she would any amount of silver or gold. An' I figger she values *me* a whole lot more'n any of that truck."

John couldn't recall a single instance when Lily had brought that young buck's name into a conversation, nor had he ever caught her stealing a glance at the burly lad. If she'd expressed the slightest interest in Jackson Dunlap—or any other young man in the settlement—John was certain he'd have noticed.

As thoughts of Lily danced across his mind, he envisioned her tearful farewell, the desperate look that tugged at his heart. The tears she'd shed had not been for the Dunlap kid or that brother of his. They'd been for—

Well, maybe not for himself directly, but certainly for his boys and for the farm they'd built together.

The raft thudded against the bank. Ian and Michael jumped ashore and went to hug Patrick. John and the others waded in to help hold the craft steady so Jackson and Frank could load the packhorse onto it.

Once everyone was aboard, eager hands grabbed hold of the ferrying rope while Ian poled the raft away from the bank. Then the older man set the pole down and stepped cautiously across the lashed logs to John.

"I kinda hoped to see Lily-girl with ye."

"With us? Why would you expect that?"

The raft lurched a bit, and the Scotsman clutched John's arm for support. "Ye dinna' hear, then? We rafted a couple backwoods fellas across the crick 'bout an hour ago. They was escortin' her back here an' lost track of her."

"*Lost track of her!*" Shocked, John used his musket to steady himself on the rocking conveyance. "What do you mean, *lost track of her*?"

Frank Dunlap's hooded eyes grew wide. "Ya talkin' about Lily? She's missin'?"

Ahead of them, Nate, Jackson, and Pat stopped tugging on the ferry rope.

Ian scanned the group with his shrewd blue eyes. "A pair of frontiersmen escortin' Lily back here to the cove rode into John's place awhile ago, hopin' the lass made it back on her own."

His jaw set like granite, John thrust his musket into the older man's hands and snatched hold of the rope, pulling the clumsy raft across the creek as hard as he could with the help of the other three men. The instant it banged against the bank, he, Nate, and the Dunlap boys grabbed their weapons and took off along the wagon trail to his farmstead.

Please, dear God, let her be there. I promise never to be jealous again. If she has a mind to marry Jack or Frank or to go live with her sister, I won't try to stop her. Just let her be safe. That's all I ask.

Despite being completely winded by the time he and the others reached his cutoff, John kept going. He turned down the wooded path to the farm, pressing a fist to the hitch in his side as he ran down his lane.

Duke, ever on alert in the distance, started barking.

Before John broke completely out of the trees, his sons rounded the house and raced to meet him.

"Pa!" Matt slammed into him. "Come quick! Lily's missing!"

All strength left John. Panting, he struggled to regain his footing. "She's not. . .here, then."

Luke tugged on his arm. "We gotta go find her, Pa, before somethin' bad happens to her."

The rest of the group arrived, breathing hard, and surrounded the boys.

"Where are those worthless maggots who lost track of Lily?" Jackson grated out, his eyes angry slits. "Let me at 'em."

Matthew gestured toward the cabin. "Back there. At the house."

The words barely left his mouth before John and the others charged toward the place. Rounding the corner, John saw two tall, lanky men in hunter's clothes sitting on the porch *like they'd come to tea*!

The strangers both rose. One had his arm in a sling. "Kinyon!" one of them hollered.

"Reynolds?" Gasping for breath, Nate frowned. "Thought you was up New York way at that Indian council, you old scapegrace."

"We was. Till we reported to Governor Denny. He tol' us—"

"Quit yer blasted jawin'!" Jackson spat. "Where's Lily?"

The red beard on the longhunter's jaw hiked upward with his scowl as he shot Jackson a surly glare. He returned his attention to Nate and clambered down the porch steps. "I know the gal's yer kin, an' all, an' we was takin' real special care of her. But when we seen some Lenape braves carryin' off two young'uns, we tol' the lass to hide whilst we went to fetch 'em back."

His cohort stood on the porch, favoring his injured arm. "The varmints heared us comin' on them dad-gum horses of ourn an' started shootin' at us. We was lucky to escape with our scalps. Winged me good, they did." He indicated his shoulder with a tip of his grizzled head, then reclaimed his chair.

"Aye." Reynolds elaborated a bit more. "We made some fast tracks outta there. Figgered they might follow us, so's we went the opposite direction from where we left yer little gal. When we finally shed 'em an' got back there, she was gone, an' so was the packhorses."

"A whole passel of moccasin tracks was all over them horse prints, too," his buddy said. "But strange 'nough, there wasn't none of hers. I never heared tell of no savage wipin' away tracks of no victim, neither."

At the end of his patience, John latched on to the nearest frontiersman. "Well, she couldn't just disappear."

Reynolds peered down his nose at his captured arm, then eyed John. "We figger she must'a heared 'em comin' an' covered her own tracks." He paused. "Would the gal know to do that, ya think?"

"Our Lily sure would." Matt took John's hand. "She ain't no stupid city girl. Let's go, Pa. We gotta find her and bring her home."

Even as he and Matt turned to head out, Reynolds raised a hand to stop them. "Hold yer horses, boy. I ain't finished. Me an' Stewart made a wide circle around where we left the little gal, an' the only sign we come across was from them Lenapes. We lit out for the Palmyra stockade, hopin' she found her way there. But nobody seen her. So we rode on back to Fort Lebanon. No luck there, neither. Then we come here, hopin' the gal'd come home."

"Pa." Matt tugged John's sleeve. "I was just goin' out to saddle up Smokey. We gotta go find her."

John turned to frontiersman Reynolds. "Are you willing to take us back there? Show us where you left Lily?"

"Don't see as how it kin help, but we'll give it a try."

"Frank." Jackson elbowed his brother. "Run over to the Shaw place. Borrow his two horses while I round us up some extra food."

As irritating as the young militiaman could be at times, John was grateful the lad and his brother weren't hesitating to help with the search.

"You can take along that packhorse we found," Nate suggested.

"An' mine." Stewart rose to his feet again. "Ya kin take my horse. My arm's achin' somethin' fierce. I'll stay here an' look after the livestock for ya."

Reynolds glanced at Nate. "Did I hear you mention a packhorse?"

"Aye. Some Injuns we was chasin' used him for a decoy. Threw us off their trail."

The longhunter wagged his head. "Prob'ly ours. Did the beast still have our gear on him?"

" 'Fraid not."

"Well, let's go." Leaping off the porch, John sprinted to the stable. Who cared about some worthless horse when Lily was who knew where?

Within the hour, John, Matt, Nate, and the Dunlaps were again unloading horses with frontiersman Reynolds on the south side of the Swatara. A disappointed Luke had been left at home with the wounded longhunter.

Nate looked at Reynolds. "Why don't you take the Dunlap boys with you? Spread out and backtrack to where you left Lily. I'll take John and Matt and head upstream. No matter what, she'll have to cross the Swatara."

Matt gave a decisive nod as John hoisted him up onto the big pack-horse. "Lily knows the Palmyra settlements are south of us. Right, Pa?"

"I'm pretty sure she does, Son." *South, southeast. Would she be able to tell the difference?* It was easy to lose one's direction in these dense woods, especially when overcast and raining, as it had been yesterday. He hefted himself up onto Smokey's broad gray back. *Please be alive, Lily. Be alive.*

Nate cocked his head at Matt as they headed upstream along a narrow trace. "Boy, stay close to your pa. I'll search a ways up the first gully, then cross over to the second. You two ride up the trace an' track across from the second to the third, then I'll take the next, and so on. We'll cover more ground that way. An' remember to keep your eyes open an' your mouth shut. We think them war parties're headed outta here, but we ain't sure." He switched to John. "If you find Lily, shoot off a ball."

"Pa." Matt reined his mount alongside. "Would it be all right if I go with Mr. Kinyon? Maybe learn somethin' more about trackin'?"

The idea didn't appeal much to John. He'd just gotten home again. Besides, it was a couple of frontiersmen who had somehow managed to lose Lily.

"I'll see the boy comes to no harm," Nate said.

"All right. But, Matt, do exactly what Nate tells you, you hear?" With that, John heeled his mount into a trot ahead of them. The sooner he reached the second brook, the sooner he could start searching in earnest for Lily. Still, he couldn't deny that, in this vast wilderness, the chances of finding her were slim. She could be anywhere.

Setting his jaw with determination, he vowed to maintain hope. No one had spoken the words, but he refused even to venture anywhere near the thought that Indians had captured her. Not his sweet Lily. He would find her. . .or die trying.

Chapter 19

John reined Smokey to a stop when he reached the Swatara. The tall trees edging the far shore were outlined with waning sunlight, and their shadows stretched across the water, making a deceptively beautiful scene. But this was not a time to appreciate God's handiwork. The sun would soon set, and Lily was still out there somewhere. He'd searched through the woods and along the creek trace for hours and hadn't found a single footprint that wasn't pocked by yesterday's rain. This area north of Beaver Creek was too rugged for settling. He had yet to pass a farmstead, so there was no place Lily might have gone for help if she was wandering lost out here. The weight of his discouragement pressed hard upon him.

Where was she?

He tried to fortify himself with the possibility that Reynolds and the Dunlaps might have already found her and were returning with her to the cove.

The sound of distant hoofbeats coming at a trot from along the trace fell on his ears. Nate and Matt must have finished searching their section and were on their way to the next one. Nate probably wanted to scour one more area before darkness set in. John waited for the pair, eager to find out if they'd come across any sign of Lily.

Within seconds the two came into view around a curve.

John waved, and his son returned a smile and a happy wave. The bittersweet sight was one more reminder of how much he had missed his children, missed being there to share their joys and triumphs, their hurts and sorrows. Two more months, and his enlistment would be up. He'd come home to them for good then—providing they still had a home left to come home to.

Despite the optimism in Matt's expression, John could tell by Nate's demeanor they'd found nothing. He spread his arms with a disappointed shrug.

Nate halted next to John's mount and spoke in a quiet tone. "How far d'ya think we covered?"

"Eight, maybe nine miles. Sound about right to you?"

"Hard to tell. Thought me an' Matt would go up an' over one more hill then call it a night. We'll meet ya at the next stream an' camp there—unless you'd rather head on home. I'll leave it to you."

John had never felt so helpless or defeated, but he couldn't give up yet. "I want to keep going for a while."

Nate reached over a big hand and gave his shoulder an encouraging squeeze. "I'm sure Lily couldn't vanish into thin air. Either Reynolds or us'll find somethin' soon."

An unwanted mental picture of Lily lying dead, her body broken and bleeding, tore at John's mind. "I told her not to come back. I *told* her."

"That's all right, Pa." Matt edged his horse nearer. "Lily's as brave as the rest of us. She learned to shoot real straight, and she never backed down at strange noises. Fact is, when me an' Luke was out away from the house doin' chores, she liked callin' us the Rogers' Rangers of Waldon Place. You know, after them rangers up in New York. They really know how to fight the Indians."

John nodded, knowing those men fighting with the English against the French and Indians had provided the bulk of the colonies' paltry victories.

"If we had more fightin' units like them," Nate added, "this war would'a been over a long time ago, 'stead a draggin' on like it is. Worst of all, it's us folks along the frontiers payin' the price, while them English generals dally around cozy an' safe, surrounded by thousands of soldiers." He popped a curious grin. "I say after we run them Frenchies outta here, let's do the same with them useless Brits."

John slanted a gaze his way. It was a radical idea, but it might make for an interesting conversation some other day. He exhaled a tired breath. "Well, reckon I'll ride up to the next stream and check it out. See you there in a while."

Moments later, as John skirted the outside of a large bend in the creek edged by a sizable hill, he realized he had yet to pass an inlet. With Nate and Matt taking a roundabout route, they wouldn't reach the next section till well after dark. He slowed Smokey almost to a stop. Maybe he should ride back and find them. The spot where they'd met awhile ago would do for the night.

"John?"

Startled, he peered up the wooded rise. Nate couldn't have caught up so soon.

"John, is that you?"

His heart jolted. A woman's voice!

Lily! Suddenly there she was, breaking past some brush high above him, half running, half sliding, as she scurried down the steep incline to him. Relief engulfed John. He leaped off his mount and started to climb up to her—then remembered the signal. He stopped and turned back, yanking his weapon from its scabbard. Hands shaking, he sprinkled black powder in the flashpan and fired the ball into the air—the loud, joyous announcement echoing across the river and back.

By the time he jammed the rifle back into its sheath and turned around, Lily, crying and laughing at once, ran into his arms.

He caught hold of her so quickly he banged his head on her musket barrel. But he couldn't have cared less. She was here, and she was. . . unharmed?

Easing her to arm's length and looking through a sheen of moisture blurring his vision, he took an assessing look. Her hair, matted and tangled, lacked its usual golden highlights. Her tattered gown was a pitiful mess of wrinkles and stains and soils. Her arms, dirtier than he'd ever seen them, were a map of scratches, scabs, and insect bites—and she'd never looked more heart-stoppingly beautiful. Noticing the muddy traces her tears were carving down her face, he took out his kerchief and dabbed at them. "I was so worried. Thank God I found you."

Then with an unexpected flash of anger, he tightened his hold on her shoulders and gave her a shake. "Why did you have to come back? I told you it was too dangerous."

"I. . ." She swallowed hard and gazed up at him, all hurt and helpless, dissolving away all his ire.

He cupped her sweet face in his palms and searched deeply into her eyes. "You had me worried out of my mind," he murmured. He brushed his lips across a nasty scratch on her cheek, then kissed another. Then he kissed her eyes with their tear-spiked lashes, tasting her salty tears. "I could've lost you, too."

"I had to come back."

Her voice was so choked with emotion, it ripped at his heart. He drew her closer, and his lips found hers. He felt her meld to him, and he couldn't help himself. He cupped the back of her head and deepened the kiss.

Lily emitted a throaty moan, and her weapon dropped to the ground as she wrapped her arms around him, making his heart ache with profound joy.

She was here.

He tightened his embrace. Vaguely, the pounding of horse hooves knocked at the edges of his mind.

"What the blazes is goin' on here!" Nate shouted. He skidded his mount to a halt.

Lily gave a shuddering breath and pushed away from John, her eyes flaring wide.

He didn't completely release her but heeled around.

Nate glared down at him from atop his tall horse. "I hope you ain't been toyin' around with my sister-in-law all this time."

Mortified beyond words, Lily stepped away from John and almost tripped over her fallen musket, compounding her embarrassment. Quickly she snatched it up. How could she have taken such gross advantage of him by turning his welcoming kiss into one of her deep passion for him!

And to think Rose's husband had witnessed her disgraceful conduct! She felt her face redden.

"Lily! You're alive!" Matt hopped down from his horse, the presence of the lad adding even more misery. He had to have seen it all as well. But he threw his arms around her with the same fervor his father had done. "Nobody said it, but we were all afraid you was dead." He gave her a smacking kiss on her cheek. "We been prayin' our heads off that we'd find you safe. Right, Pa?"

"Yes, Son. We sure have." John's words came from right behind her as he stepped close again.

"Enough chit-chat." Nate cleared his throat. "I still want an answer. What's been goin' on betwixt the two of ya?"

John rested a hand softly on her shoulder. "There is nothing going on, and no fault to be found in this wonderful lass. She's never been anything but pure and true. I was just so glad to find her, to know the Indians hadn't dragged her off to. . ." His face heated, and he lowered his gaze to the ground.

The dear man was defending her, taking the blame for her inexcusable actions. Mustering her courage, Lily raised her gaze to her brother-in-law. "If there's any blame here, Nate, it is rightfully mine. I was so overwhelmed and thrilled to be rescued, I'm afraid I lost all sense of decorum. I assure you, I shall not thrust myself on poor John in that fashion again."

Rose's husband looked from her to John and back and broke into a grin. He spread his arms. "Then come here an' give this ol' hunter a hug. I been mighty worried about ya myself."

Vastly relieved he was willing to overlook her indiscretion, Lily gladly accepted his welcoming embrace. Then he held her away a bit and regarded her. "Ya come mighty close to getting caught by them Delaware, ya know."

She nodded. "Three times. There were two groups of them. When I thought I was safe from the ones who took the horses, another bunch ran past. Thank God they never noticed my tracks. I truly believe the Lord blinded their eyes, because they crossed right over my footprints without stopping to search for me. And then to stumble upon John. . ."

Having remained behind her, John put an arm around her again and drew her close. "Well, you're safe now. We'll have you home in a couple hours."

Her expression flattened. "You mean I'm still two hours away? By horseback? I thought once I finally reached the creek I wouldn't have far to go."

A gentle smile curved his lips. "The Swatara starts turning more to the north up this way. Makes it a longer hike."

With a resigned nod, Lily looked at Matthew and smiled. "I see you brought Matt along. But where's Luke? Is he safe?"

Nate answered. "The boy's stayin' with Virge Stewart at your place."

"Mr. Stewart is at the cabin?" Lily stepped out of John's hold. "God is so good. I thought for sure my frontier guides had been killed. What about Mr. Reynolds?"

"He's fine," John said from behind her.

Matt sidled up to her. "Him an' the Dunlap boys headed back to where they left you, hopin' you'd made it to the Palmyra stockade by now. Him an' Stewart never could pick up your trail. You covered your tracks real good."

Cupping his face, Lily tipped her head and drank in the sight of him. "I did my best, just like you taught me." She then lifted her gaze to Nate. "By the by, I don't suppose any of you happened to bring along any food. I've had nothing to eat since yesterday."

"Sure did." Matt ran to Smokey's saddlebag and pulled out something wrapped in cloth. He handed it to her. "I cooked this last night for supper. Hope it's not too dried out."

Even before she unfolded the cloth, she could smell the delicious meat through the fabric. At least half a chicken lay in her hands. She squealed and barely managed to thank him before biting into a drumstick.

"Well. . ." Nate peered up at the darkening sky. "Best we git goin'. Lily can eat on the way. An' she should ride up behind the boy, to even out the weight on the horses." He darted a meaningful glance at John.

Lily realized the man was still blaming John for the kiss that was so passionate her lips still tingled. Perhaps she should divert him. After her brother-in-law hoisted her up behind Matt she turned to him. "By what miracle are you and John here?"

John hooked the bar that held the kettle of boiling water over the flames and swung it within reach as his sons brought in two more buckets of water. Using a pad, he lifted the kettle off the heat and trailed after them to Lily's room. It had been after nine when they'd arrived at the cabin, but Lily said she couldn't possibly go to bed filthy. These last batches of water should be enough.

For himself, he'd go down to the creek with Matt and Luke. Neither of them smelled any better than he did. He wondered if they'd bothered to bathe even once since Lily left for Philadelphia.

As the two emerged from her bedchamber with the empty buckets, John carried the kettle in. He found her standing before the looking glass, brushing the twigs and tangles from her surprisingly long tresses.

She glanced briefly at his reflection. "I'm such a horrid mess."

He wanted to tell her she was the most beautiful mess he'd ever seen.

She hadn't worn her hair down for years, so he had no idea it flowed so far down her back. He resisted blurting out the compliment and substituted one less personal. "A warm soak and a good night's rest will put you to rights again, I'm sure."

"John?"

He met her image in the glass.

"Thank you." Having spoken quietly, she continued to occupy herself with her hair.

He noticed that a bar of the perfumed soap she used lay on a chair next to the tub, along with some towels. The items sent his mind in a dangerous direction. Heat from the kettle's handle began to radiate through the cloth, reminding him he had yet to empty the contents into the waiting tub. Steam billowed upward as he quickly dispensed the hot water. "I'll be taking the boys with me down to the creek for a good scrubbing. That way we'll all smell like roses in the morning."

Lily turned toward him. "One doesn't realize how dear the little niceties are until one is without them."

"Them and food," he teased, grinning. He remembered how she'd devoured the chicken they'd brought with them.

She treated him to a bit of a smile. "Yes. And food."

Her smile, her eyes, her presence gave his heart a jolt. Time to get out of here. Reluctantly he started backing out of the room. "Well, I'd best get after those boys of mine." Stepping across the threshold, he closed the door. Closing himself out.

Seconds passed before it dawned on him he was just standing there staring at the door. He turned away, only to find Nate glowering at him from across the room.

"Me an' you need to talk," the big man said.

Chapter 20

Not a sound issued from the loft after Matt and Luke, bathed and utterly spent, climbed into their beds. Virgil Stewart apparently had no such leanings toward cleanliness. He used his injured arm as an excuse to avoid washing his rank self in the creek. Even now he lay in John's bed, smelling up the entire room.

John was disgusted that Lily would have to rewash the bedding she'd left clean for his use. But with her kind spirit, she'd always do what needed to be done. In any event, there was no need for anyone in the house—particularly her—to hear whatever Nate had to say to him. He handed Lily's brother-in-law a cup of tea. "Why don't we go sit on the porch?"

"Sounds good to me." Nate led the way outside and took the far chair, stretching his long legs out before him as he sipped from his mug. "It's September already. Won't be havin' too many more porch-sittin' nights this year, I 'spect."

"No, reckon not."

Not far away, a pair of bullfrogs croaked back and forth, joined by sporadic hoots from an owl and the rhythmic chirping of crickets.

It seemed Nate was going to start with pleasantries, so John took a moment to gaze up at the brilliant stars sparkling like diamonds against the blue velvet sky.

"Me an' Bob Bloom, we been gone from home since April. We've run for our lives out there more'n once. Sure hate the thought of never getting to see my little ones again, or my own Rose of Sharon."

Studying Nate's profile in the starlight, John sighed. "I know. It's stone-hard. I wish we could make a separate peace with the Indians, separate from the British, I mean."

"Won't happen. Not as long as the French keep dolin' out goodies to the tribes. The Indians want easy access to European trade goods, an' if they have to spill a little blood to get 'em, they will. The tribes been raidin' one another for supplies an' slaves for centuries. It's a way of life with 'em."

John mulled over the words and nodded. "Well then, I hope the British navy is doing a better job of blocking the mouth of the St. Lawrence River than our English generals are doing out in the field. Looks like our best hope is in stopping French supplies from coming in altogether."

Nate huffed through his nose. "Some inglorious way that'd be to win a war."

Taking a sip of tea, John grunted his agreement. "All I know is I'll do my family far more good by leaving Fort Henry in November. I was wrong to leave them here alone."

"Speakin' of that. . ." Nate turned to John. The inquisition was about to start. "No self-respectin' man would go off an' leave his wife's baby sister here in a situation like ya have here these days, neither."

"You're absolutely right." John suddenly refused to let the man continue on to where he was headed. The subject was far too painful. "I've decided to send Lily *and my boys* downriver this time. It's obvious I can't protect them from a distance."

"Glad to hear that. Then Lily'll have no obligations to come back here. Once she delivers your lads to their grandparents, she can go on to the Potomac. I know Rose'd love the company. She always set such store by young Lily."

The man was talking as if John had nothing to say about the matter. Still, he didn't want Nate to know how much this conversation gnawed at his insides. He kept his tone casual. "From what you said earlier, your place is just as vulnerable to attack as mine is. It'd be better for Lily to stay with her sister Mariah. I'm set on that."

Nate gave a slow tip of his head. "I reckon that'd be best. I been after Rose to take our children and go there, too. But she's too attached to her little yellow house, an' it's like pullin' teeth to get her to go someplace else."

"It is hard, leaving everything behind." *And everyone. Lily.* John stood, his heart aching sorely, and tossed the remnants of his tea out in the yard. He was in no mood to sit out here any longer with this accuser. "I'm done in. I'm going up to the loft to sleep with my sons. You're welcome to share my quarters with Stewart."

Nate chuckled. "If you don't mind, I'll bed down out here where it's cool—an' the air's a whole lot fresher."

Lily awakened with the melody of a hymn in her thoughts. She mouthed the words silently as the familiar tune swirled through her mind. *"O God, our help in ages past, our hope for years to come. Our shelter from the stormy blast, and our eternal home!"* She smiled, remembering how God had sheltered her when savages passed close by her not once, but thrice. And He'd sent John to bring her back here. Home.

This morning she felt anything but guilty about a kiss she probably would have given *any* rescuer—even Rose's husband had he been the one to find her.

Stretching away her stiffness, she glanced out the open window to where birds already trilled the glorious morning, even though it was nowhere near full daylight. All the better. It would give her extra time. Her men deserved a hearty breakfast after all they'd been through on her behalf.

She bounded out of bed to dress while whisper-singing another stanza of the song. *"O God, our help in ages past, Our hope for years to come; be Thou my guide while life shall last, and our eternal home."* God had been her faithful guide through the dark and dangerous woods. She'd never again doubt He was watching over her, even in these perilous times.

Remembering the two small children the war party had snatched from their home, she dropped to her knees beside her bed. "Father, forgive me for not praying for them last night. I am trusting You to take care of them as You did me. Please, keep them as safe as if they were in Your own hand. In Jesus' most precious name, amen. Oh, and thank You for bringing me home."

She finished dressing, quickly twisted her night braid into a knot, and pinned it in place. Then, grabbing her apron from a spike by her door, she hurried out to the hearth. She wanted desperately to glance up to the loft, where John slept with the boys, but she fought that desire and refrained from even the slightest peek.

But how nice it would be if he woke before the others and we could enjoy a cup of tea together. . . .

No one stirred while she got a fire going and put water on to boil. Recalling how John always bragged about her biscuits, she quietly got out a mixing bowl and all the makings and in no time at all had a batch baking in the dutch oven. Then she stepped outside to get some side pork from the smokehouse and eggs from the coop.

Closing the door quietly behind her, she spied her brother-in-law asleep at the far end of the porch. She cringed, knowing he'd caught her kissing John square on the mouth, and guilt made her cheeks burn again— as they were prone to do every time she saw him. After leaving the porch on tiptoe, she ran all the way down near the creek to the smokehouse. Maybe she'd even milk the cow before collecting the first laid eggs of the day, since the coop could be easily seen from Nate's position.

By the time Lily took the milk down to the springhouse and filled a pitcher of the creamy liquid for breakfast, Rose's husband was nowhere to be seen. She did spot Matt and Luke, however, on their way across the yard to tend to morning chores.

The younger boy caught her eye and waved. "The biscuits sure smell grand. We ain't had much of anything good since you went off."

Stopping before the duo, she grinned, knowing Luke could devour three or four biscuits with no help from anyone. "Remember, we have guests this morning. You'll need to share."

He nodded, his eyes as bright as sunshine. "How soon'll breakfast be ready?"

Lily chuckled, tempted to ruffle that shaggy mane of his. Had her hands been free, she wouldn't have resisted the impulse. "As soon as I get this side pork sliced and cooked." She held the slab aloft for them to see. "If one of you would collect the eggs for me."

"I'll get 'em." A smile splashed across half-grown Matt's face. "Soon as I let the livestock out to graze."

"Thank you. I'd appreciate that."

The boys headed toward the stable, and Lily turned back for the house. If those two were up, likely the rest of the men had risen. And no matter how much she'd lectured herself, her heart tripped over itself at the thought of facing John and her brother-in-law together at the same time. But the biscuits did need to come out of the oven before they burned. Taking a calming breath, she walked purposefully to the house.

The door swung open before she reached it.

"Good morning." John smiled and stepped back for her to enter.

"Good morning." Her voice came out in a whisper as she passed him.

"Mornin', Lily."

Her eyes widened at the sight of Nate actually setting the table. "Them biscuits smell powerful good."

Having lost her voice a second ago, she acknowledged his greeting with a quick smile and a nod, then hurried with the milk and side pork to the worktable.

John followed her. "I'll slice it for you."

He'd done that chore for her a number of times in the past, but this morning his kindness felt considerably more intimate. "Why, thank you." Glad to have recovered her voice, she hurried on to the hearth. She scanned the room. "Mr. Stewart is still asleep?"

"I reckon." Nate plunked down a plate. "It's hard to get rested up with a shoulder wound."

"I see." She stooped to haul the dutch oven out of the embers with a poker.

"We need to have us a talk, Lily, b'fore John's boys come back in."

The serious note in her brother-in-law's voice set her on edge. "Very well. As soon as I get the biscuits on the table."

To her dismay, she accomplished the task far sooner than she'd hoped.

Both men had taken seats and now stared at her.

"Sit down a moment," John urged.

She looked from one to the other. Whatever they had to say, she wasn't going to like it.

"Please." John gestured toward an empty chair.

Reluctantly, she did as he bid.

He glanced from her to Nate. "Nate and I have decided you and the boys will be leaving here tomorrow morning. And this time I mean it. You need to stay where it's safe."

"Aye." Her brother-in-law nodded. "We decided the best place for you is with your sister Mariah."

They decided. *They decided?* Lily sprang to her feet. "And *I've* decided I'm staying right here—at least until John's enlistment is up. I'm certain the boys will side with me."

"No." Raking a hand through his hair, John stood up. "Not this time. The way the Indians have started breaking into small groups and moving fast, they can strike anywhere, anytime."

"You're quite correct in that regard." She retook her seat, pulling him down as well. Then, realizing she had hold of his hand, she quickly let go.

"I'm glad ya come to yer senses," Kinyon said.

At his gloating expression, Lily hiked her chin. "I never lost them." She switched her attention to John. "I've witnessed myself how and where this group of Indians strike. They don't attack anywhere near a stockade or a populated neighborhood like ours. They sneak up like cowards on outlying farms before the families know what's going to happen, do their worst, then hightail it back into the woods. Well, the boys and I do not live off by ourselves. We'll be quite safe here. After all, we have the blockhouse just across the creek. And you did say the Dunlap brothers aren't returning to Fort Henry. That's two veteran fighters we'll have at the very next farm."

John opened his mouth as if to respond, then closed it.

Lily continued before he could utter a word. "So, as you see, I, too, have been weighing the danger. Matt and Luke want to stay and protect their inheritance, and I'll not abandon them. After seeing the sort of life they'd have in Philadelphia—and considering the life they'd be relinquishing for one less worthy—I can do no less."

Nate whacked a hand on the table so hard, the plates rattled. "By George, Waldon, this gal has spunk. An' she does make sense. Lily, girl, if you wanna stay on here, I won't be one to stand in yer way." He cocked his head. " 'Course, come the first of November, I 'spect ya to go on to yer sister's. What d'ya say, Waldon?"

Lily felt her cheeks catch fire again. She couldn't bring herself to look John directly in his eyes.

"I don't like it." He paused and heaved a defeated breath. "But you didn't mind me when I told you not to come back. I shouldn't be surprised that you won't listen now. One thing I will have your word on, though."

Her gaze slid up to his.

"If those Dunlaps start trying to get too cozy, I want you to spend your nights at the MacBride place."

"You don't have to worry none about Jackson or Frank as long as *I'm* here, Pa."

Lily swiveled in her chair.

There stood Matt, his shirt cradling the eggs, her young, rustic knight in shining armor. She could not have been more proud of him.

Chapter 21

Later that morning, Ian MacBride and neighbor Richard Shaw volunteered to ride to the Palmyra settlement to track down Hap Reynolds and the Dunlap brothers and let them know Lily had been found.

With her presence on the farmstead for the next two months settled, Lily was happy John and Nate had decided to wait for Mr. Reynolds's return before reporting to their duties at Fort Henry. Facing another stretch of time without her most wonderful of men around to do the heavy work and ensure protection, she harbored the hope it would take days for Grampa MacBride and Mr. Shaw to find Mr. Reynolds.

As the day waned, she sat on the porch shucking corn for supper. She glanced past the men's laundry flapping in the breeze and beyond to the orchard, where John, Nate, and the boys plucked peaches from the fruit-laden trees.

The heart-gladdening sound of John's laughter could be heard in the distance. Lily watched as he hoisted Luke up into a tree and handed him a bucket. A tender smile tugged at her lips. How marvelous it was to see him enjoying time with his sons. His last homecoming had been dreadful, with Emma captured by Indians and Susan's demise.

Her gaze gravitated toward the wooded rise, where grass had only begun to cover Susan's final resting place. Susan and John had loved each other since childhood, and Lily knew John still grieved for his wife. She often saw him glance in the direction of the grave, and sadness would cloud his features. Then he would fill his lungs and assume a pleasant expression.

Tearing off a handful of corn husk, Lily wondered how she could ever presume John would care for her in that way. She had not the slightest doubt he loved her, but it was the kind of love one would have for a beloved little sister, not the romantic kind that would lead to marriage and endure for a lifetime. High time she faced that fact and began thinking about another future for herself. November was a mere two months hence.

She peered down at the ears of corn still to be shucked and forced her mind onto an entirely different subject: the sweet, juicy peaches the men would soon bring in. This was the first year of a bountiful crop from the trees the Waldons had planted when they'd first arrived. Envisioning a dessert of peaches smothered in sweet cream, Lily felt her mouth water. Next month the apples and pears would be ripe, along with the bright orange pumpkins. It would be a bountiful harvest, God willing.

Having grown up in a city where folks shopped for food on market day and farmers loudly hawked their fruits and vegetables, Lily had never given thought to much else besides whether or not Rose would make a good bargain. The transfer of money had taken precedence. But there was something wonderful and fulfilling about eating the bounty from one's own labors, one's own harvest.

She could understand why ever-so-proper Rose had chosen to live on a small farm. Naturally, her sister's love for that stalwart frontiersman had played a large part in her decision, but farm work was never-ending. If the war hadn't torn Nate away, he and Rose would be laboring together to make a future for their children—working side by side, always together, laughing, loving. . . .

Suddenly Lily's mind flooded with the memory of John kissing her face, her eyes, her lips, and her heart skipped a beat. How her lips had tingled then, how her whole being seemed to come to life.

Catching herself venturing to that forbidden place again, she ripped at a corn husk with renewed fervor. Far better to think about Mariah, the black-haired, violet-eyed beauty of the family who had arrived in America determined to use her stunning appearance to attract a wealthy husband. She had done just that. But not until the Lord taught her that true beauty came from within, that knowing the everlasting love of God and showing charity for others far outweighed the importance of having an easy life. The once vain, self-centered girl had blossomed into a sensitive, loving woman, after all.

A rasping snort behind Lily drew her back to the present. Virgil Stewart was slumped in a chair at the opposite end of the porch, napping as he'd done most of the day. She smirked as another nasal rumble emitted from the dozing frontiersman.

She bundled the stripped corn in her apron and took it into the house, where earlier she'd set a big pot over the hot coals to boil. Supper needed to be ready in time to allow a nice long visit this eve. Tomorrow or the next day the men would be leaving.

John would be leaving. She heaved a morose sigh.

Midmorning the next day, John glanced out the window of his workshop and groaned in disgust as Hap Reynolds and Jackson Dunlap cantered in. With those two back, he'd have no excuse to remain at the farmstead another day. Even the wooden stock he'd been working on to replace the cracked one on Nate's musket was finished, except for the varnish that had yet to dry.

He shifted his gaze to the open doorway and spied Lily at the well, drawing up a bucket of water.

She went still, holding the handle, looking as distraught over the return of the men as John felt. *She hadn't brightened at all upon seeing*

Jackson! A gloating smirk pulled at his lips.

Abruptly she swung her gaze to his shop.

John quickly stepped back into the shadows so she wouldn't see him mooning over her. What would she think if she knew her dear Susan's husband couldn't keep his eyes—or his thoughts—off her? Especially not after having kissed her with such fierce passion. His chest still swelled as he recalled the taste of her sweet lips. With a hopeless wag of his head, he wiped the varnish from his hands and strode out to greet the men.

He stopped dead in his tracks when Jackson flew off his mount before it came to a full stop and grabbed Lily—*and kissed her right on the mouth!* John's hands curled into fists.

Nate, having emerged from the house, reached Dunlap before John got there. He jerked the upstart backward.

Angry though he was, John's main concern was Lily. To his overwhelming relief, she did not look at all pleased with the young man. She swiped at her mouth with her apron, rubbing away Jackson's kiss. She hadn't done that when *he* kissed her. He squelched the smidgen of a smile.

"That happens to be my little sister," Nate grated between clenched teeth. "An' she's not to be manhandled."

The young man looked only slightly repentant as he returned his attention to Lily. " 'Scuse me. I was just so happy to see you. We looked everywhere. We thought the Injuns took you for sure."

She planted her hands on her hips. "Well, as you can see, I'm perfectly fine. I've nothing more than a few scratches and blisters." Relaxing a bit, she glanced past him. "Where's your brother? Did he go on home?"

A lazy grin spread across Jackson's face. "Frank'll be along in a couple days. A lass at the Palmyra stockade caught his fancy. He didn't even mind that she spoke no more'n a smatterin' of English. He volunteered to stay an' help raise some cabins for the burnt-out folks."

Lily's demeanor softened. "Young lass or not, that was quite generous of him, especially since you boys haven't been home in months."

"Didn't John tell you? My enlistment's up. I'm home for good." He puffed out his chest.

Her slender brows rose, but she responded in a pleasant tone. "I'm sure your family will be most pleased to hear that."

Watching the exchange, John reminded himself that even though Jackson had just kissed her, Lily treated him with only polite regard. Nothing more.

Nate changed the subject. "Don't tell me more cabins have been set afire."

Not bothering to answer, the young man continued to stare boldly at Lily.

Hap Reynolds responded. "No. A couple a men searched the woods b'fore we got back, hopin' to pick up the trail of the little boys that got carted off. But with the rain. . ." He shrugged. "They're purty sure them raidin' parties headed back toward the Swatara Hole. Leastwise, that's what they're prayin' for."

The pleasant expression on Lily's face wilted at the news. "Those little boys. How old are they, do you know?"

"Six an' four, miss."

John watched her shoulders sag. She turned troubled eyes to him. "How horrid. Our Davy's age. We must pray for their safety every day."

Nate gave a solemn nod. "After noonin', ya feel up to headin' out again, Hap?"

The question tore John's attention from Lily.

"Sure do." The bearded hunter directed his next words to her, and he whipped off his worn hat, his face contrite. "I know we promised to keep ya safe, missy. We let ya down, an' I'm real sorry about that."

She offered him a pleasant smile. "You've no need to apologize. I don't fault you at all. You had to try to save those little ones. Anyone would've done the same. God took good care of me."

Awed by Lily's gentle response, John was dumbfounded. Heaven help him, he loved every word that came out of her mouth.

Obviously, so did Jackson Dunlap. John could see it in the young man's eyes when she turned to him.

"Jackson, I want to thank you from my deepest heart for spending so many days searching for me when you could have gone home to your family. They've missed you boys so, especially your mother. I refuse to be the cause of any further delay. So get back on that horse of yours, and don't keep the poor woman waiting any longer."

He tipped his dark head at her with an uncharacteristically tender smile. "For you. . .and Ma, I'll go. But rest assured, pretty gal, I'll be checkin' back with you real soon."

John knew that was no lightly given promise. He also knew he wouldn't be there to stop the lad.

"Pa!"

Turning toward Matt's call, John saw his boys running up from the creek with their poles and a string of fish, Duke bounding along after them. "The men. They're back already?" Panting, Matt came to a stop in front of John, with Luke a mere step or two behind. "You'll be leavin' now, won't you?"

At the pained looks on their young faces, John pulled his sons into a fervent hug and looked up at Lily.

Her eyes swam with tears.

How desperately he wanted her to stay on when he returned, stay with him and his children. But unlike that bold Dunlap rogue, he had no right to ask anything of her, no right to take advantage of her kind heart and her love for his children. After four long years of ministering to Susan and taking on the care of his children and everything else he'd thrust on the girl's slender shoulders, she deserved the chance to find a love of her own. To have her own little ones. There was only one right thing he could say. "I'll be back come November."

The cabin felt indescribably lonely when Lily rose the next morning. There'd be no sound of John's solid footsteps, no echo of his rich voice or laughter, no tender whisper after the kids were in bed. She tugged her wrapper tighter against the morning chill and pulled the bedroom window closed. The men must have taken the warmth with them when they left.

Not even Virgil Stewart, with his touch of fever, had stayed behind. "Don't like bein' closed in by jabberin' walls," he'd said. But Lily suspected it was the jabbering kids the longhunter wanted to escape. He'd turned out to be nothing but an old grumbler.

On the other hand, she was just as happy he'd taken his smelly self out of the house and out of Susan's bed. . .John's bed.

No! She could not allow her mind to dwell on that subject. Lily stopped halfway out of her bedchamber and closed her eyes. *Father in heaven, I beg you to take this awful yearning away. Help me to redirect my inappropriate feelings for John Waldon to some other man, a godly one I can love freely as my sisters do their husbands. I know You can do this. If You could blind the eyes of Indians to my footprints, surely You can blind the eyes of my heart to this man who can never belong to me.*

Slowly, gradually, a warm, gentle peace flowed through her. God loved her despite her weakness. "Thank You. . .so much," she whispered.

Realizing she could easily have been overheard, she darted a glance up to the loft, but the boys hadn't awakened. She smiled and padded to the hearth. They'd been so happy to have their papa home, even if it was for only that short time. Just two more months, and they'd have him home again for good.

At the thought, Lily's moment of peace vanished. Two months, and she'd have to leave not only John Waldon, but also the boys whom she'd grown to love. And sweet Emmy and her little scamp, Davy. How would she ever part with them all?

A Bible verse floated across the pages of her mind: *"Take therefore no thought for the morrow; for the morrow shall take thought for the things of itself."*

She sighed. Yes. Let tomorrow take care of itself.

That sweet sense of peace came flooding back.

Lily stirred the embers of the backlog to life and added a few small splits of wood, then reached for the empty water bucket. Walking outside with it, she felt a chill breeze sweep her face as she hastened toward the well. The woodshed, she noticed on the way, was already half empty.

She'd best get the boys started on filling it today. Winter could easily come early this year.

A sudden strong whiff of smoke wafted past her nose, and Lily froze. *Someone's cabin!*

She sprinted out to the center of the clearing and whirled around, trying to determine the direction of the blaze. Then, realizing the smoke issued from her own chimney, she felt utterly silly and went back to the well. Obviously, as little Emma had experienced, it would take awhile for her own terrors from the past week to fade away. But with God's help, she would overcome those frightful memories.

Still, lowering the well bucket down into the water, she couldn't help searching the woods for any sign of movement, any strange sound.

Chapter 22

Matthew and Luke moaned when Lily rousted them to feed and water the stock, but it didn't bother her. Every time they had to part with their pa, it had the same effect on them, and she knew it would take awhile for the pain to go away. Soon enough they'd turn back into the jovial helpers she knew and loved.

As she bent down at the hearth to flip the pancakes in the iron skillet, she recalled how a hymn had lifted her spirits earlier and determined to raise theirs as well. She lifted her voice to sing. "See Israel's gentle Shepherd stand with all engaging charms; Hark! How He calls the tender lambs, and folds them in His arms."

How wonderful it would have been to serve her brave lads a big helping of eggs, too. But the small flock of laying hens had failed to keep up with the demand of all the voracious eaters she'd had. At least there was plenty of butter and some peach jam she'd made yesterday after the men left. Walking outside, Lily clanged the bar around the triangle, calling the boys in to breakfast, then hurried back to pile the golden-brown flapjacks onto a platter.

Loud tromping issued from the porch. Never one to be late for a meal, Luke burst inside ahead of his brother. "What's for breakfast?"

"Pancakes, fried fish, and peach jam."

"Great! I'm starved." He flew to the table. "Sure am glad you're back."

Matt, still under a cloud, trudged behind the younger boy and plopped down at the table, his forearms resting on the surface, his shoulders slumped.

Lily's heart went out to him. "I hope you both remembered to wash up," she said brightly.

"Sure did." Luke displayed a pair of drippy hands.

"Better dry them on your napkin." Moving beside him, she forked a stack of hotcakes onto his trencher then moved to Matt's and filled his. She couldn't resist giving him a kiss on the cheek and softening her tone. " 'Tis hard, I know. But this time we can be assured he'll be back come November."

"You really believe that?" He cast a despondent glance up at her, his blue eyes dull.

"Of course I do. Your pa promised not to sign on again, didn't he?" Setting the platter down, she pulled out the chair beside him and sank onto it. "The good Lord tells us not to borrow trouble. He says we should only concern ourselves with the worries of the day."

He let out a huff. "Well, that's my worry today. An' you should be worried, too. Our Emma got took by redskins, an' then you had to run from 'em yourself, hidin' lost for days. An' Pa—he's probably out there right now chasin' after them wild savages. Anything could happen to him."

"Dear, dear Matty." Lily placed a hand on his. "It's wonderful that you care so deeply about things. It shows you're becoming a young man. But if you recall, your pa and the others were going directly back to the fort to report in."

"Aye, an' there's a whole lot of forest between here an' there where those heathens could be skulkin' around, waitin' to pounce."

"Well then, the thing to do is pray for him. Right now, while we ask the blessing for the food. Let's bow our heads." She paused. "Thank You, heavenly Father, for the bounty You provided for us this day. We lift up a special prayer for John and Nate and the two longhunters. Please surround them with angels and shield them from danger as they travel to the fort. And, again, look after the two little boys who were captured. Keep Your hand upon them while they're with the Indians and bring them safely home. We ask these things in the name of Your Son. Amen."

Matt grunted and reached for his glass of milk.

"Don't you believe God listens to our prayers?" Lily asked quietly.

"He might be listenin', but that don't mean He's gonna do nothin'."

Reaching over to him, Lily took him by the shoulders and turned him to face her. "We prayed for Emma, Matt, and God brought her back to us, didn't He? I prayed the Indians wouldn't find me, and they didn't. Surely that proves the Lord hears prayer."

"Oh yeah? I'll wager the mama and papa of them little boys prayed mornin' and night that the Injuns wouldn't come an' burn 'em out an' kill 'em an' take their little ones. But it still happened, didn't it? An' what about Mama? We prayed and prayed for her all the time, an' she still died. All them prayers didn't change nothin'."

Lily had no answer. What he said was true. Why *had* God saved her and Emma and not that other family? Still, she couldn't leave the subject there. "Tomorrow's the Sabbath. When Grampa Mac comes, we'll ask him those questions. I'm sure he'll know the reason why bad things happen to some people and not others."

Unimpressed, Matt scoffed. "He'll come up with somethin'. Probably the usual pretty words that sound good. He always comes up with those."

~

The day wore on, and Lily could not get Matt's words out of her mind. Added to that, the sweet peace she'd found early that morning had vanished. *Did God truly care about His children as much as the Bible said?* She ran the iron over the back of Luke's Sunday shirt. *Did prayer actually make a difference. . .or was it time and chance that affected the outcome of situations?*

A splintering sound broke into her thoughts, and she went to the window to check on the boys. For more than an hour now, they'd been taking turns splitting logs at the chopping stump and stacking the wood in the shed. As always, Matt's musket leaned against the wall of the woodshed, while old, shaggy Duke lay with his head on his paws, watching from nearby with his chocolate eyes at half-staff.

John's sons were good boys. Lily hoped old Mr. MacBride would have a satisfactory answer for Matt. And for her. Strange how a day could begin with such promise and then end with such doubt. It even looked like rain was headed their way. Perhaps it would be best to call the boys inside so they could work a few sums on their slates before supper.

After lifting the shirt off the workboard, she carefully folded it and set it atop Matt's, then carried the hot iron to its plate on the hearth. Unhooking the big spoon, she stirred the bubbling kettle of beans. She, Matt, and Luke would have some this eve; the rest would be shared with the neighbors tomorrow. It would be a treat to see everyone again. Lily was particularly anxious to learn how little Mary was faring now, after having been rescued with Emma. She replaced the spoon and went to summon the boys.

Suddenly, Duke's barking shattered the stillness.

Lily told herself not to be frightened. She reached above the door and took down the musket and powder horn, then poured gunpowder into the flashpan. She opened the door.

Matt and Luke were striding toward the path with Duke still barking as he loped beside them. Matt had his musket tucked under one arm, his gaze trained in the direction the dog had sensed alarm. Luke was armed now with the pistol, since Lily had purchased a musket for herself in Reading.

"Quit yapping, Duke, you mangy mutt," came a male voice in the distance.

Obviously someone they knew. Lily stepped out onto the porch to have a look.

A lone rider emerged from the dark forest.

"Aw, it's just Robby!" Matt called, tossing a glance over his shoulder to her. He jabbed a finger at the dog. "Pipe down, boy."

Robby! Why would he come here this evening, when the whole cove will attend the Sabbath service tomorrow? And with rain coming!

"Halloo the house!" Robby plodded around the corner on his old roan workhorse.

Matt and Luke went to meet him then walked alongside him until he reached the front of the cabin.

"What's up?" Matt frowned. "Somethin' wrong?"

"Sure is." Robby caught sight of Lily just then, and his whole face lit up with a smile. "I just heard you was back, Lily. I sure did miss you—I mean—*we* sure missed you. Ever'body did."

She offered him a genuine smile, though she remained on the porch. "I'm pleased to hear that. I missed all of you, too."

"Jackson Dunlap said you was all scratched up an' I shouldn't bother you yet." He swung down and casually let the reins drop to the ground as he walked toward her. He tipped his head, scrutinizing her with those big hazel eyes of his. " 'Cept for that little scratch on your cheek, you look plumb purty."

Matt cut in before she could respond. "Well, she's real wore out. Not up to a whole lot of company this evenin.'"

Robby's happy expression wavered, and he ran a hand through the short, sandy curls all the cove girls went dreamy-eyed over. "That's what Jackson said, but I needed to see for myself. I won't be stayin.'" He shuffled back toward the roan.

Lily couldn't help feeling sorry for the lad. "Since you took the time to ride down here, please, do come inside. I was just about to call the boys in. I baked two peach cobblers for tomorrow. I don't believe folks would mind if we sampled some now, while it's warm."

His grin came back full force. "Thanks. That sounds real pleasuresome."

Glancing past him to glowering Matt and Luke, however, Lily could tell that, peach cobbler or not, they didn't appreciate her invitation to Robby Randall. It would appear her young roosters didn't like anyone sniffing around their henhouse.

This was the first Sabbath Lily had spent at home since Susan died. Strange, how much faster she'd been able to finish the preparations for the service without the young ones underfoot and Susan to get ready. But the house felt empty without Davy scampering in and out and Emma helping wherever she could. Even in her weakest moments, Susan had loved to have company and always looked forward to catching up on everyone's news. Her blue-green eyes would sparkle against her pale skin. Emma had those same beautiful eyes. How were she and Davy faring now? Sadness started creeping in.

Lily swallowed against the hard knot in her throat and glanced out the bedroom window. The morning had dawned bright and sunny with not a single storm cloud in sight. A lovely day lay ahead.

Tightening the front laces of a rather ordinary day gown, she bemoaned the loss of the more stylish clothes she'd taken to Philadelphia. Likely some Indian woman was strutting about in the elaborate riding costume Mistress Gilford had given her, the scarf and bonnet plume trailing behind in the breeze. Lily sighed. No sense dwelling on what was lost.

She strode to the mirror and began dressing her hair in the simple upsweep she often wore on Sundays. She must remember to arrange a few moments alone with Elder MacBride so she and Matt could hear their much-needed explanation for why God chose to allow undeserved horrors to befall on so many good Christian people. In her four years in Beaver Cove, she hadn't met a single farmsteader who didn't attend services every Sunday. They all gladly offered a hand in Christian charity to anyone with a need.

Lily knew that actually finding a private moment with their pastor would be difficult. The neighbors would be eager to hear the latest news from Philadelphia and about her own harrowing adventure in the wilds. And if Robby Randall's attention yestereve was any indication, he'd be hovering at her side all the while he was here. So would Jackson Dunlap.

Lily still felt appalled over that bold kiss he'd planted on her in front of the men.

Well, none of that could take precedence. She'd simply have to find a way to get time alone with Mr. MacBride somehow. She pushed the last hairpin in place then pulled a few shorter tendrils loose at her temples to soften the look. Finished with her toilette, she went out into the front room, where benches already formed rows and scuffling sounds issued from the loft. "Are you two ready yet?"

Luke leaned over the railing. "Just gotta comb my hair."

"Shoes good and shiny?" *How like a mother I sound!* She rolled her eyes.

"Uh-huh." He nonchalantly rubbed the toe of one on the stockinged calf of his other leg.

Matt moved into view. "*My* shoes are clean and—"

Rapid barking interrupted his statement.

Lily shot a glance to the mantel clock. "No one should be arriving for another half hour." *And Duke gave up barking at friends and neighbors months ago.* Whirling around, she went for her weapon.

The boys scrambled down the ladder and ran for theirs as she opened the door and stepped outside.

The dog stood in the middle of the wagon lane, growling in that direction and baring his teeth. He barked again toward pounding hoofbeats.

Jackson Dunlap emerged at a canter from the dense trees.

"Quiet!" she ordered from the top step.

Duke closed his jaws and plodded back to a shady spot near the cabin.

Reaching the yard, Jackson caught sight of Lily and reined in his mount. He tipped his tricorn with a cocky grin. "You're lookin' purtier than a spring mornin', Miss Lily."

"Thank you." She kept her tone polite.

In one fluid motion, he swung his leg over the saddle and came down from the horse. A tiny cloud of dust puffed out as his boots made contact with the ground. Lily couldn't deny he was a rather good-looking young man. Months in the military had honed his formerly flabby build into one more trim and muscled. The forest-green waistcoat he wore over copper britches complemented his brown eyes, and his dark brown hair was neatly slicked back into a queue.

This was not a lad who needed mothering, like Robby. Fact was, Lily always felt in need of a mother herself whenever Jackson came close, for a chaperone. It was not a feeling she particularly appreciated, but if she had any hope of staying near the Waldon children after November, she'd do well to consider at least one of those young men as a potential suitor.

Jackson strode with assurance toward the porch. "Thought I'd come a little early, in case you needed help settin' up."

"How thoughtful." Lily tilted her head with a little smile. "However, everything's ready."

Matthew and Luke came outside just then.

The visitor eyed them up and down and laughed. "The three of you thinkin' on goin' huntin' before church?"

Suddenly remembering the musket she held, Lily smiled with chagrin.

Matt didn't seem inclined to share their mirth as he moved up beside her. "A body never knows what kinda varmint might come ridin' in."

"Right." Luke came to her other side. "Never can tell."

Lily didn't dare laugh. To think mere seconds ago she'd imagined needing a mother, when she had Matt and Luke around to protect her!

Undaunted, Jackson and his grin didn't lose any luster. He raised his hands, palms open. "No worries here, boys. I'm harmless."

"We'll see," Matt muttered.

Again, Lily felt like laughing. How would she ever be able to choose between her suitors with those boys making sure she was never left alone? Throughout Robby's visit last eve, both of them stayed glued to her side, unsmiling, listening to every word that came out of the young man's mouth.

She switched her attention to Dunlap. "Would you care to join us, Jackson? We were about to enjoy a cup of tea on the porch while we wait for the others." Anything to keep him seated and his hands occupied.

"Be my pleasure."

Once she had served them from the worktable, she led the way past the rows of benches and out to the porch. Matt and Luke dodged rudely past her, leaping over curious Duke, to take seats that would separate Jackson from her.

He outwitted them. As Lily took the chair at the far end, he picked up an empty chair and hefted it with one hand while juggling his tea in the other. He set it down facing her.

Matt's eyes narrowed to slits.

Lily cut him a stern glance then turned to their visitor. "Lovely morning, is it not?"

"Aye." He leaned forward. "Almost as lovely as yourself. Some people admire a gal who stays inside to keep her skin lily-white, but I'm kinda partial to the way that sun-kissed skin of yours makes your eyes look all the purtier."

Matt tucked his chin with a grunt of disgust.

Lily hoped Jackson didn't notice. "Such flattery." She smiled and sipped her tea.

"No such thing," he said, seemingly unfazed by the scowling boys. "I've long since admired you an' all you done to keep this place goin'."

"Well, Matt and Luke have been a tremendous help." She glanced at her young chaperones, sitting rigid on the edge of their seats, their tea obviously forgotten.

"Mebbe. But you're gonna make one fine settler's wife." His jovial smile didn't diminish a fraction. "Oh, I plumb forgot. Y'all are invited to a cabin raisin' at our place Saturday after next."

"You're adding rooms to your place?"

"No." He cleared his throat, sidling a bit closer. "I been thinkin' for some time now on havin' my own place. I chose myself a real nice spot. Purt' near flat with a couple a big maple trees to shade the porch on summer afternoons."

"That does sound pleasant." Lily kept her tone light, but was beginning to feel like prey. Jackson was definitely a man on the hunt. He was already building a house to bring his bride to. To bring *her* to.

"You prob'ly know that spot betwixt this place an' ours, where the crick makes that half-moon bend an' there's that nice sandy beach? That's where I'm gonna build."

Duke lunged to his feet, his tail wagging, and Lily began to detect the faint rattles and creaks of approaching wagons.

Matt, too, sprang up from his chair, sloshing untouched tea onto the porch boards. "Folks are comin'. It's about time." Luke stood and stretched to peer toward the wagon trail.

Expecting the pair to follow the dog out to greet their new guests, as always, Lily was surprised when they both sat back down and resumed glaring at Jackson with thunderous faces.

Jackson rushed back into his topic. "Like I was sayin', that's where my place'll be, betwixt my folks' and this one." His dark eyes sparked as he met Lily's, as if gauging her reaction.

She knew he wanted a response. "That's quite near your property marker, is it not? That's a really nice spot." Averting her gaze, she rose. "I'd better go greet the neighbors."

He got up and followed close behind her. She sensed the young man hoped his decision to build a place of his own would be far more enticing to her than the thought of living with Robby's family among that big brood of Randall children. She'd heard John say more than once the reason their father joined the militia was to get a little peace.

But was Jackson Dunlap the Lord's choice for her? She'd prayed that God would redirect her affections away from John Waldon. Perhaps this was His way of allowing her to stay within easy walking distance of the children after John returned.

On the other hand, could she ever be a proper wife to Jackson Dunlap when all the while she yearned for a man who lived a mere ten-minute walk away?

Chapter 23

Acool breeze wafted by as John sat among the rows of benches at the fort, waiting for the church service to begin. He mentally reviewed his arrival the night before, when he, Nate, and the longhunters rode in and reported for duty. John had informed Captain Busse about the Indians' change of tactics, how the war party had broken up into small raiding groups that swooped in on vulnerable cabins, then moved quickly on to others.

The commander found the news disturbing. The timing could not have been worse. Farmers needed to be on their properties to harvest their crops and preserve food for the winter. Cognizant of that need, he ordered Hap Reynolds and Virgil Stewart to leave the fort as soon as they were rested and ride through the settlements to instruct people to seek shelter at their fortifications. Armed work parties would then be sent out to take care of the harvest.

Glancing around the orderly grounds, John wondered how safe this fort was at the moment. Less than a quarter of the garrison remained here. Half of the militiamen had yet to return from Fort Augusta, and those

John had roved with had not come back yet. Would this fortification, understaffed as it was, withstand a serious assault?

The bench jolted as Bob Randall dropped down beside him. "I sure appreciate you stoppin' by my place on your way here, lettin' my family know I was safe at the fort and not out rovin'."

John chuckled at his bearded neighbor. "With you on guard duty last night, I couldn't go into detail. After I fought my way through that herd of youngsters of yours and found Edith, she didn't look too pleased to hear you were just sitting around out here."

"You don't say." A frown knitted Bob's thick brows. "I thought she'd be glad to know I wasn't in danger."

"Hardly. If anything, she's jealous. She said it's high time you came home and started helping out instead of lazing around at the fort. She feels Robby's old enough to take your place."

His friend gave a sheepish grin, but his eyes retained a spark. "Sounded put out, did she? Well, if them raidin' parties ain't left the Swatara by the time our rovers report back in, I may have to do what she wants. 'Course, with the Dunlap boys home now, I can't see as how Robby'd want to give up the courtin' field to them two. From what Edith wrote in her last letter, he's set on marryin' your Lily."

John barely had time to assimilate that disconcerting news before the chaplain's voice issued from the front of the sparse gathering.

"Let us open with prayer."

Since Bob had hit a sore spot, John heard hardly a word of the chaplain's prayer. Thoughts of Robby and those pushy Dunlap brothers nagged at him. He had no right to feel possessive, but what did any of them have to offer a gently bred and educated young lady such as Lily? If he, a man born and educated in Philadelphia, couldn't have her, why should those young jackanapes have a chance with her? As her long-time employer, he deeply appreciated the years of unselfish labor she'd provided as Susan's caretaker and second mother to his children. He couldn't justify taking advantage of her sacrificial goodness that way any longer, not when she could do much better. She deserved the best.

She must go to Mariah's.

With the chaplain's voice droning steadily in the background, John caught himself sighing. If he never had anything else, at least there was one memory he'd always treasure. Lily's beautiful image filled his mind as he reflected on that one astonishingly wonderful moment when he'd kissed her and she'd melted into him. Even now he recalled the sweet taste of her soft lips, the look of complete adoration in those gorgeous eyes, and his heart ached with yearning. But he knew that stolen moment of bliss was all they would ever have. His breath came out on a ragged rush of air, his shoulders sagged, and he closed his eyes.

"Oh, marvelous." Lily stepped around Jackson. "It's the MacBrides. I need to speak with Mr. MacBride."

"I'll go with you." Dunlap followed her off the porch.

Matt and Luke fell right in behind him, not missing a step.

Before the older man reined the team to a stop, Lily intercepted the wagon. "So nice to see you all." She included the entire family in her smiling greeting and added an extra wave for Maggie MacBride's namesake, little Margaret Rose, whose infectious grin displayed every one of her tiny teeth. "Hop down, and my boys will help Michael unhitch the horses. You'll be staying the whole day, will you not?"

Patrick's wife, Agnes, handed the toddler down to Lily, her hazel eyes shining. "We sure are. I want to hear all about Philadelphia." She tucked a strand of auburn hair her daughter had tugged free back into place beneath her lace-edged bonnet.

Moving from behind Lily as she set the wiggling tot on her feet, Jackson surprised her by helping Agnes down. Lily had never thought of him having gentlemanly tendencies, and wondered if the two years he'd spent in the militia had matured him more than she realized.

While he reached up to lift the older Maggie out of the wagon, Lily circled to the back, where Ian MacBride was helping his brunette granddaughters, Judy and Anna. Their brothers had already jumped off.

Lily relinquished Margaret Rose to big sister Judy then met the elder's gaze. "If you have a moment, I'd like a private word with you."

He set twelve-year-old Anna on her feet and turned. "Lead the way, lass."

Much to her dismay, Jackson chose that moment to join them. She managed a polite smile. "If you don't mind, I'd like to speak to the pastor a moment."

A frown furrowed his solid features. "If there's somethin' you need, I'd be happy to—"

She stilled him with a hand on his arm. "It's kind of you to offer, Jackson, but my question is of a theological nature."

He looked puzzled.

"About somethin' in the Bible," Mr. MacBride clarified.

"Oh." Somewhat stunned, the young man backed away, then quickly recouped. "After, would you do me the honor of sittin' with me durin' the service?"

Lily had little choice. "Yes. Thank you for your kind invitation. Now, if you'll excuse us. . ."

Knowing no one else would venture into Susan's room, Lily invited the pastor there for their conversation and gestured toward the chair. "Please, have a seat." She then sat on the bed across from it.

He sat down and leaned forward, resting his elbows on his knees. "Did some problem arise while ye were away, lass?"

"No. Yes. Well, not exactly." Lily felt heat rising to her cheeks under his scrutiny. "Matt asked me a question I was unable to answer, and it's been bothering me." She hesitated and gave careful consideration to her next words. "As you know, our family has had a number of, shall we say, trying events this summer."

"Aye. Ye have. We've been keepin' yer family in our evenin' prayers."

Lily smiled inwardly at the pleasant sound of r's rolling from the Scot's tongue. "I do thank you. We appreciate your prayers, truly we do. But in a way, my question has to do with that very subject."

"How do ye mean, child?"

"I was telling Matthew how God answered my prayers at the time a party of Indians crossed my path only a few feet from where I was hiding. They didn't notice my tracks, even though they crossed right over them. It was as if the Lord had blinded them momentarily."

The elder's face beamed as he straightened in the chair. "That's wonderful news. It had to be the hand of the Almighty protectin' ye."

"I thought so, too." Lily paused and moistened her lips. "But then Matt made a very disturbing point. We—all of us—prayed for Susan's healing for years. And the parents of those little boys in Palmyra who were captured most likely had prayed for their children's safety, as well. But it would appear all those prayers were for naught."

Clasping his big hands together, MacBride dipped his head with a solemn nod. "I can see where you and the lad might have a problem. For now, I'll just say the Bible tells us that it rains on the just as well as the unjust. This life isna' so much about what happens to us as it is about how we choose to respond. Then, so's we dunna' get too discouraged, God gifts us with a little miracle every now an' then, like he done for you. But now that ye've mentioned it, I'll study up on prayer an' do a whole sermon on that subject next week, if ye like. Point ye toward some scriptures that'll help."

"That would be most appreciated." She rose from the bed. "Life is really a lot harder than I thought when I was a little girl. I think my papa and older sister sheltered me from most of what went on."

"That's what we parents always want to do for our children. Ye'd be surprised how often the good Lord shelters each of His children—most of the time without us even noticin'." He stood up. "Well, lass, if ye dunna' mind, I'd like to stay here a wee moment longer an' go over me thoughts for this mornin'."

"Not at all." Lily smiled. "By the by, have I ever told you how very much I appreciate you and your dear family?"

"Now and again, but it's always good to hear." He gave her a jovial wink.

Lily found Jackson *and Robby* waiting outside the bedchamber when she came out. Both stood rigid and humorless.

"Good morning, Robby." She peered past him to the open front door. "Your family's not with you?"

He edged a step ahead of Jackson. "No. They won't leave till the twins stop fussin' with their hair. Donald'll be drivin' 'em when they do come. Could I help you with somethin'?"

Jackson nudged him aside slightly. "I already asked her. She don't need nothin'."

"She might not need help, but I do." Agnes MacBride's voice came from the hearth, as she and Maggie placed their food offerings in front of the fire to keep them warm. Agnes straightened and plucked a covered bowl from the worktable. "If you wouldn't mind, Robby, I need you to tote this down to the springhouse to keep cool till we eat."

The lad shot Lily a wounded look, then turned to Agnes. "Glad to."

As he followed her bidding, Lily caught a sparkle of triumph in Jackson's dark eyes.

"And Jackson," Maggie said, "if you plan on stayin' here with the rest of us, you might wanna put that horse of yours away. He's just wanderin' around out there."

The gleam in his eye dimmed considerably. Jaw muscles working, he gave Lily a slight bow. "Be back directly." He pivoted on his heel and hastened outside.

Snickers sputtered into laughter as soon as the door closed behind him. Lily couldn't help but join in with the MacBride women.

Maggie untied her apron and slipped it off. "Methinks maybe me an' Eva Shepard better start takin' turns stayin' here for a while again. I'll have Ian go home an' fetch some of my things afore the shootin' starts."

"*Shooting?*" A chill skittered along Lily's spine. "Have Indians been sighted?"

The older woman snorted. "Not that kind of shootin'. I'm talking about them two bucks out there. With Jackson home, I need to be here to see him an' Robby don't kill each other off. An' Frank. Ian said somethin' about him helpin' out them Dutch folk over to the Palmyra settlement for a few days. When he comes home, there'll be three of 'em trippin' over each other's feet to win your attention."

Lily's cheeks turned scarlet with embarrassment.

"Mayhap Frank won't be a problem." Agnes took Maggie's discarded apron and hung it over Lily's on the hook. "I heared tell Frank took a fancy to a young gal over that way. But then, I can't imagine that lastin' very long, with them not bein' able to talk to each other. They don't speak the same language."

The old woman gave her daughter-in-law a hug. "Agnes, girl, don't you know young folks spoonin' don't need to talk much? They say it all with their eyes. The eyes is what you gotta watch."

Suddenly Lily became keenly self-conscious and stooped down to stir a pot that didn't need stirring. How much talking did her eyes do when John was around? Undoubtedly, more than she knew. After all, the last time Maggie had seen the two of them together, the wise old woman had insisted on staying here as chaperone. Now she was planning to do that again.

La, what must Maggie think of me? Had she perceived that I was mooning hopelessly over a man who'd just laid his beloved wife to rest?

Chapter 24

If any child present had asked a question about Elder MacBride's sermon, Lily couldn't have given an answer. With Jackson on one side of her, Matt and Luke on the other, and Robby and his clan seated behind, she'd been unable to concentrate. Even the air she breathed seemed rife with hostility. . .and that during a church service! Worse yet, even though Jackson had never actually touched her, she felt as if he surrounded her. She made a solemn promise to herself not to be trapped like this again next week. She'd make sure her self-appointed chaperone, Maggie, would be sitting right beside her.

At last the final *amen* sounded. Lily sprang to her feet. "Matt, Luke, would you please help the men move the benches out while I help with the food?" She tossed the question over her shoulder as she hurried to the hearth, leaving the two rutting bulls behind to help with the chore. Not until the last child ran outside laughing and squealing and the clatter of the benches ceased did she turn to look behind her.

She grabbed some potholders and hefted up her pot of ham and potatoes, then turned to cart it to the table.

A row of women stood gawking and grinning at her.

" 'Tis not at all funny."

"Oh, but it can be so much fun." Nancy Patterson's pale eyebrows arched over her twinkling blue eyes.

"Aye," Richard Shaw's slender wife, Ruth, added, the levity of the moment adding color to her sallow complexion as she flicked a blond curl from her eyes. "Particularly now that your indenturement is over and you're free to choose whoever you wish." Puzzlement narrowed her azure eyes. "Which one *do* you fancy most?"

The last thing Lily wanted to do was keep this particular conversation alive, but her friends waited for a response. "That's a touch premature. Now that Robby's brother Donald's taken an interest in Cissy Dunlap, I'm the only unbespoken female around. Once all this war business is over, the lads will be able to look farther afield."

Robby's mother, Edith, spoke up with surprising force, considering her normally reticent personality. "My boy won't be lookin' beyond the cove. He's had his heart set on you for more'n a year now. And I'd be plumb tickled to have you on the place. I could use an extra pair of hands as capable as yours."

Millie Dunlap, Toby's wife, pursed her lips and planted her knuckles on one plump hip. "I'm afraid your boy'll have a time gettin' past mine. Jackson's so set on you, Lily, he's already choppin' down trees for your honeymoon house." A satisfied glint lit her blue eyes as she tucked a few errant strands of hair into her salt-and-pepper bun.

"I. . .uh. . .thank you both for considering me, a bond servant, with very little to bring to a marriage. But I've promised Mr. Waldon I'd remain here with his sons until he returns in November."

"I'd forgotten about the indenturement." Edith Randall tapped a forefinger on her lips in thought. "John will owe you what your contract says you're due. How much is that, anyway?"

The nosy question coming from a normally reticent woman irked Lily. She didn't appreciate anyone prying into her personal affairs. Nevertheless, she answered in an even tone. "I believe it's two pounds sterling."

"You aren't sure?"

Lily tamped down her growing anger. "Our arrangement has never been based on money. From the beginning, John and Susan treated me like family, and that's how I think of all the Waldons."

"And that's why we all love you, dear." Millie Dunlap nodded to the other ladies. "Now, I think we'd best get the food out to the servin' table a'fore it gets cold."

Utterly grateful for the reprieve, Lily lagged behind as the others walked out with their pots and platters. She'd been mistress of this household for so long, she'd never thought about living under the thumb of a prospective mother-in-law. Robby had always seemed a rather gentle young man, but his mother certainly was not. She was looking for an extra pair of hands to help her with her brood.

Then there was Jackson who had that brash way about him. His mother, though, had always been quite congenial, and so was his grandmother, Eva. Was there perhaps hidden somewhere in that young man a gentle spirit as well?

"Come along, darlin'." Maggie MacBride had remained behind. "An' stop that frettin'. I ain't gonna let nobody push you into somethin' you ain't ready for. I promise you that."

Lily was profoundly grateful to the older woman. The grandmother had shooed Jackson and Robby away and made a place for Lily at her dinner table. Now she could eat in peace between Maggie and Ian. Still, she could feel the tension between the two eager swains even after they'd taken seats at different tables.

Spearing a fat chicken breast, she spotted Matt and Luke sitting with their friends. Both sported triumphant grins. They'd managed to interrupt any attempt by Jackson or Robby to get her alone and were enjoying their meal.

But what if she *did* want some suitor's attention? Had she not asked the Lord to redirect her affections? Biting into the meat, she dismissed that thought as inconsequential. There was only one person's attention she craved, and he wasn't here.

Agnes MacBride reached across the table and touched Lily's arm. "I know Robby and Jackson are being somewhat boorish. But we all hope you'll choose one of the Beaver Cove lads and remain here with us. We already lost Susan. To lose you now would be a great sadness, indeed. Everyone here is so fond of you."

"Why, thank you." Auburn-haired Agnes was a dear, as were all the MacBrides. Lily had always been grateful that they were her nearest neighbors. "I've grown to love everyone in the cove, as well. But my own family wants me near them. I'm really quite torn." Her eyes misted lightly, and she blinked the moisture away.

Nancy Patterson's slender form leaned forward as she peered around Agnes. "It sure would be a lot safer, livin' near the coast."

"Yes, it would." Lily gave her a companionable smile. "Speaking of that, how is your little Mary faring?" She glanced at the table occupied by the younger children. "She seems a tad quieter than the other youngsters."

Nancy's light blue eyes drifted to her six-year-old. "She's still having nightmares, sad to say. We've had to take her into our bed most nights. An' durin' the daytime, she follows me like a shadow every step I take. But considerin' what happened. . ." She shrugged. "My heart cries for her. I only wish. . . ." Her golden eyebrows arched upward.

Agnes caught her hand and gave it a comforting squeeze.

Ian laid down his fork. "I'll speak to wee Mary a'fore we all leave here today, see if I can coax her to give her fears to the Lord."

Lily shot him a glance. Had he not told her more than two hours ago that the rain fell on the just and the unjust alike? He could not assure that little girl that the Indians wouldn't attack her parents' place. It did happen to be the farthest inhabited farmstead up the creek.

The dog suddenly charged out from under the children's table and bounded toward the lane, barking as he went.

Instantly everyone began untangling legs from benches to get to their feet. Men sprinted for their wagons to retrieve their weapons.

Mary ran wailing to her mother's arms.

A familiar horseman came trotting in. Frank Dunlap reined in his mount as his father and brother strode to meet him. "Looks like I made it in time for dinner. I could smell that lip-smackin' food a mile away." He swung down to the ground.

Lily's heartbeat returned to normal, and she started back to her seat.

"Thought you was gonna stay an' help with them cabin raisin's." Jackson sounded a bit accusing.

"I was. But news came that I figgered you'd wanna know. Fort William Henry surrendered to the French. An' most of the soldiers stationed there got massacred."

The strength went out of Lily. She grabbed hold of the table for support.

"What are you sayin', boy?" Toby Dunlap latched on to his younger son's shoulders.

"I'm talkin' about Fort William Henry, up in New York, Pa. The one on Lake George."

Sounds of relief drifted to Lily as the folks began to relax. It wasn't John's fort. On shaky legs, she eased down onto the nearby bench, her hand over her pounding heart, as Frank elaborated.

"Seems General Monroe was forced to surrender. The French told him he could take his soldiers an' their families on to Fort Edward, but them vicious savages killed most of 'em along the way. Worst of all, it didn't have to happen. General Webb at Fort Edward, only a few miles away, refused to send reinforcements to save the fort. The coward just sat safe behind his walls, no matter what William Johnson or anybody else told him. The dispatch rider said bodies were strung out all along the trail."

Little Mary's frightened crying grew louder.

Her mother scooped her up and carried her to the cabin. Nancy's three-year-old Sally ran after them.

"Just like last year." Cal Patterson's pained gaze followed his wife and babies to the porch.

Ian raised a hand. "Folks, let's sit down an' finish our Sabbath meal. This tragedy took place hundreds of miles away. Frank, get yourself a plate of food an' join us. But a'fore we get settled again, I'd like to say a prayer for those poor souls an' their loved ones."

After all that had just transpired, Lily found it impossible to give her attention to his words. Her insides continued to tremble, and she could still hear Mary's hysterical sobs. To think the very same horror could happen to John's fort!

Calvin Patterson stood to his feet and brushed crumbs from his trousers. "Men, whilst the womenfolk clean up, what say we walk on over to the blockhouse an' check out our supplies?"

Busy clearing her table, Lily stopped and set down the trenchers in her hand. Cal had been in the militia until he was shot in the knee, and he had the respect of all the other men. Lily was pretty sure they weren't going across the creek just to take inventory. She turned to Agnes. "Would you mind finishing here? I'm going with them."

"*Lily!*" Shock clouded Agnes' hazel eyes. "They're going to be talking about the protection of our valley. Man talk."

"That's why I'm going. I happen to be the man on my place."

"Lily—"

But she didn't wait to hear more. Ripping off her apron, she started after the men. She spotted Jackson near the front of the group. When it came to war talk, even her most determined suitor hadn't lagged behind.

No one noticed her until after they'd crossed the bridge and moved to the shade of a tree.

"Sorry, Lily-girl." Ian raised a calloused hand to ward her off. "Us men need to talk."

"As you should." She did not slow down.

"He means away from you women," Cal added as the men gathered together.

"And I would normally agree." Undaunted, Lily joined the circle. "But since I have no man on my place to speak for me, I've come to speak for myself."

Jackson came to her side. "You go on back now. I'll see to your interests."

"That's kind of you, but you don't know what I want to say."

Ian released a resigned breath. "Very well, lass. Say your piece, then shoo yourself on back."

Men. They always acted as if matters like this didn't concern anyone but themselves, when women and children were in every bit as much danger as they were. Lily stretched to her full height and mustered every ounce of authority she could into her airy voice. "Since there's been no word about our military moving against Fort Duquesne to the west any time soon, we'll continue to be under constant threat of raiding parties. If you make no other decision this day, I earnestly request that the Pattersons come and stay here with me." She turned to Cal. "I'm sure I can make room for you and your family. Your children—and most especially little Mary—need to feel safe again."

Cal eyed her momentarily and slowly shook his head. "I hate the thought of bein' run off my own place."

"You can still look after your place and get your harvest in. Please, do this for Mary."

Jackson opened his mouth as if to speak, then shut it. He obviously didn't like the idea either, and probably for his own reasons.

"I'll give it some thought," Cal finally conceded.

"That's all I ask. Now, gentlemen, I'll not hinder your *man talk* any longer." She clutched handfuls of her skirt and turned to leave, but stopped and swung back. "Except, you might consider building a stockade around the blockhouse. We do seem to be pretty much on our own." With a tilt of her head, she curtsied, as any polite woman should.

As she took her leave, she overheard Calvin muttering something. She cocked an ear, trying to make out the words.

"You lads sure you wanna wed up with somebody as bullheaded as her?"

The comment caused Lily to take an assessing look at herself. Long gone was the frightened, helpless, young gentlewoman from the genteel city of Bath. This lass had survived years of hardship and tragedy and the dangers of days alone in the wilderness. That other young girl had been replaced by a strong, capable woman who could load and shoot a musket as fast as any man.

Yes, she'd become a real frontier woman, and she liked what she saw.

Chapter 25

It was a wondrous feeling, this sense of confidence, of having worth in one's self. As Lily strolled past the springhouse, she knew she'd have to pray about her lack of humility this eve during her prayer time. For now, however, she felt marvelous.

Matt and Luke, awaiting their turn in the rope-ring tossing game of quoits, broke away from their friends and jogged toward her, intercepting her by the smelly hog pen. "What's goin' on?" Matt's stony expression did not soften. The lad rarely smiled anymore.

"The men refused to let me stay."

Luke quirked a wry face. "I'll be glad when Pa gets back so us Waldons can have a say in things, like everybody else."

Lily returned his smirk with a rather satisfied one of her own. "Actually, I did have my say before I left. By the by, I think 'twould be prudent for Mrs. Patterson and her little ones to come and stay with us for the time being, even if her husband and their older boys do not come. I figured you two wouldn't mind extra people around while things are so unsettled."

Matt met her gaze. "It'd be better if Mrs. Patterson could take Mary east to stay with family, like we did with Emma."

"That would be ideal, had they someone to go to."

An unruly lock of brown hair fell in front of Luke's eyes with his emphatic nod. A toss of his head flicked it out of the way. "That Mary is a scared little rabbit. Did you hear the way she screamed when Frank come ridin' in?"

Stepping between her two caring boys, Lily draped an arm over their shoulders and started away from the ripe animal pen. "Let's pray her papa makes the right decision, shall we?"

Matt stopped. "Speakin' of prayin', what did Grampa Ian say about. . . what I asked?"

His hair, too, looked sadly in need of a good trimming. Lily brushed aside a hank bordering his nose and tucked it behind his ear. "He wanted to study up on it a bit. He said he'd preach a whole sermon on it next week."

"Better be a good one." Matt pressed his lips into a flat line.

"I'm sure it will be." Unable to resist the impulse, she ruffled his dark brown thatch. "You need a haircut. Both of you."

Luke hiked his chin. "I like mine long, like those hunters have theirs."

Eyeing her freckled charge, Lily cocked a brow. "So, you think those longhunters look good with their hair dirty and stringing down." With a teasing laugh and a disbelieving shake of her head, she started forward again. "Come to the house with me and help me take our food over to the springhouse, would you?"

"All right if we finish playin' quoits first?" Luke asked. "So far I've made more ringers than anybody."

"You have not." Matt gave a huff.

"Well, then, my ever-so-skilled lads, I believe you need to get back to the game. You wouldn't want to lose your turn." Watching after the pair as they sprinted back to their friends, Lily felt a wave of sadness that she had to keep reminding herself they were still only children.

While the men were meeting across the creek, Lily noticed that each of the women paused at least once in clearing the table, storing leftovers, or washing dishes, to peer out the window. With no concern for her Sunday frock, flighty Cissy Dunlap even volunteered to take the slop down to the pigs. But strangest of all, these normally jabbery women spoke no more than necessary. Obviously they were all worried.

Suddenly Ruth Shaw's fears got the best of her. "I can't take it anymore. I'm plumb scared all the time. It's just me and Richard and our little ones, you know. . .and we only have that one musket. I've begged him time and again to take me back home to New Castle. But he keeps telling me to wait till harvest is over." Anxiety clouded her light blue eyes. "Seems he cares more about his precious corn than he does about me and my babies. And we all know the savages are out there. Lily saw them. Saw what they did to folks. They could be out there right now, skulking about, waiting for the right moment to swoop in here and murder us all, just like they did that family across the Swatara."

Grandma Margaret moved to her side and put an arm around her. "I know it's hard, lass, but you need to keep your voice down. Nancy's in the bedroom tryin' to get little Mary to sleep."

Ruth tightened her lips and swung a gaze to Susan's bedroom door.

"Ruthie, dear," Lily said, balancing a stack of trenchers in her hands, "the Indians are in small groups. If we all stick together—"

The young wife elevated her voice again. "So you're saying they'll only be able to scalp a couple of us before the rest of the cove's men come running!" She burst into tears.

"Shh, Ruth. Shh." Maggie nodded to Agnes, and they each took an arm and led her to the table, where they sat her down in a chair.

Eva, Jackson's grandmother, took a seat beside Ruth, and the neighbors gathered around, their expressions laced with understanding.

Lily placed the trenchers on their shelf and turned to the others. "Mayhap we shouldn't wait for the men to make our decision for us. I'd be pleased to have all of you women and your children living here with me. I've only the boys, and I'm certain we could make room." She arched her brows hopefully. "We could make a big party out of preserving our food for the winter together, peeling and pressing our apples. . ."

Jackson's mother nodded in agreement. "We could stay here until we know for sure the heathens have gone back to their villages for the winter. An' all our little ones would love bein' able to play together every day. It'd be a real treat for them."

"Please, could we do that?" Ruth's emotion-filled voice rang out as she dabbed at her eyes with the edge of her apron.

Maggie placed a comforting hand on the woman's shoulder. "What do the rest of you gals say?"

"I'm all for it." Edith Randall looked around the group. "I don't even have a grown man on my place." She shot a quick glance at Lily. "That's not to say my Robby's not holdin' his own. He is, sure enough."

Lily squelched a grin. The lad's mother wasn't about to demean her son in front of a prospective daughter-in-law and her oh-so-capable hands.

Maggie stood to her feet so quickly her mobcap went askew. "Then it's settled. When the men slack off jawin' and get back over here, we'll tell 'em what we decided."

Hearing the old woman speaking so confidently helped Lily to settle another matter in her mind. No matter how much pressure she received from any quarter, she would not allow herself to be rushed into marrying anyone. Not by Robby or his mother—and especially not by Jackson, no matter how many honeymoon cabins he built in her honor.

Upon hearing what their wives had to say, the men were less than thrilled the women had taken matters into their own hands. But by the time the neighborhood wagons started rolling out, smiles reined in abundance. Even young Mary sported a tremulous smile. The decision had been made and approved. The women would pack their necessities and, together with their little ones, would move to Lily's farmstead during the week. The men and boys would work together harvesting crops from place to place.

After she and Maggie bid the last family Godspeed and strolled back to the house, Lily noticed Jackson lounging in the shade of the porch with his legs stretched out and ankles crossed as if he lived there. Tamping down her irritation, she resolved once more that she had no intention of being pressured into a situation she didn't want. Besides, Maggie was staying the night. Confident in her assertion, she squelched a smug smile.

John's boys emerged from the house with their fishing poles. Both slanted a glare at interloper Jackson.

"Sure is nice of you, Grandma Maggie, to stay with us awhile an' keep us company," Matt said with added meaning as Lily and the older woman mounted the steps. "Okay if Luke an' me go fishin', Lily?" He cut another glower at the would-be suitor.

"That'd be fine." She tilted her head at Maggie. "I hope some fried rainbow trout sounds good to you for breakfast in the morning." Even Jackson could recognize the less-than-subtle hint that the older woman wouldn't be going away anytime soon.

"Nothin' I like more. I'll fix us up some fried taters an' biscuits to go with 'em."

"Sounds delicious." Lily nodded to the boys. "Don't stay out after dark, and don't forget your weapons." She motioned toward the firearms they'd left on the porch.

Grinning, the pair snatched up the musket and pistol and took off.

Lily gestured toward vacant chairs. "Let's sit down and rest for a while, Maggie. It's been a long day. And I do believe a nice cup of tea would be most refreshing. I'll brew some. Would you care for any, Jackson?"

"Don't mind if I do." He started to get up.

"Just relax." Lily stayed him with a hand. "I'll only be a moment."

His shrewd eyes flicked to Maggie, and he eased back down without a smile. Obviously the evening wasn't going according to his plans. Nor had the earlier part of the day, since his attempts to catch Lily alone had been to no avail.

Inside the cabin, Lily chuckled to herself as she pulled out a tray from a shelf and loaded it with cups and a few scones left over from the Sabbath get-together. Through the open window, she could hear Maggie speaking to their persistent visitor.

"I take it you got yourself set on that lass in there."

Lily paused to listen.

"That's right, ma'am. Don't want no other but her."

"She ain't no peach a body can just pluck off a tree, you know."

"She sure ain't."

There was no lack of determination in the young man's tone. Lily recognized it whenever he spoke about her or to her, and it rankled her.

Thankfully, Maggie's tenacity matched his. "I'd say you'd best trim your sails a mite, boy, if you're really serious about her. Just 'cause Lily was a bond servant, that don't mean she ain't without a lovin' family that wants her. Her folks tried to buy back her papers the first year she come to us. If it hadn't been for her carin' so much for poor sick Susan, she would'a lit out from here a long time ago."

Lily couldn't help herself. She inched closer to the window.

"Well," Jackson drawled, "she said herself she likes livin' at the cove. I'm purty sure I can talk her into stayin'. Besides, I'm a hard worker. I'll take good care of her."

His confidence made Lily's eyebrows hike upward. The guy actually believed he could make her dance to whatever tune he played! She shook her head as Maggie's voice came back into play.

"You must'a noticed them fancy duds she come here with. That gal was used to fine things, lots better than the rest of us. Her pa had a bad run of luck is all, or she wouldn't be here in the first place. An' you do know she can read an' write. That's more'n half the folks around here can do."

A span of silence followed, stretching long enough for Lily to feel sorry for Jackson. After all, it was not his fault he hadn't been schooled. Still. . .

"My pa's the best tanner and harness maker twixt here an' Reading," he finally said, force returning to his tone. "A good livin' can always be made from workin' leather. Pa learnt me a lot before the war. When it's all over, I'll be able to do right by Lily. See if I won't."

"Mm-hmm." The chair creaked as Maggie shifted her weight. "That's right good to hear. But then there *is* that quick temper of yours. I heared tell about lots of them whoppers you an' Frank got into. You two boys're known for flyin' off the hook at the least little thing."

Lily clamped a hand over her mouth to keep from laughing out loud. Bless her heart, the old woman was relentless.

But Jackson didn't back down. "Aw, that's just me an' Frank bein' brothers. But when it comes to defendin' myself an' what's mine, I ain't ashamed to say I can hold my own." He paused and spoke again in a more gentle voice. "You can ask my ma. I wouldn't harm a hair on Lily's head. . . or any other gal's. I know womenfolk are. . .delicate-like."

His statement pierced Lily's heart, and she felt ashamed to have thought ill of Jackson. He was a touch rough around the edges, but inside, he had a soft heart. She poured water into the pot and added some tea leaves.

"I have just one more question for you, boy," Maggie said.

About to pick up the prepared tray, Lily stopped again.

"Yes'm?"

"Have you prayed about this? Courtin' Lily, I mean."

He gave a snort. "Ain't no need to. I don't see Robby Randall's much competition. The lad's still wet behind the ears."

No need to pray about something as important as choosing a wife? A lifetime partner? Lily had heard more than enough. Plastering on a smile, she hastened toward the door and strode outside to join Maggie and *His Arrogance.*

Chapter 26

Neither Jackson nor Maggie wore a smile when Lily stepped out the door with the refreshments.

Jackson, however, brightened when he saw her. He sprang to his feet. "Let me help." He whisked the tea tray from her hands.

"Thank you. Put it on the side table." She indicated the one next to Maggie, then sat opposite her.

The young man plopped onto the seat next to Lily's.

His nearness irritated Lily, but she maintained her composure. She turned to the older woman. "What would you like in your tea, dear?"

"Plain'll do fine. I'm still full from that big meal we had this afternoon."

Lily dispensed some of the hot brew into a cup and handed it to her, aware of Jackson's gaze hot upon her. She reminded herself of her resolve to be strong and confident as she turned to him. "And how would you like yours, Jackson?"

"I like mine sweet an' creamy." The words sounded innocent enough, but his eyes said a whole lot more.

Once she'd handed him his tea, she poured her own plain drink and sat back, hoping to enjoy it for a moment. Alas, mere seconds passed before Jackson spoke again.

"Lily?" Balancing his cup and saucer on one knee, he leaned forward. "If you don't mind, when we finish our tea, I'd like a private word with you."

"How about now? The sun will be down soon. You can walk with me while I go shut the chickens inside their coop for the night." She set down her cup and looked at Maggie. "Would you excuse us for a few moments?"

At the woman's nod, she exited the porch, with Jackson right behind her. The coop was out of Maggie's line of view, but not so far that Lily couldn't summon her if need be.

Several fat fowl sought their roosts as Lily approached, and others came running when they saw her. Watching them scramble up the board ramp to their little house on stilts, she chuckled.

Jackson wasted no time coming to his point. "I ain't thought about nothin' but you since I was here last spring. I want you for my wife."

That was it? His proposal of marriage? Lily was tempted to give him a flat no. But what if the young man was actually God's choice for her? "I must say, that was an odd proposal." She switched her attention from the chicks to him. "Why do you want to marry me, Jackson?"

He frowned, as if that was the dumbest question he'd ever heard. "Why not? I can't keep waitin' for this lousy excuse of a war to get over. It's past time I started thinkin' on my future, an' you'd make a real fine wife. Besides. . ." He leaned closer, his breath feathering the fine hairs on her neck. "There's no other way to say it. I want you in my bed. *Real bad.*"

The intensity in his voice almost compelled Lily to holler for Maggie. She took a step back to put distance between them as she weighed her response. The young man was only being honest, and his reasoning regarding the war was logical. "Jackson, I'm honored that you would consider me for your wife. Truly I am. But before I answer you, I must spend some time in prayer and seek God's will. This is a momentous decision that would affect the rest of my life. My family expects me to join them once my indenturement is over. But even though I'll no longer be his bond servant, I promised Mr. Waldon I'd stay with his sons until he returns in November."

Jackson captured her shoulders. "You belong here with us, Lily. With me. You know you do."

"Perhaps." She reached up and gently removed his hands from her person. "Nevertheless, I believe we both need to pray about it. November is only two months hence. John will be home then."

He scoffed, and a corner of his mouth quirked upward. "We don't need to pray *or* wait. It's obvious. Who d'ya think God put you here for, anyway? Me. We could up an' marry now, an' I could stay here with you till Waldon gets home."

Lily couldn't squelch a droll smile. "You and me, honeymooning here with all the women and children from the cove? I think not. Besides, I have no intention of being rushed into the most important decision of my life. I will say this much. I will never marry a man who doesn't pray."

"Okay, okay." He took a step back and spread his hands. "If that's what you want, I'll do some prayin'. But it won't change a thing."

The following week proved to be a whirlwind of activity. By Tuesday, every entire family, not merely the women and children, took up residence in the farmhouse, the workshop, and the blockhouse. Crude canvas coverings also shrouded the wagons scattered about the Waldon clearing. The paddock was filled with milk cows. Inside the cabin, sleeping pallets were everywhere, and after bedtime, it was nearly impossible to step between them.

At dawn each morning, the men and older boys split into two groups and took their leave. One group headed downriver, the other upriver, to tend the remainder of the cove's livestock and to harvest whatever crops were ready. Lily and the neighbor women picked the last of the vegetables from her garden and began cooking them down for preserves, or drying what couldn't be stored in her root cellar. She didn't want to think about the pears and apples that soon would be ripe for picking.

By the end of the week, wagonloads of corn and vegetables from the other farms arrived to be dealt with. Lily wondered where they would put it all. The boys had cut the hay while she'd been in Philadelphia, and it was dry now and needed to be raked up and brought in.

And the corn! On Saturday evening, a weary Lily stopped with her pail of milk to stare at the bulging corn crib. Even with all she and the others had already done, tons of corn still needed to be shucked and dried and hulled. Some would need to be ground into meal at Cal's watermill. Then there was sorghum cane to be cut, pressed, and boiled down for molasses. Chestnuts and walnuts would be ready to gather soon, and then it would be hog-killing time.

Agnes, toting her toddler Margaret Rose, came to her side. "It's been a good week."

"Yes." Lily managed a smile. "Tiring, but 'tis nice to have company while we work. Lots of helping hands."

"Extra ladies help things go a lot faster. This evening, though, we have the biggest job of all to take care of."

Lily wanted to sink down to the ground and curl herself into a ball. "What are you saying?"

"Baths. You tell me how we're gonna get all them young'uns cleaned up tonight and keep 'em clean for the Sabbath."

Shoulders drooping, Lily turned toward the house and saw the Patterson twins toting water buckets to three tubs heating over fires, while Cissy Dunlap hauled more from the well for other tubs waiting to be filled. "I'm just glad Davy's not here. He'd be impossible." She laughed lightly, then sobered. "No, I wouldn't care at all. I miss him and Emmy terribly."

"So does my Joey. But soon the Indians will leave for the winter, and the children will be able to come back. Never expected I'd be looking forward to the cold months." She shook her head in disbelief.

Lily nodded in agreement. "When Jackson and Frank went out scouting, they said they didn't see any sign of war parties lurking about."

Having mentioned her persistent suitor, she had another thought. "We'll need to string up some blankets around those tubs. We womenfolk will need some privacy when our turn comes."

Agnes chuckled. "Especially you. Between Jackson and Robby, one of 'em seems to always be watching you. Personally, I think that Robby is a real charmer. And so handsome, with those cute curls and that smile of his. Don't you think?"

Knowing her friend was teasing, Lily just tucked her chin. "I think 'tis time I take this milk to the springhouse and rustle up whatever blankets I can find."

Moments later, on her return trip from the springhouse, the sight of a wagon drawing to a stop made her sigh. More work for her and the other ladies. Would it ever end? Thankfully tomorrow was the Sabbath, a most needed day of rest.

Ian, holding the reins, set the brake. Richard Shaw occupied the other half of the seat. His son Michael rode in back atop another load of corn with Matt and Luke, both of whom sported big smiles. It was good for her boys to have older men to rely on for a change, since their father was absent. At least John would return soon. Too soon, in a way, yet not soon enough for her longing heart. She knew the decision regarding her future would have to be made then.

As she walked toward them, her two lads hopped off the wagon bed. Matt waved something in his hand that looked suspiciously like. . .a *letter*! "We found some mail and a notice hooked on the nail at MacBride's dock on the river. This one has your name on." He held it out to her.

Lily took the missive and scanned the writing. *John!* Her heart leaped with joy. " 'Tis from your father."

"Thought so." Luke grinned. "The notice came from Fort Henry, so we figgered the letter prob'ly did, too."

Her joy dimmed. "Did the notice say anything of importance?"

Matt scoffed. "Nothin' much. Just that we should all do what we already done."

"Which is. . .?"

"Gather together at one place an' harvest the fields, like we been doin'. Now open the letter, would ya? I wanna hear what Pa has to say." He tapped his foot impatiently.

Glancing down at the smudged paper, Lily only hoped the news was good. But according to the notice the boys had seen, nothing had changed, so what good could there be? She broke the wax seal and unfolded the rough, heavy paper, then read aloud:

My dearest Lily, Matt, and Luke,

You are always on my mind and in my prayers. Nothing is more important to me than my children. I deeply regret that duty keeps me away from home during these dangerous times. Captain Busse has posted a notice throughout the surrounding settlements for folks to gather together for safety. I fear the people at the cove will refuse to abide by his orders, so I most urgently demand that you take the livestock to Ian MacBride's place and leave the area at once. Everything we possess at the cove can be replaced, but I could never replace you. Please do as I ask. I love all of you very, very much.

Your loving Papa, and, to Lily, your most loving friend,

J. Waldon

Lily wished she'd been alone when she read the letter. Seeing the words penned by John's hand, she'd come very close to pressing the missive to her heart. He loved her. He said it in writing.

Matt's voice interrupted her thoughts. "Well, at least we don't have to go anywheres. The cove folks already did what the notice told us to do."

Looking at the lad's dirty, dusty self, Lily smiled. "No, we don't have to leave just yet. But *I* have a demand for you two. As soon as you finish tending the livestock, I want you to go down to the creek and take a bath. Tomorrow's the Sabbath."

"Aww. . ." Luke whined. "Do we have to? I'm tuckered out."

"And be sure to take soap."

As the disappointed pair grumbled and trudged off toward the stable, Lily sought the solace of a nearby tree for a private moment. She unfolded John's letter again and drank in the message: *I love you all very, very much. . . . Your most loving friend. . .*

She ran her fingers over the treasured words. He loved her more than a mere friend. He said he was her *most loving friend.* When he'd written *I love you all very, very much,* he was trying to tell her more. For the briefest of moments, her heart flooded with joy.

Then reality set in.

It could not be. It could *never* be. John had loved Susan, had cared for her with his whole heart. It would be wise to remember that whenever thoughts of him drifted to mind. How unseemly to think anything else. John was exactly as he'd set it down on the paper, a most loved *friend.* Had it been otherwise, he'd have stated it in a way that would've left no doubt.

Still, that kiss he'd given her hadn't been that of a friend. Dared she hope it meant more? Heaven help her, she wanted desperately to cling to the hope that it did.

Chapter 27

An overnight shower brought the cool breath of autumn, but Sunday dawned bright and sparkling with fat droplets of moisture falling from the trees into puddles below. Lily smiled with chagrin at having insisted Matt and Luke bathe in the stream last eve in such brisk weather. But they looked ever so nice in their Sabbath best, their hair slicked back, as they sang with the rest of the congregation.

She appreciated having her two lads flanking her. It effectively prevented Jackson and Robby from grabbing those seats. Elder MacBride would bring a message regarding the concerns she and Matt had expressed about the Lord's supposed care of His people. She hoped the wise, older man would give the matter a perspective she could understand and accept.

The lyrics of "Hail Thou Once-Despised Jesus!" spoke to Lily's heart as she joined the other folks in the third verse: " *'There for sinners Thou art pleading, there Thou dost our place prepare; Ever for us interceding, till in glory we appear.'* " While the others continued on to the next verse, she prayed those weren't merely empty words.

The song came to an end, and Brother MacBride offered a brief prayer then motioned for everyone to be seated.

Lily reached beside her and gave Matt an encouraging smile as she took his hand, then Luke's.

The elder gazed over the congregation. "Ye've all heard that the Lord is our Shepherd, an' that we're the sheep of His pasture. So in light of recent happenings, some of ye might be wonderin' where our Good Shepherd is, that He's permittin' wolves to snatch away some of His own sheep outta the fold."

Lily squeezed Matt's hand.

"We pray for His protection, yet the wolves still circle. We're bein' stalked like animals, an' it dunna' fit with our conception of God's holy promise to be with us an' look after us. When Jesus was in the Garden of Gethsemane, he prayed"—he glanced down at the open Bible he held— " 'O my Father, if it be possible, let this cup pass from me: Nevertheless, not as I will, but as thou wilt.' Our Father in heaven allowed His own Son to die a violent death. It has often troubled me that a father would ask somethin' like that of his son. But God had a great and grand purpose beyond that death. Because of His Son's sacrifice, those who believe in Him are assured an eternal life of love an' great joy."

His faded blue eyes focused on Lily. " 'Tis a fact that all but one of the twelve disciples were martyred for preachin' the Gospel, yet their message of salvation dinna' die with them. It's been carried forth through the centuries and to every continent. The apostles fulfilled God's purpose for them in this life an' are now enjoyin' great rewards in heaven."

The elder's words far from soothed Lily's unrest. She had expected comforting words for this life, not the next.

"Now we have the privilege of piercin' the darkness of this continent with that same glorious news, the Gospel of Christ. As Christians, that is our commission while we dwell on this earth. The Lord never promised we'd all pass away gently in the midnight of our old age. The sudden death of a loved one or friend takes us by surprise, but it dunna' take God by surprise. Every death comes at its appointed time. The Bible says the

Almighty's ways are higher than our ways, an' His thoughts are higher than our thoughts. Even though we canna' understand some of the hard things, we must trust that He knows best."

Elder MacBride thumbed through the worn pages of his Bible. "I'd like to read now from Romans, chapter eight, startin' with verse thirty-five: 'Who shall separate us from the love of Christ? Shall tribulation, or distress, or persecution, or famine, or nakedness, or peril, or sword? As it is written, For thy sake we are killed all the day long; we are accounted as sheep for the slaughter. Nay, in all these things we are more than conquerors through him that loved us. For I am persuaded, that neither death, nor life, nor angels, nor principalities, nor powers, nor things present, nor things to come, nor height, nor depth, nor any other creature, shall be able to separate us from the love of God, which is in Christ Jesus our Lord.' "

Ian's voice droned on. "I'll read a few verses from chapter eight that I pray will answer more of your questions." He met Lily's gaze over his spectacles. " 'Likewise, the Spirit also helpeth our infirmities: for we know not what we should pray for as we ought: but the Spirit itself maketh intercession for us with groanings which cannot be uttered. And he that searcheth the hearts knoweth what is in the mind of the Spirit, because he maketh intercession for the saints according to the will of God. And we know that all things work together for good to them that love God, to them who are the called according to his purpose."

He closed his Bible. "Consider those last words. Are ye livin' yer life accordin' to His purpose for ye? Do ye start each mornin' askin' the Lord to guide ye through the day? Are ye servin' the Lord in whatever He asks of you? Are ye lovin' the Lord thy God with all thy heart and with all thy soul, and with all thy mind, as the Bible requires? An' are ye lovin' yer neighbor as yerself? Do ye pray for the salvation of yer enemies as well as yer friends? If ye do those things, the Lord will give ye peace in the midst of doubt and chaos."

As their spiritual leader continued reading related passages, a heavy burden of guilt pressed on Lily. Had she been praying for God's message to be sent forth? Had she even considered anything beyond her own household? No, all her thoughts had been for herself and her family, her desires and the needs of her loved ones. She'd tried to be a good servant to John and Susan, but it was all for naught unless her first purpose had been to serve the Lord. Never once had she asked God what He wanted of her on a particular day. Her prayers had always been personal wants and pleas. What an incredibly unworthy person she was. It was amazing that the Lord had bothered to save her from the Indians!

Thoroughly humiliated, she bowed her head. *Lord God, thank You for all You've done for me. I beg forgiveness for my selfishness. My mind has been cluttered with my secret hopes and desires that do nothing but war with my decision about whom I should marry, when all the time I should be seeking what You want of me. From now on I shall try to seek Your will alone. Thank You for a father and sister who tried to train me in the way I should go. And thank You for being my heavenly Father even though I've been a silly, wayward child. I pray this in Jesus' precious name. Amen.*

Lily could hardly wait for the rest of the service to end so she could find out how Matt reacted to the pastor's message. But Robby descended upon her before she had the chance.

"May I have a private moment with you, Lily?"

"Before dinner?" Lily dreaded another proposal.

He nodded. "Could we step into a side room?"

"Very well." From the corner of her eye, she saw Jackson looking daggers at Robby as she preceded him into the bedroom she now shared with several of the women.

He closed the door behind them. "Cissy overheard Jackson tell his pa he asked you to marry him."

Not appreciating being the latest topic bandied about, Lily grimaced. "I'd hoped that would remain a private matter until if and when there'd be a public announcement."

Her words did not deter Robby. "Well, did you say yea or nay?"

"I've not yet given Jackson an answer. After hearing the sermon this morning, I don't feel it's an answer I can give, as yet. Not unless the Lord directs me to do so."

He looked puzzled momentarily; then he grinned. "Whew. At least you didn't say yes. I hope that means you'd rather marry me. You must know I'd be a more pleasant fellow to live with. I'm real slow to anger, and I'd build us our own cabin just like Jackson's doin'. Far 'nough away so's you wouldn't have to listen to all the screamin' young'uns. Mr. Waldon says he's gonna let me apprentice with him, you know, so I'll be able to make us some fine furniture real soon. What d'you say?"

Lily took his hand and did her best to smile. "I must say, that was a fine proposal of marriage, Robby. However, my answer to you must be the same as it was to Jackson. I shall not marry anyone until I feel the Lord is leading me to do so." She tilted her head and searched his eyes. "Did the Lord direct you to come and propose to me?"

His gaze faltered. "I. . .uh. . .I guess not. I mean, I told God how much I want you, but I never asked if He wants me to have you."

She gave him a reassuring nod. "Well, if we're both praying for God's leading, it shouldn't take long to receive an answer. Now, if you'll excuse me, I need to help get our Sabbath dinner on the table." With a polite smile, she took her leave.

Several people stared at her when she exited the room. Lily knew it was most uncommon for an unmarried couple to go into a bedchamber alone. There was sure to be more talk.

She spied Jackson leaning against the wall by the front door, his expression morose. Thankfully, Matt and Luke were closer. She headed straight to her boys and pulled them into a hug. "Nothing's changed," she whispered. They relaxed, and their fisted hands uncoiled. "Better get these benches out to the tables now. We'll be having sweet potatoes to go with that tasty ham you boys were turning on the spit all morning."

Glancing up, Lily saw Jackson shift his attention to Robby, who carried a bench board in the direction of his seething rival.

"Jackson," she called out, hoping to forestall more fodder for gossip. "May I speak to you a moment?"

He eased his angry stance and moved away from the wall, starting toward her.

Much to Lily's relief, Robby walked on out.

She accompanied her dark-haired suitor to the relative shelter of the loft above. "I thought I should be the one to tell you Robby has asked me to marry him."

He shot a glare toward the door.

Lily caught his arm. "But I told him what I told you. If and when I marry, it will be to the person the Lord chooses for me. Especially after hearing Grampa MacBride's sermon this morning, I've no right to take matters into my own hands."

Jackson's eyes dulled with puzzlement. "God ain't talked out loud to nobody since Bible days. How d'ya expect to know for sure?"

Lily realized this young man was as confused about God and His power as Matt was. "I don't want to tell you what to do, but I believe you need to talk to Mr. MacBride about what you just asked me. Perhaps he can help you see how truly awe-inspiring our God is."

He opened his mouth to speak but apparently thought better of it and just looked at her momentarily. "If that's what you want me to do, I'll do it. But I'm gonna feel downright silly doin ' it."

"You'll not regret it. I promise."

Chapter 28

Bits of hay and yellow dust drifted down from the boards overhead where Matt and Luke raked a wagonload of hay the other lads had pitched up to the hayloft. Below them, Lily sat hunched over on the milking stool. After stripping the last of the creamy milk, she draped her apron over the pail to protect the contents from the falling debris. Then she brought the bucket out from under the cow and stretched out a kink in her back.

The boys started down the ladder. Lily had wanted to get Matthew alone ever since Sunday to ask him what he thought about Elder MacBride's sermon. She was thankful she and John's sons were no longer alone on the farmstead and vulnerable to Indian raiders, but she'd never felt so smothered in her life. People were everywhere, and they seemed to be watching her more than usual, since she'd received two marriage proposals in the same week. Everyone wondered which suitor she'd accept.

When her lads reached the bottom, Lily smiled at them. "Mercy, but you two are covered in straw." She finger-brushed bits of hay from the younger boy's hair while he and his brother dusted themselves off. "Would you mind if Matt and I had a minute to talk alone, Luke?"

His brows dipped. "Are you keepin' somethin' from me?"

"No, not at all. It has to do with a question your brother had last week about prayer. But you're welcome to stay, if you like."

"Naw, that's all right." He took the bucket from her and backed away. "I'll take this to the springhouse." Swiveling on his heel, he dashed off.

Lily had to laugh. "Next time I want to get rid of him, I'll know what to say."

Matt grinned. "Well, your talkin' about prayin' has kept Robby and that bossy *Jackson* away, that's for sure."

From his gritty utterance of Jackson's name, Lily could tell Matt was still not fond of him. But that was a topic for another day. "You may be right about them. At least they've stopped bristling every time they see each other. But getting back to that question you had regarding prayer, did Grampa Mac answer you sufficiently last Sunday?"

His expression flattened. "Imagine him wantin' us to love our enemies. *An' pray for 'em*, yet. I'll tell you how I'm gonna love any Injun that comes sneakin' in here. I'll shoot him right between his beady eyes, like I would some bobcat tryin' to get our chickens."

Placing a hand on his forearm, Lily met his gaze. "Matt, dear, 'tis right and proper to protect ourselves. But we still should pray that our enemies find the Lord. Think about it—if they came to know God, they'd realize that what they're doing is wrong. Sinful. And hopefully they'd stop doing it."

Matt's eyes narrowed to slits. "I ain't wastin' one minute of prayin' on them murderin' heathens. They deserve to go to hell." Before Lily had a chance to respond, he turned and darted out of the stable.

Watching after him, Lily wondered how to find the words that would make him understand, when many of the grown men felt exactly the same way. Yestereve, she'd overheard Cal and Richard saying they'd relish the chance to wipe out every Delaware this side of the Appalachians. She swept a look skyward. "Lord, please give me the right words and the right moment."

She strolled outside and noticed people gathering around two horsemen. She recognized the taller one as Jess Thomas, the post rider who used to come riding through with mail every three or four weeks. With the current unrest, the cove was fortunate if he arrived every two or three months. Usually jovial and quick to relate a humorous incident encountered during his travels, his light brown eyes were somber, and there were added furrows on his forehead. His partner, a short, stocky fellow with small eyes, looked equally pensive. Both men carried muskets and a brace of pistols.

Drawing closer, she could hear folks peppering the visitors with questions. The tall post rider raised a hand for quiet and waited for the chatter to subside. "Let me hand out the letters, folks. Then if you have no objections, me an' my partner'd like to stay the night. We'll have plenty of time this evenin' for swappin' news." He pulled a bundle of mail from his leather pouch and began calling out names. By the time he got to Lily's, most of the neighbors had dispersed to read their missives. Matt and Luke joined her as the rider handed her two pieces of mail.

"Is one from Pa?" Luke peered over her shoulder, trying to see as Lily studied the writing.

Matt huffed. " 'Course not, dummy. That post rider come from Reading, not from the fort."

"One's from Philadelphia," Lily answered, "the other is postmarked Alexandria. That will be from my sister. Let's go sit under the maple tree to read them, since all the chairs on the porch are occupied."

Luke grabbed her hand to hurry her along. "Let's hear about Emma and Davy first."

The boys plopped eagerly to the ground. Lily handed the letter from the Gilfords to Matt. "You read it."

He broke the seal and unfolded the paper:

Dear Lily, Matt, and Luke,
All is well here. The children are doing fine. We pray nightly that you are all equally well. Your grandfather and I want you to

know you are always welcome. Please reconsider joining us here
until after the war is over. Emma is afraid for you and misses you
terribly. Davy says Matt and Luke can stay in the room with him,
and Emma will sleep with Lily, the same as at home. They have
the details worked out quite nicely.

I dearly long to meet you, Matthew and Luke, and hope you
will come.

Your loving grandmother,
Olivia Gilford

"She's a lovely woman," Lily said. "You'll adore her when you meet her. She has that same gentle spirit your mother had."

"Really?" Luke's eyes clouded. "Let me see that letter."

As Matt handed it to him, Lily opened the one from Mariah. Knowing how blunt her sister could be, she debated whether to read it aloud. "Perhaps you two aren't interested in this one. It's probably girl talk."

"Sure we are. Anything that concerns you concerns us." Matt slanted a glance to the pasture gate, where Jackson was unhitching a team of oxen.

"Very well. But I must warn you, Mariah always says exactly what she thinks." Several pound notes fell out of the letter when Lily unfolded it. Ironically, it was more than John had paid for her indenturement papers four years ago. Lily tucked the funds inside her apron pocket and began reading:

My dear baby sister,

I am most upset with you. I cannot believe you would willingly
put yourself in danger again. If those Waldon boys were too
stubborn to go to Philadelphia with you, they should reap their
own reckless consequences. You should not have to suffer with
them. I insist you leave that perilous place at once and come to us.
I understand this letter may take weeks to reach you. But if you do
not walk through my front door within the next two months, I shall

*send men to fetch you, with or without your consent. I refuse to
celebrate another Christmas season without you.*

Your very worried sister,
Mariah

"She's right, you know," Matt commented, his eyes soulful. "You took an
awful risk comin' back here. It almost got you killed. You should go to her."

"Not without you. If I were to leave here, would you and Luke come
with me?"

Luke didn't wait for his older brother to answer. "Pa will be back in a
couple weeks. I wanna stay here for him. We're safe now, even if I do have
to share my loft with a passel of noisy fellas."

Lily ruffled his hair, shaking more bits of hay loose. "Then I reckon
we'll all stay here and wait for your pa. He should arrive before Mariah's
hired men. I don't have to decide what I'm going to do until after he
comes home."

"Right." Matt's gloomy demeanor matched his response. "Like which
one of them two jaspers you're gonna marry."

Lily inhaled a calming breath. She and the boys could have sat here
the rest of the evening without that reminder.

Lily drew her shawl tighter before taking the last bite of her supper.
Not only were the evenings growing steadily colder for outdoor eating,
but her nerves were constantly on edge. She suspected the news from
Philadelphia wouldn't be good. Both newcomers had avoided questions
during the meal, promising to convey what information they had
after supper. Post riders garnered more tidbits than any newspaper or
broadside reported, so the air crackled with anticipation.

Seated with the adult MacBrides and the Shaws, Lily noticed the
women's conversations centered on the contents of the letters they'd
received, while the men were ominously quiet. She also noted that most
everyone had finished eating as quickly as she had. The children had

already scurried off to play hide-and-seek.

The post riders, however, were taking their sweet time eating. Seated at the next table, with the Dunlaps and Pattersons, the horsemen shoveled in food as if it were their last meal. But considering the dangers of their occupation, one never knew when it might very well be.

Too anxious to sit and wait any longer, Lily untangled her limbs from the bench and rose to her feet, straightening her skirts. "I'll go prepare more tea."

She returned a few moments later with a large pewter pitcher in each hand and handed one to Agnes, then approached the cove's guests. "More tea, gentlemen?"

"That would be nice." Jess Thomas and his companion held up their mugs. "Mighty fine spread you womenfolk laid out."

"Thank you."

Lily filled their cups and mustered a pleasant expression as she moved on to Jackson. "And you?"

"Sure thing, purty lady." He didn't hold his mug up for filling, so Lily reached past him to retrieve it. Hearing his intake of breath and feeling his eyes on her, she quickly moved on, assuring herself the Lord would never expect her to marry someone so bold.

As she moved to the next table, she realized that had it been John drawing her near and looking at her the way Jackson had, she'd have been thrilled. The only thing wrong with Jackson Dunlap was her and her wayward feelings.

Cal's voice cut into her musings. "If you men would care to join us down by the crick for a smoke. . . ."

The post riders immediately rose to their feet.

They want to bring the men up to date privately! "Please!" Lily blurted out. "We women want to hear the news, too."

"That's right." Oftentimes prickly Edith Randall nodded emphatically. "Some of us don't have our husbands at home."

The stocky visitor glanced around at the men, as if seeking their consent. "You sure about this?"

Ian shook his head wearily. "Might's well tell the womenfolk. Otherwise us men won't get a lick of sleep tonight for all their badgerin'."

"If you say so." Brown-eyed Jess Thomas took a position between the adult tables. "First off, you folks are doin' the wise thing by bandin' together. The redskins are still rovin' both sides of Blue Mountain. They come in fast, burn and kill, then disappear again into the woods. One thing, though. . .you should be storin' all your harvests here where you can best protect it."

Toby Dunlap nodded. "We been storin' some of it in the blockhouse yonder, but we don't have time to build nothin' else right now. It's all we can do to git our harvest in. Mebbe in a few weeks. . ."

"Just lettin' you know, them heathens know burnin' you out before winter sets in is as easy a way of getting you out as killin' ya. Me an' Fritch here figger that's why they ain't started back to Fort Duquesne yet. They wanna destroy your food supply first."

"The only run-ins we've had here was a couple months back," Richard Shaw said, "when they snatched away two of our children. We got 'em back, though." He glanced at his anxious wife and gave her a confident tip of his head as muttering assents made the rounds.

The post rider raised a hand. "Well, you picked a lucky spot for your settlement. What with the string of forts and blockhouses guardin' along the Susquehanna not far to the west, the Injuns ain't been comin' this way. They're crossin' upriver of Fort Augusta and Shamokin an' comin' down through the Swatara and Schuylkill passes, which puts 'em quite a ways to the east of here. An' even though the Indians at Shamokin say they're loyal to us, we think some of 'em are guidin' the Delaware in."

Jackson came to his feet. "We know all that. What we wanna know now is why aren't there more militia comin' out here from Philadelphia to help? An' where are the troops from England? Why ain't them generals tryin' to take Fort Duquesne? Me an' my brother refused to reenlist this year 'cause we can do more good here protectin' our cove, since nobody else can—or will."

"I understand how you feel, lad. I did hear talk in Philadelphia that they're still considerin' takin' that fort this year."

"Considerin'?" He spat on the ground. "It's October, man. If they ain't started out by now, they ain't goin' to." Shaking his head in disgust, Jackson reclaimed his seat.

"Can't help but agree with you," Thomas said in a flat tone. "There's another rumor floatin' around that's a mite crazy. Folks are sayin' the governor wants to declare Pennsylvania its own republic and petition France to let us be under their protection. In exchange we would agree to let the Injuns freely pass through on their way to Virginia."

"Yer right about one thing," Ian said. "That *is* crazy talk."

"I wouldn't be too sure," Cal injected. "Last summer, folks on t'other side of the Susquehanna were talkin' about doin' somethin' like that. 'Course, it's too late for them. There ain't too many people left over there. Not anymore."

Jess Thomas scanned the group. "Well, like I said, your forts along the Susquehanna have been the biggest help."

"Fort Henry is pathetically undermanned." Jackson rolled his eyes. "Governor Denny won't give the order to bring our men back from Fort Augusta."

The post rider eyed him steadily. "That bein' the case, I'm surprised you an' your brother left the militia."

That raised Jackson's hackles. "We ain't cowards. But month after month we was out there chasin' ghosts. We hardly ever caught up to the marauders. We do better here, protectin' what's ours. An' me an' Frank ain't the only ones. John Waldon an' Bob Randall from here in the cove are both comin' home in November to stay. We're through havin' our families out here with no protection."

Listening to Jackson, Lily found herself impressed with the strength of his conviction. He was a much more responsible, levelheaded person than she gave him credit for. He might be a touch clumsy about courting, but if an Indian raid did come, she'd feel much safer knowing she had his protection than Robby Randall's. Jackson was militia-trained and truly cared about his family. Besides, he *was* rather nice looking, and strong. . . .

Chapter 29

N ineteen more days," Bob Randall commented. He and John scanned from beyond the fort's clearing to the forest as they slowly walked the perimeter of the watchtower.

"Soon we'll be counting the hours." John had been doing that for some time already. He prayed constantly that Lily and his sons had done as he'd pleaded in his letter and left the cove. The French and Indians had taken particular interest of late in the area between the Susquehanna and the Schuylkill Rivers.

Bob nodded. "I've been away so long, baby Laurie's cryin' will be like music to these poor ol' ears. Did I tell you she's been walkin' for months now?"

"Only about a hundred times." John quashed a wry grin.

"Sure hope Edith didn't cut off those pretty curls of hers. They're cute as anythin.'"

John shifted his stance and peered more closely at the woods. "That's right. I forgot she cut off little Charlie's when he turned one."

"Well, he *was* startin' to look like a girl. He'll be four in a couple a days. I've sure missed a lot. Don't think I'll ever want to leave home ag—" He stared hard into the distance. "Hey, somethin's out there." He pointed toward the edge of the clearing.

John wheeled around.

A figure attired in French blue stood silhouetted against the trees, a hundred yards or so away!

John peered through the spyglass. "I see him. A man in uniform." Quickly he scanned the forest shadows on either side of the enemy soldier, but saw no one else. Of all the times for Captain Busse to be downriver at the fort at Harris's Ferry. For days, the man had been too sick to make the return trip to Fort Henry.

He handed the telescope to Bob. "Watch him. If others show up, give a holler. I'll go report."

He descended the ladder and hastily covered the ground to head-quarters. Reaching the open doorway, he saw Ensign Biddle, now in command, at Busse's desk. A couple of other men stood in front. "Corporal Waldon reporting, sir. We spotted a French soldier out there. Seems to be alone."

"Where?" Biddle's chair scraped back as the stocky man lunged to his feet.

"At the edge of the forest, sir. In the southeast."

Several soldiers who'd come onto the porch after John flew by now blocked the entrance. One spoke up. "You think the bloke's come to ask us to surrender? Are we surrounded? I knew it was dumb to let 'em order so many of our men up to Fort Augusta."

"We won't have a chance," another muttered. "Not with so many of our guys out rovin' right now."

John was amazed at the outburst. Captain Busse would never abide such disrespectful conduct.

The ensign broke past the mouthy pair without a word and charged for the watchtower with John at his heels.

Once they reached the platform, Bob handed the spyglass to the commander and pointed toward the forest. "Over there, sir. Must be lost or somethin'. He just stood there watchin' the fort, then plunked hisself down. Been right there ever since."

"I see." Biddle's face scrunched up as he squinted into the spyglass. "He's armed. He's got a musket across his lap."

John prompted the ensign to issue an order. "What do you think Captain Busse would want us to do?"

"Uh—yes." Biddle returned the spyglass to Bob. "You two stay here and keep checking all around. I'll send two or three men out to learn why he's there." He shook his head. "We can't afford to weaken the fort any more than it already is." With a last glance at the French solder, he hurried back down to headquarters.

John saw Ensign Craighead and two other men dispatched in short order. From his vantage point, he could tell they weren't anxious to be going out there alone. Striding a number of feet apart, they held their weapons at the ready as they scanned the forest edge.

No one else appeared.

The Frenchman rose and strode forward, his musket held crossways above his head.

"He's surrenderin'. Don't that beat all?" Bob frowned in confusion.

"Keep watching. It could be a trick."

But it wasn't. The soldier relinquished his weapon and came quietly along with the militiamen.

Once safely inside the gates, the enemy soldier began jabbering in French. From time to time he would put his fingers to his mouth, indicating he needed food.

Militiamen converged as the soldier in the light blue coat was escorted to headquarters. One snatched away the Frenchman's tricorn, affording John a better view. Even from the watchtower, he could see the feared enemy was nothing but a shaggy-haired lad of sixteen or seventeen. Still, if he'd been wandering out there so near the fort, there could be others close by. How many? Would there be a full-scale attack?

John's heart plunged. Why now, with only nineteen days to go?

Nineteen days before he was to leave for home to be with his boys and his darling Lily, if they were still there. Once again he sent pleas heavenward for their safety and for Fort Henry.

Bob snorted. "Well, we got ourselves a prisoner, for all the good it's doin' us."

An hour had passed since the French soldier was escorted to headquarters. In the tower, John and Bob continued to survey the surrounding woods, all the while vitally interested in the information the lad was giving the officers.

John knew everyone at the fort shared his concern. Whenever he glanced down into the fort grounds, he saw fellow militiamen keeping close watch as they waited outside the building to hear what was transpiring in that room.

Suddenly the door opened, and company clerk Carson hurried out. He dashed over to the cook tent, then ran back with a trencher of food without a word to the waiting men.

Unable to hear the conversation being bandied about on the grounds, John surmised from the way the other soldiers milled around that their anxiety matched his. Everyone itched to know if an enemy force lurked nearby ready to launch an attack.

From across the platform, Bob hiked his chin. "That lad may not be so hungry once he tastes that slop we eat."

John grinned at his friend's dry humor.

He caught a movement in the distance. Placing the spyglass to his eye, John zeroed in on the spot. Just a deer. He relaxed.

Then Carson came out the headquarters' door again. "Anybody here speak French?" he yelled from the porch.

No one stepped forward.

The ensign turned on his heel and returned inside.

Bob snorted. "Well, we got ourselves a prisoner, for all the good it's doin' us."

"Too bad we don't have any English regulars here." John's gaze continued to rake the edge of the clearing. "Some of them might know that language, with England being off the French coast."

"Far as I'm concerned, the Brits an' the Frenchies should be fightin' the whole blamed war by themselves. Us colonials shouldn't have ta risk our lives over some tree-munchin' beavers across mountains you an' me'll prob'ly never cross just so's them two greedy kings over the water can fill their treasure chests."

John cocked his head in thought. "Must be hard, trying to keep hold of so much territory. But there is a bright spot. Did you read the broadside the dispatch rider posted on the board yesterday?"

"Naw. I don't work my brain that hard 'less I have to. 'Sides, if there was anything worth tellin', you would'a already told me."

"Ha! Well, there was something you might consider interesting. Seems the English have whipped the French in Bengal. Maybe some of those soldiers will now be sent here."

"Bengal? Where's that? Up north somewheres?"

"No. India."

"*India.* Are you tellin' me they're fightin' over land in India, too?"

John nodded. "And someplace in Africa called Senegal."

"Well, now. Ain't they the busy ones." Bob's tone sharpened as he studied something in the distance. "Hand me the spyglass."

John tossed it across the deck to his friend then came alongside. He strained to see what had drawn Bob's attention.

His friend lowered the telescope with a sheepish grin. "Just some leaves on one of the trees wavin'. Thought mebbe somebody might'a climbed up it. But it was just a bear scratchin' its behind."

Moments later, their relief for sentinel duty climbed up the ladder.

"You fellas heard anythin' yet?" Bob asked.

The first one to reach the platform answered. "Yep. Finally. Since nobody could understand that lad's jibberish, it took awhile to find out he was with thirty-three Indians, Delaware and Shawnee. Somehow he got separated from them."

John gave a huff. "Sounds to me like they lost him. Deliberately. They probably didn't relish taking orders from some green kid."

"Likely they won't wanna head back out without plenty of scalps, neither," Bob added.

The second man rested an elbow on the watchtower's rail. "One thing, at least. We here at the fort can relax. No thirty-three Indians would ever try to take this fortification."

John nodded and headed for the ladder. But he knew that breaking up into armed parties of five or six, those thirty-three savages could do a lot of damage, roaming the area. His urgency to return to his family intensified. Nineteen more days.

The delicious aroma of baking bread permeated the air, and now that the nights had grown chilly, the glorious colors of autumn filled the countryside. Breathing deeply of the fresh, crisp air, Lily was glad to be outdoors, despite her icy hands. Wash day had become a huge undertaking, and she appreciated sixteen-year-old Cissy Dunlap's help as the two of them pinned up the last load of wet laundry.

A wisp of light brown hair wafted over Cissy's shoulder as she peered from around a sheet flapping sluggishly in the breeze. "I really wish you'd marry up with Jackson. If you don't, he'll probably go looking for a wife somewheres else, like Frank did. He don't hardly ever come home no more since he found his Hildy."

Lily rolled her eyes. At least once a day, someone provided her with a reason why she should choose either Robby or Jackson. "The Lord hasn't nudged me in that direction as yet." She loved giving that answer, since it usually put an end to the topic.

"Well, just so's you know," Cissy persisted, jamming a pin over the draped sheet, "Jackson don't show his best side when he's out and about. When we're home, he's always good about bringin' in water and fillin' the woodbox without bein' asked. He's like that. If he sees something needs doin', he up and does it."

"That's an admirable trait." Lily shook out a dish towel to hang and changed the subject. "How are you and Donald getting along?"

Cissy's face pinkened as she brushed her bangs out of her eyes. "Oh, he can be so silly. Yesterday he gave me a bouquet. At least, that's what he called it."

"A bouquet? Where would he find flowers this time of year?"

"Aw, it was just some tree branches with pretty colored leaves. But he arranged 'em real nice. If we was at home, I could a put 'em in our blue china vase and set it on the table to look fine."

Lily averted her gaze into the distance. "I know how anxious everyone is to return to their own homes. 'Tis so crowded now that we all stay inside at night, with only the cabin, the carpenter's shop, and the blockhouse for shelter."

"You know, if I was to home, Donald could come callin' proper-like, like the fellas did for my older sisters before they married up." Cissy pulled another piece from the basket on the ground and came up with a sigh. "That's another thing that makes me sad. Esther and Betsy wed before we came out here, and I ain't seen 'em since. They both got young'uns already, too. Just think, me, an auntie." Turning to pin up the towel, she froze, and her eyes widened. She pointed with the wet article in her hand. "Look! Smoke!"

Lily spun around. A huge black cloud climbed the northern sky.

"Oh, no. Do you think it's our place?" Cissy cried.

"*Call in the children. Quick!*" Leaping over the basket, Lily ran to the house and bounded through the door. "Quick, everyone, grab what food you can and get to the blockhouse."

"What is it?" Edith came from the hearth, a large wooden spoon in her hand.

"Smoke. To the north."

The women dodged past each other as Ruth bolted to the bedroom for her baby then ran outside screaming for her other children.

"*Stop!*" Millie Dunlap hollered above the chaos, her hands on her hips. "Ever'body stop. The men are workin' at our place today, boilin' down sorghum. Remember?"

"There's far too much smoke," Lily countered. "Dear Lord in heaven, my boys are with those men. Grab all the food and bedding you can."

She lifted down her musket and hastened outside. Quickly pouring powder into the flashpan of the weapon she always kept loaded, she fired a signal round. She prayed that the Randall twins and MacBride girls would hear it. They were supposed to stay close while out picking up wild walnuts. After reloading as fast as she could, she rammed the wad down the barrel, then dashed back inside, propped the rifle against the wall, and climbed up to the loft.

Lily scooped up an armful of blankets littering the floor and threw them over the railing to the floor below. "Grab some and go to the blockhouse," she yelled to anyone still about.

Descending the ladder, she saw that the large cauldrons of food the women had been cooking for supper were already gone. She hurried to the corner by the hearth and slung a sack of cornmeal over her shoulder. Then, with a last glance around, she grabbed the musket and ran after the others, who were already disappearing beyond the springhouse.

A sudden eerie feeling made the fine hairs on her arms stand on end. She cast a glance behind her. Seeing no one, she took off again, the heavy canvas bag bouncing against her spine with every step.

She'd just crossed the creek bridge when she heard a distant gunshot. Then another. Two more. Desperate to know what was happening, she stopped, gasping for breath, as she strained to hear any others. *Matt and Luke are out there!* The thought was too much to bear.

Why, oh why hadn't she made the boys leave when she had the chance? John had been very explicit in his letter. If anything happened to them, she'd never forgive herself.

And neither would John.

"Hurry up, Lily." Edith Randall called from the blockhouse. "We need to bar the door."

Chapter 30

"Is everyone here?" Lily glanced around the shadowy blockhouse as the door closed behind her.

"Yes," Agnes MacBride said. "Ever'body's been counted."

Ruth started bawling along with her baby as she cowered in a corner, her whimpering children pulled close around her.

Others huddled in family groups, murmuring concerns to one another.

Lily's heart went out to Nancy, who held her little Mary tight. The child shook uncontrollably, her eyes huge with fright. Mary especially shouldn't have to be here.

Fifteen-year-old Judy MacBride held up hands stained with walnut hull. "Mama, how will I ever get the stain off? Did you bring the lye soap?"

Agnes ignored her whining daughter and went for the ladder in the center, hauling her ungainly weapon with her.

Slipping the sack of meal off her shoulder, Lily followed her neighbor to the top deck. Millie and Cissy Dunlap were already there, staring intently at the smoke to the north.

"It's comin' from two places now." Never taking her eyes from the sight, Millie gestured with her head. "I can't rightly be sure, but I don't think it's our place. The smoke seems to be comin' from the farmsteads the Thorntons an' the Bakers abandoned last year."

Lily joined them to stare at the two distinct and ominous black clouds billowing above the trees beyond the clearing.

"That means ours'll be next," Cissy murmured just above a whisper.

A mental image filled Lily's mind, of everything her neighbors owned being reduced to ashes. . .including the blue china vase the girl had mentioned such a short time ago. *And even my boys, if the men haven't stopped those Indians.* She squeezed her eyes shut, trying to keep them from flooding. *God in heaven, please bring back my dear boys soon. . . .*

Edith shoved her musket onto the deck and climbed up through the hole. "Any sign of our men yet? Robby and Donald's with 'em. *Not Bob, of course,*" she grated bitterly. "Duty-bound to that blasted fort, an' all."

"Donald. . . ." Cissy swung around to Edith, tears pooling.

Lily's eyes also swam.

"Ain't no time for cryin'," Edith scolded. "We gotta keep watch, make sure them heathens don't sneak up on us." She reached for Cissy and gave her a quick hug. "Our menfolk need a safe place to come back to."

"And pray." Lily used her sleeve to wipe away the moisture in her eyes. "I'll take the east side."

Millie suddenly turned around. "Did you hear that?"

"What?" Agnes stiffened.

"Another shot."

Time seemed to stand still as the sun slowly inched toward the west. Gunshots no longer echoed through the thick woods. The night air turned cold. Lily had goose bumps up and down her arms, but she wouldn't take a minute to go down and fetch a blanket as she willed the men—Matt and Luke in particular—to return. Visions of them scalped and sprawled on the ground in pools of blood, their sightless eyes staring at nothing, their mouths gaping in soundless cries, flashed through her mind. The single hope she could cling to was that the Dunlap place had not been set ablaze. Yet.

Most of the women and children had gathered on the platform and now lined the railing, quietly watching. Rarely did anyone utter a word.

Finally, as the sun disappeared behind the tallest trees, Edith slammed the butt of her musket against the deck in a resounding crack. "I'm through waitin'. I'm goin' down to saddle me a horse."

"I'll go with you." Lily headed for the ladder. Anything was better than not knowing.

"Wait!" One of the twins pointed toward the bridge. "Somebody's comin' across."

Friend or foe? Lily flew back to the creek-side edge, along with everyone else. She positioned her musket across the railing and took aim.

Breaking past the foliage, someone waved his arms as he raced across the clearing.

Luke! The boy was unharmed! *But was he being chased?*

Seconds behind him came Pete Dunlap and Michael MacBride.

Lily held her breath. *Let Matt be next, Lord. Please!*

As John's older son did indeed come into view, the sight of him brought such relief, Lily nearly dropped her weapon. He came more slowly, at a steady jog, his musket bouncing on his shoulder.

Tears streamed down her cheeks. Her knees buckled, and she sank down to the floor of the deck. Her boys were safe. Safe.

While she struggled to regain her composure, the other women scrambled down the ladder. One resolution took shape in Lily's mind. No matter how the boys felt about it, the three of them were going to take the MacBride canoe and leave this cove as soon as she could gather the needed supplies together.

Inhaling a strengthening breath, Lily rose and moved across the deck to the spot above the blockhouse entrance, waving to Matt and Luke as they neared.

People were already streaming out the heavy door. But where were the rest of the men? Surely those lads weren't the only survivors!

In the distance, Jackson and Donald emerged into view, carrying someone between them. Someone had been injured, but who was it? She couldn't see past Jackson. She could see, however, that Jackson wore no shirt, and his chest was smeared with blood. Had he been hurt as well?

Below, Edith screamed and ran toward her son.

Across the clearing, Richard appeared next. Ruthie ran to him, sobbing loudly, her baby bobbing in her arms.

Then, one by one, Toby and Ian came into sight, and finally Cal, limping awkwardly on his bad leg.

Lily could finally make out the person being carried. *Robby! Kind, gentle Robby.* Across the lad's middle, a wide leather belt held a wad of bloody cloth in place.

She propped her musket against the half-wall and scurried down the ladder. Before she reached the lower floor, Matt and Luke were already inside, reaching for her.

Sweat streaked Matt's dirty face. "We prayed all the way back that you were safe. We were afraid other Injuns would attack here while we were off chasin' the ones that burned those two empty farmsteads."

Lily tugged them both close and held them tight, weapons and all. "What happened to poor Robby?"

"He got shot." Matt's expression was hard with rage, but his voice sounded cool and steady. "We'd been chasin' them painted devils for near an hour when one of them leaped out from behind a tree and shot him. Jackson got that savage good, though. And we took care of two others back at the Thornton cabin whilst they was still torchin' the place."

Lily couldn't help noticing Luke remained silent, and he had more than just sweaty streaks down his face. He had tear tracks as well. "Are you all right, Luke?"

He buried his face against her shoulder and nodded, his breath catching as he tried to be brave. The handle of her much-too-young warrior's pistol gouged into her, but she didn't care. She held on all the tighter. She was absolutely determined to take the boys away from here as soon as she could. What a fool she'd been to insist on staying in this perilous cove.

Shadows filled the open doorway as Jackson and Donald carried Robby inside the blockhouse. His mother already had a blanket laid out. His teary-eyed twin sisters, Gracie and Patience, trailed behind, their troubled gazes fixed on their brother.

"Fetch some water an' clean rags," Edith ordered, her eyes wild as she crouched beside her fallen son.

Lily grabbed the bucket sitting atop a water barrel and partially filled it. She carried it to Edith and dropped down beside her.

Robby, barely conscious, moaned with pain. With his bloodied fingers he reached for Lily's hand. "Lily—" He started coughing and grimaced as a spasm made him gasp for breath.

"Don't talk, boy." His mother unbuckled the belt holding the makeshift bandage. Lily recognized the item as Jackson's shirt. "Gracie, where are them rags?"

"Here, Mama." She turned her head away as she handed them down to her mother.

Robby squeezed Lily's hand, drawing her back to him. Blood seeped from one corner of his mouth. "I. . .killed an Indian." He gulped. "You think. . .God will. . .forgive me?"

Lily leaned closer and brushed the hair from his pale brow as she did her best to smile. "Oh, Robby, I know He will. He loves you so—"

Robby's chest sagged as a final breath emerged. His eyes seemed to freeze in place, and his hand fell away.

He's dead. Lily swallowed hard.

Jackson plopped down beside her and grabbed Robby's shoulders. "Not now, man. You're home. You're safe." He shook the lad. "Robby! Wake up! Wake up!"

"Let him go." Edith clawed away his fingers. "Let go of my boy."

As quickly as he'd knelt down, Jackson sprang to his feet again. "I'm real sorry. I just—" He pivoted on his heel and bolted out.

Grace and Patience began crying audibly, and Donald, who had carried his injured brother in, draped an arm about each of his sisters and wept with them.

As Lily quietly moved out of the way, she noticed Matt and Luke staring at Edith, who sat crooning to her dead son as she brushed damp curls from his forehead. "Let's give the Randalls a moment of privacy." She took their hands in hers and drew them away. The stark realization that John's precious lads could as easily have been killed closed her throat till she could scarcely draw breath.

They strode out into the late afternoon light, not bothering to talk. Lily realized the sun had moved very little since she last checked the sky.

Her neighbors stood in clusters all about, the younger ones clinging to their parents, staring mutely into the blockhouse. Even the babies seemed to sense it was not a time to fuss.

Lily offered a fleeting prayer, thanking the Lord that Emma and Davy weren't there to witness this horrid occurrence.

"I brung him out as fast as I could." Still bare-chested and smeared with blood, Jackson fixed his gaze on her. "I know I always gave him a hard time about you, but I did ever'thing I could for him. You believe me, don't you?"

She nodded and attempted a smile. "Of course I believe you." All anyone had to do was look at the anguish on his face to know he spoke the truth. She took a step toward him.

His father, Toby, came to his side, looking equally distressed. "Son, you did more for Robby than any of the rest of us could. You carried him all that long way back to the wagon."

"I should'a got him there sooner. Mebbe if I had—"

Toby took him by the shoulders and looked him in the eye. "Listen to me, Son. Nothin' anybody could'a done was gonna save that boy. He was gut-shot an' bleedin' out. It was God's mercy he didn't suffer very long. Now, let's go down to the crick an' get you cleaned up a bit."

"Huh?" Jackson glanced down at his hands, then his body, as if he hadn't noticed he was covered with Robby's blood.

Lily untied her apron. "Here. Take this with you. I'll see about getting another shirt for Jackson."

She watched them stride toward the creek—the usually powerful Jackson stumbling along with his father, still staring at the blood on his hands. Obviously his guilt stemmed from the rivalry he and Robby shared, not his efforts on this most terrible of days.

Jackson's mother came up to Lily. "I'll go fetch my son a shirt." Then Millie wagged her head. "I'm startin' to believe no piece of bottom land is worth all this sufferin', no matter how rich it might be."

As Millie walked away, Lily's gaze gravitated back to the Randalls inside the blockhouse, weeping quietly and consoling each other. She drew Matt and Luke close. "She's right, boys. No land is worth a single hair on either of your heads."

Chapter 31

No sense all of us crowdin' together in that blockhouse." Cal swept a glance over Lily and the others who stood waiting for the Randall family to come out. "We run them red devils off good an' proper. They won't tangle with us again anytime soon." His light brown eyes grew soft as they gravitated to his little, golden-haired Mary. "Let's take the young'uns back to the cabin so's they can warm up."

Ian gave a decisive nod. "Cal's right. Go on back. I'll stay here awhile longer."

One by one, the women trickled inside the blockhouse and gave Edith a hug or an empathetic squeeze to her shoulder. No one seemed able to think of anything to say to comfort their grieving friend. Each neighbor emerged with a kettle or skillet of food that had been cooked earlier. Watching through the doorway, Lily wondered if Edith even noticed their presence.

Lily went in last for the sack of cornmeal. She ran a soothing palm across the heads of Robby's siblings as they sat in a circle around his body, watching tearfully as their mother worked at bandaging the unfortunate boy's wound. The lad had been the kind of son and brother any family would have been proud to have.

Backing out of the structure with the sack in one hand and an armful of blankets, Lily knew Robby would have made a wonderful husband, too.

⁓

The loaves of bread in the outdoor oven the men had constructed weeks ago had burned to black lumps during the crisis. The women quickly whipped up some less-tasty johnnycakes, and the somber neighbors gathered at two long, makeshift tables stretching almost the length of the cabin's common room. The air crackled with tension as everyone waited for Ian to fetch the Randalls for supper.

Realizing she was fiddling with her fork, Lily placed it on the table and slid a glance across to Jackson, several seats away.

Flanked by his mother and grandmother, each of whom held one of his big hands, the young man wore a clean linsey-woolsey shirt. Not a speck of blood remained on him, and his hair looked darker than usual, damp and slicked back. His eyes were downcast, but bright blotches on his face bore evidence of recent weeping.

Sudden, loud footsteps pounded on the porch.

Lily's attention flew to the door.

Edith Randall burst in, auburn curls all askew. She gulped in air as if she'd run all the way from the blockhouse.

Lily's blood turned cold. Had the Indians come back?

The woman took several gasping breaths, then let the air out in a whoosh. "I want one of you men to go get that shiftless husband of mine. You get him back here so's he can see what he let happen to my boy."

Jackson wrenched up from his seat. "I'll go fetch him right now." He threw a leg over the bench.

"No, Son," his father ordered from across the table. "Sit down. It's too late to go tonight." Toby turned his sympathetic gaze to the distraught mother. "We'd spend all our time out there just wanderin' around, Edith, lost in the dark. First light, me an' my boy'll start out." He switched his attention back to his son. "Sit down, Jackson. We'll make better time in the mornin.'"

Jackson eyed his father momentarily, then cut a glance to Robby's mother. His shoulders sagged, and he slumped back down, staring right through his trencher as if it wasn't there.

Lily's heart ached. Toby was close to sixty years old, and the trip would be hard on him. But she didn't doubt his wisdom. In Jackson's present state of mind, he'd probably run his horse near to death.

Edith glared wildly at Toby for a few moments, then as suddenly as she'd come, she charged outside again, bumping past her returning children and Grampa MacBride.

Cissy Dunlap flew to Donald's side as soon as the lad entered the room. "Come sit with me, Donald." She took his hand.

He pulled his fingers from her grasp. "Not tonight, Cis. I need to sit with my family."

"Oh. Of course." Inching back, Cissy's sad blue eyes misted as she watched him follow his siblings to vacant seats at the far end of the table. . .the same lad who'd brought her a carefully selected autumn bouquet just the day before.

At times like these, the comfort of family overshadowed the pangs of young love. Lily was utterly grateful she had Matt and Luke next to her.

If only John were here, too.

Even as that longing surfaced, so did the hope that if Bob actually were to come back, the commander would release John also. Only twelve days remained of his enlistment.

Ian's voice spoke out from between the two tables. "Let's ask God's blessing on this food and pray for Almighty God's comfort at this sad time."

Edith never left the blockhouse that night, and Lily knew that in the woman's present state, she'd have been no comfort to her other children.

The only time anyone caught a glimpse of her the next day was at dawn, when Toby and Jackson rode their mounts out of the stable. She ran up the path from the creek just as Lily and Millie brought a last cup of tea and food to the men for their trip.

Edith looked like a wild woman, her hair tangled and flying every whichway, her eyes red and swollen, bloodstains spattering the front of her day gown. Vapor clouds spewed from her mouth in the chilly air when she spoke. "Just makin' sure." She came to a stop several feet in front of the men. "You get that useless man back here right quick." Then, whirling around, she marched down the path again.

"Don't let it get to you." Millie handed the food up to her husband, then the steaming cup. "She just don't know where to put all her pain."

Lily realized Jackson could easily read something extra in her being there, and wondered if it would have been wiser to have his grandmother bring the food to him. Wishing she had awakened Eva, she gave him the cinched bag of leftover johnnycakes and sausage before passing the tea up to him.

But as he took the mug, Jackson didn't offer his usual over-confident grin. His lips moved into a merely grateful smile. He took a couple of large gulps and handed the cup back. "Tell Mistress Randall we'll bring Bob back as quick as humanly possible." Then he reined his mount around and nudged him forward. His father bent down and gave Millie a peck on the top of her head then followed their son.

The ominous, dreadful sound of nails being hammered into a coffin echoed from the workshop. With Ian busy at the chore, Lily sought a task that would take her away from the noise.

Out back in the vegetable garden, digging up potatoes with Ruth, she spied Richard and Cal rumbling away in the Dunlaps' wagon.

Ruth dropped her shovel and bolted after them. "Where you goin'?" Fear heightened her voice. Aside from Ian, these were the only two grown men left in the valley.

"We're gonna fetch the sorghum molasses from Toby's place. We left it there when—" He stopped abruptly. No one needed a reminder about the Indian attack. "Don't worry. I promise we'll be back."

Cal leaned around him. "Might be a little while. We're gonna look around a bit, too." Snatching the reins from Richard's grip, he snapped them over the horses' backs before Ruth could utter a protest.

Lily could hardly blame the man. Ruth's tendency to be hysterical was no secret. And now poor Edith. Lily gazed across the barnyard and down toward the creek. How long would she stay inside the blockhouse, secluded like that?

Only after Ian had finished the coffin and taken Donald and Michael with him to get Robby's remains did Edith leave the blockhouse. Her eyes fixed on the blanket-wrapped body, she followed as they carried the lad to the workshop. As she approached the door, her two youngest ones ran to her, but she pushed them away. Both immediately started wailing.

Gracie and Patience ran to the children and scooped them up. The twins did their best to comfort them, since their mother had nothing to offer.

The sound of more nails being hammered shattered the quiet as Ian fastened the lid in place. There would be no last viewing.

Maggie walked up between Lily and Agnes. "It's best this way. For her own good, Edith needs to be separated from the boy's body now."

But a mere closed coffin did little to deter Edith from her son. The second Ian and the lads left the building, the grieving mother shut herself inside and locked the door.

She did not come out for the rest of the day.

Calvin and Richard returned at midafternoon with the assurance that the Indians had left the area. The news provided Ruth much-needed relief. She'd gone into the house with her brood as soon as the men drove away and kept the little ones on the floor beside her stool while seven-year-old Lizzie helped at the spinning wheel. Ruth sat rigid, working fast, her flintlock pistol in her lap.

That evening, Maggie took a trencher of food and a small pot of tea out to Edith. The woman had remained sequestered in the workshop all day and wouldn't open the door to anyone, not even Maggie. Ian's wife finally sighed and left the offering on the doorstep.

Had it not been for the funeral, Lily would have taken the boys that day and left Beaver Cove.

At the close of the supper meal, Grampa MacBride picked up his Bible and motioned for everyone to remain seated. "I was hopin' Edith would be here for the readin', but I'm sure the scriptures will edify the rest of us. We all share our neighbors' great sadness."

Lily glanced along the table to Donald and the Randall children. Cissy sat beside Donald now with baby Laurie on her lap. That family needed all the comfort and help anyone could give.

"I'll be readin' from the first chapter of Philippians."

As the elder's voice filled the room, Lily put her arms around Matt and Luke. They'd done their chores without any reminders today and then found extra work to keep busy, just as she had. She hoped they'd be tired enough to get a good night's sleep.

" 'I am in a strait betwixt two,' " Ian read, " 'having a desire to depart, and to be with Christ; which is far better: Nevertheless to abide in the flesh is more needful for you.' "

A sense of peace infused Lily, that the moment Robby's soul left his body, he'd received the answer to his final question. The young man knew instantly that he'd been forgiven by God and deeply loved. He was now in the very presence of the Lord.

Ian's voice drew her back to the present. " 'And in nothing terrified by your adversaries: which is to them an evident token of perdition, but to you of salvation and that of God. For unto you it is given in the behalf of Christ, not only to believe on him, but also to suffer for his sake.' "

That last statement struck Lily. Was God calling her or any of these people to suffer here for the sake of Christ? Or should she and everyone else in the cove stop acting like fools and leave? Cal and Richard may not have found any sign of the Indians, but war parties were noted for hitting and running, attacking anywhere, anytime, at will. Any day they could all be killed. Had Robby's death furthered the kingdom of God?

She folded her arms. She would stay two more days, no more. Long enough for Bob to get here and Robby to be laid to rest. And should John return with Bob, she prayed he'd allow the boys to leave with her. She couldn't pray for anything more than that. . .not even for John.

No matter what else occupied her thoughts, they always came back to her desire for John Waldon, her dearest friend's husband. Most likely that was why she had yet to receive assurance from the Lord regarding Jackson's proposal of marriage. She'd left the poor young man dangling.

~~~~~~~

The sight of the half-moon-shaped fort came as a relief to John after the long, hard march from Tolihaio Gap. His feet felt raw and could use a few days' rest within the safety of those stone walls.

Again, as during the last ranging, all the moccasin tracks not washed away by the recent rains were days or weeks old. And all pointed eastward. The Indians always managed to slip past the patrols. John wrapped his knitted scarf tighter against the cold breeze. Would they *never* leave for the winter?

Walking a few feet from him as their roving party crossed the clearing in a wide spread, Pat gestured with his head. "Ain't that Jackson Dunlap comin' this way?" He immediately raced toward Dunlap, spurring John and Bob to follow suit. By the time they converged, John had imagined all manner of horrors. Had his family left, like he'd asked them to? Or had they stayed, been murdered, or carried off?

Pat grabbed hold of Jackson. "What happened, son? Is it my family?"

Jackson's terrible gaze slid past Pat and John, stopping at Bob.

Bob latched on to John's arm.

"It's Robby," Jackson blurted. "He's been killed. Indians."

John felt a surge of relief that it hadn't been Lily or the boys. *May God forgive me.*

"No. Please, God. No." Bob would have collapsed in grief had John and Pat not been supporting him. "I should'a stayed home." He shook his head over and over as they turned and headed back to the fort, bringing him along. "Edith's been wantin' me an' him to trade places, an' I was gonna do it. I was. A couple a more weeks, an' he would'a been here. Safe. This fort ain't once been attacked. I'd a had them make him a cook's helper or somethin' that would keep him inside. Oh, Robby, Robby." He rambled on in a flat tone the entire way back to the fort.

As they neared the gates, Toby Dunlap came out and strode up to Bob. "We're all real sorry. Just want you to know your boy weren't no coward. He shot one of them murderers before they got him."

While Toby administered comforting thumps on the grieving man's back, John sidled over to Jackson. "I need to know, lad. Are Lily and my boys still at the cove?"

He nodded. "Aye. But they're fine. All the families have been stayin' at your place for weeks. Us men took the Injuns by surprise whilst they was torchin' the old Thornton place."

"Was my pa with you?" Pat asked, leaving Bob with Toby.

"An' your Michael. We was at our place boilin' down sorghum cane."

John's breath caught. "What about my sons?"

"They was there, too. You got a real steady boy, in Matt. He shot and loaded that musket of his 'most as good as the rest of us."

John's head almost exploded with rage. His little twelve-year-old son, having to fight off Indians like a man! "I'm going home with you. And I dare Captain Busse to try and stop me this time."

Chapter 32

At the bend in the river, the silhouette of Harris's stockade and the ferry dock came as a welcome sight after a grueling day's ride from Fort Henry. The sun had set some time ago, and John had wondered if he and the others would make it there before dark.

Harris's Ferry—where before the hostilities, John had brought his wheat and corn to be ground into flour and meal, where he'd brought hardwood logs to be cut into boards for furniture. Harris's Ferry, now better known as Harris's Fort, had a stockade surrounding the store, the smithy, and cabins. The settlement's promising future as well as his own had been hanging in the balance for more than two years.

Riding ahead of him, Bob hollered over his shoulder. "Let's keep goin'. We could be home well before midnight."

"Bob." Toby emitted a weary sigh and reined his mount past John's. "The horses are tired, and we'd be goin' through the woods at night. The trace to the cove ain't marked that good."

Jackson came alongside John and called out, "We'll get an early start, Bob. Be home by midmornin.'"

The grieving father clamped his lips shut in resignation.

Once inside the gates and safe for the night, the full force of exhaustion settled into John's aching body. He'd had too many hard days in a row, and tomorrow would be worse yet.

After tending their horses and begging a supper of pork-flavored beans and fried potatoes from the militia cook, John and his three companions trudged to the blockhouse. There they laid out their bedrolls in a corner unused by the other militiamen. John noticed Toby looked as worn down as he felt himself. Hours of steady riding had taken its toll on the older man.

They eased down to the dirt floor and were starting to get comfortable when Bob regained his feet "It's stuffy in here. I'm gonna eat outside."

"The place does reek with the perfume of sweat and dirty stockings, that's for sure," Jackson quipped. They were the first lighthearted words he'd spoken since he and his father had delivered the bad news.

As Bob sauntered out, Toby lumbered up. "I better go with him. Don't want him getting no fool notions in his head—like takin' off without us." He followed his neighbor.

John watched after his friends, then, sitting cross-legged with the meal before him, he looked at Jackson. "Let's ask the blessing over the food." He bowed his head. "Father in heaven, thank You for the meal You've provided. Thank You that we reached here safely today. But mostly I want to thank You for good neighbors, men like Toby and Jackson Dunlap, who left their own family to Your safekeeping to come and fetch Bob. I pray You'll give Toby the words Bob needs most to hear. In Jesus' name. Amen."

John had barely dug into his food, when he became conscious of Jackson's gaze darting to him. The lad had something on his mind. "What is it, Jackson? What haven't you told us? Did something else happen we should know about?"

"In a manner of speakin.'"

John hoped none of his family had been injured.

"Me an' Robby both asked Lily to marry up with us."

John sat up straighter. The news came as no real surprise, since both young men had been eager for her hand. Still. . . "At the same time?"

" 'Course not." Jackson set down his spoon. "I asked her first; then the next day Robby did."

John maintained a placid expression, but this was tough to hear. "And?"

"She give us both the same answer. Said we all was supposed to pray about it. See who God wanted her to wed. And terrible as it is. . ." He glanced out the door, which had been left ajar. "Looks like God did answer. I guess what I'm sayin', sir, is I'd be plumb pleased if you'd give your blessin'."

My blessing? John swallowed. He'd been wanting Lily for himself for months, even—God forgive him—before his wife passed away. And Jackson wanted his blessing as if he were Lily's father!

He swallowed again around his tightening throat. "I can't do that, son. I need to speak to her first, learn what's in her heart. She's a free woman now. She doesn't need my blessing." He took a healthy gulp of tea.

"She's always spoke real highly of you. Your blessin' would mean a lot." Jackson leaned forward, a nearby lantern reflecting the youthful eagerness in his dark eyes. "An' I want you to know I'd take real good care of her, buy her fancies an' such. I'd never lay a hand to her. I don't cotton to a man bullyin' a woman. 'Specially someone as sweet an' purty as her. When I joined the militia, all I thought about was goin' on a big adventure. But now all I want is to go home an' make a good life for her an' me."

The lad continued to stare at him, and John knew he ought to say something. "Going home, living our lives in peace again. . .that's what we all want." He reached over and patted Jackson's knee. "Eat up so we can get some sleep. We're going home in the morning." But sleep would likely be the last thing John would be able to do.

With so many people crowded into the house since Edith had barricaded herself in the carpentry shop, the only peace one could get was before dawn. Lily sat quietly sipping her tea in a dining chair pulled close to the hearth while a number of MacBride and Randall children slept at the opposite end of the room.

She felt blessed to have Maggie MacBride and Millie Dunlap beside her. They were two of her favorite friends in the cove. She leaned toward them to whisper. "I expected the men to return last night. I woke at every little sound."

Millie's lips curved with a reassuring smile. "Only if Bob was at the fort and not out ranging when Toby and Jackson got there."

No one mentioned the always obvious possibility, *if* they made it.

Lily shifted her gaze back to the dancing flames. What if Bob was at the fort and John was not? The men wouldn't—couldn't—wait for him to return. John might not be with them. Her chest banded tight at the thought. She needed him here, now, more than ever.

"I pray the men come today," Maggie said quietly. "I don't think Edith will come out of that workshop till Bob gets here. I knew her takin' care of eight young'uns and a farm all by herself was getting the best of her. And with the ever'day threat of Injun attack. . ."

Millie darted a glance behind her at the slumbering children. "She was startin' to say some purty crazy things. An' now this. It's just too much for a body to take."

Maggie nodded. "She's gonna need a lot of extra love an' care. An' prayer."

Lily agreed. "Mercy, but I do wish she'd come out."

One of the sleeping children coughed, and Lily glanced over at the youngster before finishing her tea. "It's starting to get light. I'll go see if the hens have laid any eggs." Stepping quietly to the door, she plucked her heavy cloak from a hook and walked out into an icy mist.

Duke and the other dogs on the porch stood up, their tails swishing back and forth.

Lily untied them so they could take care of their morning business. She wouldn't be passing the carpentry shop, but still her gaze drifted to the shadowy building across the yard. The interior was dark, and no smoke issued from the iron stove inside. Edith must be freezing after locking herself inside with no more than a thin blanket around her shoulders. Lily sent yet another prayer aloft for her friend. *She needs Your care now more than ever, Father. Please look after her. And Lord, where is that joy You promised? And where is John? Is he not coming?*

⁓

The sight of the Randall children laughing and wrestling and slinging pillows with the other kids in the loft lifted everyone's spirits. The youngsters needed a few carefree moments before the afternoon's funeral service.

"Let's get them young'uns fed." Agnes MacBride set a platter of johnnycakes on the table to go with the new supply of sorghum molasses, then raised her voice. "A couple of you lads run an' fetch the families from the blockhouse."

"I'll go." Her eldest son, Michael, untangled himself from two little ones and came to his feet.

"I'll go with you." Matt went to get his musket racked high on the wall along with several other weapons.

"Don't forget your coats." Lily's reminder came seconds too late. The door slammed behind them.

"Come an' get it," Maggie called out.

The words were scarcely out of her mouth before the children clambered down the ladder and ran to one of the long tables, pushing and shoving to crowd in.

Lily scooped up the toddler, Laurie, and placed the little one on the lap of one of the twins. A ruckus sounded outside.

The dogs charged off the porch in a mad scramble, all barking at once.

Lily shot a glance to Millie. "Could it be the men this early?" She and half the household rushed out to the porch.

But the dogs hadn't gone in the direction of the lane. They were racing out back to the orchard instead! A high-pitched yelp came from one of them. Then another!

"Run!" Ian nudged the nearest children into motion. "Make for the blockhouse! Fast as ye can!"

The rest of the kids leaped from the porch, the older ones carrying the youngest. Lily and the other adults and lads charged back into the cabin for their weapons. Lily uncorked her powder horn in a frenzy and sprinkled some into the flashpan, then unhooked the ramrod and shoved the already-loaded paper cartridge wad more firmly into the barrel.

Noting that the others were already out the door, she regretted having taken that extra time. Without a second to waste, she flew off the porch and raced for the blockhouse as fast as her legs would take her.

Chilling screams and war cries pierced the air. Ominously close. The Indians must have already reached the stable! She didn't dare chance a look back.

Coming to the bridge, she caught up to Eva, who hobbled awkwardly as she ran. Not slowing, Lily grabbed the elderly woman's arm and dragged her along.

Within seconds they were past the creek undergrowth and onto the blockhouse clearing. *Out in the open!*

Deafening explosions came from both directions.

A bullet whizzed past Lily's ear.

The Indians were close! Too close!

"Hurry!" someone yelled from the door. "Hurry!"

Gasping for breath, Lily pulled Eva inside the split-log door as two bullets slammed into it.

Ian shoved it closed, and Richard dropped the heavy bar into place.

Cal shook his head. "From the number of muskets bein' fired, there must be fifteen or twenty of 'em out there. This is no small raidin' party." He headed for the ladder behind Richard. "Gotta get up top, make sure the boys don't waste their powder."

Glancing wildly around, Lily realized her two weren't among the children present. They had to be up above, *getting shot at!*

Eva's knees gave way. She started sinking out of Lily's grasp.

Millie caught hold of the sagging woman's other arm. "Are you all right, Mama?" She and Cissy took her from Lily and eased her down onto a sack slumped against a wall. "Talk to me," Millie urged, stooping before her.

The old woman's lined face was beet red. She shooed them away with a trembling hand. "Let me. . .catch. . .my breath."

"*Mama!*" one of the Randall twins wailed. "*We forgot Mama!*" She flew to the door.

Her heart sinking, Lily remembered that Edith was still out in the carpentry shop.

"Somebody has to go get her." The twin clawed at the heavy door.

Lily had to stop her. "You can't go out there, dear. You'll get shot."

"But what about Mama?" Tears streamed down Gracie's freckled face.

Taking hold of Gracie's shoulders, Lily turned the girl to face her. "With all of us running for the blockhouse, I doubt the Indians even suspect she's there."

The girl stared openmouthed as Lily's statement sunk in. She sniffed. "That's right. They're shootin' at us."

Lily nodded and eased her hold. "I'm going up top to help out now." She turned toward the ladder.

"Lily! You're bleeding!" Gracie pointed at her.

"What?" She quickly scanned her body.

"The back of your arm."

Propping her weapon against the wall, Lily tugged her sleeve around. It did have blood on it. . .and now that Gracie mentioned it, her arm started to hurt a bit. "Must've grazed me. Find a rag to wrap around it, would you?"

As the girl wrapped her arm, Lily saw that most of the young children were crowded at the back, whining and sniffing. Ruth had three little ones in her arms, nuzzling them and speaking in soft, comforting tones.

Lily arched her brows in wonder. Odd, now that the danger was actually upon them, with weapons firing from above and bullets splintering wood, Ruth's hysterics had vanished and she was admirably calm.

Lily snatched up her musket and hurried up the ladder. Seeing Matt and Luke down on the floor with other boys their age, loading weapons for the men and older lads, she nearly bawled with relief. She hunkered below the line of fire and scurried to Cal, crouched with only his musket, his hair and eyes above the half wall. "Cal?" She tapped him on the shoulder.

He sunk below and turned to her.

She leaned close to his ear, so as not to worry his son Henry, who was loading for him. "Edith's still in the carpentry shop."

"I know." Regret clouded his light brown eyes. "There's nothin' we can do about it." For a grim second or two longer, his gaze remained on Lily. Then he turned back.

Lily glanced around, counting more shooters than loaders. She dropped down beside Cal's son Sam as he rammed a shot and traded him her loaded musket for his. At fourteen, he was too young to be standing off a war party, but she knew the male in him would never allow her to swap places.

As she finished preparing Sam's musket, bullets flew across the watchtower from all directions. The blockhouse was surrounded! And no one had gone for help!

Sam fired and exchanged his spent weapon for the one Lily had finished preparing.

His father turned to him. "Did you get one of 'em?"

"I don't know for sure, Pa."

"Don't waste powder. Take sure shots."

Lily wondered if they had enough gunpowder to hold off the Indians.

Shortly, the shots coming from the war party within cover of the woods slowed to one or two every twenty or thirty seconds. They, too, were being frugal.

Across the deck, Richard tipped his head at Lily. "Don't appear as if they're gonna rush us, at least."

Cal gave a huff. "They'd be fools. They know they can bide their time. With no one knowin' we're bein attacked, they could hang around out there for days, till we run clean outta powder and food."

Ian looked from one to the other and back. "In the last couple months, we've killed seven of 'em. They're probably here for revenge."

Donald Randall hiked his chin. "Well, my pa's comin'. He'll know what to do—iff'n he don't ride into a trap."

And John? Now Lily didn't know whether or not to hope he was with the others. It was too much. All she wanted to do was cry, but she had to stay strong.

"Smoke!" Calvin raised up higher and pointed with his musket.

A shot whistled past him and he ducked.

Lily had to know. As she inched up cautiously and peeked over the edge, a bullet punched into the half-wall just below her. She hunkered back down. But she'd seen the evidence of destruction.

"It's comin' from the stable." Twelve-year-old Pete Dunlap's high-pitched voice rang out. "An' the loft's chock full of hay."

Lily stiffened. Her milk cow, Daisy, was still in there! And those savages would burn the other buildings as well.

And Edith!

Chapter 33

A thick wall of smoke roiled up beyond the trees lining the creek, eliminating all doubt. The Indians had set the buildings ablaze. Lily hadn't heard Edith screaming, but then with all the other noise and confusion. . .

Ian sat with Donald, holding the young man close as choking sobs wracked his body. For all he knew, his mother had either been hauled out by the Indians for some unspeakable manner of horrendous torture, or she was being burned alive inside, and he could do nothing to save her. None of them could.

Tears streamed down Matt's and Luke's faces as they witnessed their friend's grief. Their muskets stretched idle across their laps. Everyone up here knew.

Lily no longer tried to contain her own tears. These people were her dearest friends in the world, and like everyone else, she felt devastated and helpless.

"Ian." Cal tapped the old man's shoulder and spoke quietly. "I'm startin' to see smoke comin' from your place."

"Figures." Ian had never looked so old as when he eyed Cal over the top of Donald's drooping head.

"Mine'll be next." Richard gave a bitter laugh. "To think I made Ruthie stay here—for this."

Just then, a flaming arrow buried itself into a roof post.

As Richard stretched up to dislodge the thing and toss it off, a bullet grazed his cheek. He swiped at the blood with the back of his hand then took hold of his musket again.

Donald rubbed his red eyes and jerked free of Ian's grasp. Picking up his weapon, he slid the barrel across the railing. Mourning for his mother would have to wait.

John had expected to reach Beaver Cove earlier this morning. But a mile outside of Harris's Fort Bob's horse went lame, necessitating a return to the fort for a fresh mount. The weak sun would reach its zenith within the hour, but the day had yet to warm, and mist still dripped from the trees.

Anticipating a blazing hearth and a hot meal, he pulled off his tricorn and dumped the trapped water. The densely wooded trail had started to look familiar a few minutes back. He recognized the old lightning-struck oak and a small stream they'd crossed that fed into Beaver Creek. They'd reach Cal's place soon.

"You guys smell that?" Toby straightened in his saddle. "Smoke."

"We're getting close to home." Bob nudged his mount to a faster pace.

The Patterson clearing still lay some distance ahead when John's nerves bristled. The acrid smell floating toward them was too strong to be from a fireplace. Sounds of crackling and snapping grew louder by the second. Breaking out into the open, the evidence hit them full force. Every structure had been afire for some time. Roofs had already collapsed, and the slower-burning log walls smoldered black. The sight made him want to retch.

Gawking in shock, the others pulled out their weapons. But as they rode cautiously in, they could tell the Indians were long gone. Savages never lingered to revel in their destruction, just torched things and left as quickly as they'd come.

Toby reined alongside John. "Thank God, Cal and his family are at your place."

Bob spoke up, his tone raw with hatred. "There's more smoke to the south. They must'a got my place, too." He jammed his heels into his horse's flanks. "Come on."

With two miles separating the Patterson place from his own farmstead, John knew that even riding the animals hard, they wouldn't get to the blockhouse for twenty minutes, maybe thirty.

All too soon, they saw smoke coming from across the creek at Toby Dunlap's farm. John wondered why Richard and Cal let their property burn without running the savages off as they'd done before.

The group scarcely even slowed when they passed the smoldering, charred ruins of Bob Randall's place. From the meadow, the clear sky revealed a dense cloud filling the horizon to the south. Breathing came harder, and even the horses had to be urged onward. Had the Indians burned out the entire cove? The blockhouse?

It took all of John's better instincts not to charge full speed into the melee. He kneed his mount to the front and caught the reins of Bob's horse, pulling them to a stop, then turned to the others. "This has to be a larger war party. Let's not just ride in there like a bunch of idiots without a plan of attack."

A gunshot sounded from the south.

From the direction of the blockhouse.

⸺

Two more flaming arrows slammed into the roof.

Lily knew the men couldn't reach them without getting shot. But if the roof burned, it would collapse and crash down into the interior. They'd all be burned alive. Like Edith.

"Water!" Cal shouted. "Get buckets of water up here quick!"

Ignoring her aching arm, Lily scrambled to the ladder even as flames licked greedily at the top, spreading fast. "Water! We need water. Now!"

Another shot echoed through the woods.

The gunfire gave John a boost of hope. If someone was shooting, the blockhouse must still be standing. "Men, let's come up on the Indians from behind. Spread out. Make them think there are a lot more of us than there are. When we spot the devils, shoot your muskets, yell, and move before firing your pistols."

Jackson snorted. "An' chase the horses toward 'em to make more noise. Them savages'll think they're surrounded. They don't like fightin' if they don't got the upper hand."

Rage sharpened John's fear as he edged into position. If Lily had taken the boys away when he'd asked, he wouldn't be in such knots. He could wring her pretty neck for this.

Father God, You know I don't mean that. Keep them safe. Keep them all safe.

A feather bobbed up above the brush, moving stealthily. John moved from behind a tree to get a clear shot.

Jackson, further down, fired his weapon and gave a wild shout.

The Indian John had spotted sprang up.

John fired and hit his mark, and the painted savage crashed into some brambles.

Toby, at the rear, yelled and whipped the horses forward.

John hollered and moved as the enemy shot in his direction. Spotting the musket flash, he ripped his pistol from his belt and fired, then gave a wild yell and rolled away. He needed fifteen seconds to reload his musket and another five for his pistol.

A bullet crashed into a tree close to where he'd been seconds ago.

While he reloaded, a chilling scream followed another shot. Jackson had the best war cry.

The lad's fire was returned from two separate sources.

A musket report sounded from John's other side. Most likely Bob. Everyone knew not to shoot at once and give the enemy time to reload and charge them.

Weapon loaded, John crawled forward, passing the Indian he'd shot, sprawled facedown across a stickery bush.

A few yards ahead, another brave broke out of the undergrowth and ran off.

John fired. Missed.

The warrior never stopped. As three others popped up and sprinted after him, John berated himself for not having loaded his pistol, too.

Someone else shot at the fleeing savages and missed, but at least the marauders were on the run.

John gave a victory yell then crawled behind a tree and reloaded both weapons. He could still hear distant shots coming from the far side of the blockhouse clearing.

Crouching low, he hurried toward the building, gasping in shock when he saw flames licking up from the roof of the watchtower.

Toby came alongside. "God protect them!" he shouted and started forward.

John grabbed his pal's leg and yanked him back. "We have to stop the redskins on the other side first."

"Look!" Toby pointed. "I saw water bein' throwed on that fire. Our people are still up there."

A shot fired from the blockhouse.

An Indian fell into the clearing.

"Come on. We gotta scare those devils off." Skirting the cleared section, John led the way through the woods. Halfway around, he spotted a torch, the source of the flaming arrows. He fired.

It crashed to the ground, along with the warrior.

Another of John's comrades fired and hollered. John yelled with the others.

In a flurry of feathers and painted bodies, a dozen braves exposed themselves and raced to the west after the others. They were leaving at last!

John emptied his pistol at them then charged out of the trees toward the blockhouse, yelling and waving his musket overhead.

The structure's charred, sagging roof creaked and splintered then came crashing down. *Were the boys up there? And Lily?*

He had to get there before the fire reached below. Let everyone know it was safe. "Come out! Come out!"

He heard Bob and Jackson shouting as they emerged into the clearing. If only someone inside would hear them. Open the door.

Reaching the building, John banged on the door with the butt of his pistol. "Open up! It's safe! We're here!"

Screaming and crying erupted inside, and he heard the bar being raised. *Please let my family be there!*

Another section of the roof crashed down in flames.

The heavy door scraped inward. Frantic, John gave it a mighty shove, and people rushed out, crying and laughing.

Luke grabbed hold of him. Then Matt. He hauled them close. His boys were unharmed. *Thank You, God. Thank You. Thank You.*

But— John's heart pounded double-time. "Where's Lily? Is she all right?"

Matt lifted his head from John's shoulder. "Inside."

Why hadn't she come out? Didn't she know the roof was about to. . . ? Shoving his sons aside, John charged inside, where smoke was already drifting down through the cracks and filling the interior.

Then he saw her, kneeling with Cal beside a prone body.

Ian! The old man was conscious, but blood was staining the wad of cloth Lily pressed to his shoulder. Intent on her task, she had yet to look up.

"We had to drag him down the ladder," Cal explained.

John glanced up the length of the steps, where flames licked through a splintered board across the ladder hole. Reaching down, he took hold of Ian's arm. "Help me, Cal. We've got to get him out of here."

Lily's head jerked around. Her gaze met John's and held. She continued to press on Ian's wound while the men dragged him outside a safe distance away from the blockhouse. That's when John noticed the bandage on her arm. She'd been hurt, too.

As he and Cal gently laid Ian down, Maggie and Agnes dropped to their knees beside the old man, taking over from Lily.

"Isna' bad," the Scot assured his wife and daughter-in-law, but the strain on his face belied his brave words.

Neighbors crowded close, talking and crying and laughing at once.

"Can't abide gawkin'," Ian said, wincing with pain. "Get the supplies outta the blockhouse b'fore they burn up."

As John took a step back, Jackson caught Lily—*his* Lily—away. The young man whisked her off the ground and hugged her to him.

Lily's wild gaze flew to John.

He didn't know if she was shocked by Jackson's aggression or was embarrassed that he'd seen her and Jackson together in such a familiar way. Fists clenching, he started toward them.

"Where's Edith?" Emerging from the blockhouse with a sack of grain over his shoulder, Bob searched frantically around. "Where's my wife?"

Edith! Lily pushed away from Jackson. "Let me down. Please. I need to go to Bob."

"He already knows about Robby." Frowning, Jackson lowered her to the ground.

"But not about Edith." She scanned the crowd for him.

Several neighbors had crowded around Ian. Ruth was tending the slash across Richard's cheek. Donald and Bob's other children stood frozen in place, wide-eyed as they stared at their father. Bob's gaze searched the area.

Lily hurried to John and took hold of his knotted fist. "Please, John. Bob's going to need you now."

His hand relaxed, and he wove his fingers through hers as she led him to his friend.

"Where's Edith?" Bob asked again.

Lily placed a hand on his shoulder and prayed for the right words. "I'm. . .so sorry, Bob. Edith locked herself in the carpentry shop with

Robby's casket and wouldn't come out for anyone. We need to go and see. . . ." Unable to finish, she bit her lip.

"*What?*" Bob wrenched away from John and latched on to Lily, his fingers digging into her arms. She flinched in pain. "*You left her to the Indians?*"

"The war party came on us all at once. We had to run for our lives. It wasn't until we were in the blockhouse being shot at that we realized she wasn't with us. Believe me, there are no words to describe how terribly helpless we all felt. I'm sorry. So very sorry."

John unfurled his friend's fingers from Lily's arms and took him in a firm hold. "Let's go across and find out what happened to her. The Indians might have dragged her away with them."

"Aye." Reason began to take hold. "Aye." The man dashed madly toward the bridge with John right behind him.

Although she dreaded what they were certain to find, Lily picked up her skirts and followed, uncaring that her arm burned and ached. She was more concerned about Bob and what he would have to face. She barely noticed that Donald, Matt, and Luke caught up with her.

On the other side of the creek, Lily saw that the springhouse and smokehouse, tucked in the trees near the creek, were untouched. Likely the Indians were saving them until they had time to empty the food stores. Climbing the rise, she passed the hog pen and noticed only one hog lay dead. The other three grown ones and their spring babies were still alive. The stable and corncrib, however, were nothing but charred jumbles. And just beyond. . .

Lily stopped in her tracks.

The carpentry shop still stood! Nearby, the roof of the cabin had burned and crashed in, and the interior still smoldered. But the shop appeared to be untouched!

Bob reached the structure and pounded on the door. "Edith! Edith! Are you in there?" He swung his musket up, butt first, and used it to bang harder.

Miracle of miracles, the door swung open. And there stood Edith, haggard and weary, her hair unbound and tangled.

Her husband gaped at her for a second, then pulled her into an embrace, kissing her and murmuring over and over in her ear. "I'll never leave you again. Never. I promise."

Lily stared at the couple in wonder, so overwhelmed by God's mercy, she broke into sobs.

John immediately enfolded her trembling body within his warm, strong arms.

She clung to him, weeping, until at last she was able to regain control of herself. As Matt and Luke moved in to hug her, too, her heart ached with joy.

When her shuddering breaths eased into more natural breathing, John held her away and searched deep into her eyes. "Now, tell me. Why on earth didn't you take the boys and leave here when I asked you to?"

Lily moistened her lips and swiped at her tears, then lowered her lashes. What could she say?

Chapter 34

John's gaze pierced Lily's soul as he stared at her, his features hard as granite. "How many times did I ask you, *implore* you, to leave Beaver Cove? Look around you, Lily. Everything you risked your life for, the lives of my sons for, it's nothing but ashes."

She had no words to speak in her defense. John had every right to be furious. With nothing to say for herself, her attention shifted to his youngest son. "Luke, run back to the blockhouse and spread the word that Edith is fine. There's a good lad."

"Yes, ma'am!" The boy trotted off, happy to be the bearer of good news on this tense day.

Reluctantly, Lily raised her lashes and peered up again at John. She opened her mouth to speak, but Matthew cut in.

"It ain't all her fault, Pa. The families had already decided to stay together in one place, to keep safe. Besides, you know it was me that refused to go anywhere."

His father pressed his lips together in a grim line.

Lily could tell he wasn't ready to forgive her. She was the one in charge. She should have compelled the boys to go away with her.

John's voice held a husky quality when he responded to Matt. "You two have no idea how I felt when we got to the valley and saw all the farmsteads on fire. I was so afraid I'd lost you, I could hardly breathe."

"We know how that feels." Matt raised his chin. "We watched our place burn up while we was trapped in the blockhouse. And we was sure Mrs. Randall was bein' burned alive—or worse."

Reminded that Bob and Edith stood but an arm's length away, Lily turned to them. "Edith, dear, I have to ask by what miracle you were saved?"

Edith, composed now, but dispirited, snuggled close to her husband and tried to smile. "Them savages was in such a hurry to get in on the turkey shoot over to the blockhouse, they just broke out a window here an' tossed in a couple of torches then took off. They didn't have an inklin' I was inside. I up an' threw them fire sticks right back out. That's them layin' over yonder." She pointed at two blackened lines marring the ground. "I was so worried for y'all, I never stopped prayin'."

Lily shook her head in wonder. "We never stopped praying for you, either." Moving to her friend's side, she took Edith's hands in hers—the woman who only this morning had been so beside herself with grief that she wouldn't leave her son's coffin.

"Bob tells me all my other young'uns are fine. That so?"

"Luke went to fetch them. Any minute now you'll be able to see for yourself." Sensing John's presence behind her, Lily bit down on the inside corner of her lip as he put his hand on her shoulder.

"What about you? Your arm, I mean."

For the few moments when she'd first caught a glimpse of him and then had to deal with his anger, she'd put thoughts of pain aside. But now it returned with all its biting and burning furor. Still, gazing into his eyes, she saw only concern in the blue depths, and it strengthened her. She ignored the discomfort, knowing the injury would be taken care of soon enough. " 'Tis a bit of a slice, I believe. I didn't even realize I'd been hit till I reached the blockhouse."

Matt chuckled and shook his head. "You should'a seen Lily come racin' in, draggin' poor ol' Eva behind her." Suddenly he grew serious as he searched past her with a frown. "Duke! Duke! Come, boy!" Waiting a second or two, he ran off whistling in the direction the dogs had gone earlier.

Lily looked back at John. "The dogs charged out to the orchard this morning, barking for all they're worth. They warned us in time, but we haven't seen them since. I'm afraid the Indians might have killed them."

John let out a resigned breath. "Guess I'd better go after Matt, then." Turning, he loped past their gutted, blackened house after his boy.

Lily couldn't help but appraise the destruction around her. Years of work she and John had put in, and so little had been spared. Whatever would he do now? What would any of them do?

John strode back from the orchard with his arm about Matt's drooping shoulders. It seemed for every moment of joy, there was another of sadness. All three dogs lay dead, their bodies slashed by tomahawks and their throats cut. But Matt hadn't shed a tear. He set his jaw, his face hard with hatred.

Passing the unburned chicken coop, John wondered if the chickens would return to it this evening, considering the burnt stench coming from both sides—the stable across the barnyard and the house. He heaved a shuddering sigh. Hundreds of hours of labor gone in a morning.

The door to the root cellar near the smoldering log house remained intact. "Wait here. I want to check that out." He unlatched the door and swung it to the side, then climbed down the steep stairs into the shadowy, cave-like structure. His brows hiked at the sight of more canvas and jute sacks brimming with stores of fruits and vegetables than he'd ever seen it hold before.

"A lot of other families put their food down there, too," Matt called from above. "You should'a seen our hayloft. That's why the stable burned so fast. All that dry hay stuffed in. We been keepin' a lotta extra livestock here."

As John climbed back up, shouting and laughter reached him from out front.

Matt's sober face softened with a little smile. "Must be the Randall bunch. God gave 'em a miracle, for sure."

Rounding the corner of the rubble, John saw Bob's kids running pell-mell toward their mother. His gaze landed on Lily, who stepped away from the enthusiastic mob and started toward him. She looked from him to Matt and back, but said nothing.

"The dogs didn't make it," John said quietly.

Lily's eyes, soft with love, drifted to Matt. She reached out and brushed the hair from his brow. "Duke was a great dog, a true hero. He sacrificed his life to save us."

The boy's chin began to tremble, and he nodded. "He was the best." He sniffed. "Think folks'd mind if we buried him up on the rise beside Mama?"

She turned her beautiful, questioning eyes up to John.

"Why should anyone mind?" he asked.

"Yesterday the lads dug a grave for Robby up there. Ian also mentioned building a church on the hill after the trouble is over—providing you approve, of course."

John wasn't entirely certain he wanted to donate a patch of his hard-earned land to anyone. He tipped his head at Lily. "What do you think? That's quite a bit of property. Covers at least two or three acres."

She shrugged. "It could be used for a schoolhouse later, too. Think how handy that would be."

John couldn't help wishing she'd have said the church and school would be handy for *us,* but she was not his. Disappointment pulsed through him. He angled his head in thought. "Since we've been here, cash money has been so tight, I haven't been giving a tithe to the church, just helping folks out where the need happened to be. I suppose this could be my tithe."

A wistful smile spread across her lips. "I like the sound of that. A thank-you to the Almighty for saving us all here this day."

Standing before him with her golden hair every whichway, her day gown smudged and torn, and her delicate face streaked with dirt, Lily had never looked more beautiful. Drinking in the sight of the silver-eyed angel who had spent years of her own life caring for his loved ones, John gave a thoughtful nod. "Speaking of money, I haven't forgotten I've owed you two pounds since your indenturement contract ended. And extra, since you've stayed on since then to look after the boys."

Lily reached out a hand, then retracted it. "No. You're going to need every pence you have to rebuild. Mariah and my father sent me money from time to time during the last four years. I've more than enough already."

"But didn't it just burn with the house? The paper, the coins, they're probably melted into the rubble."

Her lips quirked into a half-smile. "Actually, with so many families living here, children running about and getting into things, I thought it best to bury it. My pouch is down in the cellar."

John realized that Lily could have bought back her papers and left Beaver Cove years ago, had she wanted to. Yet she'd stayed all that time. Hope came to life. Then he reminded himself it was for Susan and the children, not him. Even were he bold enough to ask her to marry him, how would she react to his betrayal of his wife's memory so soon? And what would the rest of the people of the cove think of him?

Looking over her shoulder, John spotted Jackson striding their way. His brash, young neighbor seemed certain Lily would marry him. If that were so, how would John deal with her living so close, knowing she could never be his?

"There you are, Lily." Jackson stopped behind her and straightened his shoulders, his expression rife with confidence.

She turned toward him. "Why, yes. Your timing couldn't be more perfect. The children are positively starved. We hadn't even had breakfast before the attack. Would you mind bringing up a ham from the smokehouse?"

"Uh. . .sure." He opened his mouth to say more, then clamped it shut and hastened off to do as she asked.

"Fast thinkin', Lily." Matt winked.

When she turned back to him and his son, John noticed a delicate tinge rise on her cheeks as she smiled at them. "Well, don't make a liar of me, Matthew. Run down to the cellar and bring up a dozen potatoes and a couple of those large squashes. And, John, would you see if you can salvage any pots and skillets from the hearth without getting burned in the process? Oh, and may I borrow your knife?"

"As you wish." He handed her his hunting knife and started around the smoldering remains of the kitchen, amazed at how his sweet, shy Lily had taken charge. With no effort at all, she'd dispatched all three of them to do her bidding. Another thought teased his consciousness. Considering Matt's remark, perhaps she wasn't quite as spoken for as Jackson Dunlap had led him to believe.

Surveying the confusion around him, John saw Ian's friends assisting the old man across the creek. His wound had been cauterized to stop the bleeding, and his wife had fashioned a sling for him. Maggie wasted no time getting her injured husband settled on a chair someone brought out from the workshop.

As aromas began wafting on the air from food cooking on open fires, Ian's wife insisted on seeing to Lily's arm. "Don't want no infection startin' in, you know," she said, clucking her tongue as she assessed the injury.

The older kids entertained the little ones near the well, and John gathered with the other men around Ian to plan the next move. He squatted down with Bob, his closest friend.

Richard Shaw still held a cloth to his cheek. He glanced at his friends and shrugged. "Still seepin' a bit. It'll stop soon 'nough."

"I believe the poker those wee womenfolk used on my shoulder's still hot." Ian's chuckle turned into a groan. Despite his pasty look, the Scot never lost his humor.

"Think I'll pass, if ya don't mind." Richard gave a one-sided grin.

"Wouldn't wanna scar up this purty face any more'n I have to."

"I don't think those savages'll tangle with the likes of us again anytime soon," Toby Dunlap said. "But what with winter breathin' down our necks, I don't see we have much choice but to send the women downriver to whatever family or friends'll take 'em in for a spell. Meanwhile, me an' Jackson'll stay here with our livestock an' get our place built back up."

"So ye plan on stayin'," Ian said thoughtfully. "I'd be obliged if ye'd look after our animals. With Pat still up at the fort an' me winged, we'll have to leave here for a while. Leastwise, till I'm fit again."

Cal met his gaze. "Would you mind takin' Nancy an' my young'uns down to Baltimore with you, Ian? I'll be stayin' here, too, with my oldest boy."

Bob kneaded his beard and focused his hazel eyes on John. "What d'ya say, my friend? You game? We could turn that workshop of yours into a barrack till we get some roofs up."

"You men really want to start all over?" John looked from one to another.

Bob shrugged. "I ain't got nothin' to go back to anyplace else. Took all I had to buy my piece of land here an' bring in my family. Donald'll stay with me, won't you lad?" He gave his second son, crouched on his other side, a hug.

"We built our places up from scratch the first time," Cal added. "Nothin' says we can't do it again. Fact is, it should be easier this time. Our fireplaces should still be good. An' think of all the clearin' an' fencin' we already done."

Richard eyed them with a bit of hesitance. "If we had some real assurance the redskins wouldn't be back, I'd stay around. I'm not sure I'll be able to convince Ruthie to come back till it's safe, otherwise."

John glanced over his shoulder at the women busily cooking over what were normally the washtub fires. Several of them, Lily included, slanted inquisitive glances his way. If he agreed to stay, he and the boys would be separated from her again. No, it would be just him and the children this time. Lily would be returning to her own family.

Disheartened, he turned his attention to the men grouped around him. "I'll stay. Me and my boys—if they want to. I came here to provide them with a future, and I intend to see it through."

"You mean you're gonna send all the womenfolk away?" Young Donald shot a plaintive look at Cissy Dunlap.

John started to smile. Then he saw Jackson lean past Richard to get a gander at Lily.

The young man rose to his feet. "If everything's settled, I'll—"

"It's not." John blurted out the words. He waited, watching until Jackson crouched down again. "There's still the matter of the rafts we'll need to build for transporting the women and children, to say nothing of supplies. They'll need as much as we can spare. We can build cabin shelters on the rafts and hire river men to take them from the mouth down the Susquehanna."

Toby nodded, his face set with determination. "Let's get started right after we eat. Shouldn't take more'n a day or two. I'm sure there must be wood we can salvage at the MacBride place."

"So, is that it?" Jackson stood up again. Without waiting for a response, he made a beeline straight for Lily.

Chapter 35

"Who do you think should say the words over our sweet Robby?" Agnes bent over a skillet to flip a sizzling ham slice, the steam adding roses to her cheeks. "Ian shouldn't have to climb that hill, wounded like he is."

Lily only heard her friend's comments on the edge of her consciousness as she tended another slice of meat. Jackson was heading straight for her.

Millie straightened, a stir spoon in her plump hand. "Toby's the next oldest here. I'll speak to him about it."

Edith, quiet once more, with her hair curls neatly brushed, moved closer to Millie and gave her a self-conscious hug. "I—I'm plumb sorry I went so crazy there for a spell. I just couldn't—"

As if he'd overheard and didn't want to intrude, Jackson stopped in his tracks.

Millie returned her friend's embrace with loving pats on the back. "We were grievin' right along with you. Now we're tickled to have you back. We were all prayin' for you."

Agnes stepped away from the fire, sincerity in her hazel eyes. "God answered our most fervent prayers. I shan't ever doubt Him again."

Lily knew she'd have to face Jackson any second, and though the answer to her friends' prayers had been obvious, Lily had yet to receive the direction she sought from God. The only thing she felt was dread every time she had to deal with Jackson, and now he was upon her again.

His glance swept the group, then focused on Lily. "Can I have a word with you?"

Mille gave her a nod. "Go ahead, dear. I'll watch your skillet."

"Thank you." Trying not to show her reluctance, she placed her spatula on one of the stones surrounding the fire pit with the reminder that Jackson's plump little mother was a sweet-natured woman no one would mind having for a mother-in-law.

Jackson led Lily away from the women at the cookfires, from the men still clustered at the woodshop, and away from the noisy children playing a game of drop the handkerchief. He steered her behind the tall hickory tree that had shaded many a Sabbath dinner last summer, then turned to her, his dark eyes intense.

She peered over her shoulder and caught John's steady gaze. What would he want her to say to Jackson?

"Lily." Jackson took her hands in his. "The men are gonna send all you women and young'uns away till we can get the cabins rebuilt. I can't wait no longer. I need your promise now. I need you to promise to return to me when I send for you."

Lord, what should I say? Please give me wisdom.

"I know your family'll try to persuade you to stay in Virginia with them. But like I said before, you belong here with us, with me. I know it, an' you know it." His grip tightened.

Be honest.

Had that come from God? How simple. . .yet somehow frightening. Lily eased her fingers from his and took a breath as she prayed for courage. Unsmiling, she looked him in the eye. "I'm afraid I cannot give you the answer you want, Jackson. I do not have the deep feelings for you that you profess to have for me. Nevertheless, I've honored your marriage proposal by praying for the Lord's leading, and He has not given me peace about making a commitment to you. You're a wonderful young man, and you deserve someone who can love you with her whole heart. That is not me. I am truly sorry to hurt you, but my answer must be no."

His demeanor hardened with confusion. "But I thought with Robby gone—"

"God never directed me to accept his proposal, either. And now the Lord is removing me from the cove altogether. Leaving here will be very hard for me. I shall miss all of you so very much."

He caught hold of her arm. "Then don't miss us. Marry me. I'll make you love me. Give me a chance."

Regarding him in silence, she stepped out of his grasp. "I must get back to work now."

As she turned away, Lily felt as if a huge weight had been lifted from her. She'd probably hurt Jackson, but he was young and would realize in time her refusal had been for the best. And even though it was inappropriate, she couldn't stop her lips from curling into a wondrous smile. The Lord had answered her. *Be honest.*

John felt deflated as he watched Lily return to the cookfires wearing a happy smile.

She'd only covered half the distance when Matt broke away from the children's game circle and ran to her. John would have given anything to do the same and run to her, tell her not to marry Jackson, to marry him instead. But that was not possible.

Matt gave Lily a quick hug then ran back to the game, all smiles himself.

A frown knitted John's brow. He could've sworn his son didn't want her to marry that young man any more than *he* did. Matt must have decided her returning to the cove at any price was better than having her go to her sister's and never come back.

His gaze remained on Lily as Millie walked up to the men seated in a circle. "How are you feelin', Ian?"

The older man glanced down at his sheathed arm. "Me shoulder's still burnin' some, an' I'm weak as an ol' dishrag. But I dunna' want ye to be frettin'. I'll be fit again in a few weeks, Lord willin'."

"You know you'll be in all our prayers." Millie rested a hand on the back of his chair. "The reason I asked is because we're fixin' to take Robby up the hill after noonin'. We don't think you should hustle up that grade whilst you're feelin' poorly. I was wonderin' if maybe Toby could say the words over the boy."

Toby's brown eyes flared wide, and his face went almost as pale as Ian's. "I ain't no good at that sort of thing." He rubbed his balding head.

John scanned the group. None of them appeared willing to take on the chore. The cove had always relied on Grampa Mac to oversee all things religious.

"John had hisself a lot more schoolin' than the rest of us," Toby hedged. "He could read the words without stumblin' over 'em."

All eyes turned to him.

He felt panic begin to rise.

Bob's gaze was the most beseeching. "I'd be much obliged if you'd say the words over my son."

How could he let his best friend down? John smiled and nodded. "I've got my New Testament in my saddlebag. Maybe Ian will show me the passage to read."

"Don't mind a'tall, laddie."

"Well then, I'll go see if I can catch my horse." John stood to his feet.

"They all wandered in awhile ago," Cal said. "I had my boys put 'em in the pasture an' unsaddle 'em. Your gear should be hangin' over the fence."

"Thanks."

John left the men and started across the barnyard toward the pasture. On his way, he noticed Jackson striding fast for the creek, his head sagging. He didn't look like a man who'd just had his marriage proposal accepted.

Matt, still grinning from ear to ear, came running. "Where you off to, Pa?"

"Going after my Bible. For the funeral service."

The lad's smile faded. "I forgot about that. I sure am glad Lily ain't gonna marry up with that Jackson."

John slowed. "She told you that?" He let go of the breath he held.

"Yep. Now she won't haf'ta leave us."

Reining in his foolish joy, John wrapped an arm around his son. "Walk with me to the fence. We need to talk."

Once they reached his saddlebag and John removed the New Testament, he turned to Matt. "Son, the other men and I have decided it's best to send the women and children downriver while we rebuild. You're welcome to stay and help out, or you can go with them. But this you must understand. When Lily leaves here, the only logical place for her will be with her family. And once she reaches her sister Mariah's and gets some much-deserved pampering, I doubt she'll want to give up the luxuries of plantation life to come back to the hardships here. She's a lovely young woman, and she deserves the best."

"But she loves us."

John averted his gaze across the heat waves rising up from the stable, to where Lily was busy spreading out blankets from the blockhouse for sitting. So much of her hair had worked loose of its pins, she'd finally allowed it to hang free. The silky waves shimmered like molten gold in the sunlight with her movements. He had to will his eyes from the glorious sight. "Yes, she does. She loves you children very much." He laid a hand on Matt's shoulder. "And if you love her as much as you say you do, you should think about her and what's best for her." *As I am trying to do.*

Matt jerked away, his jaw set. "*We* are what's best for her. If you were around more, you'd know that." He wheeled away, leaving John gaping after him.

Obviously, Lily's leaving would be as hard on the boys as it was for him. With a defeated sigh, he started back to Ian. First things first. Right now he had a funeral service to prepare.

As John neared Ian, he saw the women in the distance handing the children whatever containers for food they could scrounge and sending them to the blankets. Lily chatted happily to each little one as she forked out pieces of fried ham. He drank in the sight of his beautiful Lily. . .loved by one and all.

Ian's voice brought him back to earth. "Hold on there, laddie, b'fore ye run into me."

John turned his head forward. "Sorry. My mind was somewhere else. On. . .the need for lots of trenchers and wooden spoons."

Ian's mouth twitched up at the corner. "An' furniture, I 'spect. An' mebbe a wife?"

John's breath caught. The old man knew exactly where his focus had been.

"Time's runnin' out, ye know, laddie. She'll be gone tomorrow."

"But. . .how. . . ?" His feelings couldn't have been so obvious. How many others were aware? He crouched down before Ian and spoke in a low tone. "You know it wouldn't be proper. Decent, I mean. It's barely two months ago that we buried my wife. Besides, Lily was entrusted to my care. I'm supposed to provide for her, not lust after her."

The Scot cocked a brow. "That all ye feel for her? Lust?"

"No, of course not. There are a thousand reasons to love her. All anyone has to do is look at her, be around her for any length of time, to know that. Her sister in Alexandria probably has several suitable men in mind for her already—men with the means to give her anything she wants."

"They canna' give her you or yer children."

John eyed him for several seconds. "What exactly are you saying?"

"That wee lass has been secretly moonin' over ye ever'time ye come home, just as ye do her. This *watchin' an' longin'* betwixt the two of ye has been goin' on for months now. I know ye've both tried to ignore those feelin's, but they're plain as the nose on yer face. Why do ye 'spose me Maggie insisted on stayin' at yer place that time?"

John felt heat rising up from his collar and climbing to his hairline. So those knowing looks Maggie had given him weren't merely his imagination. "Does anyone else suspect? Does Lily?"

He shrugged. "I canna' say. But even if folks did, ever'one knows what a fine wife an' mother she'd make ye. 'Twould be a perfect fit. Besides, nobody wants to lose her any more than you do. We've all come to love the lass. 'Specially those young lads of yours. They'd move heaven and earth for her if she asked them to."

It all sounded good, but John wasn't easily convinced. "But. . .so soon after Susan?"

Ian tipped his grizzled head. "All of us know the years of sufferin' yer whole family, includin' Lily, has been through. An' the way Susan loved ye, she wouldn't want ye to be lonely for the rest of yer life. Part of ye will always belong to her, but that don't mean there's no room in yer heart for another love. There's not one among us who wouldn't be pleasured by seein' yer family experience a season of nothin' but blessin's."

John couldn't believe what he was hearing. Then he remembered Dunlap, and gave a small huff through his nose. "No one, maybe, except Jackson."

"Lily doesn't love the lad, John. An' who would wish a loveless marriage on her after the selfless, lovin' care she gave Susan? Now, hand me that Bible. We need to take care of another piece of sad business now."

Chapter 36

Lily could not have been more impressed by John as he gave a heartfelt Bible reading over Robby's grave, then offered a prayer expounding the lad's qualities and expressing the sadness of everyone who'd known him. She could tell Bob and Edith felt comforted as they stood in a solemn cluster with their remaining children, drinking in his words. Even at this sorrowful moment, Lily sensed John's sincerity and the respect his neighbors had for him. He was a man whose faith never faltered despite his trials, who'd never wavered in his love for his wife through all the years of her illness. A man who had sacrificed two years of his life in the militia to keep the residents of Beaver Cove safe.

Throughout the graveside service, she reveled in the opportunity to gaze freely upon him without worrying that someone might notice. He stood tall and confident as his rich voice offered comfort to the mourners, and Lily feasted her eyes on his strong, handsome features, the square jaw that softened whenever he smiled, the compelling blue eyes that slanted downward when he was troubled, the nicely shaped lips that had once melded to hers in a heart-stopping kiss. Knowing she was gazing upon him for what could be the last time in her life, she memorized every feature, so she could draw upon those memories in the long years to come.

At the close of the service, he stayed behind to help cover the grave. As Lily walked down the hill with Matt and Luke, she thanked the Lord for another small blessing. Jackson Dunlap had not attended the gathering. After the noon meal, he and his dismal expression had ridden to Palmyra to fetch his brother Frank home. He would not be back until the morrow.

Reaching the bottom of the hill, Lily paused to let other families pass by. She tugged Luke's coat tighter about his neck against a sporadic, light mist that threatened rain. "I see your top button is missing."

"I got it here in my pocket."

"Splendid. I'll sew it on, then." She gave a light chuckle. "If I can find a needle." She paused, serious now. "Luke, will you be staying here with the men or leaving with me?"

He glanced beyond her, past the trees to the blackened rubble. "Wouldn't be right to leave." He smirked. "But when I look at the mess we gotta clean up, it sure is a temptin' thought."

"That it is." She tilted her head. "I'd gladly stay and help."

"You would?" His sky-blue eyes brightened.

Matt scowled. Always the more somber one of the two, his tone sounded almost angry when he spoke. "There's no place for you to stay. There'll barely be room in the carpentry shop for us men."

At the lad calling himself a man, Lily could hardly contain the smile tickling the corners of her mouth. But as the words settled in, so did a grievous sadness. She would be leaving the only family she'd known for the past four years, leaving Pennsylvania for Alexandria, Virginia. She'd sorely missed her sisters when they'd been torn apart on the Baltimore wharf back then, but that nearly forgotten pain wouldn't begin to compare with the parting facing her now. This one would be forever. And she wouldn't even get to say good-bye to Emma and Davy, her precious babies.

Her gaze drifted over her half-grown boys. "You're going to be such handsome men one day."

"Aren't we, though." Grinning, Luke hiked his chin and puffed out his chest.

Matt's expression, however, crumbled. He understood.

The moment needed lightening. "Tell you what, my fine lads. Let's go on a scavenger hunt. With this damp weather settling upon us, the embers should be dying out. Maybe I'll find my needles. I remember the exact spot where I left them."

Luke turned and took off, but not Matt. Almost as tall as Lily, he entwined his strong fingers in hers and looked up at her with sad azure eyes that were heart-melting replicas of his father's. "I'll never forget you, Lily. Never."

Lily cast a despondent look down at her hands and day gown. She was black with soot. While John and the other men went to the MacBrides' to build rafts, she'd been sorting through the rubble, salvaging whatever she could for the boys before the time came to leave.

Once again she thanked God that two of the families staying at the blockhouse had a supply of lye soap and a few other necessities. Ruth and Nancy had even offered clean clothes to Lily and the other women for their trip back to civilization. More of the Lord's tender mercies.

The scent of biscuits baking in the cast-iron dutch ovens drifted her way as she walked toward the well. The overcast sky was darkening as this longest of days drew to a close. Scouring the black from her hands, she noticed that two of the wagons had been rigged with canvas tents to keep out the rain. The men would have to sleep out in the cold until the women and little ones left. Small wonder they were in such haste to build those rafts. Toby voiced the opinion that if they didn't waste time, the conveyances would be finished as early as tomorrow afternoon.

La, how she dreaded leaving here.

Returning the piece of soap to a nearby log round, she picked up the drying rag and wiped her hands before joining Nancy and Agnes at the cookfires. "I'm going down to the cellar. Is there anything you need from there?"

"No, lass." Looking every bit as spent as Lily felt, Nancy brushed a strand of light blond hair out of her eyes.

Lily put fire to a piece of kindling to light her way in the dark cellar. "I'll be back in a few minutes."

Along the way, she snagged the shovel she'd been using earlier to sort through the ashes. The sooty handle dirtied her hands again, but she sighed and took it with her anyway. She should have completed this chore before washing up.

Down in the shadowy cavern, she lit the lantern hanging from the beam and began to dig. She'd saved twenty-four pounds of the monies sent her over the years. Twenty-four pounds. Rose had needed only four more pounds to satisfy Papa's creditors when she'd indentured herself to that unscrupulous sea captain. Lily could still remember the shock and sorrow she and the family had felt upon learning of Rose's actions. She also recalled not being able to bear the thought of her older sister sailing off to some faraway land alone, and so had done the same herself—as had Mariah, but for her own reasons.

The thought made Lily chuckle. Beautiful, headstrong Mariah eventually married her dream, a rich plantation owner—but not until the Lord taught her a few hard lessons.

With the ding of metal on metal, the shovel hit the small pewter container. Wedging it up with the lip of the tool, Lily reached down to get her *buried treasure*. Four pounds would be more than sufficient to see her safely to Mariah's. The remainder she'd leave for John. So much was needed here now.

Footfalls descended the steps. Lily swung around, and her heartbeat quickened.

John! Coming down here, in this secluded place!

He wore a peculiar expression. "Nancy said you were here."

"Yes." His nearness ignited a spark of awareness of her very smudged self, even though John's clothing was far blacker than hers. Collecting her thoughts, she held out the small round container. "I came for the money."

"The money," he said absently without looking at it. Regarding her without blinking, he inhaled. "I have something to say to you, and this is likely the only privacy we'll get."

"Quite true." The root cellar, with its abundant piles of sacks and baskets of food suddenly felt closed in. Airless. And John, scarcely two yards away, seemed to fill it with his presence. "I have something to say as well." She somehow managed to speak past her tight throat.

"You do?" He took a step forward.

"Yes. And I'll not accept your refusal."

He frowned, as if puzzled over her comment.

She cleared her throat. " 'Tis the money. I shall take only enough for my trip. The rest I'll leave with you. There are so many things that need to be purchased."

He took another step closer. "Lily. . ."

She waited a heartbeat. "Yes?"

"You've always been. . .a fine, honest—" He rolled his eyes. "That's not what I came to tell you."

Baffled, Lily wondered why he was fumbling so. He'd always been so sure of himself. She took a step toward him.

Be honest with him.

"Oh, but I couldn't."

"What?" John took her hand, the tenderness in his eyes stealing her breath.

Lily's cheeks flamed. She'd actually said the words out loud! "I. . . that is, the Lord—at least, I think it's the Lord—wants me to tell you something."

He tucked his chin in disbelief.

She put her free hand over her throbbing heart. " 'Tis not the first time I've heard from the Lord today, actually." She nibbled her lip, then filled her lungs and let the words pour out like water over a fall. "Considering everything, you'll probably think I'm horrid for saying it. . .but I cannot leave here with it unsaid. I love you, John. I do. With my whole heart. This love for you has been growing inside me for months, and no matter how I try, I cannot stop—"

In an instant she was in his arms, his lips on hers, his heart pounding against her own with the same wonder, the same incredible joy that radiated through her. When at last the kiss ended, her head was spinning and her knees weak.

What had just happened?

John's penetrating eyes glistened with moisture as he cupped her face in his palms. "Ian told me not to worry about what anyone else might think. He says it's a good thing—a gift from God—that we've grown to love one another. He doesn't believe anyone will condemn us, because it's right and good."

Lily was struggling to process John's words. Had he just told her he loved her?

Then suddenly, he eased her away. "No. It isn't right. It isn't right at all."

She felt as if her whole being started to cave in. " 'Tis Susan, is it not?"

"No." He shook his head. "Maybe it should be, but it's not. I'm being far too selfish. You deserve much more than I can offer you. You'll be going off to Mariah's tomorrow, and while you're there, I want you to remember what life was like before you came to the cove. I want you to see what life could be like for you again, in a place where every day isn't a struggle. I want—"

Lily pressed her fingers to his mouth to stop him. "And if I promise to do all of that, should I want to come back here afterward, will you stop me?"

He drew her hand away and kissed her palm, his gaze searching deep into her very soul. "If you still wish to return after you've spent at least three months with Mariah, I'll not stop you. But keep in mind, my love, the danger here is far from past. The Indians could attack Beaver Cove again."

"And you keep in mind this war cannot last forever." She reached up and slipped her arms about his neck.

He pulled back slightly. "By the way, what did the Lord say to you, exactly?"

"Oh, that." Her lips spread into a grin. "Not once, but twice today, He said it. The first time was when I spoke with Jackson. This time it was with you."

A frown drew John's brows together. "Surely He didn't have you tell Dunlap you loved him, too."

"No, silly." She laughed lightly. "The Lord said, 'Be honest.' "

"Honest, you say." Smiling, John drew her close again. "Then I reckon I'll have to be completely truthful with you. I absolutely love and adore you. . .sooty nose and all." Tipping her chin up with the edge of his finger, he lowered his head and kissed her once more.

***

"Lily. . ." Luke reached out and caught her hand. "You are comin' back, aren't you?"

John tore his gaze from his son's hopeful expression. All around him, men were bidding tearful farewells to their wives and children on the ferry dock as their families boarded the three rafts. But Lily was all that mattered to John.

She raised her silky lashes to look at John over the lad's head, and those yearning gray eyes tore right through him.

One of them had to remain strong. He managed a curt nod.

She gave Luke a small smile. "Your papa made me promise not to make that decision until—"

"I know. Him an' you already told us how your other family wants you, too. But you love us best. I know you do."

The other promise John had exacted from her, not to tell his sons or the other people of the cove about the glorious confessions of love that had transpired between them in the cellar, pierced him to the core. He knew only too well that if the boys knew, they'd pressure Lily into making a commitment to return. If she did come back, he wanted it to be her decision, without regret.

He saw her lean close to Luke's ear and whisper something. *Please, Father, don't let her make a promise she may not keep.* Luke walked away with a disturbingly satisfied grin.

She then turned to Matt, who'd been waiting off to the side. Nearly as tall as Lily, he stood stiff as a ramrod, his expression beyond solemn.

Lily wrapped him in a hug. "My dear, dear Matt. You've been my rock for so long. I never could have gotten through these past two years without you. Thank you so very, very much." Easing him away slightly, she looked at his face. "Thank you for being the wonderful person you are. I'm ever so proud of you." Her gaze moved to his shaggy hair, and she ruffled it playfully with a smile. "My scissors are somewhere in the rubble. Find them. You still need a haircut."

Matt bucked his head away and smoothed down his brown thatch as he became serious again. "Come back to us," he said simply, his voice breaking. Turning, he bumped past John and bolted off.

John's heart wrenched at the sight of his son's shattered expression. He felt even worse when he looked back at Lily and saw her eyes brimming with tears. Stepping close, he took her hands in his. He couldn't afford to embrace her—he'd never find the strength to let go—or to kiss away the tear tracing a glistening path down her angelic face. The weight of all the things he wanted to say to her but didn't dare was like a chain about his heart. Mustering every ounce of fortitude he possessed, he cleared his throat. "Give my best regards to your sisters and Nate."

"Oh, yes. Nate." A delicate pink crested her cheeks. "That day when you found me, he saw us—well, you know." She moistened her lips.

Centering on those soft rosy temptations, John swallowed. "He sure did. The man knew about us even before we did. But you have to remember you've been pretty isolated here. Away from the rest of the world. There's so much more out—"

She rolled her eyes in frustration. "Will you stop? You needn't tell me again. I shall do as you say and consider the rest of the world. Not that I want to, but because you've asked it of me." She darted a quick glance around, then moved closer. "Take care of those boys. Especially Matt. He always tries too hard. . .and so do you. Take care, my love."

Those last whispered words turned John to mush. "Take care," he rasped, his voice husky. Then as Matt had done, he pivoted and hurried off the dock. Unable to watch her float away, possibly out of his life forever, he kept going.

Chapter 37

When Lily had escorted Emma and Davy to their grandparents' home in Philadelphia, she'd been amazed at how untouched by war the red brick city had been. But as she rode atop a wagon seat along the Potomac River toward Mariah's home, the expansive fields of the plantations and the opulence of the manors she passed left her awe-stricken. These aristocratic Virginia planters were far wealthier than she remembered. Even more breathtaking in this bare-tree month of November, a rainbow assortment of autumn leaves drifted placidly on the breeze as she and the driver passed beneath interlocking branches that created one glorious archway after another.

It seemed not even a whisper of the war had reached this place.

Lily knew that was not quite true. Mariah's husband, Colin, had been blinded in the first months of conflict, a full year and a half before Beaver Cove and the other settlements west of Reading ever suspected they were destined to be attacked in such vicious, wolf pack-like raids.

"Miss." The driver removed a hand from the reins and pointed. "We're coming up on the Barclay's Bay cutoff."

Lily glanced ahead to the oak-lined lane leading to the elegant manor house. She'd been here only once before—for Mariah's wedding—but the grand entrance was unmistakable. At least a dozen majestic trees graced either side of the driveway that circled a lovely fountain sitting like a diamond in the center of the expanse fronting the home.

" 'Twas such a blessing, Mr. Harris, meeting you at the Potomac ferry crossing. Otherwise I should have had to take the stage the rest of the way into Alexandria and arrange transport from there. You saved me hours, if not an entire day. I do thank you for your kindness."

The pleasant-faced gentleman guided the team onto Mariah's lane. "Nonsense, lass. For a spell now, you've provided me with the company of a lovely young miss, and it didn't put me out one whit." A jovial smile tweaked his bushy salt-and-pepper mustache.

Lily knew that as the proprietor of a general store in a small settlement farther west, above the falls, he had spoken truly. "Nevertheless, I deem it a pure blessing." She glanced ahead at the great white columns that graced the front porch and supported the balcony above. *Mariah, daughter of a mere tradesman, lived in this house of splendor.*

Mr. Harris reined his team to a halt and set the brake lever.

Lily's anticipation mounted.

Before the merchant had time to climb down and assist her, the front door opened, and a butler stepped out. Neatly attired in black and white, the tall African came to meet them. "If y'all's makin' a delivery, take yo' wagon on aroun' back. I'll fetch some boys to he'p y'all unload."

Mr. Harris chuckled. "The onliest thing I got to unload is this gal. Says she's kin to the mistress of the house."

The butler took a closer look at Lily.

She could tell he didn't recognize her. But then, she was still dressed in Nancy's homespun. "I'm Lily Harwood, Mariah's sister. I realize I'm not very presentable—"

The sudden patter of footsteps on the porch brought golden-haired Amy Barclay bounding down the steps. Taller now, and quite the lovely young maiden, she had obviously retained her youthful spirit. "Did I hear correctly? Is that you, Lily?" She turned to the butler. "Help her down, Benjamin." Then, whirling around in a rustle of buttercream flounces, she ran back up the steps and hollered into the door. "Mariah! It's your sister! She's here!"

Lily's heartbeat took up a staccato pace as Benjamin handed her down to the pebble drive. At any second, Mariah would emerge.

She'd barely circumvented the wagon when her beautiful sister came to the door, attired in a violet taffeta gown fit for a queen. But the smile she'd worn vanished as she halted where she stood. "Amy, I thought you said—*Lily? Is that you?*" With a most unladylike squeal, she grasped handfuls of her skirts and charged down the steps.

At her sister's enthusiastic welcome, emotion clogged Lily's throat. She could only manage a nod.

"Lily, Lily." Mariah drew her into a brief hug, then thrust her an arm's distance from herself and looked her up and down. "What on earth are you wearing? And your hands. . ." She picked one of them up. "They're rough and chapped. And your hair. Your complexion—why, you haven't even got a bonnet on for protection from the sun and the wind."

Lily could only shrug. "I suppose I should have taken the time to purchase more appropriate clothing, but—"

"Oh, bother." Mariah fluttered a hand as if details were of little consequence and gave her another quick hug. "You're here now. Everything else can be easily fixed. Come with me, and we'll get you in a nice warm bubble bath. And while you're soaking, you can tell me all about it." She barely paused for breath. "You do remember our darling Amy, don't you?" Flicking a glance at her young sister-in-law waiting on the veranda, she swept Lily up the steps toward the grand entry. "She's becoming quite the belle of the county, aren't you, dear?"

"So you keep sayin'," Amy answered in her airy drawl as she traipsed after Mariah and Lily across the parquet floor toward the graceful staircase.

"Now, with you here, Lily, we'll certainly be the most popular home from here to Alexandria." She slanted a frown at her. "That is, once you've had a few milk baths to turn your skin soft and creamy again. Mother

Barclay has some simply marvelous oils and creams imported from the Orient."

Mariah's enthusiasm, the splendid sights. . . Lily could hardly take everything in.

Her sister stopped halfway up the stairs. "Whatever am I thinking? Amy, run down to the kitchen and tell them we need bathwater brought up right away." She smiled and placed a hand on Lily's shoulder. "I wasn't expecting you for at least another week. Your letter said Mr. Waldon would return after the first of November, remember? But this is ever so much better. We shall have more time to get you properly outfitted before your first ball."

"My ball?"

"Yes." On the top landing, Mariah stopped in the upstairs lounge area and turned to face Lily. "I sent out invitations last week. I want to launch you properly into our little society. There's no need for anyone to know about the rustic frontier life you've been leading, unless— Did you introduce yourself to anyone in Alexandria?"

"I never went there. At the ferry crossing, I accepted a ride from a merchant who lives somewhere above the falls."

"Splendid. Oh, and Rose will arrive in a few days. I asked her to come early. I'm so excited! You, Rose, and I together again. The three of us haven't been together since my wedding, and that was such a hectic time it hardly counts." She stopped prattling, and a slow smile graced her lips as she gazed at Lily a moment, then pulled her close and gave her a longer hug.

Lily basked in the feeling of being utterly safe and loved and cared for.

When Mariah stepped back, her violet eyes glistened as she smoothed a hand along Lily's cheek. "My baby sister is back where she belongs. God is so good."

~

No amount of protesting during the next two weeks would stop Mariah and Mistress Barclay from fussing over her. Since Mariah had yet to conceive a child—a sadness she mentioned only once—Lily soon realized she was their new plaything, the new dress-up doll. Amy, who'd always been more interested in horses than fashion, whispered that she was *monstrously relieved* that attention had been diverted away from her for a change.

Lily had every intention of returning to Beaver Cove and to John and her adopted family, but she hadn't managed to find the right words to placate her sister or the lady of the house. She did enjoy the pampering, the swish and rustle of costly fabrics, the scented soaps and perfumes, to say nothing of having someone swirl her hair into amazing styles. The corset, however, was another matter. She'd forgotten how binding those torturous contraptions could be, especially considering the delicious variety of food being served at every meal.

Then a most wonderful day arrived. Hearing laughter and loud talking downstairs, Lily peeked over the railing and saw that Rose had come. . . . Rose, the older sister who had mothered Lily since she was a tender four years of age. She and her two little ones had blown into this luxurious haven on a blustery mid-November day. Gasping with delight, Lily raced down the stairs to greet them, nearly tripping over the abundant petticoats she wasn't used to wearing.

She ran right to Rose, who was attired in a fashionable dove-gray traveling costume. Lily wondered if Mariah had provided the lovely clothing, since Rose, too, lived in the much simpler surroundings of a small farm.

After reveling in hugs and kisses and cooing over pretty little Jenny, now four and a half, and three-year-old Ethan Nathaniel, Lily realized how sorely she missed Emma and Davy. She glanced at Rose. "Did Nate come with you?"

Mariah answered for Rose. "When does he ever?"

Giving her middle sister a patient look, Rose almost said something, but instead turned to Amy. "Dearest, would you mind taking my darlings to the kitchen for something to eat? They've not had a bite since early this morning."

"We'd be delighted, won't we, dear?" Mistress Barclay swept forth in all her regal elegance and took Jenny's hand, while Amy latched on to

Ethan's. "It's been months since I've had a chance to fatten these little cherubs up. Mariah, why don't you take Rose upstairs to freshen up? I'll have Cook send up a tray for you all."

"Thank you," Rose and Lily said as one while the matron ushered the children toward the butlery entrance behind the staircase.

"I received a note from Nate the other day," Rose commented, accompanying her sisters up the stairs. "He and Robert hope to make it home for Christmas."

Lily gave her an understanding smile. "Waiting can be unbearably hard."

"Yes, but Nate's family does what they can to help Star and me with the farm. They've been a real blessing to us."

"That's how the people of Beaver Cove have been to me. Like a family."

"That's lovely, you two," Mariah piped in. "But now you're both with your *real* family at long last. There couldn't possibly be anything left to harvest, Rose, so I won't take no for an answer. You and the children will stay here with us until Nate comes home." Reaching the second floor, she caught both her sisters by the hand. "We shall have a marvelous time, just like when we were young. Remember how we used to talk about attending the grand balls in Bath's assembly rooms?"

Rose chuckled. "I believe that was your dream, sister-of-mine."

"My dream, your dream, it makes little difference. Lily's coming-out ball is next Saturday, and the whole of northern Virginia is going to meet and be enthralled by the daughters of Harwood House."

Rose erupted with her wonderful throaty laugh. "*The daughters of Harwood House!* What a clever way to put it."

"I thought you'd be pleased. It has such a resplendent ring to it." She hiked her perfect nose, then broke into giggles. "Come along to my dressing room. I believe I have just the gown to set off your eyes for supper this evening."

Mariah never ceased to amaze Lily. She'd always been the beauty of the family, but so much more, as well. She possessed supreme confidence in herself. During the past months Lily had begun to attain a measure of that elusive attribute. But she now realized it was a mere shadow of Mariah's.

Even take-charge Rose was simply following along and doing her bidding.

The deeper timbre of male voices drifted up from the entry below as Mariah's husband and father-in-law returned from a few days in Baltimore. With a joyous grin, Mariah ushered Lily and Rose into her bedchamber then left to greet the men.

At last Lily was alone with Rose. She gestured toward Mariah's blue damask chaise, and after her older sister sank onto it, Lily joined her, perching on the edge. There was so much to tell Rose about John. Lily hoped to make her understand the need to return to him.

Rose took Lily's hands in hers. "Baby sister, that missive I received from Nate also mentioned you'd almost been taken by Indians. Thank God you're here now and safe with us."

Lily nodded. "Truly, Rose, I'm thrilled to be here with you and Mariah. But I wish I were still at Beaver Cove."

Angling her head, Rose searched Lily's eyes. "Nate also mentioned he saw John Waldon kiss you *on the mouth* when he found you. And this was only weeks after his wife had gone to be with the Lord, was it not?"

Lily felt her cheeks flame. "He was profoundly glad to find me unharmed. As I said in prior letters, the Waldons treated me as if I were family."

"If 'twas merely a brotherly kiss, why are you blushing?"

Lily hadn't said a word to Mariah about her intention to return to the cove, because she didn't want to be harangued day and night. But she'd never kept anything from Rose. . .until now. "I was embarrassed. Nate thought there was much more to the kiss."

"Nate." A low laugh spilled from Rose. "Is it not amazing how much a man changes once he has womenfolk to protect?"

Or how closely a woman will guard a secret when she has a love to protect. Perhaps this wasn't the time to confide in Rose, after all.

Lily's spirits sank. Mariah was determined to find her a husband here among the wealthy Virginians. A coming-out ball, no less. Still, Lily knew she'd have to tell her sisters about her and John soon. . .and somehow make them understand.

Chapter 38

As always, the richly appointed dining room with its exquisite china and silverware impressed Lily as she entered with Rose and the Barclay family. She and the others were as richly attired as the furnishings, and even the food they'd be served would be worthy of the beautiful surroundings.

Everything flowed so graciously for these people, Lily mused. The women's hands were soft and white. No blisters or calluses ever marred them, no redness from lye soap. They'd never bent to cook over a hot hearth, washed a soiled dish, or boiled and scrubbed dirt and stains from worn work clothes. They'd never spent evenings at a spinning wheel or darning stockings, spent days behind a plow or in the stable helping a mother cow give birth. So why couldn't she embrace all Mariah wanted to offer?

Lily's gaze gravitated to Mariah and her strikingly handsome husband as he flawlessly assisted his wife into her seat. Only a small scar at his temple gave evidence to the battle wound that had blinded him. And with Mariah's impeccable taste, Lily surmised her sister had some dashing, refined gentleman picked out for her, as well.

From the head of the table, Mr. Barclay spoke down the lengthy expanse in his easy Virginia drawl. "Cora, my dear, Colin and I stopped by for a short visit with Victoria on our way home. She asked how your arrangements for the ball were comin'. She and Heather are both countin' the days."

Colin chuckled. "Tori's *simply devastated* that the fabric she ordered for her gown has not come. The poor, put-upon dear had to choose some *utterly dreadful* brocaded silk."

"Colin," his mother scolded, "you shouldn't belittle your sister. It's most important to maintain a certain standing among our friends. I'm quite proud of Victoria and the added grace and elegance she's brought to that household. I can say the same about Heather, also, since her marriage to Evan Greer."

Grace and elegance. Lily suppressed a smirk. The thought of any of her cove neighbors seeking a wife to add grace and elegance to his home was laughable. Those men chose capable wives, women who could work alongside them to build a home and a life together—and fight with them to save it, should need be.

Seated next to Lily, Rose nudged her with an elbow then turned to their host. "Mr. Barclay, did you perchance hear any news of the war while you were in Baltimore?"

"No, lass. With winter upon us, things should remain quiet until next spring."

Colin turned his vacant stare in Rose's general direction. "There was that one tidbit about the captured French soldier who got separated from the Indians he was supposedly leading, and they all disappeared on him." He gave a hearty laugh. "After a week of starving, the illustrious leader stumbled onto one of the forts along the Susquehanna and gave himself up."

Lily nodded. "Fort Henry."

"I believe so. Wasn't that where your Mr. Waldon was posted?"

"Yes. Did the Frenchman give any other information?"

Colin shook his head. "Just that he'd been dispatched from Fort

Duquesne with some thirty-odd Indians to harass the settlements along the frontier."

"Which they do quite viciously." Lily swept a glance around. "Once they sneak past the string of outposts on our side of the river, they separate into parties of five or six and attack lone farmsteads in sundry places, burning and murdering as they go."

"Rather ingenious, really," Colin admitted. "A small number can keep a much larger population on edge, wondering where they will strike next."

Lily knew that all too well. "Quite. They're rather successful at frightening settlers into abandoning their homes and leaving the area."

Mr. Barclay entered the conversation. "It's imperative that our forces take Fort Duquesne next spring and stop the supply of goods that buy the services of the Indian tribes."

"Will the British generals finally do that?" Lily met the older man's gaze.

A crystal bell rang at Mistress Barclay's end as the hostess signaled for the food. "Please. No more war talk at the dinner table."

"Quite right, my dear." Her husband cleared his throat. "How are your plans for the ball coming?"

How easy it was for these people to dismiss the war and any other unpleasantness, Lily thought bleakly.

"The Kinsales have sent their acceptance," Amy said.

Across the table, Mariah raised a meaningful eyebrow. "A reply we've been most anxiously waiting for, wouldn't you say, Amy?"

The young miss turned a becoming shade of pink, a sure sign of blossoming love.

At that moment, the butler and Pansy, the maid, brought in trays of delectable-smelling food. Everyone waited as the house servants carefully dished portions of ham and glazed vegetables on each person's china plate, then left as quietly as they'd come.

No passing of heaping bowls or platters around here, Lily thought.

"Let us give thanks." Mr. Barclay bowed his head. "Our gracious heavenly Father, we thank You for Your generosity and the bounty You provide. We pray for Your continued protection over Rose's husband and all those who are fighting to save our western frontiers. Please give our British generals the wisdom and fortitude to go forth next spring and end this threat to the settlers. We ask this in the name of Your precious Son, Jesus. Amen."

As Lily raised her head, she realized the wealthy people at this table made up a fine Christian family who cared about the plight of others. She also knew for a certainty that no matter how much they wanted her to be part of them, they were not her family. She didn't need three months to conclude her family lived 150 miles away in Beaver Cove. But how would she ever find a way to make her sisters understand she wanted to give up all this luxury and safety for a life of danger and hardship?

Be honest.

"Come and get it!" The call echoed over the incessant clatter of pounding, chopping, and sawing. John glanced down from the roof of the new MacBride cabin to see Edith Randall holding her woolen shawl close as she waved an arm over her head. The noon meal was ready.

The hardworking men were eating much better since a few of the womenfolk had returned to the valley, though most meals had to be consumed outside in the damp December weather at whichever farmstead they happened to be working. As Edith's smaller children ran toward the long tables set up in the yard, the menfolk ambled from their tasks at a slower, but no less eager, pace.

"I could eat a horse," Bob commented from the other side of the roof.

Pounding a peg through a shingle, John grinned at his friend. The Randall cabin had been the first one completed, since Edith feared her aging parents in Chestertown wouldn't be able to endure her rambunctious brood for long. She and the little ones had been back for almost a month now. Millie and Cissy Dunlap came soon after, Cissy being too enamored with young Donald to stay away.

An unbidden vision of Lily, smudged nose and all, gazing up at him with those bewitching silvery eyes made John's smile die as he crossed the sloping surface to the ladder. If only. . .

He stifled a heavy sigh. This last house would be finished by day's end, giving Pat and Ian's family time to return to the cove for Christmas and him and his boys time to reach Philadelphia. The Gilfords had extended an invitation to celebrate the holy days with them, and John hoped that would perk up Matt and Luke. Their hangdog expressions showed they missed Lily almost as much as he did.

Reaching the bottom rung, he saw Cal burying his hatchet in a stump where he'd been shaving shingles. John waited for his pal to catch up, then gave him a friendly slap on the back. "Almost through."

"All of us workin' together sure has helped things go faster." Cal pulled off his canvas gloves. "Still, it's hard to believe we've rebuilt five cabins and animal shelters in seven weeks."

John nodded. "Thank heaven for all the October rains. Without them, a lot more would've burned. We were able to reuse an amazing number of logs and boards. That was a blessing."

"Wish Nancy'd change her mind an' bring the young'uns back here when the MacBride women come. There hasn't been a sign of Indians anywhere below Blue Mountain since the attack on our cove."

"That's right. I forgot you and the MacBrides came here together."

"Aye. We all hail from Queenstown."

John picked a splinter from his palm as they strode along. "I doubt Richard and his family will come back even next spring. They might after the hostilities are over, though."

"That makes three families we've lost."

"I regret the loss of Richard Shaw the most. Young as he is, he worked hard to prove up his place. Maybe if their children had been a bit older. . ."

Cal chuckled. "Ruthie, too. That li'l missy could howl louder'n a pack of wolves when she got scared."

"Not my—" John caught himself before uttering Lily's name.

The aroma of roast pork drifted toward them before they reached the table, and John's stomach growled. His boys waved him to the place they'd saved between them.

"Mind hurryin' along?" Ian stood at the head of the table. "I need to say grace."

It was good to have the older man back, even without full use of his left arm. He'd returned last week, after Pat received a three-month furlough from Fort Henry.

John had hiked one leg over the bench when he heard a dog bark in the distance. Then another. Since all the dogs in the cove had been killed, he glanced across at Toby and his grown sons.

The other men all disengaged themselves from the benches, and John and Cal bolted for the muskets they'd left leaning against the cabin wall.

The unmistakable sound of hoofbeats came from the Swatara Creek trace. Before he was able to uncork the powder horn, John heard splashing in Beaver Creek. Whoever was coming would be here in seconds.

As three large dogs bounded into the MacBride clearing, John swung his weapon around to use as a club.

On the dogs' heels came riders and horses.

"Papa! Papa!"

John lowered his musket. Davy! And Emma! They were on the first horse!

And wonder of wonders—Lily!

Leaning the weapon back against the wall, he blinked hard and looked again. Lily rode right behind the children. She'd come back! And she'd brought his babies! He didn't know who to run to first.

Before he could decide, other riders leading packhorses stopped between him and his dear ones.

"Papa!"

Dodging around the animals, he found Lily already on the ground. He caught her to him and hurried to the children, but Matt and Luke were already lifting them down. In an instant he had his whole family in his arms. His heart nearly burst with joy amid the excited childish chatter as he kissed his clinging little Emmy, who looked so much like her sweet mother. Wiggly Davy was next. Then his beloved Lily.

"What's all this stuff?"

Matt's question drew John's attention from the sparkling gray eyes that held such promise. He set the little ones on the ground, noticing that there were two men and more than a dozen horses, most of which were loaded with goods.

Neighbors, all talking at once came to join the group.

Holding Lily against his side, John ambled over to the strangers. "You are most welcome. Thank you for escorting my family here."

"Only thanks we need is to share your grub," the huge backwoodsman with rough features said.

"Aye." His stubby partner gestured with his disheveled head at Lily. "Your missus insisted we start out a'fore first light this mornin'."

Ian spoke out. "Yer welcome to partake of our vittles. Ye rode in from the Susquehanna?"

"Yep." The first one eyed the food-laden table. "A crew of rivermen poled us an' all this truck up as far as the Swatara."

"The dogs, too?" Matt knelt down to pet one that was sniffing around his legs.

"Yep. Brung them mangy curs right along with us."

"Hey, they ain't mangy," Davy piped in.

Lily laughed. "No, they certainly aren't." She glanced at John. "If you don't mind, I thought we'd keep the female and let the Pattersons and MacBrides have the other two for watchdogs."

Davy puffed out his scrawny chest. "An' when Queenie has pups, I'll give 'em to whoever wants 'em."

"Except the prettiest one." Emma planted a fist on her waist. "I get to keep that one."

"Hey, folks," Edith called from the table. "Food's getting cold. Come on an' eat. We can catch up later."

Millie and her daughter had already set more places, and everyone found a spot to sit. John still couldn't let go of Lily. He couldn't believe she'd come back.

Directly across the table, Jackson looked at both of them, then grunted and offered a lopsided grin. "Ain't no never mind. Figgered as much. 'Sides, I got my eye on the sister of Frank's gal. Don't know why he didn't pick the purtier one."

Down the way, Millie wagged her salt-and-pepper head. "We're still talkin' about them German gals. I'm not sure I like the idea of you boys bringin' home wives that can't hardly speak English."

"Wait'll you see 'em, Ma." Frank angled his head toward her with a lovesick expression. "They got hair blonder than the sun an' eyes bluer'n the sky."

Ian's voice boomed along the length of the table as he looked straight at John and Lily. "Since we're on the subject of courtin', I reckon we'll be needin' us a weddin' today, soon as we finish the cabin."

Beside John, Lily stiffened slightly.

"Either that or our Miss Lily will be spendin' the night at the Randalls.'"

John's mouth fell open. How could the old man be so crude?

"Well. . ." Lily relaxed against John again. "Since those Randall children are simply too noisy to abide, I suppose I have no choice."

Everyone laughed and started talking at once.

Amazed beyond words, John drew Lily's sweet self so close, he couldn't tell if it was his heart or hers beating with such incredulous joy.

Chapter 39

"Is that the men coming?" Lily gasped the words over the happy chatter as Edith tightened the laces on the corset Mariah had insisted on sending.

Millie opened the bedroom door of the new Waldon cabin that still smelled of fresh-cut wood and peeked out. "Aye, they're ridin' in now."

Cissy and the twins tittered behind their hands as Cissy shook the wrinkles from the exquisite gown of brocaded emerald silk Lily would wear on this, her wedding day. Their eyes grew wide as they admired the white satin stomacher with its vertical row of tiny bows, an underskirt adorned with double flounces of fine lace edged with silver, and the dropped neckline with a matching flounce. "Even puffed sleeves," Cissy breathed.

"With lacy ruffles," Gracie added, hesitant even to touch the lovely creation.

"And satin bows to hold back the skirt," Patience said softly. "I've never seen such a beautiful gown."

"Thank you." Lily smiled at the threesome. "My sister insisted on having it made for me."

"This'll be the first weddin' in the cove, and mine'll be next," Cissy declared.

Overflowing with happiness, Lily wanted everyone to share it. "We shall start a new tradition. Every bride in Beaver Cove must wear this gown on her wedding day—should she choose to do so, of course."

"You mean it?" Holding the frock against herself, Cissy whirled around, fluttering out its glory as a dreamy expression lit her eyes.

"Of course." Lily bent to pick up a package from the bed and handed it to one of the twins. "Patience, would you please take this out to John and tell him it's my wedding gift to him? It's a new outfit, since all of his clothes were burned in the fire."

"Your sister must be very, very rich," Gracie said, regarding the trunk of new clothing they'd lugged into the room.

"Her husband's family is. They are also wonderfully generous people. When they heard of our sad plight, not only did they provide crates of clothes for everyone, but bed linens, quilts, kitchen towels, and fabric for curtains. And the other packhorses are loaded down with grain and corn to help feed our livestock this winter."

"I declare." Millie wagged her head in wonder. "It's a real blessin'. I brought some grain back with me, too, but not nearly enough. We figgered before winter was through, we'd have to butcher most of the animals."

Lily stepped into the gown's pool of silk and ruffles, and Edith drew it gently up so she could slip her arms into the sleeves. Then Edith tightened the back laces. "I've another bit of good news. Mr. Gilford, the children's grandfather, is sending a barge-load of bricks and slate shakes next spring, enough for a fireproof two-story house. So should the Indians ever come again, they won't be able to burn that one. We'll all be safe inside."

Straightening the generous skirt over the petticoats, Edith glanced up. "Bob tells me he don't think the Injuns'll be back. Ever'time they came here, they lost braves. They like easy pickin's."

"That's comforting." Lily gazed down at the ruffles and bows. "Mr.

Gilford says his friend, the governor, plans to pressure the British commander into capturing Fort Duquesne in the spring. If that happens, all our men will be able to come home for good."

"Mercy me. Wouldn't that be fine." Millie began arranging Lily's hair into fancy swirls and pinning them in place. "Then our husbands can get back to why we came here in the first place: makin' a future for us an' our young'uns."

Lily turned to her. "Speaking of the future, I brought another present for John he's sure to be thrilled with. . .a box filled with fancy hinges and drawer pulls for the furniture he'll be building for us all. I can hardly wait to see his face when he sees them."

Millie wrapped her arms around Lily and sighed. "I'd hoped you'd marry my Jackson, you know, but havin' you back, wedded to John, is almost as wonderful."

Lily returned the embrace. "And so is being back here with all of you. To be quite honest, I feared you wouldn't approve of our marrying so soon after Susan's passing."

"Not at all, dear. I think she would be the first to wish you happiness, you and John."

"Truly?" Lily's eyes misted over.

"Now, now," Edith scolded. "Stop the huggin'. We don't want to crush that gown."

Lily reached around and hugged the petite woman. "I'm simply too happy to care about the gown. I'm getting married today."

꧁꧂

John flicked an imaginary piece of lint from his fine suit of clothes, feeling both dashing and thankful as he waited at the far end of the front room. His sons were attired in finery as well, the rich colors of their outfits making up for the lack of flowers for this winter wedding. Matt looked quite grown-up in sapphire, Luke in copper, and Davy in burgundy, all of which complemented John's café-au-lait frock coat and dark brown britches.

But where was Lily? He could hardly wait for her and Emma to emerge from the bedroom.

The guests, mostly men and their sons, fidgeted, too, as they sat on hastily set-up rows of benches, with Bob's daughters sprinkled about.

When John and the others first arrived from the MacBrides', his friends prevented him from going in to Lily. Bad luck, they'd said, though he couldn't imagine anything dimming the joy of this day. To think she loved him so much she'd chosen him over all the luxury that could've been hers. At long last, he'd have his life back, and so would his family.

He gazed again at his boys, flanking him on either side. They, too, watched for the door to open, knowing that from this day forth, laughter and good times would fill this home. Lily had a way of bringing such things with her.

The door cracked open.

John started forward, but Ian caught his shoulder from behind. He eased back on his heels. She was coming to him.

With a darling little giggle, Emma emerged and started past the rows of guests with practiced steps. She looked like a porcelain doll in a ruffled gown of gold silk, her red hair caught up at the crown with a matching satin bow and trailing down her back in ringlets. Her eyes fairly danced as she smiled up at him.

John bent to give his sweet daughter a kiss, then guided her beside him.

Next came Cissy in a fine gown of royal-blue taffeta that Lily undoubtedly had loaned her. Her head was bowed a little, and her shy smile was for no one but Donald.

An eternal moment later, out strolled Lily, and her glowing gaze met his and stayed there until she reached him. Looking every inch the angel she was, Lily made a breathtaking vision in emerald and white that John could hardly take in. Her hand trembled slightly as he took it in his, and he gave it an encouraging squeeze. When she looked up at him, all the love he felt for her was reflected in her eyes. What a gift she was. A gift from God.

Lily could hardly breathe for happiness. Lost in John's tender gaze, surrounded by well-wishing friends, she knew she would never forget this wondrous day. Ian's blunt but welcome words had laid the last of her fears and doubts to rest, and an indescribable sense of peace enfolded her as she looked up and met John's smile. The love they shared had been part of God's plan all along, and she knew the life they would build together would honor Him. Papa would be thankful to know that in coming to this new land, the Lord had blessed all three of his daughters with happiness and love. Rose first, then Mariah, and now His hand of blessing extended to Lily. Returning John's promise-filled smile with one of her own, she turned with him to face Ian and repeat the sacred vows that would bind them together for all time.

Author's Note

The area surrounding Blue Mountain in Pennsylvania continued to suffer random attacks in 1758 from Fort Duquesne, the southernmost French fort. In random raids, nine more people were killed, three captured, and three went missing. The fort's influence seriously waned during the year. The British naval blockade near the mouth of the St. Lawrence River stopped most of the flow of supplies and trade goods coming into Canada. Any goods that did trickle in were inflated in price and sold mostly around Quebec. None reached as far south as Fort Duquesne. Most of the Indians refused to fight without the payment of trade goods and returned to their villages.

In October 1758, the British command, along with representatives from Pennsylvania and New Jersey, invited the chiefs of thirteen tribes to a meeting. There the Treaty of Easton was signed. The Indians were given superior English trade goods in exchange for remaining neutral in New Jersey, Pennsylvania, and along a portion of the Ohio River for the remainder of the war. This brought peace to the region.

William Pitt in England was given charge of the war effort in North America. His directives changed the course of the war:

July 1758 – The British regulars and Colonial militias arrived by sea and laid siege to the French Fort Louisbourg at the mouth of the St. Lawrence River, defeating the French along with a number of their warships.

August 1758 – Lieutenant Colonel John Bradstreet defeated the French at Fort Frontenac at the east end of Lake Ontario with 150 British regulars and 2,850 colonials.

October 1758 – The Treaty of Easton (as mentioned above).

November 1758 – Only a small garrison of French was left at Fort Duquesne when they learned an English and Colonial force of six thousand was approaching. They abandoned and burned the fort.

July 1759 – The English and colonials captured Fort Niagara (La Belle Famille).

September 1759 – General James Wolf defeated General Louis Joseph Montcalm on the Plains of Abraham near Quebec City.

1762 – In the Treaty of Fontiubleau, France ceded Louisiana to Spain (an ally of England in the Seven Years' War, in which the French & Indian War was included, along with conflicts over colonies in India and Africa).

1763 – The Treaty of Paris ended the Seven Years' War. France traded all her possessions in North America for the lucrative sugar cane island of Guadeloupe.

Discussion Questions

1. Lily journeyed to the colonies with her sisters, expecting to remain with them in the new land. But the girls had barely set foot in America before they were auctioned off and split up. How do you think Lily, as the youngest, was able to accept her fate without a protest?

2. Lily admired her older sister Rose all of her life and hoped one day to emulate her. Do you think she succeeded? In what way?

3. John Waldon deeply loved his wife, Susan, and it broke his heart to watch her dying by inches, yet he never allowed himself to feel bitterness toward God. Why do you think some people find it easy to blame God for circumstances beyond their control?

4. Susan Waldon gave up the comforts of a privileged life to elope with John when they were barely twenty. She had every reason to regret missing out on the good things in life, yet her love for John remained constant. Do you know anyone who possesses that kind of sweet spirit?

5. In her four years of servitude to the Waldon family, Lily became quite attached to Susan and the children. She also grew a little too fond of Susan's husband. She knew that coveting was a gross sin—one she confessed again and again. Did she do an adequate job of keeping her attraction hidden?

6. John watched Lily turn from a frightened, wide-eyed waif of a bondservant trembling on an auction block to an engaging young woman. Even though he loved his wife dearly, he had to fight against a growing attraction for Lily. Do you think he remained completely faithful to Susan despite those unwanted desires?

7. Lily was only fourteen when John purchased her indenturement papers. Later, Mariah's husband was willing and had the means to redeem her, but she chose to stay with the Waldon family. Did you ever face a life-changing decision? How can a person know for certain that the right choice was made?

8. The little settlement of Beaver Cove was situated in an area vulnerable to Indian attacks. Only a stalwart soul would choose to live under the constant threat of danger. What qualities did Lily possess that made her want to make her home there?

9. Both John and Lily were staunch believers who lived their faith. Even though God worked in quite a roundabout way to bring them together, they eventually did find their happy ending. That doesn't always work for everyone, however. Why do you suppose that is?

10. Lily and the Waldon family prayed fervently for Susan's health to improve, yet she grew increasingly weak and finally died. Sometimes it's hard to accept that Christians aren't always protected from the bad things that happen. What promises of God comfort you during the trials of life?

11. Was there a particular character in *Lily's Plight* that you identified with? Why?

12. What will you most remember about Lily's story?

Sally Laity has written both historical and contemporary novels, including a coauthored series for Tyndale House, nine Heartsong Romances, and twelve Barbour novellas. She considers it a joy to know that the Lord can touch other hearts through her stories. Her favorite pastimes include quilting for her church's Prayer Quilt Ministry and scrapbooking. She makes her home in the beautiful Tehachapi Mountains of Southern California with her husband of fifty years and enjoys being a grandma and great-grandma.

Widowed a few years ago, Dianna Crawford lives in California's Central Valley where she is active in her local church. Although she loves writing Christian historical fiction, her most gratifying blessings are her four daughters and their families. In her spare time she loves to paint and travel.

Dianna's first novel was published in the general market in 1992 under the pen name Elaine Crawford. She was pleased when it was nominated for Best First Book by Romance Writers of America. After publishing several works by that name, Dianna felt very blessed to be given the opportunity to write for the Christian market. A number of novels have followed. She and Sally Laity were honored when their third collaboration, The Tempering Blaze, resulted in another nomination, this one for Best Inspirational by Romance Writers of America.